09/2021

**PALM BEACH COUNTY
LIBRARY SYSTEM**
3650 Summit Boulevard
West Palm Beach, FL   33406-4198

Coached
in the Act

Books by Victoria Laurie

COACHED TO DEATH

TO COACH A KILLER

COACHED IN THE ACT

Published by Kensington Publishing Corp.

Coached
in the Act

VICTORIA
LAURIE

KENSINGTON
PUBLISHING CORP.

www.kensingtonbooks.com

This book is a work of fiction. Names, characters, businesses, organizations, places, events, and incidents either are the product of the author's imagination or are used fictitiously. Any resemblance to actual persons, living or dead, events, or locales is entirely coincidental.

To the extent that the image or images on the cover of this book depict a person or persons, such person or persons are merely models, and are not intended to portray any character or characters featured in the book.

KENSINGTON BOOKS are published by

Kensington Publishing Corp.
119 West 40th Street
New York, NY 10018

Copyright © 2021 by Victoria Laurie

All rights reserved. No part of this book may be reproduced in any form or by any means without the prior written consent of the Publisher, excepting brief quotes used in reviews.

All Kensington titles, imprints, and distributed lines are available at special quantity discounts for bulk purchases for sales promotion, premiums, fund-raising, educational, or institutional use. Special book excerpts or customized printings can also be created to fit specific needs. For details, write or phone the office of the Kensington Special Sales Manager: Attn. Special Sales Department. Kensington Publishing Corp., 119 West 40th Street, New York, NY 10018. Phone: 1-800-221-2647.

Library of Congress Card Catalogue Number: 2021935213

The K logo is a trademark of Kensington Publishing Corp.

ISBN-13: 978-1-4967-3440-2
ISBN-10: 1-4967-3440-8
First Kensington Hardcover Edition: September 2021

eISBN-13: 978-1-4967-3442-6 (ebook)
eISBN-10: 1-4967-3442-4 (ebook)

10 9 8 7 6 5 4 3 2 1

Printed in the United States of America

Coached
in the Act

Chapter 1

I found Gilley in the kitchen, tearfully sniffing as he stared at his laptop screen. "Gil?" I asked, surprised to find my permanent guesthouse resident and dear friend so upset. "What's happened?"

Gilley jumped at the sound of my voice. He obviously hadn't heard me come downstairs. Once he recovered himself, he swiveled the laptop around so that I could see. There, on the screen was a video clip of M.J. Whitefeather, Gilley's best friend and former business partner, sitting in a rocking chair, with two babies cuddled against her and a towel draped over her chest. She was obviously nursing the twins.

Entering the screen to the right was a toddler, stumbling a little as she walked, obviously still half asleep. Suddenly, the voice of Heath, M.J.'s husband, could be heard. "Such a good mama, feeding the babies at five a.m.," he cooed.

M.J. glanced up at the camera, revealing dark circles and half-lidded eyes. She looked so tired, the poor love. I could sympathize. I'd had twins when I was about her age. It's not for the weak.

"Is she getting *any* sleep?" I asked Gilley.

He wiped at his cheeks with a tissue. "Not a lot," he said. "According to Heath, Skylar seems to be nocturnal, and Chase has trouble with gas or something that makes him fussy. Margot just entered her terrible twos, so the whole thing's a disaster, if you ask me."

I chuckled and came around the side of the island where Gilley was sitting to hug him around the shoulders. "You really miss them, don't you?"

"Is it that obvious?" he asked in a choked whisper. "But I especially miss M.J. We were inseparable for almost thirty years, and now the only time I get to see her is when she has the energy to call or Zoom with me, or when Heath sends me a clip, like this one."

I sat down next to Gil and took up his hand. "It's going to be really hard for her until the twins are in kindergarten," I said. "Then things will settle down, and she'll be in touch more."

"They're three months old, Cat. You're telling me I have to wait five years to connect regularly with my best friend again?"

I squeezed his hand. I understood that, deep down, Gilley was actually happy that M.J. had found her soul mate and was building a family with him, but I also knew that the adjustment of giving her up to Heath, Skylar, Chase, and Margot was exceptionally difficult.

"You could always fly out to see her," I suggested. The Whitefeathers lived in New Mexico.

Gilley scowled. "I don't do babies. The dirty diapers *alone* would have me running for the hills."

I cocked my head at him. He'd been living in my guesthouse for nearly two years now, and I was still learning new and interesting things about him. "You and Michel have never considered having a baby together?" I asked, referring to Gilley's husband.

"Nope," he said, a note of tension in his voice. Michel had spent much of the pandemic locked down in the UK, and it'd put a definite strain on their marriage. And ever since the vaccine had been widely distributed, Michel still continued to take assignments as an in-demand fashion photographer, out of the country.

"Although," Gilley continued, "I *have* been contemplating adopting a puppy."

My brow arched in surprise. "Really?"

"As long as it's okay with my landlord, of course," he said.

I waved my hand. "Of course, it's all right, Gilley."

In fact, it was more than all right. Poor Gil had been a bit lonely of late, ever since my boys went back to boarding school and I had more time to spend with my current love interest, Detective Steve Shepherd.

I realized as I stared at my dear friend that since the boys left two weeks earlier, I'd hardly spent any of my free time with Gilley. Oh, sure, we saw each other at work—he was my personal assistant—and we typically shared lunch together, but we hadn't really spent any quality time together, and I suddenly found myself feeling guilty over that.

"Gilley," I said, trying to pump a little enthusiasm into my voice. "Why don't you and I go out on the town tonight?"

Gilley slid his gaze toward me, his lids weighed down by skepticism. "Don't you have a date with Shepherd?"

"We have nothing planned," I lied, knowing I'd have to cancel our plans for dinner the moment I was out of earshot. "Come on, Gil, it's supposed to be a beautiful night, and we can go out to eat, do a little shopping, and . . . Ooh! I've got it! We could take in that hot new show at John Drew Street Theater!"

I'd wanted to catch the show everyone in town was talking about ever since I learned it was opening in late August. The show was a take on a famous classic, but with a clever twist. "You and I have both said we'd love to see *Twelve Angry Men*. Why not go tonight?"

Gilley frowned. "You're kidding, right? Tickets are impossible to get, Cat. It's totally sold out for the next three months."

Clearly, Gilley had been doing a little research into this very subject, which made my smile all the wider. "I can get us tick-ets," I said.

"You know a scalper?"

"Better. I know Yelena Galanis's best friend." Yelena Galanis was the star of the one-woman show, aptly titled *Twelve Angry Men*, in which she told the story of the twelve rich and powerful East Hamptonites she'd used and abused over the years. Word on the street suggested it was a scintillating hoot.

"You do?" Gilley said. "Who?"

"Sunny D'Angelo," I said, with a bounce to my brow. "She and Yelena go way back. I think they were college roommates or in the same sorority. And Sunny has already mentioned that she can score us tickets anytime we want."

Still, Gilley looked doubtful. With a sigh, he said, "I don't know that I'm in the mood for it, Cat."

I rubbed his arm. "Oh, come on, Gil. It's been forever since the two of us were out on the town together. Besides, what else are you going to do? Sit home and watch VH1?"

Gilley frowned, and I knew that was exactly what he'd planned on doing. "Ru's doing a special on the best of the drag racers," he said.

"Record it and watch it later," I suggested.

He made a face, but I could tell his resolve was cracking. "Where would we go to dinner?" he asked.

"Well, the Beacon is still open for another two weeks, and we haven't been there in forever. What do you say to that?"

"Hmm, I do *love* to be seen at the Beacon," Gilley said of the yacht-club bistro.

I grinned. I knew I had him. "What'll we wear?"

Gilley couldn't resist planning his outfits ahead of time. "You should wear that red, off-the-shoulder number," he said, refer-ring to the new Versace deep red dress with flared sleeves and skirt that I'd purchased only a week earlier. I'd been saving it for a special occasion out with Shepherd, but I could certainly wear it out tonight for Gilley.

"Done," I said. "And you, sir? What will you wear?"

A smile began to form on Gilley's lips. "I think," he said, tapping his lips, "that I've been looking for an opportunity to wear my new Ted Baker suit."

"The light gray plaid?"

Gilley nodded. "I've got a gorgeous black silk shirt to wear with it. The contrasts are delicious."

"Then you *must* wear it," I said, watching as Gilley began to show some enthusiasm.

"Okay," he said after taking another moment to think on it. "It's a date, Cat."

"Excellent!" I said, moving in to hug him around the shoulders. "I have a few errands to run before my client today at one, but I can call Sunny from the car and see if she can't scrounge up a pair of tickets for us."

"Cool," he said, hopping off the chair at the island. Pointing to the counter near the sink, he added, "There's a quiche that I took out of the oven a bit ago. It should be cool enough to eat by now. Let me know if we're a go for tonight so I can pull out the suit and steam out the wrinkles."

"Did you want to come with me to run the errands?" I asked.

He shook his head. "Can't. I've got a massage with Reese at ten."

My brow arched. "Again?" I asked carefully. Reese was an absolutely breathtaking man, who reminded me very much of the late Christopher Reeve at the height of his Superman career. Reese was also someone I knew Gilley had a monstrous crush on.

"Yes, *again*," Gilley said moodily.

"You've been seeing a lot of him lately," I said, undaunted, because I needed to understand Gilley's thinking here. Even though I knew he and Michel were struggling in their relationship, I felt strongly that if Gilley strayed, he'd regret it.

My dear friend sighed. "There's nothing going on, Cat."

"Okay, but *could* there be at some point, Gilley?"

Reese's sexual exploits into the beds of many of the Hamptons elite were an open secret. He was rumored to be a very . . . shall we say, *talented* lover, and he had no preference as to which team he'd pitch for on any given day. He was as sought after by women as he was by men.

Gilley glared at me. I held his eyes and didn't look away. At last, he threw up his arms and said, "I don't know. Maybe?"

"If you don't know, Gilley, then it might be best to resist the urge until you deal with your relationship with Michel. And I say that as a friend to both you and him, okay?"

Gilley nodded. "It's just nice to get some attention, you know?"

I bit my lip, the guilt of a few minutes ago returning. "I do," I said. "And I'm sorry that I haven't been paying nearly as much attention to our friendship as I should have."

The edges of Gilley's mouth quirked up in a smile. "You're forgiven."

"Good. Now, come with me to run those errands."

To my surprise, Gilley shook his head no again. "I'm going to keep my appointment with Reese." When I again arched my brow, he added, "I may be married, but I'm not dead. I'm allowed to flirt."

I held back the protest I badly wanted to make and settled for a simple nod. It was Gilley's life and relationship to work out, not mine. "I'll text you if I hear back from Sunny before I meet you at the office."

"I'll get there a little early and throw on some tea for you and your one o'clock."

"Thank you, lovey. You're a doll." With that, I leaned in to kiss him on the cheek, before I headed out the door.

As soon as I pulled out of the driveway, I called Sunny.

"Hi, Cat," she said, sounding weary.

"Sunny?" I said. I hadn't seen much of Sunny over the summer, which, I'll admit, was odd, given that she was Shepherd's twin sister. And I definitely hadn't seen much of her while the pandemic was on. As the mother of a baby—and now toddler—she'd been especially careful to protect little Finley.

"Yes, I'm here," she said, probably thinking that I hadn't heard her the first time.

"Are you okay?" I asked. Shepherd had told me that his sister had been struggling recently, and by the sound of her voice, I wondered if she might be ill.

"Yeah," she said on a sigh. "I'm fine. Just a bout of insomnia, and Finley started becoming a real handful just after his second birthday."

"Ah the terrible twos," I said. My boys had gotten up to all sorts of mischief when they were Finley's age.

"He'll be the death of me," she said, but added a tired smile.

I could tell she was trying to appear like her old self. Sunny had been very aptly named.

I grinned when I heard the old playful enthusiasm back in her voice. "Do you remember when you said that you had an in with Yelena Galanis?"

Sunny chuckled. "You want tickets, don't you?"

"Only if it won't cause you any trouble."

"It won't," she assured me. "I've been meaning to take Finley over to see her for ages. This'll give me an excuse, and Yelena always has extra seats on hand for just such an occasion."

"Have you caught her act yet?"

"Not yet. I'm waiting for Darius to come home from L.A., and then we'll go."

"Is he away again?" Darius worked in the music business, and he spent more time on the West Coast than he did at his home here in East Hampton.

It secretly upset me because it left Sunny to care for Finley for long stretches at a time without any help from the boy's father.

"Yes, but he's on his way back," she said. "He'll be here late tonight, in fact."

I let out a relieved sigh. "Well, that's good. And you promise it's no trouble to ask Yelena for a couple of tickets?"

"I promise, Cat. I'll call you in a bit to let you know, though, okay?"

I said my goodbyes to Sunny and called her brother.

"Hey there," he said, his voice warm and throaty. I shimmied a little in my seat. Shepherd could light the home fires with just a greeting, and it was a delicious thing to be the object of his affections.

"Hey there," I repeated. "Got a second?"

"For you? Always."

This was a lie, as I knew from experience. Whenever Shepherd was knee-deep into working a case, my phone calls went straight to voice mail. But I was hardly going to remind him of that at the moment. "Listen," I began. "About tonight . . ."

"Something's come up," he said, beating me to the punch.

"Yes."

"What?"

"Gilley."

Shepherd chuckled. "Ah," he said. "Our third wheel."

"Hey, he's not a third wheel, Shep, okay?" I'd adopted the nickname Shep for Shepherd after I recently discovered that was what most of the other men in blue from the East Hampton PD called him.

"Okay, okay," Shepherd said, and I could almost see him holding up his hands in surrender. "He's feeling neglected, though, right?"

"Yes," I said. "So, I've decided to take a rain check with you and focus on Gilley for tonight."

"That's fine, Cat," he said, using the nickname common to most of my friends and family, instead of the more formal Catherine, which he'd insisted on using for the first few months of our relationship.

"I'm free most of this week," he continued. "Just let me know when your schedule clears up, okay?"

"I will," I promised. "And if you want to come over late tonight, I won't say no."

Shepherd made a growling sound. "You're a temptress, you know that?"

"I do," I said, smiling wickedly. "I'll tell Sebastian to let you in if you feel like spending the night. Gilley and I should be home around eleven, I think." Sebastian was my AI butler. Much like Google Nest, but much more sophisticated.

"See you then," he promised.

A bit later, after I had run all my errands, I was headed back to the house to drop off a few packages before driving across town to my office when Sunny called me. "Hey, where are you?" she asked the moment I picked up the call.

"Um, I'm driving back to my house. Why? Do you need something?"

"I got the tickets," Sunny said. In the background I could hear Finley fussing, and there was that exhausted tone in Sunny's voice again. "Can you swing by to pick them up? Finley and I both need a nap."

"Of course," I said. "I'm rounding the corner onto your street as we speak."

"Oh, I see your car," Sunny said, and up ahead I saw her Range Rover pull into her driveway.

I parked and was out of the car first, and then I trotted over to hold Sunny's car door open so that the windy day didn't bang her door against her as she reached in to get Finley out of his car seat. The poor tyke was red faced and crying, and as Sunny backed up with him cradled in her arms, I was taken aback by the dark circles under her eyes and the sag to her shoulders.

"Thanks," she said. "The tickets are in my purse. Come on in and I'll fish them out for you."

I held my arms out toward Finley, who was kicking and fussing in his mother's embrace, and made a "gimme" motion with my hands. I'd been that overwhelmed and exhausted mother once. I knew when it was time to volunteer to take charge.

Sunny's expression was a bit apprehensive but also relieved. "He's super fussy, Cat," she said.

"Yes, which is why you should give him to me so that I can help you, instead of standing around waiting for you to be supermom and super friend all at the same time."

Sunny hesitated one more second, but then she lifted Finley away from her and pivoted him around to me. I took the tyke and held him close, relishing the feeling of holding a small toddler again. It made me miss my sons even more than usual, but it was also the right thing to do.

"Shhh, shhh, shhh," I said to Finley, bouncing him gently in my arms.

He pulled his head back, probably startled to be in someone else's arms, and that was all the opening I needed. I made a goofy face, and his expression turned from sour to unsure and then to nearly a grin.

"Who's a boogley boo?" I asked him, still bouncing him up and down playfully, while Sunny retrieved a bag of groceries from the car.

"We can go in through the garage," she said, clicking a switch on her key fob. The garage door creaked open a few feet then stopped. "Oh, come on," Sunny grumbled. "Not today!"

"What's wrong?" I asked as Sunny clicked the button on her key fob again and the door came down.

"It's the stupid garage door. It keeps sticking. Sometimes I can't get it to come down. Sometimes I can't get it to go up."

She clicked the fob a third time and the door slowly rose and this time it went all the way to the top. "Whew," she said.

I smiled, bouncing Finley in my arms as he played with my hair.

"This way," Sunny said, leading us into the garage. "Watch

your step," she added as she pointed down to a pile of supplies made up of a big carton of disposable water bottles, paper towels, laundry detergent, and various other household cleaning supplies. "I went to Costco yesterday," she explained as I waited for her to unlock the door.

"I love Costco," I said, following her through the now unlocked door into the kitchen. "Gilley and I go once a month, so if you ever need anything from there, just ask, Sunny, and we can pick it up for you."

She glanced over her shoulder as she moved to set down her groceries. "You two are my angels," she said. Then she pointed to a high chair at the table. "You can set Finley down in the high chair."

I shook my head because I wasn't about to put the child down. He was mocking my facial expressions and giggling along with me, and it was a glorious exchange that was also allowing Sunny to get herself organized.

"Oh, where did I set my purse?" she said, spinning around and looking at the counter and nearby breakfast table.

"I didn't see you bring it in," I told her.

Sunny sighed heavily. "It's still out in the car," she moaned.

"Hey," I said to her to get her attention. "When was the last time you had a proper meal?"

Sunny pushed at a stray strand of her long blond hair that had pulled free of her ponytail. The way her hair was pulled back today showed how thin she'd become since the last time I saw her. It worried me.

"I eat when he eats," she said.

"Uh-huh," I said. "And I bet it's about the same size meal too."

Sunny ignored my concern. "I'll eat as soon as I get him down."

"Or you could fix yourself a little nosh right now, my friend, and let me put him down for a nap." Not waiting for an okay from her, I edged toward the hallway leading to the stairs. "The nursery is the first door on the right past the stairs, correct?"

Again, Sunny's shoulders sagged with relief. Finley had fallen against my shoulder, the novelty of making funny faces at me having lost out to exhaustion.

"Yes," she said. "But, really, Cat, you don't have to—"

"I want to," I told her. "Now, get yourself a sandwich or something. I'll be down as soon as he's asleep."

I took Finley up the stairs slowly and carefully so as not to joust him. I'd picked up a pacifier off the kitchen drying rack as I'd passed it on the way to the stairs, and the little tot was sucking on it with heavy-lidded eyes as I crested the landing.

"Here we go," I said, walking down the hallway and heading into the nursery.

I'd last been here when Finley was a newborn, just as the pandemic was starting to exact its terrible toll on the world. I smiled as I entered, remembering the photos lining the wall that Sunny had been in the middle of putting up.

A series on the far left wall was the most inviting—it began with a breathtaking shot of Sunny, radiant in the early evening light, her hands placed protectively over her belly, as she leaned against the porch railing of the D'Angelos' old home in L.A. The twinkling lights of downtown could be seen at the bottom of the image. I knew from Sunny that Darius had taken the photo in the moments after Sunny had revealed her pregnancy to him. She'd said he'd been so excited to capture the moment that he'd insisted on the photo and every one after it, taken one a month for nine in total. The last one included a tiny baby, laid against the bare chest of his mother.

What always took me by surprise was the look of unconditional love on Sunny's face as she smiled at her husband while he chronicled her pregnancy. I didn't really understand their marriage—Darius was gone far too often for my taste—but the adoration in Sunny's expression was so obvious that it was unmistakable. They loved each other, and their marriage worked for them, so who was I to judge?

I laid Finley down in his bed, then gently eased off his shoes and socks to expose his little feet and button toes. I placed my hand around one of his feet and smiled at the feel of baby skin against my palm. My mind's eye filled with images of my sons, Matthew and Michael, at Finley's age, and I teared up a bit as I laid a blanket over the toddler, who was already asleep, his mouth still working the pacifier.

Pulling up the guard rail on his toddler bed, I moved over to the photos of Sunny through her pregnancy. Darius had quite the artist's eye for photography. The backdrop for each photo was nearly as eye catching as the central figure.

The second photo in the series, taken when Sunny was about two months along, featured Sunny perched atop the railing, staring out at the early evening view of downtown L.A., where a few twinkles of light could already be seen. It gave the viewer the impression of Sunny as the Greek goddess Aphrodite looking down from Olympus to Athens below.

A few images to the right was one of a playful Sunny clad in a tiny bikini, which even five or six months along in her pregnancy she could still pull off beautifully. She was laughing in the spray of an outdoor shower, and there was such joy on her face. I stood in front of the image and mentally noted how different Sunny looked back then compared to today.

As if on cue, I heard the sound of something behind me and turned to see her there, a weary smile on her face, watching me standing in front of the photos. "Did he go down okay?" she whispered, glancing toward the bed.

I nodded.

Sunny came over to stand next to me as I looked back to the photos. "Where was this one taken?" I asked softly.

"Here," she said, smiling at the memory. "That was the day that Darius closed on the house in L.A. and we played in the surf most of the afternoon to celebrate. That shower is so cold," Sunny chuckled. "Darius loves it but I don't think I've used it since."

"You look like you're having fun," I said, grinning too.

"Oh, he probably said something hilarious. I just remember I was so relieved to have Darius back here, and be rid of the fake, money-fame-success-focused crowd. I'd already moved back to this house, which we bought, oh, about ten years ago. It was our vacation pad, if you can believe it, but as soon as I found out I was pregnant, I packed up and moved. No *way* was I about to raise my kid in La-La Land."

"What's wrong with L.A.?" I asked. I'd been there only a few times, but I'd found it okay.

Sunny made a face. "It's full of fake people with far too much money and privilege. I didn't want our son to grow up a spoiled brat, surrounded by other spoiled brats, so I told Darius that I was headed home to New York, and I expected him to split his time between here and there. He agreed, and we sold the house, because it was a total drain on our finances. Anyway, that photo was taken the day Darius officially made his residence here in the Hamptons."

"Where does he stay when he's out there?" I asked.

"He bought a condo, and he rents out the spare bedrooms to two of his old college buddies. They're very sweet men, actually. Noah and Jason used to be lovers, but now they're just friends, and they watch over the place when he's back here with me. I like the arrangement because it keeps Darius honest. If he's living with those two, no way would they let him get into any mischief."

Sunny laughed softly, but I asked, "Mischief?"

She shrugged. "He works in the music industry, Cat. Women, desperate to sign a contract with a successful music producer, throw themselves at him all the time."

My eyes widened. "How are you okay with that?"

Sunny's lids drooped heavily, and she yawned. "I trust my husband, and so far in our fifteen years together, he's never given me a reason not to."

I placed a hand on her shoulder, knowing it was far past my time to take my leave. "I think I should let you get some sleep."

She nodded. "Thanks. I took half of a sleep-aid tablet, and it's hitting me hard all of a sudden."

"A sleep aid?" I said with concern. "Did you want me to stay in case Finley wakes up?"

Sunny yawned again. "No, it'll be okay. I took only half a dose, because I'm so exhausted by this bout of insomnia that I need something to help me get a little rest. And I called Tiffany, and she's coming over now to hang out and tend to Finley when he wakes up while I get some z's."

"Ah, the famous Tiffany," I said. Sunny raved about Tiffany. I'd never met her, but I'd heard a great deal about her over the summer, when the young woman had been touring Europe as a graduation gift from her parents.

"Yes," Sunny said, her eyes droopy. "She's finally back from across the pond, and I'm so relieved. I don't know that I could've held on one more day without her."

"I'm so glad you've got someone you can rely on to take up some of the slack."

Sunny nodded, stifling a yawn. "You know what's a funny coincidence?"

"What?"

"It was Yelena who recommended her to me. She's friends with the Blums—Tiffany's parents. She's known Tiff since the girl was a tiny tyke, so I felt good about trying her out with Finley. I never realized how well the two of them would get on together. It's like they speak the same language."

"How long was she away in Europe again?" I asked.

"Six long, impossible weeks," Sunny said, with a tired smile.

"But she's finally back, and she'll be here in ten minutes or so." Sunny again put a hand up to cover another yawn. "Sorry," she said.

"Please don't be," I told her. "You look exhausted, and I should leave you to your rest."

I was turning to go when Sunny reached out to grab my hand, and holding it, she said, "I almost forgot. The tickets are on the island counter. When I told Yelena that two of my dearest friends were hoping to attend tonight, she gave me her best two reserved seats and said that tonight was a perfect night for you guys to come, because she just might name names before the night is through."

"Ooh," I said, with an eager smile. "Sounds juicy."

Sunny giggled. "With Yelena, it wouldn't be anything but."

After leaving Sunny in the nursery, I made my way down-stairs and found the tickets in an envelope marked VIP. Taking a peek inside, I discovered that Yelena had generously offered us front-row-center seats, and I made a promise to myself to come up with a way to thank both her and Sunny for the gener-ous gift.

Looking back, I wish more than anything that I'd known then that I'd never be able to make good on my promise.

Chapter 2

After a quick pit stop home, I arrived at my office building in the heart of East Hampton's downtown. I'd purchased the building nearly two years earlier, even before my house—Chez Cat—had been built.

Charmed by the office building's historic roots and architecture, I'd invested a great deal of time and money to bring the neglected old relic to its current glorious state. And I was proud to say that every suite in the building was currently leased and bringing in a tidy income.

My office occupied the largest suite on the first floor, with an entrance onto Main Street. The building itself took up a corner lot, so its main entrance was on Pondview.

And because my suite was hemmed in by two walls of floor-to-ceiling windows, I had to ensure that it stood as the showpiece for the entire building, which was why I'd taken such care to decorate it in the most neutral but still stylish tones of stone, white, and sand. The combo gave the feeling of a fresh start, which was an important subliminal message to send to my clients, not to mention the subliminal message I was also sending to myself.

After twenty years spent building a marketing firm, which I'd sold for a tidy profit a few years back, I was now a professional life coach, and I was proud of the fact that almost all the people who'd come seeking a little wisdom were in better positions now to tackle whatever life threw at them. Slowly but surely, my client base was building, and I now had at least two to three clients on the books at any given time.

That afternoon I was meeting a brand-new client, and I was excited to see what life issues we could tackle together.

"Gilley," I said after pacing a little around the office.

"Hmm?"

"Did you confirm the time with Mr. Nassau?" Aaron Nassau, my new client.

"I sent him an email yesterday."

"Did he reply?"

"No."

I glanced at my watch. It was seven minutes past one, and I had to take a deep breath to push back the hint of irritation bubbling up from my insides. I'm a stickler for punctuality, and it drives me crazy when people show up late to their first session. I always wonder what they could be thinking, as it's their first opportunity to make a good impression on me.

Still, I realize not everyone places a high value on punctuality. But they should. They really, really should.

I crossed my arms and tapped the sleeve of my blouse impatiently while glancing out the large front windows for any sign of Aaron.

I didn't know what he looked like, but I expected at any moment to see someone hurrying toward the door, perhaps a bit disheveled and certainly out of breath.

Instead, the sidewalk was sparse of pedestrians, and those walking past hardly seemed to be in a rush.

So, with a sigh, I moved to my wing chair, took a seat, and sat back to wait. Meanwhile, Gilley was busy at his computer, going through what looked like rescue sites, in search of his new pup.

"Any of them stand out to you?" I asked into the silence.

Gilley's shoulders jumped slightly at the sound of my voice. "What?" he asked, peering over his shoulder.

"The dogs. Any of the dogs stand out to you?"

"All of them," he said wistfully. "I wish I could adopt every single one."

I made a sympathetic mewing sound. "I really get it, Gilley, but please don't."

He chuckled. "Not to worry, Cat. I'll keep it to one pup."

I headed over to stand behind him so that I could better see the screen. It was now a quarter past one, and I'd decided that Aaron had simply changed his mind and would be marked off in my book as a no-show. Bending down to have a look at the screen, I jerked when the door suddenly opened and in stepped an elegant man, whom I'd put somewhere in his midfifties, dressed in Versace loafers, silk khaki slacks, and a blue blazer with gold buttons mostly covering a crisp white shirt.

"Hello," he said, a bit flustered. "I have an appointment."

"Aaron?" I asked, taking a mental note at the hint of a European accent coming from him.

He nodded enthusiastically and stuck out his hand. "Catherine?"

"Yes," I said, reaching my own hand forward. His palm was dry to the touch, and his handshake had the perfect amount of pressure. Still, Aaron's gaze darted around the office a bit nervously.

To put him at ease, I decided not to mention the fact that he was nearly twenty minutes late and instead smiled pleasantly and motioned toward the seating area. "Won't you please come in and make yourself comfortable?"

He gave a nod to Gilley, who was eyeing him curiously, and followed me to the plush love seat and wing chair that made up my seating area. I motioned again to the love seat, and Aaron sat down with a whoosh of air escaping his lips.

I sat down, too, and leaned toward him slightly, hoping that my body language indicated that I was focused on him and intent on listening. "Can I get you something to drink?" I asked. The man had a bit of a sheen about his forehead.

"Water would be wonderful," he said. "Sparkling, if you have it."

"We do," I said and nodded to Gilley, who got up and hurried to the beverage counter.

I waited until Gilley had removed a small bottle of Pellegrino from the minifridge and brought it with a frosted glass over to Aaron before I got down to brass tacks. Taking up the yellow notepad I kept on the side table next to my chair, I said, "So, Aaron, what brings you to my little coaching corner?"

Aaron blanched as he unscrewed the cap of the Pellegrino. "I could really use some help."

"Of course," I said gently. "But about what, specifically?"

He sighed and took a sip of water. "To be honest, Catherine, I'm having some difficulty moving on after a breakup."

"Oh?" I said. "Were you married?"

"Yes, but that's not the woman I'm having trouble getting over, which is sad, given that my ex-wife and I were married for twenty years before we split. And I've dated a smattering of women, some of them seriously, since then too, so it isn't that I'm a fool for love. But recently, I split from a woman I was absolutely mad for, and I'm having a hard time getting over her."

"How long were you two together?"

"Six months."

My brow rose in surprise. "Only six months?"

"I know it seems like too short a time to develop any real feelings for a person, but I did develop feelings. Deep feelings. I'd planned to propose, and I wanted to spend the rest of my life with her."

"So, what happened between the two of you to cause the breakup?"

"I have no idea," Aaron said, with a sigh and a shake of his head. "One day we were mad for each other, and the next she wouldn't answer my calls or texts or the door when I went to check on her. It was bizarre."

"She ghosted you," I said.

Aaron's brow knit in confusion. "No, she's still alive."

I held back a grin and explained, "'Ghosting someone' means 'to cut off all contact, as if they never existed.' It's a cruel way to end a relationship, but it's becoming more and more common, I'm afraid."

"Oh," he said, his shoulders drooping. "Well then, yes, she ghosted me."

"Could there have been someone else?" I asked carefully.

"Not that I was aware of when we were together. Frankly, I don't know how the woman could've had time for another lover. We were always together, inseparable, in fact. We acted as one unit for most of our relationship."

"Ah," I said. "So, her abrupt departure from your life is part of the problem."

"What do you mean?"

"Well," I began, trying to choose my words delicately. "If you two were always together, your life as an individual morphed into your life as part of a couple. And I understand that you were very happy in your relationship with her, but when it ended so abruptly without closure or even an explanation, I can see how it would've left you feeling set adrift, without benefit of a life preserver or any way back to her."

Aaron pursed his lips, and to my surprise, his eyes watered, then leaked a tear or two. He wiped them away self-consciously. "I'm shattered," he whispered.

I inched forward to the edge of my seat in order to reach out and squeeze his hand. Behind Aaron, I heard a loud sniffle, and my gaze momentarily darted to Gilley, who was dabbing at his own eyes. He caught the look of disapproval on my face—he wasn't supposed to listen in on these private conversations with my clients—and he quickly grabbed his headphones and shoved them on to let me know he understood my look of disapproval.

Focusing back on Aaron, who thankfully seemed not to have noticed Gilley's eavesdropping, I said, "Aaron, I understand how heartbreaking this must be for you, and what I think you need is some time to ease back into your old identity as a single man with a lot to offer the world."

Aaron nodded, but his eyes were still welling up. I had to fight against my own emotions, because it was difficult to watch such an elegant, regal man be brought to tears over the insensitive, cruel, and abrupt dismissal from a woman he'd clearly loved.

"Listen," I said softly. "I know exactly what you're going through. Three years ago, my own heart was broken when I discovered the affair my husband was having with another woman. I was devastated, but after a time . . . I got through it and realized that I could have a wonderfully happy life without him. Right now, you're in the worst part, the swamp—the place where every step forward feels a little like you're also sinking into the muck—but you've also already taken the bravest and hardest step. You've come to me for help. I'm so proud of you for that, Aaron, and I promise, you won't have to move forward alone. I will help you take every step forward through the muck until you're on safe and solid ground again."

Aaron lifted his gaze then to meet mine, and the smallest hint of relief played across his expression. "Thank you, Catherine."

A bit later, Gilley came over to stand next to me as I watched Aaron cross the street after he'd left my office. "He's sweet," he said.

"He really is, the poor man. It's hard to see such a nice person get his heart stomped on by someone so callous."

"There are always two sides to every story, Cat," Gilley reminded me. "Right now, we know only his."

I pointed to Aaron's retreating form. "Agreed, but no one deserves to be simply cut off like that, Gilley. Without any explanation or even a formal goodbye. What she did was cruel, and even in the small amount of time I've spent with Aaron, I can tell you he likely didn't deserve to be treated like that."

Gilley sighed. "True," he said.

At that point Aaron had reached the side of a silver Bentley, and after unlocking it, he got in.

"Wow," Gil said next. "Aaron comes from money."

"And did you catch that accent?" I asked.

"It sounded Danish to me," Gilley said.

Gilley had traveled extensively across Europe, so I trusted that he was probably right.

He then moved back over to his laptop, lifted the lid, and began typing.

Aaron had pulled away by now, and I turned my attention to Gil. "Whatcha working on?"

"A little sleuthing."

My brow furrowed with curiosity. "Oh? What are we sleuthing?"

"I'm curious about him," he said.

"Aaron?"

"Yes," Gilley said, squinting at the screen. His eyes then widened, and he looked at me in surprise.

"What?" I asked.

"He's a count."

"A what?"

Gil swiveled the screen toward me. "I was right. Aaron is from Denmark, and he's a count from the royal house of Rosenborg."

"But his last name is Nassau."

"I know, but he's still a member of the Danish royal family, currently sixteenth in line for the throne."

"Whoa," I said. I'd never met a royal before, much less sat with one for an intimate conversation.

Gilley then looked up at me with a perplexed expression. "*Who* would dump a count?"

I shrugged. "Maybe she didn't know."

Gilley scoffed. "She knew," he said. "You're the only person left on earth that doesn't immediately Google a prospective romantic partner."

I rolled my eyes. "It's rude to snoop into someone's personal life before actually getting to know them."

"It's rude only if you get caught," Gil replied.

I sighed. On that note we'd have to disagree, and I changed the subject. "What's a Danish count doing in the Hamptons?"

Gilley shrugged, but then he said, "There's money here, so he'd be among his own kind, and a certain anonymity. I'd imagine that the members of the royal family are well known among their countrymen. Especially if they're eligible bachelors."

I tapped my lip thoughtfully. "Which, to your point, makes it odd that this ex of Aaron's would dump him without so much as an 'It's not you, it's me' speech. If you knew your boyfriend was connected to royalty and all kinds of influence, would you really want to cut ties so succinctly?"

"What do we know about the girlfriend?" Gilley asked. "I mean, it's hard to imagine someone not caring about those kinds of connections, unless she herself was even better positioned."

It was my turn to shrug. "We know nothing about her," I admitted. "I didn't think to ask."

Gilley closed the lid to his laptop and stood up. "It's probably not relevant to helping, anyway, so maybe we're better off not knowing."

I nodded. "Agreed." Changing the subject, I asked, "What's next on my schedule?"

Gilley offered me a slow blink. "You've already hit the high-light of your workday, sugar."

"Nothing?" I asked. "No calls? No emails to return?"

"Zippo," he replied.

I sighed. Launching a life-coaching business had proven to be a much more arduously slow endeavor than I'd ever expected, and while I now typically had a few clients on the books, it still wasn't enough to fill a full workday.

What was truly frustrating was that I knew that there were so many people out there in need of a little reassurance and life advice, but it was hard to get any of them to reach out to me for help. Thus, my client list was still relatively small and far less needy than I'd hoped.

"What shall we do with the rest of the workday?" I asked with a hint of exasperation.

Gilley scooted his chair in. "Let's go look at puppies," he said.

I laughed, thinking he was joking. Then I realized he was serious. "Where are we going to look at puppies, exactly?"

"The Southampton Animal Shelter, duh," he said.

I thought about telling Gilley to temper his enthusiasm until he'd had a chance to talk to his husband about bringing a dog into their lives, but then I decided there was no harm in looking. "Okay," I said.

Gilley clapped his hands happily and came around the desk to offer me his arm. I took it, and out the door we went.

Several hours later, as I was slipping into my dress, I heard the front door open and Gilley call out for me. "Yoo-hoo! Cat? Where you at?"

"Up here!" I called back.

Quick footsteps up the stairs suggested that Gilley hadn't lost any of the enthusiasm he'd arrived home with.

I pulled my dress up over my shoulders and settled it around me before he came through the doorway.

"Hey!" he said, slightly out of breath.

"Hey, yourself," I replied. Then I turned my back to him and said, "Would you help me with the zipper?"

Gilley obliged, and I could feel his hot breath on the back of my neck. I doubted the run up the stairs was totally to blame. "You seem excited," I said.

"I just finished the paperwork," Gilley said. I turned around and saw his face flush with happiness.

I reached out and grabbed his hands. "Congratulations, Papa. When does the little tyke come home?"

"Hopefully soon! Like, maybe tomorrow or the day after, which, I suppose, is okay, because it'll give me time to buy everything I need to welcome him home."

Gilley's face was aglow with happiness, and I knew exactly how magical the trip to the shelter had been for him. I was still trying to wrap my own mind around the kismet moment when, after walking up and down the aisle of adoptable dogs, Gilley had come to a pen where a small dark silver Staffordshire terrier with gorgeous blue eyes sat. The dog had immediately started wagging his tail and gazing up at Gilley while wearing—swear to God—a huge smile. Gil had stopped in his tracks and squatted down to the dog's level. There was something that passed between them in that moment, some sort of knowing, which caused goose bumps all up and down my arms. It was a sort of acknowledgment, like Gilley and the pup were destined for each other, and now that they were face-to-face, the pup actually seemed to recognize Gilley as his new human.

"This one," Gilley whispered, and that was when the pup walked forward to lick at Gilley's hands through the steel-mesh door of the pen.

The woman who'd been escorting us through the area came a little closer to gaze at Gilley and the pup. With a chuckle, she said, "You won't find a more lovable dog than Spooks."

Gilley and I turned to look at the woman, with mouths agape.

"What'd you say his name was?" I asked.

The woman—Peg, according to her name tag—pointed to the pup and said, "That's Spooks. His name when he came to the shelter was Ghost, but we changed it to Spooks because we thought it'd be cuter and make him more adoptable. Oh, but don't worry. You can change it again to whatever name you'd like. He won't mind."

Gilley and I then exchanged a look of our own, and I shook my head in wonder. Gilley had spent more than a decade as a ghostbuster, and he and his partner M.J. had come to call the ghosts they hunted "spooks," so finding such a perfect mascot seemed to be an incredibly magical thing.

"His name is perfect," Gilley said as he got to his feet. Then he added, "And I definitely want to adopt him."

We came home with a whole packet full of information, and a link to the online adoption forms. Peg had promised that as soon as Gilley filled out all the forms and submitted them, she'd make sure to process his application and check all his references quickly, in order to get Spooks to his new, "furever" home.

"It'll be exciting to have a bundle of love around here," I remarked as I reached for my wrap and clutch. "And I know you'll feel less lonely while Michel is off on his photo shoots."

Gilley bounced on his feet. "True, true," he said, but then his expression changed, and I saw a hint of worry in the creases around his eyes.

"Gil?" I asked.

"Yeah?"

"You mentioned Spooks to Michel, didn't you?"

"Not yet, but I will."

My eyes widened. "You mean you haven't even called or texted him?"

Gilley glanced down at his suit coat and pretended to pick a piece of lint off the lapel. "I need to figure out a gentle way of telling him."

"A gentle way to tell him? Why? Does he not like dogs or something?"

Gilley cleared his throat uncomfortably. "Something like that."

My jaw dropped. Michel was the gentlest of souls. If I could peg anyone for a dog lover, it would be Michel. "He doesn't?" I asked.

Gilley shrugged. "He likes little dogs, but when he was ten, a Rottweiler bit him on the leg and cheek, and he had to have surgery. He still has the scars."

I thought of Michel's handsome face and recalled the very small divot to his left cheek.

"Yikes," I said. Spooks was on the small side of medium for a dog, but his head was large. And while he certainly wasn't Rottweiler size, as he weighed only about forty-five pounds or so, I could see how he could be a little intimidating to someone who'd had a terrifying experience as a child.

"What if Michel says no?" I said, hating that I had to ask Gilley the question I knew he was dreading Michel's answer to.

"Spooks is my dog," Gilley said firmly, and it wasn't lost on me that he was already claiming ownership. And then his voice turned bitter. "Besides, he's never here, so he doesn't get a lot of say about it."

I bit my lip. I'd been married for almost twenty years before my ex-husband began an affair that led to our divorce. In those two decades I'd learned that marriage sometimes meant depriving yourself of the things you needed to live your fullest, happiest life. It was a trade-off, really. On the one hand, you received love and support. On the other hand, you sometimes had to give up something that your heart really wanted, all to keep the delicate balance of the partnership intact.

So, I understood Gilley's position, but I worried what that hard stance would do to a relationship that was already showing significant signs of strain.

I moved over to lay a hand on Gilley's arm. "Listen," I began. "I know you've already fallen hard for Spooks, and I will support wholeheartedly your efforts to claim him—even if it means adopting Spooks for you—but, Gilley, before you talk to Michel, just try to see it from his point of view. It might take him a minute or two to adjust to the idea, so give him that time before you dig in your heels, okay?"

Gilley sighed and nodded almost reluctantly. "The instant I saw him, Cat, I *knew* he was my dog. So, yeah, I'm a skosh concerned that Michel is going to give me a hard time about it."

"Then say that to Michel," I suggested. "Tell him about that immediate connection, and hopefully, he'll understand."

Gilley pushed a weak smile to his lips. "We should go," he said.

"We should," I agreed, feeling a bubble of excitement. "I'm so glad we're doing this. I've been dying to see this show!"

Little did I know in that moment that someone else was about to die for the show too. . . .

Chapter 3

We arrived at Guild Hall, home to the John Drew Theater, after a simply scrumptious meal and lively conversation. Gilley's mood had been practically giddy by the time we arrived for dinner, and the maître d' had complimented him on his choice of suit. The walk to our table had also turned a few heads, which Gilley had eaten up like free beer at a monster-truck rally. Our dinners had both been absolutely delicious, which had only added to the magic of the evening.

I had held off telling Gilley how good our seats were and delighted in his expression when the usher led us to the front-row-center seats at the foot of the stage. I felt so relieved and happy that Gilley was having such a wonderful day. He deserved it, and the change in him since that morning was readily apparent.

"I'm so excited to see the gorgeous Yelena Galanis giving it to the fat cats here in East Hampton," he gushed. "Practically everywhere I go, people are talking about who they think the twelve are."

"I wonder who we'll recognize," I said.

Neither Gilley nor I ran in any of the same social circles that many of my socialite peers did. I didn't exactly care for the "high-society" crowd, often finding them excruciatingly dull, materialistic, and shallow.

COACHED IN THE ACT

I did have a few friends in the area, of course, including Sunny and Shepherd, but most of my friends kept to the outskirts of the Hamptons' "in" crowd.

"Supposedly, Tucker McAllen was her first lover," Gilley said, which I'd also heard. "And Reese told me today that there's a rumor going around that Joel Goldberg was Lover Number Four."

Tucker McAllen was a big deal around town. The New York real estate developer owned several high-rises in the Big Apple and was always in the society papers. Gilley and I had actually had a brief encounter with him at a local eatery when McAllen had been exceptionally cruel to a female server that had dared to put the wrong dressing on his salad, berating her loudly and insulting her intelligence and her looks. McAllen had sent the young woman to the kitchen in tears, and the scene had been such an appalling display that I'd excused myself from Gilley's company, suggesting that I had to visit the powder room, and on the way there I'd stopped by McAllen's table to offer him a withering look and a very soft "Shame on you." He glowered at Gilley and me for the rest of our meal.

In an added display of solidarity with the female server, after I paid our bill and we were about to leave, I managed to intercept the young woman—who was still obviously shaken from her encounter with him—and I offered her a folded hundred-dollar bill in plain view of McAllen. Glaring hard at the insufferable ass, I told her in a loud and commanding voice, "Consider this hazard pay, my friend. And please know that my companion and I think you're doing an absolutely *marvelous* job!"

Next to me, Gilley grinned broadly, then turned to stick out his tongue at the boorish tycoon as we practically flounced out of the restaurant with our noses in the air. It was deliciously satisfying.

And, if I was honest, part of the reason I was looking forward to Yelena's show was that I wanted to take some delight in the dressing-down of Tucker McAllen.

Neither Gilley nor I had ever encountered Joel Goldberg, but we knew of him, and he was an equally big deal around town. Joel came from old money, mostly gold and diamonds. His family were some of the first and finest jewelers in the City, and they'd spent generations catering to the wealthiest citizens there and in the Hamptons. Goldberg had a fine jewelry store in every major town on Long Island, with several boutiques in Manhattan.

In the society papers, he was known to throw the most lavish parties. I had been invited to one a few weeks earlier but had sent my regrets because Shepherd had a low opinion of the man. Shep had told me in confidence that Goldberg had recently had a DWI charge thrown out, even though there was substantial evidence at the hearing that he had been quite intoxicated on the night in question. The incident had happened in East Hampton's jurisdiction, so Shepherd had been well aware of it, and he'd even done a little digging into the presiding judge's background and discovered that the Honorable Judge Waterson was a regular attendee of Goldberg's parties, where the judge's wife had been photographed wearing a new diamond pendant.

"There's a part of me that both loves the idea of this play and is also slightly repulsed by it," I confessed to Gilley.

"Oh, pish," Gilley said with a wave of his hand. "It's perfectly normal to delight in someone else's public shaming as long as that someone is a total turd."

I laughed. "Well, when you put it like that . . ."

At that moment the lights dimmed and the buzz of conversation in the packed theater came to an abrupt halt. For several seconds nothing happened, causing a palpable expectant and excited vibe to flitter across the audience. Finally, a single spotlight appeared, shining bright but empty on the center of the stage, and the excited tension in the audience ratcheted up a notch.

More seconds ticked by, and Gilley and I exchanged a look of confusion, and Gil even lifted his wrist to mimic looking at his watch. Where was the star?

Just when a low murmur began to hum out from the audience, the unmistakable sound of heels clicking against a wood floor reverberated across the stage.

I looked toward the source of the sound, but the bright spotlight made the background all the darker, and it was impossible to see anyone approaching.

And then the sound of clicking heels stopped, and more expectant seconds ticked by, until finally, the spotlight moved quickly—almost violently—several feet to land squarely on a statuesquely shapely woman in a dramatic pose, with her chin lifted and one arm raised high overhead while the other rested demurely on a hip jutted out just so.

Gilley gasped, as did many members of the audience. The sight of her standing under the spotlight was like watching the birth of a goddess.

Yelena's floor-length, sequined blush-pink dress was scintillatingly revealing, allowing her ample décolletage to bulge from the deep V at the neckline. A slit up the side from floor to hip allowed for one gorgeous leg to peek out from all that sparkling fabric. And while she stood still as a statue in that dramatic pose, her dress shimmered under the light, making it appear like a living thing adoringly wrapping itself around a celestial being.

"Oh, my goddess . . . ," Gilley whispered breathlessly.

"Indeed," I whispered back.

I'd had no idea that Yelena Galanis was such a vision, and just looking at her, I could understand why so many men reportedly fell at her feet.

I was about to say as much to Gilley when Yelena's extended arm floated down to her side, and her chin dropped, along with her gaze. It settled on us, her audience, and I felt myself subconsciously sitting a little straighter in my seat.

Gilley also shifted. Glancing at him sideways, I saw he was bug eyed, staring up at Yelena, totally entranced. In that moment, I'm rather ashamed to admit, I felt a small needle of jealousy thread its way into the pit of my stomach.

It wasn't that I had any romantic designs on Gil. . . . It was more. . . . Well, he usually wore that particular look for *me*. Not all the time, but sometimes when I'd dolled myself up extra special, he would swoon appreciatively, and it always filled me with such a lovely little ego boost.

And a further look back to Yelena told me she seemed to sense Gilley's adoration, because I swear she looked directly at him, the corners of her lips lifting in a knowing smile.

My eyes narrowed involuntarily, but I quickly pushed the expression back to neutral, just in case Gilley took his eyes off Yelena for two seconds to glance my way. I didn't want him to see the hurt and envy etched onto my face.

I needn't have worried. Gilley seemed to sense his connection with Yelena, and he leaned forward toward her and nodded. She blinked slowly, demurely, then took a step closer toward the audience.

"Lover Number One," she said, her voice low and smoky à la Kathleen Turner, "was from the mean streets of Lower Manhattan."

The audience chuckled appreciatively. Gilley giggled loudly and squirmed in his seat. Yelena came closer still, and I could see her very clearly now under the glare of the spotlight. Her long black hair shimmered in the brightness, and her delicate nose wrinkled a little distastefully when she spoke of Lover Number One, whom we all knew was Tucker McAllen.

"His trust fund was built by the timber industry," she continued drolly, holding a microphone up toward her lips, and then she turned her palm over, as if to inspect her nails. "His love-making . . . was not." Yelena let the microphone fall forward limply, and the audience roared, with Gilley laughing loudest of those around us as he also clapped his hands in glee.

And yes, even I chuckled. Still something about it felt a tiny bit shameful.

"We met at an art show," Yelena went on, swinging the microphone back to her hand while continuing to study her nails. "He liked my dress. I liked his car. He told me he called his mother twice a week, and I told him, 'What an odd name to call your mother. . . .'"

Again, the audience erupted in laughter. I giggled again, this time a little easier.

"Lover Number One was also quite the connoisseur. In par-ticular, he loved all things French . . . *du vin, la bouffe, l'art, la culture, l'architecture, les French fries, le milkshake, l'hamburger, les McDonald's* . . ."

Yelena winked at the audience, and her hand then made a curving motion out away from her trim stomach to indicate that Lover Number One had had a belly.

Gilley squealed and slapped his knee. He was eating Ye-lena's act up. It was, I thought, deliciously gossipy, but I didn't know. . . . There was something a bit too wicked about laugh-ing at McAllen so publicly. Even though he'd been absolutely wretched to that server, laughing at his expense like this didn't feel as satisfying as I had thought it would. Instead, it almost felt like we were stooping to his level.

Yelena carried on, telling us all the naughty things she'd learned about Lover Number One, winding her way through their three-month relationship and sparing him no expense. Her humor was deft. She could deliver a punch line with such casual ease that if your mind drifted for a moment, you'd be out on the joke.

Ten minutes later she'd thoroughly emasculated Lover Number One, and I had stopped giggling. I found her act more cruel than humorous, but all around me there were peals of laughter. As I glanced around at the audience, I could see people here and there mouthing, "Tucker McAllen," to each other and nodding agreeably. It was obviously no secret whom they were laughing at, and it was a bit disturbing, actually.

"Lover Number Two," Yelena announced, "had a thing for fast cars, loud music, loose women, and big money, honey."

A murmur of anticipation spread through the crowd. Yelena road out a pregnant pause, gleaming at the audience as she continued to cast her spell. "He spent his days at the house on the hill," she said, giving us another juicy clue. "Looking down his nose at all the fools that bought his act. He wasn't born into money, but he worked the phone and always came away with a generous donation or two all the same."

"A congressman," Gilley said, leaning over to whisper in my ear.

I nodded. "That'd be my guess too."

"He spent his nights cheating at cards and commitments, working his way through the wives of close friends," Yelena went on.

Gilley joined the audience's chorus of "Ooh."

"And I . . . ," Yelena said, adding another lengthy pause, "worked him out of a new Lexus and a pair of diamond earrings."

For emphasis, she offered the audience a little hip bounce and flicked her hair with a wave of her hand, exposing the bling in question.

Again, I shifted uncomfortably. I didn't like the fact that she felt so entitled to cheat men out of things. Even if those men were cads. It just didn't sit well with me.

Still, I seemed to be the only one who didn't find it amusing. The audience appeared to hang on her every word as Yelena wound her way through the sordid details of their fling.

She then moved on to Lover Number Three. "Lover Number Three thinks this show is about him, don't you? Don't you? Don't you, Lover Number Three?"

Yelena giggled as she moved over to put her mic in the stand and fluff her long black hair for effect. Blinking her eyes demurely at us, she continued. "Speaking of love, Number Three never met a camera he didn't love. Or a mirror. Or his image in any reflective surface he passed by. He spent more time preening than I do. And, honeys, let me tell you, I spend a *lot* of time preening!"

There were murmurs in the audience; clearly, everyone around us thought it was someone different. And, for his part, Gilley was pitched forward, his brow knit in concentration, as if he could tweeze out the identity of Number Three from just a few clues.

"Now, Lover Number Three is a man of traditional values, and by that I mean he enjoys a neat house, a good meal, and a boisterous romp in the hay, but only if the woman does all the work. Which is odd for a man that likes to throw his weight around so much." Yelena pretended to have an extended belly again, and she swiveled her hips back and forth, stumbling a little, as if her belly was so heavy, it was creating momentum and causing her to nearly trip.

Gilley kicked his feet as he squealed with laughter. I forced a smile, but inside I was wincing.

Yelena giggled again, clearly enjoying herself. "Ahhh, and if he were here, my dear, sweet, gossip-loving friends, he'd probably lead his introduction with a 'Do you know who I am?'"

She'd lowered her voice to quote the man and added more of the stumbling belly act, and people were laughing and laughing at her antics. Gilley looked over at me, eager to share the boisterous time he was having. I forced a laugh and nodded, intent on not spoiling his fun.

She carried on this way for another grueling half hour or so, winding her way through Lovers Four and Five and Six. Each sordid affair seemed to be worse than the last, and I stopped laughing long before Yelena waved to us, announced the inter- mission, and walked offstage to the beat of some loud, sassy music, which continued to play even as the lights flickered on and Gilley and I got up with the rest of the audience to move out into the lobby for the fifteen-minute break.

"Isn't she a hoot?" Gilley asked when we had cleared the doors into the lobby and were away from the loud music, which made it easier to speak to each other.

"She's something," I muttered, rubbing my temples. I'd de- veloped a headache during Lover Number Four, and that last wave of music ushering us out into the lobby to purchase a drink or a snack hadn't helped.

"You don't look happy. What's wrong, Cat?"

I sighed. "She's mean."

Gilley's chin pulled back in surprise. "Duh. It's what makes it all so delicious."

I shrugged. "It's just not my cup of tea."

Gil seemed to study me for a long moment. "You're probably thinking about your first days here, when you were the topic of gossip around here, am I right?"

I shrugged again. "I suppose much of it might be that, but overall, I just find her to be a narcissistic, gold-digging, self- involved bully."

"Gee, Cat, don't hold back. Tell me how you really feel."

I smiled, and my hand went to my temple again. "I'm sorry, lovey. I've been pushing back against a terrible headache for the past half hour."

"Do you have anything for it?"

"Not with me. There's a pharmacy down the street, next to the coffee shop, though."

Gilley eyed his watch, and I knew he was nervous about missing any part of Yelena's second act. "If we hustle, we can probably make it back in time."

I shook my head. "No, Gilley. I'll go. You get yourself a little wine before you head back to your seat."

"But, Cat, if you come back after the second act starts up again, they won't let you in."

"I know," I said, eyeing him intently.

It took Gilley a moment, but he suddenly understood. "You don't want to watch the second half."

"Not particularly."

Gil frowned. "Well then, I'll definitely come with you."

I put my hands on his shoulders to block him. "No, my friend. You're loving the show. I've just got too much of a headache to put off taking something for it any longer. If I don't make it back here in time, I'll wait for you in the coffee shop next to the pharmacy, okay?"

Gilley arched a brow. "Really? You think I'd actually be self-ish enough to let you wait in a coffee shop with a splitting headache while I'm back here enjoying the show?"

I grinned, genuinely amused. "In point of fact, I do."

Gilley chuckled. "You know me too well." But then he sobered and let out a sigh. "I'd feel too guilty, Cat. Let me come with you."

I took his chin in my hand and kissed his cheek. "My sweet Gilley, we're out on the town tonight for you, and just because I've got a blistering headache doesn't mean I should ruin your good time. No, you go back and catch the second act. If this is intermission, then it's only going to be another hour and fifteen minutes. I'll be fine just down the street."

"You're sure?" Gilley pressed.

"Positive," I assured him. Then, after squeezing his chin one last time, I turned and headed toward the exit.

In short order I made my way to the pharmacy, bought some pain-relief tablets and a *Town & Country* magazine, and headed outside. I looked first toward the theater and took note of the

time on my phone. I still had about three minutes left to get inside and to my seat, and I knew that it'd be close but that I
could make it, and still, I just couldn't muster up the will.

So instead, I walked the ten feet to the coffee shop—cutely
named Thanks a Latte. Entering the shop, I was immediately
charmed by the smell of baked goods and an eclectic decor.

Only one table appeared to be occupied, by a couple in their
late teens, huddled in the corner booth by the window. They
were sitting side by side, displaying lots of PDA, with eyes only
for each other.

I squashed an amused smile and looked away. *Young love is
adorable.*

After I ordered a signature latte, a bottled water, and a rasp-
berry scone, I settled down at one of the many open tables in
the middle of the shop, close to the door so that Gilley would
spot me immediately when he came to find me. After popping
two of the headache-relief tablets, I eased back in the chair,
opened up the magazine, and took a sip of the latte, prepared
for a luxurious hour spent quietly perusing the pretty pictures
and stately homes of *Town & Country*.

No sooner was I feeling an easing to the set of my shoulders
than the door opened abruptly, startling me, and in came a man
of short stature, with white, wispy hair and a wild-eyed expression, nearly completely enveloped by a raincoat that was several
sizes too large.

After the door behind him shut, he shuffled toward me a few
paces before glancing over his shoulder back at the door, and
that was when his foot seemed to catch the hem of his raincoat,
and he stumbled forward, then reached out to brace himself
against the table where I sat.

The movement seemed to startle both of us, and as our eyes
met, I asked, "Are you all right?"

"Fine," he squeaked, standing again, but he looked pale and
shaky. He wiped his brow, which was beaded with sweat, and
belatedly, I saw that his hand was smeared with blood.

"Oh, my," I said. "Did you cut yourself?"

He stared at me with those big bug eyes and furrowed brow, so I pointed to his hand.

The man looked down and quickly covered his injured appendage with his other hand. "It's fine!"

I bit my lip, concerned for him, but also fearful of making him even more agitated. "All right," I said gently. "Would you like me to get you a coffee or a bottled water?"

The elder gentleman was quivering and pale, and I was fearful he was having some sort of episode.

"No," he said, again glancing back toward the door. "I just need to get to the men's room."

It was my turn to look over my shoulder, where a sign above a dark hallway said RESTROOMS.

Pointing to the sign, I said, "I believe it's that way."

He gave a sort of half-hearted nod, glanced back behind him one last time, then headed toward the men's room.

I hoped he'd be okay and vowed to ask him to sit a spell with me so I could assess if he needed some kind of medical assistance. He'd been awfully pale, and I'd noted that his whole body had seemed to be trembling. I worried that he could be having either a heart attack or a stroke.

After getting up from my seat, I approached the counter to get another bottle of water which I intended to offer to the gentleman when he came out of the men's room, but the store's barista was nowhere to be found. Leaning over the counter, I could hear some rustling behind a curtain leading to what was likely the stockroom. At last, the curtain parted, and out came the young man who'd waited on me, carrying an armload of coffee cups in all three sizes.

"Did you need something?" he asked when he paused to set down the cups on the counter.

"A bottled water when you get a moment," I said, fishing out a five-dollar bill from my purse.

The barista got the water, took my five, and gave me change.

I went back to the table and waited for the stranger to come out, but minutes ticked by, and he didn't appear.

I bit my lip again, anxious to know if he was all right, and after another five minutes had passed, I approached the counter again and got the barista's attention.

"Excuse me," I said. The young man turned around from where he was wiping down the espresso machine to raise a brow in question. "A gentleman came into the shop about fifteen minutes ago and headed to the men's room. He hasn't come out yet, and when he went in, he looked unwell. Would you mind checking on him to see if he's all right?"

The barista blanched, and I could tell that, after hearing an older gentleman had been in the men's room for fifteen minutes, that was likely the last thing he wanted to do. "Aw, man," he said. "I hope he didn't get sick in there. I just cleaned it."

I nodded, even though it irritated me to hear the young man complain when I'd just expressed concern over a patron in the restroom. Still, he moved from behind the counter and headed toward the hallway leading to the restrooms.

I went back to my seat but turned so I could see one or both of them come out.

The barista appeared again and approached me. "There's no one in there," he said.

I blinked in surprise. "There isn't?"

"No, it's empty."

"You're sure?"

"Yes, ma'am. No one's in there."

"All right. Thank you for checking," I said.

Once the barista was back behind the counter and busy with his side work again, I slipped from the seat and quietly made my way to the hallway leading to the restrooms. It wasn't well lit, but I easily found the men's room door, first on the left. After pushing it open, I peeked inside. A vacant row of urinals and two empty stalls with the doors open showed me clearly that the barista was right. And there was no window through which the stranger could've climbed out of, either—not that he would've, but still the thought did cross my mind.

After backing out of the men's room, I made my way a bit farther down the hall to the ladies' room and pushed that door open as well.

Four empty stalls and two vacant sinks were all that were in there. While backing out of the ladies' room, I glanced a bit farther down the hallway, and there I saw a door marked with a faded EXIT sign.

I walked to the door, checked it for any OPEN ONLY IN AN EMERGENCY signs—there were none—and pushed it open, revealing a darkened alley.

A shudder went through me as I looked up and down the alleyway. It was creepy back here, but there was no sign of anyone either coming or going.

Logically, I knew that the elderly man had either bypassed the men's room and exited out the back or had used the facilities and exited out the back without my seeing him go. My back had been to the hallway leading to this exit, so it wasn't surprising that I hadn't seen him leave.

Still, something really bothered me about the entire interaction. He'd seemed to be in such a heightened state of anxiety, and when I'd looked into his eyes, there'd been the unmistakable note of fear there.

With a shudder, I closed the door and decided there was nothing more I could do for the poor man. I had no idea who he was or where he'd gone, so worrying over him was an effort in futility.

Yet, as I made my way back toward my seat, I couldn't help but worry over him. It was an unsettling encounter all around.

When I came out from the hallway, I was surprised to see a bustle of energy toward the front door. Patrons were streaming in and buzzing loudly with conversation. All were well dressed—

clearly the theater crowd—but one glance at my phone to check the time told me that Yelena was only about thirty minutes into her second act.

"What the devil . . . ?" I muttered after I reached my chair. Just then I saw someone waving out of the corner of my eye.

I glanced toward the motion and saw Gilley pushing his way through the crowd over to me, his face flush with excitement. "Cat!" he began.

"What's happened?"

"Yelena's dead!"

I gripped the top of my chair to steady myself from the shock of that announcement. "Dead? What do you mean, she's dead?"

"She's been murdered!" Gil shouted above the din of the crowd.

"*Murdered?*" I repeated. "How is that possible?"

"She was stabbed backstage during intermission!" Gilley exclaimed, still clearly excited by this turn of events. "Someone murdered her, then fled the scene!"

I stared at him with big wide eyes before looking over my shoulder toward the hallway leading to the exit. "Oh, my God," I said, focusing on Gilley again. "I think I just met the murderer!"

Chapter 4

"What?" Gilley shrieked. Several people nearby glanced our way.

I grabbed up my belongings from the table and took Gilley by the hand, and then we weaved our way through the crowd to the exit and outside. I walked with him a little way down the street until we were sufficiently out of earshot.

"Tell me everything you know," I instructed him.

"Hold on," he said, his hands finding his hips in a defiant posture. "Tell me what you meant by 'I think I just met the murderer!'"

I clenched my teeth, impatient to hear the details of what'd happened at the theater. "I will, but you tell me what you know first."

Gilley scowled at me, but he complied. "Right after the audience was seated for the second act, there was some kind of commotion that we could hear coming from backstage. After another lengthy pause, a guy showed up onstage and told us to sit tight because there'd been an incident and the police were on their way.

"One or two people got up and tried to leave the theater, but they were stopped by the ushers. It was all really unnerving until your main squeeze appeared onstage and told us that the star of the show had been violently attacked and that the police would need to get everyone's name and phone number before they'd be allowed to leave."

"He said she'd been *attacked*? How do you know she was actually murdered?"

"Shepherd spotted me, front row, center, and called me up onstage. He gave me the skinny, or as much as he knew, and then he asked where you were, and told me to come find you and take you home—*immediately*, as he put it."

"Why the rush to get me home?" I asked.

Gilley shifted on his feet. "Um, mind you, these are his sentiments and not mine, but he said that he wanted me to take you home immediately because right now there's a killer on the loose, and when trouble comes to town, you're usually at the center."

I scowled. "That's not true."

Gilley gave me a doubtful look. "This coming from the woman who just said to me that she thought she met the murderer."

I growled. "Fine. I just hate it when he's right."

"Me too," Gilley said, but I could tell he was still mocking me a little. "Now, come on, fess up. What makes you believe you've already met the killer?"

I explained my strange encounter with the gentleman at the coffee shop, and Gilley's eyes bugged wide. "Wow. He actually had blood on his hands?"

"Hand. Just the one, but truly, Gilley, the more I think about it, the more it could've been quite innocent. I mean, he was fairly short and somewhat frail to be a killer, now that I think about it. Maybe he cut himself and didn't realize it until I pointed it out to him."

"How much blood was there?"

I bit my lip. His hand and nail beds had been smeared with it. "Quite a bit, actually."

"Whoa," Gilley said. "And you say that he kept looking back over his shoulder? Like he was nervous about being caught for the crime?"

"Well, I didn't say *that*, but yes, he did seem preoccupied with who might be coming through the door at any moment. And he *did* slip out the back door into an empty alley, which probably was so that he wouldn't be seen or further questioned by me."

"Cat, I think you have to tell Shepherd about this."

"But what if I'm wrong, Gilley? What if this man was just having some sort of medical episode and is innocent of any crime?"

"What if he wasn't, though?" Gilley replied. "I mean that truthfully, Cat. What if he really *is* the killer?"

I sighed heavily, feeling the weight of the responsibility to report what I'd seen to Shepherd, but concerned that I might spark unwarranted suspicion of an innocent man.

"Listen," Gilley said, obviously sensing my indecision. "If this guy with blood on his hand who was acting all suspicious had nothing to do with Yelena's murder, then Shepherd can clear him quickly and move on to another possible suspect."

I weighed the argument out in my head one more time, then said, "Okay, Gil. Let's go find Shep."

Gilley glanced across the street, where the crowd was still snaking its way out of the theater's exits. "Good luck getting through that," he said.

After taking out my phone, I placed the call to Shepherd. It rang twice and went to voice mail. "He's not picking up," I said while the outgoing voice-mail message played.

"He's probably really busy working the case. Text him that you need to talk and it's urgent."

I hung up the call and texted Shepherd, then set the phone in my open palm so that Gilley and I could watch the screen for any telltale bubbles with his response. We waited at least two minutes in silence, and nothing but a "delivered" notification indicated that my text had gotten to Shepherd.

"Jeez, what's taking so long?" Gilley whined.

"He's probably ignoring his phone."

Gilley again looked across the street. "The crowd's starting to thin out. Should we head over and try to find him?"

"Yes," I said and took up Gilley's hand again to cross the street, now determined to tell Shepherd what I'd seen.

Gilley and I checked for traffic before trotting across the street to the theater, which was now blocked off by yellow crime-scene tape and at least half a dozen EHPD officers, who were keeping onlookers at bay.

I led us straight to a female officer, smiling as I neared her. "Officer Labretta," I said, recognizing her from the station.

"Catherine Cooper," she replied coolly. "What're you doing here?"

I pointed to the theater. "Gilley and I caught the first act, and I may have seen something suspicious at the coffee shop down the street during intermission that Shepherd would want to know. Can you ask him to come out here and meet us? Just for a minute?"

"You saw something?" she asked. "You mean, related to the homicide?"

"Maybe," I said. "Either way, it was pretty suspicious."

Labretta nodded and raised her radio, then turned slightly away to speak into it. I tried to make out what was said, but a lot of it was in police code and somewhat garbled.

Turning back to me, she put away her radio and said, "He'll be right out."

Sure enough, Shepherd appeared a few minutes later. He looked stressed and not exactly pleased to see me. "I'm working," he said quietly when he got to us. "So, if this some sort of a social visit . . ."

Gilley sucked in a breath, and I raised my brow and scoffed

at Shepherd. "You're kidding me, right?" I snapped. "Do you *really* think I'd interrupt a homicide investigation simply to say, 'Howdy-high-ho!' to my boyfriend?"

Shepherd winced. "Sorry," he said. "That crime scene has me on edge. I didn't mean to take it out on you."

But I was still a little miffed. I'd come over here with the sincerest of intentions, and it hurt my feelings that Shepherd would think me so self-involved. "Whatever," I said moodily.

Shepherd rubbed his face with his hand. It seemed like he was frustrated that I was still miffed. With a sigh, he said, "How about you tell me why you called me out here?"

"I saw something that looked very suspicious," I said curtly.

"Suspicious?"

"Yes."

"Suspicious how?"

I pointed to the coffee shop a block down the street. "I was sitting at Thanks a Latte, waiting for Gilley to finish up watching the second act of Yelena's show, when a disheveled man, who appeared to be upset, came into the shop, stumbled at my table, then dashed into the men's room before heading out the back door before I could question him further."

Shepherd blinked at me, then rubbed his face with his hand. "That's it?" he said. "Cat, are you kidding me with this?"

Again, I was taken aback by his tone, and my defenses went up. Crossing my arms, I adopted a clipped and curt tone. "Yeah, Detective, that's *exactly* what I'm doing. Kidding you. A woman was brutally murdered this evening, and I couldn't *wait* to prank you about it!"

"Cat?" Gilley said next to me.

"What?" I growled. I was in *no* mood for Gilley to take Shepherd's side.

Gilley cleared his throat. "Um . . . you forgot to mention the man had blood on his hand."

Shepherd had been wearing a scowl since I snapped at him,

but his brow lifted the minute Gilley offered up that additional clue.

"Wait a second, Cat, you saw *blood* on his hands? How much blood?"

"His left hand was smeared with it. When I initially noticed it, I thought he'd injured himself."

"Was it dried blood?"

"No," I said, making a face. "It seemed to be . . . fresh."

"And he went into the restroom?" he said, glancing down the street toward Thanks a Latte, which now had a line out the door.

I turned to look too. "Yes," I said, gulping a little.

"Damn," he swore through gritted teeth before looking to his left at Officer Labretta. Shepherd whistled loudly to get her attention, and she hurried over. Pointing to the coffee shop, he barked, "That's a possible crime scene. Take Winnacker, get those people out of there, and secure that entire area."

"Yes, sir," she said and ran to get another officer just down from where she'd been standing.

Shepherd again rubbed his face, and I could see the strain of such an unruly crime scene, one spreading out to two separate locations, with literally hundreds of possible suspects, was beginning to take a toll on him.

Still, he flipped out a little notebook he carried and a pen and asked, "Give me a description of this guy, in as much detail as you can remember."

I spent a few moments with my eyes closed, recalling every detail of the man in my memory, and described him as well as I was able to.

"You're sure he was only about five feet six or seven?" he asked me when I'd finished.

"Yes," I said. "He was right around Gilley's height." For emphasis, I looked at Gilley, who was trying to stand as straight and tall as he could in an effort to squeeze a little more height out of himself.

"I'll have you know that I'm only an inch under the average," he said.

Shepherd ignored him and kept his focus on me. "And you used the word *frail*. Did you mean *thin*?"

"Yes," I said. "There wasn't much to him. Just a little old man in an oversized raincoat."

"Did the coat have any blood on it?"

"No," I said.

Shepherd snapped the cover of his notebook shut. "None of that fits with what I've seen of the actual crime scene, Cat."

"No?"

He shook his head. "Yelena was stabbed repeatedly and in quick succession. At least six times, by my count. Believe me when I tell you that that kind of attack takes some brute strength. It also would've left more of a mark on the killer. No way did he leave the scene without a lot of blood on his clothing."

"Could the raincoat have been covering up his clothes?" Gilley asked. We both turned to look at him. "Maybe he grabbed the raincoat from somewhere to cover up the blood on his clothing."

I thought back to the stranger stumbling into the table, and for the life of me, I couldn't remember if the raincoat had been buttoned at the chest or not. It seemed like it should be an easy thing to remember, but all I could see in my mind was the man's extremely stressful expression and the bloody hand.

Finally, I shook my head. "I don't know, guys. I'm sorry, but I don't know if his clothing underneath the raincoat was bloody."

Shepherd sighed. "Okay," he said. "I'll definitely have my CSI guys check it out. For now, you two should go on home, and, Cat, I'll follow up with you later."

"Tonight?" I asked.

He shook his head. "I'm gonna be here for hours, so I won't be over tonight. But I'll make a point of finding you tomorrow, okay?" Shepherd reached out and gripped my hand for a moment. It was, I thought, a half-hearted attempt at an apology for snapping at me earlier.

I wanted to stroke his cheek and hug him, to let him know we were okay, but it wasn't the time or the place for any PDAs. "Sounds good," I said, squeezing his hand.

He let me go and turned to leave, and so did Gilley and I, but then I thought of something and turned back toward his departing form.

"Shep?" I called.

He glanced back at me. "Yeah?"

"Did you tell Sunny?"

The look of surprise on Shepherd's face at the mention of his sister told me he hadn't. "Damn it," he swore, closing his eyes, as if to rein in any further commentary. When he seemed more composed, he opened his lids and said, "I haven't. This is gonna kill her. She and Yelena go way back. They've been really close friends since college."

"Do you want Gilley and me to go to her place and break it to her?" I asked next. I hated the thought of Sunny being alone when she got the news, and there was no way Shepherd could leave the crime scene to go break the evening's tragic turn to his twin.

"Would you?" he asked hopefully.

"Yes," I said. "Absolutely. I'll text you to let you know how she's doing, and we'll stay with her until Darius gets home."

"He's in L.A.," Shepherd said, a look of disapproval crossing his features.

"Sunny told me earlier that he'd be home tonight."

The tension in Shepherd's shoulders eased a bit. "Good," he said. "If you could stay with her until he gets home, I'd appreciate it."

"Consider it done," I said.

Shepherd offered me a grateful smile and then turned back toward the theater. Gilley and I resumed our walk across the street, and I suddenly realized that Gilley was rather quiet, a pained look on his face.

"You okay?" I said to him.

"Hmm?" he asked. I'd obviously roused him from his troubled thoughts.

"Are you okay?" I repeated.

"I'm thinking about Sunny," he said. "And I'm wondering how we're going to find the words to tell her that her dear friend was just murdered."

I sighed heavily. When I'd volunteered to deliver the news, I don't think I'd thought it through as thoroughly as I should've. "I think that we should approach it with great care," I said.

"Duh," Gil replied.

"What I mean is, I think we should prepare her from the second she opens her door to us. We should say something like, 'Sunny, we have some difficult news to break to you. How about we all go inside and sit down?' and then you can guide her inside to the sofa and hold her hand while I offer her the news."

"I like that," Gilley said. "I mean, I don't *like* it, but I like the approach. We'll be gentle yet truthful, and we'll make sure to stay with her until the hubs gets home."

"Good," I said, feeling relieved that Gilley was along with me on this terrible errand.

By this time, we had reached the other side of the street and were passing by the alley on our way to the parking garage where we'd parked, when I stopped and looked down the length of the darkened alley.

"What?" Gilley asked.

"That's the alley the murderer slipped out the back door into," I said.

"So now he's the murderer?" Gilley said.

I rolled my eyes and, using air quotes, said, "Okay, the 'suspicious person.'"

"Should we check it out?"

"I don't know. It looks creepy."

Gilley pulled his chin back in mock surprise. "*That* looks creepy to you? Pish, gurl. You never would've made it on one of our ghost busts back in the day."

"Nor would I have wanted to. They sounded horrendous."

"You don't know the half of it," he said. "Come on, I'll hold your hand. Let's see if, in his haste to run out the door, he dropped something that could identify him."

I took Gilley's hand, and we crept into the alley.

"Which door is the coffee shop?" he asked.

"I think it's the one down there," I said, pointing a little way down the alley.

"Okay, let's go all the way to the end of this block. It'll let out on the right side of the parking garage, too, so this will end up being a convenient shortcut," Gilley said.

We walked along, and Gilley had the flashlight on his phone pointing toward the ground. Mostly there was just some random garbage, puddles of water, and the foul smell of a full dumpster. We passed the back door to Thanks a Latte, which was clearly marked, and continued on, with only about a quarter of the way left. Neither one of us spoke, and I began to relax, because with Gilley's flashlight, the alley wasn't nearly as creepy as it had seemed at first.

Mostly I couldn't wait to get away from the dumpster smell.

We passed another door, which led to a hardware store, and opposite the door was a tall stack of pallets. Gilley raised his flashlight to flash across the pallets, and I followed the beam as it trailed up the stack of wood. As I was waiting for it to swoop back down to the street, the beam passed over something that didn't belong in the scene.

I gasped.

Gilley made a startled squeaking sound, his beam now to the right of the pallets.

Slowly, he moved it back to the stack, my free hand now

gripping his arm, which had begun to tremble. That was how I knew we'd both seen what I thought we'd seen.

At last the beam landed on a hand that was dangling down and wedged against a torso, which was wedged against the side of the stacked pallets.

Gil and I took an involuntary step back, the beam shaking in a perfect reflection of our mutual fear.

"Hello?" I whispered, unable to make a noise any louder than that.

There was no reply.

"Hello?" Gilley tried to speak a tad bit louder than me.

Still no reply.

My own hand trembling, I moved the arm Gilley was using to hold his phone, and the bright light moved slowly left again, until it came to rest on a blood-soaked raincoat, where it froze, because I froze, and so did Gilley.

That is, we froze until the adrenaline kicked in and we both ran as if our lives depended on it.

It took me a bit to realize that we were also screaming bloody murder (pardon the pun). As we came out into the cross street, we nearly ran headfirst into Officer Labretta, who had probably come running when she heard the screams.

"What's going on!" she yelled, even though we were right in front of her.

Gilley and I both pointed forcefully back toward the alley. I couldn't seem to make my vocal cords work to form words, and neither, it seemed, could Gilley, which was doubly odd as we'd just been screaming at the top of our lungs.

Labretta pulled up her flashlight, blinding us for a moment, but then she swept the beam toward the entrance to the alley. "Someone in there?" she asked.

Gilley and I nodded. Vigorously.

"Are they armed?" she said next.

We both shook our heads. Equally vigorously.

"Did they try to hurt you?" she asked next, her eyes darting from the alley to us for a quick up-down scan, then back to the alley again.

"D-d-d-d-dead," Gilley managed as he once again pointed to the alley.

Labretta's eyes widened. "You saw a *body*?"

We both went back to the vigorous nodding thing, but I managed to add, "B-b-b-blood!"

Labretta unholstered her gun and pointed it, along with the flashlight, at the area behind us. "Anybody else in that alley besides you two?"

We both did the shaking head thing.

Labretta reached for the mic to her radio, which was snapped in place at her shoulder. She spoke in code into it, but I thought she was likely calling for backup. Sure enough, in short order the sound of pounding footsteps approached, and from around the corner emerged two uniformed police officers.

By now I thought I had some of my breathing under control, but I felt the need to clutch Gilley's arm with both of my hands. He wrapped his palm over them and inched closer to me. We were both still trembling, but the nearness of each other was comforting.

Labretta spoke to the two officers off to the side, then motioned to me and Gilley to move toward the brick wall of the building right in front of us. We shuffled over and waited as all three uniforms cautiously approached the alley, their guns drawn and their flashlights on.

Then they disappeared in the dark, but we could see the light of their beams emanating from the alley. We waited for what felt like a very long time, but it was only likely another two or three minutes, and then Labretta emerged, her gun holstered again, and a granite set to her jaw.

"Found him," she said.

Gilley and I squished together a little more.

"I radioed Shepherd. He's on his way over," she said. And then she leaned in toward us and added, "Best brace yourselves. He didn't sound thrilled that you two had found the body."

Neither Gilley nor I said a word in reply, but I saw out of the corner of my eye that Gilley wore an expression that likely matched my own: *Yikes!*

Still, I managed to square my shoulders a bit as Shepherd rounded the corner and stopped short in front of us. "*What* did you two *do?*"

I glared at him. "We used a shortcut on our way to the parking garage and discovered a dead body in an alley," I said sharply, to let him know that I wasn't about to put up with him giving us the third degree.

Shepherd ran his hand down the front of his face—a gesture he'd employed liberally tonight and one I knew he only made when he was particularly frustrated. He then seemed to consider us again and gave a half-hearted nod before leaving us standing there. We then watched as he moved in the direction of the entrance to the alley.

Labretta met him there, and the two disappeared into the darkness together.

"How long do we have to stand here?" Gilley asked.

The wind had picked up, and I was starting to shiver. I had only a simple pashmina to wrap around my bare shoulders.

"Who knows?" I said. There wasn't much more that we could offer the investigation at this point, and I was still somewhat anxious to get to Sunny before she heard the news. It was a little past nine, and I knew that Sunny would be up by now, getting ready to greet her husband when he returned home. I was worried that someone within her friend circle would learn the news and tell her over a phone call or text.

Shepherd reappeared after just a few minutes, wearing black gloves and holding his phone. He approached me and covered the face of the phone with one hand while looking critically at me. "I took a picture," he said. "The guy wasn't wearing any ID. Are you up for taking a look at his face?"

I gulped and braced myself. "Okay," I said.

Shepherd held the phone up to reveal the photo, and although he'd been very careful not to include anything gruesome in the shot, there was still a smudge of blood on the man's chin, and his eyes were half-lidded and staring sightlessly out into space. He was also very, very pale and very, very dead.

I swallowed hard. It was unsettling to look at the image of a dead man, especially one I'd spoken to earlier that night. "That's him," I said. "That's the man I saw in the coffee shop."

Shepherd pulled the phone back and slid it into his pocket. "Sorry you had to see that."

"It's okay," I said. "I understand."

"How're you going to figure out who he is?" Gilley asked.

Shepherd pulled out a small baggie from his other pocket. "He had his key fob on him. I'll have a uni walk around and see if he can find the car by pressing the alarm."

"I do that in the parking lot of the grocery store," Gilley said.

"It's effective," Shepherd replied. Thumbing over his shoulder, he added, "By the looks of it, we think this was a mob hit."

My eyes widened in shock, as did Gilley's. "A mob hit?" we both said.

"Yeah. His throat was cut, right through the carotid, hit-man style. And he's got some money on him."

"Why would having money on him indicate a mob hit?" I asked.

"The money is stuffed into the lining of the raincoat he's wearing. All hundred-dollar bills. Not sure how much he's packing, but it's a lot. We think it's counterfeit—otherwise the hit man would've taken the coat with him after doing the deed."

"Who knew that East Hampton would be such a den of Mafia murderers?" Gilley mused.

I shuddered, thinking how close I'd come to yet *another* Mafia hit man. Or hit woman. Hit person. Still, I couldn't help wondering something, so I asked, "What's the connection to Yelena?"

Shepherd shook his head slowly. "Hell if I know, honey. I've known Yelena for almost twenty years, and never once did her name come up in any investigations into mob activity around here."

"Still, it can't be a coincidence that she was killed within a half hour of this man, right?" I pressed.

"Not in my book, it can't. I'll dig a little into the guy's background once we ID him, to see what I can find out about any connection to her, but right now, these will be two separate investigations."

I shuddered again, feeling cold all over. "Did you need us to stay and give our statements?"

Shepherd's expression turned soft. "No. Sorry. You two should get going. I'll get a statement from you both tomorrow."

"Okay," I said, taking Gilley's hand, ready to leave this horrible scene on this horrible night.

"Hold on a sec," Shepherd said as we turned to go.

We stopped and waited for him to tell us why. Instead, he called out to Labretta, and she hurried out of the alley and over to us.

"Officer Labretta, would you please escort these two to their car and make sure they leave the area safely?"

"Absolutely, sir," she said.

"Oh, and take this with you and see if you can locate the vic's car."

Shepherd offered Labretta the baggie with the key fob, and she took it dutifully. "Yes, sir."

Shepherd then turned his attention back to me, and I offered him a grateful smile as I moved to give him a quick peck on the cheek, but his phone buzzed, and he lifted it out to read the display. "I gotta go," he said quickly. "They think they've found the murder weapon."

I didn't know which murder he was talking about, but after squeezing my arm, he ran past me to jog across the street toward the theater, and that told me it must've been the weapon used to kill Yelena.

Labretta walked us all the way to our car in the parking garage, and we took our leave and were off to break the heart of someone we knew and loved. Little did I know that other hearts would soon be broken too.

Chapter 5

Sunny lived only a few streets over from me, and as we wound our way there, I tried to rehearse the words that I'd need to say to break the terrible news to her as gently as I could.

"I think you should get to the point right away," Gilley suddenly suggested, like he'd been reading my mind. "She's gonna find it weird that we're showing up at her place this late at night, and we don't want her to think that something's happened to her brother."

I nodded. "Great point. There isn't any easy way to say it, though, is there?"

"No," Gilley said. "And Sunny's such a sensitive soul. This is going to be very hard on her."

"What would you say to her?" I asked.

"Well," Gilley replied, taking a moment to think about it. "I suppose I'd tell her that I had news, that it wasn't about Shepherd, but that it was still difficult news to hear. Then I'd ask for us all to sit down, and I'd take her hand and I'd say, 'Sunny, I'm so, so sorry, but your brilliant, talented, gorgeous friend Yelena has left this earth, never to return.'"

My brow furrowed. I liked most of that. "'Left this earth' sounds like she's gone on a space mission."

Gilley nodded and waved his hand poetically. "Crossed the rainbow bridge . . ."

"That makes her sound like a pet."

"Yelena has gone off to meet Jesus. . . ."

I stared at him. "*Was* she Catholic?"

Gilley's brow furrowed. "Okay, how about 'Sunny, your brilliant, talented friend Yelena has been taken from us too soon'? 'She died tonight doing what she loved best, entertaining the masses and bringing laughter and light to this world.'"

"A bit melodramatic, but that's not bad," I said.

Gilley scowled. "Everyone's a critic."

I allowed myself a small smile. "We'll tell her together as gently as we can and be there for as long as she needs us."

"Agreed," Gilley said.

We pulled into Sunny's driveway a short time later and parked near the front door. I noticed an unfamiliar car in the drive.

"Who's that?" Gilley asked.

"It could be the babysitter's car."

"The babysitter?"

"Yes. Sunny was so exhausted this afternoon that she took a sleep aid and made arrangements for Finley to be looked after while she caught some z's. Darius is coming home tonight, and Sunny wanted to be fresh and alert for her husband's arrival."

"Aww," Gilley said. "That's so romantic!"

"It's sweet," I agreed. "But it's not going to be the evening that Sunny had anticipated."

Gilley's expression fell. "Yeah. Almost forgot."

As we began to climb the steps to the front porch, I couldn't help but notice that most of the downstairs lights were on, which hopefully meant that Sunny was up.

Pausing before ringing the bell, I said, "You ready?"

"No, but let's get on with it," Gilley said.

I rang the bell, which had such a happy chime for two guests who were bringing such dark news. As approaching footsteps sounded on the wood floors inside, I squared my shoulders, prepared to keep my emotions in check, but I did take a small step back when the door was then opened to reveal a pretty young woman with a heart-shaped face, deep-set eyes, and long, dark, wet hair. She looked like she had just gotten out of the shower and had dressed quickly in a baggy XL men's sweatshirt and black leggings.

"Hi?" she said, obviously startled by our appearance.

I pushed a smile to my face. "You must be Tiffany," I said.

"I am," she said, a bit surprised, I thought, that I knew her name. "Can I help you?"

"Is Sunny home?" I tried.

"No. She went out."

"She went out?" I said.

"Yeah. I don't know when she'll be back."

"Did she say where she was going?" Gilley tried.

"No."

Gilley offered her his hand. "I'm Gilley Gillespie, and this is Catherine Cooper. We're very good friends of Sunny, and we've both heard marvelous things about you."

"Hi," Tiffany said, and she seemed to relax a bit in the presence of Gilley's charm.

"Tiffany, could Sunny have gone to pick up Mr. D'Angelo?" I asked.

Tiffany shrugged. "I don't know," she said. "She didn't say anything about where she was going when she went out the door."

"She didn't?" I pressed. This was confusing. Why would Sunny not give her sitter any information about where she was going or how long she'd be out?

Tiffany shook her head, shrugged, and said, "I was in the basement playroom with Finley, and I thought I heard footsteps above us in the kitchen and then the sound of the garage door opening and closing, but when I came upstairs to see if Sunny was up and around, she wasn't anywhere in the house, and when I looked in the garage, her car was gone."

"Did you call her?" I asked. This was very strange indeed.

"Yeah, about an hour after she left, 'cause I didn't know when she'd be back, but Sunny left her phone here."

"She . . . she left her phone behind?" Gilley asked, and he was as shocked as I was. What mother of a toddler would leave behind her phone? And if Tiffany's timeline was correct, wouldn't Sunny have realized by now that she'd left it at the house, and come back for it?

In answer to Gilley's question, Tiffany said, "Mm-hmm. I followed the sound of the rings from my call upstairs to the master bedroom. I found her cell phone on the nightstand, and I left it there, but right around nine o'clock it started ringing and pinging like crazy. So many people were calling and texting Sunny that I had to put it on silent so that it didn't wake Finley."

I turned to Gilley. "No doubt word of what happened at the theater has gotten around, and people are calling and texting her."

"Could that be why she left?" Gilley asked me.

"What word's going around?" Tiffany asked innocently, but I wondered if she didn't already have some clue about what'd happened if people had been texting Sunny. Tiffany probably couldn't access Sunny's phone due to the phone's security protocol, but she could've read the first part of the incoming texts.

Instead of answering her question, I asked, "What time did Sunny leave, Tiffany?"

"It was right before I was gonna give Finley his bath and put him to bed, so I think, like, seven thirty or eight. The weird thing is that I swear I heard her come back into the house a little after nine. I was on the treadmill in the workout room." At this admission, Tiffany's face flushed. "They let me use it as long as Finley's sleeping and I have the baby monitor with me," she added quickly. My gaze traveled to her wet hair, and she added, "And they let me shower here too."

"Hold on," Gilley said, blinking as he spoke. "You thought she came back to the house but left again?"

"Yeah. I was only into my second mile when I swear I heard someone in the laundry room, which is next door to their work-out room. It totally creeped me out, but when I went to check, nobody was there, and Sunny's car was still gone from the garage."

"That is creepy," I said.

"Right?" Tiffany agreed. "I mean, I could've imagined it, but I swear that when I passed the laundry room on the way to the workout room, the door was open, but when I went to check to see if Sunny had come back, it was closed. I could be wrong or it could be my imagination again, but it still freaked me out."

"Is Finley sleeping now?" I asked.

"Yeah. He went out like a light. I think he was pretty tired. Sunny said he hadn't been sleeping well, so I made sure to tucker him out in the playroom."

"Good thinking," I said. And then I sighed when I struggled to come up with a plan to track down Sunny.

"We could drive around and see if we spot her car," Gilley suggested, reading my thoughts.

I nodded and glanced at my phone, noted the time was now after ten. "We have no other choice. But where could she be at this hour?"

Gilley shrugged. He had no clue, and Tiffany shook her head as well.

"Are you okay to stay with Finley for another hour or so?" I asked her.

"Sure," she said. "I've got nowhere to be, and I don't have to be up early tomorrow, so I can stay as long as you need. Or until Mr. D'Angelo comes home."

"That's right," I said. "He's due back here any minute. When he gets home, could you have him call my cell?" I offered Tiffany my business card.

She took it and said, "I will. And if Sunny comes back, I'll send you a text."

"Thank you, Tiffany," Gilley said. She was a sweet, earnest young lady. I could see why Sunny trusted her to care for Finley.

"And we'll call you if we find Sunny," I suggested.

Tiffany swiped at her phone and said, "What's your number? I'll send you a text."

We exchanged information and said our goodbyes.

Tiffany went back inside, and Gilley and I made our way to the car. "She's a sweet thing," he said.

"Yes," I agreed. "And she seems to really adore Finley."

Gilley glanced over his shoulder, back at the house. "I swear I've seen her before, though."

"She might live around here," I suggested. "And she's a runner. Maybe you saw her running."

He snapped his fingers and pointed at me. "That's it," he said. "I've seen her out running." As we reached the car, he asked, "Where did you want to start?"

"Gosh, I don't know," I said, my hand on the door handle, as I looked at him over the roof of the car. "Any ideas where she could've gone?"

In answer he said, "Was there anyplace that you liked to go when the boys were with their nanny and you needed a little free time away?"

I smiled, but there was a trace of guilt to go with it. "Target," I said. "I used to go there and just walk the aisles aimlessly for an hour or two. There was something so freeing and luxurious about walking around that huge space, free of the cries and grabbing hands of toddlers."

"Motherhood wasn't your strong suit, was it?" Gilley said with a chuckle.

"Those early days with twins were hard," I admitted. "Let's see, the nearest Target is in Riverhead."

"Ugh," Gilley said. "That's an hour away, Cat."

I glanced again at my phone. "And I think they close at ten, so they've just closed."

"She could be on her way back," he suggested.

"True. Let's do a simple search of the grocery store parking lot and a few of the restaurants that we know Sunny likes to frequent."

"What restaurants are those?" he asked.

"I was hoping you'd know."

He simply shrugged.

"Well, let's start at the grocery store and work our way out from there."

"Okay," he said.

We were just getting into the car when a set of headlights turned into the drive. I held my hand up to block most of the glare and heard Gilley say, "She's home!"

But as the car turned to park next to mine, I could see that it wasn't Sunny, after all. It was Darius.

He took note of the two of us standing next to his car and offered us a little wave before getting out and grabbing his gym bag. The man was soaked with sweat, and he smelled *ripe*.

I could tell that Gilley could smell it, too, because I saw him back up a little.

"Hey, guys!" Darius said, hoisting the gym bag to his shoulder. "Were you keeping my wife company until I got home?"

I closed my door and waited for Gilley to come around the car to stand next to me. He subconsciously waved his hand in front of his nose when he got a strong whiff of Darius, but luckily, he didn't comment on it.

"Hello, Darius," I began. "We actually weren't here to visit. We came to give Sunny some absolutely dreadful news, I'm afraid."

Darius blinked, and his expression turned serious. "Is her brother okay?"

It didn't surprise me that he assumed something had happened to Shepherd. In the past two years, he had been shot twice and had ended up in the hospital both times. "Shepherd's fine," I said, quick to reassure him.

His shoulders sagged in relief, but then he asked, "What's happened, then?"

I looked at Gilley for a moment, trying to decide how to tell Darius about Yelena, but Gilley read that as a cue to spill it to him.

"Yelena was murdered," he said.

Darius blinked, his jaw fell open, and he took a step back, letting the gym bag drop to the pavement. "Yelena?" he repeated, his head shaking back and forth slightly as he took in the news. "Yelena *Galanis*?"

"Yes," I said.

Darius looked from me to Gilley and back again in disbelief. We both stood somberly while he absorbed the news. At last, he said, "When . . . How?"

"Tonight. It happened backstage, during the intermission of her show. She was stabbed by an unknown assailant," I said.

Darius stared at us with even more incredulity for a long moment, his jaw hanging open, and then he looked over his shoulder toward the house. "Did you tell Sunny?" he said hoarsely.

"No," I said. "She's not home."

He turned back to me again, his expression alarmed. "She's not . . ." Darius lifted his wrist to look at the time. "What do you mean, she's not home?"

I pointed to Tiffany's car. "Your sitter is here. Sunny went out around seven thirty, and Tiffany doesn't know where she went."

Darius shook his head some more, and I could tell he was trying to process everything that we'd just told him, and struggling to do so. He then looked over his shoulder at Tiffany's car, before swiveling his gaze back to me. "Did you call her? Did you call my wife and ask her to come home?"

"No," I said. "According to Tiffany, Sunny left her phone in the house."

Darius ran a hand through his hair and widened his eyes. "She *what*?"

I understood his shock. Sunny wasn't the type to leave her phone behind when she went out and left her toddler in the care of a sitter.

"She left her phone behind, Darius," Gilley said softly.

Darius's gaze pivoted to Gilley. "She would've noticed that she left it behind," he said. "She would've come back for it."

"Tiffany thinks Sunny came back to the house around nine so maybe she came in to look for it, couldn't find it, then went back out to see if she'd left it somewhere she'd already been."

That was the only scenario that even half made sense to me.

Darius placed both palms against his eyes, and I could tell he was trying to think and make sense of all the information we'd just given him. He then allowed his hands to drop, bent to pick up his duffel, then hoisted the strap over his shoulder again while also pulling out his phone. Tapping at the screen, he said, "I texted her when my plane landed to let her know I was gonna stop at the gym to get in a quick workout and I'd be getting in a little later than planned. I thought she was napping and that's why she didn't text back. She's been so tired lately."

"Do you know where she might be?" I asked, hoping he'd have some clue.

He started to shake his head again, but then he paused and looked toward the street. "She's been spending a lot of time at the garden of her yoga studio. She took charge of it when the yoga group came together."

"*Her* yoga studio?" Gilley asked.

Darius nodded. "She's one of five owners of a yoga studio in Amagansett. It's called Om Bliss." That was news to me. "Sunny's been working on the garden lately, trying to coax some life into it. Nobody else there cares about it, but it's one of Sunny's pet projects."

"Would she be there at night?" I asked.

Darius shrugged. "Sunny and I both like to unwind in our respective sanctuaries. For me, it's the gym, and for her, it's that garden at the yoga center. If she's not tending to it, she might be meditating or doing a little yoga by candlelight."

"We should head over and see if she's there," I suggested.

Darius nodded, but then he seemed to hesitate. "The only other place she might be is the park."

"Which park?"

Darius scratched at the widow's peak on his forehead. "It begins with an *H*," he said. "It's off of Newtown, in the center of downtown."

"Herrick Park?" Gilley said helpfully.

"Yeah," Darius said, snapping his fingers. "There. Sometimes she hires Tiffany to babysit for her while she drives over there to read for a while. She could've grabbed a book, gone there to read in her car, and nodded off, and that's why she's not back yet or worried about finding her phone."

"That makes sense," I said. Sunny always had a book handy, and I'd once seen her when she was quite pregnant doing just that—sitting in the public lot downtown, just reading in her parked car.

"Darius," I said next, "you go check out the yoga studio, and Gilley and I will try the park."

Darius nodded, then looked again toward the house; he seemed conflicted. "I gotta change," he said, pulling at his clothing. "And check in with the sitter to make sure she's okay staying with Finley."

We'd already done the latter but I understood that he wanted to check in on his son himself and change, which I was all in favor of because the man was a sweaty, stinky mess.

"Understood," I said to him before motioning to Gilley to get back in the car. "Tiffany has my business card. Send a text to my phone so that we can communicate, and if we find her, we'll text you immediately."

"Good," Darius said, opening the passenger door to pull out his carry-on and a guitar case. "I'll get on the road in the next couple of minutes."

I nodded, and Gilley and I left.

"That park isn't far from the office," I said as we got on the road.

"It's about three blocks, actually," Gil said.

I glanced at him, and he explained, "I go there sometimes for lunch when you're out with your man. It's peaceful. I like it."

"How come we've never gone together?" I asked.

"Because it's peaceful, and I like it," Gilley said, his eyelids drooping heavily.

"Ha-ha," I said just as dryly.

At that moment my phone pinged with an incoming text. Gilley lifted my phone from the cradle between the seats and read the text so that I could keep my eyes on the road. "It's Darius. He's on the road, heading to Amagansett."

"That didn't take long," I said. We'd left him less than five minutes earlier.

"He's as worried as we are," Gil said, putting the phone back in the cradle under the dash.

"I hope she's in one of the two places we're looking," I said. "I want to find her before she hears the news from someone else."

"Me too," Gilley said. "It's been a traumatizing night for everyone, I suppose."

"True that," I said. "It's not every day you're in close proximity to one murder, then stumble upon a second."

"What the heck was that all about, anyway?" Gilley said. "I mean, a mob hit in the back alley of a coffee shop just down the street from the theater where Yelena Galanis is murdered? It's too insane to be a coincidence."

"Or it's too insane not to be," I countered. "We've seen our fair share of mob hits around here, so another one wouldn't be so very surprising, other than the timing."

"True," Gilley said, shuddering. "I just want to find Sunny and get her home so that we can then go home. I need a hot bath and a big dish of ice cream to chase the blues away."

I was about to make a snarky comment when Gilley pointed ahead. "There, Cat. That's the parking lot for the park."

"Got it," I said, pulling into the lot.

As soon as I entered the lot, Gilley laid his hand on my arm and said, "Isn't that Sunny's Range Rover at the end?"

Only one car was in the lot, and it was indeed a silver Range Rover, just like the one Sunny drove. I pressed the gas a little to get us to the SUV quicker.

"Can you see if she's in the car?" I asked as we approached. Gilley's eyesight was better than mine.

"No," he said. "It's too dark."

I parked, and we got out.

"Doesn't look like she's in the car," Gilley said.

I nodded and rounded to the passenger side, just to peer in, and that was when I let out a small gasp and shouted for Gilley.

"What?" he replied, rounding the Range Rover to come to my side. "What's wrong?"

Instead of answering him, I pulled on the handle of the car, but it was locked. I banged on the window, but Sunny, who was lying on her side, her torso spilling into the passenger seat, didn't stir. As I peered through the glass, I could clearly see that she held a prescription bottle in her hand. "She's taken some pills! And, Gilley, she's not moving!"

Gilley tugged on the handle, too, and shouted, "Sunny! Sunny, wake up!"

He then joined me in pounding on the window, but it was to no avail. I stepped back from the car and looked around for something, anything that might help us. "We have to break a window!"

Gilley stopped pounding on the window and flew to the

trunk of my car. After pulling up the lid, he rummaged around for a moment and came up with a tire iron. He hurried back to Sunny's car and was about to shatter the passenger's side window when I shouted "No!" and caught his arm. "You'll spray her with glass!"

"Good point," he said. After stepping sideways, he brought the tire iron down on the rear passenger window, angling the blow toward the back of the car.

The glass didn't shatter so much as spider across the pane.

"Hit it again!" I urged.

Gilley beat the glass several more times, eventually carving out a small hole, and then he broke the rest down with a side-to-side sweeping motion. Reaching carefully through the window, he managed to stretch his arm behind the seat and tug at the rear passenger's side door handle.

When it gave way, he got in, leaned over the seat and unlocked the front passenger's side door. I pulled the now unlocked door open and leaned over Sunny, then felt along her body to find her still breathing but quite cold. "Gilley!"

"Is she alive?"

"Yes, but barely!"

"Should I call an ambulance?"

I was absolutely panicked, but I managed to devise the quickest way to help Sunny. "No," I said, waving toward the driver's seat. "Get in."

While Gilley ran around to the other side of the car, I got into the passenger seat and carefully lifted Sunny's body onto mine, pulling her legs away from the driver's side. "It'll be faster if we can drive her to the hospital," I told Gilley as he got into the car. "It's only about a half mile away."

Gilley settled into the seat and looked around the dash and on the floor. "Where's the key fob?" he asked.

"Don't worry about it! It's probably in her pocket. Just hit the START button!"

Gilley pressed the button to the side of the steering column, but nothing happened.

"Put your foot on the brake!" I snapped, the fear getting the best of me.

"My foot *is* on the brake!"

"Try again!"

"It's not working!"

"Then we need to call an ambulance!"

Gilley's hands were shaking. He jumped out, pulled his phone out of his pocket, and dialed 911.

While Gilley called for help, I shifted position, laid Sunny's head in my lap. Her hair felt damp but her skin was cool and dry. I looked her over and saw that she was barefoot and her toes and fingers were blue with cold.

Placing both hands on the sides of Sunny's cheeks, I patted them in an effort to get her to wake up. She didn't even flicker an eyelid. "Oh, God," I said, feeling tears fill my eyes. "Beautiful lady, what've you done to yourself?"

"Cat!" I heard Gilley say after he'd connected with a dispatcher.

"She's unconscious and breathing very shallow!" I yelled. There was, in fact, no need to yell, but I was now legitimately worried that Sunny might expire right in my arms. She felt painfully thin—even for her—which told me she hadn't been eating well enough. And she seemed so fragile.

"Cat!" Gilley repeated, more urgently this time.

"What?"

"Do you know what she's ingested?"

My gaze traveled to Sunny's palm, but the pill bottle had rolled out onto the passenger's side floor. "Hold on," I told him, moving awkwardly around Sunny's unconscious form to retrieve the prescription bottle.

After grabbing it and holding it up, I had to squint to see the small lettering. "Ambien," I said to Gilley and then reached across the seat to wave the pill bottle at him so that he knew to take it.

He repeated the information on the label to the dispatcher, and then he asked me, "Are there any pills left?"

The bottle was empty when I'd handed it to him, so I searched around the car, but there was no sign of any pills left. "No," I said, my voice hitching, as tears stung my eyes. Sunny had taken an Ambien around noon, so I knew she'd been in possession of the pills, but I had never thought she'd purposely overdose on them. "Gilley, tell them to hurry!"

I reached for Sunny's wrist and pulled it up from where it dangled over the seat. She was completely passive. Feeling for a pulse again I bit my lip when I found it faint and slow. Stroking her cheek I cried, "Sunny, please, please don't do this. Don't leave us, okay? Think of your son! Come on, honey, hang in there!"

The sound of a siren coming close let me know help was nearby.

"Yes, ma'am, I hear them," Gilley said. "Thank you for your help."

He hung up the phone and leaned inside the car's interior. "Oh, my," he whispered. "She's so pale!"

I nodded. Sunny's complexion in the glow of the overhead light was a ghostly white. Gilley and I both tore our glances away when a patrol car and an ambulance pulled into the small lot. An officer got to us first.

"What's going on here?" he asked.

"This is Sunny D'Angelo," I said to him. "She's our dear friend. We'd been out looking for her and found her here in her car, with an empty bottle of Ambien in her hand. She's unconscious and not responding."

He waved two paramedics over to us, and Gilley stepped out of the way while I got out of the car from the passenger's side.

Gil came around to stand next to me while the paramedics worked on Sunny.

"We need to call Darius," I said to him.

"And Shepherd," he replied.

I bit my lip. "This is the last thing he needs to be dealing with right now. Maybe I should wait until after we know she's okay?"

Gilley placed the phone to his ear. "Cat, call him. If the worst happens, he'll be furious you didn't let him know in time to get to the hospital."

I nodded and turned away to place the call to Shepherd. The phone rang four times and went to voice mail, so I left him a lengthy message, told him to call me back, and added that I'd give him any updates I could.

After hanging up, I turned back toward Gilley in time to see them loading Sunny into the back of the ambulance. She was wearing an oxygen mask, and an IV had already been inserted into her wrist. Gilley took my arm and hugged it, as if clutching it for reassurance. I leaned my head against his. "She'll be okay," I whispered, but my voice hitched again, and my lower lip trembled.

The officer approached us. "Can you two join me over here so I can get some background information?"

My breath caught. I'd thought that Gilley and I could simply follow the ambulance to the hospital, and I didn't want to let it out of my sight should Shepherd call me and ask about Sunny.

"Officer, could we be interviewed at the hospital? We'd really like to follow behind the ambulance," I said.

"No, ma'am. I'm sorry, but I'll need to take your statement here." For emphasis, he looked meaningfully at Sunny's Range Rover, with its broken window.

"That's Detective Shepherd's sister," Gilley told him angrily. "We really should be with her."

The officer's brow furrowed, and he glanced at the ambulance, which was already pulling away.

"Well then, I'm definitely going to need you to stay right here with me and tell me what happened," he said.

I wanted to sock him. "I'm the detective's girlfriend," I said, hating the adolescent sound of the word. "We were at the playhouse this evening, and Shepherd asked us to find Sunny and tell her about Yelena Galanis."

He blinked at me for a moment, clearly surprised to learn that we'd been at the scene of a homicide as well as at the scene of an apparent overdose, but then he pulled out a small notepad and a ballpoint pen. After clicking the pen, he began to scribble. "Let's start with the basics," he said. "Like your names and addresses. . . ."

Chapter 6

We got to the hospital nearly an hour later. The stupid cop had taken his sweet time jotting down every single bit of information about us he could think of, and about the events leading up to our finding Sunny. He had finally released us after we'd repeated our story to him at least three times, and it had been all I could do not to simply turn my back on his pestering questions and head to the hospital before he could give me and Gilley the okay.

We arrived at the emergency room and found Darius pacing the hall, looking worried sick. Seeing us, he rushed over.

"Have you heard anything?" he asked us.

Gilley looked from me back to Darius. "We just got here."

Darius shook his head. He seemed unable to form coherent thoughts, he was so distraught. "Right. Right. I . . . this whole night . . . she . . . Why?" he said, his eyes glistening with tears. "*Why* would she take all those pills? Why would she try to kill herself? Why?"

Hearing the words come out of his mouth hit me like a blow to the midsection. "We don't know anything other than she probably took too much Ambien, Darius. For all we know, Sunny could've taken the very last pill and it simply hit her too hard."

He shook his head. "The nurse came out to ask me about the prescription bottle found in her hand. It was mine. Sunny picked it up for me today because she knows how hard the jet lag hits me when I fly home from L.A."

"She took one this afternoon," I confessed to him. He pulled his chin back in alarm, so I was quick to explain. "She said she took only a half a pill, because she hadn't been sleeping herself. She called Tiffany and asked her to come watch over Finley while she got some rest. She wanted to be fresh when you got home."

Darius was shaking his head, as if he couldn't believe what I was saying. "No, no, no," he insisted. "She knows better than to take Ambien. *Why* would she risk that?"

"What do you mean?" Gilley asked.

Darius rubbed his eyes with his palms, and I could tell the man was exhausted both physically and mentally. "Ambien hits Sunny really hard. She's taken one of my pills before, right after Finley was born, and she went to sleep for about two hours, then woke up and started acting crazy. She got the ladder out of the garage and insisted that we needed to clean the gutters. The more I tried to talk sense into her, the crazier she sounded, and then she got so frustrated with me when I pulled the ladder out of her hands that she walked around the house and right into the ocean, fully clothed. I didn't see her until she was about neck-deep, and I had to swim like hell to reach her. When I did, she kept telling me that she was trying to catch a mermaid. I had to drag her out and lock all three of us in the bedroom together until she fell asleep again. When she woke up seven hours later, she had no memory at all of what she'd said or done."

"Oh!" Gilley said. "I've read about that. Some people who take Ambien fall into a sort of dreamlike state, where they can appear to be perfectly awake, but they're actually not. They can do all sorts of crazy things and never remember it."

Darius nodded. "I talked to my doctor about it, and he said the same thing. He said Ambien can affect women very differently than men, and for some women, it can be really dangerous."

I glanced down the hall toward the double doors of the ER, through which Sunny had, no doubt, been taken. "That would explain why Sunny didn't tell Tiffany that she was leaving and, if she in fact did come back to the house, why she left again without her phone."

"It could also explain why she took the rest of the pills," Gilley said. "She wasn't in her right state of mind."

Darius stumbled over to a chair and sat down heavily, his chin falling against his chest. "Jesus," I heard him say. "I should've picked up the prescription. If I'd known she was going to pinch one of the pills, I would've never let her pick it up from the pharmacy."

I moved over to sit down next to him. "This isn't your fault, Darius," I said. "Sunny was exhausted when I saw her this afternoon. She was probably so exhausted that she threw caution to the wind and simply gave in to the impulse."

But Darius didn't seem to hear me. He just sat there, bent over, shaking his head back and forth, no doubt continuing to blame himself.

My phone buzzed, and I got up to answer it. Caller ID said it was Shepherd. "Hi," I said, not quite knowing how to begin.

"What's happened to Sunny?" he demanded, his voice sharp with emotion.

"I need you to brace yourself," I told him.

"Just tell me," he said quietly but firmly.

I took a deep breath and dove in. "She took an overdose of Ambien, and she's now at the hospital, where the doctors are working on her."

Shepherd was quiet on the other end of the line. He was probably stunned.

I thought it best to do the talking until he could compose himself to speak and ask me any questions he wanted. "Gilley and I went to her house, just like you asked, but when we got there, we were met by the babysitter, who told us that Sunny had gone out two hours earlier and that she hadn't taken her phone. We pressed her for more details, but she didn't really have any. As we were leaving, Darius showed up. He didn't know that Sunny had left the house."

"Darius is back already?" he said, and there was an icy note in his tone.

"Yes. He got in just a little while ago. When we told him what was going on, he was upset that Sunny had left the house without her phone. We split up to look for her in the two spots she likes to go when she needs some quiet time."

"The yoga place?" Shepherd asked.

"Yes. Darius headed there, and we headed to the park."

"What park?"

"Herrick Park. It's off Newtown."

Shepherd grunted. "What's her prognosis?"

"We don't know."

"Is Darius there?"

"He is. He's beside himself with worry."

Shepherd let out an audible sigh, and I could tell he was irritated with his brother-in-law, no doubt for leaving Sunny with all the duties of rearing a toddler when she was so obviously exhausted. "I'm on my way," he said and hung up.

"What'd he say?" Gilley asked me when I turned back to him and Darius.

"He's headed here."

Gilley widened his eyes. "That man has had one busy night."

Darius looked up and said, "He's the detective assigned to Yelena's murder, isn't he?"

"He is," I said. "And there was another murder that took place this evening right across the street from the theater."

Darius's brow furrowed. "You're kidding."

I shook my head. "No. I'm not. It appears to be a mob hit."

Darius's jaw dropped. "A *mob* hit?"

I nodded.

Gilley said, "There are more of those in this part of town than you'd think."

"Laney," Darius said, mentioning Shepherd's ex-wife, who was executed by a Mafia hit woman.

"Yes," I said.

Darius put his head in his hands. "This night is freaking surreal."

I moved over to sit next to him again and awkwardly patted him on the shoulder in an effort to comfort him. "For us too."

We had sat like that for a good ten minutes when Shepherd rushed into the ER, out of breath. I wondered if he'd run from the parking lot.

"Any news?" he asked, directing his question at Darius.

"No," Darius said. "They took her back over an hour ago, and they were gonna pump her stomach and give her some meds to counteract the effects of the Ambien in her system."

"How much did she take?" he asked next.

Darius's lower lip quivered slightly. "The whole bottle, Steve."

One look at Shepherd, as his face drained of color, told me how worried he was for his twin. I stepped forward and took his hand, then guided him over to the set of chairs opposite Darius and Gilley.

He sat down heavily. "Why would she take a whole bottle of Ambien?"

Darius's expression was a mask of guilt. "She picked up my prescription from the pharmacy today. I asked her to, because I was out of pills, and I always have trouble sleeping when I come back from L.A."

Shepherd's lip curled as he angrily regarded his brother-in-law. "Then you must almost never have trouble sleeping," he said meanly.

I bit my lip and watched as Darius dropped his gaze to the floor. "I gotta work, Steve. And it wasn't my choice to move back East."

Shepherd shook his head. I had the distinct feeling there was no love lost between the two men.

"Sunny took a half a tablet earlier today, Shep," I said softly.

His gaze slid to me, and his brow arched in question.

"I visited her just before noon. She looked exhausted and thin and at the end of her rope. She called Tiffany to come watch over Finley so that she could get some sleep, and she confessed to me that she took half a tablet so that she could be sure she slept until Darius arrived home. We think that even that small amount put her in a sleepwalking state, and she likely took the rest of the Ambien while she was in that condition."

Darius said, "Remember a couple of months ago, when I told you about how she'd tried to catch a mermaid?"

Shepherd nodded absently, his stare at the floor faraway and almost disconnected. At that moment his phone buzzed, and he pulled it out to look at the display. Muttering a curse under his breath, he got up from his chair and said, "I gotta take this."

Shepherd walked down the hall, and I could tell by the tense set of his shoulders that it was official police business, very likely about one or both of the cases he'd been working tonight.

Just as he made it through the double doors to the outside, a grizzled-looking man with a short, untidy beard, thick glasses, and a crooked nose came through the double doors. He was wearing scrubs and a lab coat. "D'Angelo?"

"Yes," Darius said, getting up quickly, his hands balled into fists, as if he was trying to brace himself for bad news. Gilley and I got up too.

"Are you Mr. D'Angelo?" the doctor asked.

"Yes. Darius. I'm Sunny's husband."

"Good. I'm Dr. Papageorgiou. I've been attending your wife."

"Yes?" Darius said, more a question than a statement.

I eyed the doctor with impatience. Why didn't he put all of us obviously anxious people out of our misery and tell us Sunny was fine?

"That was a very, very close call, Mr. D'Angelo, but I believe your wife will be all right."

Collectively, all our shoulders sagged in relief.

The doctor continued. "We'd like to keep her overnight for observation. Her breathing and heart rate are still a bit sluggish."

"Sure. Of course," Darius said. "When can I—"

"And I'd also like to set up a consult with an attending psychologist tomorrow morning," the doctor interrupted. "She'll need a psych eval before I'm comfortable releasing her."

"A . . . psych eval?" Darius asked.

Dr. Papageorgiou focused an intense look at Darius. "Your wife attempted suicide, Mr. D'Angelo. You'll need to come to grips with that and support any psychological counseling, therapy, and/or evaluation at a mental health facility."

We all audibly gasped at that.

"She didn't . . . ," Darius said, shaking his head vigorously. "Doctor, I swear, Sunny isn't suicidal."

The doctor's firm tone and level gaze never wavered. "She's severely underweight, dehydrated, and exhausted, not to mention that she consumed enough Ambien tonight to kill herself. And she very nearly succeeded. Those markers alone give me great cause for concern. Still, I'll hand over the decision to have her committed to my colleague tomorrow morning. We need to be sure she no longer presents a threat to herself or others, Mr. D'Angelo."

Darius simply continued to shake his head, and for the first time, the physician's expression turned compassionate. "There's nothing you can do for her tonight. I suggest you go home and get some rest yourself."

Darius stopped shaking his head and simply stood there with his jaw agape and a dazed look on his face. It was like he couldn't form the words to insist that it'd all been a big misunderstanding. That Sunny probably hadn't been in her right mind when she took all those pills.

But then it hit me: People who were suicidal weren't in their right minds by definition. What if Sunny *had* been fully conscious when she left to drive herself to the park? She'd taken only a half a dose, and that must've worn off by the time she woke up around seven thirty or eight to leave Tiffany and Finley behind, right?

"Hey," Shepherd said, causing me to jump. He'd come right up to me, and I hadn't even been aware. "Is there news? How's Sunny?"

Darius turned to him, a pained, astonished look on his face. He didn't seem capable of answering.

"And you are?" Dr. Papageorgiou asked.

"Detective Steve Shepherd," Shep said, pulling out his badge and flashing it for the doctor. "I'm Sunny's twin brother."

"Ah," the doctor said. "She's stable but has been moved to the ICU for further monitoring through the night."

"Thank God," Shepherd said after letting out a sigh of relief. "Can we see her?"

The doctor's gaze flashed to Darius, then back to Shepherd. "I'll allow one person to visit with her briefly. Five to ten minutes only. She's stable, but I can't have her agitated or further exhausted until she's evaluated tomorrow morning."

"Evaluated?" Shepherd asked.

"I'll fill you in," I whispered to him.

Darius turned to us. "Thanks for coming, guys. I'll go back and see her. Steve, I'll call you tomorrow to give you an update."

Shepherd's brow furrowed. "I want to see her, Darius."

Papageorgiou rocked back on his heels. "As I said, I can allow only one visitor, gentlemen."

"I'm her husband," Darius said firmly.

"I'm her *twin*!" Shepherd countered. It was surprising to see him insist on cutting the line and getting in front of his brother-in-law. I was fairly certain that by way of their marriage, Darius's access to Sunny trumped Shepherd's.

"Do you have a medical directive or power of attorney?" Papageorgiou asked him.

Shepherd glared at the doctor, his lips a thin line of anger. "No, but I *am* an officer of the law."

"Is this a police matter?" the doctor retorted, and I could tell he was firmly on Darius's side.

Shepherd's jaw clenched and unclenched. "No," he finally admitted.

Papageorgiou turned back to Darius. "She's in room two-ten. Follow the green line to the elevators." Papageorgiou paused to point to a series of colored lines on the floor. "I'll let the ICU nurse know that you're cleared to visit with your wife for no longer than ten minutes."

"Thank you," Darius said in relief, and with one last defiant glance at Shepherd, Darius left us to head to the elevators.

When he and the doctor had both departed, I filled Shepherd in.

"That's ridiculous," he snapped. "Sunny isn't suicidal."

"How do you know?" I asked him, genuinely curious.

"What do you mean, how do I know?"

"I mean, Shep, that there was a time fifteen years ago when my sister was very, very depressed after a breakup, and she confessed to me later that she'd contemplated taking her life, and I never knew. There were no overt signs, other than she seemed sluggish and foggy every time I talked to her, and I always chalked it up to her being tired out because of her job."

"Her psychic work?"

"No, this was before all that. She worked at a bank back then, and there was a lot of pressure on her. Anyway, the point is that it never occurred to me that she was in such a perilous state."

"M.J. went through something like that when she was in college," Gilley said, breaking the silence. He was still standing next to me.

Shepherd and I looked at him in surprise.

He shrugged and added, "Her mom died when she was in fifth grade, and her dad started drinking right afterward. She never got therapy or counseling, and I think she pushed it all down for as long as she could, but when she was about twenty, it caught up to her, and there was a time when I made sure to stick close to her so that she didn't do anything stupid."

"How'd she pull out of it?" I asked Gilley.

"I finally convinced her to get some therapy at the university clinic, and she got on some antidepressants, which made a world of difference."

I nodded. "Abby too. She still takes them, I believe."

"Guys," Shepherd said, holding up his palms to us. "You gotta believe me, other than what happened with my parents five years ago, Sunny's life has been relatively gentle."

"Your parents passed away?" Gilley asked.

Shepherd nodded. "Mom died from ovarian cancer, and Dad passed away within six months of Mom's funeral. The strain on him through her sickness was too much for his heart."

"Did Sunny ever get counseling?" I pressed.

"Definitely. And she dragged me with her. Seriously, Sunny's on top of her mental health. Always has been."

"Maybe this time she was too quickly overwhelmed by insomnia and the duties of being a mother to a fussy toddler to recognize the oncoming depression," I suggested. "And don't forget how hard the pandemic was on everyone," I added. "I swear we're all walking around with a good case of PTSD."

Shepherd frowned and stared at the floor. "Yeah," he finally admitted. "That was kinda tough on her. Damn, I should've been paying more attention."

"We all should've," I told him. And then I reached out and took his hand. "It's not your fault, lovey."

He lifted his gaze to mine. "Then why do I feel so guilty?"

"Because that's what you do," Gilley told him. "You ride in on your white horse and save the day so often that this time it caught you off guard."

Shepherd slid a sideways glance at me. "Since when did Gilley get so wise?"

I chuckled. "Oh, trust me, Gilley is far wiser than he lets on."

Gilley beamed. "It's my side hustle," he said, adding a curtsy. "Now come on, you two. I'm exhausted, and there's nothing more we can do here. Let's get the three of us home."

Shepherd pulled me to his chest and kissed the top of my head. "I can't," he said to both of us. "I gotta get back to the scene." And then he paused a moment and added, "*Scenes.* Good God, this night is like a bad dream that just won't end."

"We'll walk you out," I said, hugging him tightly before taking both his hand and Gilley's to exit the hospital.

We parted in the parking lot, and walking to our car, I lagged behind Gil while I watched Shepherd's retreating form. He walked a little hunched over, like he carried the weight of the world on his back. I couldn't imagine being in his shoes, with so much responsibility and his own personal tragedies swirling in the mix.

"Cat?" Gilley called.

"Coming," I said absently and watched Shepherd for a few more seconds, feeling like I wanted to run to him and hug him tightly one more time.

Looking back, I really wish I had.

Chapter 7

The next morning, I woke up to the smell of coffee wafting up from my kitchen. And something else was flavoring the air with the scent of pastry and raspberries. After rolling over, I picked up my phone to check the time. It was six fifteen. On a Saturday.

I moaned and uttered a small curse under my breath, pondering if I should attempt to go back to sleep or head down to the kitchen to see why in God's name Gilley thought it a good idea to be up baking at this hour in *my* kitchen rather than his.

With a heavy sigh, I reasoned that Gilley got out the early morning baking tins like this only when something was troubling him. So, I did what any good friend would do—I rolled over and tried to go back to sleep, which worked for about fifteen minutes, or until exactly the point at which I was just starting to drift off when Gilley took his anxiety to a new level and began to loudly clang pots and pans together, creating an all-out ruckus in the kitchen.

With heavy-lidded eyes—and a glint of fury—I grabbed my silk robe from the knob behind the bathroom door and descended the stairs quietly while he kept up the racket.

I found him *literally* drumming the bottom of a saucepan with a wooden spoon, his back turned to me as he stared out the window.

"Catchy tune," I said.

Gilley jumped, then whirled around, holding the spoon like a weapon. "*Ahhh!*"

"Relax!" I said, putting up my hands. "It's just me."

"Oh," he said, immediately calming down.

A bit too quickly, I thought.

"Good morning, Cat. You're up early."

I plunked down on one of the barstools along the kitchen island. "Gee, Gilley, ya *think*?"

Gilley made a little moue face. "Couldn't sleep, huh?"

I stared dully at him. "No."

He nodded like he fully understood. "Me either."

I laid my forehead down on the island. "Why are you here, Gilley?"

"Your oven is more temperature sensitive, and I'm making a Gouda-apricot coffee cake, and the temp needs to be precisely one hundred and eighty degrees Celsius for twenty minutes, or it will overbrown."

I lifted my head to frown at him. "We have the exact same oven."

I'd personally made sure that Chez Kitty was equipped with top-of-the line appliances, just like at Chez Cat.

Gilley set down the spoon he'd been holding, and took up a dish towel. Fiddling with it, he said, "The lighting is better over here. And there's more room to spread out all the ingredients. And I was completely out of cake mix, but then I remembered you had a box in the pantry here."

"Gil?"

"Yeah?"

"Something troubling you?"

Gilley's shoulders sagged. "You know me so well."

I got up off the barstool and ambled around the island to the cabinet where I kept my French press. "Sit," I said to him. "I'll make us some coffee, and we can talk."

Gilley flounced over to a chair and took up a seat. I waited until I'd prepped the French press with fresh coffee beans and started the kettle, then set out twin mugs, cream, sugar, and two spoons before I spoke next to him. "Tell me what's on your mind."

"Michel left me a message this morning. I didn't hear my phone. I was in the shower."

I waited for Gilley to continue, but he'd paused, with a faraway look in his eyes, so I prompted him. *"And?"*

Gilley sighed. "He just said, 'I think we need to talk.'"

I winced. "Ouch."

Gilley's gaze locked onto mine. "That's bad, right?"

"Did you tell him about Spooks?" I asked, hoping that was all Michel wanted to talk to Gilley about.

"No," Gil said. "I was waiting for a good time to break the news."

I didn't confess to Gilley that I believed it was now past a good time, choosing instead to focus on a more optimistic approach. The kettle began to smoke with steam and I paused our conversation to pour the hot water over the beans in the French press. When that was done I said, "Maybe he just wants to tell you that he's booked another job and won't be home at the end of the month."

"He's already texted me that," Gilley said.

"When?"

"Yesterday, during your meeting with the count."

So much had happened in the past twenty-four hours that yesterday afternoon felt like it was ages ago. "Now I understand what led you to the Humane Society's home page."

Gilley gave me a crooked smile, but there was tremendous sadness in his eyes. "*Vogue* is going to stream fashion videos to its online subscribers. Photos of models will now become videos of models, and Michel is working to make that transition happen by teaming up with a documentary filmmaker in South Africa. He'll be gone all of October and most of November."

"Oh, Gil," I said. "I'm so sorry."

He shrugged and fiddled with his coffee spoon while staring at the counter. Sniffling, he whispered, "I really thought we'd make it."

It broke my heart to see him like this, and I quickly went around the counter to wrap him in a fierce hug.

I knew this heartbreak. It was more than simply the realization that you wouldn't spend the rest of your days with the person you'd married—it was the fact that in letting go of them, you had to let go of the dream of what you thought your life would be. The certainty of it and the comfort of that certainty were such tremendously difficult things to lose.

For a long time, I simply hugged Gilley, and I knew he was quietly weeping by the occasional sniffle and the small damp spot on the back of my shoulder that formed from his tears.

"I know, honey," I whispered to him.

I felt him nod slightly. He knew I knew.

The moment was interrupted by a bing from the timer over the oven. Gilley jerked out of my grasp and wiped his eyes. "The coffee cake is ready."

I stroked his hair and kissed his cheek. "Sit. I'll take care of it."

After moving over to the oven, I pulled out the scrumptious-looking cake and set it on the wire rack to cool. The mouth-watering aroma filled the kitchen with a heavenly scent.

"It needs to cool for about fifteen minutes," Gilley said.

I turned back to him, and he seemed more composed, although his eyes were wet and red.

"What can I do for you?" I asked him, and I wasn't talking about breakfast.

"I need a distraction," he said.

Pouring coffee into both of our mugs, I said, "We could take a day trip somewhere. Ooh! I know. We could head into the City and take a walk in the park. The leaves are just starting to turn, and I bet it'd be good for us."

Gilley sighed and shook his head. "I want to be close to home in case they call me about Spooks."

"Then how about a walk along the beach?" I pressed. Gilley needed fresh air and a little exercise. The weather had turned colder overnight, and it wasn't especially sunny out, with overcast skies, but at least it wasn't raining yet.

Gilley sighed again, as if he couldn't make up his mind. "I don't feel like it, Cat," he finally said.

"How about a Netflix marathon, then? We could stream some *Grace and Frankie*. You love that show."

"Because Jane Fonda is a living, breathing goddess, and Lily Tomlin is a national treasure!" Gilley all but yelled.

We both laughed. That was his standard line every time I mentioned the show. It felt good to see him chuckle.

But then he sobered and said, "Yeah, I don't know that I'm in the mood for that, either."

"Did you want to call Michel?" I asked gently.

"No!" Gilley snapped. I pulled my chin back in surprise, and he quickly apologized. "I'm sorry. I didn't mean to bite your head off. I just . . ."

I reached across the counter and put my hand over his. "I know," I said. I'd put off having "the talk" with Tom until he cornered me in my home office and wouldn't allow me to escape it. I'd known what he was going to say, but those were words that couldn't be walked back, and I didn't judge Gilley one bit for not being ready to hear them just yet.

"What would you like to do, then?" I asked him after a moment.

"I want to visit Spooks," he said. "Even though he's not my dog yet, I keep thinking about how lonely he must be in that kennel, not knowing that he's going to be coming home with me."

"I love that idea," I said.

"Yeah?"

"Yeah. And we can ask the shelter if it's okay to take Spooks for a walk. Maybe along the beach?"

Gilley rolled his eyes. "You really want me to get some exercise, huh?"

I cut a slice of coffee cake for him and handed it over with a winning smile. "It'll do your mind some good, lovey," I said. "And I'm sure Spooks would love it!"

As it turned out, Spooks *did* love it. We got to the shelter shortly after it opened, and inquired about taking the adorably cute puppers for a walk. The shelter was thrilled that we'd come back to bond with Spooks, and made sure we had a leash and a portable water bowl for our walk along the beach. I pocketed two water bottles into my purse, and we set off. Along the way, Gilley asked if I'd take a video of him walking his soon-to-be pup, and I happily accepted his phone to shoot the video.

As I got ready to film, however, I made the same mistake I always did, and opened up his photo app instead of the camera, and I was shocked to discover a photo taken of me inside Sunny's SUV, holding her head in my lap and giving Gilley (and the camera) a panicked stare.

"Why did you take this?" I asked Gilley. The photo felt like a betrayal of Sunny's privacy, and I couldn't figure out why Gilley would take it.

He'd been leading Spooks away, and he had a hard time bringing him back to me to look at the camera, because the dog was much more interested in moving on to scents he hadn't yet fully investigated. Still, Gilley managed it and got close enough to squint at the screen as I held it up for him.

"Huh," he said when he saw the photo. "I don't remember taking that."

"It's in your photos," I said, nearly wincing at the accusatory tone that came out of my mouth.

Gilley's gaze flicked to me, his brow furrowed in confusion.

"Cat, I didn't *intentionally* take that photo. I must've swiped left instead of up when I was trying to call nine-one-one. I was shaken up, seeing Sunny like that, and I must've accidentally taken the photo."

"Oh," I said, turning the photo back to me. "Sorry, Gil. I didn't mean to accuse you."

"It's fine," he said. "I understand."

Spooks had stopped tugging and sat down next to us to pant loudly. Gilley looked down at him and then asked me, "Hey, can you fish out one of the water bottles? I think he's thirsty."

"Sure," I said, lowering the phone to root around in my purse.

After I handed over the water to Gilley, he took the collapsible water bowl out of his back pocket and bent to offer Spooks a drink. "I'll delete the photo in a minute," he said, almost as an afterthought.

I felt guilty that I'd made him feel bad, so I merely shrugged nonchalantly and said, "Whatever."

While Gilley was squatting down to give Spooks his fill, I turned the phone back to face me because they looked very cute together that way and I wanted to take a photo of it, but I again tapped the stupid photo icon and had to look once again at the image of Sunny's prone body, her pale face, and my panicked expression.

"Gil?" I said as I stared at the screen.

"Yeah?" he said, distracted by his growing adoration for his new best friend.

I squatted down next to him and once again showed him the screen. "What's missing?"

Gil pulled his gaze away from Spooks and looked from me to his phone, then back again. "What?"

I wiggled the phone. "What's *missing*?"

"What do you mean, what's missing?"

I pointed to the screen. "There," I said. "See that?"

"See what? The middle console?"

"Yes."

"I don't see anything unusual or out of place," Gilley said.

"Exactly," I told him.

He sighed. "Can you just tell me what I'm supposed to not be seeing?"

I picked up the now empty water bottle at his feet and wiggled it. Then I watched Gilley's eyes widen. He looked again at the photo on the screen, then back to me. "How do you swallow an entire bottle of pills without any water?" he said.

"Exactly."

"Could there have been one in the driver's side door?" he said next.

"You got in on that side. Do you remember seeing one?"

Gilley closed his eyes to concentrate. "No," he said as he was imagining the scene. "I looked all around there for a key fob and there was nothing there."

I nodded. I remembered looking at the door when I pulled Sunny into the passenger seat and onto my lap. I hadn't seen it there either.

"Was it on the floor of the passenger seat?" Gilley asked. The photo allowed us to see both the driver's side floor mat and the passenger's floor mat, but parts of the mats were obscured from view.

I shook my head. "I remember looking down at the floor," I told him. "I was looking to see if she'd dropped any of the pills there, hoping she hadn't ingested the whole bottle. The floor mat was clean."

Gilley's gaze met mine. "So how did she get down an entire bottle of Ambien without water?"

"She could've simply forced the pills down," I said.

Gilley's expression was unconvinced. "Do you remember that the doctor said she was severely dehydrated?"

I let out a small gasp. "I do remember that."

"So, how do you swallow pills when you're dehydrated? It's hard enough when you're not thirsty. And Ambien comes in a tablet, not a capsule, so that'd make it even harder."

Gilley and I stared at each other until Spooks gave a small woof. He was impatient to get back to the walk.

I handed Gilley his phone, pocketed the empty water bottle, and we made our way down the beach trail in silence, each lost in thought.

"Should we tell Shepherd?" Gilley finally asked.

"Should we?" I replied.

Gilley bit his lip. "I don't know. On the one hand, you know how suspicious he is, and how likely he is to make something out of nothing, but on the other hand, how do you explain Sunny's consumption of an entire bottle of Ambien without any water?"

I continued to walk in silence next to Gil, thinking all that over, before I finally stopped and said, "She could've taken the pills when she came back to the house, Gilley."

"You mean when Tiffany thought she heard her while she was on the treadmill?"

"Yes. I mean, it sort of fits, doesn't it? Tiffany hears someone in the house, it takes her a minute to work up the courage to investigate, and when she does, no one's there. If Sunny had come back for the pills and enough water to choke them all down, then it would've taken only a few moments, right?"

Gilley handed me Spooks's leash and, after tapping at his watch for a moment, used his now free hands to pantomime opening a pill bottle, pouring out the pills into his palm, which he then slapped against his mouth, then filling an imaginary glass with water and swallowing the pretend mouthful with a loud gulp. Eyeing his watch again, he said, "Seventeen seconds."

"Even if it was thirty, that'd be quick," I said.

"So, not so unusual that there was no water in the car," Gilley said.

I nodded. "And it explains what Tiffany heard. Sunny did very likely come back to the house to take the pills."

I let out a sigh of relief, but it was somewhat forced. Thinking about Sunny willingly ingesting an entire bottle of Ambien wasn't something to be relieved over. It was something to be very, very concerned by.

We walked Spooks for another thirty minutes or so, with not a lot of conversation between us. I could tell that the facts of Sunny's overdose were troubling both of us tremendously.

When we got back to the car, with a very happy and somewhat tuckered-out pup, Gilley said, "Maybe you should call Shepherd and ask him how Sunny's doing?"

I nodded. "I was just thinking that."

I called Shepherd using the car's Bluetooth so that Gilley could listen in.

"Hey, beautiful," he said when he picked up the call, his voice a little gravelly from lack of sleep.

"Hi, there," I said, smiling at the warm tone. "Gilley's with me in the car. We want to know how Sunny's doing."

Shepherd blew out a breath. "It's not good," he said.

My grip tightened on the steering wheel, and Gilley looked at me in alarm. "What's happened?" I asked.

"Her psych eval was troubling," Shepherd said.

"What does that mean?"

"It means that the shrink thinks she should spend some time in a mental health support unit."

My eyes widened. "At the hospital?"

"No. Darius is having her committed to the EHPC. And before you ask, that's the East Hampton Psychiatric Center."

"Oh, my," I said. "For how long?"

Shepherd's voice became flat, almost void of emotion, which, I'd come to learn over the past year, meant he was struggling to keep his emotions in check. "We don't know. Until they can be assured she's no longer presenting a danger to herself or others."

I put a hand to my mouth. I'd never dreamed that Sunny was in any state to actually be committed. "So, she *did* attempt to harm herself?"

"Yeah. Darius told me she confessed to him this morning, and the hospital shrink confirmed it."

"She was aware of what she was doing, then," I said, trying to make sense of it all.

"They think so," Shepherd said, and there was a slight crack in his voice, and I knew his effort to flatten out his emotions wasn't working.

"I'm so, so sorry, Shep." I didn't know what else to say.

There was a pause, and then Shepherd said, "She's in good hands at least. And she's safe. And awake, but she's still a little groggy."

"Did you talk to her?"

"Not yet. Darius is with her. He said the shrink doesn't want her upset, and he's worried that confessing to me about what she'd done last night might trigger her in the wrong way."

I wanted to cry. I knew how close Sunny and her brother were, and this had to be killing him.

"What can we do for you?" Gilley asked.

Shepherd sighed in a way that revealed just how exhausted he was. "Nothing, Gil, but thanks. I'm just trying to focus on this case, which, thankfully, I now have a break on."

"You have a lead in Yelena's murder case?" I asked.

"I do. In fact, you guys, I gotta run. The judge is about to sign my arrest warrant, and the suspect is a flight risk, so I want to nab him before he has a chance to sneak off."

I wanted to ask him for details, but I knew that he'd likely not share much with me until after he'd made the arrest. Plus, asking him would only delay him further. "Of course," I said. "We'll chat later, okay?"

After we'd disconnected, I turned to Gilley. "That was fast."

"You know how Shepherd loves to make a quick arrest," Gilley said, with a crooked smile.

I made a face at him, but it was all too true. My boyfriend was known to flash the handcuffs first and ask questions later. "Hopefully, we'll learn all about it tonight."

Gilley twisted in his seat to look back at Spooks. "He's super adorable, isn't he?"

I eyed the pup, now fully spread out on my back seat, sleeping away, and grinned. "He is, Gilley. I'm so glad you two found each other."

When we got back to the shelter, Gilley was reluctantly about to hand over the leash to the staff worker when she grinned broadly at him and said, "Why don't you go ahead and keep that?"

Gilley's brow furrowed for a moment, but I understood exactly what she meant. Leaning over, I gave Gilley a fierce hug. "Congratulations, Papa!"

"What?" Gilley said, still confused.

"It's a dog!" I said, pointing to Spooks.

Gilley's eyes instantly welled up with tears. "I can keep him?"

The staff member nodded and clapped her hands. "Your application has been approved!"

Gilley sank to the floor and hugged Spooks, who kissed him all over and seemed to know the moment was special.

Chapter 8

A bit later Gilley, one excited pooch, and I were in the car, heading toward Spooks's new home. We'd left the shelter with a "new pawent" gift bundle that included a soft plush squeaky toy, a day's worth of dog food, a tag for a collar with Spooks's name and Gilley's cell phone number, and a certificate of adoption, which Gilley swore he was going to frame and hang above the mantel.

At Gilley's insistence, we stopped at a large warehouse-like store called the Pet Palace, where Gilley began shopping like he was in one of those *Grab and Go* game shows.

By the time we got home, it was well after lunch, and Spooks was alert and busy sniffing every corner in Chez Kitty, while Gilley and I hauled in the huge bundle of things he'd purchased for his new little buddy.

"Does he really need four separate beds?" I asked, lugging two plush, oversized doggy lounge beds, while Gilley jammed two more that were even bigger through the door behind me.

"Yes!" Gilley's muffled voice replied.

"Where do I put these?" I asked, dropping both in front of me.

"One next to the couch and one next to the kitchen counter," Gil instructed.

I set the beds where he'd instructed, while Gilley waddled to the back of the cottage with the other two beds. I then went about filling up Spooks's water dish and placed it against the wall near a side table, where it wouldn't get knocked over. I then moved over to the bags we'd already brought in from the car, and put those up on one of the kitchen chairs, where Gilley could sort through them at his leisure. I didn't think he even knew the full extent of what he'd bought, but I wasn't going to criticize. The poor pup probably hadn't been spoiled the whole time he was at the shelter—if he ever was spoiled at all.

"Sebastian," I said, pulling out another chair to plop myself down on.

"Yes, my lady?" my AI butler replied.

"Please take note that we have a new permanent resident in-house. His name is Spooks, and he'll probably set off all the motion sensors when Gilley and I are out of the residences."

"I've made a note, my lady. Your lunch has been delivered and is viewable on the front steps of Chez Cat."

I leaned sideways to look out the window toward my house, where I could clearly see the to-go order I'd placed while Gilley was being checked out at the pet supply store.

"Excellent, Sebastian. Thank you."

At that moment, Gilley came out with a satisfied look on his face. "He's all set up," he said, stopping short when he saw that Spooks had hopped up on the couch and was staring at Gilley with heavy-lidded eyes but a wagging tail.

"Spooks," Gilley said, placing his hands on his hips before pointing to the dog bed next to the couch. "Not on the furniture. You need to sleep on your brand-new bed."

The dog's gaze drifted to the dog bed, then back up to Gilley, and his short tail thumped even harder.

I held in a snicker and got up to head to the front door. "I'll bring our lunch in while you lay down the law with our newest family member."

After retrieving the bags from the front porch, I came back inside to find Gilley sprawled out on the dog bed and Spooks still firmly ensconced on the couch.

Pausing in the doorway, I said, "Yep. That's about how I thought that would go."

Gilley hopped to his feet. "I was just showing him how comfortable it is."

I glanced meaningfully at Spooks, who eyed me in return and, I swear to God, flashed me a big ole doggy smile. "He seems convinced."

Gilley made a face. "He'll get there. It's a new space. He's still getting the lay of the land."

"Uh-huh," I said.

After making my way over to the counter, I pulled out our twin Caesar salads and set us up at the table before looking back over to Gilley, who was again lying on the doggy bed, pretending to sigh contentedly and make some snoring sounds.

Spooks was also making some snoring sounds, but his were real.

"Yo, Gilley," I said softly. "Come to the table like a good boy."

Gilley scowled and struggled to get up from the dog bed. Upon arriving at the table, he pulled out his chair, and in a commanding voice, I said, "Sit!"

"Ha ha," he said woodenly.

I giggled. It was too easy.

We chatted for a bit about Spooks. Gilley was anxious to begin training his new four-legged companion, and he waxed on for a good ten minutes about the vast and varied dog collars, hats, and sweaters he'd found on Etsy, and I had a feeling Spooks would be decked out in rhinestones, glitter, leather, and feathers before too long.

At last, Gil seemed to have worn himself out from talking excitedly about Spooks's wardrobe, and I took the opportunity to say, "We should probably get some work done this afternoon."

"Work? Work on what?" Gil asked.

I shrugged. "I don't know. Maybe prep some notes for Leslie Cohen. I'm scheduled to meet with her on Monday, right?"

"Uh," Gil said, moving his eyes side to side, like he was looking for an escape. "She canceled."

"She did?" I asked, surprised. "Did something come up?"

"Don't know," Gilley said.

"When is she rescheduled for?"

Gilley avoided my gaze. "She's not."

"What do you mean, she's not?"

"She feels she's gotten all she can out of your weekly meetings," he said, so softly I had to lean in to hear him.

"Are you serious?" I asked.

Leslie was a mess. She'd graduated from Georgetown Law, only to discover she hated the thought of being a lawyer and had no idea what direction to head in next. She'd been sponging off her parents for the past two years, doing little other than socializing with friends and shopping online. She'd come to me only when her mother had insisted on it—having heard of me from one of two articles written about my practice—and had threatened to cut her daughter off financially unless Leslie met with me and redirected herself toward getting a job and making her way in the world like a responsible adult.

We'd had only three sessions together.

"Unfortunately, Cat, I am serious. The email arrived late last night, and it pretty much said exactly that."

I pressed my lips together. "I bet she comes back when her mom finds out she's no longer coming to see me."

Gilley cleared his throat and squirmed in his chair. "Mrs. Cohen was the one who sent the email."

My jaw fell open, and heat rose to my cheeks. I was embarrassed and irritated; I'd worked hard for Leslie.

"Well, I hope Leslie lives up to her potential," I said stiffly.

Gilley forced a smile and looked at me with sympathetic eyes.

"Who else is on my calendar for next week?" I said, moving on.

Gilley's forced smile turned to a grimace. "Just Chrissy," he said, referring to my longest-running client to date.

Chrissy was on her fourth marriage, and that was also headed for splitsville. She was an absolute pain in the tokus: needy, uncooperative, argumentative. And she rarely listened to my advice, much less took it. I'd been working with her for six months, and we'd made very little headway. I'd tried to fire her three times, but she had always managed to cause such an emotional scene that I'd allowed her back.

"What about Esther?" I asked, referring to one of my elderly clients.

"She and her husband are on vacation in Greece next week, remember?"

"Yes," I said. "What about Virginia?"

"She and her husband are going with Esther."

I blinked in surprise. "They are? I didn't even realize they were friends."

"They weren't until they both started seeing you."

"Wait, what?" I asked.

"Esther met Virginia while both of them were waiting on us to arrive the day that I accidentally overbooked them for the same appointment, remember?"

"Oh, yes. I do remember that. Bad day for us, being late and double-booking them."

"I've apologized a bajillion times, Cat," Gilley said moodily.

"I know, lovey. And I've accepted that. I was merely commenting on the memory of that day."

"Well, maybe it wasn't so bad, because Virginia and Esther are now buddies."

"So, nobody else is on the books?" I asked, a bit panicked. My business was an ebb-and-flow kind of deal, and truth be told, I'd seen a lot more ebbs than flows.

"Not unless Aaron Nassau wants to schedule another session."

"Did you follow up with him?"

"Not yet," Gilley said testily.

I smiled and tried to convey that I wasn't being critical. "Why don't we reach out now?" I said. "I'd like to know how he's coping after such an emotional time yesterday."

Gilley whipped out his phone and scrolled through it before finding Aaron's number, pressing CALL, and putting the phone to his ear.

A moment later he said, "Aaron? Gilley Gillespie, Cat Cooper's assistant." Gilley paused, and his expression registered concern.

"What?" I said softly.

Gilley caught my gaze and simply handed me the phone. "Something's wrong," he whispered.

I placed the phone to my own ear and heard quiet whimpering. "Aaron?" I said. "It's Catherine Cooper. I'm calling to check on you. How're you doing?"

There was loud sniffling on the other end of the call. "Not well, Catherine."

"Oh, my, Aaron. I'm so sorry. Are you still upset about our conversation yesterday?"

"I take it you don't read the papers," he said.

My brow furrowed. "Actually, I do. And if memory serves me, the markets are all up this morning, and the forecast for the rest of this year looks promising."

"Oh, I don't give a fig about the markets right now," Aaron said, his voice hitching on a small but unmistakable sob.

And then, like a big old light bulb turning on in my mind, I put two and two together and actually gasped into the phone. "Ohmigod, Aaron . . . Yelena Galanis. She was your ex, wasn't she?"

The sound of Aaron weeping absolutely gutted me. "I . . . can't . . . believe . . . she's gone!" he sobbed.

I bit my lip and realized that Gilley was staring at me with his mouth agape. I could see the sympathy in his own eyes for poor Aaron.

"I'm so, so sorry," I said to the count. "This must be such a blow."

His weeping intensified.

I looked at Gilley, absolutely pained by the fact that this poor dear man was sobbing his heart out and I was helpless to comfort him other than to speak a few words of sympathy. "What can we do for you, Aaron?" I finally said.

He didn't answer. He simply wept.

By now, Gilley had gotten up from his chair and moved to the kitchen. He brought back a pad of paper and a pen, and then he wrote out a note. It read, *Should we go to him?*

I nodded. That was exactly what we needed to do.

"Aaron," I said gently, "Gilley and I are coming over. You shouldn't be alone right now. You can expect us in twenty minutes or so." I didn't know where Aaron lived, but most people in the Hamptons were at most fifteen to twenty minutes away from each other no matter in which direction you drove.

"Okay," Aaron squeaked, and he hung up.

I got up and gathered my purse as Gilley knelt down next to Spooks and whispered in his ear. The dog's short tail tapped against the couch cushion, but he didn't move as we headed out the door.

"Do you think he'll be okay?" I asked Gil while he pulled the door shut.

"Spooks or the count?"

"Spooks."

"He'll be fine. His paperwork said he was a super-calm pup, with no obvious signs of separation anxiety."

"Good," I said, and we hurried to the car. After we got in, Gilley tapped on his phone again, then plugged Aaron's address into the car's navigation system while I backed out of the driveway.

When we got on the road, Gilley said, "He's in Amagansett, near Indian Wells Beach."

"I told him we'd be there in twenty minutes."

"We'll have a little time to spare, which is why I think we should stop and get him something to eat. He'll need nourishment and liquids."

"Great idea. What'd you have in mind?"

"How about Faye's Pho?" Gil suggested. "Pho is the ultimate comfort food. And it's fast."

"Agreed. Put in an order, will you?"

Gilley tapped at his screen some more. "Done. And I put in an order for us too. We can heat it up for a snack when we get home. That Caesar salad didn't fill me up."

After picking up the takeout, we were soon in Aaron's neighborhood, which was a particularly tony part of East Hampton.

The estates were enormous, and I was a bit jealous that they each had such a deep lot with a large section of private beach.

"Wow," Gilley said as we wound along a particularly curvy road. "This is even nicer than your neighborhood."

"It is," I said. "But probably fitting for a Danish count, right?"

"If he lives around here, he's definitely got money," Gilley said. "Big bucks."

The turn-by-turn directions pointed us to Bluff Road, and I pulled the car into one of the drives off that road. The driveway was long and sloped upward under a canopy of tall trees. At last, we stopped at a rectangular-looking structure with narrow windows and consisting of two levels, which looked like they were made of poured concrete. No, scratch that. The place looked like a prison.

"Not the friendliest-looking home," Gilley said as we came to a stop at the front door.

"No. It's not. But we're not here to criticize. We're here to offer support and comfort."

Gilley reached behind him for the carryout bag from Faye's, and we exited the car and approached the two front steps leading to the door. Gilley motioned for me to go in front of him, so I was the first to press the doorbell.

It gonged loudly from inside.

Gilley rocked back on his heels a few times while we waited. And waited.

And waited.

"Press it again," Gil said, nodding toward the doorbell.

It had made such a loud sound before that I was a hesitant to ring it again. "What if he's indisposed?"

"What if he was out back and didn't hear it the first time?"

"He knew we were coming over." I didn't want to be one of those guests who pressed the bell like an impatient pedestrian at a crosswalk.

Gilley sighed dramatically, then reached around me to press the bell himself. It gonged for a second time, and I cringed at the thought that Aaron was somewhere inside, irritated that we weren't a little more patient.

Gil and I continued to wait in silence for another minute or two, and I'll admit that I was now a bit worried that neither gong had produced the count at the door.

"You're sure you got the right address?" I asked Gil.

He eyed me with heavy lids.

"Okay, okay," I said. "Sheesh, you don't have to yell."

Gilley chuckled. "I mean, please, Cat. You've known me for how long and you still second-guess my internet sleuthing skills?"

"Right. Shame on me," I said, but I was a little distracted, as

I was looking around the drive for any signs that Aaron might be outside.

Seeing no sign of him, I glanced next at my phone and noted the time. "Where could he be?"

"Honestly, why isn't there a maid or a butler to answer the bell?" Gilley said. He then handed me the carryout bag and turned to walk back down the steps.

"Where're you going?" I asked.

He pointed toward the side of the yard, and when he disappeared around the corner, I hustled down the steps to follow him.

A concrete pathway led us to the back of the house and a narrow lap pool. The scrubby backyard fell away from the house in an open slope that allowed a spectacular view of the ocean.

"Nice," Gil said, pausing to admire the view.

I glanced at it but then focused on the pool area. There was nothing but a few patio chairs, the pool, and a grill set against the house. No sign of Aaron.

Gilley stopped admiring the view and walked right up to the twin sliding-glass doors. I squinted toward them but couldn't see anyone inside.

That, of course, didn't stop Gilley from moving right up to the doors and cupping his hands to peer inside.

I gasped. "Gilley, stop that!"

He continued to peer inside, so I hustled up to him and gave him a firm pat on the shoulder. "I'm serious!"

Gilley stepped back from the doors, clearly impatient and annoyed. "We've been out here waiting for him to answer for hours," he complained.

"Three minutes," I corrected. "But yes, I agree. It's far too long for our arrival to go unanswered."

After handing him back the carryout bag, I lifted my phone and began to tap at the screen while retracing my steps along the pathway toward the front of the house with Gilley trailing behind me.

"Who're you calling?" he asked when we reached the front of the house again.

"Aaron," I said. I put the phone to my ear and listened through the five rings. Then it went to voice mail. "Aaron? It's Catherine. Gilley and I are at your door, and we rang the doorbell twice. If you're not up for company, I totally understand, but would you at least let us know if you're all right? I'm worried."

I hung up the call and stared at my phone, waiting for a message or a call or *something* from Aaron to let me know that he knew we were there but wasn't up for visitors. After another minute or two, I took up tapping at my phone again.

"Now who're you calling?" Gilley asked.

"Shepherd," I said, then raised a finger to my lips when I heard him pick up the line.

"Hey," he said, as if he were in a rush. "I'm a little busy. Can I call you later?"

"Actually, I'm calling with a concern, and I may need an officer of the law," I said.

Shepherd's tone turned crisp with focus. "What kind of concern?"

"Gilley and I are at a client's home. We're checking on him because he's having a difficult time, emotionally speaking. And we confirmed that we'd be over within twenty minutes or so, but now he's not answering the doorbell or my calls."

"How difficult a time, emotionally speaking, are we talking?"

"Enough for me to be a tiny bit panicked that he's not answering the bell."

"I'm on it," he said. "I'll get a uniform over to do a wellness check. What's the address?"

"Actually, we're in Amagansett," I said, remembering that this town wasn't in Shepherd's jurisdiction.

"Huh," he said. "I was just in that neck of the woods, and I've got a crew headed out there now too."

"You were? You do?"

"Give me the address and I'll call over to APD and have them send a uni," he said.

"Six-one-seven Bluff Road."

There was no acknowledgment from Shepherd, so I said, "Shep? You there?"

"I'm here," he said. "Your client wouldn't be Aaron Nassau, would it?"

My eyes widened, and I pulled in my chin in surprise.

Gilley, staring at me intently, mouthed, *What?*

"Yes. Yes, that's him," I told Shepherd, getting a bad feeling. "How did you know?"

"Your client is fine," Shepherd said. "Well, relatively speaking. He's about to be charged with murder."

My jaw dropped, and I shook my head.

"What?" Gilley said. "Cat, *what!*"

"What do you mean, he's being charged with murder!" I yelled.

I hadn't meant to screech at Shepherd; it was just too preposterous to contemplate. My sweetheart was a wonderful man; however, he had one very bad habit of arresting first and asking questions later.

"Cat, listen, I can't talk about this right now. I gotta prep for the interrogation. I'll fill you in later."

"*Interrogation?*"

"Interview," Shepherd said with a chuckle. "I meant interview."

I said nothing for a moment, my mind racing furiously, while Gilley continued to look at me in earnest. And then my eyes narrowed, and I said, "Is Aaron's lawyer there?"

It was Shepherd's turn to be quiet for a moment. "No," he said softly. "He hasn't asked for one yet."

"Gotta go!"

"Cat! Wait! Don't you dare get invol—"

I hung up by pressing my finger angrily against the red button at the bottom of my phone and immediately flipped over to my contacts list.

"Let me guess," Gilley said when I placed the phone at my ear for a third time. "You're calling Marcus."

I put a hand on my hip and ground my teeth. "Damn straight I'm calling Marcus!"

Marcus Brown was the best defense attorney in all of Long Island. He'd represented me when Shepherd arrested me for murder (which I hadn't committed), and he'd also represented two other friends of mine when they'd been hauled down to the station by my overzealous main squeeze.

Marcus had easily won a dismissal in each of those cases. Shepherd's circumstantial evidence was no match for Marcus Brown in a courtroom.

"Catherine Cooper," Marcus purred, picking up the call on the first ring. "To what do I owe this unexpected pleasure?"

"Hello, my friend," I said, warmed by his greeting. "I need you."

"Personally or professionally?"

"The latter."

I heard the crinkle of paper, and I imagined Marcus turning to a fresh page on his legal pad. "Talk to me."

I told Marcus about Aaron and how Shepherd had just arrested him.

"That man never passes up an opportunity to arrest first and ask questions later," Marcus said with a sigh.

I stifled a chuckle, as I'd already thought that same thing. "Right?"

"Whose murder is he about to be charged with?" Marcus asked.

"Probably Yelena Galanis's," I said. "Shepherd was on the case last night, right after it happened."

Absolute silence filled the connection.

"Marcus?"

"I'm here," he said. But then he said nothing more.

"Are you all right?" I asked, because it was such an odd reaction.

"Fine," he said quickly. "Catherine, are you willing to Venmo me for the initial hour with Nassau? I can reimburse you once he retains me, but should he refuse my services, I won't be able to represent him in this matter."

"Of course, Marcus. I'll send that Venmo right over."

"Perfect. I'll call Shepherd and insist that he cease questioning Mr. Nassau until I get there."

"Wonderful. Thank you."

I hung up with Marcus and handed the phone to Gilley. "I need to know what a Venmo is and how to make a payment for an hour of Marcus's time," I said.

Gilley smirked.

"Stop smirking!"

Gilley's smirk turned into a giggle. "You're the mother of teenagers. How is it you don't know this stuff? Like, doesn't it ever come up in casual conversation?"

"I'm the mother of teenage *boys*. They don't talk to me. They grunt."

"Ah. Fair point."

Gilley did some stuff on my phone, tilting the screen toward me so that I could watch, but truly my mind was elsewhere, and I was simply happy when he announced, "Done. Marcus has been retained for the hour."

"Perfect," I said, beginning to walk away. "Come on," I called over my shoulder.

"I'd ask where we're going, but I already know our next stop will be to the East Hampton Police Department."

"Damn straight," I growled, balling my hands into fists.

"Cool," Gilley replied. "I love a good fireworks show."

Pulling open the driver's side door, I snapped, "Just get in!"

Gilley opened his door, placing his free hand over his mouth to suppress a giggle. "And the light show has already started!"

Chapter 9

As we turned back onto the road, retracing our way to East Hampton, Gilley remarked, "Kind of amazing that in the twenty-five minutes it took us to get here, Shepherd arrived and arrested Aaron."

"We always did have fabulous timing," I muttered.

"Are you mad at Shepherd?"

"Of course I'm mad at Shepherd!" I yelled, angrily gripping the steering wheel.

"May I ask why?"

I glanced sideways at Gilley, wondering if he was teasing me, but he had an earnest expression, which confused me. "Because he arrested an innocent man. *Again*!"

"Did he?" Gilley asked. I leveled a look at him, and he added, "I'm just playing devil's advocate, Cat, because you know Shepherd's going to give you the same argument."

"Yes, he's innocent," I said firmly. "You met Aaron. Do you think he'd be capable of murder?"

"Cat, it's been my experience that human beings are capable of anything. Even the nice ones can commit murder."

I mulled that over for a few minutes. "No," I said at last. "Yelena was stabbed to death. That method of murder requires a certain personality type, Gilley. Someone capable of snapping in absolute fury, and Aaron didn't show any sign of that. If Yelena was the woman he was still pining for, then he must have been aware of her reputation—and her show—and yet when he came to see me, he was distraught not over what she might say about him from the stage but about not having her in his life. There was no hint of jealousy or anger over being made fun of. He simply wanted her back in his life.

"Plus, you didn't hear the heartbreak in his voice when I called him earlier. He was destroyed, Gilley. Just absolutely, heartbreakingly destroyed. And it was obvious, even to you, when he picked up the line that he was distraught. How could he have faked that if he wasn't crying before we called?"

Gilley nodded slowly. "That's all true," he said. "Great point."

I smiled and squared my shoulders. I knew I was right. Aaron simply wasn't a killer. I could feel it in my gut, and my sister always said that one should always trust one's gut feelings.

Fifteen minutes later we pulled into a parking space right next to Marcus, who was just getting out of his car. He looked devilishly handsome in a tan suit with bright orange tie and cream-colored dress shirt. He lowered his sunglasses to midnose to stare at us over the rims after Gilley and I got out of the car, and I swear Gilley practically swooned with the cool silhouette Marcus cut.

"Catherine. Gilley," he said with a nod.

"Hello, Marcus," I said, adding a small wave.

"Hello, gorgeous," Gilley said.

I eyed him sharply, but Marcus covered his mouth to hide a chuckle.

"I mean, he *is* gorgeous, right?" Gilley said to me.

"He's quite handsome," I agreed, joining in the banter.

"And that suit!" Gilley added, waving at Marcus's duds. "Perfection!"

Marcus dropped his hand to give in to that chuckle, and I could tell he was pleased by the compliments. "Thanks, Gilley," he said, running his fingers along his lapel. "It's an art."

We gathered in a half circle, and I made a sweeping motion toward the door. "Shall we?"

"Whoa, whoa," Marcus said, holding up a hand to stop us. "What's this 'we' business?"

"Cat wants to yell at her boyfriend," Gilley said.

I glared at him, and he stared insolently back at me.

"No one's going to yell at anybody, at least not until I find out what the facts are," Marcus said.

"The facts are that Shepherd has *once again* arrested an innocent man," I said.

"Do you know what evidence he might have against Nassau?" Marcus asked.

"Uh . . . no," I said. "Whatever it is, it's probably flimsy."

"But you don't know that for sure?"

"Well, no. I don't."

"Okay, listen, Catherine, I know you mean well, but if Nassau agrees to retain me to represent him, then your going in there to yell at Shepherd could jeopardize my case."

I took up a stubborn stance with my hands on my hips. "How could that jeopardize your case?"

I wasn't trying to be contrarian. I simply wanted to yell at my sweetheart.

"Well, for starters, say Shepherd engages you in an argument. And say he begins to question you about your client. Did you know about the relationship between Mr. Nassau and the deceased?"

I opened my mouth to answer, closed it for a moment to think, then said, "Well, yes. But not right away. He told us that he'd dated a woman who'd dumped him flat and he was distraught over it."

Marcus nodded. "Uh-huh. When did he tell you this?"

"Um . . ." I said. "Yesterday."

"Mm-hmm," Marcus hummed. "So, the day of the murder, Mr. Nassau was agitated. Is that fair to say?"

"Upset," I corrected. "He was upset."

"I see. Thank you for that clarification. So, on the day of the murder, you saw Mr. Nassau upset at the fact that Ms. Galanis had broken up with him and was seeing other men? And that Mr. Nassau was very likely aware that Yelena Galanis had a hit show running at the local theater, where her material was comprised entirely of her dating escapades and likely featured Mr. Nassau as one of the unnamed twelve angry men. Do I have that correct, Ms. Cooper?"

I could see what he was doing from a mile away, and I hated that I'd been naïve enough to believe I could simply barge on over here, yell at Shepherd and, in doing that, assist Aaron in his situation. It was a ridiculous assumption, and one I was feeling very embarrassed for having.

"Marcus?" I said after a long, thoughtful pause.

"Yes?"

"Do give Mr. Nassau our best and tell him to reach out, should he wish to talk, once you've gotten the charges dismissed."

"Let's hope that's as far as this gets," Marcus said. "But I hear you. I'll pass on the message."

"Will you call us later with an update?" Gilley asked.

"Sure, but I'll speak to you only about what the police have on Nassau, nothing about what he tells me."

"Attorney-client privilege," I said.

Marcus nodded.

"All right. Thank you, Marcus. We'll look forward to your call."

With that, I took Gilley by the elbow, and we left Marcus to his job.

Gilley and I drove in silence for much of the ride home, until finally he said, "So you're really not going to ask Shepherd about what he was thinking arresting Aaron?"

"I can't," I said. "You heard Marcus. If I do, I could open Aaron to incrimination."

"But what if Shepherd asks you?"

I shrugged. "He can ask all he wants, but I'm not going to tell him a thing unless he calls me in for an interview, and even then, I wouldn't go without Marcus." And then I looked at Gilley, knowing he had overheard my entire first meeting with Aaron. "You have to promise not to say anything, either."

Gilley lifted a dainty pinky. "Pinky swear. And if he hauls me in, I'll call Marcus to the rescue."

"Good," I said.

Gilley jumped at the sound of his phone ringing and pulled it out from his back pocket. After glancing at the display, he simply allowed the phone to continue to ring.

"Are you going to answer that?"

"Probably not," Gilley said.

"Who is it?"

"Michel."

I raised my brow in surprise. "Ah," I said.

Gilley's phone rang one more time and then stopped. He pocketed it again, and we drove the rest of the way home in silence.

Several hours later Gilley and I were just finishing up the dinner dishes when my phone rang. Thinking it was likely Shepherd, I was actually surprised to see that it was Marcus.

"Hello, Counselor. Calling with good news, I hope?"

"Afraid not, Catherine," he said somberly.

"Tell me," I said, grabbing Gilley's arm to alert him that there was trouble.

Marcus sighed heavily. "Shepherd has some pretty damning evidence against Mr. Nassau."

"Like what?"

"Like the murder weapon for one."

"They found the knife?"

"It's a letter opener with the Danish royal family crest on it, and although the handle was wiped mostly clean, EHPD was able to lift a partial thumbprint that matches Mr. Nassau's."

"Oh, dear," I said, while Gilley's brow furrowed as he looked at me.

"There's also video footage from Ms. Galanis's doorbell camera, showing Mr. Nassau arriving at her home shortly after she left for the theater yesterday. It was around five, which was a half hour after she left for the theater. The video shows him peeking into her windows and trying the door handle."

"Oh, my," I whispered.

What? Gilley mouthed. I could only shake my head and hold up a finger, telling him to wait.

"And there's a recording on Ms. Galanis's voice mail of Mr. Nassau telling her that he can't stand to live without her, and he might do something drastic if she doesn't take him back."

"Oh, Aaron, what were you thinking?" I whispered.

"What? Cat, *what?* What was he thinking?" Gilley pleaded.

I didn't answer him, because Marcus was continuing to talk.

"And, if that weren't enough, Shepherd has video footage from a gas station two blocks from the theater where Aaron stopped to purchase a bottle of water just ten minutes before Yelena's intermission break."

I put a hand over my eyes. This was terrible. "Are you going to take the case?"

"Of course I'm going to take the case," Marcus said. "And the first thing I'll do is contact the Danish embassy to see if I can secure sovereign immunity for Mr. Nassau."

"Sovereign immunity?" I repeated.

"Yes. Since he is a member of the Danish royal family, I might be able to get Mr. Nassau an exemption from prosecution of a criminal act. He's already got it for civil acts, but I'd push for it, and if granted, he'd have to leave the country immediately, but at least he wouldn't face a murder one charge."

I took that in, struck by how much it felt like justice was being cheated in light of all the evidence that Marcus had just revealed to me. "But, Marcus . . . what if he's guilty?"

Marcus didn't answer me right away, and I felt in that moment before he spoke that he was weighing what he'd say against how I might view him. "It's not my job to determine his guilt or innocence, Catherine. It's my job to represent him legally and keep him out of jail—any way I can."

"You're right," I said. I'd almost forgotten. Still, it didn't sit well with me. "Thank you for filling me in, Marcus. I very much appreciate it."

"Have a good night, Catherine," he replied, and I swear I detected a note of relief in his voice.

When I got off the call with Marcus, I filled Gilley in.

"So, Aaron *did* murder Yelena?" Gilley said after I'd finished.

I thought about it for a long moment before I answered him. "What I can't figure out is why Aaron would leave my office yesterday, so desperate for my help in getting him to move on from the love of his life, and then, within hours of that pained confession, commit premeditated murder."

"I don't know that I'm following you," Gilley said.

"What I mean is, if you're going to kill the woman who left you, the woman you're clearly still so in love with, why would you set up an appointment with a life coach?"

"To cast doubt on your actions," Gilley said. "Maybe Aaron knew you'd testify in court to his frame of mind a few hours beforehand."

I nodded. "Agree. However, did anything about Aaron's pained session with me yesterday strike you as false?"

It was Gilley's turn to take a moment to consider that. Finally, he said, "If I'm being totally honest, Cat, no. Nothing about his manner or his story or his professed love for his ex seemed contrived. He genuinely looked and sounded heartbroken."

"Exactly," I said. "He sounded the same on the phone with me earlier. And he also said something that stuck out to me when I first asked why he was so upset."

"What?"

"He said, 'I take it you don't read the papers.'"

"The papers? You mean *newspapers*?"

"Yes."

"So, you think Aaron learned about Yelena's murder through the newspaper."

"Yes. He didn't say, 'Watch the news,' Gil. He said, 'Read.'"

"Why is that important?"

"Aaron sounded like he'd just learned of the news, but we know that Yelena's murder was the lead story on all the local news programs both last night and this morning. So if he'd been faking, he would've said, 'You don't *watch* the news,' not 'Read the news.' When we reached out to him today, he truly sounded like he'd just learned of Yelena's death, which means he'd read about it when he opened up his paper today, and not before."

Gilley nodded and pointed a finger at me. "It's a subtle distinction that lends more to truth than to fakery," he said.

"Exactly."

Gilley and I were both silent for several moments while we each contemplated what we thought of Aaron's guilt or innocence.

Finally, I said, "Say, Gil, what would you think about—"

"Yes," he said, cutting me off.

I blinked. "You didn't even let me get out my question."

Gilley rolled his eyes. "Oh, please. You were about to ask me if we should poke around a bit into Yelena's murder and do a little sleuthing of our own."

I blinked again. "How did you know that was what I was going to ask?"

Gilley grinned and reached over to tap my temple. "Because I live inside your head."

I laughed and knocked his hand away. "Whatever. Where should we start?"

"Probably with her act, don't you think? We should figure out who the lovers were in *Twelve Angry Men*. That'd at least give us eleven other suspects to focus on."

I snapped my fingers and pointed at him. "Exactly! Gilley, that's exactly where we should start." Tapping at my lip, I thought for a moment and said, "Tucker McAllen was Lover Number One, right?"

"That's the general consensus," Gilley said. "I think Joel Goldberg was Lover Number Four."

My brow furrowed. "Lover Number Four. Remind me again, what were the clues?"

"The guy who introduced her to a girl's best friend, and then she waggled that big tennis bracelet, remember?"

"Ah, yes. Now I remember, and didn't Reese tell you that the rumor was that Goldberg was Lover Number Four?"

"He did. He heard it from a woman who said she'd seen Goldberg and Yelena canoodling at a café next door to one of his jewelry stores."

Goldberg was a familiar name. His jewelry stores were very high end and dotted every town in the Hamptons.

"Thank God for your bat-like hearing," I said. I hadn't heard much other than murmurs during the show.

"Comes in handy," Gilley said, moving over to the couch to plop down next to Spooks, who had just finished his bone treat and was busy licking his paws. As Gilley put his feet up on the ottoman, Spooks got up, turned around on the couch cushion, then settled himself with his big silver head in Gilley's lap.

"Awww," I said, moving over to sit next to the pair. "He knows he's home."

Gilley stroked one of the pup's ears. "I hope so. I never, ever, ever want him to feel abandoned again."

Pointing to the dog bed in front of the couch, I said, "So, you've given up on the rule of no dogs allowed on the furniture already?"

Gilley shrugged. "I still have the receipt. We can take the beds back to the Pet Palace tomorrow."

I chuckled, then got serious again. "Okay, so do we know any of the other lovers?"

"By *we*, I'm assuming you mean *me*."

"That's what I like about you, Gil. You're so perceptive."

Gilley rolled his eyes but allowed himself a playful grin. "I got the feeling that Lover Number Five was in the navy."

"The 'six gold stripes' line?" I asked. Yelena had made a crack about Lover Number Five being cheap, saying that the only gold he paid for were the six gold stripes on his sleeve.

"Yeah," Gilley said. "She also said he was a three-star guy in a two-star suit. The gold stripes mean length of service, if I'm not mistaken, and the stars indicate rank."

"What would three stars make him?" I asked.

"Don't know," Gil said, then he pointed to his tablet, which was on the coffee table. "Would you mind?" he asked, indicating that if he bent forward to get it, he'd disturb Spooks.

I smirked but got up to retrieve the tablet and handed it to him. Gilley balanced the tablet on his lower thigh, cracked his knuckles, wiggled his fingers over the keyboard, and dove in. I waited patiently, stroking Spooks's head and smiling when the dog sighed contentedly.

"Aha!" Gil said.

"You found out what rank three stars is?"

Gilley eyed me first in confusion, then in impatience. "No. I mean, yes. That's the first thing I looked up, along with the stripes. Lover Number Five has at least twenty-four years in service, and he's a vice admiral."

"Wow. An admiral? Yelena dated a naval vice admiral?" I had no idea what a vice admiral did, but it sounded impressive.

"No, Yelena dated a Coast Guard vice admiral."

"How do you know it's the Coast Guard and not the navy?"

"Because I found out who she dated. The only vice admiral

anywhere near the Hamptons is this guy . . ." Gilley swiveled his tablet around so that I could see the photograph of a very handsome man with chiseled features, black hair that was gray at the temples, and a big, beautiful smile. He was dressed in a dark blue uniform with six gold stripes on his sleeves and three gold stars near his shoulder.

"He's pretty," I said.

Gilley swiveled the tablet back toward himself. "Right?"

"Yeah. I can see why she'd be attracted to him."

Gilley tapped the corner of his tablet and said, "Meet Vice Admiral Liam Leahy. He has a place on Shelter Island."

Shelter Island was to our north. It was a medium-sized island for these parts, sandwiched between Sag Harbor and Greenport—the two end prongs of Long Island.

"Huh," I said. "Would a vice admiral throw away his whole career out of revenge for a former lover making fun of him onstage?"

Gilley shrugged. "I'd say maybe if I hadn't heard all of that part of Yelena's act. Of all the lovers she mentioned, he was kind of the most boring."

I nodded. "Yeah. Number Five got the fewest laughs."

"So, there really wasn't anything salacious about him," Gilley said. "And a vice admiral is second in command in the Coast Guard. He's way up there in rank."

"Is he married?" I asked, thinking that if Leahy was married and he had an affair with Yelena, that could definitely end his career.

"Nope," Gilley said. "He's a divnk. Just like Shepherd, actually."

"A divnk? What's a divnk?"

"Divorced, no kids."

I blinked. "Then what am I?" I asked.

Gilley smirked. "The envy of divorcées everywhere."

I laughed. "Come on, Gilley, I'm serious."

"So am I," he insisted. "You're divorced, with two kids in boarding school, a sexy boyfriend, and all the money a person could want. You're a divrahah."

"What's a divrahah?"

"Divorced, rich, and happy as hell."

I rolled my eyes. "You make it sound like I'm happy that my sons are at boarding school."

"Oh, please, Cat. They were here the second half of the summer and had dinner with us, what? Four times?"

"Eight," I said and offered Gilley a chagrined smile. "I counted."

"Exactly my point. They were at the beach or the skate park way more than they were here."

I sighed. "I'd still rather have them home than away at school."

"But can you deny you're happy as hell?"

"No," I said. "No, I'm pretty happy."

"Exactly my point. And thank your stars you're not a man-katbed."

"A . . . *what*?"

"Mankatbed."

"What the devil is that?"

"Married, no kids, about to be divorced."

"Oh, you're right. That would be bad. Who do we know that's a mankatbed?"

Gilley eyed me expectantly.

It took me longer than I'd like to admit to realize he meant himself. "Oh, come on," I said. "Gilley, you are not!"

"Aren't I?" he said, his lower lip quivering just a tad.

I moved in for a hug, disturbing Spooks, who moaned slightly in protest. When I let go, I kept my hands on Gilley's shoulders. "I'm here for you. Day and night. Whatever you need."

Gilley nodded and pointed to his tablet. "Shall we get on with it?"

"Yes," I said, sitting back again. "Where were we?"

"Talking about Mr. Leahy. Who's divorced, no kids, and the apparent mark of a very clever, albeit very dead, lady."

"Yes, that's right," I said. "Do we know if he was recently divorced? Maybe he had an affair with Yelena and that ended his marriage, and he killed her in revenge."

"He's been divorced for six years," Gilley said, scrolling through his tablet. "At least according to my public records search."

"Let's put him on the list of suspects, anyway. We want to be thorough in our investigation."

"Agreed," Gilley said.

"Okay, so that's three out of eleven, and it's not even nine o'clock yet."

"We are good," Gilley said.

"Okay, so how do we identify the rest—especially the ones we didn't get to hear about during the second act?"

"I wish we could talk to Sunny," Gilley said. "I'm sure she'd know every guy in the show."

I shook my head. "I don't think so. She told me yesterday, when I went to pick up the tickets, that Yelena was planning to name names that night, and she gave me the impression that she didn't know who Yelena would publicly identify. She also said she hadn't yet seen the act."

"Hold on," Gilley said, swiveling to me with wide eyes. "Yelena mentioned that she was going to name names?"

"Yes," I said. I didn't know why Gilley was so excited by that. "She told Sunny when she gave her the tickets that she was going to drop a few names at the end of the show."

"Sugar," he said, "way to bury the lead."

"You think if Yelena told Sunny she was going to name names then maybe Yelena also told other people and it got back to the murderer?"

"Uh, *yeah*," Gilley said, like it should've been obvious.

"Don't be mean," I told him.

"Sorry," he said. "You're right. That was rude."

I shrugged and let it go. "How do we find out if Yelena told other people her plans for the evening?"

"We hunt down the twelve angry men and grill them about how much they knew about Yelena's show."

I nodded. "I like that. But how are we going to grill them exactly, Gilley? We don't know these men, and we wouldn't have any reason to walk right up to them and start asking them personal questions like that."

"Hmm," Gilley said. "That's true. We'll need an excuse."

We both stared at the floor while we thought about an excuse good enough to approach any of the men we identified.

"I've got nothing," I finally said.

Gilley sighed. "Me either. But not to worry. I'll think of something."

Headlights outside flashed across the room through the open blinds. I looked over my shoulder.

"Who's here?" Gilley said.

I got up and went to the front door. Spooks must've heard whoever it was outside approaching, because his head popped up and he jumped off the couch to run over to me and place himself between me and the door.

"Woof!" he barked. The sound was like a low rumble of thunder. Definitely not a bark to be messed with.

"Gilley?" we heard through the door.

Gilley had gotten up and was next to me. "Hey, Shepherd," he said through the still closed door.

"Is that a dog in there?"

"Woof!" Spooks barked in reply.

Placing a hand on the doorknob, I looked pointedly from Gilley to Spooks and back again. "Best hold on to him, Gilley. He's never met Shepherd."

Gilley knelt down next to Spooks and hugged the pup to him.

I opened the door, and Shepherd stood on the first step, hesitantly. "When did you get a dog?" he said by way of greeting.

"This is Spooks," Gilley told him. "Spooks, meet Shepherd."

Spooks had his hackles raised, and although he wasn't growling, we all understood that Shepherd needed to be on his best behavior until Spooks could approve his arrival.

"Hey, buddy," Shepherd said, kneeling low to get on Spooks's level. "He's a good-looking guy. Did you get him from the shelter?"

"We did," Gilley said, allowing Spooks to move forward toward Shepherd. "We picked him up today."

Shepherd nodded and waited for Spooks to inch forward and sniff at him. "Hey, guy," Shepherd said and very carefully lifted a hand to stroke the dog's ear. "How ya doin'? Huh? Who's a big boy? Huh? Who's a good buddy?"

I put a finger to my lips to suppress a bubble of laughter. Shepherd had completely melted at the appearance of a dog, and it was adorable.

Spooks, it seemed, had also allowed his protective heart to melt, and his stub tail was wagging back and forth furiously as he pushed his big head into Shepherd's chest. Then he had a sudden thought and bolted inside again to retrieve a squeaky toy and bring it over to Shepherd, who played tug with him for a bit out in the driveway while Gilley and I eyed each other knowingly.

At last, Shep came inside himself, still pulling on the squeaky toy while Spooks dug his heels in and tried to coax his new friend to continue playing. "Man, I love dogs," Shepherd said.

"You do?" I asked. "I never knew that about you."

Shepherd nodded. "I had a bunch of dogs growing up, three, sometimes four at a time, and they were all rescues. Rescues make the best companions. They've seen the darker side of life, and they're grateful for any love they get."

"Agreed," Gilley said, moving to the kitchen counter, where

he dug through one of the bags we'd brought inside after our trip to the Pet Palace. When he produced a large Kong, he said, "Spooks! Hey, Spooks! You want some peanut butter?"

The dog cocked his head at Gilley, the squeaky toy dangling out of his mouth. Gilley chuckled and headed into the kitchen to fill the Kong with a yummy treat. Spooks dropped the toy and padded after him, leaving me alone with Shepherd.

"How come you don't own a dog now?" I asked, feeling a sudden tension in the air between us.

"No time," he said, looking wistfully at Spooks's departing form. "I spend too many hours at the station to be a good parent to a pooch."

"Ah," I said.

"Yeah," he said.

I tried to think of another thing to say to fill the awkward silence that followed, but Shepherd beat me to it. "Thanks for butting into my case today, Cat."

My shoulders sagged. "Is that what this is?" I said, pointing to the door, then to Shepherd. "You came over here to give me a lecture?"

"Oh, come on. You knew I would," he said.

"I didn't butt into your case, Shep. I merely recommended an attorney for my client—whom you arrested based on flimsy evidence."

"It ain't flimsy, honey," Shepherd said, and his tone was dead serious. "Yelena was murdered with a letter opener that belonged to Nassau."

"How do you *know* it belonged to Aaron?" I asked.

"It has the coat of arms of the Danish royal family on it," he said easily.

"A letter opener with a coat of arms of the royal family on it can probably be found in any tourist gift shop in Denmark," I argued.

Shepherd chuckled. "I doubt a tourist gift shop sells a

fourteen-karat gold letter opener with the official coat of arms inlaid with sapphires, yellow diamonds, and rubies."

My mouth fell open. "Whoa," I said. "That has to be worth a pretty penny."

Shepherd nodded. "Our best guess is that it's worth fifty to sixty grand. Probably more."

"Probably a lot more," I said. "Which begs the question, why would Aaron use it to commit murder?"

"Because it was handy," Shepherd said, moving around me and over to the couch, where he collapsed in a tired heap.

"Do you want something to eat, Shepherd?" Gilley called from the kitchen.

"Whatcha got?"

"I made a sweet potato and chickpea curry over basmati rice."

Shepherd sniffed the air. "That must be what smells so good. Yeah, Gilley, a plate of that would be great."

"Coming right up," Gil said, and he got to work pulling the leftovers out of the fridge.

"Where did you find this letter opener?" I asked next, wanting to continue the conversation.

"At the scene. One of the techs found it under the dressing table."

"What was it doing there?"

"I dunno, Cat. Maybe Nassau threw it there after he got done stabbing my victim to death."

I looked at him crossly. "Shep," I said, "why would Aaron leave behind the most incriminating piece of evidence and not take it with him if he did in fact kill Yelena?"

"I think he panicked," Shepherd said.

"How convenient," I said drolly.

"It happens," Shepherd said.

"What did Aaron say about it when you asked him?"

"You mean, what did Marcus Brown allow him to say when I asked him?"

I pursed my lips in an effort to keep them from spreading into a small grin.

Shepherd rolled his eyes and said, "Nassau claims that he has no idea how it got in Yelena's dressing room, but he suspects she stole it the last time they were together."

"She stole it?"

"That's what he says. That's not what I believe."

"Why would she steal something worth so much money?" I said, as if Shepherd hadn't even spoken. "I mean, stealing anything over ten thousand makes it a felony, right?"

"It does," he said. "But Nassau was quick to say that if she had taken it, he wouldn't have pressed charges, because he still loved her, and as far as he was concerned, she was welcome to anything of his that he owned."

"And you don't believe him," I said.

"Of course I don't believe him. He had to add that last bit to take away the motive for murder."

"I'm missing that. What motive?"

Shepherd shrugged. "Nassau discovers his extremely valuable letter opener is missing, suspects Yelena has stolen it, heads to the theater to confront her about it, finds it, and stabs her with it when he finds the proof of her larceny."

"Why wouldn't he have simply called the police?" I asked next. "If he'd suspected that Yelena had stolen the letter opener, why wouldn't he have simply filled out a police report?"

"You'd have to ask him that," Shepherd said.

"But does that really make sense to you?" I pressed. "I mean, you're a seasoned detective. Does it make sense that a man would stab his former lover with the very object he suspected she stole, only to then throw it under a dressing table as he ran out the door?"

Shepherd rubbed his tired eyes. "I don't know what was going through his mind at the time of the murder, babe. All I know is that your guy did it. I had him set up to confess it, and then you stuck your nose into it, and now what was almost a slam dunk means I gotta work triple hard to prove my case."

"Here you are," Gilley said, handing Shepherd a steaming bowl of the delicious curry. "And here you also are," he added, pulling out a pint bottle of chilled pale ale from under his arm.

"Gilley," Shepherd said with a grin as he took the bottle from him, "you really know how to spoil a guy."

"I've had some practice at it," Gilley said, clearly pleased, as he shuffled over to a nearby chair and plopped down himself.

Shepherd tucked into his dinner, and we waited in silence for him to take a few bites. "Oh, man," he said, hovering his fork over the meal. "Gil! This is good!"

Gilley's grin widened.

"Any word on Sunny?" I asked, suddenly thinking of her.

Shepherd stopped chewing. In fact, he froze in place for a beat or two, but then he seemed to recover himself. "Nothing new," he said. "I stopped by their house on my way here. Darius had his hands full with Finley. He says that Sunny is kind of out of it. They've got her on some heavy sedatives to keep her calm until they can figure out what might've triggered the episode."

"Did you get a chance to see her?" Gilley asked.

Shepherd stared at his food and shook his head. I could see the tense line of his shoulders and knew he was terribly worried about his twin. "Darius is the only one allowed to see her right now, and he said even his visits are kept short. They don't want her upset, and they're worried that seeing me might make her upset."

"Why?" I asked.

"I don't know, Cat," Shepherd said, his voice suddenly hard. "Maybe because I'd lose it if I saw her locked up in some mental ward."

I bit my lip, regretting the fact that I'd pressed him on the point. "I'm sorry," I whispered.

He shook his head, set his fork in the curry, and reached over to squeeze my hand. "It's not you. It's this whole situation."

"Understood," I said.

We let Shepherd continue to eat his dinner in relative silence, but then he looked up at us and said, "I'm getting self-conscious with you two watching me eat. Somebody say something."

"How's that other case going?" Gilley asked.

Shepherd grunted and chewed the bite he'd taken for a moment before answering. "That one's a puzzler."

"Do you still think it was a mob hit?" I asked.

Shepherd shook his head, then shrugged. "I don't know what to think of it. I assigned the case to Santana—"

"Santa?" Gilley interrupted. "Are his eight tiny reindeers also on the case?"

Shepherd leveled a look at him. "Not Santa, Gil. *Santana*. He's the department's new detective. A hotshot out of Queens, he asked for a transfer here ''cause he likes the sea.'" Shepherd used air quotes for that last part, and he added an eye roll. "Anyway, he's worked enough homicides that I figured he could probably handle this one, and I'm keeping tabs on it 'cause I'm not ruling out that there's a link to Yelena's murder, but everything Santana's reporting back to me so far only adds to the mystery."

"Like what?" I asked.

"Well, like the fact that we were only able to identify the vic by using the key fob in his pocket to locate his car, which was in the same parking structure where you guys were parked. He left his wallet in the car, along with his phone and anything else that might identify him, and although he was wearing a women's size-ten raincoat, stuffed with two hundred thousand dollars—"

"Two *hundred thousand?*" Gilley and I both gasped.

Shepherd nodded and continued, as if we hadn't interrupted him. "In the lining. Labretta found the car. The plates were registered to a guy named Mark Purdy, and when we searched the car, we found a wallet and phone in the glove box. ID matching the vic identified him definitively.

"Purdy's on no one's list for organized crime. He's a retired estate attorney, lived in a condo overlooking the bay in Sag Harbor, and the ME says that he doesn't think the murderer used a knife to slit Purdy's throat. He thinks it was piano wire."

"Oh, God," Gilley said, his face a mask of horror. "I thought they did that only in the movies."

"Nope," Shepherd said. "They do that in real life too. It's quick and effective, and it sends a clear signal."

"So, you really do believe this was a mob hit," I said.

"For sure. What I can't figure out is the money. None of the bills are counterfeit, so why the hit man didn't take it with him is a puzzler."

"Maybe the hit man didn't know that it wasn't counterfeit," Gilley said.

Shepherd sighed and rubbed his eyes again. He seemed utterly exhausted. "Maybe," he conceded. "Santana's digging into Purdy's financials to see if he can trace the money or find any hints of a connection to organized crime."

"I don't know whether to hope for a connection or not," I said. "On the one hand, it would be a relief to know there wasn't some crazed serial killer type roaming the streets, looking for victims, and on the other hand, it'd be yet *another* Mafia hit entering our lives in a terrible way."

"How is this entering your lives?" Shepherd asked, and he was giving me that look like I'd better not even think about getting involved in an amateur sleuth kind of way.

"Well, Gilley and I *did* discover Purdy's body," I said quickly, while Gilley avoided making eye contact with Shepherd.

"Uh-huh," he said, clearly still suspicious. Wagging his finger at us, he added, "Do *not* get involved in this, you two."

"Wouldn't dream of it," Gilley said.

"The thought never entered our minds," I said.

Shepherd continued to stare at us like he knew we were big fat fibbers. Which, hello . . . we were! But no way was I going to confirm that.

Shepherd finally let up and tried to stifle a huge yawn. "Man, I am beat."

I stood up and took his hand. "Come on," I said. "Let's get you to bed."

"I'm staying over?" he asked as he got to his feet, and there was the sweetest bit of hopefulness in his voice.

"Of course you're staying over," I said, wrapping my arm around his waist and guiding us toward the door. "I'm not about to let you drive home in the state you're in."

"What state am I in?"

"Tired and suspicious."

Shepherd grinned down at me. "It's like you know me."

Chapter 10

The next day, I spent the whole day in the city with my sons. Monday morning, however, I went straight to Chez Kitty. I wanted to pick up where Gilley and I had left off on Saturday night.

Letting myself in, I called out to him, but he wasn't anywhere in the house. And neither was Spooks. There was, however, a note on the table that said that he and the pup had gone for a walk, and that I should make myself comfortable with some coffee and have the slice of quiche Florentine he'd set aside for me.

I smiled as I unwrapped the plate. Gilley was always taking care of me, and as much as I was heartbroken that he and Michel seemed to be headed for a split, I was grateful that Gilley wouldn't be leaving me anytime soon.

After polishing off the quiche and the coffee, I straightened up the living room, tossing Spooks's various squeaky toys into the toy basket, doing a bit of light vacuuming and dusting, and before I knew it, I'd also organized Gilley's spice rack.

"Where the devil could he be?" I muttered to myself when I glanced up at the time. I'd been at Chez Kitty for well over an hour.

As if on cue, the front door opened and in came Gilley and

Spooks, but leaning on Gilley and hobbling forward was none other than Tiffany—Sunny's babysitter.

"Oh, my goodness!" I said in alarm when I saw that the poor girl was sticking her right foot out in front of her in an effort not to have it touch the floor. "What happened?"

"She rolled her ankle," Gilley said, guiding Tiffany to a nearby chair.

The young woman's face was contorted in pain, and I hurried to pull the ottoman over so that she could lift her foot onto it. She winced and hissed out a breath as she very carefully placed it onto the cushion.

After hurrying to the freezer, I pulled out a cold compress and came back to the chair to see Gilley very gently putting another pillow underneath Tiffany's ankle to give it more support.

Kneeling down, I said to Tiffany, "This is going to hurt, sweetie, but we have to try and slow down the swelling."

A tear leaked down Tiffany's lovely face, and she nodded. Then she hissed a few breaths through her teeth as I slowly, slowly lowered the compress onto her ankle. "Ohmigod, ohmigod, ohmigod!" she cried as the coldness spread across her injured foot. Gilley held her hand and rubbed her fingers.

"I know it hurts," he said. "Try to hang in there for a few more seconds, and it'll get easier."

She nodded as more tears slid from her eyes. I wondered if she hadn't broken the ankle.

When Tiffany seemed a fraction less uncomfortable, I said, "What would you like for us to do, Tiffany? Is there someone we can call? Or should we take you to urgent care immediately?"

"I smashed my phone," she said, her voice hitching on the words.

Gilley produced the phone out of his pocket. The screen was smashed and dark. "I can't get it to turn on," he said. "And she can't remember her parents' numbers."

"They're just in my phone, you know?" she said. "I never have to think when I call them."

"How about where your dad works?" I tried. "If you can think of the company, maybe we could call his office and ask for him."

"He's at home today," she said miserably, and I knew that it was useless to push her for details. Her mind was clouded with pain, and she might even be in a bit of shock.

"Okay," I said gently, rubbing her arm. "Should we take you straight to urgent care, then? Or would you like us to drive you home and your parents can take you?"

"H-h-home," she sputtered, wiping the tears from her face, but more tears simply followed. The poor love was so distressed. Waving to her foot, she cried, "I can't believe I did that! I'm supposed to run the New York City Marathon this year!"

Tiffany stared at her ankle as if it'd betrayed her, and I couldn't tell if the tears were from pain or from disappointment that she'd be missing the race. Perhaps they were from both.

"Maybe it's not so bad," I said, even though her ankle was clearly swollen and turning a frightening shade of blue.

I glanced at Gilley, and he was staring at her injured foot like he was afraid some alien creature might burst out and attack him.

"We'll let you sit for a bit, and then we'll help you to the car," I told her. "Gil?"

He tore his eyes away from Tiffany's foot and looked at me with wide, almost panicked eyes. "Yeah?"

"I believe I've got a set of crutches in the garage from when Matt had that calf strain last year. They'll be short for Tiffany, but at least they'll allow her to maneuver under her own power."

"Uh-huh?" he said, not understanding what I was getting at.

"Why don't you go see if you can find them while I make room for Tiffany in my car."

"Yeah, okay," he said, and then he bolted for the door.

"Spooks," I said to the pup, who'd lain down right next to Tiffany's chair to stare up at her with worried eyes. He sat up when he heard his name. "Stay," I said, pointing to him.

He replied with a soft snort and placed his head on Tiffany's thigh.

I nodded to him. "Good boy." Then I squeezed Tiffany's shoulder and said, "We'll be right back."

She didn't respond or even acknowledge that I'd spoken. Instead, she stared into space and petted Spooks's head.

I left the pair of them and headed out to move the seats in my car so that we could ease Tiffany in without forcing her to put any weight on her foot.

Fifteen minutes later the four of us were on our way, headed northeast, and before too long we were turning into a subdivision off of Hither Lane.

"It's that one on the left," Tiffany said, pointing to a lovely French country home with neatly tended gardens and a circular drive.

I turned into the drive and pulled as close to the front door as the pavement allowed. "Gil," I said, unbuckling my seat belt, "I'll ring the bell while you help Tiffany out, okay?"

"Got it," he said.

After hurrying out of the car and up the steps, I rang the bell, and the door was opened right away by a woman with white-blond hair, big blue eyes, and a round face, who was just about my height.

"Hello," I said. "I'm Catherine. I'm a friend of Sunny D'Angelo, and we met your daughter the other night, when she was babysitting Finley."

The woman eyed me with confusion until she noticed what was happening behind me. She gasped as I was quick to explain. "My friend Gilley found Tiffany hobbling along after she rolled her ankle. We drove her home because she'd smashed her phone when she fell."

"Oh, my goodness!" Tiffany's mother exclaimed. "Charles! *Charles!* Come quick!"

I stepped aside just before Tiffany's mom rushed past me down the steps, and stayed to the side as a tall, broad presence emerged from the hallway and approached the front door.

Tiffany's dad was a surprise. He was African American, with a beard and a belly, but he stood at least six feet five. Possibly taller, as he literally had to duck his head to come outside. "What's happened?" he asked.

"Your daughter rolled her ankle on her run. We brought her home because she smashed her phone when she fell and couldn't remember your phone numbers."

Charles barely acknowledged that I'd spoken, and he hurried down the steps to join his wife while Gilley helped to prop up Tiffany, who was now out of the car.

Bending at the waist, Charles simply picked his daughter up in his arms like a rag doll and carried her up the steps and inside with ease. Gilley stayed by the car, next to Spooks, who was sticking his head out the window, and I waited for Tiffany's mother to pass me on the stairs before I made my exit, but she paused on the landing and said, "Thank you! Thank you so much for bringing her home."

"We almost took her to urgent care," I admitted. "But deferred to Tiffany about where she wanted to go."

"No, she definitely should've come home. Charles is an orthopedic surgeon."

My brow lifted in surprise at how fortunate that was for Tiffany. "Oh, good," I said. "Who better than her dad to immediately assess her injuries?"

Tiffany's mom stuck out her hand. "I'm Brenda."

"Catherine Cooper," I said, shaking her hand.

"Would you like to come in for a minute? I'm sure Charles would like to thank you for helping our baby girl home."

By now, Gilley had sidled up next to me, and, tapping his chest, he said, "Gilley Gillespie."

Brenda nodded and shook his hand. "Brenda Blum."

"We don't want to be a bother," I said.

"You're not," Brenda insisted. "Please, come in for a moment, won't you?"

I smiled and nodded, and we followed Brenda inside.

Charles had taken Tiffany to the kitchen, and she was sitting on the island, with her father kneeling down to inspect her foot as he eased her running shoe off.

Poor Tiffany cried out as the shoe came loose, and Charles looked pained as he glanced at his daughter. "Sorry, baby. I have to get a look at your foot, okay?"

She nodded, and I noticed the tears were sliding down her cheeks again. Tiffany held her breath, and we did, too, as Charles slipped off her sock. I winced when I saw how purple her whole foot was.

"Can-can I still run the marathon?" Tiffany whimpered.

Charles looked up at her again, his face sympathetic but firm. "No," he said. "Tiffy, you're going to be sidelined for the next two to three months, depending on any damage to the tendons. I'll take an X-ray at the hospital, but it looks like you've got broken second and third metatarsals."

Tiffany burst into tears, and Charles stood to hug his daughter.

I laid a hand on Brenda's arm. "Brenda, thank you so much for asking us in, but I really think it's best if we leave you to tend to your daughter."

She nodded, tears welling up in her own eyes. "You're right. I'll walk you out."

We turned and headed out the way we'd come, but at the

front door Brenda said softly, "This is just one more terrible thing to happen this week."

That was when I remembered that Sunny had told me that Yelena had recommended Tiffany to her for babysitting, and that Yelena had been friends with Tiffany's parents. "Oh, Brenda, of course," I said. "I nearly forgot that you were friends with Yelena Galanis, correct?"

Brenda blinked in surprise and said, "Yes. We knew her well. It was such a shock to find out that she'd been murdered. I'm still reeling from the news."

"I totally understand," I said. "And you have my deepest sympathies."

"Did you know her too?" Brenda asked.

"No," I said, declining to mention that we'd been at the show the night of the murder. "We'd never met, unfortunately."

Brenda nodded, and then she opened her mouth to say something, seemed to think better of it, but then whispered, "Yelena was Tiffany's birth mother."

Next to me, I heard Gilley gasp, and I knew I'd sucked in my own breath in surprise.

"She was?" Gilley said.

Brenda put a finger to her lips. "Tiffany doesn't know. We'd planned on telling her this year, because she's known Yelena her whole life. It was part of the arrangement of the adoption, actually. Yelena promised never to tell Tiffany the truth. She said she'd leave it up to us to decide if that was appropriate, and while Tiffany was in Europe this summer, Charles and I made up our minds to tell her. Yelena was supposed to come over for dinner tonight so that we could all tell her together."

I bit my lip. "I'm so, so sorry," I said.

Brenda nodded, and her eyes welled again. Glancing over her shoulder, she said, "She's been training so hard for the past three years to get fast enough to run the marathon, and she was lucky enough this year to get a lottery number. I don't even know how she'll be able to deal with the hard stuff now that she can't run. It's her coping mechanism, and it was how she got through her senior year, during the lockdowns."

Gilley and I nodded, and I thought we both sensed that Brenda was confessing all this to a pair of strangers because it was easy to confess such things to people she didn't know. It was safer to say something personal to two people you'd likely never meet again.

"If we can be of any help to you or to her, would you let us know?" I asked, reaching into my purse to pull out a card. I handed it to Brenda, then squeezed her arm in sympathy and turned to go.

"You're a life coach?" I heard her say.

"I am," I said, glancing over my shoulder. "So . . . if you or Tiffany needs someone to talk to, please think of calling me, okay?"

Brenda nodded and offered us a small smile before waving goodbye.

When we were safely back in the car and on our way back home, Gilley said, "*That* was a twist I didn't see coming."

"Right?" I said. "That poor girl, though."

"Exactly," Gilley said. "She gets a ticket to the New York City Marathon and rolls her ankle six weeks before the race *and* will soon learn that her birth mother—whom she's known her whole life but didn't know was actually her mom—was murdered three nights ago."

"I do not envy the Blums," I said, thinking of Tiffany's poor parents and the task before them of comforting their daughter through three heartbreaks.

"Do you think they'll tell her?" Gilley said.

I eyed him in surprise. "Of course. Why wouldn't they?"

Gilley shrugged. "Would it be more painful for you to think that your birth mother was some stranger out there and was never named, or that she was a woman who'd been murdered the week before the confession could be made and you would've gotten the chance to form a whole new relationship with her?"

I frowned. "I see your point."

"I wonder if Sunny knew," Gilley said next.

Again, I glanced at him in surprise. "Gosh, I don't know, Gil. She didn't give any hint about it to me, but then, she could've been protecting Yelena's privacy."

"Sunny and Yelena . . . Their history as friends goes back to college, right?"

I nodded. "That's my understanding."

"How old do you think Tiffany is?"

"Twenty. Maybe twenty-one."

"The timing fits," Gilley said.

"It does," I admitted. "Still, what does it matter now?"

Gilley sighed. "I guess it doesn't."

"How did you stumble upon Tiffany, anyway?" I asked.

"I took Spooks for a walk all the way to Indian Wells Beach, and he had a great time splashing in the waves. On the way there, we passed Tiffany going in the opposite direction. I waved at her, but I don't think she remembered me, 'cause she just kept on truckin'." Gilley laughed. "Anyhoo, when we were about a quarter mile from home, we found Tiffany on the ground, near a big ole pothole. She'd fallen in, rolled her ankle, and couldn't walk."

"The poor thing! How long was she like that?"

"She said she was there only a few minutes, and nobody stopped to help her, which is simply unacceptable, but what're you gonna do?"

"Well, *you* stopped and helped."

"I did. She said she was doing a fifteen-mile loop around

East Hampton when she took a sip of water and didn't see the pothole."

"I don't know whether I'm more pained hearing that Tiffany fell into the pothole or that she was doing a fifteen-mile run!"

"My thoughts exactly. Runners are weird."

"Candice is a runner," I said, referring to my sister's best friend and business partner, whom Gilley knew well.

"Abby's Candice?"

I nodded.

"It figures. That woman is subhuman."

I laughed. Candice was a formidable woman in every respect. I had been a member of her posse once or twice and genuinely respected her, even if I didn't necessarily want to spend a lot of time with her, because she was pretty intimidating.

"Abby says Candice is running the Vermont One Hundred next year."

"What's the Vermont One Hundred?"

"One hundred miles, mostly uphill."

Gilley blanched. "My God, *why?*"

"No idea, but I agree with you. Runners *are* weird."

We both fell silent then, lost in our thoughts, and I continued to wind my way in the direction of Chez Cat.

Breaking the silence after an idea struck me, I said, "You know what, Gil?"

"What?"

"Well, I've been trying to figure out how we can learn more about Yelena's angry men, and I think I've come up with something clever."

"Do tell," Gilley said, turning to look at me expectantly.

"Well, you know how theater people love to gossip, right?"

"I do," Gilley said.

"I'm wondering if anyone at the theater might've overheard some gossip about the identities of some of Yelena's lovers."

Gilley's grin was slow to spread, but it was ear to ear when he finished thinking about my idea. "That is brilliant!" he said. "And we know that Shepherd isn't asking them about the other men, because he believes he's got the right man in jail."

"Exactly," I said. "It's bound to be an untapped resource for suspects."

Gilley pointed to the road ahead. "The theater's three minutes away. Shall we?"

"You want to go there now?"

"I don't think we have a moment to spare. If there's anyone left at the theater who worked on Yelena's show, they'll probably be nearly finished putting away the old set and getting ready for the new act, which most definitely would've been booked in a hurry."

"You think there's a new show there already?"

"If not already, imminently," Gilley said. "A theater can't make money off of empty seats, and I'm sure they would've booked a new act ASAP."

"That just seems so . . . cold," I said.

Gilley lowered his lids, stuck his nose in the air, and adopted a British accent. "It's the theater, dahling. The show must go on!"

We arrived at the theater just a few minutes later. I parked down the street, well away from the theater's entrance.

"We passed, like, six other parking spaces," Gilley remarked. "Why are we so far away?"

"I don't want Shepherd to see my car if he decides to come back and take another look at the scene of the crime," I confessed. "He'll be miffed at me if he knows we're sticking our noses into his case again."

Gilley chuckled. "I love how adorable you are when describing Shepherd's reaction to us snooping around." Using his fingers for air quotes, Gilley said, " 'Miffed.' Ha! He'll be atomic."

"You're not making me feel better . . ."

"Nuclear!"

I glared at him.

"Apocalyptic!" And then he made a popping sound and mimed his head exploding.

"Will you stop!"

Gilley giggled. "I'll try. But they come so easily to me. Sometimes it's hard to hold back."

We got out and put some money in the meter, then headed toward the building. "I hope we can get inside," I said as we neared the entrance.

"We'll go around to the back," Gilley said. "Employees are always knocking on the back door to be let in. Just follow my lead."

I trailed behind Gilley as he led the way to the back of the building, and we were both surprised to find the backstage door propped open with a chair. Gilley gallantly stepped forward, pulled the door open wide, and bowed. "After you, m'lady."

"Why, thank you, kind sir," I said, stepping through the entryway into a darkened corridor. It took a moment for my eyes to adjust, and I felt, rather than saw, Gilley step in next to me, and then we both paused to get our bearings.

"This way," Gilley said, stepping over a bundle of electrical cords. I followed after him, lured by the sound of hammering.

We passed no one on our way toward the sound, but we could hear two men chatting away with each other about the Yankees.

As we rounded a cluttered corner of discarded theater odds and ends, I could see that we were entering backstage right, and on the stage were two men in overalls—one guy on a ladder, one on the floor—working to take down Yelena's backdrop. They stopped abruptly when they spotted us.

"You can't be back here," the man on the floor said. His tone was sharp, and it rattled me. I paused on my way toward them.

Gilley, however, was unfazed. Smiling, with the air of authority, he said, "Forgive the interruption, gentlemen, but we're from the Sharp Group."

The two men stared blankly at him.

"The personal insurance agency for the theater," Gilley said, like they should've known. He then surprised me by producing a card from the inside of his blazer pocket and extended it out to the man holding the ladder, who made no move to walk toward us to retrieve it.

"You can't be back here," the guy repeated.

Gilley swiveled his head to regard me, folded his arms, and rolled his eyes. Turning to the two men again, he said, "As investigators into the pending lawsuit brought by Ms. Galanis's heirs, we in fact, *can* be back here."

They continued to stare blankly at him, but I did notice that their aggressiveness had migrated to surprise and a look of uncertainty.

Gilley pocketed his card and folded his hands in front of him, like he was preparing to give a speech. "Now, a few questions for the two of you," he said, stepping toward them. I followed. "Were you both here the night Ms. Galanis met her . . . ?"

Gilley's voice trailed off, and both men appeared confused.

"Death?" the guy on the ladder said.

"Unfortunate end," Gilley said, adopting a tight smile.

"We were," said the man on the floor. "We were onstage, behind the main curtain, changing out the backdrop for the second act."

"And prior to intermission?" Gilley pressed. "Where were you?"

The man on the ladder pointed to just behind where we were standing. "There," he said. "In the chairs."

I looked behind me and saw the two cane chairs side by side, with a small table set between them, and on the table was a deck of playing cards. That must've been how they passed the time during Yelena's act.

"Excellent," said Gil. "And your names are?"

"Gus Webster," said the first guy; then he pointed to his buddy on the ladder. "And that's Donny Cass."

Gilley nodded, then paused before asking them his next question to size the two gentlemen up.

Rather than simply standing there, looking stupid, I decided to assist Gilley with the ruse and dug into my purse for a small notebook that I used to make shopping lists and a pen. After extracting both, I flipped to a fresh page. "Gus Webster and Donny Cass," I said, scribbling their names in the notebook.

"Gus," Gilley said, with a nod toward the man. "And Donny."

They nodded back.

Gilley placed his hands behind his back and began to walk a few paces to and fro—à la Inspector Clouseau—while peppering the men with questions, such as, Did they see or hear anything suspicious the night of the murder? Did they notice anyone who didn't seem to belong backstage? Did they personally know Ms. Galanis? Did they see anyone come into the theater after the murder to snoop around, perhaps looking for discarded evidence?

The answer to all Gilley's questions was no, save the last question, which Gus answered, "Just you two and the police."

"I see," Gilley said, as if Gus's statement was telling.

Gilley then pointed toward the direction he and I had come from. "I noticed that the backstage door is propped open with a chair," he began, and for the first time the men's demeanor changed. They became noticeably nervous. "Is that a typical practice for you two here at the theater?"

Donny looked at Gus, his eyes wide and somewhat panicked. "The door sticks, and it's easier for us to get tools and supplies out of our trucks if the door's propped open."

"Ah," Gilley said, his tone disapproving. Pursing his lips, he said, "And was that door propped open the night of the . . ."

"Murder?" Donny asked in a squeaky voice.

"Unfortunate incident?" Gilley finished.

Donny backed his way down the ladder, then turned once he'd gotten to the floor, to look meaningfully at Gus.

Gus's lips flattened into a thin line. "I don't remember," he said.

"Of course you don't," Gilley said. "But here's the thing, Gus. If you're knowingly lying to me right now, and I catch you in it, then I'll name you as a codefendant in the lawsuit, and you'll be subject to the same penalties and damages that our agency will be."

Gus gulped.

Gilley continued. "Your pension, your savings, your retirement, your house, all those things could be in play."

Gus turned pale.

"Of course, as an employee, I'd like to protect you, Gus. But only if you come clean with me. On the night of the . . ."

"Unfortunate incident," the two men said in unison.

Gilley smiled sharply at them. "*Murder*, was that door propped open?"

"It may have been," Gus admitted. And I could see he was well and truly terrified of losing his life's savings to a fictional lawsuit.

Thinking Gilley might be being unnecessarily cruel, I stepped in. "Thank you for that admission, Gus. It's an important detail that we can try to mitigate by suggesting that you had no idea that Ms. Galanis could've been in danger from one of her lovers, correct?"

Gus shook his head vehemently. "No! I swear. I had no idea the lady had anybody wanting to hurt her."

"Me either," Donny was quick to point out.

I nodded and tapped Gilley on the shoulder. "I told you they were perfectly innocent of all liability, Simon."

Gilley grinned. I could tell he liked the fake name I'd given him. "You are right again, Felicity."

I smiled too. Felicity was such a pretty name.

"Still!" Gilley said, spinning to pace away from me again. "I'm troubled that they saw no one backstage at the time of the . . ."

"Unfortunate incident?" Donny tried.

"Murder?" Gus said.

"Violent homicide of Ms. Galanis," Gilley said. "How could someone simply sneak past the two of you if you were backstage during the entire first act?"

The men stared at Gilley, as if dumbstruck.

Gilley pointed behind us. "The corridor coming from the backstage door leads directly to here. If you two were sitting in the wings, waiting to assist with the set change for the second act, how could someone possibly slip past you?"

Donny also pointed to the area behind us. "Through the secret door," he said. "It's painted black to keep it hidden. You'd miss it if you didn't know it was there."

Both Gilley and I swiveled to look behind us.

"There's a hidden door back there?" I said, thumbing over my shoulder.

"Yep," Donny said. "It's just inside the backstage door. Like I said, you'd miss it if you don't know it's there."

"And where *exactly* does it lead?" Gilley asked.

"To the dressing rooms and the hallway behind the curtain leading to stage left," Gus explained.

"Huh," I said, looking back over my shoulder again. "I totally missed that."

"If it's just inside the door, then we definitely would miss it," Gilley said. "Especially if we were coming in from outside. Remember? Our eyes needed to adjust to the change in light."

"But it was evening the night of the murder," I said softly, reminding Gilley of that one crucial detail.

"Which would've made the door all the harder to see," Gilley said, and I had to nod in agreement. He was absolutely right.

"Is that door ever locked?" I asked, just out of curiosity.

Gus nodded. "Sometimes, but never during a show."

"Is it locked now?" Gilley asked.

Gus turned red. "Uh, I don't think so."

Gilley nodded again. "Excellent. Gentlemen, we would like to thank you for your time. Please carry on with your work, and we'll be in touch should we need any further information from you."

With that, Gil turned on his heel, grabbed my elbow, and we walked away.

"I take it we're headed to the hidden backstage door?" I asked.

"Duh," Gil said, bringing out his phone.

I wondered why until we reached the door, which was indeed hard to see, and Gilley snapped several photos of it with his phone. He then tried the handle, and the door opened freely. With another gallant bow, he said, "Felicity?"

"Thank you, Simon," I said with a smile and walked through into the pitch dark. "I can't see a thing in here."

The area lit up quite suddenly with a bright light when Gilley switched on the flashlight of his phone. Upon locating the light switch to my right, he flicked it, and the hallway was illuminated.

It was a wide hallway, filled with framed playbills from previous shows and more backstage clutter.

We walked down the hallway without speaking, taking in the space, and stopped abruptly at a door with crime-scene tape across it and a placard in the shape of a star at eye level that read MS. GALANIS.

I stood back from the door and looked it up and down, and that was when I realized there were rust-colored droplets on the floor near the door. I stepped back quickly, pointing to them so Gilley could see. He made a face and also stepped back.

We both surveyed the floor—we couldn't help it—and the macabre scene unfolded as even more droplets dotted the wood planks on the floor in a gruesome series of polka dots. I followed their trail and was even more stunned to see that they weren't limited to the floor but had also stained the doorframe and the opposite wall, and then my gaze landed on the outline of a bloody handprint on the floor just beyond the door—as if Yelena had reached out for help beyond the opening but had died in the effort.

I put a hand up to cover my mouth, realizing for the first time how violent her death had been. "Good Lord," I whispered when I felt I could speak again.

Gilley's expression was equally horrified. "She must have been attacked just inside the door," he said, pointing to the arch of rusty drops.

"What a terrifyingly horrible way to die," I said.

The more I looked at the scene, the more convinced I was of one thing: Aaron Nassau did not murder Yelena Galanis. This was done by someone who was filled with rage—not heartbreak.

"Should we go in?" Gilley asked me.

"You're kidding, right?" I said, pointing to the crime-scene tape and the large sticker covering part of the door and the doorframe.

"There's no way they'd know we were the ones that broke in," Gilley said. He pointed to the ceiling covering us and the hallway. "No cameras."

I shook my head. "All Shepherd would have to do is ask Gus or Donny if we broke in, and they'd give us up in a heartbeat."

"You mean they'd give up Simon and Felicity," he said.

"From the Sharp Insurance Group." Gilley reached inside his pocket and withdrew the card he'd offered Gus. It was his card from my office. He'd gambled that Gus wouldn't come forward to take the card from him, and it'd worked.

"Clever," I said. "However, me thinks Shepherd would tweeze out the truth in a hot second, so no. We are *not* breaking in. Besides, what would be worth seeing other than more grizzly remnants of the crime scene?"

"Dunno. Which is why I say we should break in."

"No, Gilley," I said firmly.

With a sigh, he said, "Fine. But let's check out the rest of this backstage area."

I nodded and waved for him to proceed.

We moved away from Yelena's dressing-room door, then continued down the hallway past several more dressing rooms of various sizes. All were empty of anything but vanity tables and chairs.

At last, we came to the end and a tight corner, around which we could once again hear Gus and Donny, who were hammering away and continuing to talk about the Yankees' chances of winning a pennant this year.

Gilley peeked his head around the corner, then motioned for me to follow. I kept close to him as we rounded the corner and came into a large backstage left area. We were very much in shadow, so I wasn't worried that Gilley and I would be seen by Gus or Donny, but we were quiet as mice all the same.

After a cursory look around, I motioned to Gilley that we should head out, and he paused next to a small desk and a short stack of paper.

Let's go! I mouthed.

He nodded, took up the stack, and we were on our way.

We didn't speak until we had left the backstage area and Gilley had hit the light switch on his way out.

Once on the sidewalk and headed to the car, I pointed to the sheets of paper. "What's that?"

"Yelena's script," he said.

My brow shot up. "Her script?"

"Yep," Gilley said, breaking into a crocodile smile as he waved it at me. "And you know what it's filled with?"

"What?"

Gil bounced his brow. "Clues."

Chapter 11

"This is a gold mine," I said, flipping through the pages once we were home again, this time at Chez Cat, sitting at my kitchen island, sipping tea and perusing the script.

"I know, right?" he said. "Neither one of us got to see the second act, so from that standpoint alone, it's a treasure."

I read through the lines, which had felt so spontaneous coming from Yelena's lips, and marveled that she hadn't sounded rehearsed when she'd delivered all those zingers. It read exactly as it'd sounded, like a monologue—a train of thought, one lover following another through all twelve men.

"I'd really like to know who Lover Number Two is," I said.

"The legislator?"

"Yes. What we don't know is if he's a local rep or a national one."

"He'd be national. No way would Yelena date someone in the state legislature. And I'd put odds that it's a senator and not a congressman. She'd be after someone with stature."

I giggled with mirth and shook my head. "I doubt Yelena had an affair with Chuck Schumer."

"Who said it was a New York senator?" Gilley said. "*Lots* of politically powerful people have homes here in the Hamptons."

"Good point. Which widens up the field again."

"As if it weren't wide enough with eight unknown suspects," Gilley mused.

"Don't you mean nine? We only know of McAllen, Goldberg, and Leahy."

"I'm assuming Aaron is in this script somewhere," Gilley said with a sigh.

"Oh, that's right. We'll need to look for him in the script just to confirm though," I said.

After setting the script on the counter, I laid my hands flat on top of it. "We need to go through this page by page with a fine-tooth comb."

"Agreed," he said, tugging at the corners of the pages until I let him have them. He then turned several pages, stopped on one particular page, and turned it toward me. "Did you see that?"

I squinted at the page but couldn't see what had caught his attention. "What?"

Gilley tapped the bottom left corner. "See that note?"

I blinked. I'd missed it on my cursory look through the pages. "I can't make it out. Can you?"

Gilley turned the page back toward him and moved his finger to the bottom paragraph, marked *Lover Number Eight*. "See that arrow?" he said.

I did see it. It was faded, because it'd been written in pencil, but I could make it out. "You think the note is in regard to Lover Number Eight?"

"I do," Gilley said. "Her handwriting is terrible, but I believe the note says, 'Call Gene,' and then I believe that's a dollar sign."

Gilley pointed to the squiggly symbol, and I nodded. "I think you're right. So do we both agree that Gene is very likely Lover Number Eight?"

"We do," Gilley said.

"And that she was calling him for money?"

"She was."

"Like, for what? Support? Or something more nefarious, like blackmail?"

"That thought had crossed my mind," Gilley said.

"So who's Gene?"

Gilley shrugged. Then his eyes lit up. "Hold on," he said, pulling out his phone and tapping at it madly.

I refilled both our cups with more tea, waiting him out.

At last, he exclaimed, "Yes!" and then he turned the phone to face me. "Gene Bosworth."

"Gene Bosworth," I repeated as I looked closely at the screen. Then I read aloud. "Gene Bosworth, of Southampton and Manhattan, real estate developer, philanthropist, and patron of the arts, passed away on Wednesday, December twelfth, from complications of COVID-nineteen. He is survived by his sister, Kennedy June Bosworth-Murdock, and his brother-in-law, Eric Murdock, and his two nephews, Tad and Theo."

I stopped reading and frowned at Gilley. "This can't be the same Gene, Gilley. He's dead. He died last year."

Gilley nodded but then flipped through the script to the page on which began Yelena's monologue about Lover Number Eight. Holding the script up, he began to read. " 'Lover Number Eight has decided to permanently social distance himself from the rest of us—except, of course, for his dear, beloved sister, or as I like to call her, his one true love. It took me far too long to realize how much she and I look alike, and why he once called out her name in bed like a gasp for the caress of a summer's day."

"A bit poetic," I mused.

"No, Cat, don't you get it? 'Summer's day'?"

"Clearly, I don't," I said.

Gilley rolled his eyes. "His sister's middle name is *June*."

"Okay, that's a bit of a stretch."

As if challenged, Gilley went back to tapping at his phone again, and with a triumphant "Aha!" he turned it toward me.

I leaned in to stare at it and saw that he'd pulled up an image of a woman in the center of a group of people who bore a striking resemblance to Yelena. The caption under the photo read *Eric Murdock and his wife, June; Chris Fitzpatrick and his wife, Winnie; Bill O'Dowd; and Ritvik Patel at the Spring Fling Festival in Westchester.*

"She goes by June," Gilley said. Then he pointed to the script again and said, " 'He once called out her name in bed like a gasp for the caress of a summer's day.' Yelena was speaking in code. She was referring to June."

"Ew," I said.

"Right?" Gilley agreed, making a face.

"But are we really sure, Gilley? I mean, couldn't that all be a coincidence? And why would Yelena write a note to call Gene about money if he died in December? It's September—nine months later."

"I don't know. But I definitely know I want to do a little more research in this direction."

I nodded. "We should absolutely explore that angle." Then I grabbed the script and said, "Come on, I've got a scanner upstairs in my office. We can scan this in and make a copy so that we can both study it for clues."

An hour later, Gilley and I were back at my kitchen counter, having both read our copies of the script. Setting mine down, I waited for Gilley to earmark a page before I asked, "Did anything speak to you about the identity of the other lovers?"

"Number Eleven is Aaron," Gilley said. "She said the word *count*, like, fifteen times."

It was a little less than that, but I smiled at him and added a nod. "Agreed."

I got up and went to the whiteboard I'd propped up near the sink, and I wrote in Aaron's name next to the number eleven that I'd written beforehand, when Gilley and I had first come downstairs and had decided to keep track of the lovers using my whiteboard.

"So," I said, pointing to the list. "We know that Lover Number One is Tucker McAllen, the real estate developer; Lover Number Four is Joel Goldberg, the jeweler; Lover Number Five is Liam Leahy, the vice admiral; Lover Number Eight is Gene Bosworth; and Lover Number Eleven is Aaron Nassau."

"Which leaves Lovers Number Two, Three, Six, Seven, Nine, Ten, and Twelve to identify."

"Right," I said, pacing in front of the whiteboard. "Should we tackle this one by one, starting with Lover Number Two?"

"I have no clue who he could be," Gilley said. "I did a cursory search of any members of Congress that live here in the Hamptons and could find only this guy." Gilley turned the screen of his phone toward me, and I gazed at the picture.

"Oh, yeah," I said. "I voted against him in the last election."

"Me too," Gilley admitted.

"Still, he's about the same age as Yelena," I said.

"He's also got four kids, ages three to thirteen, a gorgeous wife, and a place in Eastport."

"That's a bit of a hike."

"It is. Plus, Cat, if a guy like this stepped out with a woman like Yelena, it'd be gossip central. I just don't see it."

"What do you mean?"

"I mean, if he cheated on his wife and the mother of his four kids with Yelena, no way would she not hear about it."

I tapped my chin. "That's true."

"I'm gonna do some more digging, of course, see if I can't get a handle for the representative's schedule, to see if he was even in town the night of the murder, but my gut says this ain't our guy."

I sighed. "Okay, then we'll leave Lover Number Two blank for now. Let's move on to Lover Number Three."

"Three is curious," Gilley said, lifting up the script to flip to the section on Lover Number Three. Quoting from the page, he said, "'Lover Number Three is all about the clothes. He wears them like a mask, making you think he plays for one team, when he really plays for the other.'"

"Someone in the closet," I said, guessing.

Gilley set down the script and pursed his lips. "Maybe," he said, in a way that didn't convey that he was convinced of my conclusion. He lifted his phone and began to tap at it.

"What're you thinking?" I asked.

"Yelena's dress for the show was an absolutely gorgeous creation, no?" he said.

"Oh, my God, yes," I agreed. "Stunning. And she was flawless in it."

"Custom," Gilley said. "Right?"

"The way it fit her like a second skin? Had to be."

Gilley pivoted his phone around so that I could see. It was Yelena's Instagram page. "Like this number, right?"

The photo in question showed Yelena dressed in a burgundy, sparkling, floor-length pantsuit that flared widely at the bottom and had a slit from neck to navel, allowing her ample décolletage to practically spill out. The pants were tight and tapered, and the overall silhouette of the suit and the padding of the shoulders gave her a particularly powerful look. It was absolutely a tailor-made cut and fit.

"Indeed. They look like they definitely could've been designed by the same person," I said.

Gilley scrolled to the next photo. "And here," he said.

The photo showed Yelena dressed in a rose-colored gown that fit her shape like a glove. The photo was obviously taken during the pandemic, because she was wearing a face mask made of the same material as her dress, but it was studded with Swarovski crystals.

"Yes. Another custom outfit. And I love it on her."

Gilley nodded. "When her show started causing a stir, I began following Yelena on the gram, and I remember scrolling through these, loving her style. She wears a lot of Vivace."

"Vivace?"

"Antonio Vivace. He's starting to catch fire in the fashion world. Michel is a big fan, and he's been pushing Anna's team to feature some of Vivace's designs in *Vogue*."

I smirked at the way Gilley casually dropped the name of Anna Wintour, like he was on a first-name basis with her. Though, to be fair, his husband likely was.

Gilley was silent for a moment as he continued to scroll through the photos, until he came up with what he seemed to be looking for. Turning his phone around to me again, he said, "That's him."

An impeccably dressed man with an olive complexion; a long face; big, brown, soulful eyes; and tendrils of silver hair pooling onto his shoulders stared out at me. He had the most sensual lips, set in a Mona Lisa smirk as he commanded the attention of the photographer. Meanwhile, three bare-chested male models were draping themselves over him, fawning in a way that suggested he was their *objet de désir*.

"You think he's who Yelena is referring to?" I asked Gilley.

"I do. The gown she wore for her act is obviously from him. He has a certain style that celebrates a voluptuous woman's curves that's hard to get right. You see Christian able to do it well, and maybe Zac, but the list of truly talented designers creating clothes for the Rubenesque crowd is appallingly small."

I resisted the urge to ask Gilley if he meant Christian Siriano and Zac Posen, because I knew it would only give him pleasure to say, "Duh. Who *else* would I be talking about, Cat?"

Instead, I directed the discussion back to the topic at hand by pointing to the script and saying, "So, Vivace is what . . . ? *Not* closeted and not even gay?"

Gilley shrugged. "Professionally, it would be to his advantage to be seen as someone on the LBGTQ spectrum, leaning heavily toward the G, but he could also be bi or pansexual. I've never met the man, so it's hard for me to tell."

"What other clues from the script fit?"

"Most of it," Gilley said, picking up the pages again. "I mean, if you understand that she's referring to Vivace, it makes sense. She calls him a silver-haired fox with a passion for women, wine, and walkways."

"She was a clever girl," I said.

"Indeed."

I turned and uncapped my marker. "Okay, I'll add him to the list, but we'll need to dig a little more into him as a possibility, because her clues are cryptic enough that we could be wrong."

"Agree, agree, agree," Gilley said.

"Okay, so let's look at Lovers Six and Seven and see if they offer up any clues," I said.

"Lover Seven *definitely* offers up some clues," Gilley said, and the expression on his face had me quite curious.

"What clues?"

In answer, Gilley began to read directly from the page. " 'Lover Number Seven was made entirely of chocolate. Dark, bitter, gorgeous chocolate—' "

"He was black," I said, reading between the lines.

"That would be my guess," Gilley said; then he got back to the script. " 'Willing to sell his soul for a dollar, he'd stand up for any white collar. He didn't care if you were guilty, as long as you could pay.' "

I felt the color drain from my face. "An attorney."

Gilley held up a finger and continued to read. " 'Generous in bed, certainly the second best of the lot, but unwilling to be seen putting caviar on a toast point of white bread.'"

"What does that mean?"

"I think it means that he didn't like to be seen in public with a white woman."

"Understandable," I said, feeling my defenses go up. I had a very niggling feeling that Yelena might be referring to someone I knew and cared about, and it worried me for every reason I could think of.

Gilley continued. "'When I got tired of his song and dance, I tossed him right back in the harbor.'"

"Oh, no," I said, as my suspicion was all but confirmed. "Are we both thinking the same thing?"

"Uh, that Marcus Brown fits every cryptic descriptor, including being tossed back in the 'harbor,' which is code for Sag Harbor?"

I nodded. It would explain why, when I'd called Marcus to beg him to represent Aaron, he'd been silent when I mentioned that Yelena had been murdered.

"Okay, so we're both thinking it's Marcus. Gilley, what do we do?"

"I think we need to call Marcus," he said.

I blanched. "And say what, exactly?"

"Oh, I dunno, Cat. Maybe start off by asking him how his day is going and then drift into asking him if he was the one who *murdered* Yelena Galanis?"

I made a face. "Or perhaps something more tactful."

Gilley set down the script. "I suddenly don't like this project."

With a sigh, I reached for my phone. In my heart of hearts, I didn't believe for a second that Marcus Brown had killed Yelena. But I thought it was important to ask him about her, given the fact that he was currently defending a man she had also dated, and was now accused of murdering her. To me, it was a gigantic conflict of interest, and something I was convinced would make Aaron quite vulnerable at trial.

"Catherine Cooper," Marcus said, picking up the line.

"Hello, Marcus," I said, trying to regulate my tone to something casual and breezy. "I've got you on speakerphone, and Gilley is also here."

"To what do I owe this pleasure?" he said amiably.

"Well . . ." I began collecting my thoughts hurriedly and was still unsure how I would proceed. "Gilley and I were considering helping you with the case against Aaron."

"You were, huh?" Marcus asked. "In what way?"

I cleared my throat and dived in. "This morning we took a little trip to the theater and discovered Yelena's discarded script. We've been going through it, attempting to identify the twelve angry men, you know, to give you a pool of suspects to help cast doubt upon the killer being Aaron."

"Nice," he said. "I'd like a copy of that when you get a moment."

"Of course," I told him. "While we were—"

"And I'd like to hear who you've identified when you get a decent number of names."

"Sure thing," I said. "We've made excellent progress so far."

"How many names do you have?"

"Including Aaron, we've got six," I said.

"Possibly seven," Gilley told him, eyeing me meaningfully.

"Let me guess, you got to Lover Number Seven and determined it was me?"

Gilley and I exchanged a look of surprise. "Uh . . . yes," I said.

"Is it you?" Gilley asked.

"It is," Marcus said. "I dated Yelena very briefly eighteen months ago. I thought we ended things amicably, but I might've been mistaken. I've heard through the vine that her portrait of me isn't exactly flattering."

My brow furrowed. How could he not see the problem here? "Marcus," I said, "why did you agree to represent Aaron when you're also featured in Yelena's act? Isn't that a *huge* conflict of interest?"

"No," Marcus said, without elaborating.

"Why not?" Gilley pressed.

"Because I didn't murder Yelena."

Gilley rolled his eyes and tossed up his hands. I couldn't have agreed more.

Marcus probably sensed our frustration and finally elaborated. "Listen, on the night that Yelena was murdered, I was at a poker game hosted by Judge Andrew Cordite—a New York Supreme Court justice. Also there were two other judges and a former attorney general. I was with those gentlemen all evening, from seven p.m. to two a.m., so I have about as airtight an alibi as you can ask for."

I felt my shoulders relax in relief.

But then Gilley said, "You could've paid someone to do it."

"Certainly," Marcus said. "But that could apply to any one of Yelena's lovers. Remember, she dated only the wealthy and powerful."

I shook my head, still a bit bothered by it all. "Marcus, Yelena calls you one of the angry men. If you had feelings for her, and in your investigation of this case against Aaron, you became convinced that he did it, wouldn't that compromise his defense?"

Marcus actually laughed. "Catherine, I didn't develop feelings for Yelena. She and I never had a romantic relationship of any kind. We were lovers. That was all. We didn't date, have dinner together, or spend quality time with one another on the weekends. We simply got together for a physical relationship about once every two weeks for two months or so. And while I'm saddened that she was murdered, since I broke things off with her, I honestly haven't given her another thought."

"Wait, *you* broke up with *her*?" Gilley asked. "That's not what the script says."

"I'm well aware that Yelena claims to have tossed me back in the harbor," Marcus chuckled. "I held no grudge against her for wanting to salvage her ego after our split."

I eyed Gilley in a way that silently asked him what he thought. He shrugged and nodded his head. I nodded mine too.

"Thank you, Marcus," I said. "We both appreciate your honesty. But maybe you should also come clean to Aaron. Just so that he's aware that his attorney had a prior relationship with the woman he was in love with."

"I've already done that, Catherine," Marcus assured me. "It was the first thing we talked about."

"And he was still willing to hire you?" Gilley asked.

"He was."

I said, "Okay, well, if it's good enough for Aaron, then I suppose it's good enough for—"

"Have you told Shepherd?" Gilley suddenly asked.

There was a pregnant pause on Marcus's end of the call, then, "No."

"Don't you think you should?" Gilley pressed.

Marcus sighed. "No," he said. "Not yet."

"Why?" I asked, thinking it could only help the situation if Marcus were completely forthcoming.

"Because if I can't arrange for sovereign immunity for Mr. Nassau, then I'll be using my brief affair with Yelena as a defense tactic. Mr. Nassau could hardly be considered the only suspect worth investigating if the police didn't even bother to question me—a person also featured in her act."

"Oh, that is clever," Gilley said.

"Thank you," Marcus said, with a hint of good humor. "And now I need to ask you two not to mention my relationship with Yelena to Shepherd, either."

"We won't," Gilley said quickly, but I didn't respond right away.

"Catherine?" Marcus asked.

"I'm here," I said.

Meanwhile, Gilley stared at me and mouthed, *What?*

"It's just . . . ," I began.

"Tell me," Marcus said.

"I don't want to lie to him, Marcus. We're in a committed relationship, and I feel like I'd be betraying him if I lied to him."

"I see," he said. "So you consider the act of omission a lie."

"No," I said, trying to clarify my own feelings as I spoke out loud. "But if he asked me if I knew anyone else who might've had a relationship with Yelena, I'd feel compelled to tell him."

"Well then," Marcus said, "let's hope he doesn't ask you."

"Yes," I said. "Let's."

Chapter 12

Gilley and I spent another hour going over the script, and we thought we identified two more possible names, beginning with Lover Number Six. There were multiple double entendres for football in his section of the script, and Gilley was able to cross-reference some of Yelena's social media posts to events attended by both her and an NFL legend, Brad Bosch, who had a house near Hook Pond, a stone's throw away to our west.

Bosch had played for the Giants from 1988 to 1999 and was now a featured commentator on ESPN. I'd seen him several times on the local news, discussing football with the station's sportscaster. Everything fit for a Brad/Yelena romance once we researched his background a bit.

And then we studied Lover Number Nine, in a weird coincidence, when we moved on from Brad to local news anchor Ike Chipperfield, from the very station where Brad would often make his appearances.

"She could've met Ike if she ever escorted Brad to the station for an interview," Gilley mused.

"Agreed. There's even this line, Gilley," I said, picking up the script to quote from it. "'Lover Number Nine and I were definitely behind the scenes, away from the camera and the jealous eyes of the quarterhack.'"

"'Quarterhack,'" Gilley said. "You know, I thought Yelena was deliciously clever, but now I'm wondering if she was really just cruel."

"The latter," I said.

Gilley eyed me suspiciously. "Did you really have a headache at intermission, or did you just not care to see Yelena's second act?"

"Yes," I said, winking at him.

Gilley chuckled, but then he sobered and eyed the whiteboard, where I'd just filled in Ike's name for Lover Number Nine. "What's interesting about all this is that we haven't drawn any obvious connections to the man who was murdered in the alley. . . . What was his name again?"

"Purdy," I said. "Mark Purdy."

Gilley's brow bounced. "Good memory."

"Thanks, but it's less skill than it is the fact that you're not likely to forget the name of a man you encountered minutes before he was murdered."

"I wonder if Shepherd's team has made any progress on that front."

I sighed wearily and came around to sit in the chair next to Gilley again. "I have no idea."

"Do we think he could've been one of the remaining lovers?" Gil said next.

I glanced at the whiteboard. "Well, there're only three names left, right? Lovers Two, Ten, and Twelve."

"Two is the legislator," Gilley said.

"Yes, so Purdy's out as a candidate for Lover Number Two. No history of running for office that we could find."

Gilley nodded and held up his script to read. "'Lover Number Ten treated life like a racetrack, circling the field and going nowhere fast.'"

"Does that describe a retired estate lawyer?" I asked.

"Nope. That describes a race-car driver."

I snapped my fingers. "Yes, Gilley! That's *exactly* who that would describe. Are there any local race-car drivers around these parts?"

"No one comes to mind. I'll do some research later."

"Good," I said. "But back to Mr. Purdy. That leaves only Lover Number Twelve as a possibility."

Gilley flipped a few pages and again read from the script. " 'Lover Number Twelve, you know who you are. The best of the Lovers. You had my number from the beginning, and you never failed to call. You're the son of a queen, a dreamer. A wisher. A maker of promises. But all your wishes are empty, all your promises lies, and you sit in your castle and look down your nose, and who are you really? Just another pretty face with a well-practiced line.' "

"Ouch," I said.

"She gets even meaner," Gilley said, making a face while he flipped through the last three pages. "She calls him a commitment-phobe and a lazy playboy."

"Well, she was mean about Marcus after he dumped her. Maybe Lover Number Twelve also dumped her."

"That'd be tough on someone like Yelena. Getting dumped by the two best lovers she's ever had," Gil said.

"Yeah. Which also means that Number Twelve definitely isn't Purdy."

"Why do you say that?" he asked me.

"I would've put Purdy in his late sixties to early seventies. And he was frail in stature and likely four inches shorter than Yelena. I doubt he could've kept up with her on a walk, much less between the sheets."

"In other words, we can assume that Purdy doesn't connect to Yelena's act."

"Not that I can see. Assuming all our guesses are correct, of course," I said.

Gilley frowned. "Which means both his appearance in the coffee shop and his murder in the alley weren't related to her."

I stared at the whiteboard without replying to Gilley for a long moment. "I'd agree if it weren't for two things that don't make sense."

"And they are?"

"The blood on his hand before he was murdered, and the size ten ladies' raincoat."

Gilley's eyes widened. "Yelena was probably a size ten," he said.

"That's what I was thinking. The coat was far too big for Purdy. He stumbled on the hem when he entered the coffee shop."

"Maybe he needed the extra length to fit in all the money," Gilley said.

I considered that but then said, "How thick would a stack of two thousand bills be?"

"That's right," Gilley said. "Shepherd said the two hundred thousand in cash on Purdy was all in hundred-dollar bills." After picking up his phone, he tapped at it and said, "A thousand one-dollar bills measures four-point-three inches high."

"Roughly eight-point-six inches of bills to pack into the lining of a raincoat," I said.

"Yep," Gilley said, tapping again at his phone. "A woman's raincoat is roughly one-point-eight meters of fabric."

I got a measuring tape from the drawer in my kitchen where I kept various odds and ends. Measuring it out on the counter, I said, "Even with stacks a half inch thick, he would've had plenty of room with a coat half that size."

"So, he didn't need an oversized coat," Gil concluded.

I stood back and rewound the measuring tape. "No."

"Then why was he wearing it?"

"Maybe so Yelena could walk out of the theater without drawing attention to herself while carrying a suspicious looking duffel bag stuffed with money—assuming the money in the lining of the raincoat was for her, of course."

Gilley eyed me intently before he nodded. "Do we think Purdy actually killed Yelena?"

I shook my head. "You saw all that blood on the floor backstage, Gilley. Whoever murdered her would've been covered in blood. Only Purdy's hand was smeared with it."

"Could he have been a witness?" Gilley asked next.

I pressed my lips together, thinking that through. Finally, I nodded. "If he walked in while Yelena was being murdered, he could've fled the scene in a panic, which would explain the fear I saw in his eyes when he entered the coffee shop. He might've known or assumed that the killer was in pursuit, and probably thought he was safe sneaking out the back."

"But he wasn't," Gilley said. "And if the killer was covered in blood, he couldn't have entered the coffee shop to go after Purdy without a bunch of witnesses seeing him."

"But he could've entered a darkened alley and waited for Purdy to take the side street to the parking garage, only to watch him appear in the alley itself."

"Why didn't Purdy call for help, though, if he witnessed the murder?" Gilley asked.

"He didn't have his phone on him, remember? He left it in the car," I said.

"But why didn't he ask to use the coffee shop's phone? Or even your phone, for that matter, when he bumped into your table?"

"If he was carrying two hundred thousand dollars on his person, meant for the murder victim, and his hand was smeared with her blood, I doubt he would've wanted to call attention to himself by playing the role of witness."

"Good point. Especially if he was still a licensed lawyer. Paying off someone blackmailing you probably wouldn't sit too well with the New York licensing board."

"So, what did Yelena have on Purdy?" I asked.

"Don't know," Gilley said, once again eyeing the white-board. Then he pointed and said, "Hold on. What about Lover Number Eight?"

I eyed the board myself. "Gene Bosworth?"

"Yeah. Remember? The note in the script said to call Gene for money."

"You're thinking Purdy handled Gene's estate, right?"

"I am."

"It'd be good to know that for certain and be able to put that puzzle piece in its place."

"You could call Shepherd and ask him to look into it," Gil suggested.

I cocked an eyebrow at him. "You're joking, right?"

"Yeah, I knew it was a no-go the second it was out of my mouth."

I snapped my fingers. "But you know who might be able to access that information and who would actually appreciate our super sleuthing?"

Gilley grinned. "Marcus Brown."

"Exactly. If court papers for Gene's estate were filed, Marcus could call up the county clerk and get that information easily."

Gilley waved at my phone on the counter. "What're you waiting for? Call him!"

I did just that, but instead of telling Marcus all about our the-ory over the phone, I set up a meeting for the three of us for the end of the day.

"And I'll be bringing a whiteboard," I told him.

"A whiteboard?" he said. "I have one here, Catherine. You can use mine."

"No, mine has a list of names on it that I think you'd be in-terested in, Marcus."

There was a pause, then, "In that case, by all means, bring the whiteboard."

* * *

An hour and a half later, I had changed into a pair of black skinny jeans, black Louboutin pumps, a matching Chanel sleeveless turtleneck and had topped the entire ensemble off with a pair of chic Oliver Peoples square-rimmed sunglasses.

When I breezed through the door of Chez Kitty to collect Gilley, he waved his hand up and down in my general direction and said, "Ooh, Catwoman. I like it."

I grinned. "I love that you get me."

Gilley then looked down at himself and said, "I'll change. Be with you in a jiff."

"Hurry," I called as he dashed down the hallway toward the bedroom. "We're supposed to be there in thirty minutes."

A mere four minutes later, Gilley emerged wearing tight-fitting black jeans and an equally tight-fitting T-shirt with a logo that read BAD TO THE BONE. Completing the ensemble, he wore a studded leather bracelet on his left wrist and a big gold ring on his right hand.

"Biker?" I asked.

"Badass," he countered.

I nodded approvingly. "It works. Let's roll."

I donned my sunglasses, he put on a pair of aviators, and we were off to the races.

Luck was with us as far as traffic was concerned, and we arrived at Marcus's office building right on time. The structure was interesting, made up of three stories of bright white brick standing starkly against the dull brown buildings surrounding it. Part of the first floor wasn't actually a floor, but a parking area for tenants and visitors. A set of large pylons supported the second and third floors above, giving the parking area shelter from the elements.

We parked in one of only two available spots and headed toward the main entrance. Coming through the doorway, we were greeted by a security guard.

"Who are you here to see?" he asked.

"Marcus Brown," I said.

"Names?"

Gilley and I exchanged a look. The guard held no clipboard or anything to refer to, so I wondered how he'd know we had an appointment.

"Catherine Cooper and Gilley Gillespie," Gilley said.

The guard spoke into the mic at his shoulder. "Cooper and Gillespie here to see Mr. Brown."

There was a pause, then a garbled reply that sounded like "Granted."

The guard stepped to the side and pointed to the elevator. "Third floor. Suite three-oh-two."

We nodded our thanks and proceeded to the elevator, which opened before we'd even had a chance to hit the button. What was even weirder was that when we got in the car, the button for the third floor lit up all on its own.

"That's creepy," I whispered to Gilley.

He nudged my shoulder and pointed toward the upper right corner of the elevator. A camera was aimed down in our direction. "Someone's watching us closely."

We got off the elevator and proceeded to the suite marked 302. The door had a unique design compared to the others lining the corridor—made of black walnut that had been shined and polished to really show off the beauty of the wood, it was broader than the other doors and probably quite a bit thicker.

Gilley began to reach for the latch, but the door opened on its own, swinging inward slowly so that we could enter.

After crossing the threshold, we came into a bright white room with an edgy abstract sculpture, which I thought might be a representation of Lady Liberty. She sat on the far wall, directly opposite the door, in the midsize lobby that we found ourselves in. The area was decorated with overstuffed gray couches and a few Eames side tables, but otherwise the place was fairly minimalist.

I looked around but didn't see a receptionist, or a receptionist's desk, for that matter. However, as Gilley and I exchanged *Now what?* glances, a door opened to the right of us, and a woman dressed in charcoal-gray silk stepped forward, extending her hand.

"Ms. Cooper," she said smoothly, shaking my hand, before turning to Gilley and greeting him by name as well. "I'm Jasmine Taylor, Mr. Brown's paralegal. May I ask if you'd like a cappuccino or an espresso before I take you back to meet with him?"

Gilley turned to me. "Okay. I'm impressed."

I couldn't help but grin. "Two cappuccinos would be lovely," I said, speaking for the pair of us.

"Perfect," she said. "This way please."

She led us through the door and down a hallway with two office suites off to the side. Two hard-at-work people—one woman, one man—sat at the desks within, hovered over their laptops, and didn't even look up as we passed.

At the end of the hall was a closed door, and we could hear Marcus's voice from inside. It sounded like he was wrapping up a call.

Jasmine knocked softly. There was a pause; then Marcus called out, "Come in, Jaz."

She opened the door as Marcus was saying his goodbyes. He pocketed his phone and stepped forward to greet us. "Catherine," he said, smiling wide and taking my hand.

It always gave me a little thrill when Marcus radiated warmth at me. He was a gorgeous man, powerful, in that he exuded confidence. He was someone I always hoped to have on my side.

"Marcus," I replied just as warmly, feeling a small blush touch my cheeks. I'd never, ever tell Shepherd this, but I had a tiny crush on Marcus.

As Marcus and I basked in the glow of each other's company, Gilley shoved his hand into the mix and practically shouted, "Hi, Marcus!"

Gilley's crush on the counselor *might* be a teensy bit bigger than mine.

"Gilley," Marcus said with a chuckle. Then he looked from me to Gilley and back again. "Are you both coordinating your outfits again?"

"We are, and aren't you a dream for noticing," Gilley said, swishing his hips and looking coyly at Marcus.

Marcus chuckled again and waved us over to his desk and the two chairs in front of it. "Come, sit, and tell me about this whiteboard, which, I see, you didn't bring."

"I took a picture," I told him, holding up my phone. "It was easier to get in the car."

Marcus grinned. "Excellent. Mind texting it to me?"

I did just that, and he opened the text to survey the board. "You two *have* been hard at work," he said, and I could tell he was impressed. Gilley looked over at me and bounced his eyebrows.

While Marcus reviewed the names on the list we'd compiled, I took in his office, and I found it interesting that there were no shades of gray to soften the stark contrast of the bright white walls and the dark wood tones of the furnishings.

I'd once read that the law wasn't written in black or white, but in subtle shades of gray. I thought it telling that Marcus largely surrounded himself with back-and-white tones. His view of the world seemed more pronounced and assured in that regard. Either something was right or it was wrong, and his confident assurance in one or the other no doubt helped juries to decide in his favor more often than they didn't.

Marcus set his phone down and eyed us with interest. "This list is very helpful. Thank you," he said. "How sure are you about the names on the list?"

"For most of them, we're probably eighty-five to ninety-five percent certain," I said.

Marcus nodded. "And which names are you unsure about?"

"Mark Purdy," I said.

Marcus's brow furrowed, and he picked up his phone again to glance at the list. "I don't see his name here. Which one is he? Two, Ten, or Twelve?"

"None of them," Gilley said. "Which is another reason we're here."

Marcus set his phone down. "Enlighten me."

Between us, we filled Marcus in on what we knew about Mark Purdy, including the backstory of my encounter with him on the night of Yelena's murder.

Marcus waited patiently throughout the explanation, and he didn't interrupt us once. When we finished, he said, "I heard there was a murder in the area near the theater, but I hadn't yet learned that it was timed so soon after Yelena's."

"We think there's a connection," I reiterated.

"Yes," he said. "I'm thinking there must be, especially in light of the women's size-ten coat."

"We think Purdy was paying off Yelena," I said.

"For whom?"

"For Gene Bosworth. Or rather for his estate."

"You said Purdy was an estate attorney, yes?" Marcus said, pulling up the lid to his laptop to type on it while we answered.

"Yes," Gilley said. "We think he handled the estate of Gene Bosworth." Gilley then produced his copy of the script—the original—and handed it over to Marcus. "On page twenty-eight there's a handwritten note in the bottom left corner, where Yelena wrote, 'Call Gene,' and then the dollar sign."

"Since Gene Bosworth died last December," I said, "we think Yelena wasn't saying to call Gene so much as she was reminding herself to call the trustee of Gene's estate to ask for money."

Marcus set down the script and pursed his lips in thought, and then he swiveled to type on his laptop for a few moments, before his eyes darted back and forth as he read the screen. "Purdy retired right before the pandemic got bad," he said.

I nodded. "That makes sense."

Marcus picked up his phone and hit a button. "Jaz, I know it's late, but if you call right away, you can catch the clerk's office. I need you to find out who the attorney of record was on a Mr. Gene Bosworth's estate. Good. Thank you."

"Yelena indicated in her script that she suspected Gene had the hots for his sister," I said.

Marcus's eyes went wide. "Really?"

"Yes, really," Gilley said.

Marcus again picked up the script and flipped through the pages. He stopped when he got to Lover Number Eight and read the lines while we waited. His phone buzzed, and he picked up the receiver. "Yes?" he said. Then, after a moment, he added, "You're sure?" Another moment passed, and he finished with, "All right. Thank you. I'll have a research project for you tomorrow regarding Mr. Purdy, so see me first thing when you get in, okay? Good. Good night, Jaz."

When Marcus hung up the phone again, Gilley said, "It was Purdy, wasn't it?"

"No," Marcus said.

"*No?*" Gilley and I repeated in unison.

"It was Albert Finch."

"Who's Albert Finch?" Gilley asked.

Marcus shrugged. "I'm not familiar with many estate attorneys. You don't run into them in the criminal defense law circles."

"Ah," Gil said. And then he muttered, "I really thought we were onto something there."

"You may be," Marcus said. "I'll have Jasmine check around

and see who Purdy's clients were. Maybe there's another name on the list that he's attached to."

Gilley and I both perked up. "Ooh, yes," I said. "That must be it. If Yelena was looking for cash from Gene, she probably was looking for cash from at least one or two others, right?"

"She was," Marcus said, in a way that suggested there was more to the story.

"Did she try to extort you?" Gilley asked.

"She did," he said. "Not overtly, but she did call me and suggest that she was launching her one-woman show, and if I wanted to remain anonymous, I might want to think about making a charitable donation."

"Whoa," I said. "What did you say?"

"I told her that extortion was a crime punishable by up to twenty years in prison, and she hung up. I had hoped that I'd scared her off the tactic, but obviously, I hadn't."

"We should talk to the other names on the list and see if she tried that trick with them," I said.

"How?" Gilley asked me. "Do we just call them up and say, 'Hey there! Your ex-girlfriend was brutally murdered. She wasn't by chance trying to extort money from you, was she, Suspect . . . I mean Lover Number Five?'"

Marcus chuckled. "No, we'll have to be more subtle than that."

Gilley snapped his fingers. "I know!" he said. Turning to me, he said, "Cat, what if we threw a party and invited all these guys, and once they've had a chance to imbibe a little truth serum, we ask them about Yelena?"

"Truth serum?" I asked.

"Vodka."

"Ahhh," I said. "You know, that's actually not a bad idea. The problem is, how do we get them to show up? I don't know any of them, and they'd likely decline an invite to a random stranger's party."

Gilley frowned. He'd thought he was really onto something.

"What you need is a lure," Marcus said.

We both looked at him. "A lure?" I said.

"A party honoree," he said. "Someone well known, with status."

"Like a celebrity? We don't know any celebrities," Gilley said.

Marcus shook his head. "Gilley, here in the Hamptons, celebrities are a dime a dozen. What you need is somebody rich." Pointing his finger back and forth between us, he said, "Who's the wealthiest person you know?"

"Catherine Cooper," Gilley said immediately.

I blushed and laughed. "Oh, Gilley, I am not."

"Uh, yeah you are," he insisted.

Marcus wore an amused smile on his face, and I felt my blush deepen.

"What about the Entwistles?" I said.

"Oh," Gil said. "Yeah. I forgot about them. They're definitely richer than you."

I laughed lightly and looked again at Marcus, but his amusement had turned to seriousness. "You know the Entwistles?" he said.

"Yes," Gilley and I both said in unison.

"*Julia* Entwistle?" Marcus stressed.

"Yes. And her grandson Willem," I said.

Marcus sat back in his chair and held his hands up in surrender. "Catherine, Gilley, if you could make either of them your honoree, you'd have one of the hottest tickets in town."

"Really?" I said, looking at Gilley to see what he thought. He seemed as surprised as I was. "I mean, we've been to their home, and we know they must be very comfortable, but neither of them socializes very much, Marcus. How could they be so attractive to our guests?"

"Julia Entwistle is one of the wealthiest women on Long Island, Catherine. Her money and pedigree go way back. She's blue blood, and nothing brings out the ever-social-climbing Hamptons crowd like a billionaire blue blood in attendance at a social gathering. Plus, you're right. Julia hasn't been to a social event in a decade. If you could score her appearance at your gathering, you'd get all your suspects to accept in a hot second."

I frowned. The last time I'd seen Julia she'd been bound to a wheelchair, and she'd looked quite frail. I didn't want to do anything to put stress on her. "Would Willem Entwistle be an equally appealing draw?"

"He might," Marcus said. "He stands to inherit everything, I assume, so that's a definite plus in his favor, but his influence over some of the more powerful players here in the Hamptons is far less than that of his legendary grandmother."

"How do you know all this about the Entwistles?" Gilley asked.

Marcus grinned. "It's my business to know who's who around here, Gilley. Defending big names takes big money, and I like that about practicing law in the Hamptons."

"Would you also be looking to score an introduction?" Gilley said.

Marcus's grin widened. "I wouldn't ever say no to meeting the legendary Julia Entwistle. Or her grandson."

"We'll make sure you get an invite," Gilley promised.

"Excellent," he said. "What else do you need from me?"

I raised my hand slightly and said, "Did Yelena try to extort Aaron?"

"He says she didn't," Marcus confessed.

"Why don't you look like you believe him?" I asked, reading Marcus's expression.

"Because I don't."

"He'd lie to you?" Gilley asked.

"He's still in love with her ghost," Marcus said. "He's trying to protect her."

"The poor man," I said. "How's he doing overall?"

"Not great. The odds for sovereign immunity in this case are long, and my colleague at the Danish embassy says it doesn't look good."

"When will you know?" I asked.

"Within a few days."

"What can we do for him?" I asked next.

Marcus waved his hand casually in our direction. "You're doing it. You've given me a list of eight other suspects to focus on, and you're going to throw a party where we can casually question at least a few of them. This will really help his defense."

"And don't forget about the Purdy angle," Gilley said. "If Purdy was delivering a payoff to Yelena, and if we can prove that, then that's motive pointing to one of these other guys for sure, right?"

"It is," Marcus said. "I'll know more in the next day or two about him and his client list, and I'll call you with any updates."

"Perfect," I said, getting to my feet. Extending my elbow out to Gilley, I said, "Come along, Mr. Gillespie. We have a party to plan."

Gilley bounced to his feet and looped his arm through mine. "Marcus," he said, dipping his chin demurely. "Always a pleasure."

Marcus grinned. "It is, isn't it?"

Gilley laughed, and with a wave goodbye, we left to head home.

Chapter 13

The first thing we did when we arrived back at Chez Kitty was to order dinner and feed Spooks. The dog always gulped down his food like he was afraid someone else would steal it.

"The poor thing," I said, watching him eat.

"I know," Gilley said. "He eats every meal like it's going to be his last. I read in one of the pamphlets they sent home with us that dogs who've experienced intense abuse and hunger can act like that. I'm hoping that with time and regular meals, he'll realize that he'll always get enough to eat here. Oh, and I've got to order one of those special bowls that forces him to slow down, because eating that fast isn't good for him."

"You didn't already buy it at the Pet Palace?" I said, giving his shoulder a playful knock with my own.

"That was the only thing I didn't buy."

Gilley's phone rang, and he took it out to read the display. After declining the call, he stuffed the phone back into his pocket and cleared his throat. "Spam," he said, avoiding my gaze.

"You'll have to talk to your husband sometime, lovey," I said.

"I know," he sighed. "But I just can't right now, Cat."

"Does he know that you're this worked up over the prospect of a talk?"

"I keep sending his calls to voice mail, so I'm thinking yes."

I sighed. "Okay. It's your marriage."

Gilley bent low to hug Spooks, who had finished his meal and had come over to thank Gilley for it. I watched the two of them play tug until Sebastian let me know that our dinners had been delivered and were waiting on the front steps to Chez Cat.

"Here or there?" I asked Gilley.

"Here or there what?" Gil replied, pulling hard on the other end of a braided rope, which Spooks was inching out of Gilley's hands.

"Where would you like to eat?"

"Oh, um, here is fine," Gil said. "Less to move," he added, indicating the dog bed by the couch.

"I don't know why you think we'd need to move that just to bring Spooks over. He never uses it."

"Yes, but I want him to," Gilley said.

"Do you?" I asked. I suspected that Spooks was cuddled up to Gilley at night on the bed, and I imagined that my dear friend rather liked being cuddled on the couch too.

Gilley waggled his fingers at me. "Shoo, fly. Shoo! And bring us back some dinner."

We ate our meal over talk of the party. By the end we had a wonderful idea to create a sort of *Dancing with the Stars* theme, as I really wanted to have the affair outside if the weather would cooperate.

"This weather pattern is supposed to hold for the next ten days," Gilley said, checking his phone.

"That's encouraging," I said. "Do you think next weekend is pushing it a little fast?"

"Not really," he said. "But first, you need to see when and if Willem can make it."

"Ach," I said, getting up to retrieve my purse, where I kept my phone. "I'd completely forgotten that we needed to reach out to him."

After placing the call, I waited several rings until a rather hoarse voice answered. "Catherine?"

"Willem!" I said. "Hello, my friend! How are you?"

"This is a nice surprise. I'm well, and you?"

"I'm very well. Thank you. But you don't sound well. Are you coming down with a cold?"

Willem chuckled. "No, nothing like that. You just woke me, that's all."

I looked at the clock. It was ten past eight. "I'm so sorry," I said. "I didn't realize you went to bed so early, otherwise I never would've disturbed you."

"I actually went to bed late, and you're calling early. Chanel and I are in Thailand."

"Thailand?"

"He's in Thailand?" Gilley asked, scooting his chair close so that he could hear more of the conversation.

"Yes," Willem chuckled. "We eloped!"

I gasped and stared with wide eyes at Gilley.

"What? What?" Gilley said.

"Willem and Chanel eloped!"

"Ohmigod!" Gilley squealed and grabbed the phone right out of my hands. "Willem! Congratulations! This is such amazing news!"

I pulled the phone out of his hands and laid it on the table, then pressed the speaker function.

Willem was in the middle of an explanation, it seemed. "Planned on coming here for vacation, and we had a layover in Vegas, of all places, and when we were there, I just kind of stood on my tiptoes and popped the question."

Gilley and I let out a peal of laughter. Willem was a little person, and he thought nothing of making light of his dwarfism. His new bride was a former model. She was tall and lithe and completely smitten with Willem. They made an adorable couple.

"What did your grandmother say?" I asked him. Julia Entwistle couldn't have been happy to hear the news that her grandson hadn't invited her to his wedding.

"She's fine. She's throwing us a reception when we get home," Willem said. "I'm sure you two will be getting your invites soon."

That reminded me about the reason for my call. "When will that be?"

"The reception?"

"Yes, but more importantly, your return home?"

"Save the date of October twenty-third, if you can," Willem said. "And we'll be home on the tenth."

Since it was well past September tenth, I took that to mean he wouldn't be home for another three weeks. After hitting the MUTE button, I quickly asked Gilley, "Should we wait?"

"For what? For them to get home and attend our party before attending their reception, all in the span of a week?"

I frowned.

"Guys?" Willem said. "You there?"

"Sorry, Willem. I didn't realize I accidentally touched the MUTE button," I said. "I'm so thrilled and happy for both of you, and we will definitely be attending your reception."

"Awesome," Willem said. "But was there something else? You guys called me. What's up?"

Gilley and I shrugged at each other, and then Gilley made the executive decision and said, "We were calling to invite you to a party, because we needed your help."

"My help? Help with what?"

"Cat and I are up to our old tricks," Gilley said, then added a laugh, like investigating a murder was such fun!

"Are you messing with the mob again?" Willem sounded worried.

"No," I was quick to say. "But we are attempting to help another client of mine, who seems to have gotten himself into some trouble."

I then took several minutes to explain everything to Willem. He was silent for a moment after I finished. "I think my aunt knows the count," he said.

"She does?" I said, surprised, but then not.

"Yeah. I think they've even had dinner together once or twice. My great-grandmother was Danish, and if memory serves me, Grams would be a distant cousin of Aaron's through her mother's family."

"Wow," I said. Even Gilley seemed impressed.

"Have you called her yet?" Willem said next.

"No," I admitted. "I'm hesitant to get her involved. She seemed so frail the last time we saw her."

"What's it been? Like, a year?" Willem asked.

"A year and a half," I said.

"Well, you should see her now, Catherine. She's a whole new woman. She started the RBG workout routine right after my curse was broken, and she's found herself a personal trainer, who comes to the house four days a week, and she's even ditched the wheelchair and walks three miles a day on a treadmill."

"You're kidding," Gilley said.

"No, I'm serious. She's a new woman."

"That's amazing! I'm so relieved to hear she's doing so well," I said.

"You should call her and tell her what you're up to," Willem insisted. "She'd want to help. And throwing a party in her honor would really make her happy. Every time we talk, she keeps complaining about how bored she is."

"You really think she'd come?" I asked.

"I do," he said. "And you could even throw it in honor of her eighty-fourth birthday, which is at the end of this month. Chanel and I never would've skipped out on her birthday, but

Gram bought the trip for us as a surprise and she insisted we go, so we couldn't say no."

"Ooh, I would *love* to put together a birthday celebration for your grandmother!" Gilley said, clapping his hands rapidly together.

"You'd actually be doing me a favor," Willem said. "I was starting to feel guilty about being separated from her on the thirtieth, and the only thing I could think of to do was to send her a personal chef to cook her favorite meal, but if you two want to throw the party, I'd like to insist on paying for it."

"Done," Gilley said before I could politely decline. "What's the budget?"

I stared at him in disbelief. Was he crazy? We would be using Julia as a means to an end, and because of that, we owed it to her to pay for her party.

"Start at fifty, but if you have to go up, do it. And save the receipts. I'll reimburse you as soon as I'm home."

My eyes were blinking so fast while my mind tried to take in the quick exchange between Gilley and Willem that I forgot to even protest. And before I knew it, Gilley was saying, "Perfect. I'll keep you apprised of our progress. Shoot me your grandmama's deets and we'll reach out ASAP!"

"Great. Bye, Gilley! Bye, Catherine!"

"Will—" I began, but Gilley cut me off.

"Bye, Willem! Give Chanel a kiss from us!" And with that, Gilley hit the END button and swiveled in his chair to look at me with glee.

"Why would you agree to that?" I demanded.

"What? Allow him pay for the party?"

"Yes!"

"Because I know how it feels to be away from your mom on her special day, and how you wish someone close by could make her feel special, because you can't."

I softened immediately. "When was your mom's birthday?"

"The first of April. We didn't get our second dose of vaccine until April fifth, so I couldn't go to Savannah, and I felt guilty and sad about it all day."

"Why didn't you tell me?"

"Because that was the day Shepherd surprised you with flowers and a candlelight dinner, and you were so happy. I didn't want to bring you down."

I rubbed his arm. "Oh, Gil. I'm so sorry. We'll fly to Savannah next year to surprise her on her birthday, okay?"

"Yeah?" he said hopefully.

"Absolutely," I vowed. "Now, let's call Julia and see if we can't arrange to make her birthday memorable."

We called the number Willem had sent Gilley in a text, but Julia didn't pick up, so Gilley left her a sweet voice mail. "She's probably gone to bed," Gil said, eyeing the clock. "It's just about nine o'clock."

I got up and stretched. "Okay, then," I said. "I'm headed home. I'm exhausted too."

"Lightweight," Gilley giggled.

I stuck my tongue out at him but couldn't keep down a little chuckle myself. "Good night, Gilley," I sang.

"Good night, Cat."

Spooks got up when I opened the door, and came trotting over to me. I bent to hug him and nearly asked Gilley if I could take him to Chez Cat for the night, but I knew Gilley needed Spooks's company more than I did.

"Take care of him, okay?" I whispered to the pup.

He gave me a kiss on the cheek, and I left to head to bed.

The next morning, when I entered Chez Kitty, Gilley was saying goodbye to someone on the phone. I waited for him to hang up before I asked who it was, although I was secretly hoping it was Michel and they'd worked things out.

"Perfect," he said, sounding happy. "Okay, love, I'll give you a call in the next couple of days, okay? Wonderful. Bye now." Gilley blew a kiss into the phone before hanging up, and my heart lifted with hope.

"Michel?" I asked, pointing to the phone.

Gilley let out a mirthless laugh. "No, that was Julia. She called me twenty minutes ago, and I told her all about our super sleuthing, and she is totally on board!"

"She is?" I asked, blinking in surprise.

"She is!" Gilley sang, his voice going up a few octaves. "And she's *thrilled* to attend a birthday celebration in her honor!"

"Ah, now I know why you're so giddy. You get to plan a party with a giant budget and no one to tell you no."

"Exactly," Gilley said, grinning ear to ear. "We should get started on the guest list right away," he said, hurrying to the kitchen to retrieve a pad of paper and a pen. After sitting down at the table, he began to scribble. "We'll invite all the suspects, of course, and Marcus and Shepherd and—"

I sucked in a sharp breath and clamped my hand onto Gilley's arm.

"Ow!" he said, tugging on his arm. "You know I bruise like a peach! What gives?"

"Shepherd," I said softly, letting go of him. "Gilley, *what* am I going to do about Shepherd?"

"Why is this a problem?"

"I can't invite Shepherd *and* all the men who'd dated Yelena and were featured in her show. He's bound to catch on when I start asking these men all the same questions about their relationship with Yelena."

"Just point him toward the guests and tell him to mingle. What's the big deal?"

I stared at him for a long moment before I said, "Gilley. It's Shepherd. The man who hates people, especially chatty people in fancy clothes whom he's never met before."

"Oh, yeah," Gilley said, but then he eyed me like he took

me for a simpleton. "Sugar," he said next, "you *have* to invite him. He'll be ten times as suspicious if you don't. But here's the trick. If you ask him to come, he'll want to get out of it, because snobby parties, fancy clothes, and people in general aren't his gig, and then you'll pick a fight with him that he's not support-ive enough, and if he tries to apologize, you just continue to make a big deal out of it until he tells you in a huff he's not coming."

"You know," I said, tapping the table, "that is actually a ter-rific plan." Shepherd would definitely react the way Gilley had described, and picking a fight with him was easy.

It was the making-up part that might prove problematic, but I could worry about that later.

"Okay, Gilley," I said, with new resolve. "Let's plan this thing!"

The rest of the week went by in a whirl of details, emails, phone calls, texts, mad dashes to various boutiques and restau-rants, and always another thing to do. Luckily, Shepherd was so busy working his case against Aaron that he wasn't available for much time with me. I missed him, but I didn't relish the im-pending fight I was supposed to instigate.

"Can we stop at the mailbox on Chestnut?" Gilley asked as we got in the car, ready to knock out the final errands for the party. "I have a card for Mama to mail out, and their last pickup is at four."

"Of course," I told him, making a right at the stop sign, in-stead of the left that typically took us to town. The mailbox was almost directly across the street from Sunny's house, and I felt a pang when I thought of her. I missed her and wished that she'd be released from the hospital. Shepherd had visited her a cou-ple of times, and each time he had come away unsettled, telling me only that Sunny remained in an agitated state, but nobody could pinpoint why.

We pulled up in front of the mailbox, and Gilley fished around in his messenger bag, hunting for the envelope he needed to mail out, and I looked across the street at Sunny's beautiful home. Gilley got out of the car and headed to the mailbox while I waited. After mailing his letter, he trotted back to me and opened the car door and got in just as a big Range Rover pulled past us and turned abruptly into Sunny's driveway.

I didn't know why, but Gilley and I continued to watch from the car as Darius emerged from the driver's side of the Range Rover and walked around to the rear passenger seat, where he got Finley out of his car seat. Then he balanced the little tyke on his chest as he also opened the front passenger's door.

Gil and I both sucked in a breath when Sunny stepped out onto the pavement, looking frail and unsteady. Darius was quick to close the door and wrap an arm around her waist to steady her, before the two of them moved slowly along the drive to the walkway, then up the steps and into the house.

"She's home," Gilley said softly. "She's finally home."

I nodded, wondering if Shepherd knew. I wanted to call him, but I was still working up the nerve to have a fight with him later and didn't want to jinx it.

"I wonder when we can go visit her," I said.

"Let's bring them some lasagna in the next couple of days," Gilley suggested.

Gilley made the best lasagna I'd ever tasted. "That's a great idea," I said, putting the car into drive and heading for town, with thoughts of Sunny heavy on my mind.

"Did Shepherd get his tux cleaned?" Gilley asked me after a while.

Our party was black tie and formal wear, because a party featuring the reappearance of Julia Entwistle after a decade of withdrawal from public life would demand nothing less.

"I haven't told him about the party yet," I said.

"You *what*?" Gilley said. "Cat, the party is *tomorrow*! You can't have that man showing up in a wrinkled tuxedo. Wait, *does he even own a tuxedo*? Ohmigod, what if he shows up in a plaid shirt and Dockers?"

I looked at Gilley incredulously. "What has gotten into you?" He was breathing heavily and gripping the seat belt tightly.

Gilley merely shook his head, and I thought maybe he was having a panic attack.

"Gil," I said, thinking about pulling over to tend to him and unable to see a space anywhere to do that in the crowded downtown streets. "Remember? Shepherd isn't going to come. I'm going to pick that fight with him, and he'll stomp off and not show up."

Gilley's breathing slowed almost immediately. "Ohmigod," he said, fanning himself. "I forgot that particular detail."

"Yeah, I know," I said, eyeing him again. "This will all be fine by the end of the day, okay? And then we'll have all of tomorrow to pamper ourselves and get ready. Which reminds me, I have to pick my dress up from the dry cleaner's on North Main. We can hit that after we're done picking up the extra bottles of champagne."

"There, Cat!" Gilley suddenly yelled.

I hit the brakes, thinking he was pointing to something I was about to hit. "What? What!" I looked all around and didn't see anything.

Gilley continued to point. "That spot right there!"

I realized he was pointing to an open parking space in front of a high-end boutique. "That's two blocks from our next stop," I said testily. Man, he was getting on my last nerve.

"No, pull in there!" Gilley insisted.

Frustrated that he was being so irrational, I pulled into the spot and put the car in park. I was getting ready to lecture him about toning it down a notch when Gilley jumped out of the car, looked back at me, and said, "I'll be right back."

With that, he slammed the door and ran into the boutique,

for what I couldn't imagine. He already had his tuxedo pressed and hanging on the door to his bedroom.

I waited for several minutes and was about to head in to look for him when he popped back into sight, holding a garment bag. "What in the . . . ?" I muttered.

Gilley came around to my side and opened up the rear door, where he hung the garment bag on the hook behind my seat. Then he grinned at me like he had a secret and came bounding back to the front passenger side.

"What's in the bag, Gilley?"

"Your gown, Cinderella," he said.

I furrowed my brow. "My gown? What're you talking about? Did you pick it up at the dry cleaner's and bring it down here? I hope you didn't alter it. You know it fits me like a glove."

"Yes, I know that gown, which you've worn three times since you bought it and have been seen everywhere in, fits you like a glove."

"What's that supposed to mean?"

"Sugar, you're the host of *the* best party in town this weekend. No *way* should you show up in last year's fashion."

I glanced over my shoulder suspiciously. "How much is that setting me back?"

Gilley's grin widened. "Zero dollars and zero cents."

"Come on, stop playing," I said with a sigh.

"I'm not playing. I told Willem about it, and he said that he definitely wanted to pick up the tab for the gown."

I had been about to pull out of the space with the car in reverse, but the minute Gilley said that, I put the car back into park and pointed to the boutique. "Take it back," I said firmly.

"What? Why?"

"Because I doubt it'll fit—"

"Oh, please! Like I don't have your exact measurements by now," Gilley said, with a roll of his eyes.

"*And* because you're taking advantage of Willem, and I'm not having it! We're already over budget as it is."

"By five hundred dollars," he said, crossing his arms and offering me a petulant pout.

"That's still fifty thousand five hundred dollars you've spent so far, Gil! That's outrageous!"

"Oh, please, Catherine. That's the price of a modest wedding. Willem gets it."

I glared at him. "Take the gown back."

"No."

"Fine. Then *I'll* take it back. Is the receipt in the bag?" I unbuckled myself and was on my way out of the car when Gilley stopped me by grabbing my arm.

"Cat, it's one of a kind. There are *no* returns."

My eyes widened. "How much did you spend on this one-of-a-kind creation?"

"I'm not telling," he said stubbornly.

"Then I'm not wearing it," I replied angrily, moving out of the parking spot to carry on down the street. I was furious with him for taking advantage of Willem's generosity. The gown I had waiting at the dry cleaner's was perfectly acceptable for tomorrow's festivities.

"Okay, fine. Don't wear it," Gilley said and began to whistle.

I had a bad feeling, and it was made worse by the fact that when I pulled into the lot of the dry cleaner's, Gilley began to inspect his nails. I pulled down the shade and flipped up the lid on the vanity mirror, expecting to see the ticket for my dress, but it wasn't there. "Where's my ticket?"

"Probably in a stack of other tickets in there," Gilley said, waving his hand casually toward the dry cleaners.

And then I knew. "*What* did you do with my gown, Gilley?"

"I put it someplace safe."

I let my head fall forward onto the steering wheel. "I will kill you before this day is through, you realize that, right?"

Gilley grinned wickedly at me. "Don't do that. Then you'll have to throw another party."

We didn't speak for the rest of the afternoon. Gilley tried to make small talk, but I would only glare at him. Finally, we got home, and I left the gown in the car, determined to find something else in my closet that I could wear.

A half hour later Gilley found me in my closet, sorting frantically through my formal wear for a dress or a gown even half as good as the one that he had hidden. "I'm not wearing it," I said when he entered with the garment bag dangling from his arm.

"Come on, Cat. Just look at it, will you?"

I pressed my lips together in frustration. I did in fact want to see the gown, and I hated my curiosity. But I couldn't let Gilley know that, so I simply crossed my arms and glared at him.

He dropped the lower half of the garment bag and unzipped the gown.

My breath caught at the sight of it. The garment was made almost entirely of black velvet. It had a full, floor-length skirt, a cinched waist, and a sleeveless halter top. The neckline was a deep V, and it flared wide at the top, with a collar that turned up and was made of white silk sewn onto a black silk background, and that ensemble lined the entire length of the V, with small black buttons completing the vertical trim. There were also two cuffs made of white silk that were made to be worn like bracelets.

"Oh, my," I said, breathless at the sight of such a spectacular gown.

"See?" Gilley said, moving forward to drape the gown in front of me and pivot me toward the full-length mirror. Even still on the hanger, the thing looked gorgeous next to my skin.

"Damn you, Gilley," I said, shaking my head.

"What? Cat, you'll be magnificent in this!"

"Exactly," I said, reaching up to touch the soft fabric. "There's no way I can take it back now that I've seen it."

Gilley's smile was a mile wide. "Told you so."

"But *I'm* paying for it," I said next.

"You won't like the price."

"Of course I won't like the price. How much?"

"Willem told me not to tell you."

"For God's sake, Gilley! Just tell me!"

"Take it up with Willem, Cat."

And with that, Gilley placed the hanger in my hand and began to walk out.

Quickly, I raised the collar to eye level and looked for any sign of a price tag, and of course there was none, but the small tag at the back of the collar read VIVACE.

"Gilley!" I yelled, to stop him.

Gilley looked over his shoulder and said, "How else were we going to get Antonio here? He turned down our RSVP, remember?"

He'd been the only suspect we'd identified to turn down our invite.

"You got him to come?"

"Maybe. I had a long talk with his personal assistant and made sure to tell her that Antonio would do well to attend the party, where his most gorgeous creation was about to be paraded around in front of the wealthiest woman on Long Island and all her close friends. What a shame it would be if he couldn't attend and bask in the glory of all the envious whispers his gown was about to inspire."

I shook my head and gave in to a smile. "You are one sneaky devil."

Gilley curtsied, then moseyed out the door.

I was left standing with the gown in front of the mirror, and I wanted to cry over the fact that Shepherd would miss seeing me in it.

After hanging the garment on a hook near the mirror, I looked through my shoe collection for a suitable pair of pumps, and when I'd selected those, I moved on to jewels.

"Pearls," I said to myself. "But should I wear a choker or opera length?"

"Opera length," I heard behind me, and I whirled around to see Shepherd standing there, wearing a grin on his face. "Especially if you're going to an opera."

"Hey there," I said.

"Hey, yourself. What're you picking out, and where do you want to drag me?"

I took a deep breath. It was now or never. "Actually, I've been meaning to tell you. Gilley and I are throwing a party here tomorrow night and—"

"A party? What party?"

"It's Julia Entwistle's birthday," I said.

"Julia Entwistle?" Shepherd said, scratching at his five o'clock shadow. I suddenly realized that he looked exhausted. "Sounds familiar . . ." Shepherd paused to think; then he had it and snapped his fingers. "She's Willem's mother, right?"

"Grandmother."

"Oh, yeah. That's right. She's having a birthday party here?"

"She is."

"I didn't realize you guys were that close."

I cleared my throat. "Well, Willem called with some news."

"What news?"

"He and Chanel eloped, and now they're in Thailand on their honeymoon."

I watched Shepherd's expression carefully. There was history there, which I knew was best left untouched, but I couldn't help looking for any signs that what I'd just told him bothered him.

If it did, he was careful not to show it. "Good for them," he said. "What does that have to do with Julia?"

"Willem felt bad that he won't be home in time for his grandmother's birthday, and he asked if I might throw a party in her honor."

"Oh," Shepherd said. "And you want me to come."

"Yes." I didn't elaborate, lest Shepherd ferret out the lie I was about to tell.

"Okay," he said agreeably. "Should I bring beer?"

I blinked once, very slowly. "No," I said. "Shep, this is a black-tie affair."

"Black tie? Oh, come on, Cat, you know I hate those kinds of parties."

"Yes, yes, I do," I said.

"Do you really need me to attend?" he asked carefully.

And that was my cue to blow up, and blow up I did. With very little effort, I started a fight where we were both yelling at each other, and it ended with Shepherd leaving in a huff and vowing to skip the party.

After he'd gone, I knew I should've felt relieved, but I didn't. Instead, I sank to the floor and cried.

Chapter 14

"This is quite the turnout," Gilley said as we stood in the doorway of the patio at Chez Cat, surveying the crowd. All the guests were friends of Julia, save for our suspects, of course.

"It is," I said, smiling at the excellent job we'd done putting this little soiree together in only a week.

The orchestra began to play a foot-tapping tune, and I was happy to see some of the couples taking to the dance floor. Our *Dancing with the Stars* theme seemed to be going off without a hitch, and it was a nice way for me to corner a few of our suspects and make casual conversation, which was really about sussing out any lingering anger they might still hold for Yelena, and perhaps an alibi—or lack of one—for the night of her murder.

What we needed were some viable prospects to present to Marcus. Those would be the men he'd subpoena and put on the stand—specifically targeting the question of any extortion attempts made by Yelena.

If they were caught in a lie, Marcus could subpoena their financial records and trace any unexplained large withdrawals back to similar deposits made to Yelena's bank account.

And Marcus had already had some success in obtaining a partial printout of her most recent transactions, and she had made at least three large deposits of fifty thousand dollars or more.

We suspected that one of those deposits might have come from Aaron, because the timing fit the waning days of their relationship, but there were two others that were questionable. One for the period right before Aaron and Yelena began dating, and the other for immediately after. That last deposit was for two hundred thousand, which we knew was the same amount carried but not delivered by Mark Purdy.

Since we couldn't be sure if Yelena was extorting the men she named only in her show or others from her past, it'd be necessary to question all the lovers we could identify.

"Who are you focused on?" Gilley asked me.

"I'll take Vivace, Bosch, and Chipperfield."

"Perfect. I'll take McAllen, Goldberg, and Leahy."

"Wonderful," I said. Then I scanned the crowd. "Is June here?" I asked, speaking of Lover Number Eight's sister. "I don't think I see her."

"Not yet," Gilley said. "But I'm hopeful."

"What time did Julia say she'd be arriving?"

Gilley lifted his wrist to note the time. "She should be here in the next twenty minutes. She wanted to be the last to arrive and make her entrance."

"And Marcus is bringing her, correct?"

"He is. He's going to act as her bodyguard, which means that he'll be able to overhear any conversations had by Julia and one of our suspects."

Julia was our backup plan in case we couldn't convince any of our suspects to talk, and Marcus would make sure she stayed safe in their presence.

"Okay then," I said, feeling both nervous and anxious. "Let's rock and roll."

Gilley offered his fist for a fist bump, and I obliged. I had begun to turn away when he stopped me and said, "By the way, Cat, can I just say that you are a *vision* in that gown?"

I smiled and gave him a spontaneous hug. I was still smarting from the fight that Shepherd and I had had, and it hurt that he wasn't here to appreciate how gorgeous I looked tonight. The gown fit me like a second skin, and the black velvet against my very pale white complexion was a delicious contrast. I couldn't imagine a more flattering look than the one I had on, and it was nice to hear it said out loud by someone I trusted.

"Love you," I whispered in Gilley's ear.

"Back at you," he said, squeezing me tight before letting me go.

With a deep breath, I turned to the crowd and selected my target.

I weaved my way through the cluster, stopped in front of Antonio Vivace, and smiled up at him gamely. "I've been dying to talk to you since you arrived," I said to him.

He grinned approvingly and said, "You are exactly the woman I would want to wear that gown."

I bowed my head and extended my hand. "Catherine Cooper," I said.

He took my hand and brought it to his lips. After kissing my knuckles, he said, "Antonio Vivace."

Glancing over my shoulder toward the dance floor, I said, "Antonio, may I have this dance?"

His grin widened. "Of course."

We stepped onto the dance floor, and I quickly discovered that he was a fabulous dancer. I was just okay, but with Vivace leading, I felt like a pro.

I spoke about how much I admired his creations, then segued into a casual mention of Yelena. "I discovered you through a friend of mine," I said.

"Oh?"

"Yes. She wore your creations almost exclusively, and she always looked so radiant." I then sighed sadly.

Vivace's smile faded, and his perfectly timed steps faltered for a moment. "You must be speaking of Yelena Galanis."

"I am," I said. "I didn't know her for very long, but I adored her."

The designer's gaze traveled to a spot above my head, and it was clear he was avoiding meeting my eyes. He said nothing, so I continued.

"What a terrible tragedy it is that she's no longer with us," I said.

"Mmm," he said, not quite a confirmation or a necessarily suspicious indicator.

"You knew her well, though, correct?"

"I did," he said.

"That's right," I said. "She dated you briefly, didn't she?"

Vivace's eyes met mine, and the look on his face was piercing. Suspicious. "She told you that?"

"In a roundabout way," I said. "Actually, I guessed it based on how many compliments she paid you both as a designer and a person."

"Pffft," he said. "I doubt that."

"No, it's true!" I insisted. "She only spoke highly of you, and it was in a way that made me think she had some romantic feelings and that perhaps they were returned."

Vivace offered me the tightest of smiles. "Yelena was the least romantic woman I've ever met. She wasn't who you think she was, Catherine, and if she treated you well, it was only because you hadn't known her very long."

I widened my eyes in surprise, even though I was definitely not surprised. "My goodness," I said. "What did she do to you, Antonio?"

The song we'd been dancing to ended, and he abruptly stopped moving me around the dance floor. After letting go of my hand, he offered me a deep bow, then stood straight and said, "It was a pleasure, madame."

With that, he walked away.

"Hmm," I muttered. That was interesting.

Moving off the dance floor, I next approached Brad Bosch, who was incredibly handsome and well built. "Hello," I said gamely. He was standing by himself, so my overture seemed natural.

"Hi," he said, looking relieved that someone had approached him. Then he stuck out his hand. "Brad Bosch."

"I thought you looked familiar," I said. "I'm Catherine Cooper."

"Our host," he said.

I nodded. "Are you here alone?" I asked next.

He grimaced. "Yeah. I got my invitation on short notice, and the girl I've been seeing is in the City this weekend."

"Well, it was so nice of you to come."

He shrugged. "It's not every day that you get to meet a legend," he said. "Which is why I was a little curious how I ended up on the guest list."

"Julia's idea," I said. "She gave me a list of dear friends and a list of people she'd heard of and wanted to meet, and your name was at the top."

He eyed me with renewed interest. "Did she hear about my campaign?"

"Your campaign?"

"I'm running for New York's First District next year."

I blinked in surprise. "You are?"

"Yeah," he said. "And if I got Julia Entwistle's endorsement, it could be a game changer."

"Definitely," I said. "That must be why she invited you."

Bosch's smile was radiant. "Can you get me a private audience with her?" he asked next. "I've been working on my pitch ever since I got the invite."

I returned his smile. "Of course, I can," I said, deciding there and then to allow Julia to gently interrogate Bosch. He'd probably be willing to tell her anything to gain her endorsement. She could tell him that she heard he'd suffered a recent loss with the death of Yelena Galanis, and see what reaction and information he offered in return.

Looking over Bosch's shoulder, I pretended to spot an old friend and said, "Brad, would you excuse me? I see my dear friend Ike Chipperfield is here."

Bosch's reaction startled me. He stiffened, and his expression turned to barely hidden anger. "You know Chipperfield?"

"I do," I said. "He used to date a friend of mine. She died recently, and I want to express my condolences."

Bosch nodded curtly. "Sure," he said. "I heard about that too."

I wasn't sure if he meant that he'd heard about Yelena's death or about the fact that Ike Chipperfield had dated Yelena behind Bosch's back. His quick switch to a simmering anger was pretty telling, however.

I pretended not to notice and squeezed his arm. "Thank you. I'll swing back around to take you to Julia as soon as she gets here."

"Great," he said stiffly.

With a parting smile, I left his side and moved over to Ike Chipperfield. He was standing with a couple, making small talk, but I noticed as I left Bosch that Chipperfield was glaring in our direction. Clearly, there was no love lost between these two.

Stopping in front of the threesome, I nodded to the couple and focused on Chipperfield. "So sorry to interrupt," I said. "But, Mr. Chipperfield, I have to tell you I'm such a huge fan of yours."

Chipperfield looked me up and down, and I thought I met his approval, because without even taking his leave of the couple, he offered me his arm and said, "May I have this dance?"

"Of course!" I said, taking his arm.

He moved us out to the dance floor, and we began to tango. Chipperfield was also a good dancer, not as smooth as Vivace, but still very good.

"You're a wonderful dancer," I said to him.

He beamed at me. "You're not so bad yourself, kid."

I smiled in return, even though being called "kid" got under my skin a little.

"How long have you been a fan of mine?" he asked me.

"Ever since I moved to the Hamptons," I said. "You were the first newscaster I watched in my new house, and you made me feel like I could fit in here."

"Oh, yeah?" he said.

"Yeah. You're so warm, Ike. It's like you're our friend rather than some robotic anchorperson."

"I practice my delivery to make sure I come across that way."

"Well, it's paying off. When I first offered to throw Julia a birthday party, I mentioned to her that I very much wanted to invite you, because I'd heard such good things about you, from a personal perspective."

He cocked his head a little. "From who?"

"From my friend," I said. "She just passed away, in fact. She spoke so highly of you, and inviting you here was my little way of honoring her memory."

Chipperfield's grip on my hand tightened. "Yelena Galanis?"

"Yes," I said, trying to look surprised. "I know you two knew each other, but I didn't realize you'd be aware of her death."

"I'm a newscaster," he said. "I'm aware of everything."

"Ah," I said. "Well, you should know that she adored you."

Chipperfield's mouth twitched a little. He, like Vivace, didn't believe me, either. "Is that why you invited Bosch?" he asked me.

I glanced over my shoulder in Bosch's direction. He was staring at us with daggers in his eyes. "It is," I said. "But how did you know that they used to date?"

He didn't answer me directly, but he did say something telling. "Those two deserved each other."

Again, I widened my eyes in mock surprise. "You say that like you didn't care much for Yelena."

He shrugged. "People change," he said. "She certainly did."

"Oh," I said. "I'm sorry you had that experience with her. She was nothing but kind to me."

"You must not have known her very long."

It was striking how similar that sentiment was between he and Vivace. They both clearly held the same disparaging view of Yelena. Either of them could have taken that anger and bitterness to the next level by murdering her.

Out of the corner of my eye, I saw someone waving toward me. Turning to look, I realized that it was Marcus. He stood in the doorway, with Julia out of view.

"Ike, would you please excuse me? I see that our guest of honor has arrived."

"Sure," he said. But before I could leave him, he squeezed my hand and said, "Could you arrange for a quick audience with me? Julia Entwistle is a legend, and I've always wanted to interview her. I've reached out before, but I could never get a return phone call. I figure it'll be harder to turn me down face-to-face."

"I'm sure she'd love that," I said, pulling my hand gently out of his. "I'll talk to her right away about it."

"Great," he said. "Nice meeting you."

"You as well."

I took my leave and hurried over to Marcus.

"Hi!" I said, so relieved to see him.

"Catherine," he said dipping his chin in greeting. Looking me up and down, he added, "You look beautiful."

I blushed and was quick to return the compliment. "As do you, Counselor."

Marcus was wearing a tux with Swarovski crystal buttons that had to be a custom fit, a black silk shirt, no tie, a white diamond-pattern pocket square, and gold-rimmed diamond cuff links. He bowed slightly to let me know he appreciated the compliment, then thumbed over his shoulder. "Julia is in the family room. She'd like it if you'd escort her out here."

"Perfect," I said, then turned to point to a small tent at the far end of the party area. "I've got a table and chairs set up over there so that she can receive her guests in comfort."

"Nice," he said. "You walk her out and I'll fix a plate for her."

I nodded and headed to the family room to fetch Julia.

I came up short when I saw how radiant she looked, dressed in a sheer persimmon blouse—which made her skin and eyes pop—with a black camisole and a black, shimmery full skirt that fell to her feet. Draped around her neck was an absolutely giant round black gemstone nested in a ring of diamonds and gold.

"Oh, my God," I said breathlessly. "Julia! You are *resplendent*!"

Julia batted her eyes at me. "Thank you, dear. As are you!"

"Thank you," I said, feeling that familiar blush touch my cheeks.

"Come over here and take a picture with me," she said, holding out her phone. I took it and shouldered up next to her to take a selfie of the two of us.

"Would you text that to Willem and Chanel for me, Catherine? I seem to have forgotten my glasses."

"Of course," I said, then sent the photo to Willem and then sneaked in an extra text of the photo to myself.

"How is it out there?" she asked when I handed her phone back to her.

"It's perfect, Julia. All the guests on your wish list are here."

"And the suspect pool?"

I grinned. "Nearly all of them showed."

"Good," she said, an eagerness in her eyes.

Pointing to the crowd outside I said, "Two of the suspects I've questioned so far would like a private audience with you."

"Which two?"

"Brad Bosch and Ike Chipperfield."

"The news anchor?"

"Yes."

"I never did care for his style," she said. "He's so fake."

I nodded in agreement.

Julia sighed. "I can feign interest for the evening, though, not to worry. Who's the other one?"

"Brad Bosch. He used to play for the Giants, and he's just confessed to me that he plans to run for the First District's House seat."

Julia puffed out a laugh. "Good luck in that race," she said. "Our congressman is very popular around here."

"Bosch believes that your endorsement could make the difference, and if you feign interest, I'm pretty sure you can get him to talk about his relationship with Yelena. She wasn't well liked by any of the men I spoke to."

"I don't doubt it," Julia agreed. "Anyone else I should hold a private audience with?"

"Gilley took Tucker McAllen, Liam Leahy, and Joel Goldberg. I'm not sure where he ended up with them. We haven't had a chance to talk."

"I definitely want to have a go at Goldberg," she said, fingering the gem at her neck.

I pointed to it. "His creation?"

"Yes," she said. "And he made it on short notice too. I told him I wanted the darkest sapphire he had, and he came through."

"That's a sapphire?" I asked. It had to be ten carats.

"It is," she said, smiling proudly. "I love it, so I hope he doesn't end up the killer."

I laughed. "Fingers crossed," I said. Then I offered her my arm. "Shall we?"

She took it and said, "We shall, but walk slowly, dear. I'm not as nimble as I appear."

I laughed again, and we made our way to the patio door. Julia paused to look out at the crowd of people, a few of whom had noticed her in the doorway and were looking very excited to see her.

"What a lovely setting, Catherine," she said in approval.

"Thank you," I replied. "Gilley and I worked very hard to make it special for you."

"And it shows," she said. Then she handed me the phone again. "Take another picture and send it to Willem. I want him to see the magic you've rendered."

I did as she asked, and then we proceeded forward. The crowd parted as we moved along, all eyes on Julia, and I felt so proud to be the chosen one to escort her to her table and chair.

After seating her, I realized that a couple had already sat down in the chairs opposite her. "Margot! Daniel!" she said with delight. "I'm so happy you could make it!"

I backed away from the table to leave them to each other's company and bumped into a body. Turning, I saw Marcus, holding a plate and champagne glass above my head.

"That was close," he said, motioning to the plate.

"Oh, Marcus! I'm so sorry!"

"Not to worry," he told me. "Nothing spilled." He then moved around me to discreetly set down the plate and a set of silverware for Julia, along with the glass of bubbly.

He then turned to me and whispered, "Want to fill me in so far?"

"Yes," I said. "I've made some progress, and there are a few interesting details to tell you about."

"Great," he said, offering me his arm and nodding toward the dance floor. "Do you dance?"

"I do," I said, taking his arm.

He guided me to the floor and twirled me around twice before bringing me close for our dance.

"You are good," I said, moving with him and finding it effortless.

"At most things," he said, bouncing his eyebrows.

I giggled but then turned to the business at hand and filled him in on every conversation I'd had and my impressions from all three men.

"Interesting," Marcus said when I was done. We were into our second song by now, and I was enjoying myself, even though I was technically amateur sleuthing.

"How did Gilley make out?" he asked next.

"I don't know," I said, looking around for my bestie. I finally saw him with Liam Leahy, and it appeared the two were getting along well. "I haven't had a chance to talk to him since we went our separate ways tonight, but I think he's making some progress."

Marcus glanced in the direction I was also looking. "Who's he with?"

"Vice Admiral Leahy," I said. "He also took Goldberg and he was also kind enough to take McAllen, who's simply an insufferable cad!" I hadn't forgotten McAllen's treatment of the poor server at the restaurant.

Marcus grinned. "Goldberg's the jeweler and the cad is the real estate developer?"

"Yes," I said.

"It'll be interesting to see if Gilley has the same experience with his three suspects," Marcus said.

"I'm gonna go out on a limb and say that it's likely to be a similar vibe. Yelena ended every relationship on bad terms, as far as I can tell."

"Yes," Marcus said. "Including with me."

"Julia wants to interview Goldberg herself, and she's agreed to speak to both Bosch and Chipperfield."

"I'll make sure to be near her for those conversations. No one here knows me personally, so that's a—"

"Pardon me," someone behind me said. "May I have this dance?"

I froze. I knew that voice.

"You may, Detective," Marcus said, twirling me in a half circle before releasing my hand. He then walked quickly away.

"Shepherd!" I said breathlessly. "What're you doing here?" And then I looked him up and down and couldn't believe how gorgeous he looked. His tux fit and flattered him, and he also wasn't wearing a tie, but he'd paired the deep black jacket with a band-collar white shirt. His five-o'clock shadow gave him a ruggedly handsome, yet sophisticated look, and I was smitten at the sight of him.

"I was tasked with reconsidering my choice to abstain from the evening's festivities," he said, putting a bit of poshness in his voice.

"You were tasked? By whom?"

Shepherd took me in his arms and began to sway us back and forth. "Sunny," he said.

"You spoke to her?"

"I went to see her," he said. "I had planned to stay there tonight, but when Sunny asked me why I was avoiding spending the evening with you, I had to confess that we'd gotten in a huge fight. I kinda knew she'd take your side, but I didn't count on the stern lecture and her *insistence* that I show up here to make things right."

"Wow," I said. "She must be feeling better."

"She's feeling feisty. She even gave Darius a hard time, and I've never seen Sunny give him so much as a glare."

"How'd he take it?"

"Better than I thought. He offered to loan me his tux."

"He did?"

"He did." Shepherd tugged on the jacket's lapel. "Tom Ford," he said.

"It's gorgeous on you."

"Not nearly as gorgeous as that gown is on you, pretty lady."

I smiled and blushed fully this time. "Thank you," I said. "But back to Sunny. What was she giving Darius a hard time about? He's been doting on her ever since she was checked into Stony Brook, right?"

"He has, but according to my sister, he hasn't been keeping up with the housework, and when I left her to come here, she was busy scrubbing the kitchen and doing her fifth load of laundry."

I laughed. "That sounds about right. My ex never did laundry. It would've piled up to the ceiling if I hadn't stepped in to do it."

"I suspect that's just shy of where their laundry was piled up to," Shepherd said. And then he looked at me meaningfully and said, "You are the most gorgeous woman I've ever known. Do you know that?"

I smiled, and my heart filled with love for him. "I love that you think so."

"I do. Seriously, that dress is amazing, and you're amazing in it."

Another blush hit my cheeks, and I looked down bashfully. "Stop," I said, unable to take in fully the compliment.

Shepherd bent his head to my neck and kissed me sweetly. "Stop what?" he whispered. After kissing me again, he added, "This? You want me to stop this?"

A different kind of heat filled my flesh, and I sighed and bent my head to expose more of my neck to him. "No. That you can continue."

"Goody," he said, then continued to nibble up and down my neck.

I twined my hands around his neck and felt so close to him, even though we were in the middle of a crowded dance floor. The feelings he was igniting were delicious.

"Steve!" I heard behind me. The sound made me jump.

Shepherd picked his head up abruptly and looked over my shoulder. "Sunny?" he said. "What's wrong?"

I turned to look behind me and saw Sunny standing there,

wearing a loose plaid shirt and sweatpants. The outfit made her stand out like a sore thumb. Her complexion was pale, and she'd obviously been crying, as her eyes were watery and her cheeks were wet.

"I need you to see something," she whispered.

At that moment, Darius appeared. He looked out of breath, and Finley was asleep on his shoulder. "Sunny!" he began, reaching out with his free hand to grab her arm. "Don't!"

She tugged out of his grip and held up a paper bag toward Shepherd. "I need you to look in here," she said. "I can't live with a lie. I can't live with what I've done."

A stream of tears poured out and flowed down her cheeks. Shepherd let go of me and took the paper bag, but Darius attempted to grab it away from him. Shepherd blocked the move and glared at his brother-in-law. "Don't!" he growled.

Darius looked almost panicked. "Please," he said. "Steve, don't open that bag. If you love your sister, you'll give it to me and forget we were ever here."

Shepherd's gaze flickered from Darius to Sunny, who was shaking her head and mouthing, *Please*, while pointing to the bag.

Shepherd opened the bag and looked inside. The color drained from his face, and I noticed that all the people around us had stopped to stare at the odd scene.

"What is this?" he asked Sunny.

"You know what it is," she replied. "It was me, Steve. It was me."

Shepherd let the bag drop to his waist; he seemed so stunned. I reached out and tugged on the bag. He let it go easily.

After opening it up, I peered inside and gasped at what was inside. It was the outfit that I'd seen Sunny wearing the day she'd gotten the tickets to Yelena's show for me and Gilley. But the clothing was literally covered in dried blood. It was smeared on the blouse and the joggers she'd worn that day, and there was no mistaking whose blood it was.

In that moment, everything clicked: Sunny's mysterious disappearance from the house right before Tiffany was going to put Finley in the tub, her equally mysterious return to change clothes and probably stuff the bloody clothing at the bottom of the laundry basket. And even the overdose of Ambien made sense. She had murdered Yelena and had felt so guilty that she'd tried to take her own life.

Still, it was an incredible shock to think that sweet, spiritual, gentle Sunny had committed a violent murder. The only thing I could think was that the Ambien tablet she'd initially taken had put her out of her conscious mind. That had to be the explanation, because anything else was unfathomable.

Shepherd finally recovered himself enough to take the bag from my hands and grab Sunny by the arm. "Inside," he said stiffly.

Darius looked at him like he wanted to deck him, but he followed along behind his wife and brother-in-law.

"Darius!" I called.

He looked over his shoulder with a furrowed brow.

"You can tuck Finley into Mike's bed upstairs. It butts up against the wall and there are extra pillows to hem him in while he sleeps. Third door on the left."

He nodded, and his expression turned briefly grateful; then he hurried to catch up to Sunny and Shepherd.

Before they were even inside, Marcus appeared next to me. "What happened?"

"Sunny killed Yelena," I said. I'd meant to speak softly, but my adrenaline got the best of me and my statement was a lot louder than I'd intended. In the crowd around us, several people gasped.

Murmurs began to spread through the crowd like undulating humming in a hive of bees, and Marcus took my hand and led me toward the patio doors Once we were inside, he closed the French doors and said, "Give me the details."

I explained everything to him, and he listened without interruption.

"Catherine," he said when I'd finished.

"Yes?"

"Do you have a dollar?"

I blinked. "Um, yes."

"Can you give it to me?"

I couldn't figure out what he wanted with a dollar, but I pointed toward the kitchen and led the way to the loose change jar on the counter.

Digging in the coins, I pulled out four quarters and handed them to him. "Sorry. I don't have any small bills. Will that work?"

"It will," he said, jingling the change. "You have just retained me to represent Sunny D'Angelo. Now, if you'll excuse me, I need to go where they are and stop any confession she might be making to Detective Shepherd."

I pointed toward the stairs. "I believe they went that way."

Marcus hurried toward the stairs and nearly sprinted up them. I was immediately filled with relief that he was here to take action.

Gilley then came running into the kitchen. "What's going on?" he said breathlessly. "There's a rumor going around that someone just confessed to killing Yelena."

"You didn't see?" I asked.

"See what? The last thing I saw was you and Shepherd dancing cheek to cheek."

"Sunny showed up," I said. "She confessed to murdering Yelena."

Gilley sucked in a loud breath and put his hand over his heart. "She did not!"

"She did."

"But . . . how? I mean, she was spaced out on Ambien that night. She couldn't have murdered her."

"She came here tonight with the clothing she'd worn that day. It was covered in blood. Like *covered*."

Gilley's hand traveled to his mouth, and he simply stared at me with huge, wide eyes. "What did Shepherd say?" he finally asked.

I shook my head. "Nothing. He just took Sunny upstairs to have a talk."

"Does Darius know?"

"He does. He tried to stop Sunny from confessing."

Gilley looked around. "Where's Marcus?" he asked. "We have to get Marcus to represent her!"

"He's already on the case. He's upstairs, stopping her confession."

Gilley's shoulders sagged in relief. "Thank God!" Then he turned toward the French doors leading to the patio. "What do we do about that?"

"I'm not sure," I said.

Gilley waved for me to follow him. "Come on, sugar. Let's go talk to Julia and see what she wants to do."

Chapter 15

Julia already knew about Sunny's confession. The murmurs had reached even her table. "We'll end this here," she said, taking my hand between both of hers. "Sunny is your dear friend, is she not?"

"She is," I said as unbidden tears blurred my vision.

Julia patted my hand. "There, there, Catherine," she said. "Marcus tells me he's the best attorney in the Hamptons. Send him in to defend her, and I'm sure he'll be able to stave off the worst-case scenario."

I nodded but felt such dread in my heart. "I'm so sorry that your birthday celebration is getting cut short."

"Pffft," she said. "I've had eighty-three other birthdays. They were all special in their own way, as is this one. Sometimes it's not about the length of the celebration, but the effort that went into making it memorable."

I attempted to smile at her kindness, but I was sure it was more a grimace. "May I be allowed to throw your next party, Julia?" I asked. "I'd like to make up for this one."

"Absolutely!" she said. "But we'll have it at my home next time. That way you won't be burdened with so much cleanup."

I held out my arm to her, and she took it; then we made our way out of the tent and headed toward the French doors. Julia paused to thank many of her guests and apologized for the party getting cut short.

"I'm a bit tired," she told them. "I hope you'll understand the early end to the celebration. Please help yourself to some of those marvelous hors d'oeuvres. To go, of course."

It took maybe twenty minutes to make the rounds of all the guests, and both Bosch and Chipperfield looked monstrously disappointed, but when I introduced her to them, she sharply suggested they set up a lunch date for them individually. "We'll dine at the club," she said. "Are you a member of the EHGC?"

The East Hampton Golf Club was a very exclusive club. It was rated one of the best golf courses in all the Northeast, and I wasn't surprised that Julia was a member.

"No, ma'am," Bosch replied. "But I've played there as a guest once or twice."

"Wonderful," she said.

"I'm a member," Chipperfield said, then added a sneer at Bosch. "I'm there every weekend. Name the date and time and I'll be there, Mrs. Entwistle."

Julia smiled and patted him on the shoulder. "Excellent. Have Catherine send me your contact information, and I'll be in touch."

Once I'd gotten Julia inside the house, I said, "That was very kind of you, Julia, but in light of what's happened here tonight, I don't think we need to continue to grill the men on their whereabouts the night of Yelena's murder."

"Of course we do!" she said. "Marcus should be able to use the same tactic for Sunny that he was prepared to use for Aaron."

"I doubt that will work once the jury sees her bloody clothes."

"I'm sure he'll figure out a very good defense for her, my dear," she said, patting my hand.

I walked Julia to her car—a Rolls Royce no less, and Gilley

offered to drive her home as Marcus had driven her here. She was happy to have him play chauffeur, and the two were the first to leave, but everyone else quickly followed.

Once all the guests had left, I directed the servers and bartender who'd been hired for the event to help me organize the food and bring it inside. Within short order most of the area outside had been cleared of anything edible and drinkable.

I sent the servers home with most of the food. Relatively little of it had been eaten and I certainly didn't want it to take up extra room in my fridge only to slowly spoil.

I paid everyone and saw them off then headed back inside intent on making some tea to calm my nerves.

Just as I got out my favorite porcelain teakettle, there was a loud knock at the front door.

Thinking one of the servers had left something behind, I hurried to the door and was surprised to see three uniformed police and one detective in a suit jacket and tie standing there.

"Ma'am," the detective said. "We're here to see Detective Shepherd."

I wondered who'd called the cops, but stepped back and pointed to the stairs. "He's up there," I said. "I'm not sure which room he's in, but just follow the sound of voices and you should find him easily enough."

The three unis tipped their hats at me as they filed past, and the detective gave me a nod. I didn't smile or nod back, because I had a sinking feeling about why they'd come here in force.

Busying myself in the kitchen again, I kept one eye toward the stairs, and sure enough, the four of them soon came marching down, carrying the paper bag with the bloody clothes, with Sunny in the midst of them, her hands handcuffed behind her back.

She kept her gaze firmly on the steps in front of her as she made her way down, and then she kept her gaze on the floor as the unis took her out the door and over to one of two waiting police cars.

I watched out the window as they put her carefully into the backseat, and I felt those same unbidden tears well up in my eyes and dribble down my cheeks.

The detective remained at the bottom of the stairs. He seemed to be waiting for someone. Sure enough, Shepherd came down the steps slowly, looking utterly defeated. He and the detective spoke in hushed tones for a few minutes, and then the detective tipped an imaginary hat at Shepherd and headed out to the waiting car with only one cop in it. The others had already left, taking Sunny with them.

I left the window and walked over to Shepherd. He was staring at the floor. "Hey," I said, placing a hand on his back. "How're you doing, Shep?"

"Bad," he said, his voice hitching with emotion.

"What happened up there?" I asked next.

"Sunny confessed. She said that she remembered being angry with Yelena, because she was under the firm belief that Yelena was going to hurt Finley. She remembered struggling with Yelena, and then she remembered changing clothes, but nothing more."

"She wasn't in her right mind," I said.

"I know that," Shepherd said. "If it weren't for her blood-stained clothes, I'd never believe it, but that's evidence that's hard to fake."

"What happens now?"

"They book her, then try her for murder in the first."

I bit my lip. That sounded so bad. "Is there anything we can do for her?"

"Sending Marcus up to represent her was a start. He made her stop talking the second he entered the room, but she'd already told me most of what she remembered. I interviewed

Darius, and he said that Sunny found the clothes at the bottom of the laundry basket. She freaked out, and he tried to get her to burn the clothing and never confess it to me or anyone else, but my sister isn't one to hide from her mistakes. She's always owned up to any mischief she caused, and even though this is a thousand times more serious than any prank she's ever pulled, she wasn't about to let an innocent man go to jail for something she'd done."

Marcus and Darius came down the stairs at that point. A sleeping Finley rested once again on Darius's shoulder.

Darius glared at Shepherd, and the look was so harsh that I winced. "You should've protected her," he said.

"Obstruction isn't something I'm capable of, D."

Darius turned away, clearly disgusted. Holding out his hand to Marcus, he said, "I'll get you that check right away. In fact, if you want to follow me to the house, I can write it tonight."

"You can't go to the house, D," Shepherd said.

Darius turned again to him. "Wanna bet?"

"I'm serious."

"And I'm not?"

"They'll be searching your home, Darius," Marcus said.

Darius's expression turned to shock. "What do you mean, they'll be searching my home?"

"They'll have gotten a search warrant before they came to collect Sunny. It's what took them so long to arrive," Marcus explained.

Darius glanced at Shepherd, and he nodded solemnly.

"What am I supposed to do with Finley?" Darius demanded.

"You both can stay here tonight," I said. "There's a guest bedroom at the end of the hall upstairs. It's a queen bed, so there'll be plenty of room for you and Finley. And it's an en suite, too, Darius, so you'll have total privacy."

Darius looked at me, his thoughts unreadable. At last, he

said, "Thank you, Catherine. We'll be out of your way first thing in the morning. They should be done searching my place by then, right, *Detective*?"

Shepherd nodded. "They should."

Without another word, Darius went back up the stairs, stomping as he went, clearly furious with Shepherd for upending his whole life.

Once he was safely out of earshot, Marcus said, "Are you going to charge him with obstruction?"

Shepherd shook his head. "No. Trying to talk Sunny out of confessing to me had no effect on her course of action. And I don't want Finley to go one second without a parent nearby."

Marcus nodded. "And will you be releasing my client, Mr. Nassau?"

"I'll call the D.A. first thing in the morning, Counselor. He'll be released by noon."

Marcus nodded again, then turned to me. "Did Julia make it home?"

"Gilley drove her," I said.

"My car is still at her estate. We took her Rolls here."

"When Gilley gets back, he can take you over there, you can pick up your car, and he can leave Julia's car in her driveway, and then you can drop him off back here."

"Good," he said.

As if on cue, my own drive lit up as Gilley pulled in. Marcus nodded to both of us and headed outside to inform Gilley of the plan.

Shepherd stepped to me and put his arms around me. "What a night," he said.

"Indeed. Are you staying over?"

Shepherd loosened his hold and said, "No, sweetheart. I have to go to the station and fill out some paperwork. They'll take me off Yelena's case and probably assign it to Santana, while I take over his case."

"Mark Purdy," I said.

"Yep."

"Did Santana put a few leads together?"

"He did not," Shepherd said. "Not a single lead, in fact."

"I might have a direction for you to follow," I said.

Shepherd's brow rose. "Yeah?"

I nodded. "You might want to see if there's a connection to Gene Bosworth. Or his sister."

"Who's Gene Bosworth?"

"Lover Number Eight."

Shepherd blinked in surprise. "*Yelena's* Lover Number Eight?"

"Yes."

"How do you know that?"

"Gilley and I were curious about the identities of the other lovers, so we did a little sleuthing."

Shepherd closed his eyes and sighed. "I knew you were gonna stick your nose where it didn't belong," he said.

"Then it shouldn't surprise you that we sussed out the identities of nearly all her lovers."

"You got a list for me?" he asked.

"I can send you a photo of the whiteboard we used to keep track of them."

"Do that," he said, kissing me on the cheek. "I gotta get going."

"I know," I said, wrapping my arms around him for a final hug.

When he'd gone, I headed upstairs and took off the gorgeous gown I'd been wearing and slipped into my nicest silk pajamas. After grabbing a pillow and a blanket, I made my way back downstairs and over to Chez Kitty.

I didn't want to sleep alone tonight. Even though Darius was down the hall, I craved the comfort of having Gilley close by.

Spooks looked up when I came through the door, then came bounding over to me to wriggle against my legs and make little whines of happiness that I'd come to visit him. After making my way over to the couch, I arranged the pillow and blanket before crawling under the covers. Spooks jumped up on the couch and stretched himself out so that he could lie next to me.

It was exactly the companionship I needed tonight.

I fell asleep quickly and barely woke when Gilley came through the door. He put an afghan over my blanket, covering Spooks and me, told the dog to stay, then headed off to bed.

I was left to dreams of a beautiful yellow- and orange-colored parrot locked in a birdcage, crying out her innocence.

The memory of that dream would stay with me for a long time to come.

Chapter 16

The next morning, while Gilley and I were finishing up a breakfast of fruit and yogurt, my phone rang with an incoming call from Willem.

I grimaced when I saw his name pop up on my screen. I felt terrible that the party he'd paid a ridiculous amount of money for had been shut down several hours early because of Sunny's confession.

"Willem," I said, answering the call.

"Hi, Catherine. I hope it's not too early there?"

"No, you're fine. Gilley and I were just polishing off breakfast. You've probably heard about the party, huh?"

"I did. Is there anything I can do for Mrs. D'Angelo?"

His question surprised me. I thought he'd be far more concerned with the fact that his grandmother didn't get the celebration she deserved. "That's lovely of you to ask," I told him. "But I think she's in the most capable of hands. We got her the best defense attorney in the Hamptons."

"Marcus Brown," Willem said. "Grams told me all about him. She was very impressed by him."

"I've known Marcus for two years now, and I can agree with Julia. He's definitely impressive."

"And how are you?" Willem asked next.

I shook my head, awed by his compassion. "I'm fine, Willem, thank you so much for asking. I'm sorry Julia didn't get the celebration she deserved."

He chuckled. "She had a terrific time. She couldn't stop talking about how perfect the setting was, and how much the guests seemed to be enjoying themselves until the incident. I'm so grateful to you and Gilley for going to so much trouble on her behalf."

"We'd do it again in a heartbeat."

"Speaking of which," Willem said. "She was hoping to pick your brains for ideas for our reception. Would you and Gilley be up for lunch with her today?"

I blinked and caught Gilley's eye. He wore a confused and curious expression. "I'm certainly free for lunch with her but let me check with Gilley." After placing a hand over the microphone, I said, "Julia is inviting us to lunch to pick our brains for ideas for Willem and Chanel's reception. Are you free?"

"Definitely."

Upon uncovering the microphone, I said, "Gilley would also be delighted to attend."

"Great," Willem said. "If you can get to her estate by noon, she'd appreciate it."

"We'll be there. Oh, and, Willem, one more thing. Would you send me the receipt for the Vivace gown you got swindled by my partner to purchase on my behalf?"

"Um, no, Catherine. It's my way of saying thank you for hosting the party and for now agreeing to help Grams plan the reception."

"Willem, it's too much," I insisted.

"Not in my book," he replied. "Besides, Chanel and I were blown away with how gorgeous you were in that gown."

I smiled. He was such a sweet man. "Thank you," I said. "Truly."

"Of course," he said. "It was the least I could do."

After I hung up with him, I turned to Gilley. "He's so lovely, you know?"

"I do know," Gilley said. "And I told you he wasn't going to let you pay for that gown."

"I still feel guilty about it."

Gilley shrugged. "Don't. Or if you do, maybe donate what you think the gown cost to a charitable organization."

I poked him with my finger. "That is *exactly* what I'll do!"

"See? There's a solution for every problem."

"We can drop the check off on our way to Julia's."

"Perfect!"

"Just tell me what the gown cost and I'll go fill that check out."

Gilley laughed. "Nice try," he said. "I've been sworn to secrecy, so no, I'm not going to tell you."

I pouted for a moment and then asked, "If I name a range, would you at least tell me that I'm in the ballpark?"

Gilley thought that over and said, "I think that'd be okay."

"Good. Was the gown in the range of between six and eight thousand?"

"You're in the stadium, but not yet on the field."

My jaw dropped. "Ten?" I said.

"You're in the outfield."

My eyes widened. The gift was far too generous. "Twelve?"

"You're on home base, Cat. And that's all I'll say about it."

Twelve thousand dollars was more than I'd ever paid for a gown. Even my couture wedding dress hadn't cost that much. I felt immensely guilty, even though I hadn't had a hand in the purchase.

And I also knew there was no taking it back. The only thing I could do was donate generously to my charity of choice.

After getting up from the table, I carried my dishes to the sink, gave them a quick rinse, and put them in the dishwasher. Then I moved to the door.

"You headed back to Chez Cat?"

"Yes. I want to make out that check while I still have the courage."

"You know, you don't have to donate the full twelve Gs."

I looked down at Spooks, who'd come over to lean against my legs and do his snorting routine in an effort to get me to stay. "I do, Gilley," I said, stroking Spooks's velvety head.

"I shouldn't have let you guess the price," he said.

I smiled at him. "I'm so glad you did."

After opening the door, I peered out at the beautiful day. In the driveway was Sunny's Range Rover, its rear window repaired. Darius's car was missing, though.

"Huh," I said.

"What?" Gilley said, getting up to come over to the door and peer out.

"Darius left already."

"What do you mean, he left already?"

I realized I hadn't told Gilley that I'd invited Darius and Finley to stay over. "The police obtained a search warrant for the D'Angelos' house, and he couldn't very well take Finley there while a team of strangers was turning the place upside down, so I offered to let him stay at Chez Cat for the night. He and Sunny drove separately to the party. His car was here when I came over last night, and now it's gone."

"Is that why you came here? You didn't want to be in the same space with him?"

I gave Gilley a disapproving look. "Of course not. I was unsettled by Sunny's confession and the early end to the party, and being here with you always makes me feel comforted."

Gilley nodded. "Sorry," he said. "Didn't mean to assume that Darius was a bad dude or anything."

"I don't think I would've minded the implication before Sunny tried to take her life, but after watching the way he cares for her and Finley, I've come to a different conclusion about him."

Gilley nodded. "Do you think he'll come back for Sunny's car?"

"I'm sure he'll want to, but he's probably got his hands full trying to put the house back in order after the police cleared out. If the keys are in it, and it's still here, then I think we should take it over to his house when we get back from Julia's."

"I like that plan," Gilley said. "He might know more about Sunny's case by then too."

"Yes," I said. "I'll be back here to collect you for lunch with Julia in a few hours, okay?"

Gilley saluted me smartly, clicking his heels, while I rolled my eyes and shut the door.

Three hours later we were on our way to Amagansett, but I took a slight detour south to the charity I planned to make a very large donation to.

Gilley was busy playing a game on his phone and didn't look up to see where we were headed until I pulled into the parking lot.

He gasped when he saw the building. "You're making a donation here?"

"I am," I said. "It's the least I can do to help support the place responsible for bringing Spooks into our lives."

Gilley's eyes welled up. "Oh, Cat. Thank you."

I squeezed his arm and pulled the check out of my purse. "Be right back," I sang.

"I'm coming with you!" Gilley said, and he scrambled out of the car.

We went inside and inquired about where to drop off a donation. The manager of the shelter came out of her office, and when I handed her the check, she, too, began to cry. Then she hugged me fiercely and thanked me over and over.

I was so moved by her reaction that I vowed to make a similar donation every year.

Once we were back in the car, Gilley said, "You are a *good* person, Catherine Cooper."

I grinned. "I try," I said. "It's such a deserving charity. Spooks is such a lovely boy, and all the dogs we looked at were obviously well fed and well taken care of."

We chatted a bit on our way to Julia's, mostly about mundane things, but then I realized that I'd never gotten the lowdown on any of the suspects that Gilley had questioned.

When I asked him about it, he said, "Ugh. They were a merry bunch."

"I detect a hint of sarcasm."

He nodded. "And none of them had any love lost for Yelena."

I looked at him sharply. "The same with my three," I said. "Especially Vivace. He scowled from the time I mentioned her name to the end of our dance together. He didn't reveal a lot verbally, but his body language and expression spoke for his true feelings. He didn't seem to be sorry at all that she was dead."

"But why does any of it matter now?" Gilley asked. "Sunny already confessed to the crime."

"I'm not sure I trust her memory, Gil. She was in a semiconscious state at the time she confronted Yelena, and for all we know, she could've walked in on the murderer, and a struggle ensued, where somehow Sunny got away, or she could've come in right after Yelena was stabbed to death, and tried to bring her friend back to life. In both of those scenarios her clothing would've gotten stained with Yelena's blood."

"Then our suspects are still suspects?"

I nodded. "The thing that keeps sticking out to me is Mark Purdy's murder. I just know there's a connection, but I can't figure out how."

"Have you talked to Shepherd about any of this?"

"A bit. He's certain he'll have to swap out Yelena's case for Purdy's."

"The whole situation must be impossible for him," Gilley said.

"Yeah. I'd say that it is."

At that moment we arrived at Julia's grand estate. I pulled into a spot next to the Rolls Royce she and Marcus had ridden in the night before, and we approached the door.

After climbing the steps, Gilley rang the bell, which gonged like a church bell, and the door was opened by Julia's dour-faced personal assistant, Nancy.

"Ms. Cooper," she said, with the slightest nod to me. "Mr. Gillespie," she added, acknowledging Gilley.

I offered her a grimacing smile, but Gilley took her cold greeting as a personal challenge. "Nancy!" he exclaimed, placing both hands on her shoulders and adopting a look of pure joy. "You look marvelous! Have you done something with your hair? It's stunning! And look at this figure, woman! I can see that you've trimmed down a bit since last time, hmm? Try not to lose too much weight, or you'll blow away at the slightest breeze!"

Nancy blinked rapidly, and I suspected she badly wanted to take a step backward, but with Gilley firmly gripping her shoulders, what could she do?

"Ahh, it's been too long," Gilley said when she continued to blink in alarm. "We really should catch up soon, m'kay?"

Nancy's head began to bobble a bit. I had to press my lips together to avoid bursting into laughter at her shock at being accosted by Gilley's enthusiasm and joie de vivre.

"Is Julia in?" I asked, stepping up to the threshold so that Gilley was forced to let go of Nancy's shoulders. "She invited us for lunch."

Once free of Gilley's grip, Nancy did take a step back. And then another. And a final third, just to be sure she had enough of a head start should Gilley come at her again. "She's seated on the back terrace. This way, please."

She then swiveled on her heel and began to walk quickly away. We closed the door and hustled after her.

The walk was long. And it made me appreciate just how enormous the estate house was. I guessed it was anywhere from twenty to thirty thousand square feet, as evidenced by the sheer depth of the place and the number of massive rooms—each exquisitely decorated—that we passed on the way to the back terrace.

At last, we came through a set of French doors, to appear in front of a covered terrace, with a pool to the far right and a small lake with a fountain spraying water into the air on the left.

A gorgeous teakwood table was also off to the left, and at its head was seated our favorite octogenarian, Julia herself, looking resplendent in a thick burgundy angora sweater with an overly large cowl-neck, which gave a bit more girth to her small frame.

She pressed her palms to the table at the sight of us and, with shaking arms, pushed herself out of her chair to welcome us to the table. "Hello, my darlings!"

We quickened our step, moving around Nancy, to take turns gently hugging Julia. Gilley allowed me the first hug, and Julia held Gilley's hand after he'd bent to hug her, too, and pulled on his arm to bring him around to the other side of the table, next to her on the left. I took up the chair on her right, which also had a place setting, and we all sat down, smiling broadly like old friends who hadn't seen each other in a long while, rather than friends who'd been together the night before.

"Julia," I began, "can I first simply say that I'm so sorry your birthday celebration turned into such a fiasco?"

"My dear, Catherine," Julia replied, "please do not feel sorry for an old woman who's had more than her fair share of birthday celebrations. Besides, last night's party was one for the ages! I mean, a parade of suspects all in view was stupendously thrilling. Although, poor Sunny, I feel so terrible for her."

"We do too. She's a dear friend," Gilley said.

"She's the sister to Detective Shepherd," I added.

"His sister? Oh, my, Catherine, I'm so sorry! That would make her practically family."

I was surprised that Julia seemed to remember that Shepherd and I were a couple.

"Sunny is such a gentle, loving, kind person," Gilley said, and I was surprised to see his eyes misting. "I can't imagine that she, of all people, could take the life of a friend. Especially one as close to her as Yelena."

"Oh?" Julia said, just as plates of Caesar salad and fresh, steaming-hot sourdough baguettes with pads of butter arrived and were served silently by a woman in a grey uniform with a white apron.

"She is truly a gentle person," I said. "Neither Gilley nor I think that she actually murdered Yelena."

"But she confessed, no?" Julia said.

"She did," I said with a sigh. "Which is the problem. She took an Ambien earlier in the day, and it has a history of putting her in an apparent wakeful state, but she's actually asleep and doesn't remember what she did during that time."

"Oh, dear," Julia said. "It's all so tragic."

I nodded in agreement. "Still, my gut says she didn't do it. Gil and I think either she walked in while Yelena was being attacked, and tried to stop it, or she walked into her dressing room right after and tried to do CPR or something."

Julia tsked a few times and shook her head. "If she didn't kill Yelena, who did?"

"That's what we'd like to know," I said.

"I take it you two are still investigating, then?"

"We are," I confirmed.

"Good," she said. "I'll help."

"How?" Gilley asked.

"I've set up two lunch dates with Mr. Football and Mr. Full of Himself."

Gilley's brow furrowed.

"Brad Bosch and Ike Chipperfield," I said.

"Ahhh," Gilley said. "Well done, Julia."

"I don't want you to probe them for clues alone, though," I said. "Is it all right with you if I ask Marcus to tag along?"

"Of course!" she said. "I so enjoyed his company last night."

"Great. And, on that note, Julia, do you think you could arrange a meeting with another suspect?"

"Who?"

"A woman named June Murdock. She didn't show up last night even though she sent an RSVP."

Julia pursed her lips distastefully. "June," she said.

"Do you know her?" Gilley asked.

"We're acquainted," she told him in a clipped tone.

Gilley and I exchanged a look, and I could tell we were both trying to decide whether or not to press the issue. "It doesn't sound like you think much of her," Gilley finally said, much to my relief.

"True," Julia said, and she began to poke at her salad like she was spearing fish.

Gilley and I again exchanged a look. He shrugged subtly, like he didn't know what else to say to get her to open up.

I was just about to try to prod Julia gently when she set down her fork, sighed heavily, and said, "June had an affair with my husband."

I gasped, and Gilley dropped his fork. It clattered against his china lunch plate. "Sorry," he said, wincing.

Julia's mouth worked from angry pursed lips to a sad frown and back again. At last, she said, "Richard was a good husband for over fifty years. He had one slip the whole time we were married. I knew immediately when it happened. I also knew that June had targeted my husband specifically, because of his friendship with her brother, Gene."

My eyes widened as Gilley asked, "Why would your husband's friendship with Gene Bosworth provoke June to target your husband?"

Julia snorted derisively. "To make Gene jealous, of course."

I bit my lip to prevent a bubble of excitement from leaking out of me. "So, it's true," I said. "Gene and his sister were . . ." I didn't think I could even finish the sentence, their illicit relationship so disgusted me.

"Involved in an incestuous relationship?" Julia said. "Yes. Yes, they were."

Again, Gilley and I traded looks of eager excitment. "Julia," I said, treading as carefully as I could. "We believe that Gene was Lover Number Eight in Yelena's show, and that June was paying off Yelena to keep her quiet about her true relationship with her brother."

"Doesn't surprise me," Julia said. "After June got married and began to refuse her brother, he tried to get even with her by courting the most glamorous loose young women who would have him. Yelena would've fit that profile perfectly.

"Tell me," she said, placing her elbows on the table and leaning in toward me. "What does June's payoff to Yelena have to do with her murder?"

"We're not sure," I said. "But a man named Mark Purdy was wearing a ladies' size-ten raincoat—Yelena's size—lined with two hundred thousand dollars when he was found dead in the alley behind the coffee shop down the street from the theater. We suspect there was a professional relationship between Purdy and June, and we also believe that the money lining Purdy's raincoat came from her."

"And this Mr. Purdy was murdered the same night as Yelena?"

"Yes," I said.

Julia sat back in her seat and subtly shook her head. "My, my," she said. "What a tangled web."

"Agreed," I said.

"Was the weapon used to kill Yelena also used to murder Mr. Purdy?"

"No," I said. "The method of death for him was exsanguination. From a piano wire across Mr. Purdy's neck."

Julia's eyes again widened, and Gilley made a slashing motion across his neck. A bit macabre for the moment, but that was Gilley.

"That's horrible," Julia whispered.

"It is. And it's the second reason that we don't believe that Sunny murdered Yelena. It's unfathomable to us that she'd be able to commit not one, but two murders back-to-back. And one by way of piano wire?" I shook my head. "I'm not buying it."

"You're right," Julia said. "Sunny appeared far too fragile to have overpowered a man."

"So, you see why we're trying so hard to find an alternative theory," Gilley said. "One that checks all the boxes."

"Indeed," Julia said, and I could tell she was trying to put the pieces together herself by the faraway gaze she held while looking down the length of the table. And then her eyes came back into focus, and she said, "It's a mystery within a mystery. Sunny D'Angelo's confession and the bloody clothes really throw a monkey wrench into things, don't they?"

"In a huge way," Gilley said.

"Gilley," Julia said. "Tell me again which of Yelena's lovers you questioned last night?"

"One, Four, and Five," he said.

"Tucker McAllen, the real estate developer; Joel Goldberg, whom you've met; and Vice Admiral Liam Leahy," I reminded her.

"What did you learn from them?" she asked Gilley.

"Not much, other than they seemed to feel no remorse for Yelena's passing."

"That's curious," Julia said, tapping her chin.

"None of the men on my list cared much about her, either," I said.

Julia sighed. "Which means that any one of them could've been her murderer."

"It does," I agreed.

"Is there anyone on the list you haven't identified?"

"Lover Number Two, Lover Number Ten, and Lover Number Twelve," Gilley said.

"Are you completely stumped on their identities, or do you suspect who they might be?"

"We suspect a few things about them," I said. "Lover Number Two, we believe, is a congressman. Lover Number Ten, we think, is a race-car driver, and Lover Number Twelve is the son of a queen, a lazy playboy, a commitment-phobe."

"That's an interesting crowd," she said. "Twelve sounds like someone connected to royalty."

"It's not Aaron Nassau," I said quickly. "He's Lover Number Eleven."

"Could she have repeated herself?"

"You mean, could she have used the same man twice in the script?" I asked.

"Yes."

I looked at Gilley. He shrugged. He didn't know. "I suppose anything is possible," I said.

"But you don't think she did, correct?"

"No," I said. "Aaron is neither a playboy nor a commitment-phobe. He is wealthy, but he's not the son of a queen. I mean, you know him, Julia. He's what, sixteenth in line to the Danish crown?"

Julia nodded. "Something like that. But to your point, yes, that description does sound significantly different than who I know Aaron to be."

"Until we can identify the three remaining suspects, we're stuck with only probing the other eight," I said.

"Not Aaron?" she asked, and I could tell she was playing devil's advocate in asking me that.

I shook my head. "Of everyone we've talked to so far, he's the only one who showed remorse upon hearing about her passing. What's more, he wouldn't admit that Yelena tried to extort him, and he said that the reason his letter opener was discovered in her dressing room and used as the method to kill her was that he allowed her to take it."

"And you don't believe that he allowed her to take it?"

I shook my head. "The letter opener is worth at least fifty thousand dollars. It's inlaid with precious gemstones and made of fourteen-karat gold."

Julia sat back in her chair as if she was satisfied. "All right," she said. "I trust your judgment and my own regarding Aaron. I'll do my best to ferret out any information from Mr. Bosch and Mr. Chipperfield, and perhaps I'll even pay Mr. Goldberg a visit. Now that I've purchased something rare and expensive from him, he might be inclined toward some small talk."

"Gilley?" I said. He looked at me expectantly. "Are the other two on your list worth investigating any further?"

Again, Gilley shrugged. "I don't know, Cat. They clearly weren't sad that Yelena was dead, but I didn't really get a murder vibe off of them. Especially the vice admiral. He struck me as a very by-the-book kind of guy. You know, like Shepherd."

"Huh," I said. "If he's like Shepherd, no way is he the killer."

"McAllen would have far too much to lose," Julia said. "He's an absolute pig of a man, but I don't see him doing something so irrational that could jeopardize his future. Not when he's at the peak of his power."

"Good point," I said. "So, really that just leaves Bosch, Chipperfield, and Goldberg to focus on."

Julia reached out to pat my hand. "You let me worry about them. The two of you should focus on discovering the identities of Two, Ten, and Twelve."

Gilley and I both nodded, and Julia took the napkin from her lap and stood up carefully.

"Now, shall we walk the grounds and plan my grandson's wedding reception?"

"We shall," I said, getting up along with Gilley.

"This will be fun!" he said, clearly excited.

And we set off on an afternoon of party planning.

Chapter 17

Pulling into my driveway after a wonderful afternoon spent with Julia, Gilley and I both saw that Darius hadn't yet come to retrieve his wife's car.

"Fingers crossed the keys are inside the Range Rover," Gilley said.

"Hopefully, they're not still with Sunny," I agreed, thinking that could be why Darius hadn't come back for the car. If he didn't have a spare key fob, then Sunny's car could be sitting in my drive for quite a while.

Gilley hopped out and went over to the Rover to have a look. He pulled up on the door handle and discovered that the car was unlocked. Looking back at me he bounced his eyebrows.

I rolled down my window and said, "That's a good sign."

He then got in, looked around, looked at me, and shrugged. Then he leaned forward to press the START button, and the Range Rover came to life.

"It's about time that worked," I said.

Gilley closed the door and buckled up, and I let him take the lead over to Sunny's house while I followed behind. He pulled the SUV over to the garage, and to my surprise, the garage door began to lift. Gilley pulled forward, parked the Range Rover, sat there for a moment then got out of the car and exited the garage, hurrying over to my car but he didn't get in.

"The garage door won't go down," he said.

"Yeah. It sticks apparently. It did that when I came over to get the tickets to Yelena's show."

Gilley pointed to Darius's car parked in the drive near the door. "He's home. Let's go tell him we dropped off Sunny's car and parked it in the garage," he said.

"Good idea," I said, getting out of the car.

Together we approached the front steps, but as we got close, we could hear music coming from the backyard.

Gilley and I exchanged curious looks, and I pointed to the back gate, which was open. As we neared the source of the music, it became clear that Darius was playing one of his acoustic guitars and singing a lullaby.

"Oh, wow," Gilley whispered. "He's good!"

He was good. His voice was husky and deeper than his speaking voice. He had perfect pitch, and it was such a pleasure to hear him sing that both Gilley and I stopped to listen to the whole song.

Every few chords, we'd hear Finley cackle with laughter and clap his hands. Now we knew who Darius was singing to.

When he finished the song, Gilley and I finally stepped around the corner and called out to him. "Hi, Darius!" Gilley yelled.

Darius jumped but quickly recovered himself. "Hey, guys," he said. "Sorry! Did you knock, and I didn't hear you?"

I shook my head. "No, we brought Sunny's car back and parked it in the garage but we can't get the door to close so we came looking for you and heard that gorgeous singing voice of yours and had to investigate."

Darius broke out into a bashful grin. "I have always loved to sing," he said. "Just not in front of an audience."

"Such a shame. Because you are good!" I said, sitting down in one of the patio chairs next to Darius.

Gilley walked toward Finley when he saw the little tyke

make eye contact with him, and he stuck out his arms, like he was coming in for a hug.

Finley, who was seated in his toy car, let out a squeal of delight and held his own arms out too.

Darius and I watched them in silence as Gilley picked Finley up and began to dance with him.

I chuckled, and so did his dad. Gilley whirled in a series of spins that took him off the patio and onto the beach. It was clear that Gil wanted to play with Finley for a minute, so I took the time to ask Darius about Sunny.

"How's our girl holding up?"

Darius shook his head and stared at the ground. "It's like a nightmare," he said. "I keep thinking she's gonna come home and walk right out here to tell me that it was all one big mistake."

I bit my lip. I couldn't imagine how hard this might be for him. If Sunny was convicted, he'd have to raise Finley alone.

"Has Marcus said anything about her defense?" I asked.

"Not much. He asked me to put him in touch with her doctor, to get a history of her Ambien-induced amnesia. And he said he might be going with an insanity defense—which, ha, I can't *even* wrap my mind around."

"If it keeps Sunny out of jail . . ."

"That's just the thing, though, Catherine. She'd be out of prison, but she'd be imprisoned in a mental health hospital. Probably for life."

I felt like Darius had just gut punched me. Sunny's options weren't really options. "Gilley and I have been looking into other suspects," I said.

Darius looked at me in surprise. "Other suspects?"

I nodded. "We found a copy of Yelena's script, and we've been able to identify nine out of twelve of her lovers."

"You think one of them did it?"

"I do. I think that Sunny might've walked in on Yelena when she was being murdered, and Sunny probably rushed in to help, which is how she got the blood on her clothes, and then she ran out of there, and whoever committed the murder tossed the letter opener aside and ran after her, but she got away. She then went home, changed, got back in her car, and drove to the park. The guilt of not being able to save Yelena caught up with her, and she swallowed your entire prescription."

The expression on Darius's face told me he doubted my explanation. "You think a jury's going to believe that?"

"If we can catch one of the lovers in a lie, I think they just might."

"Who've you identified so far?" he asked.

I reached into my purse and pulled out the script and also pulled up the photo I'd taken of the whiteboard. Showing them both to Darius, I said, "This is who we've got so far."

Darius read sections of the script and eyed the list of names. "I know she dated some of these guys," he said. "I'm a Giants fan, and Yelena bragged that she was dating the quarterback. I knew she wasn't dating Jones or McCoy. They're too young and too successful to have gotten involved with her, so Bosch makes sense."

I squinted at him. "Is there anything you might know about the three missing names?"

Darius studied the opening lines for each of those lovers for a moment. "Okay, so Lover Number Ten is gonna be Killington Cavill."

"Who's that?"

"He's a Scottish race-car driver. He's really good. He came to the States to drive a car for Team Penske. Sunny and I saw Yelena and Cavill dining outside at the end of the summer about a year ago. Sunny said that Yelena was really into Cavill, but she was worried that the relationship was starting to go downhill, because Cavill was talking about going back to Scotland."

"Did he go back to Scotland?" I asked.

"I think so," Darius said. And then he squinted at something in the text of the script, and I heard him take in a sharp breath.

"What is it?" I asked.

He tapped the script. "I know who Number Two was."

"Was? Or is?"

"Was," he said, and he looked sad.

"Who?"

"My uncle Roy."

It was my turn to sound surprised. "*Your* uncle?"

"Yeah. 'Fraid so."

"Yelena dated your uncle?"

"For about four months. She came over one Sunday for barbecue, and Uncle Roy stopped in to say hi. They met and hit it off, and I tried to warn him about Yelena, how she went through men, but he was diggin' the fact that this pretty, much younger woman was attracted to him, so he didn't listen. He got his heart broken when she called it off with him. He died of a stroke about two months later."

"Oh, Darius, I'm so sorry."

"It's okay. He had a good life. He made a bundle, retired, and moved out here to be closer to me and Sunny. He was more my dad than my own dad, actually."

"Was he a congressman?" I asked.

"A congressman? No. What made you think that?"

I pointed to the line in the script. " 'He spent his days at the house on the hill.' "

Darius let out a short laugh. "No, Uncle Roy was a stockbroker for thirty years. He moved into a house up there." Darius pointed to a bluff overlooking the ocean. "It's up a steep hill," he said.

"Ahhh," I said. "Okay, I get it." Then I pointed to the script again. "Any guesses about Lover Number Twelve?"

Darius read the lines and shook his head. "No clue," he said.

"Ever since COVID ended, I've been working a lot in L.A., so I haven't been around. I could ask Sunny if she knows."

"Would you?"

"Sure," he said. "If this will help her case, then I'll definitely try to get the name from her."

"You are a gem," I said happily. Darius had solved two riddles in about five minutes, and I felt such a wave of relief knowing that the two men he identified had been out of the picture at the time of Yelena's murder—although I'd have to have Gilley look up Cavill and make sure he was still in Scotland.

Next to me, on the table, something buzzed. I looked down and saw that it was Darius's phone.

"Andrew is calling," I said, picking up the phone and offering it to him.

"Great!" he said, handing me the script and my phone, then taking up his own. "He's my real estate guy. Excuse me." Darius moved off toward the house to speak privately, and I sat in one of the Adirondack chairs and watched Gilley run around Finley as the toddler stood still and laughed and laughed at Gilley.

It was good to see Finley so unaffected by his mother's absence. I knew that was unlikely to last, but the boy was young enough that it might not be as awful as you'd expect.

After another few minutes, Darius came back over to me and sat down again. "Sorry about that," he said. "I'm selling my place in L.A."

"The condo?"

He pulled his chin back in surprise. "You know about the condo?"

"I do. Sunny told me. Why're you selling it?"

Darius's gaze traveled to the ground again. He was clearly embarrassed. "I'm trying to raise money for Sunny's defense. Marcus told me it could be as much as a half a million."

"Yikes," I said.

"Yep," Darius said, looking sadly at Finley and Gilley playing together. "I'd pay anything to get Sunny off the hook. She's the love of my life." His voice hitched as he said the last part.

"We'll do whatever we can, Darius," I said softly. I really felt for him.

"Thanks," he said, then offered a grateful smile.

A moment of awkward silence followed, and I asked, "Do you and Finley have enough to eat?"

"You mean for dinner and stuff?"

I nodded.

"Yeah. I guess. He's got plenty of food, but I haven't been very hungry."

"We'd like to make you a lasagna. Would that be okay?"

"You kidding? Lasagna is my favorite. That'd be great, Catherine. Thank you."

Gilley came up to us, holding Finley on his hip. "Whew!" he said. "This tyke has got some energy!" Gilley poked Finley's belly button, and the boy squealed in delight.

Darius stood and held his arms out. "It's almost dinnertime for him," he said.

I got up too. "We'll leave you to your daddy duties, but we'll see you soon, okay?"

"Great. And, Catherine?"

"Yes?"

"Thank you. And I mean that."

I grinned. "Of course, Darius. Of course."

When we were once again on the road, I said, "Is it okay with you if we stop at the grocery store?"

"I've got all the supplies I need for dinner, sugar."

"What're we having?"

"Chicken Veronique."

"Ooo," I said. "I love your chicken Veronique. But I was hoping we could pick up all the ingredients to make your famous lasagna tomorrow."

"You know that takes me all day, right?"

"I'll be there to help," I said. "I want to make it for Darius and Finley."

Gilley's brow shot up. "Oh yeah," he said. "I totally forgot about bringing them over something easy to heat up so they wouldn't have to worry about dinner. Thanks for reminding me. And yes, we will absolutely make that tomorrow."

"Yay!" I said, happy that he was willing to put in the time to make his famous dish.

We arrived at the grocery store, and just as I slid into a spot, my phone rang. "It's Marcus," I said.

"You talk. I'll shop," Gilley said.

I nodded, and Gilley hustled out of the car.

"Marcus," I said happily. I always enjoyed talking to him.

"Catherine," he said. "Got a minute?"

"I do. What's up?"

"A couple of things."

"Tell me."

"For starters, the D.A. just sent over some exculpatory evidence that the new detective—"

"Santana?"

"Yeah, that sounds right. That Detective Santana found when he subpoenaed Yelena's phone records."

"What did he find?" I asked, knowing it was bad.

"A series of phone calls between Yelena and two numbers, both registered to Sunny D'Angelo, placed approximately twenty, ten, and five minutes before the start of her show."

"Sunny had *two* phones?"

"It looks that way."

"I've only ever called her on the two-four-two-four number," I said, remembering the last four digits of Sunny's number because my birthday was on the twenty-fourth of the month.

"She had another number listed with a three-eight-three-eight subscriber number."

"What's a subscriber number?"

"The last four digits of a telephone number."

"Ah," I said but then got back to the topic at hand. "So Sunny was calling her from both her phones?"

"And Yelena was calling her back at both numbers."

"How long did the conversations last?"

"A minute or two for the first two calls, placed by Yelena to the three-eight number, then another call out to Sunny at the two-four-two-four number, and that one lasted ten minutes, but the last call was from Sunny's phone to Yelena, and that lasted thirty seconds."

"Could Sunny have left a message?"

"It's possible. Still, it doesn't bode well for Sunny's case that she and Yelena were having phone calls back and forth with each other in the hours before Yelena's murder. And it bodes even less well that the three-eight-three-eight number has been disconnected."

I blinked. "It was disconnected?"

"Yes. The morning of the day Sunny confessed to murdering Yelena."

"Whoa," I said.

"Agreed," Marcus said.

"Did you ask Sunny about it?"

Marcus sighed, and I could tell he was tired. "I did."

"And?"

"And she's all but catatonic, Catherine. She won't respond to any of my questions. She just sits there, staring at nothing, and cries."

I closed my eyes and felt tears sting the back of my lids. I couldn't imagine what Sunny's mental state was right now. I felt so bad for her.

"So, what are you going to do?" I asked.

"I'm going to call Darius and see if he can meet me at the county lockup and try to coax her out of her despondency. I'm hoping he can get her to answer my questions at least."

"That's a good plan," I said. "He's really worried about her. When are you going to go back for another talk with her?"

"Tomorrow, after we finish up at the EHCP and I drop Julia off at her home."

"You're accompanying her to the club," I said.

"Yes. She works quick and dirty, and I like her style."

"Good, Marcus. That's good. Make sure she stays safe, okay?"

"Definitely. Now, tell me about any progress you've made."

"Well! Darius has actually shed some light for us on that front. He's helped me identify two of the remaining three mystery men."

"Which ones?"

"Two and Ten."

"The man you think is a member of Congress and the race-car driver?"

"Yes. Good memory."

"It comes in handy," he said. "So, who are they?"

"Two was Darius's uncle Roy."

"Darius's *uncle* dated Yelena?"

"He did. Roy was loaded, and that was all that mattered to Yelena, apparently."

"Was he a congressman?"

"No. Turns out he actually lived on a hill. It's not far from their home, in fact."

"Where is he now?"

"Dead. Darius said he died a year ago."

"Natural causes?"

"Stroke," I said. "Anyway, Lover Number Ten is a guy named Killington Cavill."

Marcus grunted. "I'm familiar with that name. He drove for an oil company."

"Tire," I said. "Penske."

"Okay, so where is he now?"

"We think he's back in Scotland. I'm going to have Gilley look into it tonight, see if he can't pinpoint if that's true and for how long Cavill has been back in his homeland."

"Good," Marcus said. "No luck with Number Twelve?"

"No," I said. "Darius couldn't fit the description to anyone he knew that Yelena had dated."

"It would be nice to have all the names locked down," Marcus said.

"It would. Gilley and I won't give up, but for the moment, that guy remains a mystery."

"All right, Catherine. Really good work so far. I'll be in touch."

With that, Marcus was gone. A moment later, Gilley appeared with a grocery cart brimming with paper bags. I got out and helped him load up the car.

"We really need all this just to make lasagna?"

"The best ingredients make the most delicious meals, sugar."

"Good point."

On the way home, I filled him in on my conversation with Marcus.

"I hope they can coax Sunny out of her despondency," Gil said. He looked as worried as I felt.

"If anyone can do it, it'll be Darius."

"Not Shepherd?"

"No," I said. "I doubt Marcus would allow Shep anywhere near Sunny right now."

"Why do you say that?"

"He's the cop that turned her in. If she confesses even one detail that helps the murder charges against her, he'll report it to Santana."

"He'd do that to his own *sister*?"

"He's already done it to her," I said.

Gilley sat with his arms crossed as he fell silent and stared out the window. I could tell he wanted to say something judgmental and was holding it back.

"What?" I asked.

"Nothing."

"Gil," I pressed. "Say what you're going to say."

"Fine. Do you think dating someone who's capable of throwing his twin sister in jail is a good idea?"

"What was he supposed to do?" I asked him. "She confessed to murder in front of him and fifty other people standing close by. It's not like he could've pretended that she hadn't said what she'd said *and* hadn't backed that up with a paper bag full of bloody clothes."

Gilley scowled and went back to staring out the window. "Well, *I* could never date someone like that."

"Come on, Gil," I begged. "Shepherd's a good guy caught in an impossible situation."

"I still don't like it," he insisted.

"I don't, either, but I'd rather date a principled, honest, decent man than a liar and someone unprincipled. I had that in my last relationship. I don't need it in this one."

"Maks?" Gilley asked in surprise, referring to a man I'd briefly dated before Shepherd.

"No, not Maks," I said. "Tom."

"Oh, your ex."

"Yes."

Gilley sighed. "Okay, Cat, it's your life. Live it however you want."

We arrived at Chez Kitty a few minutes later, and Spooks greeted us warmly at the door, with lots of tail wagging and wiggling against our legs.

"Poor guy," I said, setting down the groceries and then bending to give Spooks a hug. "He's been home alone all day."

"I gotta get a walk in for him," Gilley said, looking through the window at the darkening sky.

I pointed to the door. "Go," I said. "I'll put the groceries away and start the pasta and cut the grapes for the chicken Veronique."

Gilley grabbed Spooks's leash and kissed me on the cheek. "You're a lifesaver," he said. "I'll be back in twenty minutes."

I spent the next five minutes just hauling in all the bags from the car and unpacking them. Then I put hot water from the hot water spigot into a pot, set it on a burner, and turned the flame to high. I then got out a knife, a cutting board, and the green grapes in the fruit bowl on the counter. Checking on the water for the pasta, I was happy to see it beginning to boil. I got some penne pasta out of the cupboard and dumped the whole box in. After setting the timer on my watch, I picked up the knife. I had cut exactly two grapes when I heard the front door open.

"That was fast," I called out to Gilley.

"What was fast?" Shepherd replied.

I whirled around. "Oh!" I exclaimed. "I wasn't expecting you tonight."

Shepherd rubbed his eyes and blinked several times. "I know. I should've called, but I really wanted to see you and couldn't handle it if you'd said no."

I set down the knife and hurried over to him, then hugged him fiercely. "I'll always have room for you here, Shep."

He hugged me back just as tightly, swaying the two of us back and forth. "Thank you," he said softly. Then, with a big inhale, he said, "Hey, good lookin'. Whatcha got cookin'?"

"Chicken Veronique. Would you like some?"

"Depends on what *Veronique* means."

I laughed. "It's a dish made with chicken, pasta, green grapes, white wine, and lots of cream."

"That sounds good," Shepherd said, and he looked surprised.

"Gilley's recipe," I admitted, pointing to a seat at the table before I returned to the grapes. "Sit," I told him. "And tell me how your day was."

"Exhausting," he said.

"Did you work on the Purdy case?"

"I did. All damn day. Went in circles on it. There's technically no phone record on Purdy's phone or in his records that matches up with any of the guys on your suspect list."

"Oh! I have another name for you."

"Who?"

"Killington Cavill."

"The race-car driver?"

"Everybody knows this guy but me," I said.

"He's a really good driver," Shepherd said, getting up to go to the fridge and peer inside it hopefully.

"Bottom of the door," I said. "On the left."

"Ahhh," he said, bringing up a bottle of pale ale. "You two really know how to spoil a guy."

"Back to Cavill," I said. "We think he went back to Scotland a year ago."

"You haven't checked?"

"Not yet."

"I'll look into it," Shepherd said. "How'd you pinpoint the name?"

"Darius. I showed him the script, and he told me that Yelena had dated his uncle, and he remembered seeing her with Cavill during the pandemic."

"Hold on," Shepherd said. "Yelena dated Darius's uncle Roy?"

"You knew him?"

"I did," he said. "Sweet old guy. Had a ton of money."

"Which is probably why Yelena found him attractive."

Shepherd grunted. "Yeah. That seems to have been her pattern. How's D doing, anyway?"

"He seems to be holding up," I said. "Or as well as can be expected. When we saw him today, he was singing a lullaby to Finley."

"He was?"

"You sound surprised."

"That just sounds really nurturing, and I never took Darius for the nurturing type."

"Why not?" I asked.

He shrugged. "Darius didn't have much of a home life growing up. His parents split when he was four, and his mother moved through husbands like a beaver through wood."

"Really?" I said. "That's sad. Does she live around here too?"

"Nah," he said. "She's in Singapore, on husband number six. Or maybe seven. Each one of them she takes to the cleaners when she files for divorce, but this latest husband made her sign a prenup."

"A gold digger like her signed a prenup?" I said.

Shepherd tipped his beer at me. "I found that curious, too, until Darius told me that they actually worked out a compromise. If his mom stays with this husband for the next ten years, she'll get half his money."

"Wow," I said. "Why do kind men always end up with the worst women?"

"Don't know," he said. "Still, Darius's mom isn't *all* bad. She's made Finley the heir to her fortune."

"Well, that's comforting," I said. "Finley will never want for anything."

"Except his mother," Shepherd said. I stopped slicing the grapes and went to him, hugged him around the shoulders and kissed the top of his head. "I love you," I said. "And I'm so sorry you and your family are going through this."

"My hope is that Santana bungles the investigation. I'm counting on Marcus to seed some doubt into the jury."

"He will," I said. "He will."

Shepherd patted my arm and said, "Back to the Purdy case. It turns out the counselor wasn't as retired as he let on."

"He was still seeing clients?"

Shepherd held up three fingers while he took a long pull from the bottle.

"Only three?" I asked.

"Yeah. Two are elderly women with too much money and too many squabbling family members. I talked to both of them. They know each other, and the one recommended the other. They were really upset to hear that Purdy died."

"I bet," I said.

"He was well liked by his clients," Shepherd continued. "I called a few from the last couple of years. They all raved about him."

"Who was the third client?" I asked.

"That's some shell company, which I'm having a heck of a time tracking down. It's gonna take me a week of red tape to come up with a name connected to it."

I looked up from the cutting board, having cut a nice pile of grapes. "I have faith," I told him, moving to the stove to stir the pasta.

"Where's Gilley?" Shepherd asked. "And Spooks?"

"They're on a walk. They should be back any minute."

"Aw, man," Shepherd moaned. "I am starving. I was hoping you guys would already have dinner made."

"We're not the only ones who can cook, you know."

"Are you looking at me?"

"Yep."

"Cat, you *know* I can't cook."

"Anyone can cook, lovey. You just need to commit to learning how."

Shepherd got up and came over to me. "Okay, Obi-Wan. Teach me."

I got out all the ingredients from the fridge, including the chicken tenders, and began to heat them in a frying pan. I showed Shepherd how to tell when the chicken was done by pressing on his palm, then on the chicken, so that he could compare the two pressures.

When the chicken was done, I had Shepherd slice the tenders up into bite-sized pieces while I stirred a quarter cup of white wine into the still hot pan. It bubbled almost immediately.

"Would you hand me that?" I asked, pointing to the flour jar on the counter closer to him.

Shepherd slid it over to me. "Whatcha gonna do with that?"

"Make a roux."

"What's a roux?"

"It's when you add a little bit of melted butter to a little bit of flour, stir until the butter is absorbed, then add a little more melted butter, and a little more and more, until the roux is the consistency of cream soup."

"Okay. My next question is, why?"

"It's what we're going to use to thicken the sauce," I said before showing him how I did it. I put some butter in a small dish, placed the butter in the microwave, and melted it. Then I filled another small dish with a generous teaspoon of flour, pulled the butter from the microwave, swirled it around to melt the last bit of it, then added a little to the flour and stirred that until it was absorbed. I continued adding butter until the roux was the consistency of soup.

Shepherd then watched while I poured a whole cup of cream into the pan with the bubbling wine and stirred it to keep it from overheating. Then I folded in the roux and stirred until it thickened the sauce right before tossing in the grapes, and waited for them to heat up a bit. Once they were just starting to soften, I tossed in the chicken tender pieces, finishing it all off with a bit of salt and pepper.

Shepherd stuck his finger into the sauce to taste it. "Mmm," he said. "That's good!"

I smiled and removed the sauce from the heat, drained the pasta, and had Shepherd set out three place settings while I loaded up three plates with pasta then sauce.

"I'm sorry!" Gilley called out as he burst through the door. "Spooks saw a cat and pulled the leash right out of my hand! I had to chase him for, like, a mile before I got him to come back."

Shepherd and I turned to look at Gilley, then Spooks, then Gilley again.

Spooks was panting and looking rather proud of himself.

Gilley was panting and looking rather frazzled.

"Come," I said to him, picking up two of the plates and bringing them to the table. "Sit. We'll eat, and you'll feel better."

"Thank God you made dinner," Gilley said. "I'm starved!"

"Feed Spooks first, though," I said.

Gilley snapped his fingers and got out Spooks's new bowl, poured a half a cup of kibble into it, and set it on the floor. The pup went right to it, and he would've gulped it down, but the new bowl was a maze of curved ridges, which allowed him to eat only one bit of kibble at a time.

At last, we all sat down and ate together, and I didn't remember ever feeling more comforted by the presence of these two men.

Just as we were finishing up, Shepherd's phone buzzed. He took it out of his pocket and looked at the display, his brow knitting when he read the caller ID.

After getting up, he walked a few steps away and took the call. "Lieutenant," he said.

"Oh, God," I whispered to Gilley. "I hope he's not in trouble again."

"Why would you think that?"

"Why else would Shep's lieutenant be calling if not to bawl him out for some petty thing?"

We both watched Shepherd intently as he ran a hand through

his hair and was obviously rattled by whatever his boss was telling him. "When?" he asked sharply.

Gilley and I exchanged a nervous look.

"Where's he now?"

There was a set to Shepherd's shoulders that told us the news was bad. Just how bad, I thought, we'd soon find out.

"All right. I'll head there now."

Clicking off the call, he turned to look at us, and something in his eyes made my own eyes well up. The news wasn't just bad. It was personal to us.

"What?" I said, my voice cracking.

Shepherd came back to the table and sat down. Taking up my hand, he said, "There's been a car accident."

My first thought was that it had to do with my sons, and the tears overflowed and slid down my cheeks. "Wh-wh-who?" I said.

"Marcus," he said.

I blinked and shook my head a little, unable to take in fully what Shepherd was telling me. "Who?" I repeated.

"Marcus Brown," Shepherd said.

I put a hand to my mouth, and Gilley stared at Shepherd in stunned silence. "But I just talked to him," I squeaked.

"When?" Shep asked.

"Like, an hour and a half ago."

Shepherd nodded. "I'm going to the hospital," he said.

"He's in the hospital?" Gilley said, his own eyes watering.

"Yeah, Gilley. It's bad. They had to use the Jaws of Life to get him out of his car."

"Did he lose control?" Gilley asked and I was surprised to see he, too, was crying.

Shepherd shook his head. "It was a hit-and-run. We think Marcus may have been targeted."

I was also shaking my head. This couldn't be happening. I adored Marcus, and I didn't want him hurt. I didn't even want him scratched.

"We'll go with you," Gilley said, jumping to his feet.

Shepherd nodded. "We need to go now, though."

I got up and grabbed all three plates, hustled them to the sink, then hurried to get my coat and purse. "I'm ready," I said while Shepherd was slipping into his.

Gilley didn't even bother with a coat. He just headed to the door and hurried outside.

"Are you okay to drive?" Shepherd asked me.

"Why? You're not taking us there?"

"I'll be working the case all night, Cat. You'll need your car."

I was panting with worry. "I'll be okay," I said.

Shepherd kissed the top of my head, and we moved on out the door.

Chapter 18

We arrived at the hospital and followed Shepherd inside. Gilley and I were both silent and numb. I'd prayed all the way over, and while I walked behind Shepherd, I continued to pray.

Shepherd came to a stop at the information desk. He spoke softly, but I still heard him and saw him flash his badge as he asked about Marcus.

The information desk clerk pointed to his left and said, "That way, past the elevators to the end of the hall. Then turn right and follow that hallway to the end. The trauma unit is through the double doors, and you can ask the nurse on duty for more information about Mr. Brown, Detective."

"Thanks," Shepherd said, then thumped the counter between them two times before turning away, back to us. Pointing ahead, he said, "This way, you two."

Again, we trailed behind Shepherd, who was following the clerk's directions. At last, we came through a set of doors, and immediately, I felt the energy shift to one of urgency. Doctors and nurses were rushing around in a no-time-to-waste kind of way.

Gilley inched closer to me and took up my hand. I squeezed it to reassure him, but I felt so vulnerable and scared in that moment, so I stopped several feet behind Shepherd, who approached the nurses' desk with his badge out.

He and the nurse spoke; then he nodded and came back to us.

"He's in surgery," Shepherd said. "He's got a collapsed lung and some internal bleeding. The nurse will have the surgeon come out and speak to us as soon as they're done operating."

I swallowed hard, barely managing to hold down a sob.

Shepherd stood across from me and Gilley, and then he opened his arms wide and said, "Get in here, you two."

We both rushed forward and wrapped our arms around him and each other, and that hug did me a world of good.

Afterward, we sat quietly in the waiting area, where a TV with the sound off but closed-captioning on played a sitcom.

As the time closed in on 9:00 p.m., a woman in scrubs, booties, and a surgical cap walked in and said, "Detective?"

Shepherd got up, and Gilley and I did too. He moved forward to walk a few feet away with the surgeon; we held back but took up holding each other's hands again.

Shepherd spoke to the surgeon at length, and I saw him taking down the details on the small pad of paper he always kept on him.

At last, they nodded to each other, and she walked away, while he turned back to us.

"He's stable," he said.

Gilley and I both let out a huge whoosh of air. "Oh, my God," I said, putting my free hand to my chest, where my heart was thumping wildly inside. "Thank God!"

Gilley put both his hands together in prayer and looked skyward, then shook his praying hands at the ceiling. "Thank you, thank you, thank you!" he said.

Shepherd also looked relieved. "He's in the ICU right now, and they'll keep him sedated for at least the next twenty-four hours, but the surgeon said she was able to stop the bleed and repair and expand his lung again. She also needed to put a few pins into three of his ribs to support the rib cage and keep it from collapsing again. He's also got a pretty good head wound, but the CT scan didn't look too bad, she said. He's probably got a solid concussion but no brain bleed."

"That all sounds so horrible!" I said.

"It couldn't have been fun," Shep agreed. Then he sighed and said, "Now that you know he's okay, why don't you two head home? I've got to get to the scene and take a look at the car and get an estimate for how fast the other car was going, and from which direction."

"There were no witnesses?" I said.

"I don't know that yet, Cat. That's why I've got to go."

I nodded. "Understood. But will you monitor his condition and let us know if anything changes?"

"I will," he said. "Do you guys know who to contact about getting a number for his next of kin?"

"His paralegal is named Jasmine, but I don't know her last name," Gilley said.

"Taylor," I said, recalling her introduction to us.

"Terrific," Shepherd said, jotting that down before closing his little notebook and putting it back in his blazer pocket. "I'll call her next, tell her what's happened, and be in touch."

"Oh!" I said, remembering Julia's get-together with Marcus the next day. "Can you tell her to make sure Julia knows that Marcus won't be available to accompany her to the club?"

"What club?" Shepherd asked.

"The EHGC. They were going to have lunch tomorrow."

"They know each other?"

"They do," I said.

"Yeah, okay. I'll pass along the message. You guys drive safe, and I'll be in touch."

With that, we went our separate ways.

When we got back home, Gilley and I got out of the car and he said over the hood, "Would you like to stay over again?"

"I would," I said.

"Good. But this time, sleep in the spare bedroom, okay?"

"I don't like to put you out by sleeping in a bed where you'll have to change the sheets and remake the bed."

"Cat," Gilley said, as if he found the notion ridiculous. "Come on. Sleep in a bed tonight. Washing sheets is no big deal."

"I'll wash them tomorrow," I said. "I have to wash the linens in the room Darius and Finley slept in tomorrow too."

Gilley sighed. "Whatever makes you feel more comfortable," he said.

I went to Chez Cat and changed into the same silk pajamas I'd worn the night before and headed back over to Chez Kitty.

Gilley was already in his robe and pajamas too. He yawned and said, "Did you want to stay up a bit?"

"No," I said. "I'm exhausted."

"Me too. See you in the morning?"

"Yes."

"You'll come get me if Shepherd calls with any news about Marcus?"

"I will. I promise."

"Good night, Cat."

"Night, Gilley," I said before shuffling into the guest bedroom. I was asleep almost as soon as my head hit the pillow.

The next morning, I woke up to the smell of coffee. I grabbed my phone to make sure I hadn't missed any calls from Shepherd—I hadn't—and made my way to the kitchen.

"It's so early," I whispered when I found Gilley at the table, staring into space and sipping on a steaming cup of coffee.

"I woke up and couldn't get back to sleep," he said.

It was 4:00 a.m., and while I didn't feel fully rested, at least the hours of sleep I'd gotten were restful.

"Any news from Shepherd?" Gilley asked.

"Not a peep," I said, moving over to the French press to pour my own mug of brew.

"No news is good news, right?"

"It is."

"Who could've done that to him, Cat?"

I sat down and sighed. "I don't know, Gil. He's a defense attorney, and from what I understand of that profession, it's not an especially safe one. A client loses in court, gets some jail time, and comes back for revenge when freed. I mean, you saw his office, right? It was all top-notch security, and I'm thinking there was a reason for that."

"You're right," Gil said. "I just feel so helpless. I wish there was something we could do."

I knew what he meant. I felt helpless too. But then I had an idea about how we could fill our morning with purpose. "Hey," I said, tapping his arm. "What do you think about making not just one lasagna for Darius and Finley, but three? One for the D'Angelos, one for Tiffany and her parents, which will give us a chance to check up on her, and one for Aaron. I've wanted to call him since yesterday, when he was released."

"I think that's a great plan," Gilley said, with an eager eye.

I stood. "Then let's hop to it!"

We spent the next several hours making the lasagnas. Gilley even insisted on making the noodles from scratch. "What's the point of having a pasta roller and a noodle drying rack if you're just gonna go store bought?" he'd said when I'd questioned his laborious methods.

While Gilley tended to the pasta, I got started on his recipe for meat sauce, which was a complex series of steps, but when it was finally simmering, it filled Chez Kitty with an aroma that was heavenly.

Gilley placed two small fans in front of and behind the perfectly made pasta noodles and sniffed the air. "You did great," he said, squeezing my shoulders in a one-armed hug.

"How long will the noodles have to dry?"

"The fan cuts the time in half, so about six hours."

I looked at the time on the stove. "We can start assembling at eleven thirty, then?"

"Yep. It'll take about forty minutes to assemble all three, and another forty to forty-five minutes to bake, and then I'd give it at least a half hour to cool, which means we'll be good to go around two o'clock."

"What should we do while we wait for the pasta noodles to dry?"

"Make breakfast and take a nap."

"I love that idea," I said, grinning.

Gilley put together a quick quiche while I sent a text to Shepherd in the hopes that he might be up. His reply was quick.

"Is Shepherd up?" Gilley asked me. He'd obviously seen me sending a text.

"He is. He's heading out to the car lot to inspect Marcus's car, and he'll call me later."

"Did you ask him about Marcus?"

"I did. He says there's no news."

Gilley paused to wipe his hands on a dish towel and looked at me earnestly. "Do we still think no news is good news?"

"We do," I said, willing myself to believe it.

"Okay, then I won't worry more than I already am."

We ate breakfast together and talked over some ideas for Willem and Chanel's reception. We'd given our first impressions to Julia, but now that we had a chance to discuss the event between us, we were coming up with new ideas and jotting them down to send to her later this afternoon, after we got done spreading some lasagna cheer along the way.

Around nine o'clock I yawned. So did Gilley.

"Nap time," he said.

I grinned and asked, "Can I cuddle with Spooks?" Gilley

had, of course, claimed the pup the night before, but Spooks gave me such comfort that I couldn't resist asking.

"Of course," Gilley said.

We headed back to our bedrooms, Spooks following me, and once again I fell asleep quickly.

By eleven thirty we were back in the kitchen, both feeling much more rested, and we got to work assembling the pasta.

"These noodles are perfect," Gilley said.

"They feel amazing," I told him. Soft and velvety, they covered the layers of meat sauce and cheese perfectly.

"Do you think we'll have enough for a small lasagna for us?"

"We should," Gilley said. "You made plenty of meat sauce."

"But is there enough pasta?"

"There is," he said. "If we cut the noodles in half and use a small casserole dish."

"I've got the perfect size at Chez Cat."

"Fantastic," Gilley said. "You can take all the ingredients over there and assemble our dinner, and put this third one in your oven while you're at it."

"Sebastian," I said.

"Yes, Lady Catherine?"

"Please preheat the oven at Chez Cat to three hundred seventy-five."

"Preheating initiated," Sebastian said.

"I love Sebastian," Gilley said.

"I love you as well, Sir Gilley."

That made us both giggle.

Gilley helped me across the driveway with all the ingredients for our small pan pasta and announced that he had to take Spooks for a walk.

"Careful he doesn't pull the leash out of your hand this time," I said.

"Trust me, from now on I'm holding on to that leash with a death grip."

He left, and I put the third lasagna into the oven, then assembled ours and was so pleased that the leftover ingredients were the exact amount I needed. After setting that completed casserole dish in the refrigerator, I peered through the oven glass and smiled at the bubbling concoction. Then I glanced at the time and hurried upstairs to take a shower and change before I had to pull the lasagna out.

When I stepped out of the shower, I got a text from Gilley, asking me to pull out the lasagnas at his place because he wouldn't be back in time.

I growled. He was cutting into my schedule now, but I donned a robe and dashed across to Chez Kitty just in time to hear the timer go off on the stove.

After carefully removing both casserole dishes, I set them on cooling racks, then hurried back across the drive to Chez Cat, looked at the timer on the stove, and said, "Sebastian, will you please let me know when the stove timer goes off?"

"I will, Lady Catherine."

After dashing up the stairs, I shimmied into a pair of leggings, a long-sleeved olive dress that fell just below my knees, and some low-heeled black boots.

I was almost finished drying my hair when Sebastian told me that the timer had gone off on the lasagna, so I abandoned the hair dryer and raced downstairs to pull the lasagna out of the oven. After setting the casserole dish on a cooling rack, I went back upstairs and finished making myself presentable.

By 1:15 p.m. I was ready for the day, but I didn't have a lot to do until the pasta cooled enough to be transported.

Making my way to the family room, I noticed how dirty the floor was, and so I hauled out the vacuum cleaner and got up most of the debris, which had been brought in by the birthday party guests. I then took the cordless vacuum upstairs, started in on the carpet in the hallway, and made my way to the boys' rooms.

Opening the door to Matt's room first and then to Mike's, I sighed. "I've raised slobs," I said. The boys' rooms were a mess!

I started cleaning their rooms by pulling off the sheets and tossing them into the washing machine and starting the load. I then moved to the guest room and found it neat as a pin. Darius had kindly made up the bed. After pulling those sheets off, I dumped them in the basket in the laundry room, making a mental note to wash them with the sheets at Chez Kitty when the first load was done.

Peeking at the time on my watch, I saw that I had twenty minutes left before meeting up with Gilley, so I headed to the worst disaster—Matt's room—and started sorting clothes scattered about the room into piles of darks and lights. It was as I was checking to see if anything had been shoved under the bed that I saw his duffel bag. After pulling it to me, I unzipped it and spread the flaps, only to be assaulted by the most god-awful stench.

His running shoes and sweaty clothes had been percolating ever since he left for school three weeks before.

"Oh, my God, child of mine," I said, pinching my nose and gingerly taking out the shoes and the clothes.

And that was when it hit me.

And everything clicked.

All of it.

I could see it laid out perfectly, each such a tiny clue, but leading to the final conclusion.

"Oh, my God," I whispered, rushing to my bedroom, where I'd left my phone. Snatching it off the bed, I realized that there were half a dozen texts from Gilley, sent only fifteen minutes before.

Ohmigod! I—shower—gone for ten minutes! He ate the whole thing!

Why aren't you answering your phone????
Headed to emergency vet!

Immediately I called Gilley.

"*Where have you been?*" he yelled.

"Honey, I'm so sorry! I was vacuuming and didn't hear my phone! What's happened?"

Gilley was sobbing. "I've killed him, Cat! *I've killed him!*"

I gasped. "Oh, no! Gilley, you mean Spooks . . . he's . . ." I couldn't form the words.

"In the back, with the vet," he said, still crying. "They're doing an ultrasound. He ate the whole damn lasagna, Cat! He figured out how to push a chair to the counter climbed up and *ate the entire thing*!"

I bit my lip. "Do you need me to come there?"

"No," he said. "No. I'll call you if I get news. But it might be a while. They're busy here today."

"Okay, sweetie. I'll wait to hear from you."

Clicking off the call, I stared at my phone. I hadn't wanted to add anything to Gilley's brain, because he was so undone.

So I called Shepherd. I got his voice mail. Then a text, with the words **Can't talk right now.**

I got up and began pacing the room. An idea was forming to confirm my suspicions, and I wondered if I could pull it off safely.

"I'll just slip in and take a few pictures," I said. "I've already got a distraction. I'll be fine."

Still, I paced just a little bit more before reaching for my laptop and conducting several searches just to satisfy any lingering doubt. "The theater is only two miles from the park," I mumbled. "That's an easy run for someone so in shape."

I then looked up the safety features in Range Rovers and found what I was looking for easily. Next, I searched for a name that flashed through my memory, found it and, scrolling the associated web page, landed on the very item that tied every single thing together.

Standing up from my place on the bed, I settled on the endeavor before I lost my nerve. After dashing down the steps, I carefully placed my phone in my purse with the camera facing outward, put the lasagna in a warming bag, and rushed out the door.

Chapter 19

When I pulled into the drive, the garage door was up, but no car was in the bay, and there wasn't one to the side, either.

I had sat there for a beat, wondering what to do, when I saw a car pull into the drive right behind me. My pulse quickened, but I didn't let the fear get the best of me. I reached for the lasagna and my purse, got out of the car, and smiled all friendly-like.

"Catherine!" he said, smiling at me, as if he was genuinely happy to see me.

"Hello, Darius." I lifted the lasagna and said, "We promised to bake you one, remember?"

Darius opened the back door of his car and unbuckled his son, who was barely awake and fell limply against his father's shoulder.

"Aww!" I said, happy that things had also fallen in my favor. "He's so sleepy!"

Darius rubbed his son's back. "It's his nap time," he said, walking toward me.

I held out my free hand. "Can I?" I asked.

"Sure," he said and placed Finley against my shoulder while he took up the lasagna. "This smells amazing."

I grinned and shifted Finley to a more comfortable position for him. "Gilley insisted on homemade noodles."

"Wow!" he said, getting out his keys to open the front door. "I get the VIP treatment, huh?"

I laughed softly. "Well, mostly Finley, but also you."

Darius laughed. "Yeah, I get it."

He unlocked the door and held it open for me, but I pointed toward the garage. "Your door sticking again?"

He shook his head and sighed. "That stupid garage door never did work right. I gotta get a guy out here to get a whole new system put in."

I walked into the home and swiveled on my feet as Darius was closing the door. Whispering, I said, "Can I put him down? I miss my sons so much, and it would give me great comfort to lay him down for his nap."

Darius seemed to hesitate for just a moment. "Sure," he said. "Don't mind the mess in the nursery, though. I'm reorganizing a few things."

I smiled at him. "You're a wonderful father, Darius."

"Thank you," he said, and I could see the set to his shoulders relax a fraction. "This thing is still really warm. Should I put it in the fridge until we're ready to eat it?"

"I'd put it on a cooling rack for another thirty to forty minutes. Let it cool to nearly room temperature before you put it in the fridge and risk any other food spoiling."

He pointed a finger gun at me. "Gotcha," he said, then made a clicking sound. When he turned to move into the kitchen, I took Finley up the stairs and into the nursery.

The place was a mess. Much of Finley's clothing had been pulled out and strewn on the floor. Almost all of it for cold weather. After moving to the crib, I laid Finley down quickly but carefully.

I then snapped a photo of the room, then hurried out into the hall on tiptoe, and eased open the door directly opposite the nursery.

Two large suitcases were standing upright against the wall, and various guitars in different states of repair were also set about the room. The guitars were the link between the two murders. Purdy hadn't been killed with a piano wire. He'd been killed with a guitar wire. Most definitely from the guitar that Darius had pulled from his car when we'd approached him in the drive the night of the murders.

I snapped two more pictures, one of the suitcases and one of the guitars. And then something else caught my eye. On the wall where the suitcases were set were a series of framed photographs of Darius, grinning next to a woman who, in each photo, was wearing a different wedding dress but atop her head in each photo was the same elaborately-sized tiara. Every image showed the same pose for the two subjects, but clearly, they had been taken at different stages in both of their lives. I realized belatedly that the woman must be Darius's mother at some of her many weddings.

"Married to a queen," I whispered. I snapped a picture of the series of photos on the wall too and then tiptoed back into the nursery and up to another photo, this time of Sunny standing on the porch of her old home overlooking L.A.

The view was the same one shown in the listing that I'd found by looking up Andrew Yamanski, Darius's "real estate guy."

There was no condo. There never had been. This was the house on the hill that Yelena had been referring to. Lover Number Two wasn't Darius's uncle. He was Darius.

And Darius was also Lover Number Twelve. He was the lover that Yelena had pretty much begun and ended her show on. His mother had dressed like a queen at her wedding. She was wealthy and powerful, and willing to leave a giant portion of her money to her grandson.

And, no doubt, with her financial support, Darius had been

able to keep the house in L.A. as a love nest for himself and Yelena. "Phoning for donations wasn't a political campaign reference. It was a reference to Darius calling his mother for money,"
I said to myself.

I snapped a quick photo of the image on the wall. And then I
noticed a small photo in a frame nestled on a table with a lamp.
I hadn't seen it before when I was here with Sunny, or I
might've put things together sooner.

The photo was of the two of them, Darius and Sunny, taken
in the early days of their relationship. Sunny was stunning, and
she looked about twenty, as did Darius, but his hair was longer,
his face thinner than it was now, and he resembled his daughter
so much that there was no mistaking that he was Tiffany's birth
father.

And Tiffany had been the fly in the ointment. I was certain
that Yelena not only would've told Tiffany that she was her real
mother but also would've given her the identity of her father.

And that was why, in her drug-induced subconscious state,
Sunny had left her home after getting a call from her "dear"
friend. Yelena had called to tell her that she and Darius had a
daughter. The very woman babysitting her child.

Of course, Sunny would've translated that as a threat to her
son. Finley stood to inherit a sizeable portion of his grandmother's money, but if the queen living in Singapore knew she
also had a far older granddaughter, she could revise the terms of
her will and switch the financial assets to Tiffany, which would
no doubt be somewhat controlled by Yelena.

Darius must've known that his mother would make him her
executor, giving him full control over her finances until Finley
turned of age. He'd have a lot less money to be in control of if
his mother recognized her granddaughter as family, since
Tiffany was already of age.

That was why he'd killed Purdy. He'd been trying to pay off
Yelena with the estate lawyer he'd hired through his shell corp

and assigning him the task of delivering two hundred thousand dollars to her.

But Yelena had called him and told him of her plans. She'd called him on a phone registered to Sunny, because Sunny had opened up a family plan for the two of them. I'd checked the number on my one text from Darius when the three of us split up to go find Sunny. His subscriber number was 3838, the same subscriber number that Marcus had told me was in Sunny's plan.

And recalling the night Darius had sent me the text, it wasn't lost on me that he'd purposely pointed us toward the park, knowing we would likely find Sunny dead.

And the park was only two and a half miles from the theater. An easy run for a man in Darius's physical condition.

The clue had come from my son's duffel bag. The night of the murders, when Darius had gotten out of his car, he'd smelled terrible. Just as terrible as Matt's clothing when I'd opened up the duffel. I knew now that Darius's other clothes had been covered in blood, but he had had his duffel in the car and had changed into his dirty workout gear to hide his bloody clothing.

As I stood in Finley's nursery, I saw the murders unfold in my mind's eye like a movie: Yelena calls Darius and tells him of her plans to reveal his name during her performance that evening and alerts him to the fact that his wife's dear friends will be sitting front row center.

Panicked, Darius tries to buy her off with the two hundred grand. She accepts the terms, and he catches the first flight home from L.A. He then makes a withdrawal from his trust fund—which wouldn't have Sunny's name on it—for the two hundred Gs. He then goes shopping and buys the raincoat and personally packs it with the money before dropping it off to Purdy so that the elderly man can take it to Yelena. He then calls Sunny, and in that conversation, Sunny admits to taking some Ambien, but she also lets him know that Tiffany is there with Finley.

Darius goes about his day, hiding from anyone who might recognize him, and just before he's set to go home, he gets a call from Yelena. She tells him the deal is off, and she's already told Sunny everything. She demands that he introduce his daughter to his mother, or she'll do it herself.

Furious, Darius hangs up on Yelena and frantically tries to reach Sunny. She has already gone to the theater and has left her phone behind. When she doesn't answer, Darius assumes she believes Yelena, so he goes to the theater to get his revenge.

He plans on sneaking in and waiting for her in her dressing room, but when he gets there, he finds Sunny is already waiting. Maybe she's still loopy, or maybe she's out of it, and Darius thinks he has a good chance of getting her out of the theater and convincing her, should she remember anything, that it was all an Ambien dream.

As he's pulling Sunny along out of the dressing room, Yelena appears backstage and is enraged to see both of them there. She and Darius get into a physical fight. He grabs the nearest weapon he can find, which is Aaron's letter opener, and he stabs Yelena.

Sunny becomes lucid enough to try to get between the pair, but she manages only to smear blood on herself as Yelena collapses.

As he throws away the letter opener, Darius grabs Sunny's hand—they've got to get out of there—but as they're leaving through the exit door, covered in blood, they literally bump into Purdy, smearing his hand with Yelena's blood.

Putting two and two together, Purdy realizes that Darius has killed Yelena, and he makes a run for it.

Darius quickly moves Sunny to his car, grabs the guitar wire, and chases after Purdy, but he can't catch up before Purdy ducks into the coffee shop.

Darius sees him through the window, lit up from the lights inside, and he watches him move to the back of the shop. That's when Darius rushes to the alley to wait and see which way Purdy will go.

After washing off the blood in the restroom, Purdy goes out the back way, and Darius, hiding in the shadows, jumps out and wraps the guitar wire around Purdy's neck and kills him. He then shoves Purdy's body into the crevice between the wall and the stack of pallets. But he doesn't have time to grab the cash, because he has to get back to his wife, and so he rushes back to his car.

She's in the car and a little out of it, but she's also now a probable witness to murder, so Darius drives her to her car. Maybe it's parked down the street, or maybe in the parking garage, but he finds it and places Sunny in the car, grabs his gym duffel from his own car, and heads toward home, but not before he coaxes Sunny to take a few more Ambien.

When he gets home, he probably didn't park in the driveway, but at the curb down the street from the house. Darius then sneaks over to the house and uses the outdoor shower to rinse off and change into the workout clothes he has in his duffel bag. He shoves his bloody clothes into the duffel and heads back to the car to remove Sunny's bloody clothes and shoes. Taking these with him he returns to the house, this time sneaking around to the back and looking in the well-lit windows to see where Tiffany is. He spots her on the treadmill, so he sneaks inside through the garage, hurries down the hallway and into the laundry room. There he rummages through the laundry basket for some clothes for him and Sunny, but he can't find any clothes that don't stink for himself because he's been gone for a month and Sunny would've done his laundry weeks earlier, so he's stuck wearing what he's already changed into.

He can't stay long inside the house, lest Tiffany discover him, so he shoves Sunny's bloody clothes and her shoes to the bottom of the laundry basket and takes whatever's on top for her to change into.

Once he's back at the car, he coaxes Sunny to the outdoor shower and rinses her off, getting his clothing wet in the process. What I had mistaken for sweat was actually the water from the shower. And it's also the reason Sunny's hair was damp and she was barefoot when Gilley and I found her in her Range Rover at the park.

Once Darius has got Sunny rinsed off and changed, he takes her back to the car and drives her to the park. After he's got them parked in a spot at the end of the lot, he forces Sunny to take all the rest of the Ambien with the bottle of water that he takes with him from the supplies in the garage. Then he places the empty pill bottle in Sunny's hand, removes the water bottle with his fingerprints on it and leaves the key fob in the car, but he can't lock it that way, because the car won't let you lock the doors if the engine is off and the key is inside the car. So he takes the key fob with him, shuts the door, locks the car from the outside, and jogs back to his own car, parked somewhere near the theater.

On the drive home he plans on sending Tiffany away, before waiting until perhaps the next day for the call that tells him that his wife has committed suicide in her car parked downtown.

But Gilley and I are already in his driveway when he shows up, spoiling his plans.

Seeing another angle that will push any suspicion away from him, he sends us to the park, knowing that's exactly where he's left Sunny's car. He knows we're the ones that will find her dead body, and he can then play the role of grieving husband.

Complicating things is the fact that Sunny is not dead when we find her, so Darius holds his breath until he can privately question her about any memories she might remember of that evening. Maybe she confesses to a terrible dream, or maybe she doesn't, but Darius is prepared for any memory that might bubble up by playing up her depression to her doctors. Which is what keeps her so long inside that mental health facility.

Darius thinks he's totally in the clear when Sunny arrives home, as another man has already been charged in Yelena's murder, but then Sunny discovers the bloody clothes at the bottom of the laundry basket which he has forgotten all about until she presents them to him.

Darius tries to talk Sunny out of confessing, if only to keep the suspicion as far away from him as possible, but Sunny cannot let an innocent man go to jail when she believes she murdered Yelena. So she sneaks away from Darius long enough to drive to my house with the bloody clothes, where she confesses to her brother in front of a large crowd.

Darius must be relieved when he learns the case against Sunny is so solid. He's happy to let her take the blame, all the while playing the role of distraught husband and devoted father perfectly.

While he's thinking about what to do next, Marcus keeps him informed of all the details in the case, which is why, after Marcus calls him yesterday to ask him to come along for the interview with Sunny so that she can explain the two phone numbers associated with her name, Darius knows he has to take care of Marcus first, to slow down the case, and he has to make a run for it—with Finley and probably to Singapore—because the walls are closing in.

I snapped a picture of the framed photo. "And so they are," I whispered.

Downstairs I found Darius in the kitchen, already eating a piece of lasagna.

"Sorry," he said through a big bite of warm pasta. Chewing quickly, he added, "It's so good!"

I laughed, waving my hand nonchalantly. "No, please, eat away!"

Darius took another huge bite and pointed to the casserole dish and looked at me, as if asking me if I wanted a bite.

"I'm fine. I just ate lunch," I lied. Switching topics, I said, "I folded up all the clothes on the floor of the nursery and set them in piles."

I hadn't, but it was a good excuse to explain why I'd taken so long upstairs.

"Thanks," he said. "Taking care of a toddler is hard work."

"Don't I know it," I said. "I raised twin boys, although I had help. I can only imagine how much more difficult it must be for you now that Tiffany can't babysit."

Darius eyed me carefully but said nothing. I had no doubt that he hadn't heard about Tiffany's fall and broken foot.

"I really hope her foot and ankle heal up quickly," I said into the awkward silence. "That was quite a spill she took, and her ankle and foot swelled up so fast."

Darius's expression relaxed. "Yeah, tough break for that kid."

I pretended to look around the kitchen for another topic and then said, "Say, what happened to Sunny's car?"

Again, that quizzical, careful expression returned to his features. "Her car?"

"Yeah. You know, her Range Rover. It's not in the garage."

Darius was sweating a little, and his face was a little flushed. "The rumors are true," he said, pushing a playful smile to his lips. "Those cars spend more time in the shop than they do on the road."

I knew there was absolutely no chance Sunny's car was in "the shop." It was someplace hidden. Like a junkyard. The police were, after all, looking for the car that'd hit Marcus's and might still have some of the car paint from Sunnys's car on the fender.

"Ahh," I said. "Yeah, I told Sunny that model had a terrible maintenance record, but there was no talking her out of it."

"She wanted one bad," he said. "I wanted her to get a Mercedes."

"You love yours, huh?"

"I do."

"Good," I said. "Oh, and did you sell your condo yet?"

Belatedly, I realized that I'd probably asked one question too many, because Darius's look turned from playful to suspicious. It was subtle, but it was definitely there.

"Not yet," he said, setting down his plate. His eyes flickered to the knife block across the kitchen. It was a very quick movement, but I saw it.

I was about to announce that I had to dash when my phone rang. Relieved beyond measure, I snatched the phone out of my purse and opened up the screen. After placing it to my ear, I said, "Shepherd! What a coincidence that you'd call right when I was chatting with your brother-in-law!"

"What?" Gilley said. "Cat, it's *me!*"

I laughed loudly and winked at Darius. "No, he's taking wonderful care of Finley, not to worry. The tyke is upstairs in his crib, and we're down here in the kitchen, chatting while Darius has some of Gilley's lasagna." I wanted to let someone know where we were should I need the cops to break in and rescue me.

"What the heck are you talking about?!" Gilley shouted.

"Of course I'll save you a piece, lovey. What time will you be home from all that detecting you're doing?"

There was a pregnant pause on the other end of the call, and then Gilley said, "Are you in trouble?"

"Yes, yes, I am. I'm looking forward to it too."

Gilley sucked in a breath.

Across from me, Darius stared at me with narrowed eyes. I might've been trying too hard to appear casual. "Let me talk to him," Darius said softly, holding his hand out for the phone.

I couldn't help my immediate reaction, which was to widen

my eyes in fear. Recovering quickly, however, I said, "Hold on, Shep. Darius wants to talk to you."

Before I handed over the phone, I pressed my thumb on the END button. The phone made a small beeping sound, and I pulled my hand back in surprise. "Oh, no," I said. "He must've hung up."

Darius crossed his arms. "Show me your list of recent calls, Catherine."

I could feel the blood draining from my face. I knew he knew that I hadn't been talking to his brother-in-law.

"Why?" I asked.

"To prove that it was him on the line."

"You think it wasn't him, Darius?"

"I do."

"Well, that's not very nice. In fact, it's downright rude! And here we made you such a delicious feast." I settled my purse on my arm and took two steps toward the front door. Darius took three. He was bigger, stronger, and faster than me, and I knew he could get to the door before I even made it out of the kitchen.

Feeling a panic settling in, I couldn't think of what to do! And then my phone rang, and I gasped both in surprise and relief. "Oh, look!" I said, swiveling the face of the phone toward him. "See? It's him calling back."

I had punched the green TALK button, ready to clue Shepherd in, when Darius snatched the gadget from my hands.

Before I could even recover from the shockingly fast move, Darius took my phone and slammed it facedown into a corner of the kitchen island.

It broke apart into at least a dozen pieces. Then I watched in abject terror as Darius reached for me. I ducked and spun and managed to twist my way toward the hallway leading to the front door, trying to move as fast as my feet could possibly go as I made a break for it.

I had gotten only a few feet when Darius's hand clamped down on my shoulder and pulled me back right off my feet.

My head hit the wood floor with a loud whack, and my vision darkened to gray, with lots of sparkles. Putting my hands up in front of my face protectively, I did my absolute best to remain conscious, but that was about all I could manage.

I then felt cruel hands grip my shoulders, lift me off the floor, and place me on my feet. I wobbled and felt my knees weakening, but Darius kept me upright while he pulled me forward.

My vision was still blurred, though some of the darkness had lessened.

I tried to form words, but all I could get out was a low moan.

Still, Darius pulled me forward. Suddenly the light was too bright, and I brought my arms up to shield my eyes. Darius responded by shoving me hard. I would've fallen flat on my face if he wasn't holding tight to my arm.

I heard a car door open, and I was shoved inside, smacking the middle console before crumpling onto the front passenger seat in the fetal position.

The car door opposite me opened, and Darius got in. "You got your key fob with you?" he asked.

My head throbbed with pain while I twisted around to sit sideways in the seat with my back against the door and my knees pulled up to my chest protectively. As I looked dully at him, I could see that Darius's expression was filled with deadly intent, and it was startling to see in someone who played the Dr. Jekyll part of his character so well.

"Whah . . . ," I said, still unable to form coherent words.

Darius pressed the START button, and my car hummed to life.

In the distance I heard the wail of sirens, and I thought, *Oh, God! I'm saved!*

Darius put the car in reverse and stomped on the gas while pulling hard on the wheel, spinning the car around, and I bounced against the passenger side door, nearly blacking out again.

"I bet you think you're safe, huh?" he said.

I could only blink my lids slowly at him.

"You'd be wrong," he said. "You're about to have the same accident my wife's car had."

I tried to make sense of what he was saying. Was he about to hit someone else with my car?

But then, as we sped down the road before taking a sharp left, all the while those sirens drawing closer, I realized where he was taking me. I could feel the immediate incline as the car sped up the hill.

The same hill his uncle had lived on.

"So that's what you did with her car," I said. Realizing I'd actually spoken coherently, I wanted to smile, but my mind's ability to move my body wasn't exactly cooperating.

"Yeah. It was beautiful. I didn't think the Rover would make it. It got smashed up pretty good, but it did. All the way off the cliff."

My chin drooped while I looked up at him with half-lidded eyes.

He looked at me and scowled. "I was gonna take the flight to Singapore tomorrow, but I guess taking it tonight doesn't make much of a difference."

Again, I blinked at him, all the while my head drooping on my neck.

I knew we had to be near the top of the hill by now, so I turned my head ever so slightly to stare out the windshield. The sirens were no longer approaching. They'd stopped. No doubt the police had arrived at Darius's house.

But I wasn't there.

And in a moment, I wasn't going to be anywhere.

Suddenly there was a whoosh of air, and I turned my head again to see Darius had opened the car door and was beginning to lean out while gripping the steering wheel with one hand. My feet were resting on the seat while I was lying back against the door.

Using all my willpower and strength, I lifted my legs and slammed my feet into Darius's arm. He let go of the wheel immediately and went tumbling away from the car.

And then I barely managed to lift my hand, clamp down on the wheel, and turn the car to the left. I had no idea if this would save me or kill me, but I had to try something to save my life.

The open door swung wide, then came whooshing back and slammed shut. My car bobbled along, shaking the interior—and me—and then slowed down, until it bumped into something and stopped.

Panting hard, I picked my head up and looked around, blinking furiously all the while. My car had hit something that was out of sight. Probably a rock. Thank God the airbags hadn't deployed.

After pulling myself up into a sitting position, I crawled into the driver's seat and was just about to turn the engine off when, out of nowhere, Darius's bloody and dirt-stained face appeared in the windshield to the left of the car.

"*You stupid bitch!*" he screamed.

The rush of adrenaline helped to clear my thoughts. Darius was already scrambling forward to reach for my door handle, so I threw the car in reverse, punched the gas and turned the steering wheel left again, hard. Darius was thrown away from the car once again, and I raced away.

Somehow, I managed to get back down the cliffside road, and I thought it was probably a good thing I didn't actually know how close I'd come to going off the top of the cliff.

When I got to the bottom and the main road, I hit the brakes and just sat there, panting heavily again. I felt nauseous and dizzy and unable to drive even an inch farther. So I laid my head down on the steering column, reaching up to push weakly on the horn with my left hand.

The horn bleeped, and I let up on the pressure and then pressed down again to give another short beep, then three long beeps and three short beeps. I kept that pattern up through sheer force of will until there was a knock on my door.

I stopped hitting the horn and gasped, thinking it was Darius again, come to finish me off.

"Cat?" Shepherd said.

Lifting my head ever so slightly and opening one eye, I saw him wearing a frantic look and trying the door handle, but the automatic locks had kicked in.

"Cat! Let me in!" he said.

I turned my face away, closed my eyes, and fumbled around for the door handle. After pulling on it, I felt the door open and a rush of fresh air hit my cheek.

"Cat?" Shepherd said, laying very gentle hands on my shoulders. "Cat?"

"I need help," I squeaked. Tears leaked out of my closed lids.

"I'm here," he said. "I'm here."

Chapter 20

I was on a solid week of bed rest and bored out of my mind. Gilley propped me up with a dozen pillows, and every four hours he fed me a little something to help with the lingering nausea. I'd sustained a terrible concussion, and the doctors had told me I'd need at least a week of bed rest until my dizziness subsided, and then I'd have to take it easy for the next few months, while my brain healed.

The CT scan hadn't shown any bleeding, thank God. That would've been a fine kettle of fish.

Shepherd came to stay with me every single night, after he got off from work. He and Santana had been able to put all the pieces together once I told them how I thought both Yelena and Purdy's murders had gone down.

Even better, when they found video of Darius purchasing the size ten raincoat from a local department store, *and* discovered that he'd withdrawn two-hundred thousand dollars from his private savings account on the day of Yelena and Purdy's murders, they knew they had Darius dead to rights with the circumstantial evidence.

When presented with all the evidence, and the fact that only the worst attorney in the Hamptons would take his case after what he'd done to Marcus, Darius had confessed, simply to save himself from ending up at Rikers. The deal he made with the DA meant he'd be sent to another maximum-security prison in Kentucky.

Sunny had been cleared of all charges, and at least Darius had insisted that she'd had nothing to do with any of the murders. She was back home, still recovering from the shock of discovering that her cheating husband had fathered a child out of wedlock, murdered one of her closest friends, had attempted to kill her, Marcus, *and* me, and had allowed her to take the blame for at least one of those murders.

Let's just say it was a *lot* to process.

Gilley had floated between Chez Cat and Sunny's house, playing nursemaid and helping her with Finley. He would sweetly bring Spooks up the stairs to me every time he was about to leave me go to Sunny's for a few hours.

"How're we doing today, sugar?" he asked when he brought in my breakfast tray, Spooks padding along faithfully behind him.

I patted the bed, and Spooks jumped up and took up his usual spot, on the pillows next to me, his head resting on my shoulder.

"I'm feeling better each day, Gil."

"That's good!" Gilley said, setting the tray table down across my legs.

"How's Sunny?" I asked.

"She's getting better every day too. I think she's over the shock and finally moving on to angry."

"Let's hope she doesn't stay angry for too long."

Gilley crossed his fingers with one hand and removed the silver covering to the plate on the tray, revealing the most delicious set of blintzes I'd ever seen.

"Blueberry's your favorite, right?"

"Oh, my God," I said, clapping my hands in delight. I am a huge fan of blintzes.

Gilley flipped out a cloth napkin and placed it over my lap. "Pain pill today?"

"No," I said. "I'm starting to crave them, so . . . no."

"Good idea," he said, pocketing the vial. "I'll take these back to the pharmacy to be properly disposed of tomorrow, after I know that you don't still need one before bed."

I took a bite of a blintz and moaned. "That is insanely good, my friend."

"The trick is to have two pans going. You don't want your first crepe to dry out before you've cooked your second."

I wrapped my hands around one of his. "Thank you."

"You're welcome," he replied, swishing his hips happily. "Oh, and Marcus would like to come over for a visit."

I stared in shock at him. "Marcus? Marcus Brown?"

Gilley smirked. "The one and only."

"He's already out of the hospital?"

"Oh, yeah. He got out two days ago. He's allowed to move around for short periods of time. He's hired a driver and a nurse, and he wants to check in on you and Sunny, of course."

"Please tell him I said absolutely yes."

"I will," Gilley said. "Now, if you'll excuse—"

Gilley's phone rang, and he and I both jumped at the sound. After taking his cell out of his pocket, he stared at the screen.

"It's Michel, isn't it?" I said.

Gilley nodded.

"Gil, please, please talk to him. Please put the two of you out of your misery."

Gilley looked up at me, took a deep inhale, then pressed the TALK button. "Hey," he said.

Then he walked out of the room, taking my best wishes for him and Michel with him.

THE
COMING
REVOLUTION
IN
SOCIAL SECURITY

HD
7125
RC2
.1581

THE
COMING
REVOLUTION
IN
SOCIAL SECURITY

A. HAEWORTH ROBERTSON

RESTON PUBLISHING COMPANY, INC.
A Prentice-Hall Company
Reston, Virginia

Copyright © 1981 by A. Haeworth Robertson.

All rights reserved. No part of this publication may be reproduced, stored in a retrieval system, or transmitted, in any form or by any means, electronic, mechanical, photocopying, recording, or otherwise, without the prior written permission of the publisher, except by a reviewer who may quote brief passages in a review.

This publication is designed to provide accurate and authoritative information in regard to the subject matter covered. It is sold with the understanding that the publisher is not engaged in rendering legal, accounting, or other professional service. If legal advice or other expert assistance is required, the services of a competent professional person should be sought.

From a Declaration of Principles jointly adopted by a Committee of the American Bar Association and a Committee of Publishers and Associations.

In this book, the masculine pronoun "he" has occasionally been used to refer to both sexes for the sake of simplicity.

Manufactured in the United States of America
Composed by Science Press, Ephrata, Pennsylvania

Originally published under the same title by Security Press, Inc.

Library of Congress Cataloging in Publication Data

Robertson, A. Haeworth
    The coming revolution in social security.

    Includes bibliographical references and index.
    1. Social security—United States. I. Title.
HD7125.R62   1981   368.4'3'00973   81-4700
                                                    AACR2

ISBN 0-8359-0880-1

To
my parents
Al and Bonnie Robertson
and my children
Valerie, Alan, and Mary
two distinct generations
with immeasurable influence
on the preparation of this book

Social Security is an enormous program providing financial support to millions of people. Yet, only a very few people understand the system in all its complexity. Who is eligible for benefits and why? Are benefits "earned" and how are they financed? What is the effect of the system on the economy? Where is Social Security headed in the decades ahead? *The Coming Revolution in Social Security*, by Mr. A. Haeworth Robertson, is a candid look at Social Security that provides insight into each of these questions. Mr. Robertson uses "straight talk" to unravel the complexities and the misunderstandings surrounding Social Security. While not everyone will agree with its conclusion, I am confident that everyone can benefit from reading *The Coming Revolution*. It is a timely and important book that comes to us during a crucial period in the history of Social Security.

Senator Bob Dole
Chairman, Committee on Finance
United States Senate

Contents

CONTENTS

PART THREE
COMMENTARY ON SELECTED TOPICS

CONTENTS

PART FOUR
THE FREEDOM PLAN

List of Charts

List of Tables

LIST OF TABLES

Preface

In 1975, only six months after becoming Chief Actuary of the United States Social Security Administration, I concluded that the most important problem confronting Social Security in the immediate future was the widespread lack of understanding of the program—its basic rationale, the type and level of benefits it provides, the method of financing, the significance of its high future cost, and the tenuous relationship between taxes paid and benefits received by an individual. For the most part, people's ideas about Social Security were wrong. It was natural, therefore, that the program could not satisfy their expectations. Furthermore, it was evident that as taxes continued their inexorable rise this frustration and disenchantment would get worse and not better.

Immediately I began trying to clarify these issues by talking with anyone who would listen to me—inside or outside the government. People were thirsting for knowledge about Social Security, yet there was no single source of written information concerning the many questions being asked. As time went by and I developed simplified answers to these never-ending questions, I decided the most effective way to communicate with a broad audience would be to write a book on the subject—a book that could be read and understood by nontechnicians.

At first I thought a mere explanation of what Social Security really is would suffice. In fact, that is all I could do while working as an actuary responsible for estimating the future costs of Social Security. It was not appropriate for me to criticize Social Security or propose major changes. One night in

Atlanta, however, after I had addressed a group of actuaries and other businesspeople, the audience was almost frantic in asking, "What do we do to resolve these problems?" They virtually demanded a solution. This experience, repeated over and over, demonstrated that any book on Social Security should also include suggestions for change—and a new dimension was added to my mission. I soon developed a personal sense of urgency about my "outreach project," as the Commissioner of Social Security used to call it, and in 1978 left the Social Security Administration to have the time and freedom to prepare this book.

Some of the material in the book is an elaboration of ideas advanced orally while serving as the William Elliott Lecturer, College of Business Administration, The Pennsylvania State University, in April 1978, and presented in writing in a commentary entitled *Social Security—Prospect for Change,* prepared for the National Chamber Foundation and presented at the Sixty-sixth Annual Meeting of the Chamber of Commerce of the United States on May 1, 1978.

Many people encouraged and assisted me. I am grateful to the consulting firm with which I am associated, William M. Mercer, Incorporated, for the many accommodations necessary to develop and write the book. Chapter 3, in particular, draws heavily upon a summary of the Social Security Act published semi-annually by Mercer. I wish to acknowledge the cooperation of the actuarial staff of the Social Security Administration, headed by Chief Actuary Dwight K. Bartlett and Deputy Chief Actuaries Harry C. Ballantyne and Francisco R. Bayo, and the actuarial staff of the Health Care Financing Administration, headed by Roland E. King, Acting Director, Office of Financial and Actuarial Analysis. The actuarial work performed by these staffs is crucial to ensure that we are able to honor our commitments to future generations.

Although it is not practical to acknowledge everyone who helped me with this particular work as well as with prior endeavors that made this book possible, I would mention a few individuals who were of particular assistance: Richard S. Foster, Actuary, Social Security Administration; Maynard I. Kagen, Director of Research, Railroad Retirement Board; and Robert W. Kalman, Consultant/Public Employee Benefits,

William M. Mercer, Incorporated. Valerie L. Robertson, my
daughter, provided the invaluable talent needed to prepare an
accurate and consistent manuscript. The views expressed
herein are strictly mine, of course, and not necessarily those of
my employer or anyone else who helped me.

It is unfortunate that the public perception of Social Security
has been allowed to grow so far apart from the reality. This has
created a serious dilemma for Social Security. If public misunderstanding is allowed to persist, confusion and disappointment will worsen because Social Security will continue its
failure to match most of the public's expectations; and this will
result in a frenzied cry for change. On the other hand, if the
misunderstanding is eliminated it is probable that the public
will not like what it sees and thus will demand significant
revision. In either event, therefore, a big change is on the
horizon. *There is a coming revolution in Social Security.*

This book is dedicated to the premise that any new Social
Security system should arise from a clearheaded appraisal of
our existing system and not from our present state of bewilder-
ment. This should permit a more reasoned transition, even if it
is no less traumatic.

Washington, D.C.   A. Haeworth Robertson
January 20, 1981

THE
COMING
REVOLUTION
IN
SOCIAL SECURITY

Part One
Introduction

*"What you don't know won't hurt you" may be an appropri-
ate maxim in many situations, but Social Security is not one of
them. There is widespread misunderstanding about Social
Security, an institution having a pervasive effect on our lives
and the lives of our children. Part One raises questions to
heighten the awareness of the need to learn more about Social
Security—before it is too late.*

1
The Slumbering Giant Awakens

Social Security, a slumbering giant for the last forty years, is finally awakening—rapidly and noisily. Is it friend or foe? Without a closer examination we cannot be sure.

Most of us don't understand what Social Security is all about. The general purposes of Social Security, the types and levels of benefits it provides, how it is financed, the relation between an individual's taxes and benefits—all of these areas are sources of confusion or uncertainty to many people.

Most of us don't realize how large Social Security has become or how rapidly it will grow in the future. In 1940 the Social Security program paid out less than $1 billion in benefits and administrative expenses; in 1979 it paid out $138 billion; in 1990 it will pay out an estimated $387 billion. During the next ten years, 1981 through 1990, it is estimated that about $2,734 billion will be paid out in benefits and administrative expenses.[1] In December 1979 Social Security monthly cash benefits were paid to 35 million persons, one out of every seven Americans.

But what Social Security pays out in benefits it must first collect in taxes.

In 1979, 114 million workers paid about $65 billion in Social Security taxes, an average of roughly $570 per person. For many American workers, probably at least a fourth, their Social Security tax is greater than their federal income tax. Ten years

3

ago (1970) the average Social Security tax paid by each taxpayer was about $220; ten years from now (1990) it is estimated that it will be $1,450.

In addition to these taxes paid directly by individuals, an approximately equal amount was paid by their employers.[2] Total income to the Social Security program in 1979, most of it from taxes of one kind or another, was some $138 billion ($138,455,480,515.72 to be precise).

Some Questions

What do we get for our money? What do you know about your own Social Security benefits? How much, if anything will you receive if today you become disabled and are unable to work any longer? Can you work part time and still collect disability benefits? Are your benefits higher if you are married? And have children? If Social Security benefits are not adequate to support you and your family, and if your spouse goes to work to supplement your income, will any of these benefits be forfeited?

If you die tomorrow will any benefits be paid to your spouse, children, parents? If so, how much? How long will the benefits be paid? Will this be enough to support your family? Will your spouse be able to work without forfeiting these benefits? Should you buy life insurance to supplement your Social Security benefits? If so, how much should you buy?

If you stay in good health and work until age 65, will you be eligible for a retirement benefit from Social Security? If so, how much will it be? Are there any strings attached to its payment? Can you continue working after age 65 and still receive your Social Security benefits? Can you collect the benefits if you move to another country when you retire? Will these benefits be enough to support you and your family? Should you have your own private savings program in order to supplement your Social Security benefits?

How much will you personally pay in Social Security taxes this year? Did you know that your employer will also pay this same amount? To get an idea of how much you and your employer pay in Social Security taxes, examine the following figures which show the amount of such taxes paid in 1980 for three employees with different levels of pay.

	Social Security Taxes		
	Paid by	Paid by	
Earnings in 1980	Employee	Employer	Total
$ 6,000	$ 367.80	$ 367.80	$ 735.60
$12,000	$ 735.60	$ 735.60	$1,471.20
$25,900 or more	$1,587.67	$1,587.67	$3,175.34

The maximum tax paid by the employee and employer combined is estimated by the Social Security Administration to rise from $3,175.34 in 1980 to $8,078 by 1990, just ten years from now. This increase is due in part to a scheduled increase in the tax rate and in part to a projected increase in the maximum amount of earnings subject to tax (an estimated $52,800 in 1990).[3]

A person who is self-employed and thus doesn't have an employer to share the cost pays somewhat higher taxes than those paid by an employee (but lower than the total taxes paid by employees and employers combined). The following figures show the Social Security taxes paid in 1980 by three self-employed persons with different levels of earnings.

Self-Employment Earnings in 1980	Social Security Taxes
$ 6,000	$ 486.00
$12,000	$ 972.00
$25,900 or more	$2,097.90

The maximum tax paid by self-employed persons is estimated by the Social Security Administration to rise from $2,097.90 in 1980 to $5,676 by 1990.

Do you spend this much money for anything else and know so little about what you get for your money? Whose fault is it that you do not know more about your Social Security benefits? Did you know that there are millions of people in the United States who do not participate in Social Security and thus do not pay its taxes and receive its benefits?

Is Social Security going bankrupt? Will there be enough money to pay your benefits when you retire? In 1950 the Social Security Trust Funds had enough money to pay benefits for twelve years (at the rate benefits were being paid in 1950); in 1960 there was enough money to pay benefits for about two years; at the beginning of 1980 there was enough money left to pay benefits for only about three months. What happened to all the money you and your employers paid into the Social Security Trust Funds?

If you don't know the answers to any or all of these questions, don't feel left out. Not many people know the answers. Social Security is one of the least understood, perhaps I should say most misunderstood, programs around. This misunderstanding of Social Security is not unique to us in America. In my travels and work with social insurance programs around the world, I have found this confusion everywhere—in sophisticated industrial economies as well as in emerging agricultural economies.

The Problem

Social Security has been roundly criticized in recent months. Complaints are heard about its financial condition, the inadequacy of its benefits, the overadequacy of its benefits, the fact that some persons receive more in benefits than they pay in taxes, the fact that some people receive less in benefits than they pay in taxes, and so on. Although some of these criticisms are valid, many are not. And none of them poses a real threat to Social Security at this time.

The most serious threat to Social Security in the immediate future is the widespread misunderstanding of the program. Why is this misunderstanding a threat? Because the very survival of Social Security depends upon our continued ability and willingness to pay the taxes necessary to support the benefit payments. It is not reasonable to expect this support to continue if we do not understand and approve of the Social Security program.

The Social Security program is not what most people think it is. It is not what many critics think it is. Because of this, it does not always behave the way we think it should. Therefore, it is natural for us to resent the program, the Congressmen who adopted it, the Social Security Administration and the Health Care Financing Administration which administer it, and most of all the tax collectors who take our hard-earned money and use it in ways that are different from the ways we thought it would be used.

The Social Security program does not have a chance of being successful until we understand it. Once we know what the program is and we decide what we believe our income security needs are, we can compare what we have with what we want. If they are the same, then we can congratulate ourselves and our leaders who designed Social Security over the years and be content. If they are different, we can set about to change the program to better suit our needs. Until then—until we really understand what the present Social Security program is—all discussions of the program will be chaotic and most of the proposed changes will be nonsensical.

The Solution—The First Step

Part Two of this book presents basic background information on Social Security and has one purpose: to help you understand the Social Security program in its present form. This is the first step toward accepting the program as it is or revising the program to make it what you want it to be.

This book is intended to be constructive. It is intended to be based on facts and objective analysis, not on fantasies and uninformed opinions. It is intended to explain the Social Security program as it is, not as others would like us to believe it is.

Many of you will not like what you read. Some people have been shocked at the explanations in this book. Some will consider the book an exposé of Social Security. The book will probably be looked upon with disfavor by certain special interest groups and by some planners and administrators of social insurance. Some will view the book's publication as heresy and not in the best interest of the public.

Why would anyone object to this book? In some cases, because "they" know what is best for you; because you (the public) do not know enough to decide what is best for you; and because, in order to enact and perpetuate a social insurance program which "they" believe is best for you, it is acceptable to do whatever is necessary to sell the program to you—the consumer—and to the Congress which must enact it. If half-truths, omissions, or misleading statements are necessary, some will use them on the theory that the end justifies the means.

Does the End Justify the Means?

In our complicated and technical society, there are undoubtedly issues that can be fully understood and evaluated only by a small group of informed experts. In these cases, the public must place substantial trust in its leaders.

For example, how is an average person to know for certain how much money should be spent for defense in order for America to remain a free and independent nation? What is the real threat to our freedom from other countries with different ideologies, food shortages, land shortages, or demagogic leaders?

How is an average person to know what our national energy policy should be if we are to avoid crippling shortages in the future? Should we have gasoline rationing, higher gasoline taxes, restrictions on oil imports, improved public transportation facilities, smaller cars, increased nuclear and solar energy capabilities, or should we take some other action?

What about the current debate over environmentalism? How do we balance the trade-off between continued industrial growth and a less healthful environment? How much is our increasingly crowded and polluted environment threatening our physical, emotional, and spiritual health?

In all these and many other areas we must rely heavily upon experts, people who study these matters full time. But we ourselves should also be as fully informed as possible. We must not leave important decisions exclusively to the experts or to the politicians who act, sometimes solely, on their advice. This would seem obvious from recent revelations concerning activities by the government and its various agencies where decisions were made by individuals and select groups of experts who did not think they were accountable to the public and who did not think the public knew what was best for it.

But what about the Social Security program? Is it so difficult a subject that only the experts can understand it? Is it so complex that we have no choice but to leave it to the experts and politicians to decide what is best for us without our being told the facts? I don't think so.

Certainly, Social Security is complicated. Many aspects of Social Security are neither fully understood nor agreed upon by experts who have spent years studying it. Despite its complexity, there is no excuse for the failure to explain in plain words as much as possible about the program. It is time for us all to stop hiding behind the mystique created by the double-talk explanations that make it so difficult to understand Social Security. Let's tell it like it is. Let's make as many people as fully informed as possible about the Social Security program. Then if we do not like what we see, let's change it. The sooner the better.

Not a Textbook

This is not intended primarily to be a textbook on Social Security or a treatise on the mathematics of pensions and insurance. I hope it doesn't sound like one. Accordingly, it does not have many footnotes and citations and it skips over some details that are not essential for a general understanding of Social Security.

This book is written for people who pay for and benefit from the Social Security program—people who want to understand how their Social Security program works. My sincere hope is that this book will help you gain the understanding of our Social Security program that will be necessary if you and the Congress and the Administration are to get together and cause the program to be changed so that it will meet our needs in a logical way and in accordance with our ability to pay for it.

If we do not gain a better understanding of our Social Security program and then either accept it or change it to satisfy our desires, the consequences are frightening.

Part Two
Basic Background
Information

For most of us, our knowledge of Social Security is based upon a hodgepodge of information we have gathered from radio, television, newspapers, magazines, employers, and friends. This is a difficult way to learn, especially when many of the fragments of information are misleading or even incorrect. It is no wonder that myths and misinformation abound.

Part Two is designed for the reader willing to discard all past information and misinformation received about Social Security and start with a clean slate. Chapters 2 through 7 present systematically the basic background information necessary to understand what Social Security is, how it works, and what it costs.

2
Social Security—
An Overview

Congress passed the Social Security Act in 1935 and it became effective on January 1, 1937. The original legislation has been amended many times since then and has become a complex maze of laws, rules, and regulations governing and influencing the lives of all Americans in one way or another. Some of these influences are obvious; others are not. Some of these influences are favorable; others may or may not be depending upon your viewpoint. This chapter gives a brief overview of some but not all of the many aspects of Social Security.

What Is Social Security?

Mention Social Security to a dozen people and they will conjure up a dozen different ideas—and for good reason. The *Social Security Handbook*[1] published by the government contains 530 pages of explanation of the Social Security Act and then refers the reader to thousands of additional pages of explanation contained in other volumes. In describing Social Security, this handbook makes a general statement,[2] which may be paraphrased fairly as follows:

> The Social Security Act and related laws establish a number of programs that have the basic objectives of

13

providing for the material needs of individuals and families, protecting aged and disabled persons against the expenses of illnesses that could otherwise exhaust their savings, keeping families together, and giving children the opportunity to grow up in health and security. These programs include:

    Retirement Insurance (frequently referred to as
        Old-Age Insurance)
    Survivors Insurance
    Disability Insurance
    Medicare for the aged and the disabled:
      Hospital Insurance
      Supplementary Medical Insurance
    Black Lung Benefits
    Supplemental Security Income
    Unemployment Insurance
    Public Assistance and Welfare Services:
      Aid to needy families with children
      Medical assistance
      Maternal and child-health services
      Services for crippled children
      Child welfare services

The federal government operates the first six programs listed above. The remaining programs are operated by the states with the federal government cooperating and contributing funds.

This book limits itself to a discussion of the first four programs listed above and refers to them collectively as Social Security. This is partly for simplicity but largely because these four programs are financed primarily by the Social Security payroll taxes paid by employees, employers, and self-employed persons, and thus are usually thought of by the public as Social Security. (The Supplementary Medical Insurance program, "Part B" of Medicare, is not financed by payroll taxes but rather by premiums paid by those electing to be covered and by general revenue.)

Who Participates in Social Security?

Who is covered by Social Security and is therefore eligible for Old-Age, Survivors, Disability, and Medicare benefits?

When Social Security took effect in 1937 it applied only to workers in industry and commerce and covered only about 60 percent of all working persons. Since then there has been a steady movement toward covering as many workers as possible under Social Security, and universal coverage has clearly been the ultimate goal. In the 1950s, coverage was extended to include most self-employed persons, most state and local government employees, household and farm employees, members of the armed forces, and members of the clergy. Approximately 90 percent of all jobs in the United States are now covered by Social Security. Chart 2.A illustrates the growth in coverage over the years.

The principal groups that are not now covered automatically by Social Security are as follows:

> Civilian employees of the federal government (military employees are covered by Social Security)
>
> Employees of state and local governments
>
> Employees of religious, charitable, and other nonprofit organizations
>
> Farm and domestic workers with irregular employment
>
> Low-income, self-employed persons

Chart 2.A

Workers in Covered and Noncovered Employment, 1940 and 1978

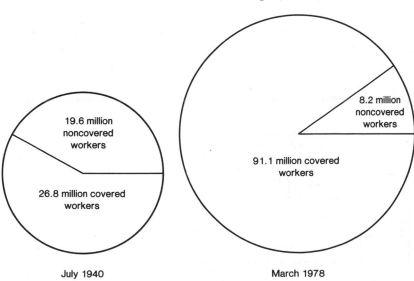

19.6 million noncovered workers

26.8 million covered workers

8.2 million noncovered workers

91.1 million covered workers

July 1940

March 1978

Chart 2.B illustrates the number of persons in these categories whose jobs are not covered by Social Security.[3] Considerable publicity has been given to the fact that most employees of the federal government are not covered by Social Security as a part of their government employment. Participation is optional for employees of state and local governments and for employees of nonprofit organizations. The fact that some employees of state and local governments have recently "opted out" of Social Security has given rise to considerable controversy. A typical reaction is, "If they can opt out, why can't I?" A few words of background on some of these employee groups may help explain the situation.

Federal Government Employees

In 1920 the civil service retirement system was established to provide retirement and other benefits to civilian employees of the federal government. It was not particularly unusual, therefore, when Social Security began operation on January 1, 1937,

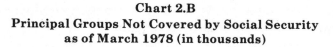

Chart 2.B
Principal Groups Not Covered by Social Security
as of March 1978 (in thousands)

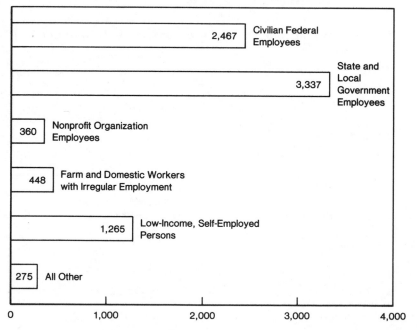

that federal government employees were excluded from it. On the other hand, it would have been logical to include federal government employees in Social Security and to adjust the benefits under the civil service retirement system accordingly. This is what most private employers did and still do; that is, they coordinate, or integrate, their private benefit systems with Social Security so that the two systems taken together provide the desired benefits.

Federal government employees have long been opposed to entering Social Security. One reason for this opposition is that the process of coordinating the two systems has not been explained adequately. Many federal employees believe, without justification, that if they entered Social Security their civil service retirement system would be abolished completely. Other employees believe, without justification, that they would receive full benefits—and pay the full employee costs—of both Social Security and the civil service retirement system. Still other employees believe that if they entered Social Security the assets of their civil service retirement system would be used to rescue an ailing Social Security. No one is considering such a consolidation of assets, however; and even if they were, it would be fruitless since the total assets of the civil service retirement system would be enough to provide only about 2 percent of the total Social Security benefits that will be paid in the next ten years.

There are other reasons that federal government employees have opposed entry into Social Security. The long-service career employees who qualify for benefits under both systems enjoy a distinct advantage that would be lost if they participated fully in Social Security, and paid taxes, throughout their career. Also, government-employee unions have vigorously opposed participation in Social Security—in part, probably, because they would then have influence over a smaller segment of the employee benefit area (if the civil service retirement system were reduced in order to coordinate with Social Security).

State and Local Government Employees

When Social Security was enacted in 1935 it was considered unconstitutional for the federal government to tax state governments. And since Social Security is financed from taxes paid by employees and employers, state and local government employees were not included.

In keeping with the steady movement to make Social Security coverage as universal as possible, legislation was enacted in 1950 and later to provide that employees of state and local governments could be covered under Social Security on a voluntary basis under certain conditions. For example, Social Security coverage was made available on a group voluntary basis through agreements between the Secretary of Health, Education, and Welfare and the individual states. After coverage of the employees of a state, or of a political subdivision of the state, has been in effect for at least five years, the state may give notice of its intention to terminate the coverage of such employees. The termination of coverage becomes effective on December 31 of the second full calendar year after such notice is given, unless the state withdraws the notice of termination within such period. Once the termination becomes effective, however, it is irrevocable and the same group cannot be covered again under Social Security. So, state and local employees can opt in; they can then opt out; but they cannot reenter Social Security after having gone through such a procedure.

Approximately 10 million state and local employees, about 75 percent of the total, are covered by Social Security under voluntary participation arrangements. Compared with these 10 million participants, the number of employees who have voluntarily terminated is very small. A total of about 130,000 employees have terminated during the program's entire history through June 1980. Most of these terminations have occurred within the last five years. There is still a relatively large number of pending terminations, hence this trend may continue for awhile longer. More detailed information on voluntary terminations is contained in Chapter 17.

In mid-1980 several states had never elected to enter Social Security: Colorado, Louisiana, Maine, Massachusetts, Nevada, and Ohio. Three of these states—Colorado, Maine, and Nevada—include teachers in their general state retirement systems; hence their teachers are not covered by Social Security. In ten states or jurisdictions with statewide teachers' systems, teachers are not covered by Social Security: Alaska,

California, Connecticut, Illinois, Kentucky, Louisiana, Massachusetts, Missouri, Ohio, and Puerto Rico.

The states that have not elected to enter Social Security maintain programs of retirement and other benefits for their employees that are more liberal than Social Security in some respects and less liberal in others. A strict comparison of benefits is difficult because of the basic differences between Social Security and most public employee systems. For various reasons, some states prefer to continue their own employee benefit programs and to remain outside of Social Security.

Alaska is the only state that has elected to cover its employees under Social Security and then terminated such coverage. The Alaska termination became effective December 31, 1979, and affected approximately 14,500 employees.

Employees of Nonprofit Organizations

Nonprofit organizations were not required to participate in Social Security when it was enacted, because of their tax-exempt status. Imposition of the employer Social Security tax on the organization would have violated this tax-exempt status.

Legislation has been enacted over the years to permit nonprofit organizations to be covered by Social Security on a voluntary basis. Today approximately 90 percent of the 4 million employees of nonprofit organizations have elected to be covered by Social Security.

Increased Possibility of Universal Coverage

As already indicated, during the entire history of the Social Security program the trend has been toward broader coverage. The increasing attention given in recent years to the question of Social Security coverage, how widespread it is and how widespread it "should be," was reflected in the Social Security Amendments of 1977. In these amendments, Congress directed the Secretary of Health, Education, and Welfare to undertake a study of the "feasibility and desirability" of covering federal employees, state and local government employees, and employees of nonprofit organizations under the Old-Age and Survivors Insurance, Disability Insurance, and Hospital Insurance programs on a mandatory basis. This study,[4] completed in March 1980, presented and discussed several options for achieving universal coverage but stopped short of recommending any specific option. Several other advisory groups and commissions are studying this question, and it is possible that their findings will result eventually in virtually universal coverage of the nation's work force by the Social Security program.

What Benefits Are Provided?

Because of the complexity of Social Security this chapter will give only an overview of the benefits provided. More detail is included in Chapter 3. The idea at this point is to explain how Social Security works in general, not to enable you to determine the benefits you would receive in a particular case. If you need specific information concerning your own situation, it is normally best to contact your local Social Security Administration office.

In a nutshell: *Social Security replaces a portion of the earnings that are lost as a result of a person's old age, disability, or death, and pays a portion of the expenses of illness of aged and disabled persons.*

The benefits that are provided under the Old-Age, Survivors, and Disability Insurance programs (usually referred to as OASDI) are as follows:

> Monthly benefits for workers who are retired or partially retired and are at least 62 years old, and monthly benefits for their eligible spouses and dependents
>
> Monthly benefits for disabled workers and their eligible spouses and dependents
>
> Monthly benefits for the eligible survivors of deceased workers
>
> A lump-sum death benefit payment for each worker

To be eligible to receive these benefits at the time of retirement, disability, or death, a person must satisfy several conditions that are different for each type of benefit. In addition, a person's spouse and dependents or survivors must satisfy a variety of requirements to be eligible for benefits. These requirements, which are somewhat complex, are described in more detail in Chapter 3.

As of June 30, 1979, approximately 35 million persons were receiving monthly Social Security benefit payments. That was more than one out of every seven persons since in mid-1979 there were approximately 231 million persons in the United States.[5] Total cash benefit payments in fiscal year 1979 amounted to $101 billion. Chart 2.C illustrates for fiscal year 1979 the numbers of OASDI beneficiaries and the amount of their benefits in each of the various categories.

The Medicare program has two parts, Hospital Insurance (HI) and Supplementary Medical Insurance (SMI). The Hospital Insurance program, which is compulsory for those covered by Social Security, provides benefits for persons aged 65 or older and persons receiving Social Security disability benefits for more than twenty-four months. The program helps pay for inpatient hospital care and for certain follow-up care after leaving the hospital.

The Supplementary Medical Insurance program, which is voluntary, is offered to almost all persons aged 65 and over. In addition, the program is offered to all disabled Social Security beneficiaries who have received disability benefits for more than twenty-four months. The program helps pay for doctors' services, outpatient hospital services, and many other medical items and services not covered by the Hospital Insurance program.

During 1979, an average of 24.1 million persons aged 65 and over were covered under the Hospital Insurance program (that is, were eligible for hospital benefits in the event of illness). This represented 95 percent of all persons aged 65 and over in the United States and its territories. Another 2.9 million disabled persons under age 65 were covered by Hospital Insurance.

Approximately 23.8 million persons aged 65 and over were covered under the Supplementary Medical Insurance program in 1979. Again, this represented about 95 percent of all persons aged 65 and over in the United States and its territories. Another 2.7 million disabled persons under age 65 were covered by Supplementary Medical Insurance.

It is estimated that the total benefit payments in 1978 of $24.9 billion under the Hospital Insurance and Supplementary

Chart 2.C

OASDI Beneficiaries as of June 30, 1979 and Amount of
Benefits in Fiscal Year 1979, by Type of Beneficiary

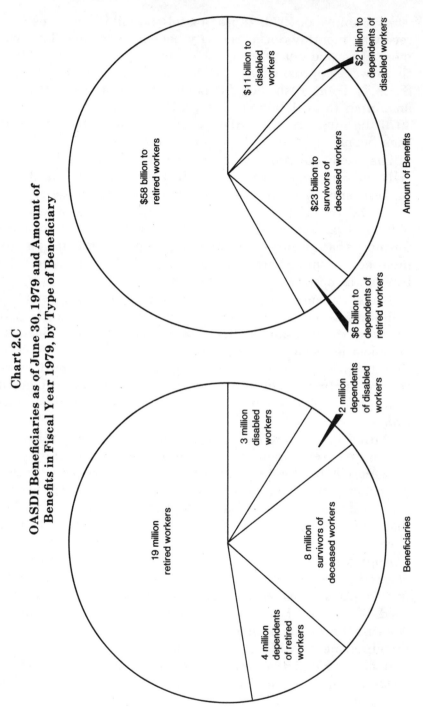

Medical Insurance programs represented approximately 45 percent of the total medical expenses of the persons participating in the two programs.[6]

Who Administers Social Security?

Social Security is administered by the Social Security Administration and the Health Care Financing Administration. For fiscal year 1979, these agencies of the Department of Health, Education, and Welfare accounted for roughly 60 percent of the total employees and 75 percent of the total expenditures of the Department.[7] Even more important, they accounted for approximately 27 percent of total government expenditures.[8]

The Social Security Administration (SSA) administers the Old-Age, Survivors, and Disability Insurance program, along with several other programs not included in our present discussion of Social Security; for example, the Supplemental Security Income program and Aid to Families with Dependent Children. The determination of eligibility for disability benefits is handled by state agencies under contract to the Social Security Administration.

The Health Care Financing Administration (HCFA) administers the Medicare program, both Hospital Insurance and Supplementary Medical Insurance. It also oversees Medicaid, a program providing hospital and medical expense benefits for the needy—not considered part of Social Security in our present discussion. Prior to the formation of HCFA in March 1977, Medicare was administered by the Social Security Administration and Medicaid was administered by the Social and Rehabilitation Service.

Social Security taxes are collected for the Social Security Administration and the Health Care Financing Administration by the Internal Revenue Service. The Department of the Treasury issues the benefit checks, at the direction of the Managing Trustee of the Social Security Trust Funds, on the basis of benefit certifications by the Social Security Administration and the Health Care Financing Administration.

The Social Security Administration had 1,325 district and branch offices in operation around the country in 1978, facilities normally shared with the Health Care Financing Administration. Most administrative contact with the public is handled by these district and branch offices which issue Social Security cards, process benefit claims, provide information about the program, and help resolve participants' problems. The local offices are supervised and assisted by ten regional offices. In addition, about thirty "teleservice centers" around the country provide assistance to participants by telephone, in order to give more prompt service and reduce the need for visits by the public to local offices.

The Social Security Administration's national headquarters, or central office as it is called, is located primarily in Baltimore, Maryland (with some offices in Washington, D.C.). The central office maintains the records of the millions of participants and oversees and directs the operation of the OASDI program and all its regional and local offices. The Health Care Financing Administration is also headquartered in Baltimore and Washington. To operate these offices and administer the Social Security program, there is a staff of some 80,000 people including about 20,000 in the central offices. This is not an unduly large administrative staff relative to the size and complexity of the program involved. Administrative expenses for the OASDI and Medicare programs combined were $2.5 billion in 1979, only 1.9 percent of total benefits paid during the year. With an appropriately increased budget, the Social Security Administration could provide better administrative service and do a more thorough job of explaining Social Security to the public, something that is certainly important at this critical time in the history of Social Security.

Conclusion

Any overview of Social Security reveals it to be almost overwhelming in size and complexity. Directly or indirectly, Social Security touches the lives of virtually every resident of the U.S., and it is startling to become more aware of its growing influence on our lives, individually and collectively as a nation. Social Security's significance to us and our children must not be underestimated if we are to retain any control over our lives.

3
Social Security Benefits

Social Security is simple in concept but complicated in actual operation. Essentially, Social Security replaces a portion of earned income that is lost as a result of a person's retirement, disability, or death; and it pays a portion of the hospital and medical expenses of aged and disabled persons. The complications arise in determining:

> when a person is eligible to *begin* receiving benefits;
> the amount of the benefits; and
> when a person is no longer eligible to *continue* receiving benefits.

To explain all this in an efficient way requires that a few definitions and explanations be given at the start. This will also make the subsequent commentary on benefits easier to follow. You should probably not expect to learn how to calculate your exact benefits and the precise conditions under which they will be payable. On the other hand, you should understand Social Security well enough to know when you and your family members may be eligible for benefits and the approximate amounts of such benefits. This will enable you to obtain maximum advantage from Social Security and your tax dollar.

Eligibility for Benefits to Begin

Monthly benefits can be payable to a wide variety of persons, or beneficiaries as they are sometimes called. Benefits can be paid to you as a worker, as well as to your spouse, children, grandchildren, and parents. They can even be payable to a divorced wife, a stepparent, a foster parent who adopted you before age 16, a stepchild, a legally adopted child, and an illegitimate child.

Various requirements must be met before benefits are payable to you or members of your family. An important underlying requirement for the payment of most benefits is that you have paid Social Security taxes for certain minimum periods called "quarters of coverage." During each year before 1978 a quarter of coverage was given for each calendar quarter in which you paid Social Security taxes on at least $50 of wages for employment covered under the law. In 1978 one quarter of coverage was credited (up to a total of four) for each $250 of wages on which you paid Social Security taxes. After 1978 this $250 amount is subject to an automatic increase each year to reflect increases in average wages of the nation's workers. For 1979 the amount was $260, for 1980 it was $290, and for 1981 it is $310. It will continue to rise in future years as average wages increase. For self-employed workers, quarters of coverage for 1978 and later are earned on the same basis as for employees. Prior to 1978, four quarters of coverage were earned for any year in which at least $400 of self-employment income was reported.

An individual has different levels of "insured status" depending upon the number of quarters of coverage that have been credited and the recency with which they have been earned. Different benefits require different levels of "insured status." There is a "currently insured" status, a "fully insured" status, and a "disability insured" status. All of this special terminology is the same as that used by the Social Security Administration.

Currently Insured Status

To be "currently insured" an individual must have at least six quarters of coverage in the thirteen-quarter period ending with the quarter in which death or entitlement to old-age or disability benefits occurs. This level of insured status is easily maintained by a steady worker in employment covered by Social Security.

Fully Insured Status

To be "fully insured" an individual usually must have at least one quarter of coverage for each year after 1950 (or, if later, the year of attainment of age 21) and before the year of death, disability, or attainment of age 62, whichever occurs first. A minimum of six and a maximum of forty quarters of coverage is required. Once fully insured status for retirement benefits is acquired, it continues throughout life and no further work in covered employment is needed. The attainment of this permanent fully insured status relates only to *eligibility* for benefits and not the *amount* of the benefits. The quarters of coverage do not have to be earned during the period used to define the required number of quarters. They can be earned also before or after that period.

Disability Insured Status

To be eligible for disability benefits, an individual must be both fully insured and:

> have earned at least twenty quarters of coverage during the forty-calendar-quarter period ending with the quarter in which disability begins; or

> if disability begins before age 31, have earned at least one half the quarters of coverage possible during the period after the attainment of age 21 and the quarter in which disability begins. (A minimum of six quarters of coverage earned during the preceding three years is required if disability begins before age 24.)

For an individual who meets the statutory definition of blindness, only the fully insured requirement need be met.

In addition to the insured status requirements, other conditions must be met before benefits will be payable to you or your dependents. These will be mentioned later when the various specific benefits are discussed.

Amount of Benefits

The amount of monthly cash benefits paid by Social Security is based principally upon the following factors:

> The average earnings upon which you have paid Social Security taxes, excluding earnings for certain years

and adjusted for changes over the years in the average
earnings of the nation's workers

The number and kind of your family members

Consumer Price Index changes that occur after you become
eligible for benefits

Furthermore, the amount of monthly cash benefits may be
reduced, or even terminated, as a result of earnings by you and
your family members after becoming eligible for benefits.

Medicare benefits, on the other hand, are the same for
everyone who is eligible for them and are not affected by
average earnings on which you have paid Social Security taxes,
or earnings after becoming eligible for benefits.

For the time being, let us concentrate on the amount of
monthly cash benefits initially payable to any given beneficiary,
ignoring subsequent upward adjustments because of changes in
the Consumer Price Index and downward adjustments because
of an individual's earned income.

The key factor in determining monthly cash benefits initially
payable is the Primary Insurance Amount. All monthly cash
benefits are based upon the Primary Insurance Amount. The
Primary Insurance Amount (PIA) is the monthly benefit
payable to a disabled worker or to a worker at the normal
retirement age of 65 before application of any delayed retirement credit. For those who attain age 62, become disabled, or
die in 1979 and later, the PIA is determined by a formula
applied to the individual's Average Indexed Monthly Earnings.
(Some individuals becoming eligible for benefits before 1984
may have their benefits calculated under an alternative procedure to permit a smoother transition to this new calculation
method.) Determination of the Average Indexed Monthly
Earnings is somewhat complicated; it is computed for retirement and disability benefits approximately as follows:

Only earnings on which Social Security taxes are paid are
used. Thus, earnings in excess of the maximum taxable
earnings in each year are not included. Table 6.2 in
Chapter 6 lists the maximum taxable earnings for each
year in the past. The amount has increased from
$3,000 prior to 1951 to $29,700 in 1981, and will
continue to increase in the future as average wages of
the nation's workers increase.

Only earnings after 1950 (or, with some exceptions, after the year a person reached age 21, if later), and up to and including the year before entitlement to old-age or disability benefits, are used (except as noted below).

Earnings in prior years are "indexed" by applying a ratio to the individual's earnings for each year. The ratio is the average earnings of all the nation's employees in the second year before the year of the individual's eligibility for benefits, divided by the average earnings of all the nation's employees in the year being indexed. For example, an individual with $3,600 of taxable earnings in 1951 who reached age 62 in 1979 would have these earnings indexed to become $12,577.34, thus adjusting the old earnings approximately to their equivalent value today.

The average of these indexed earnings is then computed, substituting years of actual earnings at age 61 and later if it increases the resulting average indexed earnings, and leaving out as many as five years of the lowest indexed earnings.

This is a rather complicated process intended to produce average earnings that are representative of the value of today's dollar and today's earnings. It is important to note that average earnings are based on virtually an entire working career; accordingly, years of no earnings or low earnings can result in reduced average earnings and thus in reduced benefits. People sometimes erroneously assume that if they are *fully insured* they are eligible for *maximum benefits.*

There is a limit on the total amount of benefits payable in any month to members of one family. This limit varies according to the level of the PIA; while difficult to calculate exactly, it is generally in the range of 150 to 188 percent of the PIA in retirement and survivor cases. In disability cases it can vary from 100 to 150 percent of the PIA. In January 1980, the family maximum benefit for an age 65 career maximum earner was $1,000.60. Benefits for family members other than the primary beneficiary are reduced proportionately to the extent necessary to stay within the family maximum.

In considering the amount of Social Security benefits payable, it is important to note that they are not subject to federal, state, or local income tax. Also important is the fact that after benefits commence, they are increased automatically to reflect increases in the Consumer Price Index. Generally speaking, benefit increases are made in June each year if an increase of at least 3 percent is indicated.

Eligibility for Benefits to Continue

Once benefits begin, their continuation hinges upon a variety of conditions being satisfied, depending upon the particular benefit. In every case benefits to an individual stop upon his or her death. A disability benefit normally terminates shortly after the disability ends (at age 65 it is converted to an old-age benefit). Benefits payable to children stop at age 18 (age 22 if a full-time student), but not if the child was disabled before age 22; children's benefits also stop if the child marries. Benefits to widows and widowers who are caring for young children terminate when the children reach 18 (unless they are disabled). Benefits payable to widows and widowers sometimes cease upon remarriage, but frequently do not.

Benefits usually stop or are reduced if the individual receiving the benefits has earnings in excess of specified amounts. This is because of the provision in the law usually referred to as the earnings test or earnings limitation. Only earned income can result in a loss of benefits; unearned income (such as investment income, rental income, pensions and retirement pay) is not taken into account. The amount of the earnings limitation is different for beneficiaries under age 65 than for those aged 65 or older. An individual aged 72 or older can have unlimited earned income and continue to receive full Social Security benefits. Beginning in 1982 this age will be lowered to 70.

An individual between the ages of 65 and 72 (age 70 in 1982 and later) can have earned income of $5,500 in 1981 without affecting the receipt of Social Security benefits; however, benefits will be reduced by $1 for every $2 of earned income in excess of $5,500. This earnings limitation will increase to $6,000 in 1982 and it will increase thereafter to keep up with increases in average earnings of all the nation's employees.

An individual who is under age 65 can have earned income of $4,080 in 1981 without affecting the receipt of Social Security benefits. Benefits will be reduced by $1 for every $2 of earned income in excess of $4,080. This earnings limitation increases each year to keep up with increases in average earnings of all the nation's employees.

In the case of a worker and dependents receiving Social Security benefits as a result of taxes paid by the worker, earnings of the worker in excess of the earnings limitation will reduce the benefits of both the worker and the dependents. On the other hand, earnings of a dependent in excess of the earnings limitation will reduce only the dependent's benefits.

This earnings limitation applies to earnings of dependent beneficiaries of a disabled worker but not to earnings of the disabled worker. Different criteria than this earnings limitation are used to determine continued eligibility for disability benefits.

Retirement Benefits

An individual must be "fully insured" to be eligible for retirement benefits under Social Security (sometimes referred to as old-age benefits since that terminology is used in the law). Monthly retirement benefits can begin as early as age 62 and are payable for life. The starting date depends upon the individual's election and the individual's earned income after the starting date selected.

For retirement at age 65, the benefit payable to a fully insured individual is equal to his Primary Insurance Amount. This amount is subject to a "regular" minimum benefit, and a "special" minimum benefit designed for individuals with low earnings but many years of employment. For an individual retiring at age 65 in January 1980, the retirement benefit ranges from the regular minimum of $133.90 to a maximum (in normal circumstances) of $572.00 per month. The higher the worker's average earnings, the higher the benefit. The monthly benefit for an individual whose career earnings had always been the average for persons covered by Social Security would be approximately $450.00. After the retirement benefit begins, it increases with the benefit escalator provisions of the law.

If retirement is delayed beyond age 65 or if benefits are withheld under the earnings test, the benefit otherwise determined at actual retirement date is increased for each month that retirement is delayed. For individuals born in 1917 or later, the amount of the increase is $\frac{1}{4}$ of 1 percent for each month benefits are not received between ages 65 and 70. For individuals born before 1917, the amount of the increase is $\frac{1}{12}$ of 1 percent for each month (after 1970) that benefits are not received between ages 65 and 72. The increase applies to old-age benefits and widow's and widower's benefits only, and not to benefits to other family members.

Retirement may be elected as early as age 62 with the Primary Insurance Amount reduced by $\frac{5}{9}$ of 1 percent for each month that retirement precedes age 65.

Benefits are subject to reduction or complete withholding between ages 62 and 72 if the individual's earned income exceeds the earnings limitation mentioned previously. In 1982 and later this reduction in benefits will be applicable only through age 70.

Disability Benefits

An individual must be "disability insured" to be eligible for disability benefits under Social Security. Disability generally means the inability to engage in any substantial gainful activity by reason of any medically determinable physical or mental impairment that can be expected to result in death or has lasted, or can be expected to last, for a continuous period of not less than twelve months; or after age 55, blindness which prohibits an individual from engaging in substantial gainful activity requiring skills or abilities comparable to those of any gainful activity in which he previously engaged with some regularity over a substantial period of time.

The disability benefit is payable following a waiting period of five consecutive calendar months throughout which the individual has been disabled. The disability benefit is equal to the Primary Insurance Amount, computed as though the individual had attained age 62 in the first month of his waiting period. Accordingly, the amount of the disability benefit is the same as the age-65 retirement benefit, if the average earnings on which benefits are based are the same. Since average earnings vary with the age at disability, however, so does the amount of the disability benefit. For an individual becoming disabled in July 1979 and thus eligible for benefits in January 1980, the minimum benefit is $122.00 per month and the maximum benefit is $596.30 per month. The disability benefit increases with the benefit escalator provisions in the law.

If a disabled individual is under age 62, the total disability benefits paid to him and his dependents may be reduced if he is receiving workers' compensation benefits. Social Security disability benefits plus workers' compensation benefits cannot exceed 80 percent of "average current earnings" prior to disability. Average current earnings for this purpose means actual earnings, not merely Social Security-taxed amounts, and is usually defined as the individual's best year in the period consisting of the calendar year in which disability started and the five years immediately preceding that year. If applicable state law provides that workers' compensation benefits are reduced by Social Security disability benefits, there will be no reduction in Social Security disability benefits.

An individual's disability benefits end with the month preceding the earliest of (a) the month in which he dies, (b) the month in which he attains age 65, and (c) the third month following the month in which disability ceases. The retirement benefit at age 65 for an individual entitled to a disability benefit until then generally will be equal to the Primary Insurance Amount on which the disability benefit is based.

An individual who applies for disability benefits, whether he receives monthly benefits or not, is considered for rehabilitation services by his state vocational rehabilitation agency. These services include counseling, teaching of new employment skills, training in the use of prostheses, and job placement. Benefits may be denied for any month in which the worker refuses to accept such rehabilitation services.

The earnings limitation that applies to retirement benefits does not apply to the payment of disability benefits. Instead, special limitations are used which are intended to measure the continuation of disability on an all-or-none basis.

Wife's or Husband's Benefits

At age 65 a wife or husband will receive 50 percent of the spouse's Primary Insurance Amount, a benefit which is payable, of course, only if the spouse was fully insured or disability insured and is receiving benefits. Payments may commence before age 65 (as early as age 62), but in that event will be reduced by $25/36$ of 1 percent for each month in the reduction period. This same benefit is payable to a divorced spouse with at least ten years of marriage. Payments will cease with the month before the month in which (a) either spouse dies, (b) they are divorced (except if the duration of the marriage was at least ten years), or (c) the primary insured individual is no longer entitled to disability benefits and is not entitled to retirement benefits.

A wife or husband under age 65 may also be eligible for spouse's benefits if she or he is caring for a child of the worker entitled to a child's benefit, provided the child is not receiving his benefits solely because he is a student. The spouse's benefit in this case is 50 percent of the worker's Primary Insurance Amount. Benefit payments will cease with the month before the month in which (a) either spouse dies, (b) the primary insured individual is no longer entitled to disability benefits and is not entitled to retirement benefits, or (c) there is no longer a child entitled to benefits. If benefit payments cease as a result of the death of the worker, the surviving spouse may be entitled to widow's or widower's benefits, or mother's or father's benefits as described below.

Widow's or Widower's Benefits

At or after age 65 a widow or widower will receive 100 percent of the Primary Insurance Amount of the deceased spouse, provided that such spouse was fully insured and had not received a reduced old-age benefit before death. Payments may commence before age 65 (as early as age 60) but in that event will be reduced by $19/40$ of 1 percent for each month in the reduction period. If the deceased spouse was receiving a reduced old-age benefit at the time of death, the widow's or widower's benefit may not exceed the greater of (a) the amount of the reduced old-age benefit of the spouse, and (b) 82½ percent of the spouse's Primary Insurance Amount. Severely disabled widows or widowers are entitled to a percentage of the spouse's Primary Insurance Amount at or over age 50 (50 percent at age 50, grading up to 71½ percent at age 60 and graded further to 100 percent at age 65). The disability must have occurred within seven years after the death of the spouse (or, if later, seven years after the last eligible child attains age 18 or ceases to be disabled). This same benefit is payable to a surviving divorced spouse with at least ten years of marriage. These benefits cease with the month before the month in which the surviving spouse dies or remarries (prior to age 60). Under certain circumstances a widow's remarriage prior to age 60 will not cause benefits to terminate.

Child's Benefits

Every child of an individual entitled to old-age or disability insurance benefits, or of an individual who dies while fully or currently insured, is entitled to a monthly benefit equal to 50 percent of the individual's Primary Insurance Amount if the individual is living, or 75 percent of his Primary Insurance Amount if he is deceased.

Payments cease with the month preceding the earliest of (a) the month in which such child dies or marries, (b) the month in which such child attains the age of 18 and is neither disabled nor a full-time student, (c) the earlier of a month during no part of which he was a full-time student or the month in which he reaches age 22 (under certain circumstances benefits may continue through the current semester in which he is enrolled), and (d) if the child's entitlement was based solely on his being disabled, the third month following the month in which he ceases to be disabled.

A grandchild can qualify as a "child" of a grandparent if both parents are disabled or dead and if the grandchild is living with and being supported by the grandparent.

Mother's or Father's Benefits

A mother's or father's benefit is payable to the surviving spouse of an individual who dies while fully or currently insured, provided the surviving spouse (a) is not remarried, (b) is not entitled to a widow's or widower's benefit, and (c) at the time of filing an application is caring for a child of the deceased spouse entitled to a child's benefit, provided the child is not receiving his benefit solely because he is a student. This same benefit is payable to a divorced wife (and, as a result of court decisions, to a divorced husband) even though the marriage did not endure ten years, provided she or he has not remarried. The mother's or father's benefit is equal to 75 percent of the Primary Insurance Amount of the deceased individual. Benefit payments will cease with the month before the recipient remarries, dies, becomes entitled to a widow's or widower's benefit, or has no child of the deceased individual entitled to a child's benefit.

Parent's Benefits

A parent of an individual who dies while fully insured is entitled to monthly benefits if such parent (a) has attained age 62, (b) was receiving at least one half of his support from such individual, (c) has not married since the individual's death, and (d) has filed an application for parent's benefits. Generally, the parent's benefit is equal to 82½ percent of the Primary Insurance Amount of such deceased individual. For any month for which more than one parent is entitled to parent's benefits, the benefit for each parent is equal to 75 percent of the Primary Insurance Amount. The parent's benefits cease upon death or, in certain circumstances, remarriage.

Maximum Limit on Family Benefits

The law limits the total of monthly benefits payable to a family entitled to benefits on the basis of wages of an insured individual. In retirement and survivor cases this maximum is about 175 percent of the individual's Primary Insurance Amount, except that for low-wage earners the percentage varies between 150 and 188 percent. In disability cases the percentage varies from 100 percent at very low wage levels to 150 percent at higher wage levels.

Generally, when benefits are subject to reduction because they exceed the limits on maximum family benefits, each monthly benefit except the old-age or disability benefit is decreased proportionately.

Lump Sum Death Payments

If an individual dies while fully or currently insured, an amount equal to $255 is normally paid to help meet the cost of burial expenses. Application for the payment must generally be filed within two years after the death of the insured individual.

Nonduplication of Benefits

An individual entitled to benefits both on his own earnings record and as a dependent or survivor of another worker may receive only the larger of the two benefits.

Medicare Benefits

The Medicare program consists of Hospital Insurance (HI) and Supplementary Medical Insurance (SMI), frequently referred to as Part A and Part B, respectively. Hospital Insurance provides partial protection against the cost of inpatient hospital services as well as a number of other services such as those provided by a skilled nursing facility or a home health agency. Supplementary Medical Insurance helps pay for the cost of physician services plus certain other expenses such as outpatient hospital care and home health agency visits. Not all medical services are covered by Medicare, the major exceptions being routine care, outpatient drugs, eyeglasses, and dental care.

HI benefits are payable automatically once you reach age 65 if you are entitled to a Social Security benefit as a retired worker, spouse, widow(er), or other beneficiary. HI benefits are available even if your monthly cash benefit is withheld completely because of earnings in excess of the earnings limitation. If you are not receiving monthly cash benefits at age 65, however, you may have to apply specifically for HI benefits.

The SMI program is voluntary and requires payments of $9.60 per month after July 1, 1980. (These premiums are subject to increase in the future as the cost of medical care increases.) If you are receiving a Social Security monthly benefit, the SMI premium will be deducted automatically from your benefit unless you specifically elect *not* to participate in the SMI program.

If you have been receiving Social Security benefits as a disabled beneficiary for at least twenty-four months (or twenty-nine months under the Railroad Retirement system), you are eligible for Medicare benefits, even if you are under age 65. Medicare benefits are also available if you (or one of your dependents) have chronic kidney disease requiring dialysis or kidney transplant.

Under the HI program, the cost of a hospital stay is reimbursed after certain deductible and coinsurance requirements are met. Hospital services for up to ninety days in a "spell of illness" are covered; furthermore, you have a "lifetime reserve" of an additional sixty days that can be drawn on if you stay in a hospital for more than a total of ninety days in one spell of illness. (A "spell of illness" ends once you have remained out of the hospital or skilled nursing facility for sixty days.) The hospital is usually reimbursed directly for the cost of your care over and above the amount you are required to pay. You must pay the first $180 of expenses (the "HI deductible" for 1980, subject to future increases) and you must pay $45 per day if your hospital stay lasts longer than sixty days and $90 per day if you use any of your "lifetime reserve" days. These "coinsurance" amounts of $45 and $90 are also subject to increase in future years.

If you have been hospitalized for at least three days and then enter a skilled nursing facility for follow-up care within two weeks after leaving the hospital, the services provided by the facility will be covered in part by the HI program for up to 100 days in a spell of illness. For days 21 through 100 you must pay a daily coinsurance amount of $22.50 (subject to future increase). In the first year after hospitalization, up to 100 home health agency visits are provided under HI.

The SMI program helps pay for the costs of physician services, outpatient services by hospitals and clinics, and home health agency visits. Reimbursement is on the basis of "reasonable charges" for such services, that is, maximum amounts that Medicare can, according to the law, pay for services covered under SMI. You pay the first $60 of reasonable charges each calendar year (a deductible that is *not* subject to automatic increase) and coinsurance of 20 percent of reasonable charges in excess of the deductible. You also pay all amounts in excess of Medicare's reasonable charges. In some cases the physician or other person or organization who provides covered services may agree to bill Medicare directly and accept as payment in full the amounts determined to be reasonable charges, in which event there will be no excess charges. The deductible is on a calendar year basis, and expenses incurred in the last quarter of a year can be carried over and applied toward meeting the deductible in the following year.[1]

Conclusion

This relatively brief description makes it obvious that Social Security is so complicated that it is not possible to explain in detail in just a few pages all the benefits and all the conditions surrounding their payment. It is possible, however, to give a general idea of the type of benefits payable, how they are determined, and who is eligible to receive them. With this information you should be able to work more effectively with your local Social Security office in making sure that you get maximum advantage from the program and receive all the benefits to which you are entitled. Getting the most possible value from Social Security is discussed further in later chapters, particularly Chapter 21.

4
How Much Do Social Security Benefits Cost?

There are several ways to state the money cost of Social Security. For the purpose of this chapter let us use a simple definition: The cost of the Social Security program in any given year is the amount paid in benefits and administrative expenses for that year—a simple but valid definition.

For many years after a social insurance program is adopted, costs can be expected to rise. This is true for several reasons. During the first year of a new program very few retired persons receive benefits (persons who are already past the retirement age when a program is adopted are not usually eligible for benefits). During the second year of a program there are a few more retired persons receiving benefits, the third year a few more, and so on. Eventually the retired persons begin to die, but there is still a net increase in the number of retired persons receiving benefits for many years after a new program is adopted. The same is true of benefits paid to survivors of deceased workers: the number of survivors receiving benefits increases steadily for many years after a program is adopted.

Costs also increase as new benefits are added. For example, disability benefits were added to the Social Security program in 1956. The predictable result was a steady increase in the number of disabled persons receiving benefits for many years to

41

Table 4.1

Social Security Beneficiaries at End of Selected Calendar Years

| | *Number of Persons (in thousands) at End of Year Who Were* | | | |
| | *Receiving. . .* | | *Eligible for Benefits under. . .* | |
Calendar Year	Old-Age and Survivors Insurance Benefits	Disability Insurance Benefits[a]	Hospital Insurance Program[b]	Supplementary Medical Insurance Program[b]
(1)	(2)	(3)	(4)	(5)
1940	222	—	—	—
1950	3,477	—	—	—
1960	14,157	687	—	—
1970	23,564	2,665	20,361	19,584
1979	30,348	4,777	26,800	26,700

[a]The Disability Insurance program was enacted in 1956 and began operation in 1957.
[b]The Medicare program was enacted in 1965 and began operation in 1966. Figures represent the average number eligible for benefits in the year shown.

come. Medicare benefits, paying part of the hospital and other medical expenses of retired persons, were added in 1965. As a result, the number of persons receiving Medicare benefits should increase along with the increase in the number of persons receiving retirement benefits.

Social Security costs can be expected to increase for other reasons, such as an increased number of persons covered by the program and increased benefits (as a result of inflation as well as benefit liberalizations). Accordingly, it is predictable and not at all unusual for the total cost of a new social insurance program to increase steadily for many years after it is adopted.

How does this theory hold up in light of past experience? Table 4.1 shows the number of persons who were receiving various types of Social Security benefits at the end of selected calendar years. As was to be expected, the number of beneficiaries has increased steadily since Social Security was enacted. The total number of beneficiaries is not meaningful and is not shown since some persons receive more than one type of benefit (for example, both Old-Age and Medicare benefits).

Just as an increase in the number of beneficiaries was to be expected, so was an increase in the amount of benefits paid. Table 4.2 shows the amounts that were paid in benefits and

Table 4.2

**Amount of Benefits and Administrative Expenses Paid
during Calendar Year
(in millions of dollars)**

Calendar Year	Old-Age and Survivors Insurance Program	Disability Insurance Program[a]	Hospital Insurance Program[b]	Supplementary Medical Insurance Program[b]	Total
(1)	(2)	(3)	(4)	(5)	(6)
1940	$ 62	—	—	—	$ 62
1950	1,022	—	—	—	1,022
1960	11,198	$ 600	—	—	11,798
1970	29,848	3,259	$ 5,281	$2,212	40,600
1979	93,133	14,186	21,073	9,265	137,657

[a]The Disability Insurance program was enacted in 1956 and began operation in 1957.
[b]The Medicare program was enacted in 1965 and began operation in 1966.

administrative expenses for the four separate parts of the Social Security program during selected calendar years. There has been a spectacular increase in costs since Social Security began: from $62 million in 1940 to $137,657 million in 1979. These figures are almost meaningless, however, taken by themselves. It is more appropriate to view them in relation to the size of the U.S. population, or the Gross National Product (the total amount of goods and services produced by the population), or some other measure of the population affected by Social Security.

As we will see in a later chapter, our Social Security program is financed primarily by taxes based upon the earnings of the active working population that participates in Social Security. Therefore, it is convenient and meaningful to compare the cost of Social Security with the total earnings of persons covered by Social Security, excluding that portion of earnings exempt from the Social Security tax.

This procedure may be illustrated with the following statistics for calendar year 1978. Approximately 110 million persons worked in employment that was covered by Social Security. Their total earnings in such employment were about $1,091 billion. But the portion of an individual's earnings in excess of $17,700 per year did not count for Social Security purposes;

Table 4.3

Amount of Benefits and Administrative Expenses as a Percentage of Effective Taxable Payroll[a] during Past Calendar Years

Calendar Year	Old-Age and Survivors Insurance Program	Disability Insurance Program[b]	Hospital Insurance Program[c]	Total for OASDHI	Supplementary Medical Insurance Program[c]	Total for OASDHI & SMI
(1)	(2)	(3)	(4)	(5)	(6)	(7)
1940	0.19%	—	—	0.19%	—	0.19%
1945	0.48	—	—	0.48	—	0.48
1950	1.17	—	—	1.17	—	1.17
1955	3.34	—	—	3.34	—	3.34
1960	5.59	0.30%	—	5.89	—	5.89
1965	7.23	0.70	—	7.93	—	7.93
1970	7.32	0.81	1.21%	9.33[d]	0.51%	9.84
1975	9.29	1.36	1.69	12.32[d]	0.69	13.01
1979	8.95	1.36	2.00	12.31	0.88	13.19

[a]"Effective taxable payroll" consists of the total earnings subject to Social Security taxes, after adjustment to reflect the lower contribution rates on self-employment income, tips, and multiple-employer "excess wages." This adjustment is made to facilitate both the calculation of contributions (which is thereby the product of the tax rate and the payroll) and the comparison of expenditure percentages with tax rates. This effective taxable payroll is slightly different for OASDI and HI because of the tax treatment of self-employed persons; however, it does not materially affect the comparisons.

[b]The Disability Insurance program was enacted in 1956 and began operation in 1957.

[c]The Medicare program (both SMI and HI) was enacted in 1965 and began operation in 1966. Although the SMI program is not financed by payroll taxes, its cost is shown for comparative purposes as a percentage of payroll that is taxable for HI purposes. Participation in SMI is optional and is financed by premiums paid by the enrollees, and by general revenue.

[d]The total is not the exact sum of the preceding columns because of "rounding."

that is, it did not count for computing benefits and it was not subjected to tax. Only about 84 percent of total earnings, or $913 billion, was subjected to Social Security tax. Total expenditures in 1978 for benefits and administrative expenses amounted to about $96 billion under the Old-Age, Survivors, and Disability insurance programs. This was some 11 percent of the total taxable payroll of $913 billion.

Table 4.3 shows the cost as a percentage of taxable payroll for the four separate parts of the Social Security program during selected calendar years in the past. It is important to note that the Supplementary Medical Insurance program is not financed by a payroll tax; nevertheless, this method of expressing costs is used in order to have a convenient method of comparing the cost of this program and its growth with the other parts of the Social Security program. In reviewing Table 4.3 it may be useful to note that the percentage of the total earnings subject to tax has not always been 84 percent. Table 4.4 indicates what these percentages have been for selected years in the past as well as what they are projected to be in the future. It should also be noted that in 1978 the total amount of covered earnings of persons participating in Social Security represented about three-fourths of the total earnings of all workers in the United States.

A review of Tables 4.2 and 4.3 substantiates the obvious. The cost of Social Security has grown by leaps and bounds not only in dollar amounts but also in relation to the earnings of those who are covered by Social Security.

How long will the cost of Social Security continue to rise? As a matter of fact, barring major legislative changes, costs will continue to rise until the population of active workers and

Table 4.4

Percentage of Total Earnings in Covered Employment That Is Subjected to Social Security Payroll Tax

Calendar Year	Percentage
(1)	(2)
1940	92
1945	88
1950	80
1955	80
1960	78
1965	71
1970	78
1975	84
1978	84
1979	88
1980	89[a]
1981 and later	90[a]

[a]Estimated.

beneficiaries (retired workers, disabled workers, surviving spouses, etc.) reaches a mature stage—that is, at least seventy-five to one hundred years after the program is adopted. Another way to think about it: the program and the population covered by the program reach a mature stage when the program has existed unchanged for the entire adult lifetime of every person who is covered by the program, and when the characteristics of the population (birth rates, death rates, retirement ages, etc.) have remained unchanged for the entire lifetime of the existing population. A further requirement for the maturity of the program is that there have been no large fluctuations in the economic experience (wage increases, Consumer Price Index changes, unemployment, etc.) during the working lifetime of every person who is covered by the program.

These conditions make it seem as if our Social Security program will never mature, and it probably will not; but for all practical purposes we can assume that it will mature approximately seventy-five years from now. In the year 2050 most of the active workers and the retired workers and other beneficiaries will have participated in the program throughout their entire working lifetime. Of course, we have no assurance that population characteristics, economic conditions, and the program itself will remain stable throughout this period, but if they should do so, then we could expect program costs to level off around the middle of the next century.

It is possible to obtain a more specific idea of future Social Security costs. Every year the Board of Trustees of the Social Security program issues reports based on studies made by the actuaries of the Social Security Administration and the Health Care Financing Administration. These reports include projected future costs of the program for as long as seventy-five years in the future. The projected costs, based on the 1979 Trustees Reports and on a limited number of unpublished studies, are summarized in Table 4.5. Total expenditures for benefits and administration are projected to increase from about 13 percent of taxable payroll in 1979 to approximately 17 percent by the year 2000 and to 26 percent by the year 2025, remaining approximately level thereafter.

Do these figures surprise you? Do you believe them? It is

Table 4.5

**Projected Expenditures for Benefits and Administration as a
Percentage of Effective Taxable Payroll[a] during
Future Calendar Years**

Calendar Year	Old-Age and Survivors Insurance Program	Disability Insurance Program	Hospital Insurance Program	Total for OASDHI	Supplementary Medical Insurance Program[b]	Total for OASDHI & SMI
(1)	(2)	(3)	(4)	(5)	(6)	(7)
1980	9.16%	1.40%	2.12%	12.68%	0.95%	13.63%
1985	9.12	1.38	2.73	13.23	1.18	14.41
1990	9.27	1.42	3.51	14.20	1.39	15.59
1995	9.13	1.54	4.27	14.94	1.57	16.51
2000	8.90	1.74	4.92	15.56	1.60	17.16
2025	13.49	2.18	7.52	23.19	2.35	25.54
2050	14.02	2.13	8.20	24.35	2.43	26.78

[a]"Effective taxable payroll" consists of the total earnings subject to Social Security taxes, after adjustment to reflect the lower contribution rates on self-employment income, tips, and multiple-employer "excess wages." This adjustment is made to facilitate both the calculation of contributions (which is thereby the product of the tax rate and the payroll) and the comparison of expenditure percentages with tax rates. This effective taxable payroll is slightly different for OASDI and HI because of the tax treatment of self-employed persons; however, it does not materially affect the comparisons.

[b]Although the SMI program is not financed by payroll taxes, its cost is shown for comparative purposes as a percentage of payroll that is taxable for HI purposes. Participation in SMI is optional and is financed by premiums paid by the enrollees, and by general revenue.

difficult *not* to believe the figures that are shown in Table 4.3 for the forty years from 1940 through 1979, because this is past history. What about the future—is it possible for the total cost of the Social Security program to be as high as 25 percent to 30 percent of taxable payroll? Yes, it is not only possible, it is quite likely if there are no significant changes in the present program.

These figures are no surprise to an actuary who is familiar with the Social Security program. It is no surprise that they increased rapidly in the past and it is no surprise that they are expected to increase in the future. It may be of interest to note that the early actuarial studies in 1938 indicated that the cost of retirement benefits under Social Security would rise steadily from 0.2 percent of taxable payroll in 1940 to 9.35 percent of taxable payroll by 1980.[1] These figures are quoted not to prove the accuracy of long-range projections, but rather to illustrate that from the very start of Social Security, actuaries have been providing information about the trend and level of future costs.

What Is an Actuary?

A short digression about actuaries may be in order. What is an actuary? I have heard it said that somewhere in the Congressional Record the statement is made that an actuary is a person who is "always taking the pessimistic view by looking many years into the future." It is true that the actuary's job is to look into the future; however, whether this is a pessimistic exercise is in the eye of the beholder. If you like the result that is projected, you would probably consider it optimistic; if you don't like the result, you would probably consider it pessimistic.

The most widely accepted standard of professional qualification in the United States for actuaries who work with life insurance, health insurance, pensions, and social insurance is membership in the Society of Actuaries. There are other actuarial organizations designed to serve the specialized needs of their membership: American Academy of Actuaries, Conference of Actuaries in Public Practice, Casualty Actuarial Society, and American Society of Pension Actuaries.

The Society of Actuaries is a professional organization of actuaries whose purpose is to advance the knowledge of actuarial science and to maintain high standards of competence within the actuarial profession. At the end of 1979, there were 6,997 members of the Society of Actuaries, of whom 3,955 were Fellows (the ultimate membership designation). In mid-1980, the Social Security Administration employed eighteen members of the Society of Actuaries and the Health Care Financing Administration employed thirteen members.

In its publication describing the actuarial profession, the Society of Actuaries states:

> An actuary is an executive professionally trained in the science of mathematical probabilities. He uses mathematical skills to define, analyze, and solve

complex business and social problems. He designs insurance and pension programs which meet the public's needs and desires, and which are financially sound. He forecasts probabilities and he commits his company or his client to long-range financial obligations for a generation or more.

One of the principal jobs of the actuaries of the Social Security Administration and the Health Care Financing Administration is to make long-range forecasts of the cost of the present Social Security program, as well as any proposed changes, and thus provide the information that will enable the program to be financed on a sound basis both now and in the future.

Long-Range Forecasts

In making long-range forecasts of the amounts that will be paid out in benefits under the Social Security program, actuaries must make assumptions regarding a host of factors, including:

    mortality
    disability
    immigration and emigration
    birth rates
    wages and salaries
    Consumer Price Index changes
    unemployment rates
    age at retirement
    participation in work force by males and by females
    marriage rates

For a given set of assumptions, projections of future costs can be made with a reasonably high degree of accuracy. But it is obvious that no one can accurately select these assumptions, particularly those concerning wages, the Consumer Price Index, and birth rates, all of which are important determinants of future costs. By expressing future costs as a percentage of future taxable payroll, rather than in dollar amounts, the predictability of future costs is greatly improved. Nevertheless, the overall level of certainty of long-range cost projections for a program like Social Security is still less than we might hope for.

The trustees of Social Security, as well as the government actuaries, recognize that it is impossible to predict the future accurately. They also recognize, however, that it is essential to adopt one or more sets of assumptions about the possible future social and economic environment and then to project future income and outgo under Social Security to determine whether or not it would be financially sound under those conditions.

In recent years the trustees have employed three alternative sets of assumptions about the future, usually labeled optimistic, pessimistic, and intermediate. Projections of future expenditures under the optimistic and pessimistic assumptions indicate a broad range within which it might reasonably be expected that expenditures will fall during the coming years. Projected expenditures based upon an intermediate set of assumptions are normally used for planning purposes since it is too cumbersome to deal in every instance with a range of future costs. The projected expenditures, as well as the projected income, shown throughout this book are based upon the intermediate assumptions used in the 1979 Trustees Reports, unless indicated otherwise.[2] The Appendix contains a summary of the more important of these assumptions.

Table 4.6 and Chart 4.A illustrate the range of projected expenditures for Social Security under the optimistic, pessimistic, and intermediate sets of assumptions. Expenditures include both benefits and administrative costs for all elements of the Social Security program that are under consideration here: Old-Age, Survivors, and Disability Insurance and Medicare (Hospital Insurance and Supplementary Medical Insurance). While it may be reasonable to assume that actual experience will fall within the range defined by these alternative projections, particularly during the first twenty-five years of the projection, there can be no assurance that this will be the case because of the high degree of uncertainty in the selection of assumptions for long-range forecasting.

Accordingly, the future costs shown in Table 4.6, particularly the costs after the turn of the century, should not be viewed as absolute amounts but rather as trends based upon assumptions

Table 4.6

Projected Expenditures for Benefits and Administration of the Social Security Program[a] under Alternative Demographic and Economic Assumptions,[b] Expressed as a Percentage of Effective Taxable Payroll[c]

Calendar Year	Optimistic Assumptions	Intermediate Assumptions	Pessimistic Assumptions
(1)	(2)	(3)	(4)
1980	13.54%	13.63%	13.95%
1985	13.75	14.41	15.03
1990	14.38	15.59	17.09
1995	14.57	16.51	18.89
2000	14.61	17.16	20.54
2025	19.73	25.54	35.95
2050	18.31	26.78	47.50

[a]Amounts shown include expenditures for OASDI, HI, and SMI combined.
[b]See text and Appendix for discussion of alternative sets of assumptions.
[c]"Effective taxable payroll" consists of the total earnings subject to Social Security taxes, after adjustment to reflect the lower contribution rates on self-employment income, tips, and multiple-employer "excess wages." This adjustment is made to facilitate both the calculation of contributions (which is thereby the product of the tax rate and the payroll) and the comparison of expenditure percentages with tax rates. This effective taxable payroll is slightly different for OASDI and HI because of the tax treatment of self-employed persons; however, it does not materially affect the comparisons. Although the SMI program is not financed by payroll taxes, its cost is shown for comparative purposes as a percentage of payroll that is taxable for HI purposes. Participation in SMI is optional and is financed by premiums paid by the enrollees, and by general revenue.

that seem reasonable to us at the present time. By updating the cost projections on a regular basis and by revising the assumptions in the light of emerging trends, actuaries can provide extremely important information for making sound future financial plans for the Social Security program. We should not ignore these future cost estimates just because they will affect *future* generations and not us, or just because we know that actual future costs will not be exactly the same as projected future costs.

As Table 4.6 and Chart 4.A indicate, under all three sets of assumptions, expenditures are projected to rise slowly until the turn of the century and to grow much more rapidly thereafter. The relatively small increase in costs between now and about

Chart 4.A

Projected Expenditures for Benefits and Administration of the Social Security Program[a] under Alternative Demographic and Economic Assumptions,[b] Expressed as a Percentage of Effective Taxable Payroll[c]

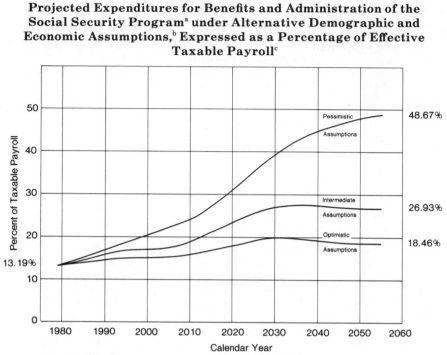

[a]Amounts shown include expenditures for OASDI, HI, and SMI combined.

[b]See text and Appendix for discussion of alternative sets of assumptions.

[c]"Effective taxable payroll" consists of total earnings subject to Social Security taxes, after adjustment to reflect the lower contribution rates on self-employment income, tips, and multiple-employer "excess wages." This adjustment is made to facilitate both the calculation of contributions (which is thereby the product of the tax rate and the payroll) and the comparison of expenditure percentages with tax rates. This effective taxable payroll is slightly different for OASDI and HI because of the tax treatment of self-employed persons; however, it does not materially affect the comparisons. Although the SMI program is not financed by payroll taxes, its cost is shown for comparative purposes as a percentage of payroll that is taxable for HI purposes. Participation in SMI is optional and is financed by premiums paid by the enrollees, and by general revenue.

the year 2010 is attributable primarily to the Hospital Insurance and Supplementary Medical Insurance programs[3] and, to a lesser extent, to the Disability Insurance program.

The much larger increases during the twenty-year period following the year 2010 are attributable primarily to the large number of persons then attaining age 65 (from among the children born during the post-World War II "baby boom" period from 1946 to the mid-1960s). The birth rate among these baby boom generations has been and is expected to continue to be lower than that of their parents, resulting in an eventual increase in the size of the older benefit-collecting population relative to the younger tax-paying population. Chart 4.B compares the size of these two segments of the population at three points in time: 1950, 1979, and 2025. The figures for 2025 are estimates based upon the intermediate set of birth rate and mortality assumptions.

As indicated in Table 4.6, the costs under the intermediate assumptions are projected to rise rapidly after the turn of the century to about 26 percent of taxable payroll before leveling off some fifty years from now. This is twice the current expenditures of about 13 percent of taxable payroll. Under the more optimistic assumptions, costs would still rise substantially above current levels but to an ultimate level of only about 18 to 20 percent of taxable payroll. Under the more pessimistic assumptions, projected expenditures would rise to about 36 percent of taxable payroll by the year 2025 and would continue increasing to some 48 percent by the year 2050. We are probably deluding ourselves by relying unduly on "optimistic-intermediate" assumptions rather than truly intermediate assumptions and by failing to emphasize that future costs can be predicted only within a broad range. Although it is a matter of judgment, I believe that future Social Security costs are much more likely to be higher than lower than the intermediate cost projections.

The so-called pessimistic assumptions selected by the Board of Trustees do not represent the most pessimistic view that it would be reasonable to take in determining whether Social Security will be viable in the future. For example, it can be argued that improvements in life expectancy will continue at a faster rate than has been assumed; or it is possible that average wages will not increase much, if any, faster than the cost of living, reflecting a marked slowdown in the steady improvement in the standard of living to which we have become accustomed—and which has been assumed for the future. Either of these events would result in much higher future Social Security costs (expressed as a percentage of taxable payroll).

Furthermore, none of the customary projections takes into account a variety of significant events that are conceivable, but

Chart 4.B

Past, Present, and Projected Retired Workers and Other
Social Security Beneficiaries, and Covered Workers

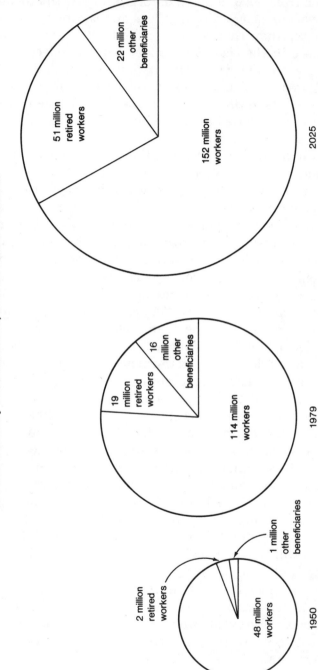

22 million
other
beneficiaries

51 million
retired
workers

152 million
workers

2025

16 million other
beneficiaries

19 million
retired
workers

114 million
workers

1979

2 million retired
workers

1 million other
beneficiaries

48 million
workers

1950

that would not ordinarily be expected. Unfortunately, there is no obvious way to prepare in advance to cope with some of these events. A significant improvement in health at the older ages is one of the easiest to comprehend of such possible events. People who were aged 60 in 1980 could expect to live another twenty years, on average, or until about age 80. It should be emphasized that 80 is the average age; some persons will live to age 100, others will die soon after age 60. About 90 percent of persons aged 60 in 1980 will die before reaching age 93. Fifty years ago in 1930, persons aged 60 could expect to live to age 75, on average. Fifty years from now in the year 2030, the projections assume that persons who are then aged 60 can expect to live to age 83, on average (according to the intermediate set of assumptions). It is entirely possible, however, that the average life span for persons aged 60 could be somewhat higher in the future, say 85 or 90; and with major breakthroughs in health care or improved understanding of the aging process, it could even be 95 or 100. Even if there are no remarkable increases in our average life span, we can expect generally improved health during our old age. Some analysts predict that life-extending techniques will become so developed in the twenty-first century that we may live well beyond 100 years, perhaps for 200 years or more! Major improvements in the health of the elderly or significant increases in life span would make our present Social Security system totally inappropriate.

Another example of a possible event that is difficult to comprehend, much less assess the impact of, is cataclysmic change in the earth resulting from volcanic eruptions, earthquakes, or polar shifts. These would lift large areas of land, submerge others in the sea, change underwater currents and tides, revise weather patterns, and generally transform the nation's coastal areas and mountain regions. Such changes would undoubtedly have a dramatic effect on human life, not only the size of the population initially surviving these disasters but also the population's ability for continued survival.

A still different type of development that is almost impossible to understand or predict the consequences of is the social evolution going on in this country and throughout the world. If this evolution should turn into a revolution, we could easily find our present Social Security system as well as most other institutions to be completely obsolete and all of our projections about future costs to have been of no avail.

None of this is to say that we should ignore the future because it is not predictable with certainty or because it may be calamitous. We must make every effort to design our institutions, including Social Security, so that they:

> appear to be appropriate in a future environment that we can postulate and comprehend; and
>
> are adaptable to non-calamitous future change.

Long-term projections such as those presented in this chapter provide information that is vital to our long-range planning and to our assessment of whether the present Social Security program is appropriate for the future. The projections indicate that future costs will continue to rise in the future no matter what assumptions are employed; it is just a question of how much they will rise. It is clearly inappropriate, therefore, to rely upon some undefined good fortune to enable us to continue our present Social Security program without paying substantially higher costs. Unfortunately these long-term projections and their significance do not appear to be widely known and understood by the public or the Congress or the Administration. Continued failure to heed these indications of the future could prove disastrous.

5
How Is the Money Obtained to Pay for Social Security Benefits?

In the last chapter we saw how the cost of any social insurance program can be expected to rise steadily as it matures. And we saw, in particular, how the cost of our Social Security program has grown in the past and how it is likely to grow in the future.

The question we turn to now is how we obtain the money necessary to pay these costs in order to fulfill the promise of the Social Security program to pay the various benefits outlined in Chapter 3. Obviously, we must levy some kind of tax against some segment of the population.

Sources of Federal Government Income

There are numerous ways taxes can be assessed. Chart 5.A illustrates the major sources of income to the federal government in fiscal year 1979 to operate all our government programs (not just Social Security).

Federal Income Tax

The federal income tax is the tax we are most familiar with. It is paid by most individuals and businesses. In fiscal year 1979

Chart 5.A

Federal Government Income by Source, Fiscal Year 1979

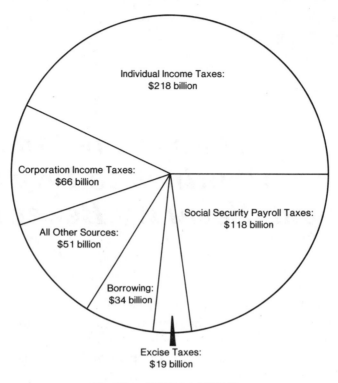

Individual Income Taxes:
$218 billion

Corporation Income Taxes:
$66 billion

Social Security Payroll Taxes:
$118 billion

All Other Sources:
$51 billion

Borrowing:
$34 billion

Excise Taxes:
$19 billion

Fiscal Year 1979 Total: $506 billion

the federal government received $218 billion in personal income taxes paid by individuals, and $66 billion in income taxes paid by corporations. This was 56 percent of all income received by the government.

Miscellaneous Taxes

A variety of special taxes of one kind or another are collected by the federal government: excise taxes (on alcohol, tobacco, gasoline, and entertainment, for example), gift taxes, estate taxes, licensing fees, customs taxes, and so on. In fiscal year 1979, the total of these miscellaneous taxes amounted to $70 billion, or 14 percent of all income received by the government.

Borrowing

The money to pay for federal programs does not necessarily have to be collected immediately in the form of taxes. Any excess of appropriations for expenditures over tax income constitutes a "budget deficit" and is made up by borrowing additional money from the general public. This borrowing is carried out by the sale of U.S. government securities, with the repayment of principal and interest to be made from future income (from taxes or further borrowing). In fiscal year 1979, an additional $34 billion was borrowed. This represented about 7 percent of total federal government income.

General Revenue

The total of the federal income taxes, the miscellaneous taxes mentioned above (excluding amounts specified by law for a particular purpose, such as the Highway Trust Fund), and newly borrowed amounts is sometimes called "general revenue." General revenue is available to the government to spend for general purposes; that is, there is not usually a direct connection between the source of the tax and how it is spent. Last year, general revenue was spent for national security, interest on the public debt, veterans' services and benefits, welfare (Supplemental Security Income, Medicaid, Food Stamps, Aid to Families with Dependent Children, etc.), operating the federal government, and other purposes. Approximately 70 percent of total income to the federal government in fiscal year 1979 (including the amounts borrowed from the public to finance the budget deficit) represented "unallocated" income or general revenue.

General revenue is used to pay for a relatively small part of the total Social Security program. In 1979 about 6 percent of the total expenditures for Social Security ($8.2 billion out of total expenditures of $137.7 billion) was accounted for by general revenue.

General revenue is used to pay a relatively large portion of the cost of the Supplementary Medical Insurance part of the Medicare program. In 1979 approximately 70 percent of expenditures for Supplementary Medical Insurance was accounted for by general revenue; the other 30 percent came from contributions, or "premiums," paid by those who elected to have this benefit. General revenue is also used in cases where special benefits are granted a person even though he has not paid the normal Social Security taxes to be eligible for such benefits. If Supplementary Medical Insurance is excluded, only about 1 percent of the cost of Social Security is financed by general revenue.

Payroll Tax

Sometimes special taxes are assessed based on a worker's gross earnings without any exemptions or deductions. They are referred to as payroll taxes and are usually earmarked for special purposes.

This is the way the money is raised to pay for most (94 percent) of the cost of the present Social Security program. In 1980 an employee paid taxes of 6.13 percent of his earnings; his employer also paid taxes equal to 6.13 percent of the employee's earnings (but this amount was not deducted from the employee's earnings); and a self-employed person paid taxes of 8.1 percent of his earnings. In each case, no tax was payable on earnings in excess of $25,900 in 1980. Payroll taxes such as these, which are collected by the Internal Revenue Service, and the relatively small amounts of general revenue referred to earlier are placed in special trust funds that are invested in U.S. government securities until they are used to pay Social Security benefits. These taxes can be used only to pay Social Security

Table 5.1
Social Security Taxes Payable in 1980 with Respect to Selected Individuals

| If Your Earnings in 1980 Were | Your Social Security Taxes Were | | | If You Are Self-Employed Your Social Security Taxes Were |
	Paid by Employee	Paid by Employer	Total	
(1)	(2)	(3)	(4)	(5)
$ 6,000	$ 367.80	$ 367.80	$ 735.60	$ 486.00
12,000	735.60	735.60	1,471.20	972.00
25,900 or more	1,587.67	1,587.67	3,175.34	2,097.90

benefits (and related administrative expenses) and cannot be used for any other purposes. Table 5.1 shows the Social Security taxes payable in 1980 by several individual workers and their employers, as well as by self-employed persons.

Why Do We Pay for Social Security the Way We Do?

When Social Security was adopted, only about 60 percent of the working population was eligible for its benefits. There was apparent justification, therefore, in assessing a payroll tax on the segment of the population eligible for its direct benefits rather than using general revenue paid by a broader segment of the population. The use of a payroll tax was also consistent with the notion that there was a strong relationship between taxes and benefits for an individual under the Social Security program. Now, even more than when Social Security was enacted, this logic is more apparent than real. More than 90 percent of the working population is currently covered by Social Security. Furthermore, the relationship between taxes and benefits for an individual is so tenuous as to be virtually nonexistent.

There is no particular reason an employee and his employer should share equally the cost of Social Security; that is, there is no reason the worker and his employer should pay the same amount in Social Security payroll taxes—except that it happens to be the law. Also, there is no particular reason the tax rate should be the same for all levels of earnings. The Social Security tax rate could be variable rather than constant. It could increase or decrease as the level of earnings increases. In fact, Social Security could be financed by general revenue or some form of tax other than the present payroll tax.

If there is no particular theoretical reason why we should pay for most of our Social Security benefits with a tax that is a constant percentage of payroll and that is paid in equal amounts by an employee and his employer, why do we do it this way? Why do we use a payroll tax instead of general revenue? Many justifications can be given and many theoretical arguments can be constructed; but in fact, the reasons seem to be rather arbitrary.

It may be interesting to note the recollections of a member of the staff of President Roosevelt's Committee on Economic

Security which made the recommendations in 1934–35 leading to the adoption of the Social Security Act on August 14, 1935:

> From the first, we assumed that contributions to old age insurance should be "in equal shares by employer and insured employee" as stated in the September 13th draft. A "fifty-fifty" ratio seemed to us to be justified by an "esthetic" logic difficult to controvert. I remember proposing this ratio to William Green, then president of the American Federation of Labor, as we were going to the White House for the President's reception on November 14th. He agreed that labor should go along with an equal sharing of the cost of old age insurance. . . . There never was any objection from the labor movement against equal contributions to old age insurance.[1]

> Departing from European tradition, we proposed the use of a uniform percentage of wages in determining the amount of contribution rather than a flat dollar amount or a series of amounts by wage classes.[2]

The above memoirs are not quoted to suggest that the decisions made in 1934–35 were anything less than well thought out and sound. Undoubtedly there were other considerations than those reflected in the memoirs. One of those considerations is suggested by an observation made by President Franklin D. Roosevelt in responding to a visitor who complained about the economic effect of the tax:

> I guess you're right on the economics, but those taxes were never a problem of economics. They are politics all the way through. We put those payroll contributions there so as to give the contributors a legal, moral, and political right to collect their pensions. . . . With those taxes in there, no damn politician can ever scrap my social security program.[3]

How High Will Future Tax Rates Be?

As indicated in Chapter 4, projections have been made of the future cost of Social Security. If the benefits are not changed and if Social Security continues to be financed the way it is now, future tax rates are projected to be approximately as indicated in Table 5.2 for the Old-Age, Survivors, and Disability Insurance and the Hospital Insurance portion of the Medicare program (i.e., the part of Social Security that is currently financed by the payroll tax). It should be noted that the rates shown represent the tax rates required to finance Social Security adequately (based on the intermediate assumptions in the 1979 Trustees Reports) and are not always equal to the actual tax rates scheduled in present law.

The tax rates in Table 5.2 from 1980 through 1990 are the tax rates scheduled in present law. It is possible that these tax rates will be barely sufficient in the aggregate; however, if each segment of Social Security is to be financed adequately, some reallocation of taxes will be necessary. In October 1980, a law was enacted providing for a reallocation of taxes in 1980 and

Table 5.2

Projected Tax Rates Necessary to Finance Present Social Security Program[a]

| Calendar Year | Tax Rates for Employed Persons | | | Tax Rates for Self-Employed Persons |
	Paid by Employee	Paid by Employer	Total	
(1)	(2)	(3)	(4)	(5)
1980	6.13%	6.13%	12.26%	8.10%
1981	6.65	6.65	13.30	9.30
1982–84	6.70	6.70	13.40	9.35
1985	7.05	7.05	14.10	9.90
1986–89	7.15	7.15	14.30	10.00
1990	7.65	7.65	15.30	10.75
2000	7.80	7.80	15.60	10.75
2010	8.60	8.60	17.20	11.50
2020	10.55	10.55	21.10	14.10
2030	12.30	12.30	24.60	16.40
2040	12.35	12.35	24.70	16.40
2050	12.20	12.20	24.40	16.20

[a]Figures from 1980 through 1990 are the tax rates scheduled in present law. The figures for the year 2000 and later represent the tax rates necessary, based on the intermediate assumptions in the 1979 Trustees Reports, to finance benefits and administrative expenses assuming no change is made in present law. This does not include the taxes necessary to support the Supplementary Medical Insurance program, which is not financed by payroll taxes.

1981 (an increase in OASI taxes and a corresponding decrease in DI taxes). Further tax reallocation or interfund borrowing will probably be necessary in 1982 and later; also, it appears likely that additional taxes in the aggregate will be necessary beginning in the mid-1980s.

The tax rates in present law are scheduled to rise between now and 1990 to the amounts shown in Table 5.2 for the year 1990 and then remain at that level in the future. If benefits are to be paid after 1990, however, the payroll tax rates must continue rising as indicated in the table from the year 2000 to 2050. The "financial deficits" for the next century (the difference between the tax rates that are scheduled in law and the tax rates that will be required to pay benefits) are given remarkably little attention. Yet just as costs have risen in the past, they will rise in the future. Ignoring the projected high future costs will not change them. These deficits are explored in more detail in Chapter 7.

The tax rate is applied to a worker's earnings subject to an upper limit called the "maximum contribution and benefit base." For 1980 the maximum was $25,900; thus the portion of an individual's earnings in excess of $25,900 in 1980 does not count for computing benefits and was not subjected to tax. This maximum is scheduled to be $29,700 in 1981 and to increase thereafter at the same rate as the average wages and salaries of the nation's workers increase. Consequently, although the dollar amount of the maximum taxable wage base will increase in the future, it will remain approximately constant relative to its 1981 level.

The Supplementary Medical Insurance portion of Medicare is an optional program available to most persons aged 65 and over and to certain disabled persons. About 95 percent of those eligible for this program have elected to participate. The cost of SMI benefits is not financed by payroll taxes as is the rest of Social Security. The cost of SMI benefits was met originally by premiums paid by the participants and approximately matching payments from general revenue; at the present time, however, about 70 percent of the total cost is being paid from general revenue because premiums have been prevented by law from rising as rapidly as total costs have risen. The percentage of the total cost paid by general revenue can be expected to

Table 5.3

Projected Supplementary Medical Insurance Expenditures and Proportion Financed by General Revenue

Calendar Year	Supplementary Medical Insurance Expenditures in Dollars (in billions)	Supplementary Medical Insurance Expenditures as a Percentage of Hospital Insurance Taxable Payroll[a]	Percentage of Total Financed by General Revenue
(1)	(2)	(3)	(4)
1980	$10.6	0.95%	71%
1990	34.2	1.39	82
2000	b	1.60	90
2010	b	1.70	92
2020	b	2.11	93
2030	b	2.50	94
2040	b	2.48	95
2050	b	2.43	96

[a]Although the SMI program is not financed by payroll taxes, its cost is shown for comparative purposes as a percentage of payroll that is taxable for HI purposes.
[b]Dollar amounts are not shown in the distant future since they tend to lose their meaning except when related to an index such as taxable payroll.

increase in the future, probably to as much as 90 percent by the year 2000 and 96 percent by the middle of the twenty-first century.

The SMI Trustees Report normally shows projected expenditures only for a three-year period; however, the same demographic changes in the population that will cause the projected OASDI and HI program costs to accelerate rapidly after the turn of the century will also cause the SMI program costs to increase rapidly. Table 5.3 illustrates the projected expenditures under the SMI program for the next seventy-five years. Although the SMI program is not financed by payroll taxes, its cost for comparative purposes has been computed as a percentage of the payroll that is taxable for Social Security purposes. On this basis, as shown in column (3) of Table 5.3, the expenditures under the SMI program are projected to increase from the equivalent of 0.95 percent of taxable payroll in 1980 to 2.50 percent in the year 2030. Within ten years (by 1990) the cost of Supplementary Medical Insurance will equal the present cost (in 1980) of the Disability Insurance program. Congress is very concerned about the costliness of the Disability Insurance program (witness the recently enacted Social Security Disability Amendments of 1980) and numerous groups are studying ways to reduce the cost. On the other hand, no one seems to be aware of, much less concerned about, the cost of SMI.

General Revenue versus Payroll Tax Financing

As indicated previously, approximately 99 percent of the cost of the Old-Age, Survivors, and Disability Insurance and Hospital Insurance programs is financed by payroll taxes; the other 1 percent is financed by general revenue. With respect to the Supplementary Medical Insurance program, approximately 30 percent is financed by premiums paid by the participants and the remaining 70 percent is financed by general revenue.

There is an ongoing debate about whether these financing methods are proper and whether we should rely more on general revenue and less on payroll taxes. It is not the purpose of this section to discuss the relative advantages of general revenue and payroll tax financing or other forms of taxation. A few general statements, however, may be helpful in establishing a perspective on financing.

It is important to note that if more general revenue and less payroll tax were used it would not change the total cost of Social Security or the total amount of taxes collected—it would simply change the way the tax is spread among the taxpayers, and some people would pay more and some would pay less than they do now.

To the extent that payroll taxes are used to finance Social Security, the taxes are paid by the same groups of persons who receive benefits. That is not to say that each person receives the exact benefits that can be "purchased" by his taxes. The relationship between the value of taxes paid and benefits received is discussed in Chapter 11.

To the extent that general revenue is used to finance Social Security, the taxes are paid by the entire population without regard to whether they participate in Social Security. Consider, for example, an employee of the federal government who never works in employment covered by Social Security. Such a person will never pay Social Security taxes and will never be eligible for

Social Security benefits (unless he enrolls in the SMI program at age 65). Nevertheless, the federal income taxes he pays contribute to general revenue which is used to pay for 6 percent of total Social Security benefits.

One of the most important drawbacks of general revenue financing as currently practiced is that it seems to facilitate ignoring the future. The Supplementary Medical Insurance program provides a good example. The government does not make long-range plans to finance the Supplementary Medical Insurance program. Provision is made only two years in advance. There seems to be a feeling that since the program is financed primarily by general revenue there is no need to be aware of the future cost or to make any advance plans to finance future benefits. The theory is apparently that "We can always increase general taxes enough to pay for SMI, so why worry about it." This viewpoint is clearly inappropriate in a program like Social Security, under which it is entirely possible to promise more in future benefits than the nation will be able and willing to pay for when they fall due.

Conclusion

In summary, Social Security benefits must be financed by taxes of one kind or another. The particular tax that is selected is important because of the way in which it spreads the burden among the various segments of the population. It is important psychologically because the taxpayer may be more willing to pay one form of tax than another. Finally, it is important because of the degree of fiscal responsibility it encourages—or discourages—among the Congress and other policymakers, as well as the taxpayers.

6
When Do We Pay for Social Security Benefits?

In Chapter 4 we saw how expenditures for benefits and administration under a social insurance program can be expected to grow steadily until the program matures—that is, for at least fifty to seventy-five years after it begins. In particular, we saw how expenditures under our Social Security program have grown in the past and how they are likely to grow in the future. For convenient reference this pattern of expenditures is shown in Table 6.1 for the Old-Age, Survivors, Disability, and Hospital Insurance parts of the Social Security program (i.e., everything except Supplementary Medical Insurance, which is optional and is financed principally by general revenue). The dollar amounts in column (2) are shown only through 1990 since the figures in the later years tend to lose their meaning except when related to an index such as taxable payroll. The projected future costs are based upon the "intermediate" set of assumptions as discussed in Chapter 4, and actual future costs may be higher or lower than those indicated in Table 6.1.

In Chapter 5 we discussed the various kinds of taxes that could be collected to pay for these benefits and saw that traditionally a payroll tax, shared equally by the worker and his employer, has been used as the principal means of financing our Social Security program.

Table 6.1

Expenditures for Benefits and Administration under the Old-Age, Survivors, Disability, and Hospital Insurance Program for Selected Years

	Expenditures Expressed as a...	
Calendar Year	Dollar Amount (in millions)	Percentage of Taxable Payroll[a]
(1)	(2)	(3)
1940	$ 62	0.19%
1945	304	0.48
1950	1,022	1.17
1955	5,079	3.34
1960	11,798	5.89
1965	19,187	7.93
1970	38,388	9.33
1975	80,765	12.32
1980	146,330[b]	12.68[b]
1985	235,967[b]	13.23[b]
1990	352,928[b]	14.21[b]
1995	c	14.94[b]
2000	c	15.57[b]
2025	c	23.19[b]
2050	c	24.35[b]

[a]Taxable payroll is adjusted to take into account the lower tax rates on self-employment income, tips, and multiple-employer "excess wages" as compared to the combined employer-employee rate. Taxable payroll is slightly different for OASDI and HI because of the tax treatment of self-employed persons; however, it does not materially affect the results.
[b]Estimated.
[c]Dollar amounts are not shown in the distant future since they tend to lose their meaning except when related to an index such as taxable payroll.

In this chapter we will discuss the question of how the amount of payroll tax to be paid by a worker and his employer at any given time is determined. In 1940 a worker paid taxes of 1 percent of the first $3,000 of his earnings, a maximum of $30.00; in 1980 a worker paid 6.13 percent of the first $25,900 of his earnings, a maximum of $1,587.67. How was it decided that the tax rate would be 1 percent in 1940 and 6.13 percent in 1980? How was it decided that a worker would pay tax on $3,000 of earnings in 1940 and $25,900 of earnings in 1980? What will these amounts be in the future?

Current-Cost Financing Method

There are a variety of "financing methods" available to pay for a social insurance program just as there are a variety of financing methods available to pay for automobiles, houses, life insurance policies, and almost everything else we buy.

The most obvious financing method for a social insurance program is what is sometimes called the pay-as-you-go method, or the "current-cost method." Under this method, just enough taxes are collected each year to pay the benefits and administrative expenses which fall due that year—the "current costs." Since it is difficult to estimate the exact amount of expenditures for a given year, it is usual to plan to collect slightly more in taxes than is likely to be needed. This excess amount of taxes is set aside in a reserve fund, or a "trust fund," to be used in years when benefit payments are higher than expected or tax collections are lower than expected or a combination of both. Under current-cost financing the trust fund never becomes very large since it serves merely as a contingency fund.

What is the pattern of tax collections that can be expected under a current-cost financing method? Basically, it is about the same as the pattern of program expenditures illustrated in column (2) of Table 6.1. The current cost of benefits and administration started very low at $62 million in 1940 and rose steadily to an estimated $146,330 million by 1980. Column (3) of Table 6.1 expresses these costs as a percentage of taxable payroll and permits a more meaningful comparison from year to year.

A few words of review about the "taxable payroll" may be of help in interpreting the figures in Table 6.1. The taxable payroll in a given year is the total earnings subject to Social Security tax for persons who pay Social Security taxes during that year, but it does not include earnings for any individual in excess of the "maximum contribution and benefit base," sometimes loosely referred to as the "maximum taxable earnings base." In 1980, for example, this maximum was $25,900; thus the taxable payroll was the total earnings subject to Social Security tax for all persons who paid Social Security taxes in 1980, but it did not include earnings in excess of $25,900 for any individual. Reference was made to "earnings subject to Social Security tax" to

Table 6.2

History of Increases in the Maximum Taxable Earnings Base

Calendar Year	Maximum Taxable Earnings Base
(1)	(2)
1937–50	$ 3,000
1951–54	3,600
1955–58	4,200
1959–65	4,800
1966–67	6,600
1968–71	7,800
1972	9,000
1973	10,800
1974	13,200
1975	14,100
1976	15,300
1977	16,500
1978	17,700
1979	22,900
1980	25,900
1981	29,700

recognize that some earnings are not taxable: earnings in jobs not covered by Social Security and investment earnings, for example.

From 1937 to 1950 the maximum earnings subject to Social Security tax was $3,000. It is estimated that 97 percent of the persons covered by Social Security earned less than $3,000 in 1937, and 71 percent earned less than $3,000 in 1950. Table 6.2 illustrates how this maximum taxable earnings base has increased from time to time. Under present law, the maximum taxable earnings base will increase automatically after 1981 to keep up with increases in the average wages and salaries of American workers.

In 1980 an estimated 92 percent of those covered by Social Security earned less than the maximum earnings base and thus had all of their earnings taxed under the Social Security program. It is estimated that this percentage will be 93 percent in 1981, and that it will remain at about that level unless the law is amended to provide otherwise. It is estimated that 90 percent of total earnings in covered employment in 1981 and later will be subjected to Social Security tax.

Table 6.3 shows the total amount of taxes needed to meet the current costs compared with the actual tax rates used in the past under our Social Security program. The table covers the Old-Age, Survivors, Disability, and Hospital Insurance parts of the Social Security program; the Supplementary Medical Insur-

Table 6.3

Comparison of Current Costs and Tax Rates, and Trust Fund Levels, under the Old-Age, Survivors, Disability, and Hospital Insurance Program for Selected Years

Calendar Year	Current Costs: Expenditures as Percentage of Taxable Payroll[a]	Actual Tax Rate[b] as Percentage of Taxable Payroll	Amount in Trust Funds at Beginning of Year	
			Dollar Amount (in millions)	Multiple of Expenditures during Year
(1)	(2)	(3)	(4)	(5)
1937	c	2.00%	$ 0	—
1940	0.2%	2.00	1,724	27.81
1945	0.5	2.00	6,005	19.75
1950	1.2	3.00	11,816	11.56
1955	3.3	4.00	20,576	4.05
1960	5.9	6.00	21,966	1.86
1965	7.9	7.25	21,172	1.10
1970	9.3	9.60	36,687	.96
1971	10.6	10.40	41,270	.93
1972	10.4	10.40	43,468	.87
1973	11.0	11.70	45,710	.76
1974	11.2	11.70	50,881	.73
1975	12.3	11.70	55,005	.68
1976	12.7	11.70	54,859	.60
1977	12.9	11.70	51,738	.50
1978	12.8	12.10	46,303	.41
1979	12.3	12.26	43,223	.34

[a]Taxable payroll is adjusted to take into account the lower tax rates on self-employment income, tips, and multiple-employer "excess wages" as compared to the combined employer-employee rate. Taxable payroll is slightly different for OASDI and HI because of the tax treatment of self-employed persons; however, it does not materially affect the results.
[b]Combined tax rate paid by employee and employer.
[c]During 1937–39 no benefit payments were made except a return of employee taxes in the event of death.

ance program is discussed later. Although tax collections began in 1937, no benefits were paid from 1937 through 1939 except a return of the workers' taxes in the event of death. The tax rates indicated in column (3) are the combined worker and employer tax rates. For example, in 1937 the workers' tax rate was 1 percent and the employers' tax rate was 1 percent, or a combined tax rate of 2 percent.

Self-employed persons first became covered in 1951 and pay taxes in amounts larger than the workers' tax and smaller than the combined worker and employer tax. For convenience of presentation, the figures in Table 6.3 have taken these different tax rates into account by expressing the current costs in column (2) as a percentage of a "hypothetical taxable payroll." This payroll was constructed so that the application of the worker and employer tax rates to such payroll would yield the same total taxes as would the application of the actual different tax rates to the actual taxable payroll in each category of employment. This procedure also adjusts for other minor deviations in the financing.

A study of the figures in Table 6.3 indicates that during its first twenty years of operation Social Security collected considerably more in taxes than it paid out in benefits but that during the past twenty years or so the taxes have been approximately equal to the current expenditures. The years since 1974 have been an important exception, and expenditures for benefits and administration have exceeded tax collections, thus requiring previously accumulated funds to pay a portion of the benefits. During the next few years, provision has been made for increased taxes that will approximate projected expenditures, although there still may be some deficits unless further tax increases are made.

The Supplementary Medical Insurance program has always been financed on a current-cost basis, so far as is practical. Participants pay premiums specified by law, and Congress appropriates whatever amount of general revenue is necessary to pay the balance of the cost each year. Of course, this is done on an estimated basis and income and outgo do not always come out even; therefore, a small trust fund balance is maintained. Also, provision is made for medical expense claims that begin in one year but carry over into the next year.

For all practical purposes, therefore, Social Security is financed on a current-cost basis; and the trust funds are intended to reflect all financial transactions and to serve as contingency funds in absorbing temporary differences between income and expenditures. The trust funds are adequate to pay only about 2 percent of the benefits during the next ten years and thus play a relatively minor role in ensuring the payment of future benefits; it is the ongoing collection of Social Security taxes that is the most important factor in providing benefits under the program.

Although the trust funds are relatively small, some background information on how they are invested may be useful in understanding certain aspects of the financing questions to be discussed later. The portion of each trust fund that, in the judgment of the Secretary of the Treasury (the Managing Trustee of the trust funds), is not required to meet current expenditures for benefits and administration is invested on a daily basis in one of the following types of security:

> Interest-bearing obligations of the U.S. government, including special public-debt obligations utilized only by the trust funds
>
> Obligations guaranteed as to both principal and interest by the United States
>
> Certain federally sponsored agency obligations designated as lawful investments for fiduciary and trust funds under the control and authority of the United States or any officer of the United States

The trust funds earned interest amounting to $3.5 billion during fiscal year 1979, equivalent to an effective annual rate of about 7.6 percent on the total assets of the trust funds.

Alternatives to Current-Cost Financing

There are alternatives to the current-cost financing method. Instead of collecting just enough in taxes each year to pay the benefits for the year, we could collect more in taxes than needed to pay current benefits and place the excess contributions in a reserve fund or a trust fund. The higher the taxes, the larger the trust fund. This procedure is usually termed "advance funding." There are different levels at which advance funding can take place, depending upon the theory being followed as well as certain practicalities. Columns (4) and (5) of Table 6.3 indicate the extent to which Social Security was advance funded during its early history.

Why would we want to collect more in taxes than we need to pay current benefits? Why would we want to accumulate sizable trust funds? There are advantages and disadvantages to both the current-cost and the advance-funding methods, some of which are obvious but many of which are not.

Current-cost financing is easy to understand. Simply collect enough taxes each year to pay the benefits falling due that year. Most governmental programs are financed in this way. The taxes are low in the early years of the program and increase gradually as the public "gets used to paying the taxes." There is no sizable fund to invest, thus numerous investment problems are avoided. If a large fund were to exist, the public might misunderstand the purpose of the fund and believe that benefits could be expanded more than was in fact economically sound.

On the other hand, current-cost financing may mislead the public. The public may think the low cost in the early years will continue indefinitely and thus may demand or be enticed into accepting a Social Security program that is more generous than will be affordable at some time in the future. Steadily increasing tax rates which are an integral part of the current-cost method may not be desirable. The public may prefer to have tax rates that are more predictable and that remain the same for several years at a time.

If the Social Security program were a private system, under normal circumstances it would be considered desirable to collect more income than is necessary for current benefit payments and to accumulate a substantial fund. This is in fact the normal procedure for a private employee benefit system for reasons which include the following:

> *Security of benefits.* The existence of a large fund gives the employees some assurance that if the system terminates and no future income to the system is available, the benefits accrued to date can in fact be paid, at least to the extent the accumulated fund is adequate. (The Employee Retirement Income Security Act of 1974 requires

that most private pension plans accumulate a fund in order to give employees this added security.)

Reduction of future contributions. The amount of investment earnings on the trust fund can be used to pay a portion of future benefits and thus permit a reduction in the amount of future contributions otherwise required to finance the benefits.

Allocation of costs to period during which they are incurred. Even though benefits may not be paid until some future date, the cost of these benefits can be considered as having been incurred gradually over an employee's working lifetime as he earns the benefits. The recognition of this principle through payment of sufficient contributions to fund the benefit obligations as they accrue will generally lead to the accumulation of a substantial fund.

Although these are valid reasons for the advance funding of a private pension system, they are less valid for national compulsory social insurance—such as the Social Security program—covering substantially the entire population.

With respect to security of benefits, it is usually assumed that the Social Security program will continue indefinitely and that the taxing power of the federal government is adequate assurance that the benefits will be provided. This is probably a justifiable assumption provided that the Social Security benefits, together with all the other benefits and services supplied through the government, that have been promised for the future are not unreasonable.

With respect to reduction of future contributions, the accumulation of a fund for Social Security would have a paradoxical effect. Higher Social Security taxes would be required from today's generation of taxpayers, but tomorrow's generations of taxpayers, considered as a whole, would pay the same total amount of taxes to support Social Security—Social Security and general—as if there were no fund. This is true because Social Security trust funds are invested in government securities, the interest on which is paid from general revenue; therefore, the accumulation of a fund would result in lower future Social Security taxes but higher future general taxes. In other words, the total future cost of Social Security would be the same but would be distributed differently within each generation and would be paid not only by persons who pay Social Security taxes but also by those who do not pay such taxes. On the other hand, the accumulation of a trust fund that is invested in government securities could serve to reduce the amount of government securities issued to other parties to finance government activities. Accordingly, the total outstanding government securities, including those issued to the trust fund, could be the same before and after the accumulation of a trust fund. In this event, total general revenue paid in the future to the government for all purposes would be unaffected by the accumulation of a trust fund, Social Security payroll taxes would eventually be lower, and the nation's total tax burden would be reduced.

With respect to the appropriate allocation of costs to the periods during which they are incurred, an argument can be made (under a national social insurance system as well as under a private pension system) for recognizing that a liability is accruing during a person's active working lifetime, even though the benefits and the costs thereof may not be paid until a later date. Recognition of this liability does not necessarily take the form of accumulating a fund that is related to the value of the benefits being accrued.

An argument is being made in some quarters these days for advance funding of the Social Security program for a reason that does not apply to an individual private pension plan. It goes something like this: Since a large part of a person's retirement needs are met by the Social Security program, his private saving for retirement is reduced; the result is that the nation's capital accumulation needs are partially unmet; to offset this reduced saving by the individual, the Social Security program should collect more in taxes than is needed for current benefits payments and thus accumulate a sizable trust fund; the assets of the trust fund would be invested in government securities; thus the amount of government securities held privately would be reduced and more private savings would be freed for use in developing the economy. Elaboration of this argument will not be made here. It should be noted, however, that this argument for funding is a controversial one, and it is difficult for various experts to reach agreement on the extent, if any, to which the Social Security program has resulted in a reduction in private saving.

With respect to the general question of funding, whatever the rationale, it is important to note the difficulty of assessing the effect on the economy, particularly over the longer term, of collecting higher taxes from today's generation of taxpayers and the same or lower taxes from tomorrow's generations. The effect would depend in part upon how the government utilized the additional funds placed at its disposal as well as the ways in which private saving would in fact be affected. These matters are extremely difficult to evaluate retrospectively; they are even more difficult to evaluate in advance.

In assessing the financial stability of Social Security, much more is involved than the question of whether to use current-cost or advance-funding methods. The most important test of financial soundness for Social Security is whether the future income (taxes and interest on the trust funds) can reasonably be expected to equal future benefits and administrative expenses.

This condition does not prevail uniformly for the various segments of the Social Security program. Under the Old-Age, Survivors, and Disability Insurance program, projected future income is approximately equal to future outgo for the next fifty years, on the average, according to the intermediate assumptions described in the Appendix; however, more recent projections indicate that relatively small deficits (less than 1 percent of taxable payroll) may be expected throughout the 1980s. On the other hand, substantial deficits are expected during the second quarter of the next century as the children of the post-World War II baby boom reach retirement age. Under the Hospital Insurance program, deficits are projected to begin to occur within ten years and to continue in rapidly increasing amounts each year thereafter. Under the Supplementary Medical Insurance program, there are no earmarked taxes scheduled beyond the next three years; hence it is difficult to define the deficit. Nonetheless, substantial increases in expenditures are projected for the next fifty years or so.

The matter of future financial deficits in the Social Security program is extremely important and is discussed in more detail in Chapter 7.

Trillion Dollar "Actuarial Deficits" and "Accrued Liabilities"

Actuarial Deficits

As discussed in Chapter 6, Social Security operates on a pay-as-you-go financing basis, sometimes called a current-cost basis. The trust funds are not large, relative to expenditures, and serve only as contingency funds, not as guaranty funds. The financial stability of Social Security depends, therefore, upon the ability and willingness of the nation's workers and employers to continue to pay the taxes necessary to support the benefit payments. Accordingly, it is essential that we constantly monitor estimated future income and expenditures to determine whether they are still in "actuarial balance" and whether our Social Security program is still viable. When projected future income and expenditures are not in balance, an "actuarial deficit" or an "actuarial surplus" exists—depending upon whether projected expenditures are greater than income, or vice versa. Actuarial projections made during the past several years, including the most recent projections, indicate that Social Security has a significant actuarial deficit. This deficit is

81

discussed in the following sections for each of the major portions of the Social Security program.

OASDI Deficit

In determining the actuarial balance of the Old-Age, Survivors, and Disability Insurance program, projections have been made customarily during a seventy-five-year future period. This covers the remaining lifetime of most current participants in Social Security.

Chart 7.A shows graphically the projected expenditures and tax income under the OASDI program based upon the 1979 Annual Report of the Board of Trustees.[1] Expenditures are shown based upon the "intermediate" assumptions contained in this report and would, of course, have been lower or higher if the "optimistic" or "pessimistic" assumptions had been depicted. Table 7.1 gives the corresponding numerical comparison of the projected expenditures and tax income, and the resulting differences, over various periods. For convenience of presentation, both the chart and the table ignore the trust fund balances since they play a relatively small role in the financing of a current-cost system.[2]

As indicated in Chart 7.A, tax income rises in steps in accordance with increases scheduled under the law. The expenditures rise in dollar amounts but generally decline as a percentage of taxable payroll from 1978 to 1981. This is because of the gradual expansion of the taxable payroll during that period from 84 percent of total payroll in covered employment to 90 percent. Expenditures then remain relatively level for the next twenty-five years, reflecting the combined effect of a projected rise in Disability Insurance expenditures and an expected temporary decline in Old-Age Insurance expenditures as small birth cohorts of the Depression years reach retirement age. Expenditures start rising rapidly early in the twenty-first century as the children of the post-World War II "baby boom" begin reaching retirement age. Around the year 2035 after all the children of this baby boom period (which ended in the 1960s) have reached retirement age, expenditures decline slightly and then level off.

Under the intermediate assumptions, OASDI tax income is

Chart 7.A

Projected Expenditures and Legislated Tax Income for Old-Age, Survivors, and Disability Insurance Program[a] Expressed as a Percentage of Effective Taxable Payroll[b]

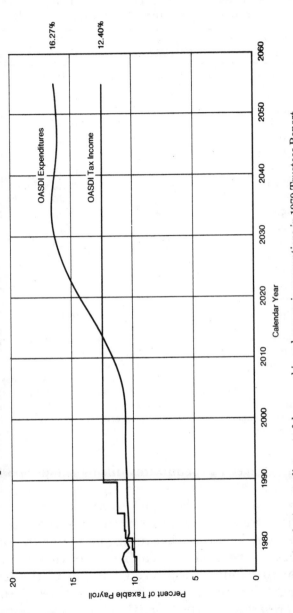

[a]Projected under intermediate set of demographic and economic assumptions in 1979 Trustees Report.

[b]"Effective taxable payroll" consists of total earnings subject to Social Security taxes, after adjustment to reflect the lower contribution rates on self-employment income, tips, and multiple-employer "excess wages." This adjustment is made to facilitate both the calculation of contributions (which is thereby the product of the tax rate and the payroll) and the comparison of expenditure percentages with tax rates.

Table 7.1

Projected Expenditures and Legislated Tax Income for Old-Age, Survivors, and Disability Insurance Program,[a] Expressed as a Percentage of Effective Taxable Payroll[b]

Calendar Year	OASDI Expenditures	OASDI Tax Income	Difference[c]
(1)	(2)	(3)	(4)
1979	10.31%	10.16%	−0.15%
1980	10.56	10.16	−0.40
1985	10.50	11.40	0.90
1990	10.70	12.40	1.70
1995	10.67	12.40	1.73
2000	10.65	12.40	1.75
2010	11.58	12.40	0.82
2020	14.29	12.40	−1.89
2030	16.44	12.40	−4.04
2040	16.29	12.40	−3.89
2050	16.15	12.40	−3.75
25-year averages:			
1979–2003	10.59	11.76	1.17
2004–2028	13.26	12.40	−0.86
2029–2053	16.30	12.40	−3.90
75-year average:	13.38	12.19	−1.20

[a]Projected under intermediate set of demographic and economic assumptions in 1979 Trustees Report. Figures for 1979 represent actual experience.
[b]"Effective taxable payroll" consists of total earnings subject to Social Security taxes, after adjustment to reflect the lower contribution rates on self-employment income, tips, and multiple-employer "excess wages." This adjustment is made to facilitate both the calculation of contributions (which is thereby the product of the tax rate and the payroll) and the comparison of expenditure percentages with tax rates.
[c]Negative figures represent deficits.

projected to exceed expenditures during the period from 1981 until the year 2015.[3] At this time the combined OASDI trust funds are projected to be equal to about three years' outgo. Thereafter outgo will exceed tax income, requiring that the interest earnings on the trust funds, and later the principal of the trust funds, be used to make benefit payments. By the year 2025, the trust funds are projected to fall to the level of one year's outgo, thus requiring an increase in taxes at that time in order to preserve the trust funds' ability to act as contingency reserves.

The actuarial balance of the OASDI program may be summarized during the next seventy-five years as follows: an actuarial surplus during the first twenty-five years of the seventy-five-year projection period, an approximately offsetting actuarial deficit during the second twenty-five-year period, and a substantial actuarial deficit during the latter third of the seventy-five-year period.

The average annual amount by which expenditures are projected to exceed tax income over the entire seventy-five-year projection period is 1.20 percent of taxable payroll. This actuarial deficit represents about 9 percent of average expenditures of 13.38 percent of taxable payroll.

Another way to express the actuarial deficit is as a single-sum amount—$800 billion as of January 1, 1979—determined by computing the excess of expenditures over tax income (sometimes positive and sometimes negative) in each of the next seventy-five years and discounting these amounts at interest[4] to the present time, and then reducing the sum of these amounts by the value of the trust fund at the present time.

If the actuarial deficit determined in 1979 is to be eliminated by the payment of additional taxes, it could be achieved, at least in theory, in one of two ways. A single-sum amount of $800 billion could be placed in the trust funds immediately, and the resulting trust funds together with interest thereon, supplemented by the currently scheduled Social Security taxes, would be sufficient to pay all benefits falling due in the next seventy-five years. At the end of that period, the trust funds would have returned to a relatively low level as at present.

As an alternative to this obviously impossible solution, additional taxes could be collected over the next seventy-five years. The average additional taxes would have to be equivalent to 1.20 percent of taxable payroll (approximately 10 percent of the average scheduled taxes of 12.19 percent). If it is desired that the trust fund be maintained at a relatively low level to serve as a contingency fund—as in recent years—the additional taxes would not be constant throughout the next seventy-five years but would be variable so as to approximately match emerging expenditures. In this event, average taxes (paid by the employee and employer combined) would be about 1 percent of taxable payroll less than already scheduled until the turn of the century, about 1 percent more than already scheduled during the first quarter of the next century, and about 4 percent more than already scheduled thereafter.

In summary, the actuarial deficit is simply the amount by which projected future expenditures for benefits and administration exceed the projected income and the value of the trust funds. The actuarial deficit can be stated in various ways, some of which make it appear more formidable than others. There should be no question, however, about the necessity of eliminating any significant actuarial deficit that may appear from time to time. Otherwise, scheduled benefits cannot be paid.

HI Deficit

In determining the actuarial balance of the Hospital Insurance program, projections have been made customarily during a twenty-five-year future period. There is no valid justification for limiting the projection period; it should be the same seventy-five-year period that is used in determining the actuarial balance of the OASDI program. Hospital Insurance is in effect a deferred retirement benefit commencing at age 65 (or after the receipt of twenty-four months of disability benefits). It is similar to an old-age retirement benefit except it is not paid in cash but in the form of partial provision of hospital services. The demographic changes in the population that will cause the OASDI program costs to increase rapidly after the turn of the century will also cause the HI program costs to increase rapidly.

Accordingly, the actuarial balance of the HI program is presented here for a seventy-five-year period. The figures for the first twenty-five years are based upon the 1979 Annual Report of the Board of Trustees,[5] and the figures for the ensuing fifty years are based upon information prepared by the Health Care Financing Administration actuaries but otherwise unpublished.

Chart 7.B shows graphically the projected expenditures and tax income under the HI program. Expenditures are based upon the "intermediate" assumptions employed by the trustees. Table 7.2 gives the corresponding numerical comparison of the expenditures and tax income, and the resulting differences, over various periods. For convenience of presentation both the chart and the table ignore the trust fund balances since they play a relatively small role in the financing of a current-cost system.

Chart 7.B
Projected Expenditures and Legislated Tax Income for Hospital Insurance Program[a]
Expressed as a Percentage of Effective Taxable Payroll[b]

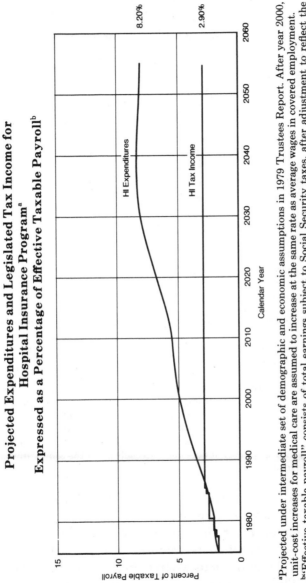

[a]Projected under intermediate set of demographic and economic assumptions in 1979 Trustees Report. After year 2000, unit-cost increases for medical care are assumed to increase at the same rate as average wages in covered employment.
[b]"Effective taxable payroll" consists of total earnings subject to Social Security taxes, after adjustment to reflect the lower contribution rates on self-employment income, tips, and multiple-employer "excess wages." This adjustment is made to facilitate both the calculation of contributions (which is thereby the product of the tax rate and the payroll) and the comparison of expenditure percentages with tax rates. This effective taxable payroll is slightly different for OASDI and HI because of the tax treatment of self-employed persons; however, it does not materially affect the comparisons.

Table 7.2

Projected Expenditures and Legislated Tax Income for Hospital Insurance Program[a] Expressed as a Percentage of Effective Taxable Payroll[b]

Calendar Year	HI Expenditures	HI Tax Income	Difference[c]
(1)	(2)	(3)	(4)
1979	2.00%	2.10%	0.10%
1980	2.12	2.10	−0.02
1985	2.73	2.70	−0.03
1990	3.51	2.90	−0.61
1995	4.27	2.90	−1.37
2000	4.92	2.90	−2.02
2010	5.60	2.90	−2.70
2020	6.77	2.90	−3.87
2030	8.13	2.90	−5.23
2040	8.39	2.90	−5.49
2050	8.20	2.90	−5.30
25-year averages:			
1979–2003	3.64	2.78	−0.86
2004–2028	6.27	2.90	−3.37
2029–2053	8.28	2.90	−5.38
75-year average:	6.06	2.86	−3.20

[a]Projected under intermediate set of demographic and economic assumptions in 1979 Trustees Report. After year 2000, unit-cost increases for medical care are assumed to increase at the same rate as average wages in covered employment. Figures for 1979 represent actual experience.

[b]"Effective taxable payroll" consists of total earnings subject to Social Security taxes, after adjustment to reflect the lower contribution rates on self-employment income, tips, and multiple-employer "excess wages." This adjustment is made to facilitate both the calculation of contributions (which is thereby the product of the tax rate and the payroll) and the comparison of expenditure percentages with tax rates. This effective taxable payroll is slightly different for OASDI and HI because of the tax treatment of self-employed persons; however, it does not materially affect the comparisons.

[c]Negative figures represent deficits.

Tax income rises in steps in accordance with increases scheduled under the law. Expenditures rise throughout the period before leveling off after the children of the post-World War II baby boom have reached retirement age. An actuarial deficit first occurs in the mid-1980s when expenditures begin to exceed tax income. Thereafter, an actuarial deficit is projected to occur each year in the future.

The average annual amount by which expenditures are projected to exceed tax income over the entire seventy-five-year projection period is 3.20 percent of taxable payroll, or about 53 percent of average expenditures of 6.06 percent of taxable payroll. Expressed as a single-sum amount, this actuarial deficit is about $2,500 billion as of January 1, 1979.

Accordingly, if the HI actuarial deficit is to be eliminated by the payment of additional taxes it could be achieved by:

placing a single-sum amount of $2,500 billion in the trust fund; or

paying additional taxes that would average about 3.20 percent of taxable payroll over the next seventy-five years (an increase of approximately 112 percent of the average scheduled taxes of 2.86 percent).

Assuming the trust fund is to be maintained at a relatively low level to serve only as a contingency fund, the additional taxes would not be constant throughout the next seventy-five years but would be variable so as to approximately match emerging expenditures. In this event, average taxes (paid by the employee and employer combined) would be about 1 percent of taxable payroll more than already scheduled until the turn of the century, about 3.5 percent more than already scheduled during the first quarter of the next century, and about 5.5 percent more than already scheduled thereafter.

This is a formidable deficit no matter how it is presented: a lump sum of $2,500 billion, or increased taxes averaging more than 3 percent of taxable payroll. Furthermore, the HI actuarial deficit is three times the size of the OASDI actuarial deficit, yet it is not formally acknowledged by the Board of Trustees, the Congress, the Administration, or the Health Care Financing Administration which has administered the HI program since March 1977.

OASDI and HI Combined Deficit

The preceding discussions of actuarial deficits for OASDI and HI were based upon the intermediate set of demographic and economic assumptions used by the Social Security actuaries in making projections for the 1979 Trustees Reports. The actual situation could be better—or it could be worse. Chart 7.C depicts the projected expenditures for OASDI and HI combined under the optimistic and pessimistic assumptions as well as the intermediate assumptions used in the 1979 Trustees Reports. Tax income expressed as a percentage of taxable

Chart 7.C

Projected Expenditures for Old-Age, Survivors, Disability, and Hospital Insurance Programs Combined under Alternative Demographic and Economic Assumptions,[a] and Legislated Tax Income, Expressed as a Percentage of Effective Taxable Payroll[b]

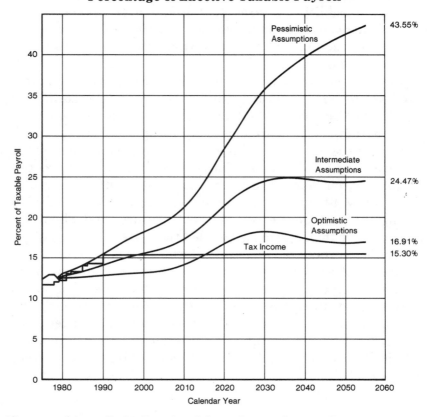

[a]See text and Appendix for discussion of alternative sets of assumptions.

[b]"Effective taxable payroll" consists of total earnings subject to Social Security taxes, after adjustment to reflect the lower contribution rates on self-employment income, tips, and multiple-employer "excess wages." This adjustment is made to facilitate both the calculation of contributions (which is thereby the product of the tax rate and the payroll) and the comparison of expenditure percentages with tax rates. This effective taxable payroll is slightly different for OASDI and HI because of the tax treatment of self-employed persons; however, it does not materially affect the comparisons.

payroll remains the same under all sets of assumptions. Table 7.3 gives the corresponding numerical comparison of the average expenditures and tax income, and the resulting deficits, over various periods for each of the three sets of assumptions.

Based upon the intermediate assumptions, the actuarial deficit for the OASDI and HI programs combined is 4.39 percent of taxable payroll on the average over the next seventy-five years (equivalent to $3,300 billion as of January 1, 1979). The optimistic assumptions produce an actuarial deficit of 0.38 percent of taxable payroll on the average over the next seventy-five years (equivalent to $300 billion as of January 1, 1979). The pessimistic assumptions produce an actuarial deficit of 12.00 percent of taxable payroll on the average over the next seventy-five years (equivalent to $6,800 billion as of January 1, 1979).

The taxes that are scheduled under present law (a tax rate for employees and employers combined that will increase by 25 percent from 12.26 percent in 1980 to 15.30 percent by 1990) will not be adequate to provide future benefits even under the optimistic assumptions. Under the pessimistic assumptions, scheduled future tax rates are woefully inadequate; that is, they are sufficient to provide only about half the benefits that will become payable during the coming seventy-five years.

At least one thing seems clear from examining these actuarial deficits. Only the foolhardy would continue to ignore the longer range financial problems projected for the Social Security program. It is not a question of whether future costs will be higher; it is a question of whether they will be so much higher as to be unaffordable. It is a question of whether we are making promises we will not be able to keep.

SMI Deficit

The question of the actuarial balance of the Supplementary Medical Insurance program is a difficult one because of the way in which the program is financed and the way in which future costs are presented (or not presented). Participants in SMI pay monthly premiums which account for about 30 percent of the current cost of the program. This percentage is expected to continue declining and to be about 10 percent by the year 2000. The amount of these premiums is determined for one year at a

Table 7.3

Projected Expenditures, Tax Income, and Deficits for Old-Age, Survivors, Disability, and Hospital Insurance Programs Combined, under Alternative Demographic and Economic Assumptions[a] Expressed as a Percentage of Effective Taxable Payroll[b]

Calendar Year	OASDHI Expenditures under...			Scheduled Tax Income	Tax Income Less Expenditures under...[c]		
	Optimistic Assumptions	Intermediate Assumptions	Pessimistic Assumptions		Optimistic Assumptions	Intermediate Assumptions	Pessimistic Assumptions
(1)	(2)	(3)	(4)	(5)	(6)	(7)	(8)
1979	12.31%	12.31%	12.31%	12.26%	-0.05%	-0.05%	-0.05%
1980	12.59	12.68	13.00	12.26	-0.33	-0.42	-0.74
1985	12.68	13.23	13.81	14.10	1.42	0.87	0.29
1990	13.11	14.21	15.38	15.30	2.19	1.09	-0.08
1995	13.34	14.94	16.89	15.30	1.96	0.36	-1.59
2000	13.41	15.57	18.42	15.30	1.89	-0.27	-3.12
2010	14.20	17.18	21.27	15.30	1.10	-1.88	-5.97
2020	16.91	21.06	28.16	15.30	-1.61	-5.76	-12.86
2030	18.50	24.57	35.66	15.30	-3.20	-9.27	-20.36
2040	17.34	24.68	39.66	15.30	-2.04	-9.38	-24.36
2050	16.78	24.35	42.52	15.30	-1.48	-9.05	-27.22
25-year averages:							
1979–2003	13.02	14.23	15.71	14.54	1.52	0.31	-1.17
2004–2028	15.84	19.53	25.73	15.30	-0.54	-4.23	-10.43
2029–2053	17.45	24.58	39.71	15.30	-2.15	-9.28	-24.41
75-year average:	15.43	19.44	27.05	15.05	-0.38	-4.39	-12.00

[a]See text and Appendix for discussion of alternative sets of assumptions. Figures for 1979 represent actual experience.

[b]"Effective taxable payroll" consists of total earnings subject to Social Security taxes, after adjustment to reflect the lower contribution rates on self-employment income, tips, and multiple-employer "excess wages." This adjustment is made to facilitate both the calculation of contributions (which is thereby the product of the tax rate and the payroll) and the comparison of expenditure percentages with tax rates. This effective taxable payroll is slightly different for OASDI and HI because of the tax treatment of self-employed persons; however, it does not materially affect the comparisons.

[c]Negative figures represent deficits.

time, approximately one year in advance. The balance of SMI costs is paid with general revenue.

Annual reports of the Board of Trustees on the financial condition of SMI include projections of income and expenditures for only three years. This limits any formal statement about the actuarial balance of the SMI program to a three-year period. SMI costs (relative to the payroll of active workers) may be expected to continue their rise until becoming nearly three times their current level early in the next century, yet no formal provision has been made to collect the taxes necessary to pay for these benefits. The theory seems to be "what we don't know won't hurt us."

Chart 7.D shows graphically the projected expenditures under the SMI program under the intermediate set of assumptions consistent with those used for the OASDI and HI programs. Also shown is the projected income from participants' premiums. Table 7.4 gives the corresponding numerical comparison of the expenditures and premium income, as well as the differences that must be drawn from general revenue during selected time periods. These amounts are expressed as a percentage of the payroll that is taxable for HI purposes even though the SMI program is not financed by payroll taxes. This is done to facilitate comparison with the other parts of the Social Security program. For convenience of presentation, both the chart and the table ignore the trust fund balances since they play a relatively small role in the financing of the SMI program.

The actuarial deficit could well be considered to be the amount by which projected future expenditures for benefits and administration exceed the projected income from premiums paid by the participants. Under this theory, future general revenue would not be taken into account since it has not been earmarked in any way to ensure its availability. Using such a definition, the actuarial deficit over the next seventy-five years would average approximately 1.78 percent of the payroll taxable for HI purposes. Expressed as a single-sum amount, this actuarial deficit is about $1,400 billion as of January 1, 1979. A range of possible future SMI costs is illustrated by Chart 7.E which shows projected expenditures under the three alternative sets of assumptions consistent with those used for

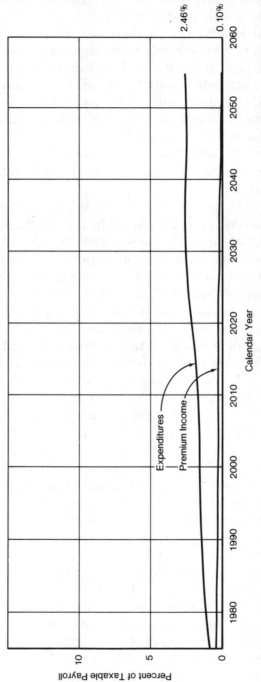

Chart 7.D

Projected Expenditures and Premium Income
for Supplementary Medical Insurance Program
Expressed as a Percentage of Effective Taxable Payroll[a]

[a]Although the SMI program is not financed by payroll taxes, its cost is shown for comparative purposes as a percentage of payroll that is taxable for HI purposes. Participation in SMI is optional and is financed by premiums paid by the enrollees, and by general revenue.

Table 7.4

**Projected Expenditures, Premium Income, and General Revenue
Requirements for Supplementary Medical Insurance Program[a]
Expressed as a Percentage of Effective Taxable Payroll[b]**

Calendar Year	SMI Expenditures	SMI Premium Income	Amount to Be Drawn from General Revenue
(1)	(2)	(3)	(4)
1979	0.88%	0.26%	0.62%
1980	0.95	0.26	0.69
1985	1.18	0.24	0.94
1990	1.39	0.21	1.18
1995	1.57	0.19	1.38
2000	1.60	0.16	1.44
2010	1.70	0.15	1.55
2020	2.11	0.14	1.97
2030	2.50	0.13	2.37
2040	2.48	0.12	2.36
2050	2.43	0.10	2.33
25-year averages:			
1979–2003	1.36	0.21	1.15
2004–2028	1.97	0.14	1.83
2029–2053	2.47	0.11	2.36
75-year average:	1.93	0.15	1.78

[a]Projected under intermediate set of demographic and economic assumptions in 1979 Trustees Report. Figures for 1979 represent actual experience.
[b]Although the SMI program is not financed by payroll taxes, its cost is shown for comparative purposes as a percentage of payroll that is taxable for HI purposes. Participation in SMI is optional and is financed by premiums paid by the enrollees, and by general revenue.

the OASDI and HI programs. There is no assurance, of course, that actual future costs will fall within this range.

The most important conclusions to be drawn from these statements about the actuarial deficit of the SMI program are that:

significantly larger costs can be expected for the future; and

these costs should be estimated, acknowledged, and some formal procedure adopted to assure their payment.

The present procedure of not formally acknowledging these future costs is unfair to present and future taxpayers and beneficiaries. It makes it too easy for us to make promises of future benefits that we may not be able and willing to finance.

Chart 7.E

Projected Expenditures for Supplementary Medical Insurance Program under Alternative Demograhpic and Economic Assumptions[a] Expressed as a Percentage of Effective Taxable Payroll[b]

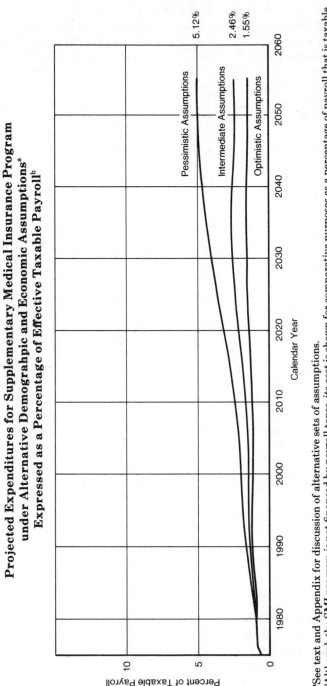

[a]See text and Appendix for discussion of alternative sets of assumptions.

[b]Although the SMI program is not financed by payroll taxes, its cost is shown for comparative purposes as a percentage of payroll that is taxable for HI purposes. Participation in SMI is optional and is financed by premiums paid by the enrollees, and by general revenue.

The Need to Eliminate Actuarial Deficits

Substantial actuarial deficits exist for all segments of the Social Security program. The OASDI deficit has been determined and acknowledged; but since it will not become significant until the children of the post-World War II baby boom begin to retire about twenty-five years from now, it has not yet been taken seriously. The HI deficit during the next twenty-five years has been determined but not very well acknowledged. The more significant HI deficit projected to occur early in the next century is not even computed and formally reported to Congress by the Board of Trustees. SMI deficits—or high future costs if you will—are not computed, they are not communicated to Congress, and they are not even worried about by anyone except a few knowledgeable and concerned individuals.

The total amount of these actuarial deficits for the Social Security progam (OASDI, HI, and SMI combined) is a staggering sum: $4,700 billion, or $4.7 trillion. These actuarial deficits must be eliminated. Indeed, they *will* be eliminated sooner or later. *It should be obvious that gaps between income and outgo (actuarial deficits) will be closed eventually by either raising taxes or lowering benefits.* It is simply a question of whether we plan in advance the best way to close these future gaps or wait until it is so late that we have no desirable options available to us.

The only prudent action is to eliminate the actuarial deficits now: to revise the benefits or the financing procedures, or both, so that anticipated future expenditures will equal anticipated future income on the basis of the best information available at this time. To do otherwise is to court disaster.

Accrued Liabilities

Once the actuarial deficits have been eliminated and Social Security is in actuarial balance—with anticipated future income equal to anticipated future expenditures—there is still the question of the "accrued liability." This is a completely separate issue from the "actuarial deficit." The existence and the amount of the accrued liability has no relationship whatsoever to the actuarial deficit, although these two terms are frequently confused.

The accrued liability can be defined as the present value of benefits that have been earned or accrued as of a given date but that will not actually be paid until a later date. This concept is discussed in the following sections for each major portion of the Social Security program.

OASDI Accrued Liability

At the beginning of 1979 there were 35 million persons receiving monthly Social Security benefits of about $105 billion per year under the OASDI program. All conditions had been met for these benefits to be payable in the future, thus the benefits may be considered to have been fully earned or accrued. The present value of these future benefits is estimated to be about $950 billion; that is, a fund of $950 billion invested at interest would be just enough to pay all the future benefits to these persons and the fund would be exhausted at the time the last benefit payment fell due. Accordingly, the accrued liability for benefits payable to these 35 million persons may be said to be $950 billion.

It is more difficult to define the accrued liability for the more than 100 million persons who have participated in the Social Security program at some time in the past and who are potential recipients of benefits at some time in the future. Because of their earlier participation, these persons may be considered to have earned or accrued a certain portion of the benefits that will be paid to them at some time in the future. It should be emphasized, however, that these benefits are not vested from a legal point of view because, in theory at least, the entire program could be terminated by Congress at any time. Section 1104 of the Social Security Act provides that "The right to alter, amend, or repeal any provision of this Act is hereby reserved to the Congress." As a practical matter, however, it is more reasonable to assume that Social Security will continue without abrupt change. A variety of methods can be used to calculate the amount of benefits and the value thereof that should be assigned to this earlier participation. According to a recent study made by the Office of the Actuary of the Social Security Administration,[6] it is reasonable to consider this accrued liability as of January 1, 1979 to be approximately $2,750 billion.

When that amount is added to the accrued liability of $950 billion for those persons already receiving benefits, the result is a total accrued liability of some $3,700 billion. Since the OASDI trust funds had assets of about $32 billion on January 1, 1979, the "unfunded accrued liability" could be considered to be about $3,668 billion, or $3.7 trillion. The unfunded accrued liability as of any given date may be viewed as the amount by which benefits, paid or promised with respect to earlier years of participation in the system, exceed the amount of taxes paid during those years by employees and their employers.

HI Accrued Liability

There has been little, if any, concern expressed about the accrued liability under the HI program. Yet, the HI program is similar to the OASDI program in most respects that are relevant to an accrued liability. Hospital Insurance is, in effect, a deferred benefit commencing at age 65 (or, if earlier, after the receipt of twenty-four months of disability benefits). The benefit is not paid in cash but rather in kind in the form of partial provision of hospital services. An individual may not be hospitalized and thus may not appear to receive tangible benefits; nevertheless, benefits are received just as surely as if cash benefits were paid to the individual in the amounts necessary to purchase the Hospital Insurance benefits. The program is financed by a portion of the Social Security taxes paid by active workers. To be eligible for HI benefits, a retired worker must be eligible for monthly old-age benefits, which in turn requires a certain minimum period of tax-paying participation in Social Security.

At the beginning of 1979, there were approximately 26.5 million persons eligible to receive partial reimbursement for hospital costs in the event of their illness. All conditions had been met for these benefits to be payable in the future, thus the benefits may be considered to have been fully earned or accrued without further payment of Social Security taxes by the individuals eligible for benefits. The present value of these future benefits is estimated to be about $400 billion; that is, a fund of $400 billion invested at interest would be just enough to pay all the future benefits to these persons and the fund would be exhausted at the time the last benefit payment fell due. Accordingly, the accrued liability for benefits payable to these 26.5 million persons may be said to be $400 billion.

Similarly, it is reasonable to assume that an accrued liability exists for the more than 100 million persons who have participated in the Social Security program at some time in the past and who are potential recipients of benefits at some time in the future. Because of their earlier participation, these persons may be considered to have earned or accrued a certain portion of the HI benefits that will be paid to them in the future, although these benefits are not vested from a legal point of view. No formal estimates have been made of this accrued liability by the actuaries of the Health Care Financing Administration; however, it is probably of the magnitude of $1,100 billion. When that amount is added to the accrued liability of $400 billion for those persons already eligible for HI benefits, the result is a total accrued liability of about $1,500 billion. Since the HI trust fund had assets of $11 billion as of January 1, 1979, this would still leave an "unfunded accrued liability" of $1,489 billion, or about $1.5 trillion. Just as with the OASDI program, the unfunded accrued liability as of any given date may be viewed as the amount by which benefits, paid or promised with respect to earlier years of participation in the system, exceed the amount of taxes paid during those years by employees and their employers.

SMI Accrued Liability

The accrued liability for the SMI program is somewhat more elusive and difficult to define because of two features that distinguish it from the OASDI and HI programs:

Participation is voluntary, although some 95 percent of those eligible are in fact participants.

Eligibility does not depend upon whether past Social Security taxes have been paid; rather, it depends upon whether "premiums" are paid after eligibility for benefits commences. Anyone eligible for the HI program is eligible for SMI, but anyone aged 65 and over with at least five years' residence in the United States is also eligible.

These differences are more of form than substance, however. Virtually everyone who becomes eligible will undoubtedly elect to participate in SMI, and participation will continue throughout his remaining lifetime. Furthermore, although eligibility does not depend upon the payment of Social Security taxes, the premiums required for eligibility are so insignificant it seems reasonable to assume that the right to receive SMI benefits after age 65 accrues ratably during a person's working lifetime prior to age 65.

At the beginning of 1979 there were approximately 26.3 million persons eligible to receive partial reimbursement for medical costs covered under the SMI program. All conditions had been met for these benefits to be payable in the future provided only that the participants continue to pay nominal premiums. For this group of participants, the premiums represent less than 20 percent of the total cost of future benefits; therefore, it is virtually certain that present participants will continue their eligibility by paying premiums.

The present value of the portion of these future benefits that will not be financed by the participants' premiums and thus will be paid from general revenue is estimated to be about $100 billion. This may be termed the accrued liability for these 26.3 million participants.

Similarly, it seems reasonable to assume that an accrued liability exists for the more than 100 million persons who are in the active work force paying taxes (personal income taxes, not payroll taxes) to support the SMI program and who will be eligible for SMI benefits when they reach age 65. Just as with the other parts of Social Security, from a strictly legal point of view there are no vested benefits or accrued liabilities because the entire program can be terminated at any time. It seems more reasonable, however, to assume that the SMI program will continue without abrupt change.

Although no formal estimates have been made of this accrued liability by the actuaries of the Health Care Financing Administration, it is probably of the magnitude of $300 billion. When that amount is added to the accrued liability of $100 billion for those persons already eligible for SMI benefits, the result is a total accrued liability of about $400 billion. Since the SMI trust fund had assets of $4 billion as of January 1, 1979, this would leave an unfunded accrued liability of $396 billion, or about $0.4 trillion. The unfunded accrued liability as of any given

date may be viewed as the amount by which benefits, paid or
promised with respect to earlier years of participation in the
system, exceed the amount of premiums paid by participants
and general taxes paid by all taxpayers (and allocated to the
SMI program) during those years.

The Significance of the Accrued Liability

The total accrued liability as of January 1, 1979, under Social
Security (OASDI, HI, and SMI combined) is some $5,600
billion, or about $6 trillion. The total assets of the Social
Security trust funds are only $48 billion, thus the *unfunded*
accrued liability is also approximately $6 trillion.

This unfunded accrued liability is based upon the intermediate set of demographic and economic assumptions used by
the Social Security actuaries in making projections for the 1979
Trustees Reports. It would not be markedly different based
upon the optimistic or pessimistic assumptions referred to
previously. Compared with the actuarial deficit, there is relatively little variation in the unfunded accrued liability based
upon the alternative assumptions. This is true, in part, because
the unfunded accrued liability is related to a closed group of
existing participants in Social Security and is thus independent
of future birth rates.

As indicated in Chapter 6, if the Social Security program
were a private system, it would be considered desirable to begin
to collect more income than is necessary for current benefit
payments and to accumulate a substantial fund in order to
transform this *unfunded* accrued liability into a *funded*
accrued liability. But, as also discussed in Chapter 6, it is not
necessary to fund the Social Security accrued liability if it is
assumed that Social Security will exist forever and that its
promised benefits, together with other national commitments
for the future, are consistent with the nation's ability to
produce in the future. In other words, an unfunded accrued
liability is not necessarily unacceptable for the Social Security
program.

The existence of an unfunded accrued liability is significant,
however, and should not be dismissed lightly—as some observ-
ers are wont to do. As already noted, an accrued liability
represents the value of benefits that have been earned or

accrued as of today but that will not be paid until a later date. A small part of the accrued liability is funded but most of it is unfunded. The unfunded accrued liability represents the value of benefits that have been promised as a result of service to date but that have not yet been paid for.

In other words, persons who have participated in Social Security the past forty years or so have received benefits (some of which will not be paid until later) of considerably greater value than the taxes they have paid. This excess value is equal to the unfunded accrued liability or approximately $6 trillion. Is it any wonder that we heard so few complaints about Social Security during its first forty years of existence? If taxpayers had paid the full cost of benefits accruing the past forty years, their taxes would have been about five times as much as were actually paid.

Some critics advocate terminating Social Security, part of their reasoning being that it will resolve its financial problems. If Social Security were terminated today *and* if we satisfied the promises made to date, we would have to pay benefits to millions of people currently receiving benefits or expecting to receive benefits in the future (only the benefits earned because of past service and excluding benefits that would have been earned in the future). This would require a lump sum amount today of $6 trillion (the unfunded accrued liability) or an equivalent amount spread over future years. The nation thus has a "hidden liability" of approximately $43,000 for every adult now between ages 20 and 65, or more than $24,000 for every living man, woman, and child regardless of age. This is seven times the estimated national debt of $800 billion as of January 1, 1979, the government's officially acknowledged liability.

The fact we must face is that we have made promises worth $6 trillion more than we have collected in taxes in the past. The choices are not many. We can make good on the promises by collecting higher future taxes than would have been required otherwise, or we can renounce some of the promises already made. Some would favor continuing to hide this unfunded accrued liability; but, whether hidden or explicitly acknowledged, it represents a significant lien on the nation's goods and services to be produced in the future.

Conclusion

We have seen that the existence of an unfunded accrued liability is not necessarily a sign of financial weakness in our Social Security system, provided we have arranged for future tax collections that are adequate to pay future benefits. In the final analysis, the future financial stability of Social Security depends upon the ability and willingness of the nation's workers and employers to continue to pay the taxes necessary to support the benefit payments.

The combined tax rate in 1980 was 12.26 percent of taxable payroll (6.13 percent from the worker and 6.13 percent from the employer). The combined tax rate is *scheduled* to rise to 15.30 percent by 1990, although the taxpayers have not yet demonstrated their willingness to pay these increased taxes.

The actuarial deficits under our present Social Security program imply *tax increases above and beyond those already scheduled.* To eliminate these substantial actuarial deficits, it seems likely that the combined tax rates under the OASDI and HI programs must rise to at least 24 percent within the next forty or fifty years: that is, double the present tax rates. Under more pessimistic assumptions, these tax rates must be triple the present rates. In addition, substantial but as yet unrecognized future taxes will be required to support the SMI program.

Painful as it may be to communicate this information to the taxpayer, it must be done. Since the financial stability of Social Security is based upon the taxpayer's *ability and willingness* to pay future taxes, we have a compelling obligation to keep the taxpayer informed about how high those taxes may be. If we are not willing to so advise the taxpayer, we have no right to use a current-cost financing method whose very foundation is the taxpayer's *ability and willingness* to make future tax payments.

Part Three
Commentary on
Selected Topics

Part Two contained basic descriptions of the Social Security program and the way it works. It gave the background information to permit a more informed discussion of Social Security—the way it is now and the way the reader may wish it to be in the future.

Part Three is designed to answer in a more direct way some of the questions that are frequently raised about Social Security. Also, it presents a commentary on aspects of Social Security that are ignored too frequently. In some cases the commentary will stand on its own; however, in others it will be more meaningful if Part Two has been read previously. To the extent the commentary on a topic is self-contained, it may duplicate other sections of the book.

8
Public Understanding of Social Security

The most important problem confronting Social Security in the immediate future is not the program's high cost, mismanagement, inappropriate benefits, unfair treatment of participants, or any of the other charges directed at it by critics. The major problem facing Social Security is the widespread lack of understanding of the program—its basic rationale, the type and level of benefits it provides, the method of financing, the significance of the high future cost, and the tenuous relationship between taxes paid and benefits received by an individual. The average individual does not know what Social Security is really all about. He does not know what to expect from Social Security. Should he expect it to meet all of his needs (and those of his dependents) in the event of old age, disability, death, or sickness? Or should he expect it to be merely a floor of protection in meeting these needs, a floor upon which he and his employer should build through supplemental private saving and insurance and some form of retirement program? Apart from his expectations, what type and level of benefits does Social Security actually provide in meeting these various needs? Most people don't know.

Social Security was enacted on August 14, 1935, some forty-five years ago. It is not a new program and no sudden and dramatic revisions have been made. The Social Security Administration has published millions of pamphlets explaining Social Security. The news media—radio, television, magazines, and newspapers—have issued billions of words and pictures on the subject. Hundreds of books have been written about every aspect of Social Security. So how did this public misunderstanding come about? It is probably a result of the following combination of factors.

First, in explaining Social Security over the years the government has employed certain rhetoric that has contributed to the confusion. The use of words and phrases like "insurance," "trust fund," "account," "contributions," and "earned right," while not necessarily wrong, has sometimes conveyed the wrong impression. Although the government may not have deliberately misled the public, it certainly has not been in the forefront of a movement to explain to the public the rationale of the Social Security program.

Moreover, during the first forty years of the program, the public did not devote very much effort to finding out what Social Security was all about. Taxes (euphemistically called "contributions") were fairly low; benefits to a retiring individual were high in relation to the taxes that had been paid; it almost seemed like something for nothing. That should have been reason enough to provoke a few more penetrating questions by the public than were actually asked. Over the past two or three years, however, this public apathy has evaporated just as rapidly as Social Security taxes have risen. A significant number of people pay more in Social Security taxes than they do in federal income taxes. In 1980 an employee who earned $25,900 or more paid $1,587.67 in Social Security taxes. This was matched by his employer, resulting in total tax payments of $3,175.34. By the year 1990 this tax for a high wage earner will have increased to an estimated $4,039.20 for the employee and another $4,039.20 for the employer, or a total of $8,078.40. No longer will the public be indifferent to Social Security—the taxes paid and the benefits received.

Lastly, the media should assume some responsibility for the misunderstanding. It takes considerable time and effort to learn enough about Social Security to report on it in a meaningful way. Not enough people have been willing to invest that-much time, and the result has been an undue amount of incomplete and confusing media coverage of the program.

If this general misunderstanding of Social Security continues, the inevitable result will be growing dissatisfaction and frustration among the taxpayers, and increasing reluctance to pay the taxes required to support the program. There is no excuse for permitting this lack of understanding to continue. Widespread understanding of the Social Security program may result in a certain amount of trauma and even disruption among the public, but even more disruption will result if the current misunderstanding is allowed to continue.

It is unlikely that rational changes can be made in the Social Security program as long as the present low level of under-standing of the program exists. In the future, public under-standing or misunderstanding will play a much more critical role in determining the shape of the program than it has in the past when the payroll tax was relatively low and when the taxpayer was in a less questioning frame of mind. If people understand Social Security, there is a much greater chance that the program will be modified to coincide with their desires and thus gain the public acceptance obviously necessary for a program that will pay benefits, and require tax collections, of almost three trillion dollars during the next ten years.

Accordingly, a careful analysis should be made of the Social Security program, as well as the various other governmental income maintenance programs, to determine exactly what policy is inherent in such programs. This rationale, once deter-mined, should be explained clearly to the public. Everyone should understand the extent to which an individual is respon-sible for himself and his dependents in the event of his retire-ment, disability, death, or sickness and the extent to which the government (supported by the resources of the working segment of the population) is responsible.

In addition to the rationale, the cost of Social Security both now and in the future should be acknowledged and explained clearly to the public. No further attempts should be made to conceal the cost, to minimize the importance of the cost, or to apologize for the cost. Such efforts will not change the cost in any way.

After having been informed of the rationale, the cost, and other features of the Social Security program, the public will then be in a position to reaffirm the program or ask that it be revised. It seems likely that some change will be called for as the real cost and significance of Social Security become known. It is entirely possible that the public will reverse the trend in recent years of increasing governmental intervention in private affairs and decide that the "government should provide" only those benefits that can be provided in no other way, and that the individual should be responsible for himself and his dependents to the fullest extent possible.

9
The Need for a Periodic Benefit Statement

When you reach age 65 there is a good chance that you will be eligible for a monthly retirement benefit from one or more sources: Social Security, employer-sponsored retirement plan, personal insurance and annuity policies, and so on. If you become disabled prior to retirement, you may be eligible likewise for disability benefits from several sources. Moreover, if you die your spouse and children may be eligible for various "survivors benefits."

It is obviously important that you and your family know, at least approximately, the type and level of benefits that will be payable in these various events. Such knowledge will enable you to make private arrangements to fill any needs that may not be satisfied by Social Security and the various employee benefit programs in which you participate. Without full knowledge of the benefits that may be payable by programs outside your immediate control, it is almost certain that you will either overprovide or underprovide for your own future needs and those of your family.

It is difficult to obtain this information about your eligibility for future benefits. The prospects have brightened in recent years, however, and the future looks even better.

Private Pension Plan Benefits

Some employers have always done a good job informing employees about details of their employee benefit plans; others have not.

Congress passed the Employee Retirement Income Security Act (ERISA) in 1974 which required, among other things, that the administrator of a private pension plan make available to the employees copies of the plan and related documents as well as a summary of the essential features and provisions.

The Internal Revenue Code has long required that a qualified pension plan be reduced to writing and communicated by appropriate means to the plan participants and their beneficiaries. It was ERISA, however, that first required the plan administrator to furnish each participant and beneficiary a summary plan description written in a manner "calculated to be understood by the average plan participant or beneficiary." This is important since a plan document is usually complex and written in legal jargon.

The summary plan description must include the important plan provisions, a description of benefits, the circumstances that may result in disqualification or ineligibility, and the procedures to be followed in presenting claims for benefits under the plan. Upon the request of a plan participant or beneficiary, the plan administrator must provide, on the basis of the latest information available, the total benefits that have accrued in respect of the participant, as well as those that have vested, that is, become nonforfeitable. No more than one request per year may be made by a participant or beneficiary for this information. When an employee terminates from a plan with vested benefits, the employer is obligated to provide him without request a statement of the amount of his vested benefits.

This level of information disclosure is a vast improvement over practices that prevailed in the past. There is still much room for improvement, however, in providing information that is complete enough to be of value yet simple enough to be understood. Public employee retirement plans (covering employees of federal, state, county, and municipal governments) are not subject to these ERISA disclosure requirements;

hence, the amount of information disclosed varies considerably among public employee groups. Some public employees are well informed about their benefits; others are not.

Social Security Benefits

Social Security is another matter. Information is available (for those who seek it out) about the type and level of benefits that are payable in general. Very little information is available, however, about the benefits that may become payable to an individual in a particular situation. The average employee covered by Social Security does not know the amount of monthly benefits that would be payable to his spouse and children if he should die. Neither he nor his spouse realizes that some or all of these benefits may be lost if the surviving spouse works in paid employment after his death. Hardly any employee knows how much, if anything, would be payable in disability benefits if he should become unable to work any longer. This lack of information extends to almost every participant in Social Security and to every benefit provided.

In some instances, when employers provide estimates of private plan benefits that will be payable at retirement they also provide estimates of Social Security retirement benefits, particularly when there is an interrelationship between the benefits. Seldom, however, is detailed information provided about Social Security benefits that may be payable other than at retirement or, in some cases, disability.

Information Provided by the Social Security Administration

Very little, if any, information is provided automatically to taxpayers about the specific benefits they may expect to receive from Social Security. It is possible for a taxpayer to go through life without receiving a single communication from the Social Security Administration (SSA) about his or her potential benefits.

This is not to say that the Social Security Administration tries to hide information about the program. Thousands of pamphlets are printed and distributed every year describing in general terms the benefits that are available. Radio, television, and newspapers often have public service announcements urging people to apply for benefits if they believe they are eligible. The Social Security Administration has hundreds of employees in offices throughout the country giving speeches to civic meetings and various groups of employees to explain Social Security. Nevertheless, this is a small effort compared to the large numbers of people who need more information: 35 million people currently receiving benefits and 115 million people (and their employers) paying taxes.

The Social Security Administration does make a concerted effort to see that benefits are paid to everyone who is eligible. District offices of Social Security throughout the country are responsible for developing and maintaining outreach activities with organizations and institutions having knowledge of potential claimants so they can be contacted by SSA representatives. In many cases a death claim is filed by a funeral home or other party that has paid the burial expenses. When such a claim is filed (the maximum death benefit is $255), SSA usually follows up to see if any survivors benefits are payable (sometimes worth hundreds of thousands of dollars). SSA representatives in many areas make routine visits to hospitals to determine whether anyone may be eligible for disability or other benefits.

The Medicare program poses a particular problem of making certain that everyone who is eligible for benefits actually receives them. Medicare becomes available at age 65 whether you are retired or still working. When you apply for retirement benefits, this is an automatic application for Medicare. If you do not retire by age 65, you must apply for Medicare separately. If someone is within three months of age 65 and has not applied for benefits, SSA has generally attempted to contact such person to advise of his eligibility for Medicare. SSA is handicapped in this area, however, since its records do not indicate current addresses (only the address at the time the Social Security number was issued). SSA used to obtain many of these addresses from the Internal Revenue Service files of individual income tax returns; however, recent privacy legislation prohibits sharing of personal information among the government agencies, and SSA no longer has access to current addresses of its taxpayers.

By one means or another most persons learn eventually of their eligibility and receive most of the benefits to which they are entitled. The most common loss is probably from filing a late application and losing benefits because of limits on making retroactive payments.

In contrast to the information it furnishes automatically, the Social Security Administration provides a much broader range of information to those who request it. Unfortunately, not enough people realize the burden is on them to ask for information and even fewer know how to articulate their requests.

Consider the following example of special information that can be obtained. You can file a form with SSA (Form OAR-7004, available at any Social Security office) and request "a statement of your Social Security earnings." You will then receive a statement showing the amount of earnings on which Social Security taxes have been paid in each of the past three years, as well as the total for your lifetime. It is important that you request this earnings statement and verify your records at least every three years so that any errors can be corrected. In general, an earnings record can be corrected at any time up to three years, three months, and fifteen days after the year in which earnings were received. SSA used to encourage people to check their earnings statements regularly but, for some reason, no longer does this.

There is not much use for the information in the earnings statement except to verify SSA's records of your earnings. It will not enable you to determine your current eligibility for benefits or to calculate the amount of such benefits. You can request additional information, however, when you file Form OAR-7004 by appropriately annotating the form. For example you could ask for:

> The number of quarters of coverage on your record. This would help you determine whether you meet the requirements for various benefits.
> An itemized record of your covered earnings by employer and calendar quarter beginning with your first quarter of employment and continuing to the present. This would help you compute the approximate amount of benefits to which you may become entitled (except

this is such a complicated calculation that it requires an expert to do it).

An estimate of the amount of benefits you can expect to receive at retirement. SSA frequently computes this benefit estimate by assuming that you have no covered earnings in the future—an assumption that tends to underestimate your benefits. Furthermore, SSA prefers to provide this information only for persons within five years of retirement, that is, aged 57 or older.

Of course you can visit (or call or write) a local Social Security office at any time and request any information you desire. Chances are, if you have a reasonable request, it will be satisfied. SSA offices are probably best equipped to help you at the time you actually apply for benefits. It is in furnishing information prior to eligibility for benefits that SSA is most deficient.

The Need for More Information

The procedures currently followed by the Social Security Administration fall short of satisfying the following reasonable objectives:

A worker and family should know enough details about the type and level of benefits to enable them personally to provide such supplemental benefits as they believe necessary in the event of retirement, disability, illness, or death of the worker or the worker's spouse.

Workers and their employers should receive an accounting that is compatible with the substantial amounts of taxes they pay to support Social Security—total taxes per person of as much as $3,175 in 1980 and $3,950 in 1981 (and an estimated $8,078 in 1990).

Some of the current public dissatisfaction with Social Security is because people do not fully realize the scope of benefits payable. Better understanding would almost certainly result in better acceptance of Social Security.

There are subtle yet important dangers of not providing periodic benefit statements and not properly explaining Social Security. One of these dangers is that a person may begin to assume that "someone else" is making provision for his retirement, disability, illness, or death. Then, when he actually needs the benefits he may find that "someone else" has not done the job to his satisfaction. The high taxes we are paying make it easy for us to build up unreasonably high expectations for benefits from Social Security. Such benefits are expensive, however, and the fact is that if Social Security met *all* of our economic security needs, substantially higher taxes would be required.

On the other hand, the opposite of unexpectedly small benefits may occur. "Someone else" may begin providing you with benefits that you do not particularly need or want and at a cost that you may not be willing to pay. As taxpayers, we need to assert more control over the size and shape of the Social Security program, and an important beginning step is to have a better understanding of the benefits being provided.

All of this points to a simple conclusion. The Social Security Administration and the Health Care Financing Administration should be providing all participants—taxpayers and benefit recipients alike—with comprehensive periodic benefit statements.

Each person who is receiving Social Security benefits should be given clear and simple information about:

   The amount of benefits and the conditions under which they will continue to be payable. Particular care should be taken in explaining how hospital and medical expenses will be shared by the beneficiary and the Medicare program.

   Events that will change those benefits (death of one of the beneficiaries, changes in the Consumer Price Index, remarriage, changes in average hospital and medical costs, earned income in excess of specified amounts, etc.). Increases in deductibles and coinsurance under Hospital Insurance, and increases in SMI premiums, should not come as a surprise. Reductions in monthly benefits because of earned income should not come as a surprise. In fact, nothing should come as a surprise to a beneficiary.

   The way in which such benefits are financed. If taxes (payroll or other) are increased to continue providing benefits, this should be noted. If benefits are increased

(or reduced), this should be explained and any associated increase (or decrease) in taxes should be noted.
The status of the trust funds should be included in this
financial report. Media headlines should not have to
be relied upon for this information.

Each person who is paying Social Security taxes and who will
not receive benefits until some future date should be given clear
and simple information about:

The approximate amount of Social Security benefits that
would be payable if the taxpayer should die or become
disabled during the coming year, the conditions under
which such benefits would continue to be paid, and the
events that would change the benefits.

The approximate amount of Social Security benefits that
would be payable when the taxpayer becomes eligible
for retirement, the conditions under which the benefits would be paid, and the events that would change
the benefits in any way.

The amount of Social Security payroll taxes paid by the
individual taxpayer and the amount of earnings
recorded for use in future benefit computations, for
the most recent accounting period. This would permit
ready verification by the taxpayer of information vital
to the computation of future benefits.

The financial status of the various parts of the Social
Security program. If Social Security payroll taxes were
not adequate to pay benefits for the most recent
accounting period and if general revenue were used,
the amount should be noted. If the government
borrowed money to pay current benefits, this should
be noted and an explanation given of when and by
whom the debt will be repaid. If tax increases (or
decreases) or benefit increases (or decreases) are
imminent, they should be reported and explained. The
taxpayer deserves more than media headlines.

The preceding list of items for possible inclusion in a periodic
benefit statement is not exhaustive. It is given to illustrate the
kind of information that taxpayers and beneficiaries might find
useful in evaluating Social Security and making personal plans
for their future financial security.

Some may argue that providing this information is too costly—that it will require more government employees and thus will require higher taxes. This is true but is also largely irrelevant. Administrative expenses for Social Security currently amount to only about 2 percent of benefit payments. A relatively small increase in expenses in order to advise us about our benefits would not jeopardize the program; on the contrary, it would strengthen the program and make it more valuable to us.

Some may argue that Social Security is too large to permit the provision of individual benefit statements to 35 million beneficiaries and more than 100 million taxpayers—that the system would drown in its own paperwork. If this is true, and if Social Security has become so large and complex and difficult to administer that it cannot even provide taxpayers with details about what they are receiving for their tax dollars, then it should be transformed into a system that is manageable and understandable. There is a frightening possibility that this is, in fact, the situation and that in due time it will become evident to all concerned that Social Security has become so cumbersome that it cannot be administered—that an "administrative breakdown" is on the horizon.

These arguments notwithstanding, there is no excuse for the Social Security Administration not to provide periodic benefit statements that keep us informed about the benefits we can expect to receive in the future.

10
A Program of Future Promises—Fulfilled or Broken?

The actuary's job is to make forecasts about the future. Many other people do this in addition to the actuary: crystal ball gazers, seers, fortune tellers, economists, weathermen, and so on.

All of these people have one thing in common. When they forecast good news, their audience is grateful and happy. When they forecast bad news, their audience is unhappy and sometimes even belligerent. Moreover, people are so reluctant to believe bad news that they usually either refuse to listen or they label the forecaster as a panicmonger.

The actuary frequently has a thankless task. When he is making forecasts about possible future costs of pension benefits, his conclusion is almost always that future costs will be much higher than they are at present, that they will be much higher than most people expect, and that it may be difficult to pay for such pensions.

Why is it important to forecast the future costs of a program like Social Security? *Social Security is a program of future promises.*

Consider a retired man and his dependent wife who are both aged 65 and receiving a monthly Social Security check of $600.

Social Security promises to continue paying this monthly check as long as both the man and his wife are alive; the program also promises to pay $400 a month as long as the man lives after the death of his wife; or to pay $400 a month to the wife as long as she lives after the death of her husband.

But that is not all; Social Security promises to increase these monthly benefits so that they will keep up with the cost of living as measured by changes in the Consumer Price Index. If the cost of living increases 5 percent a year, in just fifteen years this $600 check will more than double to $1,247. If the cost of living increases 8 percent a year, this $600 check will more than triple to $1,903 within fifteen years.

This is a substantial promise which involves a lot of money (its "present value" is roughly $100,000) and a long period of years (benefits could still be payable thirty to forty years from now).

Let's take another example. Consider a male worker aged 20 who is just now entering the work force in employment covered by Social Security. The Social Security program makes the following promises:

> If the worker dies at an early age, leaving behind a dependent wife and children, monthly benefits will be paid, not necessarily continuously, during the next fifty to seventy-five years.
>
> If the worker becomes disabled at an early age, monthly benefits will be paid to the worker (and possibly to his wife and children) during the next fifty to seventy-five years.
>
> If the worker lives to retirement at age 65 (forty-five years from now), monthly benefits will be paid to the worker for the remainder of his life (and possibly to his wife, if she survives him, for the remainder of her life), promises spanning the next seventy-five or more years.

In each of these cases, benefits will be related to the worker's average monthly earnings in the future, and benefits, once commenced, will be adjusted for changes in the cost of living.

Hundreds of other promises are made about benefits that will be paid during the next seventy-five to one hundred years. When we make these promises about the benefits Social Security will pay during the next seventy-five years or so, with respect to the millions of people now living and paying Social Security taxes, it is essential that we make every reasonable effort to determine whether we can make good on the promises. There are two basic approaches we can take.

The first one is what I call the "head-in-the-sand" approach. We can determine the type and level of benefits that we think people *need*. We can determine the costs of paying such benefits during the next *two or three years,* and if these costs don't seem too high, we can adopt the benefits and *let the future take care of itself.* Sad to say, many policymakers prefer this approach although they might not describe it in quite these terms.

The other approach is to make a reasonable effort to look ahead throughout the period over which the promises have been made and determine their likely future costs. It can then be decided whether or not we can afford the cost of such promises, not only for the next two or three years, but for the period of approximately seventy-five years during which we will have to make good on our promises.

This is the task of the actuary: to do the best job possible of forecasting future expenditures under the program over a long period of years to determine whether it seems reasonable to make such promises in view of the income that is similarly forecast over the same period. It cannot be concluded, of course, that today's projections of future Social Security expenditures will be highly accurate. The cost of the program will depend on a variety of changeable factors such as the rate of future economic growth and future fertility levels. Social Security actuaries realize this fact, however, and make projections on the basis of alternative sets of economic and demographic assumptions that span a range considered reasonable by most professional analysts.

Our knowledge of the future is limited, to be sure; but it is not as limited as many people assume. Consider the following:

> Eighty-five percent of the people who are going to receive old-age retirement benefits at any time during the next seventy-five years are alive today.
>
> These people will receive 96 percent of the total old-age retirement benefits that are paid during the next seventy-five years.

> Of the total Social Security taxes that will be paid during the next fifty years, 81 percent will be paid by people who are now alive. For the first twenty-five years the figure is 99 percent.

Thus, while many of the projection factors are subject to substantial variation, the basic numbers of people who will be tomorrow's workers and beneficiaries can be determined today with reasonable certainty. The purpose of long-range projections is not to predict the future with certainty (no one, obviously, can do that) but rather to indicate how the Social Security program would operate in the future under a variety of economic and demographic conditions, any of which could reasonably be expected to occur. Such projections provide a valuable test of the reasonableness and long-range viability of the Social Security provisions that we enact today.

The extent to which we are interested in projections of future income and outgo of the Social Security program and the prospects for its continued financial health depends in part upon our own age. A person just now retiring at age 65 may be content to worry about Social Security's financial health for about the next twenty years or so. On the other hand, a person now aged 40 should be concerned about Social Security's financial health during the next fifty years at least. The Veteran's Administration is keenly aware of the long-range nature of pension promises. In mid-1979 the VA was still making monthly benefit payments to 103 widows and 142 needy children of Civil War veterans, both Union and Confederate.

The "head-in-the-sand" approach is taken by far too many people. I have watched in amazement as prominent politicians, policymakers, and labor leaders have taken this approach. It is understandable, perhaps even forgivable, for a layman to take this approach, particularly if he has never had the situation properly explained to him. It is completely irresponsible, however, for a politician or a labor leader or a policymaker to take such an approach, especially when he has been informed about the long-range consequences of promises inherent in a social insurance program. There is no excuse for persons in responsible positions not to familiarize themselves with the possible long-range consequences of their actions.

It is important to note that the Board of Trustees of the Social Security program has not been consistent in assessing our nation's ability to fulfill the promises we have made under the various parts of Social Security. Specifically, consider the following:

Old-Age, Survivors, and Disability Insurance Programs: Projections are made for seventy-five years; however, there is steady pressure from the "head-in-the-sand" devotees to reduce this to as short a period as twenty-five years and thus to ignore the consequences of the inevitable transition from the present youthful population to a future older population.

Hospital Insurance Program: Projections are made for only twenty-five years. Hospital Insurance benefits are paid principally for persons aged 65 and over; thus Hospital Insurance benefits may be viewed as a form of retirement benefit. Accordingly, it is just as important that seventy-five-year projections be made for these benefits as it is for the old-age benefits.

Supplementary Medical Insurance Program: Projections are made for *only three years.* These benefits are paid for substantially the same persons who receive Hospital Insurance benefits and thus are just another form of retirement benefit; hence, it is as important that seventy-five-year projections be made for these benefits as it is for the cash old-age benefits and the Hospital Insurance benefits. Any report that the SMI program is in "sound financial health" is practically meaningless since projections are made for only three years.

It seems clear that we should do a better job of recognizing the cost implications of the longer term promises we have made under our Social Security program. As indicated in Chapter 4, the present Social Security program makes promises that we cannot keep unless tax rates are at least doubled within the working lifetime of today's young people. We must examine our Social Security program carefully in the light of its possible long-range costs and make whatever changes we believe are advisable.

The purpose of the long-range cost estimates made by an actuary is not to scare people or to cause unrest about the future viability of Social Security. The purpose is to provide the information necessary to ensure that we do not make promises we cannot keep. The purpose is to make certain that Social Security is a program of *fulfilled promises*, not a program of *broken promises*.

11
Do We Get Our Money's Worth from Social Security?

A question that is being asked more and more often is "Do we get our money's worth from Social Security?" This question can be answered from several different points of view and each produces a different answer.

Taxes, Benefits, and Administrative Expenses

First, consider the Social Security program from the viewpoint of the nation as a whole, taking into account only the dollars involved. The total income and outgo, including interest earnings and administrative expenses, of the trust funds since the program's inception are summarized in Table 11.1 for the three parts of Social Security that are supported primarily by payroll taxes. Table 11.1 shows that over the years about $1,000 billion has been collected in payroll taxes. Normally, as these taxes were collected, they were used almost immediately to pay benefits. This procedure is known as "current-cost" or "pay-as-you-go" financing and is one of the fundamental characteristics of our Social Security program, as discussed in Chapter 6. For a variety of reasons, the taxes collected plus other trust fund income are not exactly equal to benefits and administra-

Table 11.1

**Summary of Cumulative Income and Outgo under the Old-Age,
Survivors, Disability, and Hospital Insurance Programs, 1937–79
(Amounts in Billions)**

	Old-Age and Survivors Insurance[a]	Disability Insurance[b]	Hospital Insurance[c]	Total
	(1)	(2)	(3)	(4)
Payroll Taxes	$796.0	$100.6	$127.7[d]	$1,024.3
Interest Earnings	32.4	4.7	5.5	42.6
General Revenue	6.1	0.9	8.4	15.4
Total Income	$834.5	$106.2	$141.6	$1,082.3
Benefit Payments	$796.8[e]	$ 97.0[f]	$125.2	$1,019.0
Administrative Expenses	13.0	3.6	3.2	19.8
Total Expenditures	$809.8	$100.6	$128.4	$1,038.8
Excess of Income Over Expenditures (Value of Trust Funds on 12-31-79)	$ 24.7	$ 5.6	$ 13.2	$ 43.5

[a]Taxes were first collected in 1937; monthly benefits were first paid in 1940.
[b]Taxes were first collected and benefits first paid in 1957.
[c]Taxes were first collected in January 1966; benefits were first paid in July 1966.
[d]Includes $1.3 billion in net transfers from the Railroad Retirement Fund and $0.06 billion in HI premiums paid by uninsured voluntary enrollees.
[e]Includes $14.6 billion in net transfers to the Railroad Retirement Fund and $0.07 billion in payments for vocational rehabilitation services.
[f]Includes $0.4 billion in net transfers to the Railroad Retirement Fund and $0.6 billion in payments for vocational rehabilitation services.

tive expenses paid in a given period. Any excess of income over expenditures is maintained in the appropriate trust fund for the payment of future benefits during periods when income is less than outgo. As indicated by Table 11.1, total income to the OASI, DI, and HI trust funds from 1937 through 1979 exceeded total expenditures by $43.5 billion—and this amount was present in the three funds at the beginning of 1980.

Trust fund assets are invested in U.S. Treasury securities, primarily special issues yielding interest at the same rate as the average of all outstanding long-term Treasury securities. During the twelve months ending June 30, 1979, the effective annual rate of interest earned by the combined assets of these three trust funds was approximately 7.5 percent. Total OASDHI interest earnings in 1937–1979 were $42.6 billion. The reason the interest earnings appear relatively small compared to the $1,000 billion in tax income is that the amount in the trust funds at any given time has been small relative to the total amount of benefit payments. The relatively low level of trust fund assets at any given time is consistent with the fund's purpose as a contingency reserve to cover any temporary short-falls that occur as a result of current-cost financing. Table 11.1 also indicates that administrative expenses have been low, amounting to only 2 percent of the benefit payments for all three trust funds combined.

Table 11.2 summarizes similar information on income and outgo for the Supplementary Medical Insurance trust fund. This program is not supported by payroll taxes, but rather by premiums paid by those electing to participate and by general revenue derived from all taxpayers (not just Social Security taxpayers).

Table 11.2

Summary of Cumulative Income and Outgo Under the Supplementary Medical Insurance Program, 1966–79 (Amounts in Billions)[a]

Premiums from Enrollees	$21.3
General Revenue	35.1
Interest Earnings	1.4
Total Income	$57.8
Benefit Payments	$48.3
Administrative Expenses	4.6[b]
Total Expenditures	$52.9
Excess of Income Over Expenditures (Value of SMI Trust Fund on 12-31-79)	$ 4.9

[a]Premiums were first collected in January 1966; benefits were first paid in July 1966.
[b]SMI administrative expenses are higher (relative to benefits) than under OASDI or HI due to the many benefit claims, often involving small amounts.

There is no mismanagement of the trust funds, there is no significant waste in administering the programs, and there is no significant misapplication of the funds. That is, benefits are generally determined correctly and are paid to those who are entitled to receive them according to Social Security law. Mistakes are made, of course, but most of the spectacular stories of fraud and abuse that have appeared in recent years are about Supplemental Security Income and Medicaid, welfare programs which are more difficult to administer than the Social Security benefits being discussed here. Accordingly, an examination of the past financial operation of the four major parts of the Social Security program could easily lead one to conclude that "Yes, we do get our money's worth from Social Security."

Individual Equity

A second viewpoint from which to consider whether we get our money's worth is the viewpoint of the individual. Chapter 3 explained the types of benefits that are payable under Social Security, and Chapter 5 explained how taxes are assessed in order to pay for those benefits. A careful reading of those sections will indicate that there is relatively little connection between what an individual pays in taxes and receives in benefits. The system was not designed to pay benefits to an individual that are equivalent to his tax payments. Accordingly, it is a futile exercise (perhaps even a waste of time) for individuals to attempt to determine whether they can expect to receive benefits from Social Security that are commensurate with their tax payments. The answer is "No." As illustrated below, many participants can expect to receive much more in benefits than can be provided by their taxes and many can expect to receive much less. This does not mean the system has failed because it is "unfair"; it means simply that the system was never designed on the principle of individual equity or "fairness" for each participant—even if many people thought it was.

Therefore, if one ignores the value to the nation as a whole of the existence of our Social Security program and is concerned only with the direct value a particular individual receives in terms of benefits or benefit protection, the answer to the question of whether we get our money's worth from Social Security is "No. Some get more and some get less."

Ample support for this conclusion is provided in a recent study by actuaries at the Social Security Administration. This study[1] considered the value of benefits payable under Social Security throughout the lifetime of more than 100 hypothetical workers. The study took into account only the principal benefits: those payable in the event of retirement, death, and disability, including benefits payable with respect to a spouse and children, as well as to the worker. "Secondary benefits" were not taken into account by this study; for example, benefits to dependent parents or divorced spouses. These secondary benefits, although valuable to those who receive them, are not a significant part of the overall cost of Social Security. Medicare benefits were excluded to simplify the calculations.

After the value of the benefits was computed, it was determined how much the worker and the employer would have to pay in taxes to finance such benefits. The cost was expressed as a level percentage of the worker's earnings that are subject to Social Security tax. Administrative expenses, which amount to less than 2 percent of benefit payments, were ignored.[2]

The results of this study are not surprising to anyone who understands how Social Security works; however, they will be astonishing to those who think "you get what you pay for" when you pay Social Security taxes. Table 11.3 briefly describes four hypothetical workers[3] and shows the tax rates that would be payable by each worker and his employer if total taxes were equivalent to the total benefits during the lifetime of the worker and his dependents. *The theoretical tax rate is as low as 2 percent of earnings for some workers and as high as 26 percent of earnings for others.* In each case the employee tax would have to be matched by an equal employer tax. By way of contrast, the actual tax rate for all employees is 5.35 percent for 1981 (with a matching employer tax rate) and is estimated to be about 8 percent by the end of the working lifetime of today's new entrant to the work force. Of course this tax rate excludes Medicare taxes since Medicare benefits were excluded from the benefit values used in preparing Table 11.3. While these examples may not be typical of persons covered by Social Security, they do show that it is only sheer coincidence when a worker receives benefits that are equivalent to the taxes that he or she pays. This statement is true whether we consider employee taxes only, employee and employer taxes combined, or taxes of the self-employed.

It should be noted that the calculations shown in Table 11.3 are strictly theoretical, and it cannot be assumed that an

Table 11.3

Theoretical Tax Rate Payable by Workers and Employers, Each, If Taxes Are to Be Equivalent to Benefits for Selected Workers Entering the Work Force[a] in 1978

Brief Description of Worker[b]	Tax Rate Payable by Worker (with Matching Rate Payable by Employer)
Unmarried male who enters work force at age 22, works in steady employment at the maximum taxable earnings under Social Security, remains single, retires at age 70	2%
Unmarried female who enters work force at age 25, works in steady employment at the average earnings level for all workers covered by Social Security, remains single, retires at age 65	6%
Married male with dependent wife and two children, who enters work force at age 22, works in steady employment at the federal minimum wage, retires at age 65	12%
Married male with dependent wife who enters work force at age 52, works in steady part-time employment at high salary (that produces same annual income as full-time employment at the federal minimum wage), retires at age 65	26%

[a]In employment covered by Social Security
[b]Retirement age shown in each example represents age at which worker is assumed to retire if he or she has not died or become disabled prior to that age.

individual or a group of individuals with the characteristics indicated in Table 11.3 can duplicate Social Security benefits by means of private savings and insurance for the costs that are shown. Many benefits provided under Social Security are virtually impossible to duplicate outside a system covering practically the entire working population and having the assured tax revenue inherent in such a system. Chapter 17 discusses this and related points in more detail.

Equity Among Generations

A third viewpoint from which to consider whether we get our money's worth is that of the various generations of persons covered by Social Security. Under the current-cost method of financing used for the Social Security program, the amount of taxes collected each year is intended to be approximately equal to the benefits and administrative expenses paid during the year plus a small additional amount to maintain the trust funds at an appropriate contingency reserve level. This means that the taxes paid by one generation of workers are used to provide the benefits to an earlier generation of workers. Therefore, the taxes paid by a particular generation of workers are not necessarily equivalent to the cost of the benefits that generation will eventually receive.

For example, if benefit levels are increased over time (in addition to adjustments made for inflation), then any particular generation may receive benefits of greater value than the taxes it paid to become eligible for such benefits. On the other hand, if benefits are decreased or "deliberalized" over time, any particular generation may receive benefits of lesser value than the taxes it paid to become eligible for such benefits.

Also, the size of the working population relative to the retired population, now and in the future, is an important determinant of whether a given generation will receive benefits equivalent to the taxes it pays. Even if benefits are not increased from their present levels in relation to preretirement earnings, current projections indicate that future generations of workers must pay considerably higher tax rates than today's workers (at least 50 percent higher) because in the future the ratio of beneficiaries to taxpayers will be higher.

From the viewpoint of one generation compared with another, past generations have done extremely well. The case of Miss Ida Fuller is one well-known and extreme illustration. The program's very first beneficiary, Miss Fuller paid only about $22 in Social Security taxes prior to her retirement but lived to collect more than $20,000 in retirement benefits. Most early participants, of course, did not receive "actuarial bargains" of this magnitude. Still, on average, they have done remarkably well. Specifically, during the first forty years of Social Security's existence, the total taxes paid by employees and employers combined have amounted to only one-fifth of the value of the benefits that have been paid or promised with respect to this period of participation. In other words, during the past forty years, if the Social Security tax rates had been five times what they were, they would have been adequate to pay for the benefits that were "earned" during that period. This concept is discussed in more detail in Chapter 7.

Present and future generations will not fare as well. Social Security actuaries have estimated that the generation of workers currently entering the work force will receive benefits that in total are roughly 15 percent greater than those that can be provided by their Social Security taxes and those of their employers (based upon taxes scheduled by present law and ignoring Medicare benefits and taxes). Future generations should probably expect to receive less in benefits than can be provided by the total of employee and employer Social Security taxes; however, this will depend to some extent upon the timing of future changes in the benefits and upon fluctuations in future birth rates.

This question of equity among various generations is not as simple as it seems and it should be considered from a broad point of view. In recent American history, for example, each generation has enjoyed a better standard of living than the prior generation. At least some of the credit for this steady improvement in the standard of living should be given to the work, savings, and sacrifice of prior generations. Thus, it could be considered that the receipt by today's beneficiaries of benefits of greater value than could have been provided by their past taxes is a partial repayment for the sacrifices they made which resulted in a higher standard of living for later generations of workers. The point in mentioning this question of intergenerational equity is not to resolve it but rather to note that any consideration of money's worth from Social Security should be viewed from a broad perspective, taking into account much more than Social Security taxes paid and benefits received by a particular individual or group of individuals.

Are Benefits Appropriate?

There is yet a fourth point of view from which to consider the question of money's worth: whether we are buying the proper benefits with our Social Security tax dollars. Just because there is no significant waste in administering the Social Security program, it does not follow automatically that we get our money's worth from our tax dollars. Similarly, just because we may not be discontent with questions of equity among generations or among individuals within each generation, it does not follow automatically that we get our money's worth.

Perhaps we are providing the wrong benefits to the wrong people. To the extent that this is true, it can be said we do not get our money's worth from Social Security. It is difficult, if not impossible, to find a simple answer to questions about whether we are collecting the right taxes from the right people and paying the right benefits to the right people. The answer depends upon one's philosophy of right and wrong and, for better or for worse, there is no agreement among all Americans as to exactly what this philosophy should be.

I would suggest that the answer to the question "Do we get our money's worth from Social Security?" depends upon the ultimate effect of Social Security on the American social and economic structure. Will the effect be favorable or unfavorable? Will the effect be what we intended or will there be unforeseen consequences? My opinion is that we will get our money's worth from Social Security if it is designed to be consistent with the following principles:

> An individual should have freedom of choice to the fullest extent possible consistent with the interest of the nation as a whole.
>
> An individual should be afforded maximum opportunity and incentive to develop and utilize his abilities throughout his lifetime.
>
> A government (federal, state, or local) should provide those benefits, and only those benefits, that an individual (acting alone or as part of a group of individuals utilizing some form of voluntary pooling or risk-sharing arrangement) cannot provide for himself. In meeting this responsibility, the government should become involved to the least extent possible consistent with the interest of the nation as a whole.

The development of a system like the Social Security program is a continuing and evolutionary process. A program that was appropriate for yesterday is not appropriate for today. A program that is appropriate for today will not be appropriate for tomorrow. The present Social Security program is a product of decisions made by past generations of policymakers who lived in a different social and economic environment and who were trying to resolve problems different from those that will exist in the future. When Social Security was enacted some forty-five years ago, the nation had been in a serious depression for almost six years. The social and economic conditions existing at that time included the following:

> More workers than jobs and a consequent high unemployment rate
>
> A small elderly population relative to the younger potential working population
>
> Relatively undeveloped reliable institutions through which an individual could invest and save for the future
>
> An almost completely undeveloped system of private pensions and other employee benefits provided by employers

When the bulk of today's population approaches retirement some thirty to fifty years in the future, social and economic conditions can be expected to be quite different from what they are now or were forty-five years in the past. Accordingly, the nation need not and should not be forever influenced by past decisions made to solve past problems. On the contrary, it is the responsibility of today's generation to begin now to make any changes that may be necessary so the Social Security program will be appropriate for the probable future social and economic environment. In designing a Social Security program for the future, full recognition should be given to the extent to which the design of the program itself will influence the future environment, to ensure that more problems will not be created than resolved. It must be borne in mind that a social insurance system, if not properly designed and communicated, can:

> effectively dictate the retirement age patterns followed by the nation and thereby encourage earlier retirement at a time when later retirement may be in the best interest of the nation;
>
> discourage individual initiative and private saving for retirement, yet fail to provide adequate retirement benefits; and

create unrealistic expectations for retirement which, when unfulfilled, will result in frustration and dissatisfaction.

In my opinion, our present Social Security program exhibits these unsatisfactory characteristics in varying degrees.

So, what is the answer? Do we get our money's worth from Social Security, from the viewpoint of whether the program is appropriate to society's needs? With regard to the past forty years: PERHAPS, but it does no good to worry about what is past. With regard to the next forty years: NO, not unless we change the program.

Even if the present Social Security program were appropriate for the conditions that existed in the past, it will not be appropriate for conditions that are likely to exist in the future when the young working population of today is ready to retire. Although the present Social Security program may have given us our money's worth in the past, it will not give us our money's worth in the future because, unless the program is changed, *we will be using our tax dollars to buy benefits that are inappropriate for the future.*

12
The Earnings Test

You work and pay taxes all your life and finally retire on Social Security and a company pension. Things are going all right until you encounter some unexpected medical expenses—and inflation. You locate a temporary job that will put your finances in order, but then learn that because of your new job you must forfeit some of your Social Security benefits and you will not be as much better off as you thought.

You are a widow with small children and are glad to be receiving Social Security benefits but would like to resume your career. This will give you extra money to send the children to college and will also make your future life happier. But then you find out that since you are so successful in your job, you will lose most of your Social Security benefits and you will not have as much extra money for the children's college as you had planned.

The culprit is the "earnings test," sometimes called the retirement test, an often misunderstood feature of Social Security designed to reduce or even eliminate benefits when a beneficiary has more than nominal earnings.

The earnings of a retired worker can reduce both his own benefit *and* the benefits of dependent beneficiaries, but the earnings of a dependent beneficiary or a survivor beneficiary can reduce only his own benefit and not the benefit of any other beneficiary. The earnings test does not apply to disabled beneficiaries; other standards are used to determine the continuance of disability. Also, eligibility for Medicare benefits is not affected by the earnings test.

The earnings test is complicated but its essential features can be summarized as follows:

> The test applies only to beneficiaries under age 72 (age 70 beginning in 1982) whose benefits are not based on disability.
>
> Certain types of income are not counted in applying the earnings test (investment earnings, rental income, pension benefits, etc.).
>
> A beneficiary may have annual earnings up to a specified amount—the annual exempt amount—without having any benefits withheld:
>
> > For people aged 65 to 72 (70 starting in 1982), the annual exempt amount is:
> >
> > > $5,000 in 1980
> > > $5,500 in 1981
> > > $6,000 in 1982
> >
> > automatically adjusted after 1982 to reflect increases in average wage levels.
> >
> > For people under age 65, the annual exempt amount is $4,080 in 1981, automatically adjusted after 1981 to reflect increases in average wage levels.
>
> If earnings of a beneficiary exceed the applicable annual exempt amount, $1 in benefits is withheld for each $2 of excess earnings. For example, a beneficiary over 65 who earned $6,000 in 1980 would have $500 withheld from his benefits because his earnings exceeded his annual exempt amount ($5,000) by $1,000.
>
> Beneficiaries can have relatively high earnings and still get some benefits.
>
> > A beneficiary could earn an amount equal to the total of the applicable exempt amount and twice his annual benefit before all his benefits would be withheld.
> >
> > A 65-year-old worker who elects to begin receiving benefits in 1980, having had average earnings during his career, could earn $16,724 in 1980 before all his benefits ($5,862) would be withheld.
> >
> > If the above beneficiary has a spouse (also 65) receiv-

ing dependent's benefits, their combined benefits would be $8,793 and he could earn $22,586 before all their benefits would be withheld.

There is a provision that permits a person who retires to receive benefits in the remainder of the year regardless of his earnings before retirement. In the first year a beneficiary has a nonwork month, that is, a month in which he earns less than one-twelfth the annual exempt amount, and does not provide substantial services in self-employment, benefits are not withheld in any nonwork month even if annual earnings exceed the annual exempt amount. (Prior to 1978, the monthly measure applied in all years of benefit payment. It is currently applied in some years of benefit payment to certain types of beneficiaries such as children and young widows.)

Since the exempt amount of earnings is a flat amount for all beneficiaries, it favors the lower paid workers. For example, a worker who has always earned something less than the federal minimum wage is not affected by the earnings test and can continue working at the same earnings level after age 65 and receive full Social Security benefits. On the other hand, a worker who has always earned the maximum taxable amount under Social Security and who continues to work past age 65 at the same earnings level will receive no benefits at all while still working prior to age 72.

The reason for the earnings test lies in the traditional view of the purpose of the Social Security program; namely, to replace, in part, earnings that are lost when a worker becomes disabled, dies, or retires in old age. The earnings test is used as a measure of whether a loss of income has occurred. The test also applies to dependents and survivors who have earnings, although the rationale for this is not clear. It is sometimes stated that earnings of dependents and survivors offset partially the loss of a worker's income to the family. This reasoning is faulty, however, in the case of dependents and survivors who worked prior to becoming eligible for benefits. Perhaps the reasoning follows the general concept that Social Security benefits are based partly on "presumed social need." Thus dependents or survivors with significant earnings of their own are assumed not to need Social Security benefits as much as dependents or survivors without earnings.

The original earnings test in 1940 was simple but stringent: If monthly earnings in covered employment were $15 or more, the entire monthly benefit was forfeited. Over the years the retirement test has been liberalized continually as a result of public pressure for change.

There is no provision in the present Social Security law that is subject to such consistent public and Congressional criticism as the earnings test. In each session of Congress in recent years, well over 100 bills have been introduced to change the earnings test.

The reason for this public criticism and misunderstanding of the earnings test is not hard to find. For forty years the government has employed rhetoric to describe Social Security that has led people to believe that their "contributions" were placed in a "trust fund" under an "insurance program" to create an "earned right" to benefits payable upon old age, disability, death, or illness. Little emphasis was given to explaining that the "earned right" was to a benefit payable only if the beneficiary did not have substantial earnings. After awhile the public began to believe that they had in fact "bought and paid for" their benefits (as they believed them to be defined) and that it was inconsistent with forty years of rhetoric, if not downright unfair, to withhold benefits just because the beneficiary continued to work (particularly if the work was to supplement an inadequate benefit in a time of frustrating inflation).

The result of this misunderstanding of the nature of Social Security should not be surprising: pressure by the public to liberalize the earnings test, a yielding to this pressure by Congress, and a substantial change in the very nature of Social Security (to conform more with what the public thought Social Security was all along). This process will probably continue until the earnings test is eliminated altogether and the original design of this part of the Social Security program is transformed completely. There comes a time when misunderstanding is too deeply imbedded to be reversed.

In theory, at least, the original concept of the earnings test was a sound one. In effect, it provided for a flexible retirement age for each individual. Retirement benefits were not to be paid to everyone at an arbitrarily determined age; rather they were to be paid whenever a person was no longer both willing and able to work (but not earlier than age 65 originally, reduced later to age 62).

The purpose of the earnings test was to facilitate changes in the size of the work force as the nation's work opportunities vary. Such changes are necessary because of shifts in the relative size of the aged and young populations caused by fluctuations in the birth rate and because of changes in the nation's production needs. We shall see a striking need for higher effective retirement ages during the first half of the next century as today's youth reach their sixties and the size of the work force (as we now define it) declines relative to the total population.

It is tempting to suggest that the trend toward elimination of the earnings test be reversed and that the original concept of a strict earnings test be restored. This could be achieved simply by freezing the exempt amounts of earnings at present levels instead of raising them as average wages increase, and retaining age 72 as the maximum age for applying the earnings test instead of continually reducing it. In a relatively short time, inflation would effectively restore a strict earnings test to Social Security, which would then provide flexible retirement ages to accommodate the nation's changing needs. This would, of course, also reduce the high retirement costs after the turn of the century by reducing the ratio of beneficiaries to active taxpayers. It may be too late to restore a strict earnings test, however, since that would require the population to view Social Security in a considerably different way than they have become accustomed.

13
Sex and Social Security

What does sex have to do with Social Security? Plenty, according to those who complain that women are not being treated fairly by Social Security as a result of their sex. In reality, Social Security has discriminated in favor of women based upon their sex more often than it has discriminated against them. Paradoxically, however, Social Security satisfies income security needs less adequately for women than it does for men. To understand this situation requires some background explanation.

The overall social and economic environment in America makes it easier for independent men than for independent women to support themselves during their active healthy lifetimes, and it provides more support for independent men than for independent women in the event of their inability to work because of age or disability. This environment is a reflection of the different roles played by men and women in this country during the early twentieth century. A considerable amount of work and effort is required to sustain a family, and the roles traditionally played by married men and women in performing this work may be stated simply as follows:

> The man works full time outside the home for cash wages which he uses to support himself and his family.
> The woman works full time caring for the home and family and receives no cash wages.

This division of responsibilities, which used to be the norm, was a workable arrangement, particularly during a lasting marriage. Until recently, divorce was relatively infrequent.

When Social Security was designed and adopted in the 1930s it was intended to recognize and be compatible with this environment. By doing so it served to reinforce and perpetuate such an environment, even though it did not create the environment.

This environment has changed, however, and it will continue to change. Women are increasingly combining paid employment with family life. The percentage of married women in the labor force increased from 20 percent in 1947 to almost 50 percent in 1980. It has been estimated that by the end of the 1980s, two-thirds of all married women under age 55 will be working, including over half of all mothers with young children. Women in paid employment already outnumber women who work at home without pay—slightly more than half of the female population over age 15 is working for pay. As the frequency of divorce has increased, so has the number of women supporting themselves and their children.

Changes in the Social Security program have not kept pace with changes in the economic role of women and in the institution of marriage that have occurred since Social Security was enacted. This has led to charges that Social Security discriminates against women, or that it is unfair or inequitable in its treatment of women.

The women's issue is often misunderstood. There is no significant discrimination against women in the current Social Security program. Any discrimination, now as well as in the past, is more often against men than against women. The 1979 Advisory Council on Social Security, which devoted more time to women's benefits than any other issue, summarized their findings on discrimination as follows:[1]

> ... the social security law is largely sex-blind. With few exceptions (which the Administration and the council recommend be eliminated), benefits are not paid on the basis of sex, but rather on the basis of labor force attachment and family status. The council also notes that as a group, women get as good a return on

the social security taxes they pay as do men. Indeed, if separate systems were established for men and women, women workers would have to pay social security taxes that are about 9 percent higher than men would pay. Because the average wages of women are lower than men's, a greater portion of their wages is replaced by benefits because of the weighting in the formula for low-income workers. Also, because women tend to live longer, they collect more benefits than men. These two factors outweigh the fact that more dependents' benefits are paid on the basis of men's wage records than are paid on the basis of women's wage records.

It may be useful to list the circumstances in which men and women receive different treatment under the Social Security program. In some cases women are favored, while in others men are favored. This information was taken from the report of the 1979 Advisory Council on Social Security.[2]

Nine Remaining Gender-Based Distinctions

1. Divorced Men and Women. Although benefits are provided for aged divorced wives, aged divorced widows, and disabled divorced widows, the statute does not provide benefits for aged divorced husbands, aged divorced widowers, or disabled divorced widowers (*Social Security Act,* Sections 202(b)(1), (c)(1), (e)(1), and (f)(1)). (Although still in the statute, this provision is no longer implemented for aged divorced husbands because of a successful challenge in the courts, *Oliver v. Califano.*)

2. Young Fathers and Mothers. Benefits are payable to young wives, widowed mothers, and surviving divorced mothers who have children entitled to benefits in their care, but not to young husbands, widowed fathers, or surviving divorced fathers in similar circumstances (*Social Security Act,* Sections 202 (g)(1), (b)(1), and (c)(1)). (Although still in the statute, this provision is no longer implemented for widowers with an entitled child in their care because of a successful challenge in the courts, *Weinberger v. Wiesenfeld.*)

3. Remarriage of a Surviving Spouse Before Age 60. A widow who remarries before age 60 may receive benefits on a deceased husband's earnings if she is not married when she applies for benefits, while a widower who remarries before age 60 cannot get such benefits, even if the subsequent marriage has terminated (*Social Security Act*, Sections 202(e)(1) and (f)(1)).

4. Transitional Insured Status. When Congress enacted the transitional insured status provisions in 1965 to provide special payments for persons who had not been able to work in covered employment long enough to qualify for benefits, wife's and widow's benefits were included in the provisions, but husband's and widower's benefits were not *(Social Security Act,* Section 227).

5. Special Age-72 Benefits. When both members of a couple are receiving special age-72 payments, the wife's payment is equal to one-half of the husband's payment even though each member must qualify for the payment individually (*Social Security Act*, Section 228(b)).

6. Benefits for Spouses of Disabled Beneficiaries. If a disabled male beneficiary who is married to a dependent or a survivor beneficiary ceases to be disabled, the benefits of his spouse are terminated; however, if the disabled beneficiary is a female whose disability ends, the benefits to her spouse do not end (*Social Security Act,* Section 202(d)(5) et al.). For example, when two beneficiaries who have been disabled since childhood marry, their benefits continue; if the male recovers from his disability, both benefits are terminated, while benefits for the male continue if the female recovers. Similarly, when a disabled worker is married to an aged survivor and recovers from his or her disability, termination of the spouse's benefits depends on the sex of the worker.

7. *Determination of Illegitimacy.* In the few juris-dictions in which an illegitimate child does not have the right to inherit the intestate personal property of his mother, a woman's illegitimate child cannot qualify for Social Security benefits under the same conditions as a man's illegitimate child can (*Social Security Act,* Section 216(h)(3)).

8. *Waiver of Civil Service Survivor's Annuity.* A widow can waive payment of a federal benefit attribut-able to credit for military service performed before 1957 to be able to have the military service credited toward eligibility for, or the amount of, a social secu-rity benefit, but a widower cannot (*Social Security Act,* Section 217(f)).

9. *Self-Employment in Community Property States.* The income from a business operated by a husband and wife in a state which has a community property statute is deemed to belong to the husband unless the wife exercises substantially all of the management and control of the business (*Social Secu-rity Act,* Section 211(a)(5)(A)).

Although the number of gender-based distinctions in the present law is not large, it is obviously preferable that they be removed so as to eliminate any lingering confusion about discrimination in the Social Security program. In some cases it has not been feasible to correct, retroactively, past discrimina-tion based upon sex. One example is the less liberal treatment of men than women born before 1913 in the computation of benefits and insured status (not mentioned in the previous listing of gender-based distinctions since it does not apply to those currently becoming eligible for benefits). No consider-ation is being given to correcting this discrimination because of the large short-term costs it would entail and because the courts have upheld the provision currently in the law.

If the Social Security program does not discriminate directly against women, why are there so many complaints about its unfairness? To some degree, the complaints are due to misun-derstanding and lack of knowledge about program provisions. But valid reasons also exist for unhappiness concerning the design of Social Security in relation to the nature of women's careers. Women suffer certain disadvantages during their working life that result in lower benefits under Social Security. As a general rule, women earn less than men of comparable age, education, and prior experience. One reason for this is the historically weaker job commitment of women, e.g., working irregularly and changing jobs frequently. This was, of course, a natural consequence of fulfilling the role of motherhood and traditional family life. In addition, there has been an occupational segregation which effectively divides labor into that "typically" done by women (e.g., nurses, teachers, secretaries) and that done by men (e.g., doctors, professors, managers).

Much of the criticism of the way Social Security treats women is in reality a criticism of the way our social and economic environment treats women. Accordingly, it is inappropriate and probably even futile to attempt to use Social Security as a vehicle to achieve social, economic, and political parity of women and men. More appropriate tools for this purpose would appear to include the Equal Pay Act of 1963, Title VII of the Civil Rights Act of 1964, the Equal Employment Act of 1972, and various affirmative action programs.

This is not to say that the present Social Security program properly meets the needs of women and that no change is appropriate. It is to say, however, that much of the criticism regarding the benefits Social Security provides women is ill-founded. Rational changes can be made only in response to rational analysis and criticism.

One of the alleged inequities in the benefits provided by Social Security is not because of a conflict between men's and women's benefits. Rather, it is a conflict between benefits provided women who work in paid employment, and women who work at home and are married to a person covered by Social Security. The homemaker who pays no Social Security taxes may receive as much or more in Social Security benefits as the woman who works in paid employment and pays Social Security taxes. An alternative way to view this situation is that, for many years women who were not in paid employment got something for nothing; that is, they received certain Social Security benefits without paying any taxes therefor. Now that they are in the paid work force, however, women are treated just like any other working person—except they receive the *larger* of benefits based upon their own work record and benefits based upon their being a dependent.

Since approximately half the married women are in paid employment and half are not, there are obvious difficulties in modifying Social Security to satisfy the desires and needs of all women simultaneously. Marriage as an institution is not dying, rather it is evolving. People still get married although perhaps at later ages. Most families still have children, even though a smaller number. The frequency of divorce has increased but most divorced people remarry. Accordingly, it would be ill-advised to revise Social Security dramatically so as to accommodate the needs of this relatively new female role, at the expense of the traditional female role. Any change in Social Security must make suitable provision for both extremes of the female role as well as the many variations in these roles that currently exist or that may develop in the future.

It is common to criticize Social Security on the grounds that benefits are disproportionate to taxes for certain taxpayer groups, e.g., women in two-wage earner families. As indicated in Chapter 11, Social Security was not intended to be a savings plan under which an individual receives benefits commensurate with his or her tax payments. Accordingly, it is not appropriate to use "individual equity" as a yardstick by which to measure Social Security's fairness to women or to any other group. Social Security will always fail this test, providing more than a fair return on taxes for some and less for others.

Women are coming to view their home and childcare activities as being as valuable as their husbands' work for cash earnings and to believe that disability and retirement benefits should be provided based on the value of such activities. The basic nature of Social Security—as presently constituted—is to provide benefits only when there has been a loss of cash earnings; hence, it will be a very difficult philosophical transition for Social Security to provide benefits based upon non-cash-earning activities, homecare or otherwise.

It is increasingly pointed out that Social Security gives insufficient protection for divorced women. Even though the law was recently changed to lower the number of years divorced wives must have been married to their former husbands (from twenty years to ten years) in order to receive benefits, the complaint still persists that ten years is too long a marriage prerequisite for receipt of benefits. A woman need be married to her husband for only one year (and sometimes less) in order to receive a wife's or survivor's benefit based on his record, yet a marriage that lasted nine years is of insufficient duration to allow for the payment of a similar benefit to a divorced wife. A complaint is sometimes made that the level of benefits for divorced women is inadequate since it is the same as the wife's benefit, which is intended as supplemental income for a second household member and not as sole support for a single household member.

In considering the appropriateness of these complaints, it should be noted that any deficiency in benefits is not the result of discrimination against women; on the contrary, in the areas just mentioned, any discrimination that exists is against men, not women, since divorced men generally receive less favorable treatment than divorced women. Furthermore, charges that benefits provided by Social Security are inadequate should be viewed in light of the premise that Social Security is intended to provide only a basic minimum benefit and is not intended to be sufficient by itself.

In summary, there is no overt discrimination against women in the Social Security program. On the other hand, Social Security is structured to reward work patterns that fit men better than women. Furthermore, Social Security is structured to reward life patterns (e.g., male breadwinner and female homemaker, and lifelong marriages) that are becoming much less representative of modern life. The net result is that Social Security is not meeting the income security needs of women in today's world as well as it did some forty years ago. The need for some kind of change is irrefutable.

14
Integration of
Private Benefit Plans
with Social Security

Social Security was *not* designed to meet all the financial needs that arise from a person's old age, disability, death, or illness. It is still necessary to supplement Social Security with personal savings and employee benefit plans. Supplemental employee benefit plans are sometimes designed without regard to the benefits provided under Social Security. It is preferable, however, to correlate any supplemental plans with Social Security so that the combined benefits from all sources will form a rational package. This process of correlation is usually called "integration."

In theory, integration is not very difficult. In practice, however, it is quite complicated, largely because of:

the design of the Social Security program itself; and

the requirements of the Internal Revenue Service that supplemental plan benefits be designed in certain ways in order to be a "qualified plan" and thus be accorded favorable tax treatment.

A discussion of the integration of supplemental retirement benefits and Social Security benefits upon retirement at age 65 will illustrate some of the problems.

153

Social Security retirement benefits are based largely upon the principle of "social adequacy" and thus provide benefits for persons with low average earnings that are higher, relative to preretirement earnings, than for persons with high average earnings. For example, consider four workers retiring in January 1980 at age 65 after a steady work history, each at a different level of earnings. A worker whose past earnings have always been at about the minimum wage level would receive benefits during the first year of retirement of approximately 71 percent of his or her average earnings in the three years prior to retirement. This percentage is frequently called a "replacement ratio" because it represents the proportion of average preretirement earnings that is replaced by the retirement benefit. This replacement ratio would be 55 percent for a worker whose past earnings have equaled the average earnings of all employees covered by Social Security, 39 percent for a worker whose past earnings have equaled the maximum taxable wage base in effect during prior years, and 20 percent for a worker whose earnings have been twice the maximum taxable wage base in effect during prior years. These replacement ratios represent the basic benefit payable to a worker alone. For a worker with an eligible spouse (also aged 65), the replacement ratios become 106 percent for the low wage earner, 83 percent for the average wage earner, 59 percent for the maximum wage earner, and 29 percent for the high wage earner (one earning twice the maximum taxable wage base). These replacement ratios for the various categories of workers retiring at age 65 in 1980[1] may be summarized as follows:

| | Annual Earnings in 1979 | Social Security Benefits as a Percentage of the Last Three Years' Average Earnings | |
		Worker Alone	Worker and Spouse
Minimum wage	$ 6,032	71%	106%
Average wage	11,479	55	83
Maximum taxable wage	22,900	39	59
High wage	45,800	20	29

An examination of these figures makes it obvious that income replacement needs at retirement are not met uniformly for all of the workers in the example and that for most workers some kind of supplemental plan is called for. This need for supplementation is not a deficiency of the Social Security program; it was always intended that Social Security provide a basic floor of protection upon which additional protection could be built. Furthermore, it has always been a characteristic of Social Security to provide more adequate benefits for workers earning lower than average wages than for workers earning higher than average wages.

It is not unusual to find a supplemental retirement plan that provides benefits that are a uniform percentage of average preretirement earnings and that are the same whether the worker does or does not have a spouse. Such a plan *supplements* Social Security, yet it is not *integrated* with Social Security. As an example, consider a supplemental plan that provides a career worker with retirement benefits of 60 percent of average earnings in the three years prior to retirement. The benefits under such a plan are summarized below for the same workers used as an example in the preceding table:

	Annual Earnings in 1979	*Supplemental Plan Benefits as a Percentage of the Last Three Years' Average Earnings*	
		Worker Alone	*Worker and Spouse*
Minimum wage	$ 6,032	60%	60%
Average wage	11,479	60	60
Maximum taxable wage	22,900	60	60
High wage	45,800	60	60

If this supplemental plan is superimposed on the Social Security program, the total benefits may be summarized as follows:

	Annual Earnings in 1979	*Total Benefits as a Percentage of the Last Three Years' Average Earnings*	
		Worker Alone	*Worker and Spouse*
Minimum wage	$ 6,032	131%	166%
Average wage	11,479	115	143
Maximum taxable wage	22,900	99	119
High wage	45,800	80	89

This table illustrates the wide discrepancy in benefits relative to preretirement earnings that can occur when a supplemental retirement plan is simply *added to* Social Security but not *integrated with* Social Security. Such a situation is not uncommon, particularly among supplemental plans covering public employee groups.

If a supplemental retirement plan is to be integrated with Social Security, the plan must comply with the Internal Revenue Code as well as with rules and regulations of the Internal Revenue Service if the plan and its participants are to be accorded favorable tax treatment. The Internal Revenue Service requirements for integration permit a supplemental plan to provide benefits, relative to preretirement earnings, that favor more highly paid workers in order to offset the effect of the Social Security program which favors lower paid workers.

Assume, for example, that the benefit level of 80 percent of the final three-year average earnings shown in the preceding table for a high wage worker with no spouse is considered to be the desired goal for all workers regardless of their earnings level. Assume further that the supplemental plan benefits are modified toward that goal within the limits of the integration rules of the Internal Revenue Service (using the "offset" method[2] of integration). The benefits under such a plan may be summarized as follows:

	Annual Earnings in 1979	Supplemental Plan Benefits as a Percentage of the Last Three Years' Average Earnings	
		Worker Alone	Worker and Spouse
Minimum wage	$ 6,032	18%	18%
Average wage	11,479	30	30
Maximum taxable wage	22,900	44	44
High wage	45,800	60	60

If these integrated supplemental plan benefits are added to Social Security benefits, the total benefits may be summarized as follows:

	Annual Earnings in 1979	Total Benefits as a Percentage of the Last Three Years' Average Earnings	
		Worker Alone	Worker and Spouse
Minimum wage	$ 6,032	89%	124%
Average wage	11,479	85	113
Maximum taxable wage	22,900	83	103
High wage	45,800	80	89

A review of this table indicates that it is not possible to achieve simultaneously for all employee categories the stated goal of replacing 80 percent of the final three-year average earnings. Even if a supplemental plan is integrated to the full extent permitted by Internal Revenue Service requirements for a tax-qualified plan, there is still a wide variation in benefits. Lower wage earners receive relatively larger benefits than high wage earners. Workers with spouses receive relatively larger benefits than single workers. If adequate benefits are provided the high-wage single workers, excessive benefits must be provided all other workers.

The problem is made even worse by a factor not yet mentioned in order to simplify the discussion. Death and disability benefits provided by Social Security favor the lower wage earner just as does the age-retirement benefit. Death and disability benefits provided under a supplemental retirement plan can be integrated with those provided under Social Security; however, if they are so integrated the permissible degree of integration of age-retirement benefits is lessened. This would further aggravate the imbalance in benefits illustrated in the preceding table.

Of course, not everyone would agree that the combined benefits from Social Security and a supplemental retirement plan should be a uniform percentage of gross preretirement earnings. Some would argue that it is "equitable" for such a percentage to decline as average earnings increase—to reflect, if for no other reason, the progressive nature of the federal income tax and the nontaxability of Social Security benefits. These features tend to make a declining replacement ratio for gross preretirement earnings equivalent to a level replacement ratio for net (after tax) preretirement earnings. In any event, it would seem that more uniformity of retirement benefits relative to preretirement earnings is desirable than is permitted by current integration requirements of the Internal Revenue Service.

This entire subject may seem complicated, and it is. Nevertheless, the following observations seem reasonable:

Social Security alone does not meet all the financial needs that arise from a person's old age, disability, death, or illness. It meets those needs more completely for lower wage earners than for higher wage earners and more completely for married workers than for single workers.

Supplemental plan benefits must be provided if income replacement needs are to be met adequately. Supplemental benefits should be *integrated with* and not just *added to* Social Security benefits. Otherwise, the unevenness with which financial needs are met will be continued but at a higher level.

Under present laws and regulations, it is not possible to integrate supplemental benefit plans with Social Security to the extent necessary to satisfy uniformly the financial needs of all workers at the various earnings levels. If appropriate benefits are provided for workers with average earnings, less than adequate benefits are provided for the more highly paid workers; if adequate benefits are provided for the more highly paid workers, excessive benefits will be provided for lower paid workers. This situation can be corrected only if the Internal Revenue Service integration rules are revised, or if the Social Security program is revised, or both.

Many employee groups that do not participate in Social Security (civilian employees of the federal government and a portion of the employees of state and local governments and nonprofit organizations) have established employee benefit plans that satisfy uniformly the financial needs of all participants regardless of their earnings level. If these employee groups elect to participate in Social Security or are required to do so, significant revisions will be necessary in their existing employee benefit plans if rational balance is to be maintained in the benefits provided employees at the various earnings levels. The extent to which these revisions can be implemented is seriously hampered by the Internal Revenue Service laws and regulations, assuming they are in fact applicable to public as well as private employee benefit plans.

Providing rationally correlated benefits under two systems, Social Security and supplemental employee benefit plans, is quite difficult in view of the nature of Social Security itself and the Internal Revenue Service rules for integration. Nevertheless, proper correlation of benefits is essential if income replacement needs are to be met at an affordable cost. To achieve this correlation within the framework of the present laws and regulations requires that:

tax-qualified supplemental employee benefit plans be integrated as completely with Social Security as is allowed by Internal Revenue Service rulings; and

death and disability benefits for all employees, and a portion of the retirement benefits for the more highly paid employees, be provided separately from tax-qualified retirement plans so as to minimize the limiting effect of integration rulings.

It is unfortunate that federal tax laws are not more consistent and are not more conducive to the formation of rationally conceived supplemental employee benefit plans. Many tax laws are designed to encourage the adoption of supplemental plans while others tend to discourage their adoption. The Internal Revenue Service integration rules in particular make it virtually impossible to design a supplemental retirement plan that fits together with Social Security to form a sensible combination of retirement benefits. On the other hand, many supplemental plans are not as completely integrated with Social Security as is permitted under existing tax laws, imperfect though such laws are.

15
Inflation and Automatic Benefit Increases

Social Security payments for 35 million beneficiaries were increased by 14.3 percent in June 1980. This benefit increase corresponded with the increase in the Consumer Price Index of 14.3 percent from the first quarter of 1979 to the first quarter of 1980 and was granted automatically in accordance with Social Security's automatic adjustment provisions. These provisions were enacted in 1972 and were scheduled to take effect in January 1975, but it was June 1975 before they were permitted to operate without modification. Increases in Social Security benefits in the course of payment for each year since 1974 are summarized in Table 15.1.

These benefit increases have provided valuable protection against inflation for Social Security beneficiaries. The cumulative increase in benefits during the seven-year period from 1973 to 1980 was 81 percent. At first glance, the automatic adjustment provisions may appear to have solved the problems of inflation. There are many factors to consider, however; and in attempting to alleviate the various problems caused by inflation, the government faces a dilemma because not all of these problems can be resolved simultaneously. In fact, resolving one problem often aggravates another—as indicated below.

161

Table 15.1

Automatic Increases in Social Security Benefits

Calendar Year of Benefit Increase	Percentage Benefit Increase
(1)	(2)
1974[a]	11.0%
1975	8.0
1976	6.4
1977	5.9
1978	6.5
1979	9.9
1980	14.3

[a]Automatic benefit increases did not become effective until 1975. The 1974 benefit increase shown is approximately the same amount that would have resulted if the automatic increase provision had been in effect.

Responsibility and Opportunity

It can be argued that the government has a responsibility to maintain the purchasing power of any Social Security benefit it provides if the program is to carry out the purpose for which it was established. The individual pensioner did not cause the inflation which is robbing him of purchasing power. In most cases, at least some of the blame must be placed on governmental economic policies. To the extent that external forces or actions by the nation's active workers have caused inflation, it is true that the government may not have played a role—but then neither did the individual pensioner. Consequently, the government may still be considered responsible for finding a solution.

Moreover, the retired pensioner is out of the active work force and usually is powerless to protect himself against inflation. The government is the only logical protector of pensions provided by Social Security. The government enacted the Social Security law in the first place; it is the government that can and must amend the law as necessary to preserve the pensioner's standard of living. Finally, if the government does not protect pensioners against inflation, who will do so?

These are powerful arguments in favor of governmental action, and they do in fact usually lead to governmental intervention such as Social Security's 1972 automatic adjustment provisions. But what does governmental intervention entail? Can the government really solve the problems caused by inflation?

Who Bears the Burden of Inflation?

It is easy to make casual references to "governmental responsibility" or having the "government pay" for all or part of a social insurance program, without pausing to realize what this truly means. The government has no magic wand. If social insurance benefits are made inadequate by inflation and the government responds by increasing benefits, this simply means that the active workers and their employers must pay higher taxes to provide such benefits. Many analysts believe that higher payroll taxes result in more inflation and that increased benefits to pensioners will reinforce, if not aggravate, inflation. If this is true, the net result is still further increases in pensions and further increases in inflation, resulting in an ever-increasing upward spiral. This is particularly so if wages of active workers are adjusted for inflation. And if the government adjusts *pension benefits* for inflation, to be consistent it must endorse adjustment of *wages* for inflation.

The problem of maintaining the purchasing power of the active worker is a difficult one. It requires wage increases *in excess of the rate of inflation* to offset the progressive income taxes that must be paid on gross income. Social Security benefits are not taxable; therefore, if both wages and pensions are increased by the same percentage amount to compensate for inflation, the pensioners' standard of living will increase relative to the active workers' standard of living.

Table 15.2 compares the average increase in earnings of persons who pay Social Security taxes and the increase in the Consumer Price Index during recent years. Historically, average wages have increased faster than prices. This is a reflection of increased productivity of the nation's workers and thus an improved standard of living. For example, from 1952 through 1972, average wages increased faster than prices by an average annual amount of more than 2 percent. This was not true during the period 1973–1979 when, as indicated in Table 15.2, average earnings of Social Security taxpayers generally

Table 15.2

Comparison of Yearly Increase in Consumer Price Index and Average Earnings of Social Security Taxpayers

Calendar Year	Percentage Increase in Consumer Price Index[a]	Percentage Increase in Average Earnings of Social Security Taxpayers[b]
(1)	(2)	(3)
1973	6.2%	6.9%
1974	11.0	7.5
1975	9.1	6.6
1976	5.8	8.4
1977	6.5	7.1
1978	7.6	8.1
1979	11.5	8.4[c]

[a]The figure for 1973 represents the relative increase in the average CPI for 1973 over the average CPI for 1972, and so on.
[b]The figure for 1973 represents the relative increase in the average earnings for 1973 over the average earnings for 1972, and so on.
[c]Preliminary estimate.

increased less than the Consumer Price Index (by an average annual rate of 0.6 percent). A comparison of the increase in net earnings after taxes (instead of gross earnings) with the Consumer Price Index would show a substantially larger gap, or loss of purchasing power among the active workers.

On the other hand, Social Security benefits have been adjusted fully to reflect increases in the Consumer Price Index—putting the Social Security recipient at an advantage over the active worker. If this phenomenon continues, the result will be an eventual conflict between the working and nonworking populations, since it will not be possible to protect the nonworking population against the ravages of inflation, except at the expense of the working population. Similarly, there can easily be a conflict among the various segments of the working population, since it is virtually impossible to distribute the burden of inflation "equitably." If inflation continues, these realities will be more widely recognized and strong efforts will be made to require all segments of the population to share more equally in bearing the cost of inflation. This could result in less than a full adjustment in Social Security benefits for inflation.

There are other problems in adjusting pensions and wages for changes in the cost of living. For example, some methods of compensating for inflation may, in fact, overcompensate and thus accelerate the very inflation for which adjustment is being made. In some cases this is because of faulty methods in designing the cost-of-living index; in other cases it may result from failing to apply different adjustments to the active and the retired populations, although there is little reliable information available on whether different adjustments should be applied. Accordingly, extreme care must be taken in constructing an index (or indices) to be used in adjusting pensions and wages.

The Real Solution

Although the problems posed by inflation are complex, it is clear they must be addressed in some way. It is becoming generally accepted that the purchasing power of social insurance pensions (and other benefits) should be restored if eroded by inflation. Increasing the benefits, however, should be viewed as a temporary stop-gap measure. A government cannot simply increase social insurance benefits and thereby presume to have resolved the widespread problems caused by inflation, or even to have alleviated them, except temporarily for a limited segment of the population.

In the final analysis, there is only one action a government can take that will be in the best interests of the most people and keep social and economic turmoil to a minimum. The government must identify the underlying *causes* of inflation, attack those causes, and keep inflation under control to the maximum possible extent. This is a large order, but to do otherwise will be to permit inflation to fester into such a complex problem that there will be no acceptable solutions.

16
Should Social Security Cover Everyone?

Approximately 75 percent of the nation's workers are in jobs automatically covered by Social Security and are therefore required to pay Social Security taxes. Of course this entitles them to receive Social Security benefits if they meet the eligibility requirements. Roughly 5 percent of the nation's workers are in jobs that are not covered by Social Security, hence they neither pay Social Security taxes nor receive its benefits. The remaining 20 percent of the working population have the option of paying or not paying Social Security taxes and thus receiving or not receiving its benefits. About three-fourths of the workers with this option have chosen to participate in Social Security. (Generally speaking, the option must be exercised by groups of employees and not by individuals.) The reasons for this varying treatment of different segments of the population are outlined in Chapter 2.

Is this situation of nonuniversal and partly optional coverage by Social Security a fair arrangement? Is it in the best interest of the nation?

The purpose of Social Security is to ensure that everyone with a significant work history is assured a basic standard of living in the event of retirement because of age or disability and that the dependents of every such worker are also assured a basic standard of living in the event of the worker's retirement,

167

disability, or premature death. In theory it may be acceptable to exclude a portion of the population from the protection offered by Social Security, provided there is reasonable assurance that this excluded segment will have alternative protection and thus not become a "charge on society." Most of the persons who do not participate in Social Security do in fact have a variety of employee benefit programs that provide much of the benefit protection offered by Social Security. Of course, no alternative system can be as financially stable as Social Security, publicity to the contrary notwithstanding. Furthermore, even though a person may be protected adequately under an alternative system, there is no assurance that such protection will continue as long as it is needed: either the system may change or employment may terminate. Accordingly, it should be anticipated that some of the persons who do not participate in Social Security and who rely upon other systems of benefit protection will die or become disabled or reach old age without receiving benefits equivalent to those that would have been afforded under Social Security. This will in turn create some situations in which society (more specifically, the taxpayers) will have to step in and provide financial support through one of the welfare programs—the very situations that Social Security was adopted to prevent.

Another point to consider is the fairness, actual as well as perceived, of a nonuniversal system. If Social Security were a system whereby an individual received benefits with a value approximately equal to his tax payments, then it might be considered fair, or "actuarially sound," to permit optional participation or to exclude certain groups from participation. As we saw in Chapter 11, however, this is not the case. Benefits are not equivalent to taxes. It is natural, therefore, for persons for whom participation is optional to select their options in such a way as to take maximum advantage of Social Security, leaving the bulk of the taxpayers—who have no choice in the matter—to make up any extra cost this may entail. This is in fact what is happening. When a group of municipal employees opt out of Social Security, they take with them the right to receive future benefits of considerably greater value than the taxes paid to the date of withdrawal. When a career federal civil servant takes a part-time job in employment covered by Social

Security, he receives benefits of considerably greater value than his tax payments. When a policeman or fireman retires at age 50 and then works in a job covered by Social Security, upon his "second" retirement he receives benefits of much greater value than his tax payments. This is not the fault of the municipal employee or the career federal civil servant or the policeman or fireman; it is the fault of the Social Security system which was designed to cover all of the nation's workers but which, because of a series of "loopholes," leaves out a significant portion of the population.

If groups of employees in different parts of the nation were given the option of continuing to support the national defense effort by electing either to continue paying the necessary taxes or to discontinue paying such taxes, it would be reasonable to expect that certain groups would "opt out" of paying the taxes used to support the defense effort. Similarly, if persons were given the opportunity to "opt out" of providing any support for the nation's educational system, it would be reasonable to expect that some persons would elect to discontinue paying taxes that are used to educate our youth. In both of these cases, persons who elected to discontinue tax payments would none-theless receive benefits, admittedly indirect and difficult to perceive, from the national defense effort and the national educational effort, since both of these efforts would be continued by other taxpayers—perhaps at a slightly reduced level because of slightly reduced tax receipts. The difference between these examples and the option for certain groups of persons to withdraw from Social Security is not very great. Although a person who opts out of Social Security and discon-tinues paying Social Security taxes may suffer a reduction in benefits, it is not a complete cessation even though the payment of taxes ceases completely. First, the withdrawing employee will in most cases receive at least some Social Security benefits in the future as a result of the payment of Social Security taxes in the past. Second, there is an indirect, although substantial, benefit by virtue of the Social Security system's continuing to pay benefits to some 35 million persons—retired and disabled persons and their dependents, as well as widows and orphans. Were it not for the Social Security program, the burden of supporting a large proportion of these beneficiaries would fall directly upon all taxpayers regardless of whether they paid taxes to the Social Security program.

Social Security was not designed to be a neatly defined package of benefits that a particular group of persons could elect to buy or not buy in exchange for the payment of Social Security taxes. It was designed to provide a wide range of benefits to the bulk of the nation's workers and their dependents based upon their presumed need. The benefits are based upon prior earnings levels, the worker's type and number of dependents, the ability of the beneficiary to work, and so on. Benefits are not related, except incidentally, to the taxes paid by the participant. Since the program is operated on a pay-as-you-go basis, the taxes paid by one generation of workers are used to provide benefits for an earlier generation of workers. Therefore, the taxes paid by a particular generation of workers are not equivalent to the cost of the benefits that will be provided eventually to that generation of workers.

These characteristics of Social Security result in a significant redistribution of income: intragenerational transfers as individuals within each generation receive benefits with a different value than the taxes paid by such individual, and intergenerational transfers as benefits received by one generation taken as a whole are more or less than the value of the taxes paid by such generation.

The provisions regarding optional participation for certain groups of workers were designed as if the employee group concerned would pay taxes equivalent to the benefits it receives. This is obviously not the case under our present Social Security program; hence such provisions are poorly conceived and inappropriate. Apparently when the provisions were designed it was presumed that most persons for whom participation is optional would elect to participate and that they would not decide to withdraw at a later date.

One of the reasons frequently given for requiring everyone to participate in Social Security is that it will solve Social Security's financial problems. This is not an appropriate reason. For one thing, if more people are added to Social Security, they will not only pay more taxes but will also receive more benefits. The net effect of bringing everyone into Social Security would be to decrease the required tax rate paid by employees and employers by less than ½ percent each on the average over the next seventy-five years. This is not very much compared with the present tax rate of 6.65 percent and the much higher tax rates of 8 to 12 percent that will be required during the early part of the next century if no changes are made in the program. But this phenomenon of reduced payroll tax rates deserves closer study. Even though universal coverage may result in slightly lower payroll tax rates, and thus may appear to alleviate Social Security's financial problems, *it would not reduce the total tax burden—direct and indirect—imposed on present participants to support Social Security.* On the contrary, it would most likely *increase* the tax burden.

This paradox may be explained as follows by considering the effect of bringing federal employees into Social Security. Federal employees would pay the same Social Security tax rate as all other participants; however, because of the characteristics of federal employees, their Social Security taxes relative to their benefits would be higher than the average for all other participants, yielding a "gain" to Social Security. This gain would result in lower average benefit costs relative to taxable payroll and lower average tax rates for all participants. It should be obvious, however, that the cost of benefits for present participants would not be lowered by adding federal employees; it is simply that "excess" Social Security taxes paid by federal employees would permit slightly reduced taxes by present participants. But who pays the Social Security taxes for federal employees, including any "excess" taxes? It is the taxpayers of the nation. Accordingly, any reduction in Social Security payroll taxes made possible by including federal employees would be offset by an exactly corresponding increase in general revenue paid by all taxpayers.

One might argue that the federal employee—not the general taxpayer—would pay half the Social Security tax, hence there would be a saving to the general taxpayer. Any such tax saving would be unlikely for the following reasons. Federal employees already contribute 7 percent of their salary to their own retirement system. Inclusion of federal employees in Social Security would almost certainly be made on the basis of no increase in employee cost; hence existing employee contributions to the civil service retirement plan would be reduced by the amount of any Social Security taxes imposed on federal employees. There- fore, federal employees would not pay any more under Social Security and the civil service retirement plan combined than they now pay under the civil service retirement plan alone. (A minor exception, perhaps, is with respect to short-term employees, since Social Security taxes are not refundable as are contributions to the civil service retirement plan; therefore, some short-term employees would in effect pay higher contri- butions if participating in Social Security.) Any diversion of present employee contributions from the federal civil service retirement plan to Social Security would have to be restored by added general revenue paid by the nation's taxpayers.

One might argue that civil service retirement plan benefits could be reduced by the amount of any Social Security benefits newly provided, resulting in a saving to the general taxpayer. It is true that the substitution of pay-as-you-go financed Social Security benefits for advance-funded civil service retirement plan benefits may give an apparent reduction in costs in the short run, but it cannot reduce costs in the long run; it can only shift part of the costs to later generations. Providing identical benefits through different vehicles cannot change the cost, taking into account the time-value of money.

Finally, universal coverage would actually increase the total tax burden because civil service retirement plan benefits can be reduced by some but not all the benefits provided by Social Security. This is because Social Security provides some benefits that are not provided by the civil service retirement system. Therefore, if federal employees are included in Social Security on the basis of not receiving lower total benefits than the present benefits provided under the civil service retirement system, it follows that there would be an increase in total benefits (to the extent Social Security provides benefits not provided by the civil service retirement system). This increase in benefits for federal employees would result in increased costs for the general taxpayer.

The same general reasoning concerning the financial implica- tions of requiring federal employees to participate in Social Security also applies to the inclusion of employees of state and local governments, although the particular taxpayers affected may be different. For example, lowered Social Security taxes may be offset by increased state and local income taxes or increased real estate or other taxes. Inclusion of employees of nonprofit organizations in Social Security could result in lower Social Security costs for existing participants if the characteristics of such employees result in a "gain" to Social Security. This would be true because employer-paid and employee-paid Social Security taxes of nonprofit organizations would not be provided from general revenue. The financial impact of including all nonprofit organization employees is minor, however, compared with the financial impact of including all federal, state, and local government employees.

In summary, with regard to the financial aspect of universal coverage, although there are certain financial inequities in nonuniversal coverage, which should probably be corrected, universal coverage cannot possibly reduce the total tax burden—direct and indirect—of supporting Social Security (unless, in the process, someone suffers a benefit reduction). Universal coverage can result only in the shifting of Social Security costs among taxpayers brought about, generally speaking, by substituting general revenue for part of the payroll tax. In addition, universal coverage could result in a shift among generations of some of the costs of the affected public employee retirement systems. This would result from substituting part of the Social Security benefits for part of the public employee retirement system benefits, which could in turn cause a change in the financing patterns since Social Security is financed on a pay-as-you-go basis (for all its participants) and a given public employee retirement system may be financed on a pay-as-you-go basis (for its particular participants) or some form of advance-funded basis. Universal coverage could also result in higher long-range total costs of benefits for public employees since they would, in some cases, receive a broader array of benefits by participating in Social Security.

Universal coverage would, of course, pose many problems. Most employee groups not now covered by Social Security have their own employee benefit programs. These programs would need to be revised in the event of universal coverage so that the employees affected would receive neither smaller nor appreciably larger benefits after inclusion in Social Security than before inclusion. There would also be certain technical as well as legal problems in revising existing employee benefit plans. All of these problems can be resolved, however, should coverage under Social Security become universal.

Based upon the present design of Social Security, there should be no optional participation: everyone should participate in both the payment of its taxes and the receipt of its benefits, direct and indirect. If it is desired that participation be optional, one of the following types of change should be made:

> The Social Security program should be redesigned so that the benefits paid to each group of workers are approximately equivalent to the taxes paid by such group.

> The provisions regarding optional participation should be revised so that a group of workers electing first to participate and then to opt out would receive benefits more closely related to the taxes paid during its period of participation in Social Security.

Unless one of these basic changes is made, there can be no satisfactory basis for optional participation. On the other hand, compulsory participation of all federal, state, and local government employees and employees of nonprofit organizations does not appear likely in the near future because of the strong opposition to mandatory participation by government employees not now participating, as well as legal questions regarding the constitutionality of mandatory participation of state and local government employees. Accordingly, the debate over this issue can be expected to become more and more heated and confused and acrimonious. This issue cannot be resolved to the mutual satisfaction of everyone involved based on the present design of Social Security.

17

Should You Opt Out of Social Security If You Can?

As indicated in Chapter 2, there are about 10 million employees of state and local governments and 4 million employees of nonprofit organizations who participate in Social Security on a voluntary basis. These employees can elect to withdraw from, or "opt out" of, Social Security. The decision to opt out cannot be made on an individual basis but must be made for groups of employees.

An increasing number of these voluntary participants have considered opting out of Social Security as taxes have continued to rise, as misunderstanding of Social Security has increased, and as more people have become disenchanted with the federal government and its huge programs that, to some people, are unnecessarily paternalistic.

This chapter presents some of the many considerations to be taken into account by employee groups that are considering opting out of Social Security. In order for the chapter to stand on its own as much as possible, there is some duplication of material contained in other parts of the book.

General Background Information

The Social Security Act originally excluded from Social Security coverage all employment for state and local governments because of the question of whether the federal government could legally tax such employers. Also excluded was work for most nonprofit organizations, which were traditionally exempt from taxes.

Legislation enacted in 1950 (and later) provided that employees of such organizations could be covered by Social Security on a voluntary basis under certain conditions. For example, Social Security coverage is available to employees of state and local government systems on a group voluntary basis through agreements between the Secretary of Health and Human Services (formerly Health, Education, and Welfare) and the individual states. After coverage of the employees of a state or of a political subdivision of the state has been in effect for at least five years, the state may give notice of its intention to terminate the coverage of such employees. The termination of coverage becomes effective on December 31 of the second full calendar year after such notice is given, unless the state withdraws the notice of termination within such period. However, once the termination becomes effective, it is irrevocable and the same group cannot be covered under Social Security again. Nonprofit organizations may terminate coverage similarly except that the notice of intention to terminate cannot be given until coverage has been in effect for at least eight years and termination of coverage becomes effective at the end of the calendar year quarter occurring two years after the notice is given.

Approximately 75 percent of the 13 million state and local employees and 90 percent of the 4 million employees of nonprofit organizations are covered by Social Security under these voluntary participation arrangements.

In the past few years there has been an increase in the number of terminations of coverage among state and local government employees. Table 17.1 compares the number of newly covered employees with the number of terminations during each of the past seven years. The number of employees who terminated during the seven-year period 1973–1979 was 113,423, compared with total terminations of about 130,000 employees during the program's entire history through June 1980. Coverage groups in Alaska, California, Louisiana, and Texas account for 86 percent of the terminations.

Table 17.1

**State and Local Government Groups and Employees—
Comparison of Number Newly Covered and Terminated during
the Period 1973–1979**

| Year | Newly Covered | | Terminated | |
	Number of Groups	Number of Employees	Number of Groups	Number of Employees
(1)	(2)	(3)	(4)	(5)
1973	709	20,231	32	4,287
1974	821	21,281	68	8,680
1975	1,057	17,010	46	13,014
1976	762	20,000	54	7,940
1977*	675	17,000	137	25,242
1978*	722	17,050	112	20,515
1979*	601	13,293	79	33,745
Total	5,347	125,865	528	113,423

*Estimates prepared by the Social Security Administration.

As of early 1980 there were 255 coverage groups representing 77,289 employees who had given their two-year notice of intention to terminate but had not yet terminated. The filing of such a notice by a state does not necessarily mean that coverage will be terminated, however, since the state may withdraw the notice at any time before the termination becomes effective. Coverage groups in four states account for most of these potential employee withdrawals: California (16,301), Georgia (14,436), Louisiana (9,109), and Texas (25,147).

The State of Alaska is the first and only state to withdraw all of its employees from Social Security. The termination of the coverage agreement for Alaska state employees became effective December 31, 1979 and ended participation for about 14,500 employees.

The increasing attention given in recent years to the question of Social Security coverage, how widespread it is and how widespread it "should be," was reflected in the Social Security Amendments of 1977. In these amendments Congress directed the Secretary of Health, Education, and Welfare to undertake a study of the feasibility and desirability of covering federal employees, state and local government employees, and employees of nonprofit organizations under the Old-Age and Survivors Insurance, Disability Insurance, and Hospital Insurance programs on a mandatory basis. The final report on this study was issued on March 25, 1980. Although the report did not make a definite recommendation, it concluded that universal coverage was feasible and at least implied that it was desirable. The chairman of the study group, in his letter of transmission to the Secretary of HEW, clearly supported universal coverage as both feasible and desirable. Furthermore, universal coverage was considered by the 1979 Advisory Council on Social Security, which issued its final report on December 7, 1979. The Advisory Council found that "our nation's income security goals can be achieved fully and equitably only if all employment is covered by social security." Universal coverage will probably be considered by other recently appointed income maintenance study groups, and it appears likely that they, too, will support universal coverage or, at least, not be opposed to it.

Financial Importance to Social Security of Participation by Groups Not Now Covered or for Whom Participation Is Optional

In fiscal year 1979, Social Security taxes received by the Old-Age and Survivors Insurance, Disability Insurance, and Hospital Insurance trust funds representing amounts paid with respect to coverage of state and local government employees amounted to $12.1 billion, about 10 percent of the total taxes received. If a large proportion of such employees should withdraw from the system, tax income would be reduced substantially and immediately. There would be little immediate reduction in benefit payments to such employees; however, over a period of time (twenty-five years or so) the reduction in liability would be more substantial.

Because outgo now exceeds income under the Social Security program and the trust fund balances are relatively small, the withdrawal of a large number of state and local employees would have a significantly adverse effect on the system, especially in the short term, thus requiring relatively large immediate tax increases in one form or another.

Over the long term, however, the average cost of the Social Security program would be affected relatively less than in the short term by changes in participation among persons not now covered or for whom participation is optional. It is estimated that the average seventy-five-year cost of the cash benefits part of the Social Security program (OASDI) will be about 13.4 percent of taxable payroll under present law (assuming that all presently participating groups continue to participate). If all state and local groups that now participate should withdraw from the program, the average seventy-five-year cost would increase to about 14.3 percent of taxable payroll (a relative increase of 7 percent). On the other hand, if all state and local groups, as well as federal employees, not now participating should become participants in the program, the average seventy-five-year cost would decrease to about 12.8 percent of taxable payroll (a relative decrease of 4 percent).

The Hospital Insurance portion of Social Security would also be affected financially by increased or reduced participation by groups for whom participation is optional. It has been estimated by the Health Care Financing Administration actuaries that if all state and local government and nonprofit organization employees who now participate should withdraw from coverage, the average twenty-five-year cost of the Hospital Insurance program would increase by about 0.4 percent of taxable payroll (a relative increase of 10 percent). Alternatively, if all employees not currently covered should become participants in Social Security, the average twenty-five-year cost of the Hospital Insurance program would decrease by about ¼ percent of taxable payroll (a relative decrease of approximately 6 percent). The longer range effect has not been calculated, but it would probably be less significant.

Changes in the level of participation in Social Security by groups for whom participation is optional would have a financial impact on the entire economy, not just on Social Security costs, as indicated in Chapter 16. It is not possible to describe the exact financial impact on every aspect of the economy. It is possible, however, to conclude—as explained in detail in Chapter 16—that the inclusion in Social Security of all federal, state, and local government employees would not decrease the total tax burden of supporting Social Security. Generally speaking, it would only substitute general revenue for part of the payroll tax.

The financial impact on the Social Security program of participation or nonparticipation by groups for whom participation is optional is probably less important than the effect on the employees themselves of gaining or losing the diverse benefit protection offered by the program.

Difficulties in Making Cost Comparisons of the Social Security Program with Alternative Private Systems

Social Security provides many benefits and has many characteristics that are difficult, if not impossible, to duplicate for subgroups of the population. It is only through a mandatory program with practically universal coverage that it is feasible to provide many of the benefits that are available under Social Security. Therefore, it is almost impossible to make a valid comparison of the cost of Social Security benefits as provided under:

> the Social Security program financed through its payroll taxes; and

> a private program providing the "same benefits" but financed in a different way.

Some of the characteristics of the Social Security program that make it virtually impossible to duplicate are listed below.

> Benefits increase automatically as increases occur in the Consumer Price Index, in the average wages of the nation's employees, and in the average covered wages of a particular employee.
>
> Benefits in course of payment increase with the CPI.
>
> Survivorship benefits, as well as benefits that may become payable upon future age-retirement or disability-retirement, increase automatically:
>
>> Benefit formula is revised as changes occur in the average wages of the nation's employees.
>>
>> Average earnings of a particular employee for purposes of computing benefits ("indexed earnings") change as his own earnings change and as

average wages of the nation's employees change, usually resulting in eligibility for increased benefits.

Type and level of benefits change automatically as an employee's family status changes (without any change in the Social Security taxes payable). For example:

Single male marries.

Family has children.

Couple divorces after ten years of marriage (former wife continues to be eligible for certain benefits).

All of these changes—and others—result in automatic extensions in benefit protection. Certain other changes in family status result in contractions in benefit protection.

When an employee changes employers, he takes his "accrued benefits" with him regardless of his length of service. If he has satisfied part but not all of the participation requirements for a particular benefit (say the disability benefit) and his new employment is covered by Social Security, his previous participation will be added to his new participation in determining eligibility for future benefits. Changes back and forth between employed and self-employed status have no effect on benefits (but do affect Social Security taxes paid).

Survivorship protection and disability protection are provided without regard to an individual's health, occupational and avocational hazards, or other factors affecting his "insurability status." The same amount of Social Security tax is paid by an individual regardless of any of these factors.

Medicare benefits are payable to persons aged 65 and over who are entitled to monthly cash benefits under Social Security and to disabled persons under age 65 after they receive disability benefits for twenty-four months. Special medical expense benefits are payable to an insured person or to his dependents in the event of kidney disease.

Social Security benefits are not subject to federal income tax and are usually not subject to state and local income tax. The value of this tax-free feature to the individual depends upon the type and amount of his other income.

Social Security benefits for retired and disabled persons, their dependents, and their survivors are, in general, either reduced or not paid when the beneficiary is engaged in substantial employment or self-employment. Whether benefits are eliminated completely or simply reduced depends upon the individual's level of earnings. Different earnings levels apply for persons under age 65 than apply for persons between ages 65 and 72. This "earnings test" is no longer applied after an individual reaches age 72. (After 1981 references to age 72 will become age 70.) There are special rules, which include medical considerations, for disabled beneficiaries who work.

The Social Security program has experienced dramatic changes over the years with the addition of survivors benefits, disability benefits, Medicare, automatic adjustment provisions, and so on. Although future changes are certain to occur, they cannot be predicted with certainty.

Nature of Social Insurance: Social Adequacy

Because of the characteristics of Social Security listed above, it is probably possible to find a group of employees who could rightfully maintain that they receive less in benefits relative to their Social Security taxes than some other group of employees. For example, compare the following two hypothetical Groups A and B. (This example is for illustrative purposes only; it is not suggested that groups having precisely these characteristics exist.)

Group A

Women employees married to men who are in employment covered by Social Security.

Relatively high salaries for the husbands and low salaries for the wives.

Relatively small number of children.

Short working career for the wife.

Group B

Male employees.

Hazardous working conditions.

Nonworking wives with a relatively large number of children.

Relatively low wages.

Obviously more will be paid in benefits with respect to Group B relative to their Social Security taxes than will be paid with respect to Group A. Is this fair? It depends upon your standard, the yardstick by which you measure.

According to social insurance standards, it is fair and just that Group B receives relatively more from the program than does Group A. Social Security is a program of social insurance. It emphasizes social adequacy. It pays benefits according to presumed need: A married male who dies leaving behind a wife and three young children is presumed to have a need for survivorship benefits; a single person who dies—male or female—is presumed not to have a need for survivorship benefits (unless there are dependent parents). Yet, the Social Security tax rates paid by single and married persons are the same. That is social insurance.

It costs more to provide survivorship protection and disability protection for persons in Group B than it does for persons in Group A, yet the Social Security tax rates are the same for Group A and Group B. That is social insurance.

In a social insurance program that emphasizes the principles of social adequacy, no attempt is made to relate the benefits that a particular group of persons receives to the taxes paid by that group of persons to become eligible for such benefits.

There is, of course, a relationship between the taxes an individual pays and the benefits he receives since benefits are related to the earnings on which taxes are paid—among numerous other factors. But this relationship is more tenuous than most people have realized and this misunderstanding contributes materially to the public's current dissatisfaction with the Social Security program.

Can a Particular Group of Persons Duplicate Their Social Security Benefits at a Lower Cost than Their Social Security Taxes?

It follows from the preceding comments that some groups of employees could argue that they could obtain the same benefits that are provided by the Social Security program but at a lower cost than their Social Security taxes. While this seems reasonable, and while it may be true in theory (because of the way in which a social insurance program works), as a practical matter it is not true because it is not possible for a small group of employees to obtain many of the benefits that are available under the Social Security program.

If a group of employees drops out of the Social Security program, at least some of the employees will lose some benefits because some Social Security benefits are irreplaceable. The value of the benefits that are lost may well be offset by the reduced cost for the group as a whole; however, with respect to the individuals who are affected by the lost benefits, the reduced cost may not offset the value of the lost benefits.

Furthermore, just because the Group A employees may receive less in benefits than the Group B employees, it does not necessarily follow that Group A can duplicate its benefits at a lower cost than the Social Security taxes that it currently pays or will pay in the future (including the taxes paid on behalf of the employees by the employer).

Under the current-cost method of financing used for the Social Security program, the amount of taxes collected each year is intended to be approximately equal to the benefits and administrative expenses paid during the year plus a small additional amount to maintain the trust funds at an appropriate contingency level. This means that the taxes paid by one generation of workers are used to provide the benefits to an earlier generation of workers. Therefore, the taxes paid by a particular generation of workers are not necessarily equivalent to the cost of the benefits that will eventually be paid to it.

For example, if benefits are liberalized over time (in addition to adjustments made for inflation), then any particular generation may receive benefits of greater value than the taxes it paid to become eligible for such benefits. On the other hand, if benefits are deliberalized over time, any particular generation may receive benefits of lesser value than the taxes it paid to become eligible for such benefits.

Also, the size of the working population relative to the retired population, now and in the future, is an important determinant of whether a given generation receives benefits equivalent to the taxes it pays. Even if benefits are not increased from their present levels in relation to preretirement earnings, current projections indicate that future generations of workers must pay considerably higher tax rates than today's workers (at least 50 percent higher) because in the future the ratio of beneficiaries to taxpayers will be higher.

Relative Financial Stability of Social Security Program and Private and Public Systems

Despite the financial problems—specifically the need for additional income—the Social Security program will face during the coming years, there is little reason to expect that private and public employee benefit systems will not also face difficult financial problems, particularly if they attempt to provide benefits roughly comparable to those provided under the Social Security program. The financial problems of many of these private and public systems have become evident recently as a result of the maturing of some of the systems and as a result of the preparation of appropriate actuarial studies for others.

It stands to reason that a national social insurance program supported by the taxes of and operated for the benefit of 90 percent of the working population has greater financial stability and has a greater chance of meeting any financial challenge it may face than any smaller system covering only a few hundred or a few thousand employees in a limited geographical area or in a single industry.

Dilemma of Irrevocability of Election to Discontinue Participation

If a group of employees opts out of the Social Security program, the decision is irrevocable and future employees of this group will never again be eligible for coverage under present law.

It may be advantageous to the present employees of a particular group to opt out if they have sufficient quarters of coverage to be permanently and fully insured. The reduction in benefits may be more than offset by the exemption from future taxes (because of the weighted benefit formula, the minimum benefit, and the eligibility for Medicare benefits). For new employees of the group who have *no* Social Security coverage, however, the benefits that are relinquished may be equal to or greater than the taxes not required to be paid.

In other words, while it may be advantageous to present employees in a particular group to opt out of the Social Security program, it may *not* be advantageous to future employees to relinquish participation in the Social Security program. It is natural for present employees—or their representatives—to make decisions on opting out based on their own self-interest. But what about future employees whose self-interest is to participate in the Social Security program? Are they to be banned from participation in a program that provides benefits they need (and will probably desire) just because of action taken by their predecessor-employees? The government would undoubtedly come under pressure to permit any disadvantaged group of future employees to participate in the Social Security program, present law notwithstanding.

Another possibility to keep in mind is that a portion of the cost of the Social Security program may be financed by general revenue at some future time. If so, the general revenue paid by all segments of the population will be used to provide benefits to a limited segment of the population (participants in the Social Security program). In this event, also, the government would come under pressure to permit groups that had opted out to participate again in the Social Security program.

For these and related reasons, it seems unlikely that a group that opts out and is thereby irrevocably ineligible for future participation will in fact be forever excluded from the Social Security program. This means that a group that opts out now in accordance with present law will have been given advantages not afforded similar groups at other points in time—and thus could be considered to have received unfair advantage.

Better from Whose Point of View?

Consideration of whether a particular group of employees should opt out of Social Security should take into account the viewpoints of a number of interested parties, some of whose preferences can be expected to be conflicting:

Employer

Present employees with past Social Security coverage and their families

Future employees with no Social Security coverage and their families

Taxpayers and financial supporters of nonprofit organizations

Nation as a whole

Miscellaneous Considerations

The provision that enables a group of employees to "opt in" for a few years and then "opt out" creates a one-time opportunity for such a group to take advantage of the program—and of the participants for whom participation is compulsory. This is because of the "inequity" of the present law which pays to short-term participants benefits that are disproportionate to their period of participation, when compared with benefits earned and taxes paid by persons who participate in the program throughout their entire working career. This feature of the law also makes it possible for persons whose primary employment is not covered by Social Security—and who thus participate for a relatively short period—to receive benefits that are relatively large compared with their tax payments. To the extent that flaws in the design of the program create opportunities for the Social Security program to be taken advantage of, it is likely that the program will be redesigned. The Social Security Amendments of 1977 took limited steps in this direction by modifying the minimum benefit as well as certain dependent's benefits.

At the time a group of employees elects to participate in Social Security the individual employees usually have a voice in the decision; however, a subsequent decision to "opt out" of Social Security can be made unilaterally by the employer, at least in theory, without obtaining consent of the employees (present and future) who are affected. It would seem imprudent for an employer to make a unilateral decision to "opt out" of Social Security without consulting the employees who would be affected. On the other hand, even if all employees should favor "opting out," it may well be imprudent for the employer to honor the employees' wishes because of gaps that may then occur in employee benefit protection—as a result of the adverse impact on future employees who would be deprived of Social Security benefits as well as the possible long-range adverse, but unforeseeable, effect on present employees.

By one means or another it appears likely that virtually all persons will be covered by the Social Security program within ten to fifteen years and possibly sooner. If this is true, then a group that opts out of Social Security now and makes the necessary changes in its employee benefit program (not only the retirement plan but also the various death and disability benefit plans) will be faced with still further turmoil when it reenters the Social Security program and must again redesign its employee benefit program. Employee benefit programs that provide age-retirement, disability, and survivor benefits are long-range programs that need not and should not be revised frequently and substantively.

Conclusion

Groups of persons for whom participation in the Social Security program is optional face a predicament: whether to discontinue participation, if they are currently covered by Social Security, or to initiate participation, if they are not currently covered by Social Security. The problem is complex and its resolution depends upon diverse factors and future events, many of which cannot be predicted with certainty. Furthermore, because of the different interests of the various parties involved, a decision that appears to be advantageous for one party may not be advantageous for another party. Accordingly, there can be no assurance that a particular decision will turn out to be "correct" in the long run for the majority of persons much less for each person affected.

With respect to the original question posed in this chapter, "Should you opt out of Social Security if you can?": If a one-word reply is required I would answer "No." If a two-word reply is required I would answer "Probably not." If a one-sentence reply is desired, I would answer "No, but in the case of some employee groups, it may be preferable to opt out, taking into account the average of all points of view; however, if a group opts out, some individuals and their families will lose some benefits and thus be worse off."

It is vexatious to ponder a question with no clearly preferable answer. As indicated in Chapter 16, this dilemma arises because Social Security was designed to be compatible only with universal, mandatory participation. The imposition of optional participation on such a system cannot have been expected to work for very long—and it did not.

18
Should You Opt
Into Social Security
If You Can?

There are almost four million workers whose present jobs are not covered by Social Security—jobs that could be covered if the workers and their employers so desired. For the most part these are employees of state and local governments and nonprofit organizations. They include all state employees in Colorado, Louisiana, Maine, Massachusetts, Nevada, and Ohio, and all state teachers in Alaska, California, Colorado, Connecticut, Illinois, Kentucky, Louisiana, Maine, Massachusetts, Missouri, Nevada, Ohio, and Puerto Rico. State employees of Alaska are not covered by Social Security, but they are not eligible to elect coverage because they were once covered and elected to withdraw.

On the other hand, there are approximately ten million state and local government employees, including state teachers, and almost four million employees of nonprofit organizations who *are* covered by Social Security.

Which group made the correct decision—the fourteen million workers who decided to participate in Social Security or the four million workers who decided not to participate? The total benefit protection—in the event of retirement, disability, or death—enjoyed by each of these two groups is different since, as was indicated in Chapter 17, it is virtually impossible to duplicate the benefits provided under Social Security.

Should these decisions, many of which were made some thirty years ago, be reevaluated? Just as a significant portion of the fourteen million workers are considering whether to opt out of Social Security, perhaps many of the four million workers should be considering whether to join Social Security.

Chapter 17 outlines the many factors to be considered in deciding whether to opt out of or continue to participate in Social Security. These same factors should be studied by groups that wish to consider joining Social Security. In addition, it is possible to make "quantitative studies" that will compare the benefits and costs of various alternative benefit programs for a particular group of employees considering joining (or opting out of) Social Security. Although these studies will give important guidance for making such decisions, they will not eliminate the role of judgment—as well as a certain amount of luck—in predicting the future course of Social Security and the actions and needs of the particular employees affected. The following miscellaneous comments may give added perspective to the question of whether to elect participation in Social Security.

Social Security has changed considerably in the thirty years since optional participation first became possible. These changes may make participation more desirable than it was when the last serious consideration was given by a particular group to joining Social Security. Disability and Medicare benefits have been added. A new method of determining benefits (based on indexed earnings) has been adopted and benefits in general have been increased. Automatic cost-of-living benefit adjustments have been in effect since 1974—a significant change in this era of inflation. Some of Social Security's benefits may be more important now than they were in the past; for example, benefits for divorced wives and tax-exempt benefits in a time of high taxation. All things considered, Social Security offers a very different package of benefits now than it did several years ago.

For some groups of employees it may be desirable to replace an existing system of employee benefits—partially, if not completely—with the Social Security program. Characteristics of the employee group may have changed since the decision not to participate was made. The financial situation of the employer may have changed. And, as already noted, Social Security has changed.

Despite the adverse publicity in recent years, Social Security is a good buy for many groups. For some employees, it may provide almost all the employee benefits that are needed. Also, there are some employee groups that still have no pension plan and would be well-advised to consider Social Security along with the other systems available. A small group of employees, most of whom have average earnings or less, should look seriously at the option of joining Social Security. If the group has a limited number of employees with higher earnings and special needs, supplemental benefits outside of Social Security can be arranged easily.

Groups with a relatively large number of employees nearing retirement age would probably find Social Security a particularly good buy. Some groups may find it advantageous to join Social Security for a few years and then opt out after a majority of employees have acquired certain minimum benefit rights. Some risk would be involved in such a course since Congress may change the law permitting withdrawal, particularly if the trend toward opting out accelerates.

Not participating in Social Security is sometimes a handicap in hiring the more experienced and mature employees who are employee-benefit-plan conscious and whose former jobs were covered by Social Security.

Most employees of employers whose jobs are not covered by Social Security have had some covered employment in the past and are thus entitled to some Social Security benefits. An employer that wants to integrate its supplemental plan benefits with these Social Security benefits may have difficulty in justifying such procedure if not participating in Social Security and may thus have to provide larger benefits than otherwise necessary.

Every year Congress considers financing some part of Social Security with general revenue. If and when this happens, and it almost certainly will, more of the cost of Social Security will be borne by the general body of taxpayers and less of the cost will be borne directly by the participants themselves. In such an event, Social Security will become a much better buy for the participants (considering only the direct payroll taxes). In fact, if a large enough portion of Social Security is financed by general revenue, the only sensible course of action for an employee group—from an economic viewpoint—would be to participate in Social Security.

In view of the above commentary, it would seem desirable for each employee group to reevaluate its position regarding participation in Social Security—the four million nonparticipants as well as the fourteen million participants. It would be unfortunate if sheer inertia prevented a group of employees from modifying past decisions—made under past conditions to solve past problems—and thus prevented the group from more appropriately satisfying the employee benefit needs of tomorrow.

A final word to prevent any misunderstanding: The reader can conclude fairly that I would recommend participation in Social Security for many employee groups not now covered. Later in the book I recommend significant change in Social Security so it will better serve our future needs. There is no conflict in these recommendations. Social Security should be changed; but until it is, we should take maximum advantage of the present system.

19
The Fortunate Eight Percent

This chapter is for a limited audience: the approximately 10 million men and women who will pay the maximum taxes and receive the maximum benefits under Social Security. All the comments and examples in this chapter apply to persons who have always had earnings equaling or exceeding the maximum earnings base used in computing benefits and taxes under Social Security and who will continue to do so in the future. By thus limiting the applicability of the chapter, we can reduce the number of examples and figures that you, the fortunate eight percent of Social Security participants, must examine in order to know how you personally—not someone else—will be affected by Social Security. Of course there will be some duplication of other sections of the book.

Your Taxes

Table 19.1 shows for an individual the maximum amount of earnings that have been subjected to tax for selected years since tax collections began on January 1, 1937. This is also the maximum amount of earnings used in determining benefits; hence the maximum is referred to as the "contribution and benefit base." Table 19.1 also shows the tax rates and the maximum taxes during these selected years. Figures are shown

Table 19.1

**Contribution and Benefit Base, Tax Rate,
and Maximum Tax for Selected Years**

Calendar Year	Contribution and Benefit Base	Employees[a]		Self-Employed[b]	
		Tax Rate	Maximum Tax	Tax Rate	Maximum Tax
(1)	(2)	(3)	(4)	(5)	(6)
1937	$ 3,000	1.0%	$ 30.00	—	—
1950	3,000	1.5	45.00	—	—
1960	4,800	3.0	144.00	4.5%	$ 216.00
1970	7,800	4.8	374.40	6.9	538.20
1980	25,900	6.13	1,587.67	8.1	2,097.90
1981	29,700	6.65	1,975.05	9.3	2,762.10
1990	52,800[c]	7.65	4,039.20[c]	10.75	5,676.00[c]

[a]A matching amount of taxes is paid by the worker's employer.
[b]Self-employed persons were not covered by Social Security prior to 1951. In 1951 the tax rate was 2.25%, and the maximum tax was $81.00.
[c]Amounts for 1990 are estimates prepared by the Social Security Administration.

separately for employed persons and for self-employed persons. In the case of employed persons, a matching employer tax is also payable. Figures for 1990 are on an estimated basis (the tax rate is specified in law but the contribution and benefit base will depend upon future changes in average wages). The Social Security taxes shown in Table 19.1 represent combined OASDI and HI taxes.

Table 19.1 indicates that the annual taxes for an employee have grown from $30.00 in 1937 to $1,587.67 in 1980 and that they will increase to an estimated $4,039.20 by the year 1990. For a self-employed person taxes have risen from $81.00 in 1951 (the first year the self-employed were covered) to $2,097.90 in 1980, and they will grow to an estimated $5,676.00 by the year 1990. These figures demonstrate, if nothing else, why the fortunate eight percent of Social Security taxpayers are paying more attention than ever before to Social Security.

This dramatic increase in taxes during the next ten years will be caused by two factors. First, the tax rate itself is scheduled to increase from 6.13 percent in 1980 to 7.65 percent in 1990 for employees as well as for their employers (a relative increase of 25 percent). For self-employed persons the tax rate is scheduled to increase from 8.10 percent in 1980 to 10.75 percent in 1990 (a relative increase of 33 percent). Second, the maximum taxable wage base is scheduled to increase from $25,900 in 1980 to $29,700 in 1981, and it is scheduled to increase thereafter at the same rate that average wages increase for the nation's workers.

For the next ten years or so following 1990, it is unlikely there will be significant increases in the amount of taxes relative to earnings. The maximum taxable wage base during this period is scheduled to rise in direct proportion to the rise in average earnings; hence, this will not result in any "real" increase in taxes. The tax rate for employees (and employers) will probably have to be increased from the scheduled rate of 7.65 percent in 1990 to about 8.0 percent by the year 2000, a relative increase of only 5 percent. Thus, the bulk of the tax increases for the remainder of this century will probably take place within the next ten years—that is, by 1990. The next round of substantial tax increases will not be required until some twenty-five years hence, around the year 2006, when the post-World War II baby boom begins to reach age 60. During the twenty-year period from 2006 to 2025, as this generation reaches retirement age, the tax rate for employees will have to increase from about 8 percent to about 12 percent. The tax rate for self-employed persons must increase from 10.75 percent in 1990 to about 11 percent in the year 2000 and to about 16 percent in the year 2025.

Please remember that these taxes for the future are estimates based upon the intermediate assumptions mentioned in Chapter 4. Actual future tax rates could be lower or higher than these estimates, depending upon actual experience. It seems more likely, however, that they will be higher than lower.

There has been increasing resistance among taxpayers to these higher payroll tax rates. This has resulted in proposals that payroll tax rates be held down and that more general revenue be used to finance Social Security. This procedure would not reduce the total taxes collected for Social Security purposes; it would simply redistribute the tax burden. Lower *payroll tax rates* would result in higher *total taxes* for persons with above-average earnings. The reasoning for this statement is as follows. General revenue consists primarily of personal and corporate income taxes. Personal income tax rates increase as income increases, while Social Security payroll tax rates are constant and are not even applied to an individual's income in excess of the contribution and benefit base. Accordingly, the use of general revenue to raise a given amount of taxes would result in higher taxes for high wage earners than would the use of payroll taxes.

The effect on employer costs of substituting general revenue for payroll tax is more complex. Employers with above-average profits could expect to pay higher total taxes; employers with above-average labor costs could expect to pay lower total taxes; nonprofit organizations and state and local governments participating in Social Security would pay none of the added general revenue, yet would benefit from the reduced payroll tax. Using general revenue would result in a further redistribution of the tax burden since it would impose taxes for Social Security purposes on individuals not covered by Social Security and thus not benefiting directly from Social Security. These and other effects of introducing general revenue and thus redistributing the tax burden are seldom mentioned when the panacea of general revenue is proposed.

Questions are frequently asked about the total Social Security taxes that have been paid in the past. An employee who paid the maximum tax from Social Security's inception on January 1, 1937 through December 31, 1979 would have paid a total of $11,203. This same amount would have been paid by the employer. A self-employed person would have paid total taxes of $14,987 during this period. In considering the value of Social Security taxes paid in the past, it is more appropriate to assume that they were invested and earned interest. In making calculations that involve interest, Social Security actuaries usually assume that funds can be invested to yield 2½ percent more than the rate of inflation each year (although this is relatively more difficult to achieve in years of high inflation). Based upon this assumption, the cumulative employee taxes of $11,203 augmented by interest become $27,760 (not including employer taxes which would have accumulated an equal amount). The cumulative self-employed taxes of $14,987 augmented by interest become $32,820.

Table 19.2 summarizes these figures as well as similar figures for more recent periods. Because of the relatively higher taxes

Table 19.2

Maximum Cumulative Taxes Paid during Selected Periods by Employees and Self-Employed Persons

Period	Total Taxes Employees[a]	Self-Employed	Taxes Accumulated With Interest[b] Employees[a]	Self-Employed
(1)	(2)	(3)	(4)	(5)
1937–1979	$11,202.97	$14,987.10	$27,760	$32,820
1960–1979	10,056.97	13,920.60	19,550	27,530
1970–1979	7,811.77	10,619.70	12,150	16,620

[a]An equal amount of employer taxes was paid during this period.
[b]An interest rate of 2½ percent more than the Consumer Price Index increase during each year was assumed for this purpose.

in recent years, the bulk of the tax has been paid during the past ten years. As will be indicated later, extreme care must be taken in interpreting these accumulated taxes lest erroneous conclusions be drawn.

Your Benefits

Contrary to popular belief, your benefits are not based primarily upon the Social Security taxes you have paid. Taxpayers have been led to believe that there is a strong connection between their tax payments and their benefits because of forty years of propaganda about "contributions" paid to a "trust fund" under an "insurance program" thus creating an "earned right" to benefits payable upon old age, disability, death, or illness. The fact is that benefits are based upon many factors, principally the following:

The average earnings upon which you have paid Social Security taxes, excluding earnings for certain years and adjusted for changes over the years in national average earnings. (But benefits are not uniformly proportional to earnings. Benefits relative to earnings are higher for low wage earners than for high wage earners.)

Your need as measured by your earning power after becoming eligible for benefits.

The number and kind of your family members, including their need as measured by their earning power after becoming eligible for benefits.

The following sections give examples of benefits payable under various circumstances. Not every benefit is mentioned, just the principal benefits most often payable. Keep in mind that Social Security benefits are not subject to federal, state, and local income taxes. On the other hand, Social Security taxes paid by individuals are not tax deductible; that is, they are paid from earnings on which normal federal and state income taxes have been paid.

Retirement Benefits

Social Security retirement benefits can begin as early as age 62 or as late as age 70 (age 72 until 1982), depending upon the circumstances. Examples are given first for retirement at age 65; then earlier and later retirements are discussed.

To be eligible to receive retirement benefits, you must be "fully insured." You obtain "insured" status by earning "quarters of coverage." In 1981, one quarter of coverage is obtained for each unit of $310 that you earn in covered employment and pay Social Security taxes on during the year. (No more than four quarters of coverage can be earned in any given year.) In future years this amount will increase automatically in step with increases in average wages. Prior to 1978 a quarter of coverage was obtained for each quarter in which you had wages of at least $50. If you were self-employed prior to 1978, you earned one quarter of coverage for each unit of $100 of self-employment income (maximum of four per year). To be "fully insured," you must have as many quarters of coverage as there are years in the period beginning with 1951 (or the year you became age 22, if later) and ending with the year before the year in which you become age 62. This period is inclusive: for example, a worker reaching age 62 in January 1980 would need 29 quarters of coverage to be fully insured for retirement benefits (one quarter for each of the years 1951 through 1979).

If you quit working at the end of 1979 and attained age 65 in January 1980, you were eligible for a retirement benefit of $572.00 payable each month from January 1980 until your death (no benefit is payable for the month in which death occurs). This monthly benefit will be increased automatically to take into account increases in the Consumer Price Index. Generally speaking, benefit increases are made in June each year if an increase of at least 3 percent is indicated. This automatic adjustment feature has considerable value. With inflation of 5 percent per year, the $572.00 monthly benefit would become $730.30 after five years and $932.30 after ten years. With inflation of 10 percent per year, the $572.00 monthly benefit would become $921.50 after five years and $1,484.40 after ten years—and $2,390.90 after fifteen years.

These full benefits may not be paid, however, if you continue to work after age 65 and receive earned income (as distinguished from investment income, rental income, and the like). In 1980 you can receive earned income of $5,000 without affecting your retirement benefits; however, benefits will be reduced by $1 for every $2 you earn over $5,000. Therefore, if your earned income is $19,873 or more in 1980 you would not receive any Social Security retirement benefit for 1980. (This computation is based on total benefits in 1980 of $7,436.60 reflecting the June 1980 cost-of-living benefit increase.) Earned income of more than $5,000 and less than $19,873 would result in the loss of some but not all Social Security retirement benefits. The "earnings limitation" increases from $5,000 in 1980 to $5,500 in 1981 and $6,000 in 1982. Thereafter the earnings limitation is increased to keep up with increases in average wages of all the nation's employees. After you reach age 70 there is no earnings limitation, and you will receive your total Social Security retirement benefit no matter how much you earn. During the calendar year in which you reach age 70, your earnings during the month of your 70th birthday and thereafter are excluded in determining your benefits for the year. (Until 1982 the earnings limitation applies until age 72.)

This example makes it clear that Social Security does not make an unconditional promise to pay benefits beginning at age 65. If you continue working at full salary, benefits will not commence until age 70 (age 72 until 1982). A substantial reduction in salary may entitle you to receive partial Social Security benefits; however, full benefits are payable prior to age 70 (age 72 until 1982) only if your paid employment virtually ceases.

Just as Social Security does not unconditionally provide benefits at age 65, it does not specify the age at which you must retire to receive Social Security retirement benefits. Benefits may commence as early as age 62 or as late as age 70 (72 until 1982). However, age 65 is the "normal retirement age." If benefits commence prior to age 65, they are reduced; and if benefits commence after age 65, they are increased.

Benefits commencing earlier than age 65 may be smaller for several reasons. First, you may have smaller average earnings as a result of not working until age 65. Second, a reduction factor will be applied to the benefits otherwise payable because you will receive more monthly benefit checks since they will begin sooner. This reduction factor is 5/9 of 1 percent for each month that you receive your benefits before age 65. If benefits begin at age 62, for example, they will be reduced by 20 percent. Furthermore, the annual amount of earned income you can have between ages 62 and 65 without giving up Social Security benefits is only $3,720 (in 1980), in contrast to the $5,000 earnings limit after age 65. This may result in a further effective reduction in benefits commencing earlier than age 65.

Benefits commencing later than age 65 may be larger for two reasons. First, you may have larger average earnings as a result of working beyond age 65. Second, an increase factor will be applied to the benefits otherwise payable to reflect your expectation to receive fewer monthly benefit checks since they will begin later. If you reach age 65 before 1982, the increase factor is 1 percent of your benefit for each year after age 65 that you postpone receipt of your benefit (1/12 of 1 percent for each month). If you reach age 65 in 1982 or later, the increase factor is 3 percent of your benefit for each year (1/4 of 1 percent for each month). The increase factor, be it 1 percent or 3 percent, is much less than it would be if full adjustment were made to compensate for the later commencement of benefit payments.[1]

Money-Saving Hints

If you reach age 65 in January 1980 and plan to work until March 1, 1980, you should still apply for Social Security retirement benefits as of January 1, 1980. If your earned income for January and February combined is less than $5,000, you can still receive Social Security benefits for January and February ($1,144 of tax-free income you might otherwise overlook). Even if you retire later than March 1, 1980, and your earned income exceeds $5,000, it may still work to your advantage to apply for benefits as of January 1. You may want to take into account the offsetting effect of the increase for delayed commencement of benefits which you will forego; however, in most cases it is to your advantage to start your benefits as soon after age 65 as possible.

Even if you do not start your retirement benefits at age 65, you should apply for Medicare benefits at age 65. Medicare is available at age 65 even if you continue working after age 65, *but only if you apply for the benefits.*

Benefits for Family Members When You Retire

When you retire and begin receiving benefits, other members of your family may also be entitled to benefits based upon your participation in Social Security, even though they may not have paid Social Security taxes. As in the above example, it is assumed that you quit working at the end of 1979, and attained age 65 and began receiving a monthly retirement benefit in January 1980 of $572.00.

If your spouse were aged 65 or older in January 1980, he or she is eligible for a benefit of $286.00 payable each month that both of you are alive. This benefit, too, will increase automatically as the cost-of-living increases. After your death, your spouse's benefit will increase to your basic benefit of $572.00 per month (plus any cost-of-living benefit increases that have been granted) and will be payable for his or her remaining lifetime.

If your spouse is between age 62 and 65, there is a choice to make:

> Defer commencement of benefits until age 65, in which event the full $286.00 will be payable (adjusted for cost-of-living increases that have occurred in the interim).

Start receiving benefits immediately on a permanently reduced basis. (For example, if benefits commence at age 62 they would be reduced by 25 percent and would be $214.50.)

If your spouse is not yet age 62, you can arrange for benefits to commence at any time between ages 62 and 65. The exact amount will depend upon the age at which benefits commence and the cost-of-living increases that have occurred in the interim.

If your spouse has had government employment in a position not covered by Social Security, his or her spouse's benefit from Social Security will generally be offset by the amount of any pension benefit derived from such employment. An exception is made that permits the payment of spouse's benefits without the offset if the spouse were eligible for the noncovered-employment pension prior to December 1982 and would have been eligible for the spouse's benefit under the law in effect in January 1977. (This is a situation where precise details should be furnished the local Social Security office for a determination of the exact benefits payable.)

Your spouse will be eligible to receive benefits *prior to age 62* if he or she is caring for an "eligible child" under age 18 (or any age if disabled before age 22). The benefit would depend on how many children were also receiving benefits. If there is one such child, the spouse's benefit would be $214.30 per month payable until the child reaches age 18. Your spouse's benefits would then stop, and start again any time your spouse elects between ages 62 and 65.

Each eligible child will also receive benefits until reaching age 18, or age 22 if a full-time student, or until death if disabled before age 22. An eligible child must be one of your natural children (legitimate or illegitimate), adopted children, dependent stepchildren or dependent grandchildren (if their parents are deceased or disabled), and must be unmarried. The amount of the benefits payable to your children depends on how many of your family members are eligible to receive benefits. For example, if only one child is eligible for benefits as your dependent, and no one else, his or her benefit would be $286.00 per month. If there are additional beneficiaries, the amount per beneficiary would be lower because of the limit on the total amount of benefits payable in any month to members of one family. For a worker retiring in January 1980 at age 65, this maximum family benefit was $1,000.60. Benefits for family members other than the primary beneficiary are reduced proportionately to the extent necessary to stay within the family maximum.

The examples of monthly retirement benefits given above are summarized in Table 19.3 along with the "replacement ratio" corresponding to each of the illustrative monthly dollar benefits. The replacement ratio is defined here as the ratio of the total benefits payable for 1980 (including the benefit increase for June and later) to the average annual maximum taxable earnings (gross earnings before taxes) during the three-year period 1977–1979. This is an arbitrary definition; average preretirement earnings could have been net of taxes, or they could have been averaged over a longer or shorter period than three years.

A projection of future replacement ratios gives an indication of the extent to which Social Security will replace preretirement income, and thus the extent to which Social Security must be

Table 19.3

Estimated Social Security Retirement Benefits for Workers Retiring at Age 65 in January 1980, Having Had Maximum Career Earnings

Beneficiary[a]	Monthly Benefit Amount	Replacement Ratio[b]
(1)	(2)	(3)
Worker only	$ 572.00	39%
Worker and spouse aged 65	858.00	59
Worker and one child	858.00	59
Worker and two children	1,000.60	68
Worker, spouse, and one or more children	1,000.60	68

[a]Benefits shown in family examples assume that each family member is dependent on the retired worker for support. See text for discussion of benefit eligibility requirements for family members.

[b]This figure is the ratio of the total benefits for 1980 to the average annual maximum taxable earnings during the three-year period 1977–1979; thus, it is the percentage of the final three-year average earnings that is replaced by Social Security benefits during 1980.

supplemented (by private savings and employer-provided pensions) to sustain any given standard of living. If the Social Security law is not revised, the replacement ratios shown in Table 19.3 will decline somewhat for persons retiring in the near future but will then rise and eventually stabilize at about 85 percent of the amounts shown in Column (3). This information is quite valuable in making advance provision for retirement. It should be kept in mind that the replacement ratios in Table 19.3 relate to the maximum taxable earnings covered by Social Security and not to actual average earnings, which may be larger.

The payment of benefits shown in Table 19.3 is subject to the earnings test mentioned earlier. Earnings of the worker may reduce benefits of both the worker and family members. Earnings of individual family members may reduce only their individual benefits.

The benefits payable to family members will be increased to reflect changes in the Consumer Price Index in the same way that benefits payable to the retired worker are increased.

Your divorced spouse (or spouses) may be entitled to benefits as early as age 62 if married to you for at least ten years. Benefits will not be payable unless you are also receiving benefits. In some cases remarriage of your spouse will disqualify him or her from benefits.

The benefit examples outlined above for family members by no means cover all the possible cases. A spouse may have earned benefits based on his or her own work record. If so, this benefit or the benefit payable as a family member, whichever is larger, will be payable. To be eligible for a wife's benefit, a woman must have been married to a retired or disabled worker for at least one year, but there are exceptions. There are countless fine points to consider in determining benefits. While this section provides information on the general level and nature of Social Security retirement benefits, your local Social Security office should be consulted once you near retirement age for a complete analysis of the various benefits payable and the particular rules involved.

Disability Benefits

To be eligible for Social Security disability benefits, you must be unable to engage in any substantial gainful activity because of some medically determinable physical or mental impairment that can be expected to result in death or has lasted, or can be expected to last, for a continuous period of at least twelve months; or, after age 55, if blindness prohibits you from engaging in substantial gainful activity requiring skills or abilities comparable to those of any gainful activity in which you previously engaged with some regularity over a substantial period of time.

In addition, you must have acquired quarters of coverage—that is, paid Social Security taxes—for a specified period of time which varies with your age. To be eligible for benefits in 1980: if you were born after 1956, you must have acquired at least six quarters of coverage in the last three years; at the other extreme, if you were born before 1930, you must have twenty-nine quarters of coverage, twenty of which were acquired in the last ten years; and if you were born between 1930 and 1956, inclusive, the required number of quarters of coverage falls within these extremes. For blind persons the requirements are somewhat less stringent.

There is a waiting period of five full consecutive calendar months before disability benefits begin. For example, if you became disabled in July 1979, benefits would first be payable for January 1980. (The benefit check would actually be received approximately February 3.)

Just as for retirement benefits, your basic disability benefit depends upon the average earnings upon which you have paid Social Security taxes—with certain adjustments. Your average earnings for this purpose vary with your attained age; therefore, benefits vary somewhat depending upon your age at disability. Accordingly, disability benefits for a person first eligible to receive them in January 1980 could be as low as $498.00 or as high as $552.40 depending upon the age at disability—the higher the age, the lower the benefits. If you became eligible for disability benefits payable beginning in January 1980, and you were then aged 35, your monthly disability benefit would be $528.90.

Monthly disability benefits are increased automatically to take into account increases in the Consumer Price Index, just as the age-retirement benefit is increased, and the benefits are also tax free. The payment of benefits ends with the earliest of:

the month in which you die;

the third month following the month in which disability ceases; and

the month in which you attain age 65.

At age 65, normal old-age retirement benefits become payable in an amount that is usually equal to the disability benefit.

The earnings limitation that applies to age-retirement benefits does not apply to the payment of disability benefits; however, other restrictions apply. A disabled person may be offered rehabilitation services by a state vocational rehabilitation agency. If so, benefits may be denied for any month in which such rehabilitation services are refused. There is a certain amount of judgment involved in determining when disability ceases. To encourage rehabilitation, earnings of up to $300 per month (as of 1980) are generally allowed without affecting the payment of disability benefits. Furthermore, a disability beneficiary is allowed nine months of trial work without affecting the right to benefits.

After you have received disability benefits for twenty-four months you will be eligible for Medicare benefits. Hospital Insurance benefits (Part A of Medicare) are provided free of charge. Supplementary Medical Insurance benefits (Part B of Medicare) are optional and require a monthly premium of $9.60 after July 1, 1980 (subject to annual increases as average medical expenses increase). If you or your dependent has chronic kidney disease requiring dialysis or kidney transplant, Medicare is available without the twenty-four-month waiting period.

Money-Saving Hints

Benefits are not paid automatically, they must be duly applied for. If you make late application for benefits, they can be paid retroactively but only for twelve months, beginning with the months after the five-month waiting period. In some cases where a disabled worker dies without having filed for disability, benefits may be claimed retroactively.

As early as possible you should establish the fact that disability has begun in order to minimize any dispute about when the disability has lasted five full months.

Disability benefits may begin with the first full month of disability if it arises within five years after an earlier qualifying disability has ended.

Benefits for Family Members If You Become Disabled

If you become disabled and begin receiving benefits, other members of your family may also be entitled to benefits based upon your participation in Social Security, even though they may not have paid Social Security taxes. In general, the rules for payment are the same as if you receive age-retirement benefits. As in the above example, assume that you became eligible for disability benefits payable beginning in January 1980, that you were then aged 35, and that your monthly disability benefit is $528.90.

If you are married but have no eligible children (defined later), no spouse's benefit will be paid until he or she reaches age 65. At age 65, your spouse's benefit would be $264.50 adjusted for cost-of-living increases granted between January 1980 and the spouse's attainment of age 65. Stated another way, your spouse's benefit at age 65 will be 50 percent of your benefit at that time. Your spouse may elect to receive benefits as early as age 62, in which event the benefits would be actuarially reduced to take into account the longer period over which they would be payable.

If your spouse has had government employment in a position not covered by Social Security, his or her spouse's benefit from Social Security will generally be offset by the amount of any pension benefit derived from such employment. An exception is made that would permit the payment of spouse's benefits without the offset if the spouse were eligible for the noncovered-employment pension prior to 1983 and would have been eligible for the spouse's benefit under the law in effect in January 1977.

If you should die—again, with no eligible children—a monthly benefit would be payable to your spouse when he or she reaches age 65. The benefit would be $528.90 adjusted for cost-of-living increases granted between January 1980 and the spouse's attainment of age 65. In other words, your surviving spouse's benefit at age 65 would be the same as would have been payable to you had you survived. Your surviving spouse may elect to receive benefits as early as age 60, in which event the benefits would be actuarially reduced to take into account the longer period over which they would be payable.

If you have eligible children, additional benefits may be payable not only to the children but also to your spouse regardless of age. An eligible child must be one of your natural children (legitimate or illegitimate), adopted children, dependent stepchildren or dependent grandchildren (if their parents are deceased or disabled), and must be unmarried. The amount of the benefits payable to your children and your spouse depends on how many of your family members are eligible to receive benefits since there are limits to benefits payable to a single family.

The following examples assume, as before, that you became eligible for disability benefits payable beginning in January 1980, that you were then aged 35, and that your monthly disability benefit is $528.90.

If you have a spouse who is caring for an eligible child under age 18 (or any age if disabled before age 22), each of them will be eligible for monthly benefits of $198.40, or a total of $396.80. This amount, together with your monthly benefit of $528.90, totals $925.70, which is the maximum family benefit in January 1980. If there is more than one child, the $396.80 payable to your family members would not be increased; rather, each family member would receive a smaller portion of the total. The spouse's benefit will cease when the child reaches age 18. The child's benefit will cease at age 18 except that if the child is a full-time student, benefits will continue, in most circumstances, through the semester or quarter in which the child reaches age 22. If the child is a full-time student, the child's benefit would increase to $264.50 at age 18 (when the spouse's benefit ceases) because the family maximum would no longer be limiting.

If you should die while these benefit payments are being made to your spouse and child, the benefits would continue just as if you were still alive and disabled, except they would be larger: $396.70 for your spouse and $396.70 for your child, or a total of $793.40 per month. Benefits to your spouse would cease when the child reaches age 18 and would resume when the spouse reaches age 65 (or age 60 if reduced benefits are selected). The spouse's benefit at age 65 would be $528.90 adjusted for cost-of-living increases granted since January 1980. Benefits to your child would cease at age 18 (22 if a full-time student).

Table 19.4 gives examples of monthly disability benefits payable in several situations along with the replacement ratio corresponding to each of the illustrative monthly dollar benefits. For workers only, these replacement ratios will not change significantly unless the law is amended; hence, they can serve as a guide to how much Social Security benefits must be supple-

Table 19.4

Estimated Social Security Disability Benefits for Workers Becoming Eligible for Disability Benefits in January 1980 at Various Ages, Having Had Maximum Career Earnings[a]

Beneficiary[b]	Monthly Benefit Amount	Replacement Ratio[c]
(1)	(2)	(3)
Worker becoming disabled at age 25:		
Worker only	$552.40	44%
Worker, spouse, and one or more children	966.80	76
Worker becoming disabled at age 35:		
Worker only	528.90	42
Worker, spouse, and one or more children	925.70	73
Worker becoming disabled at age 55:		
Worker only	498.00	39
Worker, spouse, and one or more children	871.60	69

[a]Public Law 96-265 (enacted June 9, 1980) made a number of changes in the way benefits are calculated for disabled workers and their families. The disabled workers in this example would not be affected; however, benefits would be reduced somewhat for persons becoming eligible for family disability benefits in the future.
[b]Benefits shown in family examples assume that each family member is dependent on retired worker for support. See text for discussion of benefit eligibility requirements for family members.
[c]This figure is the ratio of total benefits for 1980 to the average annual maximum taxable earnings during the three-year period 1976–1978, the last three full years of earnings prior to disablement. In each example the worker is assumed to become disabled in July 1979 and to begin receiving benefits in January 1980.

mented to sustain any given standard of living. For workers becoming disabled after June 1980 and becoming eligible for *family benefits*, however, replacement ratios would be somewhat smaller than indicated here. Please note that the replacement ratios relate to the maximum taxable earnings covered by Social Security and not to your actual average earnings, which may be larger.

The payment of the benefits shown in Table 19.4 is subject to the continued disability of the worker as well as to the continued eligibility of the spouse and children. The earnings test, which applies to retired workers, does not apply to a disabled worker. The earnings test does apply, however, to family members, whose benefits are thus subject to reduction if their earnings exceed certain specified amounts.

Your divorced spouse (or spouses) may be entitled to benefits as early as age 62 if married to you for at least ten years. Benefits will not be payable unless you are also receiving benefits. In some cases remarriage of your spouse will disqualify him or her from benefits.

The benefit examples outlined above for family members by no means cover all the possible cases. A spouse may have earned benefits based on his or her own work record. If so, this benefit or the benefit payable by virtue of being a family member, whichever is larger, will be payable. To be eligible for a wife's benefit, a woman must have been married to a retired or disabled worker for at least one year, but there are exceptions. There are numerous details to consider in determining benefits payable in a particular situation. A thorough consultation with your local Social Security office is highly recommended.

Survivors Benefits

A variety of benefits may be payable under Social Security in the event of your death. To be eligible for some benefits you must be "currently insured"; for others you must be "fully insured."

You are currently insured if you have acquired at least six quarters of coverage—that is, paid Social Security taxes—in the thirteen-calendar-quarter period ending with the calendar quarter of death.

You are fully insured if you have as many quarters of coverage as there are years in the period beginning with 1951 (or the year you become age 22, if later) and ending with the year before your year of death.

You are eligible for a lump sum death benefit of $255 if you are *either* currently insured or fully insured. The benefit will be paid to your surviving spouse if living in the same household at your death; otherwise it will be paid to the funeral home director or such other person who paid the funeral expenses.

Upon your death one or more of the following types of monthly survivors benefits may become payable:

Mother's or father's benefit. A monthly benefit payable to a widow or widower, regardless of age, who is caring for at least one of your children under age 18 or disabled before age 22. A divorced wife can qualify for this benefit if the child in her care is her natural or legally adopted child. You must have been either currently insured or fully insured.

Child's benefit. A monthly benefit payable to a child who is under age 18, or over age 18 but disabled before age 22, or between ages 18 and 22 and a full-time student. The child must have been considered your dependent and must be unmarried. You must have been either currently insured or fully insured.

Widow's or widower's benefit. A monthly benefit payable to a widow or widower aged 60 or older who is not entitled to an old-age or disability benefit that is larger than the widow's or widower's benefit. A divorced wife can qualify for this benefit if married at least ten years before the divorce. In some cases a widow or widower who is disabled can start receiving survivors benefits at any time after reaching age 50. You must have been fully insured.

Parent's benefit. A monthly benefit payable to a parent aged 62 or older who was dependent upon you for support and who is not entitled to an old-age or disability benefit that is larger than the parent's benefit. You must have been fully insured.

The monthly survivors benefits outlined above have many

other conditions governing their initial and continued payment. The amount of the benefits depends upon a variety of factors, including the average earnings on which you have paid Social Security taxes (which is related, in part, to your age at death), the maximum benefits payable to a family, and the earnings of the beneficiaries once they are eligible for benefits. There are so many possible combinations of benefits that it is not feasible to cover all of them here.

Table 19.5 gives numerical examples of benefits payable in selected cases. The initial monthly benefit amount is stated in dollars. The total benefits payable for 1980 are stated as replacement ratios: that is, the benefit in relation to the average annual maximum taxable earnings during the three years preceding death. Also shown is the actuarial present value of these survivors benefits (explained later in this chapter in more detail). Consider the middle example in Table 19.5 of a worker who died in January 1980 at age 35, having had maximum career earnings and leaving as survivors a spouse aged 35 and two children aged 5 and 10. Assume that you, the worker, were a male and the spouse a female. (The actuarial present values are different for male and female spouses; for the other figures in the table, the sex of the spouse is irrelevant.) Based on all these assumptions, your wife and children would receive a monthly benefit of $928.80, or 63 percent of your average gross earnings during the three years prior to your death. Ignoring cost-of-living adjustments for the moment, this amount would continue for twelve years; that is, until your older child reaches age 22 (assuming the child was a full-time student). It would then reduce to $796.20 and continue for another year until your younger child reaches age 18. Monthly benefits for your wife would stop at this time (your wife would then be aged 48). Your younger child, if a student, would receive $398.10 for another four years, until age 22. When your wife reaches age 65, monthly benefits of $530.70 would be payable to her for the remainder of her life. Alternatively she could elect to receive reduced monthly benefits beginning anytime between age 60 and 65. If benefits commence at age 60, they would be $379.50 per month. All of these benefits would be increased to reflect changes in the Consumer Price Index, a very important feature.

Table 19.5

Estimated Amount and Value of Social Security Survivors Benefits for Survivors of Workers Dying in January 1980 at Various Ages, Having Had Maximum Career Earnings

Beneficiary[a]	Monthly Benefit Amount	Replacement Ratio[b]	Actuarial Present Value of Future Benefits[c]
(1)	(2)	(3)	(4)
Worker dying at age 25:			
Spouse aged 25 with one child	$849.00	58%	$189,800[d]
Spouse aged 25 with two or more children	990.60	68	221,300[d]
Worker dying at age 35:			
Spouse aged 35 with one child	796.20	54	155,100[e]
Spouse aged 35 with two or more children	928.80	63	172,000[e]
Worker dying at age 55:			
Spouse aged 55 with one child	739.20	50	100,100[f]
Spouse aged 55 with two or more children	862.50	59	103,000[f]

[a]Benefits shown in family examples assume that each family member is dependent on retired worker for support. See text for discussion of benefit eligibility requirements for family members.

[b]This figure is the ratio of the total benefits for 1980 to the average annual maximum taxable earnings during the three-year period 1977–1979; thus, it is the percentage of the final three-year average earnings that is replaced by Social Security benefits during 1980.

[c]This figure represents the amount that, if placed in an interest-bearing account on January 1, 1980, would be just sufficient to pay all monthly benefits as they fell due. It assumes that the family members have average life expectancies and that interest will be earned at a rate equal to the cost-of-living increases each year plus 2½ percent.

[d]Estimate assumes children are ages 1 month and 2 years as of January 1, 1980, and will remain in school until age 22. Single-child estimate assumes child is at lower age. Estimate includes present value of future widow's benefits to spouse, beginning at age 60, of $30,000.

[e]Estimate assumes children are ages 5 and 10 years as of January 1, 1980, and will remain in school until age 22. Single-child estimate assumes child is at lower age. Estimate includes present value of future widow's benefits to spouse, beginning at age 60, of $36,300.

[f]Estimate assumes children are ages 15 and 20 years as of January 1, 1980, and will remain in school until age 22. Single-child estimate assumes child is at lower age. Estimate includes present value of future widow's benefits to spouse, beginning at age 60, of $58,900.

The value of all these future benefits payable to your widow and children is approximately $172,000 as of January 1980 when they commence. In other words, a lump sum amount of $172,000 invested to earn interest (at 2½ percent more than the increase in the Consumer Price Index) would be sufficient, on the average, to provide the future monthly income outlined above. These survivor benefits, therefore, may be viewed as a death benefit of $172,000. As indicated in Table 19.5 for other examples, the effective death benefit ranges from some $100,000 to $221,000. Of course, a worker with no survivors would have no death benefit (except for the $255 lump sum benefit).

There are several factors that could affect the payment of these future benefits and thus decrease (in some instances, increase) their value. If the children do not continue as full-time students, their benefits will stop at age 18. If one of the children marries, the child's benefit will stop. If one of the children becomes disabled before age 22, the child's benefit and the mother's benefit will continue indefinitely (so long as your wife is caring for the disabled child). If your wife becomes disabled, she may qualify for benefits as early as age 50 (otherwise, between ages 48 and 60 she would not be receiving benefits). If your wife remarries after age 60, it has no effect on her benefits; but, if she remarries before age 60, in most cases she would forego all future benefits (but the children's benefits would not be affected). If your wife or either of your children should work, their earnings could result in a reduction of their Social Security benefits—because of the earnings limitation discussed previously. It is important to note, however, that the earnings of a particular survivor affect only his or her benefit and not the benefits of any other survivor. If your wife has government employment in a position not covered by Social Security, her survivors benefit will generally be offset by the amount of any pension benefit derived from such employment. An exception is made that permits payment of benefits without the offset to widows (and widowers) *if* they were eligible for their noncovered-employment pension prior to 1983 and meet all the requirements for entitlement to survivors benefits that existed and were applied in January 1977.

Money-Saving Hint

When a retired worker and spouse apply for benefits, the spouse will automatically be paid the higher of the benefits he or she would receive as either a spouse or as a retired worker. The spouse cannot apply only for spouse's benefits or only for retired worker benefits—the application for either is treated as an application for any and all benefits payable. In the case of a widow or widower, however, the applicant can choose to apply for either survivors benefits *or* retirement benefits. If the widow(er) is retiring before age 65 and is in good health, it could be greatly to her or his advantage to apply for reduced widow(er)'s benefits only, and then at age 65 apply for *unreduced* retirement benefits. In some cases the reverse procedure may yield greater value; that is, an application for reduced retirement benefits followed by an application at age 65 for unreduced widow(er)'s benefits.

An example will illustrate the potential windfall from restricting one's application. Suppose a male worker died in January 1980 at age 62, leaving a widow the same age. Assume that both the husband and wife had maximum career earnings in Social Security covered employment. The widow could begin to receive a monthly survivors benefit of $408.60 based on her husband's work record. She would also be eligible for a *reduced* retirement benefit of $402.80 based on her own work record—*but she doesn't have to apply for it at this time.* Instead she can collect the reduced widow's benefit of $408.60, plus cost-of-living adjustments, for three years and then apply for her *unreduced* retired worker's benefit of $503.40 per month, plus any intervening cost-of-living benefit increases. The actuarial present value of her net gain (or loss, if she simply continues to receive reduced widow's benefits) is approximately $15,000.

In other examples where there is a difference between the husband's and wife's earnings, it could still be to the surviving spouse's advantage to file for reduced benefits of one type and then convert to unreduced benefits of the other type at age 65. Of course, this assumes that the surviving spouse intends to retire prior to age 65 anyway—it would not necessarily be an advantage to stop working before age 65 just to receive three years of extra benefits. Careful examination of the facts is necessary in many of these cases to determine the best procedure since it is not always obvious.

There are many types of survivors benefits payable, and the preceding paragraphs merely summarize the more common ones together with the basic rules governing their payment. Social Security is obviously a very complicated program. If you are in doubt about your family's eligibility for Social Security benefits in the event of your death, you should consult with a local Social Security office—and do some studying on your own.

Medicare Benefits

You become eligible for Medicare benefits once you reach age 65 and fill out the appropriate applications. You are also eligible for Medicare benefits—even if you are under age 65—if you have been receiving Social Security benefits as a disabled beneficiary for at least twenty-four months, or if you or a dependent has chronic renal disease requiring dialysis or kidney transplant.

The Medicare program consists of Hospital Insurance (HI) and Supplementary Medical Insurance (SMI), frequently referred to as Part A and Part B, respectively. Hospital Insurance provides partial reimbursement for the cost of inpatient hospital services as well as a number of other services such as those provided by a skilled nursing facility or a home health agency. Supplementary Medical Insurance helps pay for the cost of physician services plus certain other expenses such as outpatient hospital care and home health agency visits. Not all medical services are covered by Medicare; the principal exclusions are routine care, outpatient drugs, eyeglasses, and dental care.

HI benefits are provided automatically once you reach age 65 as long as you are entitled to a Social Security benefit as a retired worker, spouse, widow(er), or other beneficiary. HI benefits are available even if your monthly cash benefit is completely withheld because of "excess earnings" under the retirement test. The SMI program is optional and requires premium payments of $9.60 per month after July 1, 1980. These premiums are subject to increase each July 1 in the future as the cost of medical care increases. If you are receiving a Social Security monthly benefit, the SMI premium will be deducted automatically from your benefit unless you specifically elect not to participate in SMI.

Under the HI program, the cost of a hospital stay is reimbursed once certain deductible and coinsurance requirements are met. Hospital services for up to 90 days in a "spell of illness" are covered; in addition you have a "lifetime reserve" of another 60 days that can be drawn on if you stay in a hospital for more than 90 days during one spell of illness. A "spell of illness" ends once you have remained out of the hospital or skilled nursing facility for 60 days. The hospital is usually reimbursed directly for any costs in excess of the amount you are required to pay. You must pay the first $180 of expenses (the "deductible") plus "coinsurance" of $45 per day if your hospital stay lasts longer than 60 days and $90 per day for any "lifetime reserve" days that you use. These deductible and coinsurance amounts apply to 1980 and will increase in future years as average hospital costs increase. In addition you must pay for certain costs not covered by the Hospital Insurance program: for example, the extra cost of a private room as distinguished from a semiprivate room.

If you have been hospitalized for at least three days and then enter a skilled nursing facility for follow-up care within two weeks after leaving the hospital, the services provided by the facility will be covered in part by the HI program for up to 100 days in a spell of illness. Days 21 through 100 will require that you pay a daily coinsurance amount of $22.50 (subject to future increase). After discharge from a three-day stay in a hospital or from a skilled nursing facility, up to 100 home health agency visits are provided under HI.[2]

The SMI program pays the "reasonable charges" for physician services, outpatient services by hospitals and clinics, and home health visits, after you have paid the first $60 of such services (this $60 deductible amount is *not* subject to automatic increase). You must also pay 20 percent of expenses in excess of the deductible as well as all expenses not considered "reasonable charges."

This is not a complete description of the benefits provided by the Medicare program. Chapter 3 contains somewhat more detail. You should consult with your local Social Security office (or your hospital and physicians) if you have particular questions.

All participants in the Medicare program are eligible for the same benefits regardless of the level of earnings on which they have paid Social Security taxes or the length of time such taxes have been paid. Approximately 70 percent of the cost of the SMI portion of Medicare is financed by general revenue which is paid by all taxpayers, including those not participating in Social Security. Accordingly, there is virtually no "individual equity," or relation between taxes paid and benefits received, under the Medicare program.

Money-Saving Hints

You should contact your local Social Security Administration office a few months before you reach age 65 and apply for benefits even if you have no intention of retiring at 65 and will not be able to receive cash benefits for some time. The application will ensure that you are eligible for Medicare benefits immediately at age 65. If your spouse is older than you and not eligible for retirement benefits based on his or her own earnings record, you should apply for cash benefits when he or she is about to reach age 65 (provided you are at least age 62). This action would establish your spouse's entitlement to Medicare benefits even if you yourself are not yet eligible. Medicare protection for your spouse could be valuable should hospital insurance coverage provided by your employer terminate or reduce upon a spouse's attainment of age 65.

Medicare does not pay for hospital and medical care outside the United States (except in Canada for U.S. residents living nearby and in a few other limited cases). Accordingly, if you depend normally upon Medicare and you plan to travel abroad, you should make alternative arrangements for temporary health insurance.

You should definitely enroll in the optional SMI program unless you have similar coverage provided without charge. As a taxpayer, you are already paying for most of the cost of SMI, whether or not you elect to receive its benefits. Currently only about 30 percent of the program's total costs are met from enrollees' premiums—the balance is paid from general revenue, the bulk of which comes from personal and corporate income taxes. In the future, premiums will represent an even smaller portion of total costs, probably no more than 10 percent by the year 2000.

You have a lifetime reserve of 60 hospital inpatient reserve days. Reserve days can be used one time only and are not renewable for a second benefit period as are the first 90 days of benefits. If you have other hospital insurance, you may want to save your reserve days for a later time when such other insurance may not be available. If you do not want to use your reserve days, you must notify the hospital before the end of your first 90 days of hospitalization.

Many private insurance companies have policies designed to complement Medicare by covering the cost of Medicare deductibles and coinsurance. Unless you are in poor health, it probably would be to your advantage to self-insure for these relatively small amounts rather than buy the complementary insurance policies. You should, however, consider such an auxiliary private policy if it includes reimbursement for costs in excess of "reasonable charges" and if it includes "catastrophic coverage" for hospital stays lasting longer than 150 days (or 90 days if you have used your lifetime reserve days under HI). Extended, high-cost illnesses are rare, but they can be financial catastrophes when they do occur.

Do You Get Your Money's Worth?

This is an easy question to ask but a difficult one to answer. Chapter 11 discusses this subject and concludes that the answer may be yes or no depending upon the viewpoint from which the question is being asked. The present chapter considers the question only from the viewpoint of the benefits received compared with the taxes paid for a given individual—a narrow yet quite legitimate viewpoint.

It is always tempting to compare the retirement benefits one may expect to receive with the taxes that have been paid. This is an interesting exercise, but much more complex and sophisticated studies are required to answer the money's worth question. Just to satisfy our curiosity, however, here are a few incomplete comparisons of the type sometimes made.

As shown in Table 19.3, a person retiring at age 65 in January 1980, having had maximum career earnings, would receive a monthly benefit of $572 payable for life. The value of these future benefits depends upon whether the retired person is male or female, the health status, and so on. For an average male, the present value of this benefit when it commences at age 65 is $77,800. In other words, this amount, if placed in an interest-bearing account on January 1, 1980 to yield the Consumer Price Index increase each year plus 2½ percent, would be just sufficient on the average to pay lifetime monthly benefits of $572, increased as the Consumer Price Index increases.

If this same illustrative male worker had a wife aged 65, the monthly benefit would be $858 during their joint lifetime and $572 during the remaining lifetime of the survivor. The present value of these benefits when they commence at age 65 is $143,100. If this couple also had two children, aged 16 and 18, who continued as full-time students until age 22, the monthly benefits would be even higher. The present value of such benefits would be $158,800.

The big question then is how do these present values ranging from $77,800 to $158,800 compare with the taxes that have been paid. Reference to Table 19.2 will provide the answers. An employee would have paid total taxes of $11,202.97, at the most, from 1937 through 1979. Invested to yield the Consumer Price Index plus 2½ percent, these taxes would have amounted to $27,760.00. Total taxes paid by employee and employer combined would have been at most $22,405.94, or $55,520.00 accumulated at interest. For a self-employed person, total taxes accumulated at interest would have been $32,820.

Accordingly, no matter what tax payments are considered they are substantially less than the value of the retirement benefits for persons and their families who live to age 65. But that is not the entire story. If you continue working full time after age 65, no retirement benefits will be paid until age 72 (or when you stop working, if sooner); this would cause a substantial reduction in the large present values of retirement benefits just illustrated. If you die just before reaching age 65 and have no dependents, only $255 would be payable. On the other hand, if you die at a young age and leave several survivors, total benefits worth more than $200,000 could be payable. The value of disability benefits and Medicare benefits must be considered—and a host of possible benefits to dependent parents, a divorced spouse, disabled children, and so on.

So, it is interesting to make these simple comparisons of retirement benefits and taxes, but they should not be mistaken for more thorough actuarial studies comparing all potential benefits with all potential taxes.

A recent study[3] on this subject by the actuaries at the Social Security Administration considered the value of the principal benefits payable under Social Security throughout the lifetime of several hypothetical workers. These values were then compared with the value of payroll taxes scheduled in present law. Standard actuarial procedures were employed, taking into account interest earnings, probabilities of death and disability, and so forth. To simplify the calculations, Medicare benefits and taxes were excluded from the comparison (although this is a significant benefit which should also be studied). Here is a summary of the results for several hypothetical employees entering the work force in 1978 at age 22. In each example, the person's status—married or single—is assumed to remain unchanged (except if affected by death). As in the rest of this chapter, the examples are for persons who receive maximum taxable Social Security earnings throughout their career.

> An unmarried male employee could expect, on average, to receive benefits equivalent to 92 percent of his taxes (but only 46 percent of the combined taxes paid by his employer and himself). Unmarried self-employed males could expect, on average, to receive benefits equivalent to 61 percent of their taxes.

> An unmarried female employee could expect, on average, to receive benefits equivalent to 125 percent of her taxes (63 percent of the combined taxes paid by her employer and herself). For an unmarried self-employed female, the expected value of benefits is equivalent to 83 percent of her taxes.

> A married male employee (with a wife the same age and not in paid employment, and two children, 25 and 27 years younger) could expect to receive benefits equivalent to 210 percent of his taxes (105 percent of the combined taxes paid by his employer and himself). Such a married self-employed male could expect to receive benefits equivalent to 140 percent of his taxes.

> A married couple, both of whom work and are the same age, with two children of ages 25 and 27 years younger, could expect to receive benefits equivalent to 125 percent of their own taxes (and 63 percent of the combined taxes paid by their employers and themselves).[4]

Whether persons currently entering the work force get their money's worth depends on which of the above categories they fit into, and whether they consider just their own taxes or those of their employer as well. Furthermore, it is difficult to be sure that a person now in one of these categories will remain permanently in that category; hence, a final answer to the money's worth question can be given only in retrospect after all the facts are in. Among the simplifying assumptions used in the above examples is that retirement occurs at age 65. If retirement should occur later than age 65 (a more likely assumption for persons entering the work force today) the ratio of benefits to taxes would be much lower than stated above.

Generally speaking, highly paid employees entering the work force today—and their employers—cannot expect to receive their money's worth from Social Security; that is, the value of their benefits will probably be less than the value of the taxes they and their employers will pay. On the other hand, persons retiring throughout the past forty years of operation of Social Security generally received much more than their money's worth. For the generations between these two extremes, the answer to the money's worth question is also in between. As discussed in earlier chapters, Social Security significantly redistributes income, not only within each generation but also from one generation to another. Accordingly, the younger members of the fortunate eight percent of Social Security participants to whom this chapter is addressed must look elsewhere for satisfaction than to an equitable return of benefits for their Social Security tax dollar. Chapter 11 mentions some of the broader issues to consider when asking the money's worth question.

20
Is Social Security Enough?

Social Security is a complex program providing a vast array of benefits which very few people comprehend. It is costly and will become even more costly. Accordingly, much of the public has come to believe that the government (through Social Security) is providing, or should provide, for most of our needs in the event of retirement, disability, sickness, or death.

Despite its complexity and cost, however, Social Security does not meet all of these needs uniformly for all sectors of the population. Some needs are met more adequately than others; for example, retirement needs are better satisfied for low income workers than for high income workers. Some needs are not met at all; for example, income maintenance during short-term illness and long-term partial disability. Some needs that appear to be satisfied may not be met in reality; for example, survivors benefits which are forfeited if the survivor has earnings in excess of the "earnings limitations."

It should be noted again, of course, that there are some eight million employees who are not covered by Social Security except through occasional employment (mainly, employees of federal government, state and local governments, and non-profit organizations; low-income, self-employed persons; and farm and domestic workers with irregular employment). This discussion of whether Social Security by itself provides adequate benefits obviously does not apply to these eight million employees.

For an individual to determine the status of his protection, a careful analysis of benefits from all sources—not just Social Security—is necessary. This is a difficult task, however. The Social Security Administration can provide valuable information on Social Security benefits, but it is not prepared to do so routinely for all participants. The personnel department of your employer can usually give information about employer-provided benefits (group life insurance, disability and sickness benefits, retirement benefits, etc.) but may or may not be equipped to provide detailed information about Social Security benefits. Your employer may also be able to give you information about benefits under programs it does not directly administer such as workers' compensation and state cash sickness plans. Your life insurance agent can provide information about any individual life insurance, disability insurance, health insurance, or retirement policies you may have. Putting all this information together is not an easy matter, but it is something you must do if you are to meet your various needs and those of your family on the most economical basis possible.

Where do you start? If your income is high, you may want to hire a financial advisor—a new breed of consultant specializing in analysis of your total financial picture. Some life insurance agents are qualified to help you organize your financial affairs. You stand a better chance with an experienced, well-trained agent—perhaps one who has completed the study program offered by the American Society of Chartered Life Underwriters and has thus received the C.L.U. designation. It is reasonable to expect your employer—probably through the personnel department—to provide some help in comparing your financial needs with coverage offered under employer-provided plans. In the final analysis, however, you will have to get heavily involved in comparing what you have with what you need, and thus be able to fill any voids that may exist. The following sections of this chapter are intended to help you identify these voids in income security for you and your family. Although the emphasis is on gaps in protection, in some cases there may be duplications that can be eliminated. The threats to income security are presented under four general headings: sickness, disability, death, and retirement.

Sickness

It is possible, of course, for you and members of your family to become ill or suffer an accidental injury at any time throughout life. This can result in loss of income because of inability to work, as well as hospital and medical expenses. This section deals only with the expenses of illness or injury; loss of income is covered in the following section on disability.

It should not be surprising that Social Security provides less protection against expenses of illness or injury than it provides against loss of income upon retirement, disability, or death. Social Security, as originally designed, was intended to replace a portion of lost income upon retirement and not to provide any reimbursement for expenses of illness. It was only when Medicare was added in 1965 that Social Security began to pay any of the costs of illness. Medicare benefits are provided only in the following relatively limited circumstances:

> For a person after he or she reaches age 65 if entitled to cash payments under the Social Security (or Railroad Retirement) program.

> For the spouse (aged 65 or older) of a person entitled to such cash payments, or the widow or widower of someone who had been entitled to such payments.

> For a disabled person less than age 65 after having been entitled to Social Security benefits for twenty-four months. (This could be a disabled worker, a disabled widow or widower, or a person receiving childhood disability benefits. A person who has received a disability annuity under the Railroad Retirement Act for twenty-nine months is also eligible.)

> For a person of any age with chronic kidney disease who is fully or currently insured under Social Security (including the afflicted spouse or dependent child of a person so insured).

Generally speaking, therefore, you and your spouse will be eligible for Medicare benefits after each of you reaches age 65 but not before. Your healthy children will never be eligible for Medicare benefits. This leaves many circumstances in which hospital and medical expenses are not covered by Social Security and in which supplementary health care arrangements may be advisable for you or your family members. Here are a few examples:

> If either you or your spouse is less than age 65 and you do not have adequate employer-provided health insurance (covering family members as well as yourself).
>
> If you are older than age 65, but your spouse is less than age 65 or you have dependent children.
>
> If you are younger than age 62, but your spouse is aged 65 or older and is excluded from employer-provided health insurance yet ineligible for Medicare.
>
> If you are older than age 65 and you live outside the United States or travel abroad.
>
> If you are older than age 65 and are an alien with less than five years' permanent residence in the United States (and thus are ineligible for Part B of Medicare).
>
> If you retire earlier than age 65 and your employer-provided health insurance terminates.
>
> If you become disabled earlier than age 65 and your employer-provided health insurance terminates.
>
> If you are a federal employee covered by a government-provided health insurance plan (under the Federal Employees Health Benefits Act of 1959).

In most of these situations you would be well-advised to make arrangements for supplementary health care coverage. This could be in the form of individual or group health insurance, Blue Cross-Blue Shield coverage, or group prepaid health care such as is offered by a health maintenance organization. If you are a regular full-time employee of an established company, you probably have such health insurance as one of your fringe benefits. Supplemental coverage is sometimes advisable even if health care benefits are provided by your employer, particularly to protect you in the event of a catastrophic or extended and high-cost illness.

After you reach age 65 and are covered by Medicare (Supplementary Medical Insurance as well as Hospital Insurance) you will probably still need to make special provision for the expense of illness. This is because Medicare does not pay the total health care expenses of those who participate. By way of example, here are just a few of the expenses *not* paid by

Medicare (the dollar amounts apply in 1980 and are subject to increase as average costs increase):

The first $180 of hospital expenses.

$45 per day for hospital charges for the 61st day through the 90th day and $90 per day for the 91st through the 150th day, and all costs thereafter plus all hospital room charges that exceed the cost of a semiprivate accommodation. (If you have previously exhausted your lifetime reserve of 60 days, you must pay all hospital costs after the 90th day.)

$22.50 per day for skilled nursing facilities charges for the 21st day through the 100th day, and all costs thereafter.

The first $60 of covered medical expenses plus 20 percent of subsequent covered medical expenses and all costs in excess of "reasonable charges" as determined by the Health Care Financing Administration.

The cost in excess of $250 per year of outpatient treatment for a mental illness.

These hospital and medical expenses that are not covered by Medicare can easily amount to thousands of dollars, particularly in an extended illness. Accordingly, even if you are covered by Medicare it is advisable to obtain supplemental protection against catastrophic illnesses.

Furthermore, you will still need a cash reserve to pay for part of the expenses of illness, even if you are covered by Medicare and even if you have appropriate supplemental health insurance coverage. Most insurance programs have features of "non-covered services," "deductibles," and "coinsurance" which require that you pay at least a portion of the costs.

Social Security is not intended to provide for all hospital and medical expenses in your old age. Furthermore, it provides for virtually none of those expenses for you and your family during your working years. In order to protect yourself and your family against the high costs of illness, as well as to ensure that proper medical care is available, it is essential that you make appropriate arrangements for supplemental health care insurance of one kind or another and that you accumulate a suitable cash reserve.

Disability

The financial problems caused by disability, particularly long-term permanent disability, are sometimes more severe than those accompanying death, or even old age. Yet, acquiring protection against disability usually receives the lowest priority. In this section, disability means the inability to perform part or all of one's normal work as a result of sickness or injury; hence, disability may be partial or total. Also, it may be temporary, lasting only a few days or weeks, or it may be permanent, lasting a lifetime.

Social Security began providing disability benefits in 1957. Since then eligibility for benefits has changed from time to time. Currently, the provisions may be summarized as follows (stated in a negative way to highlight the conditions under which benefits will *not* be available):

Disability benefits will not be paid unless you are so severely disabled that you cannot perform any substantial gainful work, and the disability is expected to last at least twelve months or result in death.

Disability benefits will not be paid until you have been disabled for five full consecutive months. Since the benefit for a particular month is not paid until the end of that month, the first benefit payment will not be made until sometime between six and seven months after the disability begins.

Disability benefits will not be paid unless you have paid Social Security taxes for a specified number of quarters, the number varying based upon your date of birth and disability. This is usually referred to as acquiring "quarters of coverage." For example, if you become disabled in 1980 the approximate requirements are:

Age at Disability	Quarters of Coverage Required
50	29 with 20 earned in last 10 years
40	20 earned in last 10 years
30	19 earned after age 21
20	6 earned in last 3 years

Therefore, you will not be eligible for disability benefits until you have paid Social Security taxes for at least one and one-half years and, possibly, as long as seven and one-fourth years. For disabilities occurring after 1980, even more quarters of coverage may be required.

You can see that there are many circumstances in which you could become disabled without being eligible for Social Security benefits. These voids in disability income protection may or may not be filled by other disability benefit programs in which you participate.

Many employers have formal or informal sick-pay plans which continue part or all of one's pay in the event of short-term sickness or disability. Some employers have sick-pay plans that provide benefits for six months, after which Social Security is presumed to be effective—at least for severe and probably long-lasting disabilities. Still other employers have comprehensive arrangements that meet a large proportion of the financial needs of a disabled person throughout his lifetime. The period of time during which employer-provided disability benefits are payable usually increases as the employee's service with the employer increases.

Five states (California, Hawaii, New Jersey, New York, and Rhode Island) and Puerto Rico require that employers participate in mandatory state-operated cash sickness benefit programs or establish comparable programs on a private basis. Employees are usually required to pay a large part of the cost of such plans. These programs provide cash payments for short-term periods (up to twenty-six weeks) in the event of sickness or injury that is not work connected. All fifty states require that employers participate in state-operated workers' compensation programs, or otherwise provide comparable benefits to compensate employees for job-related injuries, sickness, or death.

Few plans that provide disability benefits take into account the number and type of dependents of a worker. Social Security is a notable exception. Furthermore, hardly any program except Social Security provides disability benefits for members of a worker's family who become disabled.

Even after you meet all the eligibility requirements for Social Security disability benefits, you may still need to make special provision for supplemental disability benefits. This is because Social Security benefits are sometimes adequate but sometimes not. It depends upon your earnings level, family responsibilities, and—to a certain extent—your age at disability.

Table 20.1 illustrates the wide range of benefits payable under various circumstances. In each case it is assumed the worker becomes disabled in July 1979 and begins receiving benefits for January 1980. Benefits are not shown in dollar amounts, but rather as a percentage of average earnings during the three full years of work prior to commencement of benefits (1976–1978). This percentage is referred to as the replacement ratio. Since Social Security disability benefits are not taxable

Table 20.1

Ratio of Initial Social Security Disability Benefits to Average Earnings Prior to Disability for Illustrative Workers[a]

| Earnings Level of Worker[c] | Replacement Ratio[b] When Disability Began at. . . | |
	Age 25	Age 50
(1)	(2)	(3)
	Single Worker	
Minimum	70%	70%
Average	54	53
Maximum	44	39
Twice Maximum	22	20
	Married Worker with Eligible Family[d]	
Minimum	110%	110%
Average	99	97
Maximum	76	69
Twice Maximum	38	34

[a]Public Law 96-265 (enacted June 9, 1980) made a number of changes in the way benefits are calculated for disabled workers and their families. The disabled workers in this example would not be affected; however, benefits would be reduced somewhat for persons becoming eligible for family disability benefits in the future.

[b]Replacement ratio equals the disability benefits payable in the first year divided by the average of the last three full years of earnings prior to disablement. In each example the worker is assumed to become disabled in July 1979 and to begin receiving benefits in January 1980.

[c]"Minimum" denotes earnings equal to the minimum wage in each year. "Average" means earnings in each year equal to the average wages of all covered employees. "Maximum" and "Twice Maximum" refer to the level of the maximum contribution and benefit base under Social Security.

[d]Family is assumed to consist of worker, spouse, and one or more children.

and since many work-related expenses are eliminated, a replacement ratio of less than 100 percent will usually maintain the pre-disability standard of living (depending, of course, upon the level of medical care required).

Assume, for example, that you are a single worker who becomes eligible to receive disability benefits in January 1980 at age 50. Assume further that you have participated in Social Security throughout your adult lifetime and have always had maximum earnings covered by Social Security. Your monthly disability benefit during the first year would average $539.60, or about 39 percent of your average earnings during the three full years prior to disability. This benefit, taken by itself, is probably *not* adequate to support you and it will certainly not preserve your pre-disability standard of living; therefore, supplemental disability benefits should be provided through a pension plan, group or individual disability insurance plan, accumulation of personal savings, or by some other means. If your average earnings during the three-year period prior to disability had been $33,000 (twice the average maximum amount taxable for Social Security earnings), your disability benefit would be the same dollar amount but would be only 20 percent of your pre-disability average earnings. In this example, supplemental disability benefits are essential unless a substantial decrease is made in the standard of living.

In other situations, the Social Security disability benefit— once it commences—may be adequate, or even more than adequate, to continue the pre-disability standard of living. Consider a worker who earned the minimum wage and who becomes disabled at age 25 with a spouse and one or more small children. Social Security disability benefits during the first year would average $460.20 per month, or about 110 percent of average earnings during the three years prior to disability, assuming the spouse and children did not have earnings at a high enough level to forfeit any of their benefits because of the "earnings limitation."

For a person who begins to receive Social Security disability benefits in January 1980, the monthly benefit could be anywhere between $122.00 and $966.70, depending upon the circumstances.

An examination of the figures in Table 20.1 indicates a need to revise the Social Security benefit structure to eliminate inconsistencies and provide more equitable treatment of various categories of workers. There is no good reason an older worker should receive lower benefits than a younger worker if both of them have had the same level of pre-disability earnings. And the differentiation between benefits paid a single worker and a married worker with dependents appears to be greater than is reasonable. Recent amendments made a number of changes in the way benefits are calculated for disabled workers and their families (Public Law 96-265, enacted June 9, 1980). These amendments have no significant effect on the benefits shown in Table 20.1 for a single worker becoming disabled in the future. For married workers with families, however, benefits for future disabilities will be reduced about 15 percent, relatively speaking, from those shown in Table 20.1 (except for minimum wage earners, for whom the reduction is only 5 percent).

It is a rare case when an employee is adequately protected, from the first day of employment, against the various kinds of disability he may suffer. It is even more rare for family members to be protected against the possibility of their becoming disabled. The risk of loss of income because of disability may well be the most neglected area of personal financial planning. It is time-consuming and difficult, but not impossible, to summarize the benefits provided from all sources in the event of disability: Social Security, employer plans, workers' compensation, personal insurance, etc. Such a survey must be made, however, to identify gaps in coverage and enable you to obtain the supplemental disability insurance and plan the personal savings program necessary to protect you and your family from the catastrophe of disability.

Death

When someone who has been contributing to the support of a family dies, a variety of expenses may have to be met: burial costs, liquidation of personal debt (including home mortgage repayment), estate taxes, transitional costs while the surviving family adjusts to a different standard of living, and so on. If the decedent provided the principal support to a family, it may be necessary to replace part or all of the lost income for an extended period.

Social Security, as originally enacted in 1935, provided no death benefit except a guaranteed return of employee-paid Social Security taxes. In 1939, this type of death benefit was eliminated; instead, a lump-sum benefit and monthly benefits to survivors were adopted. Subsequent legislation broadened and extended these benefits so that, today, Social Security provides much more in death benefits than is commonly realized. In fact, the value of the death benefit ranges from $255 to $200,000 or more, depending upon the circumstances.

The lump-sum death benefit paid by Social Security is $255. This was the maximum benefit payable in 1954 and was intended to cover only the expenses of a modest funeral; however, the benefit has not been increased since then.

Survivors benefits, on the other hand, are relatively substantial and can be paid to:

a spouse caring for an eligible child;

a divorced spouse caring for an eligible child;

an eligible child;

a spouse aged 60 or older (50 or older, if completely disabled);

a divorced wife aged 60 or older (50 or older, if completely disabled), if the marriage lasted at least ten years; or

dependent parents aged 62 or older.

The amount of the benefits and the conditions for payment are based upon a seemingly endless set of conditions. These conditions are discussed briefly here and in more detail in Chapter 3. Eligibility for some death benefits requires that you be "currently insured," while eligibility for others requires that you be "fully insured."

To be currently insured, you need six quarters of coverage during the last thirteen quarters ending with the quarter in which you die. This would qualify your survivors for the lump-sum death benefit and monthly benefits for an eligible child and a spouse (or divorced spouse) caring for an eligible child.

To be fully insured, you must have between six and forty quarters of coverage depending upon when you were born and when you die. This requirement is not difficult to meet if you have been working in fairly steady employment. Fully insured status would qualify your survivors for monthly benefits for a spouse or a divorced wife and dependent parents, as well as the benefits mentioned above for currently insured participants.

Table 20.2 presents examples of benefits for several illustrative workers and their families. Benefits are expressed as replacement ratios; that is, the ratio of the first year's benefits to the average earnings in the three years prior to death. Consider, for example, a 25-year-old worker who has always had

Table 20.2
Ratio of Initial Social Security Survivors Benefits to Deceased Worker's Average Earnings Prior to Death for Illustrative Surviving Families

Earnings Level of Worker[b]	Replacement Ratio[a] Where Worker's Death Was at. . .	
	Age 25	Age 50
(1)	(2)	(3)
Surviving Spouse and Two or More Children		
Minimum	101%	100%
Average	90	88
Maximum	68	59
Twice Maximum	34	29
Surviving Spouse and One Child (or Two Surviving Children)		
Minimum	95%	95%
Average	75	73
Maximum	58	50
Twice Maximum	29	25
One Surviving Child		
Minimum	48%	48%
Average	37	36
Maximum	29	25
Twice Maximum	14	13

[a]Replacement ratio equals the survivors benefits payable in the first year divided by the deceased worker's average earnings in the last three years prior to death. In each example the worker is assumed to die in January 1980.

[b]"Minimum" denotes earnings equal to the minimum wage in each year. "Average" means earnings in each year equal to the average wages of all covered employees. "Maximum" and "Twice Maximum" refer to the level of the maximum contribution and benefit base under Social Security.

earnings equal to the average amount earned by those covered under Social Security and whose family consists of a spouse (who is not currently working in paid employment) and two children. Such a worker who has at least six quarters of coverage would be both currently insured and fully insured, and death in January 1980 would result in a lump-sum benefit of $255 and monthly benefits payable to the family of 90 percent of the worker's average earnings in the last three years. Since Social Security benefits are tax free, this benefit would exceed the worker's average take-home pay.

The amount of this benefit, payable in future years, would vary depending upon many factors. It would increase as the Consumer Price Index increased. It would reduce as each child reached age 18 and would terminate altogether when both children reached age 18 (except that a benefit would continue until age 22 for each child who remained a full-time student). Benefits would resume to the spouse at age 65 (or as early as age 60 if a reduced benefit is elected). The monthly benefits payable to any of these beneficiaries would be reduced by $1.00 for every $2.00 of earnings *by that beneficiary* in excess of the "earnings limitation" (in 1980, $3,720 for beneficiaries under age 65 and $5,000 for beneficiaries aged 65 and older). Finally, the remarriage of the surviving spouse or the marriage of a child beneficiary would normally terminate benefits for that beneficiary.

The survivors benefits in this example are substantial and are worth about $175,000 at the death of the worker. In other words, on the average, it would take approximately $175,000 invested at interest to provide these survivors benefits. Most of the surviving family's needs in this example are well satisfied by Social Security in the early years following the worker's death. Once the children have reached maturity, there will be a period when the spouse will have no income (from about age 40 or 45 until age 65). At age 65 benefits to the spouse would resume at about 50 percent of the worker's average earnings in the last three years (adjusted for changes in the Consumer Price Index occurring since then). Supplemental income for the spouse during this period before age 65, as well as after age 65, may be necessary since Social Security benefits alone will not be adequate to maintain the earlier standard of living.

This particular example was chosen to illustrate a situation in which Social Security almost "does it all." Other situations require substantial provision for supplemental benefits through private saving and private insurance, either group or individual. Most workers with above average income need supplemental benefits unless their family's living standard is to suffer in the event of their death. The examples in Table 20.2 illustrate that the initial replacement ratio ranges from 13 percent to 101 percent, depending upon the circumstances of the worker and his or her family; for persons with higher earnings than illustrated, the replacement ratio can be even lower than 13 percent. Obviously, the amount of survivors benefits payable under Social Security can vary widely and is not easy to determine; however, a basic understanding of such benefits and their payment provisions is essential in determining an appropriate level of supplemental coverage.

Many employees are covered under group life insurance plans sponsored by their employers (partially paid for by the employee in some cases). Some people obtain group life insurance benefits through membership in unions or professional organizations, purchase of "credit insurance," and so forth. Many persons buy individual life insurance to supplement their other benefits or to cover specific obligations such as home mortgage loans. Life insurance benefits are normally described by their face amount, such as $10,000 or $50,000, but in most cases a variety of payment methods is available in the event of death. In determining your supplemental insurance needs, it will be helpful to determine the monthly income that can be provided by these insurance policies. This can be added to the monthly income paid by Social Security to indicate any gaps that should be filled to protect your family adequately. Remember that Social Security benefits and most life insurance benefits are tax free and that family expenses are usually lower after the death of a breadwinner.

When deciding how much supplemental life insurance protection and personal savings should be provided, several key decisions must be made regarding the surviving family's lifestyle. Would a spouse who was not working in paid employment begin working? Would the family's house or other major possessions be kept? How long are the children likely to need support, and what financial arrangements will be necessary for their education? Once these and other personal decisions are worked out within the family, attention can be turned to evaluating the overall financial needs that would result from a breadwinner's death, the level of benefits payable by Social Security, employee benefit plans, etc., and the need for any supplemental benefit protection. The effect of future inflation must also be considered. What might seem like an adequate benefit in the first two or three years could prove to be inadequate in later years.

Just as in making contingency plans for sickness and disability, in planning for the possibility of death you must absorb an array of facts and figures to decide what financial alternatives should be devised. Your responsibility in making such plans is more awesome, of course, since you will not be around to modify any arrangements that need adjusting.

Retirement

Retirement is somewhat different from the events just discussed—sickness, disability, and death—which result in extraordinary expenses or loss of income. Barring premature death, everyone will experience old age and for most of us there will come a time when retirement must be considered, and probably will be necessary for one reason or another. Knowing that we must one day retire, however, does not make it any easier to plan for and make the necessary financial arrangements. A person who reaches age 65, a common retirement age at the present time, can expect to live another fifteen to twenty years, on the average, and perhaps as long as thirty-five years or more. This uncertainty itself makes planning for retirement difficult.

Social Security, as originally enacted, was designed solely to replace a portion of the income that was lost because of old age. Social Security has expanded over the years and now provides a wide variety of benefits in the event of a worker's retirement; for example, benefits may be paid to:

a retired worker aged 62 or over;

the spouse aged 62 or over of a retired worker, if the retired worker is also receiving benefits;

the wife of a retired worker who is receiving benefits, if the wife is under age 65 and caring for an eligible child;

a divorced spouse aged 62 or over, who was married to the insured worker for at least ten years, if the insured worker is receiving benefits; or

an eligible child.

Table 20.3 illustrates the benefits payable upon the retirement of a worker at different retirement ages and in different family situations. The examples reflect the actuarial reduction of benefits for retirement before age 65 and the effect of the "delayed retirement credit" for retirement after age 65. Benefits are shown as a percentage of average earnings in the last three years before retirement, hence are referred to as replacement ratios. Benefits are assumed to commence in January 1980; examples for later years would show slightly less variation for different ages at retirement.

As indicated in Table 20.3 there is an extremely wide varia-

Table 20.3

Ratio of Initial Social Security Retirement Benefits to Average Earnings Prior to Retirement for Illustrative Workers

Earnings Level of Worker[b]	Replacement Ratio[a] for Worker Retiring at...		
	Age 62	Age 65	Age 70
(1)	(2)	(3)	(4)
	Single Worker		
Minimum	51%	71%	79%
Average	39	55	63
Maximum	28	39	44
Twice Maximum	14	20	22
	Worker and Spouse		
Minimum	74%	106%	116%
Average	57	83	94
Maximum	40	59	65
Twice Maximum	20	29	32

[a]Replacement ratio equals the retirement benefits payable in the first year divided by the average of the last three years of earnings prior to retirement. In each example, the worker is assumed to attain the indicated age in January 1980.

[b]"Minimum" denotes earnings equal to the minimum wage in each year. "Average" means earnings in each year equal to the average wages of all covered employees. "Maximum" and "Twice Maximum" refer to the level of the maximum contribution and benefit base under Social Security.

tion in the replacement ratios, depending upon the age at retirement, earnings level, and family status. The replacement ratios shown range from 116 percent for a low wage earner who retires late to 14 percent for a high wage earner who retires early. The replacement ratio would be even lower for persons with higher earnings. The replacement ratio that is necessary to permit suitable retirement depends upon a variety of factors including preretirement earnings level, family status, and postretirement standard of living. Also, Social Security benefits are tax free, income taxes are lower for persons over age 65, Social Security taxes stop when earned income stops, expenses associated with employment cease, personal savings after retirement may be lower, medical costs for the elderly are usually higher, and so forth.

If one's preretirement standard of living is to be maintained, retirement benefits of some 60 to 85 percent of average preretirement earnings are probably necessary—depending upon the factors mentioned above. Furthermore, these benefits must be adjusted periodically to reflect changes in the cost of living. Social Security benefits satisfy these criteria reasonably well for workers with average earnings or less, provided they retire at age 65 or later. Even for these workers, there is some need for supplementation through private saving or a job-related retirement plan. This need, however, is relatively small compared with that of the above-average wage earner for whom substantial supplementation is needed if preretirement living standards are to be maintained.

Supplemental retirement income is available from several sources. The majority of full-time permanent employees in private employment are covered by a pension or profit-sharing plan sponsored by their employer. Most public employees are covered by employer-sponsored retirement systems. Many self-employed persons have so-called "Keogh" or "HR 10" retirement programs. An increasing number of people are establishing Individual Retirement Accounts. Many people have cash value life insurance, as well as endowment and retirement income insurance policies that are earmarked for retirement purposes. Finally, personal saving (investments, equity in a home, etc.) is accumulated for general purposes but may be used eventually for support in retirement years.

Just as in analyzing the needs discussed earlier, it is quite difficult to compare your retirement needs with the various sources of income that will be available and thus to determine what level of supplementation is required. In studying your needs it is well to keep in mind that Social Security and other benefits may be less than they appear, as indicated by the following examples.

A wife may appear to be protected by Social Security by reason of her marriage to a person in Social Security covered employment. An untimely divorce (particularly before ten years of marriage) would normally terminate this financial protection. The payment of Social Security benefits is subject to the earnings limitation discussed earlier; and if you or your dependents or survivors work in order to supplement Social Security benefits, it may result in a reduction or complete loss of such benefits. A retirement income that is adequate for a couple may be reduced upon the death of one of the members (as is the case with Social Security), leaving the survivor with an inadequate income. Retirement benefits that are not adjusted for inflation (unlike Social Security which is so adjusted) may be adequate at their inception but inadequate just a few years later because of continuing inflation.

If you receive a pension under a government pension plan as a result of being an employee of a federal, state, or local government (this includes policemen, firemen, and public school teachers) and you were not under Social Security in such employment, you may not receive Social Security benefits you thought you would receive. This is because Social Security benefits payable to you as a dependent or survivor will be reduced by any benefits under such a government pension plan, thus reducing or completely eliminating your Social Security benefits. This provision was enacted in 1977 and does not apply to:

> anyone entitled to Social Security benefits before December 1977; or
>
> women (or men who can prove dependency on their wives) who are eligible to receive a government pension any time between December 1977 and November 1982.

The net result of an analysis of Social Security retirement benefit protection is that most persons need some supplemental protection, and workers with above average earnings need substantial additional benefits unless a significant reduction is made in their preretirement standard of living. Even workers with average earnings or less need to make provision for supplemental retirement benefits if they desire to retire earlier than the standard set by Social Security.

Conclusion

In the event of the sickness, disability, death, or retirement of any member of your family, the family's financial situation will change—sometimes drastically. None of these events can be predicted with certainty. The only certainty is that at least one such event will occur, probably at a time it is least expected.

It is tempting to assume that one's financial needs in time of crisis will be met by Social Security or some other governmental program or by a job-related fringe benefit program. This is a dangerous assumption and is not one that can be relied upon.

To protect your family from financial stress you must compare what you need with what you have—much easier to say than to do. If you provide the principal financial support for your family, define your needs and those of your family if you should become sick, disabled, die, or retire. Do the same for other family members who provide financial support. Also define the needs that will arise if a member of your family becomes sick or disabled.

Then analyze all the programs that will provide benefits in any of these events: Social Security and other government programs, job-related fringe benefit plans, personal insurance and saving, and so forth. A surprising number of unmet needs will be revealed. In some cases there may be duplications in benefit protection. You can then set about to fill the gaps in protection and eliminate the duplications.

You can get help in making this analysis and taking corrective action; but in the end, you must get heavily involved and do much of the work yourself. Perhaps this is as it should be. Your family financial situation is a unique and personal matter, and you cannot expect a stranger to have the same level of interest as you.

21
How to Take Advantage of Social Security

The government has a thorough method of collecting Social Security taxes. Even without any initiative on your part, the government will almost certainly find you and collect the taxes you owe.

Getting your benefits is another matter. The government does not take the initiative in locating you, determining your eligibility, and then paying any benefits to which you may be entitled. It is up to *you* to take the first step and apply for the benefits. Before you can do this, of course, you must know enough about Social Security to apply for the right benefits at the right time.

Know Your Social Security Benefits

The first step then to take full advantage of Social Security is to obtain all the benefits to which you and your family are entitled. To do this you must learn as much as possible about the benefits: the various events in which benefits may be payable (old age, disability, illness, or death); the eligibility requirements you must meet; the events that may terminate the payment of benefits; and the basis for calculating benefits (so you can take the steps necessary to maximize benefits).

As a bare minimum you should know when to ask your local Social Security office whether you are eligible for benefits. A recent Social Security publication suggests that you get in touch with a Social Security office if:

> you are unable to work because of an illness or injury that is expected to last a year or longer;
> you are 62 or older and plan to retire;
> you are within two or three months of 65, even if you don't plan to retire; or
> someone in your family dies.

Many other events can affect the type and level of benefits to which you and your family may be entitled. These events include marriage, divorce, bearing of children, a child's reaching age 18 (22 if in college), disability of family members, job change, moving from the United States and its possessions, and your parents' becoming dependent upon you. Learn as much as possible about Social Security benefits, and when in doubt, ask questions of your local Social Security office.

Eliminate Gaps and Duplications

There is another reason that becoming familiar with the benefits provided by Social Security will enable you to take full advantage of it. On the one hand, you can more easily avoid costly and wasteful duplication of benefit protection; and on the other hand, you can more easily fill the gaps in benefit protection which, unfilled, could leave you or your family in serious financial trouble. By way of illustration, consider the following examples.

If you should die, in some cases Social Security would pay monthly benefits to your surviving spouse and children. In addition, you may be eligible for death benefits under a group life insurance program provided by your employer. Under some circumstances the total death benefit protection thus provided may be adequate to meet the needs of your spouse and children, yet you may be buying added life insurance on a personal basis—insurance which you cannot easily afford and which you do not really need. Under other circumstances the death benefits provided by Social Security and employer group life insurance may be less than adequate and you may need additional personal life insurance to protect your family adequately.

The same principle applies to all the contingencies against which you must protect yourself and your family: old age, disability, illness, and death. Disability protection is often found to be inadequate. Old-age retirement protection is frequently less than desirable. The starting point to eliminate these gaps and duplications in benefit protection is to be thoroughly familiar with benefits provided under Social Security and employer-sponsored fringe benefit plans.

Under ideal circumstances, you will be able to tailor your personal security plans so as to eliminate the gaps and duplications in benefit protection. In some situations, however, this will not be possible because of the particular combination of benefits provided under Social Security and employer-sponsored plans. To correct any such inconsistencies will require the cooperation of both employer and employees in making appropriate modifications in the employer-sponsored benefit plans.

Ways to Increase Your Benefits

There are numerous ways to get the most benefits from Social Security for your tax dollar. In some cases the local Social Security office will help you. Most of the time it will be up to you, however, to take at least the first steps. Here are some examples of how to maximize your Social Security benefits.

Satisfy Minimum Eligibility Requirements

As indicated in Chapter 3, you must satisfy a variety of requirements to be eligible for benefits. These can include having paid Social Security taxes for a minimum number of quarters, satisfying certain marital status requirements, keeping earned income within specified limits once benefits commence, filing a timely application for benefits, and so forth. In some cases you may almost, but not quite, meet all these requirements. With a relatively small effort you may be able to satisfy the minimum eligibility requirements and obtain extremely valuable benefits.

A classic example of this is the person whose principal career employment is not covered by Social Security—for example, most employees of the federal government and some employees of state and local governments and nonprofit organizations. Such persons can work in covered employment on a part-time basis during their careers and qualify for Social Security benefits worth many times their Social Security taxes.

Another example is the woman who worked in employment covered by Social Security but left her job to rear a family prior to becoming permanently entitled to retirement benefits. Just a few more months in covered employment, even on a part-time basis, may be enough to qualify her for significant benefits.

To qualify for disability benefits, you must have a recent attachment to the work force, hence you cannot leave covered employment and be permanently eligible for benefits. Generally speaking, five years' continuous absence from covered employment will cause a loss in the right to disability benefits. These rights can be maintained, however, by working part time every few months in covered employment.

Verify Your Earnings Record

The government (Internal Revenue Service) collects taxes on your earnings that are subject to Social Security tax. The Social Security Administration keeps a record of these earnings and uses it to determine whether you are eligible for benefits and the amount of such benefits. Obviously, if the records are wrong, your benefits will be wrong. Mistakes do happen and you should do everything possible to make certain that the government's records of your earnings are correct.

Each year you should review carefully the Form W-2 Wage and Tax Statement supplied by your employer and determine that Social Security taxes have been paid on the correct amount of earnings. The items on the form that relate to Social Security are entitled "total FICA wages" and "FICA tax withheld." FICA is the acronym for Federal Insurance Contributions Act, a less than obvious reference to Social Security.

This annual review of your Form W-2 is only a beginning step to check your records and does not ensure that the government's records are correct. To verify this, you can file a form with the Social Security Administration (Form OAR-7004) and request a statement of your Social Security earnings. You will then receive a statement showing the amount of earnings on which Social Security taxes have been paid in each of the past three years, as well as the total for your lifetime. It is important that you request this earnings statement and verify your records at least every three years so that any errors can be corrected. In general, an earnings record can be corrected at any time up to three years, three months, and fifteen days after the year in which earnings were received. After that it is still possible—though more difficult—to have a mistake corrected.

Someday, perhaps, the government will take the initiative in confirming the amount of earnings on which you have paid Social Security taxes (as recommended in Chapter 9). Until then, you are on your own.

Do Not Overlook Military Service

If you were on active military duty at any time from September 16, 1940 through December 31, 1956, you may be eligible for special wage credits of $160 for each month of service. These wage credits do not appear on your Social Security earnings record maintained by the government. It will be up to you or your survivors to notify Social Security about this service at the time application for benefits is made. The Social Security representative will then ask for a record of service if this will result in higher benefits. It would be particularly easy for survivors to overlook this military service and thus be deprived of benefits to which they are entitled.

There is yet another item regarding military service that does not appear on the government's records of Social Security earnings. For each quarter in which you have active duty pay after 1956 and before 1968, you are to receive additional earnings credits of $300. Although these free credits do not appear on your earnings statement, they are supposed to be considered in figuring monthly benefits. Similar earnings credits are provided for military service in 1968 and later, but these amounts are shown directly on your earnings record. At the time your benefit is determined you should verify that you have in fact received all such earnings credits.

Apply for Benefits Even If Not Retiring

You should consider applying for benefits at age 65 even if you do not actually quit working until later. There are several reasons this may yield unexpected benefits.

The earnings test (described in Chapter 12) permits you to have a limited amount of earnings without losing any Social Security benefits. This exempt amount of earnings is a flat dollar amount regardless of your level of benefits or preretirement earnings. Accordingly, low wage earners may be able to continue working beyond age 65 in the same job for the same pay *and* collect full Social Security retirement benefits.

For example, consider a low wage earner reaching age 65 in 1980 who earns $5,000 per year and is entitled to the "special minimum benefit" of $252.80 per month. Such a worker could continue working and receive full wages *and* Social Security benefits. Higher wage earners who continue to work beyond age 65 would not fare as well and would lose some or all of their Social Security benefits because of earnings above $5,000; however, you should consider applying for benefits regardless of your earnings level, particularly if you have family members entitled to benefits on your earnings record, because of the possibility of receiving unexpected benefits.

If you plan to retire during the early part of the year, you should apply for benefits earlier than you actually stop working, even if you are a high wage earner. For example, if you were aged 65 at the beginning of 1980 and quit working March 1, 1980, you could have had total earnings of $5,000 in January and February and still collected full Social Security benefits for January and February (because of the exempt earnings amount in 1980 of $5,000). Social Security benefits for these two months could be as much as $1,716 for a retired person with an eligible spouse. These are tax-free benefits which could be overlooked easily.

You are eligible for Medicare benefits at age 65, even if you have not retired and are not receiving monthly cash retirement benefits. You are also eligible for Medicare after you have received Social Security disability benefits for twenty-four months or if you have chronic kidney disease requiring dialysis or a kidney transplant. But this valuable Medicare coverage is not automatic; you must apply for it.

Get the Most from Medicare

Medicare has two parts: Part A (Hospital Insurance) helps pay for inpatient hospital care and for certain follow-up care after leaving the hospital; Part B (Supplementary Medical Insurance) helps pay for doctors' services, outpatient hospital services, and many other medical items and services not covered by Part A.

If you are aged 65 or older and are entitled to Social Security (or Railroad Retirement) benefits—even though you may not be receiving them—you are eligible for Part A of Medicare. You need not pay any specific additional contributions or taxes since Part A is financed by Social Security taxes paid by active workers.

Part B of Medicare is another matter. It is optional and requires premium payments of $9.60 per month after July 1, 1980 (subject to increase in the future as the cost of medical care increases). These premiums finance only about 30 percent of the cost of Part B. The balance is financed from general revenue; that is, general taxes paid by everyone, whether or not they participate in Social Security or receive Part B benefits. By the year 2000 it is estimated that individual premiums will pay for only 10 percent of the cost of Part B, with general revenue paying for the remaining 90 percent.

Since Part B provides needed medical benefits and since an individual pays directly for less than 30 percent of the cost, you should have some very good reasons if you elect not to be covered. When you become covered by Part A, you will be covered automatically by Part B and the monthly premium will be deducted from your regular Social Security or Railroad Retirement checks unless you advise Social Security that you do not want Part B coverage.

If you have not been a regular participant in Social Security (or the Railroad Retirement system) and thus are not eligible automatically for Part A benefits, you can elect to be covered by Part A by paying a premium of $78 per month after July 1, 1980, subject to increase in the future as the cost of hospital care increases. To make this election, you must be a resident of the U.S. and a citizen or an alien lawfully admitted for permanent residence who has resided in the U.S. continuously for five years. This election may be made during the month you reach age 65 or during the three months before or after that month. If you do not enroll at this time, you may enroll later during the "general enrollment period" from January 1 through March 31 of each year. If you are not eligible automatically for Part A of Medicare and you do *not* elect to be covered thereunder, you should have some very good reasons. The cost may appear to be high, but it is consistent with the average cost of benefits. Furthermore, the cost is a bargain if your health is worse than average. If you elect to be covered by Part A, you must also elect to be covered by Part B. You can enroll in Part B without enrolling in Part A, but this would not be a wise decision except for a person assured of alternative hospital insurance for his or her remaining lifetime.

If your spouse is older than you, there may be some advantage to filing an application for retirement benefits when you reach age 62, even if you do not actually receive benefits until a later time when you stop working. This establishes your "entitlement" to retirement benefits and thus affords Medicare protection for your spouse after he or she attains age 65. The provision of Medicare protection for your spouse could be valuable should hospital insurance coverage provided by your employer terminate or reduce significantly upon a spouse's attainment of age 65.

Medicare does not pay for hospital and medical care outside the United States, except in Canada for U.S. residents living nearby and in a few other limited cases. Accordingly, if you depend normally upon Medicare and you plan to travel abroad, you should make alternative arrangements for temporary health insurance.

Consider Effect of Marriage on Benefits

Many Social Security benefits are paid as a result of a person's being a wife, husband, widow, or widower. The state of marriage has an important bearing on whether benefits become payable and whether they continue to be payable. This should be duly considered when decisions are made about whether and when to marry, remarry, divorce, and, perhaps, whom to marry. Even though eligibility for Social Security benefits may not affect these basic decisions about marriage, it should certainly be taken into account in arranging personal financial affairs.

Significant gaps in income security protection usually occur when changes are made in marital status. Chapter 22 gives examples of some of the many ways in which benefit protection can be affected by such changes in status.

Maximize Survivors Benefits

Benefits paid to your widow or widower and children may require supplementation if their standard of living is to be maintained. Yet, if one or more of your survivors earns more than a nominal amount, it may result in the forfeiture of Social Security benefits, thus requiring even further supplementation (because of the "earnings test" described in Chapter 12 and mentioned elsewhere). One way to prevent your surviving spouse from having to work while caring for young children (and then losing Social Security benefits as a result of such work) is to buy an appropriate amount of life insurance. Life insurance benefits payable after your death will not reduce Social Security benefits and, for the most part, are not taxable.

Maximize Educational Benefits

The child of a retired or disabled worker is entitled to a benefit of as much as $286 per month (early in 1980). The child of a deceased worker is entitled to a benefit of as much as $429 per month (early in 1980). Payment of these benefits normally stops at age 18; but if the child is a full-time student, payment continues until age 22 (until the end of the semester or quarter the child reaches age 22 provided an undergraduate degree has not yet been received).

The earnings test described in Chapter 12 applies to student beneficiaries. Accordingly, to avoid the loss of student benefits it may be preferable for a student to borrow (rather than earn) a portion of the additional funds needed to continue in school. Appropriate life insurance benefits provided by a deceased parent would permit the continued education of a student without the necessity of work that may result in loss of Social Security benefits.

Be Persistent in Applying for Disability Benefits

If you are denied Social Security disability benefits but believe your claim to be legitimate, you would be well-advised to consider appealing and, perhaps, using an attorney to help you pursue your claim.

The number of hearings requested by Social Security claimants after being denied benefits has grown at a substantial rate in recent years. Currently, about two-thirds of all disability claims are denied initially. More than half of all appeals are reversed, and the chances of winning an appeal seem to be greater if an attorney is involved.

Control Timing of Earnings

Prior to 1978, benefits could be paid for any month you earned one-twelfth or less of the annual exempt amount and performed no substantial work in your own business. Accordingly, there was a tendency for persons who could do so to concentrate their earnings in certain periods and keep income low in as many months as possible. This technique was blocked by imposing an "annual measure" of earnings instead of a "monthly measure."

Nevertheless, it is still advantageous to control the timing of earnings so as to minimize the effect of the earnings test and reduce the forfeiture of Social Security benefits. This is because the monthly measure is still used during the first year benefits are paid; earnings after attainment of age 72 (age 70 after 1981) are not considered in applying the earnings test; and earnings can be shifted from one year to another (instead of from one month to another as in the past). Self-employed persons sometimes facilitate this shifting of income by carrying out their business activities in a corporate form rather than a proprietorship.

Maximize Purchasing Power of Pension

After you have done everything possible to receive the maximum benefit available, the next logical step is to reside in a locale where the dollar has maximum purchasing power. Some areas of the United States have markedly lower costs of living than others, particularly in the South and Midwest. In the past twenty years the number of Social Security beneficiaries living abroad has tripled. According to the latest count, there are more than 300,000 beneficiaries residing in 130 foreign countries and receiving approximately $800 million per year in benefits.

There are some restrictions on the payment of benefits to those living abroad, particularly to aliens. The restrictions are relatively lenient, however, except for those living in the following countries that are currently on the U.S. Treasury Department's restricted list: Albania, Cambodia, Cuba, North Korea, Vietnam, East Germany, and the Russian zone of Berlin. Aliens who qualify for Social Security benefits can often retire to their homeland and enjoy a comfortable and less expensive life among old friends and family. Despite the vicissitudes of the dollar in recent years, it is still a sought-after currency in many countries. It is sometimes converted into a local currency at a rate more favorable than the official tourist rate and it is sometimes spendable in hard-currency shops that sell popular Western goods.

There are many considerations in deciding whether to retire abroad, not the least of which is the availability and cost of hospital and medical care. As already mentioned, Medicare generally does not provide benefits outside the United States. This disadvantage may or may not be compensated for by lower cost hospital and medical care in the country being considered.

There may be another advantage in living abroad as a result of conditions relating to the continued payment of benefits while working. If you live in the United States, because of the "earnings test" your earnings in excess of the exempt amount will result in a forfeiture of part or all of your Social Security benefits. If you live abroad and have foreign earnings (that are not covered under the U.S. Social Security program), the "earnings test" is different. It is not based upon the amount of your *earnings* but upon the amount of *time* employed. If you are employed on seven or more days during a month in a foreign country, the benefit for that month is completely withheld; otherwise, you receive the entire benefit. Accordingly, you might be able to maximize benefits by concentrating your work during selected days or months during the year. As once observed by a noted authority on the subject, thorough administration of such a provision is difficult and depends to a considerable extent on the good conscience of the individuals involved.

In the final analysis the selection of a place to live in retirement is a personal decision in which economic factors are only part of a multitude of considerations. It would be imprudent, however, not to take these economic factors into account.

Benefits That May Be Overlooked

A host of unique benefits are provided under the Social Security program. It is not feasible to list every conceivable situation that will result in benefit payments; however, the following examples will alert you to some of the types of benefits frequently overlooked.

Benefits Payable to Children

A child may be entitled to monthly benefits in the event of the retirement, death, or disability of one of his parents who is covered by Social Security. The child must be unmarried and:

less than 18 years old;

between 18 and 22 years old and a full-time student; or

18 years old or older with a severe physical or mental disability that began before age 22.

It is not necessary that a child be living with or receiving support from a parent in order to receive benefits based upon the parent's earnings record. Furthermore, a child can receive benefits based upon a stepparent's earnings record if the child lives with the stepparent *or* receives half his support from the stepparent.

Consider, for example, a child living with his father and stepmother, both of whom are covered by Social Security. Assume also that the child's natural mother is covered by Social Security. If any one of the three parents should retire, die, or become disabled, the child could be eligible for a benefit. It would be easy to overlook the availability of a child's benefits based upon the earnings record of a natural mother or father with whom the child does not reside.

A child may be able to receive benefits based on one parent's Social Security account even though the other parent is working and furnishing his support. An example would be when the child is entitled to benefits because of the death of his mother who was a covered worker. The fact that the child's father was supporting him would not matter.

A child may be eligible for benefits based on a grandparent's earnings record. The grandparent must have provided at least half the child's support; the child's parents must be dead or disabled; and the child must have begun to live with the grandparents prior to age 18.

Disability After Early Retirement

If you begin receiving Social Security retirement benefits before age 65, they will be reduced somewhat to offset the expectation that they will be paid over a longer period than if they had commenced at age 65. If you become disabled (seriously enough to meet disability benefit requirements) after benefits commence but prior to age 65, you should ask Social Security to switch your benefits from age-retirement to disability benefits. Disability benefits will be greater than the reduced age-retirement benefits you were receiving, since the early-retirement reduction will be eliminated with respect to the period between disability and age 65.

The net result will be larger monthly benefits for the remainder of your life and, in some cases, larger benefits for your widow or widower after your death. The total value of this increase in benefits could be as high as $15,000. It would be easy to overlook this opportunity for increased benefits since the disability would not be related to a cessation of work.

If family benefits are payable, however, the question of whether to apply for disability benefits becomes more difficult. This arises because maximum family disability benefits are generally lower than maximum family retirement benefits. As is true in all cases of actual benefit eligibility, it is advisable to consult your local Social Security office.

Retroactive Disability Benefits Paid After Death

It is possible for a person to become disabled and die without ever filing for disability benefits, even though all eligibility requirements have been met. In such cases it may be possible to establish retroactive eligibility for disability benefits and thus receive such benefits for as much as twelve months. Although an application can be filed within three months after the death of a disabled person, it should be filed as early as possible to prevent possible loss of benefits.

Earnings While Disabled

The rules governing work by disabled persons receiving Social Security benefits are surprisingly liberal, purportedly in an attempt to encourage rehabilitation.

A disability beneficiary is allowed unlimited earnings for as much as nine months of trial work without losing any disability benefits. (Disabled widows and widowers receiving benefits on the basis of a spouse's earnings record are not eligible for this nine-month trial period.) Even after it has been determined that disability ceased, full benefits are paid for that month and for the next two months.

Furthermore, a person who is disabled and receiving Social Security benefits can generally have earnings of up to $300.00 per month indefinitely without losing any benefits. This was the limit in effect in 1980; it will probably be increased in the future. Social Security sometimes reviews disabled persons' earnings in *covered employment* to determine whether they are disqualified from receiving further disability benefits. It is more difficult, if not impossible, for Social Security to discover any earnings in *noncovered employment*.

Benefits for Divorced Wives

Divorced wives (including surviving divorced wives) are entitled to certain Social Security benefits based on their former husband's earnings record provided the marriage lasted for ten years. This ten-year requirement was effective for benefits payable for months after December 1978. For benefits payable earlier, it was required that the marriage last twenty years. Accordingly, there may be many divorced wives married between ten and twenty years who became eligible for benefits in January 1979 but who are not aware of it.

Until recently, a divorced woman was not eligible for benefits based on her former husband's earnings record unless he contributed to her support after the divorce. This support requirement was eliminated in 1972; therefore, a woman denied benefits because of this support requirement may now be eligible for benefits.

Benefits for Widows and Widowers

As the result of a recent change in the law, remarriage of a surviving spouse after age 60 will not reduce the amount of widow's or widower's benefits with respect to benefits for months after December 1978. Accordingly, many widows and widowers who married after age 60 but prior to December 31, 1978 first became eligible for benefits in January 1979. For the most part, these benefits are being paid automatically; however, there may be some widows and widowers who are not aware of their eligibility.

A widow who remarries before age 60 may receive benefits on a deceased husband's earnings if she is not married when she applies for benefits. A widower, however, who remarried before age 60 cannot get such benefits even if the subsequent marriage has terminated (except in certain cases where the new wife is a beneficiary).

A widower with an entitled child in his care can receive benefits payable based on the earnings record of his deceased wife. The law does not read this way but it has been so administered since a successful challenge in the courts in 1975 (Weinberger v. Wiesenfeld).

An aged divorced husband can receive benefits payable based on the earnings record of his wife. The law does not read this way, but it has been so administered since a successful challenge in the courts in 1977 (Oliver v. Califano).

Several other changes have been made recently in the law or the way it is administered with respect to males, married as well as divorced; for example, the finding in 1977 that a man does not have to be financially dependent on his wife in order to receive husband's or widower's benefits based on his wife's earnings record. It is likely that these changes made some males eligible for benefits of which they are still unaware.

Benefits for Persons Aged 72 or Over

A person who reached age 72 before 1969 (in some cases, 1972) may be eligible for small monthly benefits even if the normal requirements for insured status have not been met. As in the case of all benefits, the local Social Security office should be consulted first to determine whether benefits are payable. Since this is a unique benefit, however, you should make a special effort to ensure that your case receives proper consideration.

Ways to Decrease Your Taxes

There are not many ways to decrease your Social Security taxes; however, they do exist. They usually involve a reduction in earnings on which Social Security taxes are paid, hence a reduction in benefits. Careful study is necessary, therefore, to determine whether the reduction in taxes is offset by the reduction in benefits (perhaps considering both employer and employee taxes).

Refund of Excessive Tax Payments

In each calendar year there is a maximum amount of earnings on which you must pay Social Security taxes. In 1980 this maximum was $25,900, and in 1981 it is scheduled to be $29,700. It will increase each year thereafter as the nation's average wages increase.

If you work for more than one employer in a calendar year and if your total wages exceed this maximum taxable amount, you will probably pay more Social Security tax than is required. This is because each employer determines the maximum taxable wages without regard to earnings from other employers.

Assume, for example, that you earned $40,000 in 1980: $30,000 from employer A and $10,000 from employer B. Employer A would have withheld taxes on the first $25,900 of the $30,000 of earnings; and employer B would have withheld taxes on the entire $10,000 of earnings. Thus, you would have paid Social Security taxes on $35,900 of earnings. Your total taxes would have been $2,200.67, or $613.00 more than you were required to pay.

If you are aware that you have overpaid your taxes you can get a refund. One of the lines on Form 1040 of the U.S. Individual Income Tax Return is entitled "Excess FICA and

RRTA tax withheld (two or more employers)." You can enter any excess Social Security tax payment on this line and it will be applied toward any federal income taxes that are due, and refunded to the extent not needed to pay such taxes.

In this example, your two employers also would have paid $2,200.67 in Social Security Taxes, or $613.00 more than if you had received all your earnings from just one employer. No refund of these "excess" taxes will be made, however, with respect to the employers' taxes. An exception to this treatment of taxes paid by multiple employers was made by the 1977 Social Security Amendments; namely, two or more financially related employers are not required to pay more in Social Security taxes for any given employee than if the employee were on the payroll of a single employer. This requires compliance with several technicalities that are relatively simple.

Incorrectly Collected Taxes

In some cases an employer may deduct Social Security taxes from an employee's wages and determine later that such taxes were not in fact payable. For example, domestic workers must receive cash pay of $50 or more in a calendar quarter before Social Security taxes are payable; and agricultural employees must receive cash pay of $150 or more in a calendar year (or meet certain other employment tests). If an employer begins withholding before these tests are satisfied and later finds out that the employee does not meet the test, the employer must repay the Social Security taxes deducted or, if the employer cannot locate the employee, send the incorrectly collected taxes to the Internal Revenue Service. Under these circumstances an employee would be well-advised to verify that the correct Social Security taxes have in fact been collected.

Method of Payment of Social Security Taxes

Social Security taxes are normally paid by employees as well as employers. It is possible, however, for the employer to make these employee tax payments from its own funds on behalf of the employee and reduce the employee's gross earnings by the amount of such tax payments. The tax payments must be included in the employee's income for federal tax purposes; however, the tax payments are not counted as wages for Social Security tax purposes. In this way an employer can reduce the wages that are taxable for Social Security purposes (with respect to employees whose wages after being reduced by Social Security taxes are less than the maximum taxable earnings base), and thus reduce both employee and employer Social Security taxes payable with respect to such employee. Total Social Security taxes for such employees can thus be reduced by an amount equivalent to about 0.88 percent of payroll in 1981. The percentage saving will rise in the future as the Social Security tax rate increases.

This procedure will, of course, reduce future Social Security benefits to the extent that an employee's average earnings—on which such benefits are based—are reduced. The procedure of reducing the wages subject to Social Security tax also reduces the wages subject to unemployment insurance tax, resulting in additional saving in taxes. Furthermore, the reduction in cash earnings brought about by this procedure may result in a reduction in other fringe benefits (and the costs thereof) that are related to cash earnings—for example, group life insurance and disability benefits. Finally, the personal income taxes paid by an employee may be reduced slightly (by the amount of personal income tax on the reduction in Social Security taxes payable on behalf of the employee).

The option for the employer to pay the employee Social Security tax and thus reduce certain taxes was available for *all* employees until the enactment of the Omnibus Reconciliation Act of 1980. This act eliminated the tax-saving effect of the option for all employment except domestic service in a private home and agricultural labor—effective in 1981 for private sector employees and in 1984 for public sector employees (provided the public sector practice was in effect on October 1, 1980).

Method of Payment of Unemployment Insurance Taxes

In three states (Alaska, Alabama, and New Jersey), employees must pay taxes to help finance a state-administered unemployment insurance program which provides partial income replacement for a limited period to persons who become unemployed. The employer can make these employee tax payments from its own funds on behalf of the employee, and reduce the employee's gross earnings by the amount of such tax payments (not necessarily directly and immediately). The employee's income for federal income tax purposes will not change (since unemployment insurance tax payments made by the employer on behalf of the employee are taxable); however, the tax payments are not counted as wages for Social Security tax purposes. In this way an employer can reduce the wages that are taxable for Social Security purposes (with respect to employees who earn less than the maximum taxable earnings base), and thus reduce Social Security taxes payable by the employee and the employer. This procedure will, of course, reduce future Social Security benefits to the extent that average earnings—on which such benefits are based—are reduced.

If the unemployment insurance tax is levied on total cash income (not including the unemployment insurance tax payments made by the employer on behalf of the employee), this procedure would reduce the total unemployment insurance taxes paid by both employer and employee. In some cases it would also reduce unemployment insurance benefit protection that is related only to the cash income.

Until enactment of the Omnibus Reconciliation Act of 1980 the tax advantages of the optional payment of unemployment insurance taxes was available for all employment. Effective in 1981 for the private sector and in 1984 for the public sector (provided the practice was in effect on October 1, 1980), the option is available only for employment in domestic service in a private home and in agricultural labor.

Taxes on Sick Pay

Most employers and employees pay Social Security taxes on all their wages, even though some of these "wages" may be legally exempt from such taxes (and, in some cases, exempt from federal unemployment insurance taxes). This overpayment is done for convenience in some cases; but, in others, it is probably out of ignorance of the law.

Payments made to an employee under a sick-pay plan (which

meets certain requirements) are not subject to Social Security taxes. There is no exemption, however, for payments for unused sick leave since such payments are not made "on account of sickness or accident disability." Taxes that have been paid in error can be recovered for up to four years in the past (Internal Revenue Code, Section 3121 (a)(4)). A decision to recover or not to recover past overpayment of taxes can mean thousands of dollars to an employer and its employees. Any recovery of past tax overpayment attributable to withholding from employee earnings is, of course, refundable to the employee. It is possible that such amounts would be considered owed by the employer to the employee, even if they are not recovered by the employer, since the payment of Social Security taxes on qualified sick pay is a mistake, though perhaps well-intentioned.

This reduction in taxes, including any retroactive recovery, would affect only employees whose earnings (excluding sick pay) were less than the maximum taxable earnings base for the year under consideration. Since a reduction in taxes results from a reduction in earnings on which taxes are payable, future Social Security benefits would be reduced also.

Taxes on Stand-by Pay

Once you reach age 62 any pay you receive for periods in which you perform no work is not considered earnings subject to Social Security tax (except for vacation and certain sick-leave pay). This could include stand-by pay, subject-to-call pay, idle-time pay, and the like.

Convert Taxable Earnings Into Nontaxable Earnings

There are numerous ways to convert earnings that normally would be subjected to Social Security tax into forms of income that are not considered subject to such tax. The validity of some but not all of these conversions is questionable.

One method that is reportedly used by small groups of individuals who are in business together is as follows: The individuals incorporate as a small business corporation and then arrange to receive dividends but little or no salary. Dividends are not subjected to Social Security tax, hence Social Security taxes *and benefits* are reduced.

It is ironic that at the same time some people are trying to keep their income from being subjected to Social Security tax, others are trying to make their nontaxable income subject to Social Security tax so they will be eligible for additional benefits.

Opt Out of Social Security

Of course, the ultimate way to decrease taxes is to opt out of Social Security altogether. Generally speaking, the only persons eligible to opt out of Social Security are employees of state and local governments and nonprofit organizations, and members of certain religious groups. Less than fifteen percent of the work force is eligible to do this, and even then such an option can be exercised normally only by an entire group of employees and not by an individual.

Chapters 17 and 18 contain more details about groups for whom participation in Social Security is optional and the many considerations involved in making a decision to participate or not participate. Even though withdrawal from Social Security is a way to save Social Security taxes and thus may be of advantage to some persons, it is not necessarily the best way for most persons to take advantage of Social Security.

Domestic Workers

Failure to pay Social Security taxes on work performed by domestic workers is *not* a good way to decrease taxes. Domestic workers and casual workers, as well as their employers, may be less inclined than those in a more formal employer-employee relationship to follow the cumbersome administrative procedures and pay all the Social Security taxes required by law. This may be due in part to a misunderstanding of their taxpaying obligations, but also to a lack of appreciation of the value of Social Security benefits.

It is easy to depreciate Social Security benefits when the taxes fall due, but these benefits will be quite valuable at the time of old age, disability, illness, or death. The most prudent course, especially for workers with a casual attachment to the labor force, is to qualify for the maximum possible benefits afforded by Social Security. An employer who deprives employees and their dependents of needed benefits by failure to carry out an obligation to pay Social Security taxes may be taking unwarranted legal risks. This is entirely apart from the moral obligation of the employer to the employee to afford this needed protection.

Conclusion

There are several things you can do to take maximum advantage of Social Security. Learn as much as possible about the benefits provided by Social Security so that you can supplement those benefits appropriately with your own personal arrangements for financial security. There are ways to decrease Social Security taxes as well as to increase benefits. Extreme care should be taken in arranging a decrease in taxes, however, since this usually results in a decrease in benefits. Apply promptly for any Social Security benefits to which you may be entitled since, in general, benefits cannot be paid retroactively for more than six months (twelve months for certain disability benefits). Periodically verify your earnings record maintained by the Social Security Administration to be sure your record is accurate. Notify the Social Security office of any changes in your personal situation and that of your family members. The benefit provisions are complicated and are ever changing; thus you cannot be certain about your eligibility for benefits. If the answers you get from Social Security do not seem reasonable, double-check them. More and more mistakes are being made as Social Security becomes increasingly complicated and every precaution should be taken to prevent you and your family from being an innocent victim of an innocent mistake.

22
Social Security as a Determinant of Behavior

Most people think of Social Security as a program that collects taxes from the active working population and provides benefits in the event of old age, disability, illness, or death. This is certainly true, but it may be useful to look at Social Security from another point of view that may be of even greater importance in the long run.

Social Security is in effect a complex system of rewards and penalties for various kinds of social and economic behavior among its participants. As such, it is an important determinant of the behavior of the individual participants; thus it will ultimately shape the habits of the nation as a whole. Here are some examples of how Social Security affects our behavior.

Normal Retirement Age

We usually think of age 65 as the "normal retirement age." If we retire before age 65 it is called "early retirement." If we retire after age 65 it is called "late retirement."

Why is age 65 the normal retirement age instead of 66, or 67, or 70, or 60? It is because the planners of Social Security back in the 1930s thought this was a good compromise between the high cost of paying full benefits at age 60 and the limited usefulness of a retirement age of 70 for combatting unemployment. Since then, Social Security has been changed to permit retirement benefits to commence as early as age 62, but on a reduced basis. Age 65 remains the normal retirement age, the earliest age at which unreduced benefits are payable.

Most private and many public employee pension plans have followed the Social Security practice of normal retirement at age 65. This is partly for convenience and consistency but also because the Internal Revenue Service regulation of private pension plans is related to the standards set by Social Security.

Social Security, then, started it all and has effectively defined the retirement age pattern for the nation. After forty-five years of being told that normal retirement is at age 65, most people have begun to believe it. In fact, many people believe that it is their inalienable right to retire at age 65 and that it is absurd to suggest they should work longer, even if they are in good health.

Whether or Not to Work

Decisions about whether or not to work depend largely upon a person's financial situation, state of emotional and physical health, and the availability of work the person considers suitable. Social Security plays an important role in this decision by virtue of the benefits it provides or does not provide. Furthermore, the existence of Social Security has influenced significantly the birth and growth of the private pension movement. Social Security, directly and indirectly, has thus spawned an entirely new way of thinking about work and retirement.

The influence of Social Security on our acceptance of age 65 as the normal retirement age has already been noted. Through its various provisions concerning the payment of benefits, Social Security also influences early and late retirement practices. Social Security pays full benefits at the "normal retirement age" of 65. Benefits may commence as early as age 62, in which event they are "actuarially reduced" to offset their expected payment over a longer period of time; however, the method of calculating benefits favors retirement at age 62, and the worker receives greater total value in relation to Social Security taxes paid by retiring at age 62. The commencement of benefits may be deferred until after age 65, in which event benefits will be increased to reflect partially, not fully, the shorter remaining lifetime during which they will be paid. The worker thus receives relatively less value if benefits commence after age 65.

Chapter 12 discusses in some detail the retirement test, or earnings test. If the worker begins to receive benefits but also continues in paid employment, his Social Security benefits are reduced if his earnings exceed certain "exempt amounts." These exempt amounts are lowest under age 65, next lowest between ages 65 and 72, and are highest after age 72 when there is no limit on earnings. The provisions of the current law would seem to encourage a person to retire at age 62, to engage in limited paid employment until age 65, to increase the level of his activity in paid employment from age 65 to 72, and then to work in full-time paid employment after age 72—an apparent irrational set of provisions. (After 1981 references in this paragraph to age 72 should read age 70.)

Spouses and children who receive benefits based on the work record of a retired worker, or because of the death or disability of a worker, are also subject to the earnings test. Accordingly, they may lose part or all of their benefits if their earnings exceed the exempt amount. In cases where the maximum family benefit is in effect, however, a family member could earn more than the exempt amount and lose part of his or her own benefit without causing a reduction in the total amount received by the family. This is because the reduction in family benefits as a result of excess earnings is made before the maximum family benefit is determined.

The influences exerted by Social Security on the decision of whether or not to work are subtle and are different for each type of beneficiary. Unfortunately, many of the beneficiaries, particularly the worker's family members, are not aware of the effect of their working on the receipt of benefits early enough to make informed decisions about related financial matters.

Whether to Marry or Remarry

Many benefits are paid under Social Security to wives, husbands, widows, and widowers. Of course the payment of such benefits presupposes that marriage has taken place. Even though common-law marriages are recognized, this is frequently an ambiguous situation. Just living together will not necessarily create an entitlement to these benefits—benefits which may be quite important in the event of death, disability, or illness, particularly if dependent children are involved. The failure to formalize a de facto marriage could result in substantial financial hardship.

If you are the widow (nondisabled) of a worker covered by Social Security, your eligibility for widow's benefits will cease if you remarry prior to age 60 (except if you marry a person who is entitled to a widower's, father's, parent's or disabled child's benefit, or if you are receiving a mother's benefit and you marry another Social Security beneficiary). Remarriage at age 60 or later does not affect a widow's benefit.

If you are receiving benefits as a result of being a dependent parent of a worker covered by Social Security, your benefits will cease if you remarry after the worker's death (except if you marry a person who is entitled to a widow's, widower's, mother's, father's, divorced wife's, parent's, or disabled child's benefit).

If you are receiving benefits as a result of being a divorced widow of a worker covered by Social Security, your benefits will cease if you remarry at any age (unless you marry a person who is entitled to a widower's, father's, parent's, or disabled child's benefit).

If you are receiving benefits as a result of being a divorced wife of a worker covered by Social Security, your benefits will cease if you remarry someone other than the worker; however, your benefits will not be terminated if you marry an individual entitled to widower's, father's, or parent's monthly benefits, or an individual aged 18 or over who is entitled to childhood disability benefits.

Some children receive benefits because one of their parents is receiving retirement benefits (as a result of disability or having attained age 62), or because one or both of their parents have died. To continue receiving these benefits, such a child must be *unmarried* and:

> under age 18;
> under age 22, if a full-time student; or
> any age, if disabled before age 22.

In any of these circumstances, marriage could result in a substantial loss of benefits.

Whom to Marry

Some people marry to attain financial security. If this is your objective, all other factors being equal, it may be preferable to marry someone who will work in employment covered by Social Security. This excludes about 10 percent of the nation's workers at any given time: some nonprofit organization employees, some governmental employees, some members of religious orders, and so forth.

If you are a divorced wife who was married at least ten years to a man who will become entitled to Social Security benefits, you may eventually be entitled to benefits yourself based upon his work record. You will retain this benefit if you remarry someone receiving Social Security benefits as a widower, father, parent, or disabled child. You will lose this benefit if you marry anyone else.

If you are a disabled person aged 18 or over and are receiving benefits as a result of being a child of a worker covered by Social Security, your benefits will cease if you marry (except if you marry another disabled child aged 18 or over who is receiving child's benefits, or if you marry a person entitled to old-age, widow's, widower's, mother's, father's, parent's, disability, or divorced wife's benefits).

These comments about whether and whom to marry, taking into account the Social Security benefits that may be gained or lost, may appear to be somewhat overdrawn. There is, perhaps, an element of satire in the exposition in the sense it is "used for the purpose of exposing folly." Consider, however, Chart 22.A, which is a copy of page 322 of the following government publication: *Social Security Handbook,* U.S. Department of Health, Education, and Welfare, Social Security Administration, HEW Publication No. (SSA) 77-10135, July 1978.

Whether (or When) to Divorce

A divorce at any time will result in a potential loss of future benefits. A divorce *prior* to ten years of marriage can result in a *total loss* of benefits a person may have become eligible to

Chart 22.A

1856. The Effect of One Beneficiary's Marriage to Another Beneficiary is Summarized in the Following Chart:

Male beneficiary	Female beneficiary									
	Retirement insurance benefits	Disability insurance benefits	Divorced wife	Child under 18 and child 18 or over in school	Disabled child 18 or over	Widow under 60	Widow 60 or over	Surviving divorced wife	Mother	Parent
Retirement insurance beneficiary	←C	←C	←CT[1]	←CT	←C	←CT	←C½*	←CT	←C	←CT
Disability insurance beneficiary	←C	←C	←CT[1]	←CT	←C[2]	←CT	←C½*	←CT	←C[2]	←CT
Child under 18 and child 18 or over in school	←TC	←TC	←T	←T	←T	←T	←TC½*	←T	←T	←T
Disabled child 18 or over	←C	←C	←C[2]	←T	←C[2]	←C[2]	←C[3]	←C[2]	←C[2]	←C[2]
Widower under 60	←TC	←TC	←C	←T	←C	←C	←C	←C	←C	←C
Widower 60 or over	←C½*	←C½*	←C	←C½T*	←C	←C	←C	←C	←C	←C
Father	←C	←C	←C	←T	←C	←C	←C	←C	←C	←C
Parent	←TC	←TC	←C	←T	←C	←C	←C	←C	←C	←C

"T" means Termination; "C" means Continuation of benefit; the arrow indicates the beneficiary affected.

*½ means that, effective with the month of marriage, the benefit of the widow or widower, while not terminated, is reduced to 50 percent of the deceased worker's primary insurance amount. This reduction is effective for months prior to 1979. As of January 1979, there is no reduction because of the remarriage of a widow(er) age 60 or over.

[1] The divorced wife's benefits end unless the retirement insurance or disability insurance beneficiary is the insured worker on whose earnings record her benefit is based.

[2] If the male's benefits terminate for any reason other than his death or his entitlement to retirement insurance benefits, female's benefits will also terminate. However, termination of a female disability or childhood disability benefit will not terminate any benefit which her husband is receiving on another earnings record.

[3] If, subsequent to the marriage, the male's childhood disability benefit terminates for a reason other than death or entitlement to retirement insurance benefits, the widow's benefit is reduced to 50 percent of her former husband's primary insurance amount for benefits payable before 1979. Beginning January 1979, there is no reduction.

receive based on the other person's coverage by Social Security. A divorce *after* ten years of marriage will result in a *partial loss* of such benefits. From the standpoint of receiving Social Security benefits, it is obviously preferable to divorce after ten years and one month of marriage rather than after nine years and eleven months. The difference in a few days could amount to a loss of thousands of dollars.

Consider, for example, a divorced wife aged 30 with one child aged one month, whose former husband died in January 1980 leaving her with maximum Social Security benefits. The actuarial value of these benefits at the time of the former husband's death would be as follows (the actual dollar amount payable over the years would be more than four times these amounts):

Divorced Mother's benefits	$ 72,000
Divorced Widow's benefits	33,000
Child's benefits	85,000
Total	$190,000

This example assumes that the divorce occurred after at least ten years of marriage. If the divorce had occurred just prior to ten years of marriage, no divorced widow's benefits would have been payable and $33,000 worth of benefits would have been lost, probably unwittingly. The divorced mother's benefits would still be payable but would usually terminate upon remarriage. The child's benefits, worth about $85,000 and payable in any event, would be controlled by whichever party is given custody of the child.

Generally speaking, a divorced wife of a marriage that endured at least ten years will receive the same benefits as if the divorce had not occurred. There are, however, at least three exceptions:

The wife of a person entitled to disability or retirement benefits will receive monthly benefits if she is caring for a child entitled to benefits if under age 18 or disabled, even if the wife is less than age 62. A divorced wife in these circumstances will receive no such benefit.

A widow who remarries prior to age 60 loses any benefits to which she is entitled on her husband's earnings record; remarriage after age 60 does not result in such loss of benefits. A surviving divorced wife loses such benefits if she remarries at any age, even after age 60.

The wife's benefits may be reduced if the total family benefits would otherwise exceed the family maximum. A divorced wife's benefits are not subject to such a reduction.

Therefore, the benefits payable to a divorced wife may be equal to, less than, or greater than, the benefits payable if the divorce had not occurred, depending upon the circumstances. Even though a divorced wife may be entitled to the same benefits as if divorce had not occurred, these benefits can be forfeited completely in the event of her remarriage; and the amount of Social Security benefits resulting from the remarriage may be equal to, greater than, or less than, the benefits forfeited.

A divorce frequently has significant financial consequences as a result of lost Social Security benefits. Oftentimes, these consequences are not fully recognized until it is too late to prevent the loss (sometimes they are never recognized), in large part because the myriad of benefits provided by Social Security is not widely appreciated.

Whether to Recover from Disability

Social Security pays disability benefits to persons who are so severely disabled, mentally or physically, that they cannot perform any substantial gainful work. Needless to say it is not always possible to determine conclusively whether a person is disabled. Subjectivity is sometimes involved, not only on the part of the administrator who is assessing the disability but also on the part of the potential beneficiary.

I shall ignore the question of whether a potential beneficiary feigns disability just to collect benefits. Undoubtedly some do, but most people are not inclined to go to such lengths and are not aware of the relatively generous benefit levels, so let us assume most disabilities are determined fairly at their inception. Once benefits commence, however, there may not be sufficient incentive to recover.

Consider the following example: A married couple, both aged 35, with two children under age 18. Each adult earns the same as the average person covered by Social Security: that is, $11,479 in 1979 for combined gross earnings of $22,958 per year. The annual net take-home pay after federal, state, and Social Security taxes is $17,734 (based on the standard deduction and an average of representative state tax rates). Assume that one of the spouses qualifies for disability benefits early in 1980 of $9,581 per year payable monthly (for the disabled spouse and the children). The disability benefit is not taxable of course. The net take-home pay after federal, state, and Social Security taxes is now $19,490. This is $1,756 per year more than when both parents worked. After disability benefits have been paid for two years the disabled spouse also receives Medicare, free of charge except for a nominal premium for Supplementary Medical Insurance ($9.60 per month in July 1980). Furthermore, the disabled spouse is not subject to the earnings test applied to retired persons; and under rules followed by Social Security, a disabled person can earn about $300 per month without jeopardizing the disability status. Finally, the disability benefits are automatically and fully adjusted for changes in the Consumer Price Index—which may be more than can be said of the working spouse's earnings.

Some attempt is made by Social Security to rehabilitate disabled workers. For such an attempt to be successful in the example given, however, the rehabilitation effort would have to be Herculean, the disabled person would need an overwhelming desire to reenter paid employment, and both the man and wife would need to perceive Social Security as a fair program and not one that they should try to take advantage of.

Social Security was amended in 1980 (PL 96-265) to reduce disability benefits somewhat for persons first becoming eligible on July 1, 1980 and later. The change was not great enough, however, to have a material effect on the incentive to recover from disability.

Which Employer to Select

Social Security has the potential to influence our selection of employers in many ways. If it does not, frequently it is because of our failure to appreciate how much variation exists in the employee benefit plans provided in various jobs and how this may affect our future security.

Suppose you are a public school teacher in a state that provides Social Security coverage for its teachers. Suppose further that you would like to move to another state and continue teaching, and you believe that Social Security provides appropriate benefits for you because of your circumstances at this time (and there are many valid reasons this can be true). There are twelve states you may not want to consider any further because their teachers are not covered by Social Security. Alternatively, perhaps you would like to leave the teaching field and get a job in state or local government. There are six states that do not provide their public employees with Social Security. Perhaps you are considering a job with the federal government in the new Department of Education. If so, remember that civilian employees of the federal government do not participate in Social Security. True, federal employees have their own benefit plans, but these may not provide adequate benefits for short periods of service and you may not plan to make a career with the federal government.

On the other hand, you may not now be in a job that is covered by Social Security, but you may want such a job at some point in your career so you can obtain at least some of the benefits Social Security provides. For example, you may be a career employee with the federal government who plans to retire from government service at age 55 but work in other employment until age 65. In this event, you would probably choose your next job to be one that is covered by Social Security.

In some cases a person may want to spend the last few years of his career in a job *not* covered by Social Security, particularly if covered by Social Security during the first part of his career. The reason is that such employment frequently provides larger retirement benefits than employment covered by Social Security. Accordingly, the total benefit at retirement may be larger than if work continued in jobs covered by Social Security.

Each year thousands of employment decisions are made that reflect, or should reflect, factors similar to those mentioned.

To Save or Not to Save

The existence of Social Security discourages individuals and their employers from saving for their eventual retirement needs. Whether this affects the total saving habits of the nation is debatable; however, it seems reasonable to assume that it does.

Imagine that your employer does not provide a pension plan and that there is no Social Security program. Under these conditions would you save any of your current earnings for a time when you may not be able to work because of poor health or old age? Any prudent person past middle age would almost certainly answer yes. On the other hand, if you participate in Social Security do you make less provision for your retirement than if you were not covered by Social Security? Again, the only reasonable answer is yes.

If you are covered by Social Security and your employer also provides a pension plan, are the benefits lower under this employer plan than they would be if you were not covered by Social Security? Once again, the most common answer is yes.

Accordingly, it seems clear that the existence of Social Security results in individuals' and employers' making less provision for retirement than if there were no Social Security. And this means less saving by individuals and employers for retirement. This reduced saving by individuals and employers is not offset by increased saving under Social Security since Social Security is operated on a pay-as-you-go basis and does not generate saving.

Since the existence of Social Security results in less saving for retirement purposes, it is logical to assume that total national saving for all purposes is reduced. This has not been, and probably cannot be, proven conclusively. Furthermore, if there is no capital shortage in the nation, it may not matter whether total national saving is reduced. However, if there is a capital shortage in the nation, now or in the future, the negative influence exerted by Social Security on saving may be very important.

Whether to Feel Responsible for Oneself and One's Family

Social Security is changing our attitudes about our responsibility for saving and providing for our own future needs and those of our extended family. Part of this change in attitude is justified by the facts about how Social Security is now satisfying some of our financial needs. Another part of this change in attitude is not justified by the facts, rather it is based upon confusion about what Social Security is all about.

The average individual does not know what to expect from Social Security. Should he expect it to meet all of his needs (and those of his dependents) in the event of old age, disability, death, or sickness? Or should he expect it to be merely a floor of protection in meeting these needs, a floor upon which he and his employer should build through supplemental private saving and insurance and some form of retirement program? Apart from his expectations, what type and level of benefits does Social Security actually provide in meeting these various needs? Most people don't know. Under a system as complex as the present Social Security program, it is doubtful that a clear delineation of such responsibility will ever be possible—*a situation almost certain to result in people's expecting more and thus eventually receiving more from the government (that is, from the active working taxpayers).*

A number of factors, not the least of which is the general misunderstanding about the role of Social Security, have caused more and more people to believe that their economic needs in time of adversity should and will be met by someone else, namely the government. This change in attitude about responsibility for self is frightening. Its consequence has been and will continue to be a decline in individual initiative and self-reliance and thus a decline in the productivity of the nation as a whole.

Conclusion

Our Social Security program plays an important role in satisfying the population's economic security needs. While satisfying these needs, Social Security exerts strong influences, both good and bad, on the social and economic behavior of the nation's citizens. We must recognize that the design of Social Security is not only a reflection of our nation's existing social and economic structure, it is an important determinant of that structure in the future.

The nation must decide the extent to which it wants its citizens to have freedom of choice and the extent to which it wants to regulate their activities. It can then design an appropriate public policy as to the optimum roles to be played by the three natural sources of retirement income: government, employers and trade unions, and individuals. By properly designing and implementing such a policy, the nation can ensure that its citizens' basic economic security needs are met by methods that are consistent with the social and economic environment in which the nation will flourish, not wane. The challenge of finding and implementing the optimum mix that is the most favorable to this given end is considerably greater than merely satisfying the population's economic security needs during the next few years.

23
The Great American Retirement Dream

Many Americans believe that if they work until about age 60 or 65 they will then be able to live the balance of their lives in carefree and leisurely retirement, occupying themselves with hobbies, sports, and travel—activities for which they had neither the time nor the money in their earlier years. They believe this will be possible because of some combination of Social Security benefits, employer-paid pension benefits, and private savings in one form or another (a paid-for house, personal life insurance and annuities, etc.).

Not everyone really believes that this period of carefree and leisurely retirement will actually occur; however, most people want it to happen, hope that it will happen, and after a few years of nourishing such wants and hopes begin to believe that it *should* happen—that they are *entitled* to a leisurely retirement after having worked a lifetime in a job they consider difficult, or frustrating, or boring, or unsatisfying in some way. Indeed, this Great American Retirement Dream serves as a kind of opiate in making life more tolerable in the face of a sometimes onerous job, not to mention the everyday difficulties of living.

The Great American Retirement Dream has failed to materialize for most people in the past. Those who live to the "normal retirement" age of 60 or 65 are frequently disappointed because of the ill health of themselves or their immediate family, the loss of friends and relatives, or their inability to disengage from work-related activities and substitute new activities. In addition to these problems, most people experience significant financial difficulties. In an inflation-plagued economy, fixed pension benefits lose their purchasing power, and the cost of maintaining a "paid-for house" escalates unduly as real estate taxes and other costs increase; increased sickness in old age and skyrocketing medical costs combine to produce extremely high health care costs; personal savings do not prove to be as significant as planned, dissipated perhaps by unexpected health care expenses or high education costs for children; Social Security benefits and employer-provided pension benefits prove to be less than hoped for.

Just as the Great American Retirement Dream has failed to materialize in the past, it will probably fail in the future. It is not a goal that can be achieved for the majority of the population. It is not affordable, at least at a price the nation will be willing to pay. It is not a healthful concept, particularly if there is so little chance it can be achieved. It is a sad commentary on our way of life that anyone would spend most of his or her adult years looking forward to retirement.

The nation's concept of work, education, leisure, and retirement must be revised. It must be presumed that an individual will engage in gainful employment suitable to his physical and mental condition until well beyond age 60 or 65 and possibly until the end of his life. A trend toward later retirement may be a natural development as health and life expectancy improve and as the growth in the work force slows because of the low fertility rates now being experienced and expected to continue in the future. For this trend to be consummated, however, significant changes will be required in existing social and economic arrangements. Jobs must be structured to be more meaningful and satisfying to the individual. Persons must undergo training and retraining to enable them to have not just second careers, but third and fourth careers. In some instances jobs must be designed to fit the capabilities of the human resources available. For older persons as well as disabled persons, less strenuous jobs and part-time employment must be made available. Significant advances will be required in our ability to match persons with jobs. Sometimes this complete utilization of an individual can be achieved with one employer, but in some cases it will involve many different employers and may require geographical relocation as well. Attitudes must change to make these new concepts possible.

These changes must begin to take place during the next ten years, and they must be well underway by the turn of the century when the children of the post-World War II baby boom begin to reach their forties and fifties. Bringing about these changes will be a slow process that will require the cooperation of many institutions, not just Social Security.

The first step in the process is the recent action by Congress prohibiting an employer from imposing mandatory retirement at an age lower than age 70 (with certain exceptions). This action was coincidental and was just another step in the direction of eliminating job discrimination altogether. Nevertheless, it fits in well with the need for a more complete utilization of the nation's human resources. As time goes by and the health of the elderly continues to improve, further increases in the mandatory retirement age will probably be adopted. In fact, mandatory retirement may one day be eliminated (as it has been already for federal civilian employees).

The next step is to revise the Social Security program so that it is consistent with a policy of more complete utilization of the nation's human resources. It is sometimes said that the Social Security program has no particular influence on the nation's retirement policy since it does not specify the age at which a person can retire and it does not impose a mandatory retirement age. Nevertheless, the Social Security program effectively dictates the retirement policy of the nation.

It does this in part through the manifold and complicated conditions under which benefits are payable. Full benefits are payable at age 65, the "normal retirement age" selected somewhat arbitrarily in the 1930s by the program's designers. Benefits may commence as early as age 62, in which event they are "actuarially reduced" to offset their expected payment over a longer period of time; however, the method of calculating benefits under the present law favors retirement at age 62, since the worker receives greater total value by retiring at age 62. The commencement of benefits may be deferred until after age 65 in which event benefits will be increased to reflect partially, but not fully, the shorter remaining lifetime during which they will be paid. The worker thus receives less value if benefits commence after age 65.

If the worker continues in paid employment, his Social Security benefits are reduced if his earnings exceed certain levels. These levels of "permitted earnings" are lowest between ages 62 and 65, next lowest between ages 65 and 72, and are highest after age 72 when there is no limit on earnings.[1]

The Social Security program's influence on other retirement systems and thus on the nation's employment practices is pervasive. Private and public employee pension plans must as a practical matter follow the retirement patterns fostered by Social Security. Internal Revenue Service regulation of private pension plans is related to the standards set by Social Security. Practices followed by Social Security in determining eligibility for disability benefits influence the practices of private pension plans and private insurers.

Although the Social Security program is influencing the retirement policy of the nation through these many complicated provisions, it is rather difficult first to determine and then to state in a concise way exactly what that retirement policy is. The provisions of the current law would seem to encourage a person to retire at age 62, to engage in limited paid employment until age 65, to increase the level of his activity in paid employment from age 65 to 72, and then to work in full-time paid employment after age 72.[1]

Of more significance, however, the mere existence of the Social Security program sets a standard, and thus creates an expectation that fosters a presumption of entitlement, for retirement in a person's early to mid-sixties, regardless of the condition of his health and his ability to continue as a productive and useful member of society.

This retirement policy, which is inherent in the Social Security progam and which effectively sets the nation's retirement policy, should be reviewed carefully to determine whether it is in fact the retirement policy that is appropriate for the nation at this time as well as in the future. Moreover, and more importantly, careful attention should be given to the question of the extent to which the Social Security program should set the retirement policy for the nation and the extent to which such policy should be determined otherwise. The nation's retirement policy must vary from time to time depending upon a variety of factors, not the least of which is the fluctuating birth rate which causes shifts in the proportions of the population that are aged and young—the principal reason for the substantial projected Social Security cost increase beginning about thirty years from now. The present Social Security program may not be flexible enough to accommodate a variable retirement policy. In this connection it should be noted that one important reason for adopting Social Security in the first place was to alleviate the hardships of the widespread unemployment that prevailed in the 1930s. Much of the present design of the program is thus attributable to conditions that existed forty-five years ago.

Finally, work must begin on training and retraining individuals to meet existing job opportunities, as well as designing and redesigning jobs so they can be performed by available human resources. More sophisticated ways must be developed to appropriately match individuals and jobs.

The nation should provide an environment in which the capabilities of each individual can be utilized effectively, an environment that fosters meaningful activity, not empty idleness. Both the incentive and the opportunity should exist to enable every individual to work and produce throughout his lifetime in a series of endeavors compatible with his changing physical and mental abilities. Governmental policies should be directed toward these goals and not toward the removal from the active work force of able-bodied persons who must then be supported by the remaining active workers.

It will not be easy for the nation to move in this direction of full utilization of its human resources. The alternative will be continued high unemployment and underemployment, an ever-increasing pool of idle "disabled persons" and "aged persons," and a total cost to society that will become increasingly unbearable and that will eventually become destructive.

24
What Is the Outlook for Social Security?

The public is frequently given official assurance that the Social Security program is in sound financial condition during the foreseeable future and that there is nothing much to be concerned about. Such statements overlook the dramatic effect on costs of the growth in the aged population relative to the active working population shortly after the turn of the century. They also ignore the financial condition of the Hospital Insurance program which is financed by a portion of the Social Security payroll tax. Projections of future costs prepared by Social Security actuaries—contained in unpublished as well as published studies—indicate that the tax rate for the Old-Age, Survivors, Disability, and Hospital Insurance programs will at least double within the working lifetime of today's young workers: that is, it will rise from 6.13 percent in 1980 to about 8 percent by the year 2000 and 12 percent by the year 2025. The maximum wages to which these tax rates apply are also scheduled to increase: from $25,900 in 1980 to $29,700 in 1981, rising thereafter in proportion to increases in national average wages. Of course these are just the employee taxes; the employer pays a matching tax. The tax rate for self-employed persons is projected to rise from 8.10 percent in 1980 to about 11 percent in the year 2000 and 16 percent by the year 2025.

These projections assume that the Social Security law is not changed (except to increase tax rates enough to pay benefits), that present financing practices are followed, and that current patterns of retirement continue. Such assumptions will probably not materialize, particularly in view of the large projected tax increases as well as the increase that will occur in the average age of the population if the present relatively low birth rates continue. As has been highly publicized in recent years, this aging of the population will result eventually in only two workers paying taxes for every one person receiving benefits— in contrast to the present situation of three workers for every beneficiary.

What Changes Lie Ahead?

What kinds of change can be expected in the present law and in the behavior of the population covered by that law because of these projected rising costs, the aging of the population, and various other factors? The following seven points seem to be reasonable expectations for the future. They may or may not be desirable, depending upon your point of view.

First, taxpayers must become accustomed to paying higher taxes for Social Security benefits unless benefits are reduced substantially from current levels. It is just not possible to pay for the current Social Security program with the taxes now being collected or even those scheduled in the current law.

Second, it seems unlikely that the payroll tax will continue to be the primary source of tax revenue for the program. Taxpayers are increasingly asking what benefits they receive for their Social Security tax payments. As it becomes more evident that the relationship between taxes and benefits is tenuous for any given individual (that is, the program gives more emphasis to social adequacy than to individual equity), there will be increased resistance to payroll tax rate increases. This will probably result in the use of some form of nonpayroll tax (such as general revenue or a value-added tax) for at least one-third of Social Security expenditures sometime before the turn of the century. It seems unlikely that present Social Security payroll tax rates will be reduced significantly; the new form of taxation will represent additional taxes.

Third, all state and local government employees and federal civil servants will eventually become participants in the Social Security program. Perhaps participation will be made compulsory for such employees. Alternatively, if and when nonpayroll taxes are used to a significant degree to finance Social Security, these employees may insist on being covered by Social Security in an attempt to obtain their money's worth from their general taxes. Also, as the real costs of existing public employee retirement systems become more evident, there may be an inclination to reduce benefits under such systems and integrate them with the Social Security program. Full participation by all state and local employees and federal civil servants would permit a reduction in the average tax rate paid by employees and employers of less than one-half percent each.

Fourth, beginning about twenty-five to thirty-five years from now, employees will be working longer and retiring at higher ages. This will be a natural development as health and life expectancy improve, and as the growth in the work force slows because of the low fertility rates. For this to be feasible, present socioeconomic arrangements must be revised to make it easier for persons to continue working until advanced ages, perhaps in less strenuous jobs or part-time employment. This development could lessen the financial problems of the Social Security program during the next century since a later effective retirement age, other things being equal, is tantamount to a reduction in benefits. The cost effect of later retirement, however, could well be offset by increased longevity. Also, further liberalizations in the retirement test or further increases in the delayed retirement credit would negate any cost savings resulting from later retirement.

Fifth, social and economic changes in the nation will result in substantial revision of the program. The changing role of the family unit and of women; changing patterns in the incidence of work, education, and leisure throughout a person's lifetime; lengthening life expectancy and improved health in old age; and increased (or reduced) need to work in order to maintain the desired standard of living—all of these changes and more will require that significant revisions be made in the benefit structure if the evolving economic security needs are to be satisfied appropriately. The net effect of all these changes will not necessarily be an increase in costs.

Sixth, if the nation experiences sustained inflation at relatively high levels, it is likely that the portion of an individual's economic security needs that are met by the private sector will decrease over time; the needs must somehow be met; and the federal government (probably through an expanded Social Security program) will be left as the only entity with the audacity to make unqualified promises to pay benefits seventy-five to one hundred years in the future based upon indeterminable cost-of-living increases. Obviously, the cost of an expanded Social Security program would be correspondingly higher.

Seventh, the Medicare program as well as the nation's entire health care system will be changed beyond recognition during the next twenty-five years. This will be the inevitable result of diverse attempts to make more adequate health care available to society at large, but at the same time prevent total health care costs from continuing to rise as a percentage of the Gross National Product. Early in 1977, the management of Medicare and Medicaid, the nation's two largest health care programs, was consolidated under the newly formed Health Care Financing Administration. These two programs will be reshaped in various ways and will probably evolve into a comprehensive national health insurance program.

These seven areas in which Social Security and the behavior of the nation's citizens can be expected to change are stated only in general terms. The exact nature of the changes will depend upon a variety of future events: demographic shifts in the population (affected, in turn, by birth rates, health care developments, and immigration), the nation's economic health, inflation, conditions throughout the world over which we may have little control, and so on. Moreover, public understanding or misunderstanding will play a much more critical role in determining the shape of Social Security in the future than it has in the past—when the payroll tax was relatively low and when the taxpayer was in a less questioning frame of mind. It is obviously preferable for changes to arise from a clearheaded appraisal on the basis of an understanding of our present system rather than from a frenzied cry for change on the basis of misunderstanding and frustration.

Even though a variety of future events—some of which we cannot control—will influence the Social Security of the future, it would be a mistake to be fatalistic. It is still up to us to shape Social Security so that it is appropriate for tomorrow's environment—so that it provides a system of benefits consistent with our needs and our ability to pay for them.

The outlook for Social Security, then, is whatever we desire—and have the courage to achieve.

25
Can Social Security Be Abolished or Changed Drastically?

More and more often questions are being asked such as, "Can't the Social Security program be abolished?" or, "Isn't there some alternative to Social Security?" or, "Wouldn't I be better off if I quit Social Security and invested my tax payments in the stock market?" These questions are usually prompted by concern over the seemingly endless rise in Social Security taxes, dissatisfaction with the benefits a particular individual expects to receive in relation to his tax payments, misunderstanding about how the program actually works, general antipathy for any large governmental program, fear that the present Social Security program is going bankrupt and will be unable to make good on its promises, and so on.

What are the facts? Are there any real alternatives to the present Social Security program?

Without question the present program can be revised and it should be revised—slightly now and significantly later. There are certain practical limits, however, concerning the extent to which changes can be made as well as the speed with which they can be implemented. Complete termination of the Social Security program, as suggested by some, is out of the question.

Some form of national social insurance is absolutely necessary. There is virtually no alternative in a nation that is so large and diverse and that is based on an industrial economy and a highly mobile and dynamic society. The days of the static, agrarian society, built around an extended family with all its attendant mores, are over. In any society it is inevitable that there will be persons unable to work and care for themselves because of conditions virtually beyond their control. In an orderly society, provision must be made in an organized manner for some minimum level of support for such persons. Some form of social insurance must fill this role in modern industrial society.

The present Social Security program, supplemented by an array of welfare programs, is an important element in providing this minimum level of support. To the extent it fills this role, the Social Security program cannot be terminated. It can be revised, consolidated with other components of the total welfare system, or called by another name; but it must continue to exist in one form or another.

The present Social Security program, however, provides not only this *minimum level of support* but also, in some instances, a much higher level of support. The portion of the Social Security program that provides these "supplemental" or "discretionary" benefits is not necessarily essential to the well-being of the nation. Social Security may or may not be the best vehicle by which to provide these "supplemental" benefits depending in part upon:

> the freedom of choice desired by the people in providing for their discretionary needs;
> the practical alternative means that are available to provide for such needs; and
> the differing effect on the economy of these alternative means.

In any event, the portion of the Social Security program that provides for discretionary needs is certainly amenable to study and revision.

In considering any revision in Social Security, an extremely important factor is the long-term promises, express or implied, that have been made to millions of Americans who have paid Social Security taxes in the past. In 1981, monthly cash benefits of approximately $140 billion will be paid to over 35 million people—retired and disabled workers and their dependents, widows and orphans, and dependent parents. One of every seven Americans is receiving a monthly Social Security benefit check. Millions of people who are just a few years from retirement have built their plans around the present Social Security program. Furthermore, over 100 million people have worked and paid Social Security taxes in the past and have some expectation of future benefits.

But that does not mean Social Security cannot be changed. It can be changed, and it can be changed significantly. We are often too quick to say that Social Security is so large and complex and that it has been in existence so long that it will be difficult, if not impossible, to make substantial revisions.

Consider the following important statistics—numbers not called to our attention by those who insist that Social Security should not and cannot have major revisions. The post-World War II generation, approximately 135 million persons under age 35, now (in mid-1981) comprises 65 percent of the total population that is less than age 65. In other words, at least 65 percent of the population that is not yet retired is still young enough to adjust to any retirement policy they decide is appropriate for them. These young persons will begin reaching their sixties just twenty-five years from now in the year 2006. It is today that a general framework should be constructed regarding the retirement of this generation—the type and level of benefits to be provided, the source of benefits, the approximate age at which benefits will commence, and so on. In making these choices we need not be influenced unduly by decisions made in the past for different generations of people living under different circumstances. The only reverence we owe these past decisions is to fulfill the promises made to date to our older population.

It is entirely reasonable, therefore, that we give serious consideration to a completely new type of social insurance system for the relatively young segment of our population, even if we continue the present system for the older segment of the population. Significant change is possible if we really want such change.

Remember this astonishing statistic: 65 percent of the present population that is not yet retired is less than age 35. This youthful population of 135 million persons has had more influence on our way of life than any group of youngsters in modern history. Are they not entitled also to decide the ground rules that will apply to their retirement, provided only that they not disturb the promises already made to our older population?

Part Four
The Freedom Plan

Presumably, the reader of the first three parts of this book will have concluded that Social Security should be changed— or, at least, that pressures are building that will indeed cause it to be changed, like it or not. Assuming this is true, it is important to do whatever is necessary to ensure that any change be conceived and implemented on as rational a basis as possible.

Part Four offers suggestions for a new Social Security program—the Freedom Plan—intended to satisfy the essential income security needs of our nation's citizens within an environment that affords maximum freedom of choice.

26
Social Insurance in Perspective

A particular system of social insurance is good or bad only in relation to the yardstick by which it is measured. Most people have a set of standards by which they judge Social Security, although the standards are not usually stated explicitly. Unfortunately, this set of standards is not always consistent, either internally or with standards used to judge other aspects of our social and economic life. In thinking about any revised system of Social Security, it is well to consider for a moment the nature of social insurance and the standards we wish to govern our behavior. Of course, even among persons with consistent and well-articulated sets of standards, there will not always be agreement as to which set of standards should apply.

The Meaning of Government Sponsorship

Many of us have fallen into a bad habit of referring to "government sponsored" programs, "governmental responsibility," and having the "government pay" for things. Sometimes we behave as if the "government" not only *should* be ready to help us in time of financial need, but that the "government" *owes* us something—a retirement benefit, support for our dependents if we die, and so forth. When something in our lives goes wrong, the first place many people look for help is to the government.

Who is this "government" we keep looking to for help?
Where does it get its money? We all know the answer: the
government is simply a system we have established and a group
of people we have hired or elected to carry out our wishes.
Bureaucrats and politicians do not have any money to give us
except what we ourselves have paid in taxes. When we demand
a benefit from the government, we are demanding it from our
friends and neighbors.

There is a basic truth of economics that people frequently
overlook and that some people never even knew existed: Before
the government can give one dollar to anyone, it must confis-
cate that dollar from some other person who has earned it. And
to earn a dollar a person must produce something.

If the government sets up a program to give someone food
stamps worth $100, the government must do two things:

Find someone who is willing and able to perform work for
which he or she will earn $100; and

Convince such working person that he or she should give
the government (by paying taxes) this $100 (plus
governmental administrative expenses).

This reasoning is equally true whether we are considering
food stamps, or disability benefits, or retirement benefits, or
any other "income transfer" program the government uses to
redistribute the production of America's workers.

It cannot be emphasized strongly enough that casual references to "governmental responsibility" or having the "government pay" for all or part of Social Security are extremely
misleading. Stripped to its essentials, a governmental program
like Social Security is just an agreement among the people of
the nation that one segment of the population will receive
certain benefits and that another segment of the population will
pay for such benefits (with a certain amount of overlapping).
The government may administer and enforce compliance with a
program but, in the final analysis, any governmental program is
paid for by and is for the benefit of the people of the nation.
The government is simply the intermediary that carries out the
wishes of the people.

Who Should Assume Responsibility?

Assume, for the moment, that you live in a typical small
community of 25,000 people. Most of the people work and

support themselves in a variety of jobs. A few are retired, others are in school, some are unemployed from time to time. A few are rich, some are poor, and most are somewhere in between.

What if your family doctor came around one day and announced he was only aged 62 and still in good health, but he was tired of working; he wanted you and the rest of the townspeople to take up a collection and pay him a monthly pension so he could spend full time fishing and hunting. It is doubtful that you and the other citizens of the community would feel any obligation to honor this request. Would it be any different if it were the butcher or the baker? Probably not, if they were in good health and capable of working.

What if the cashier at the bank died leaving behind a wife and two young children? Would the community have an obligation to support the survivors? Would it matter if the local life insurance agent had tried in vain to get the cashier to use part of his earnings to buy life insurance to protect his family, and the cashier had said, "Let them fend for themselves after I'm gone; I'd rather spend my money for a new motorcycle"?

What if a young fireman became totally and permanently disabled while fighting a fire that threatened to destroy the town? What if the town librarian reached age 70, was unable to work any longer, and had lost all his or her savings in a stock market recession? Would the community have an obligation to support these individuals? If so, what level of support should be provided?

Questions such as these deserve much thought, and they are not always easy to answer. Social Security, however, answers all these questions and many more. It defines the circumstances in which benefits will be paid, the amount of the benefits, and who will pay the taxes required to provide the benefits. It does all this on an impersonal basis not only for people in your community but also for people throughout the land. It is so impersonal, in fact, that we sometimes forget who pays for the benefits.

This Part Four of the book, The Freedom Plan, presumes that Social Security no longer answers all these questions the way the majority of the public would like them answered. In designing new answers, of course, we need a set of standards to follow. Proposals for the revision of Social Security as presented in Part Four are based upon the following set of principles (previously mentioned in Chapter 11):

An individual should have freedom of choice to the fullest extent possible consistent with the interest of the nation as a whole.

An individual should be afforded maximum opportunity and incentive to develop and utilize his abilities throughout his lifetime.

A government (federal, state, or local) should provide those benefits, and only those benefits, that an individual cannot provide for himself. In meeting this responsibility, the government should become involved to the least extent possible, consistent with the interest of the nation as a whole.

What are the economic security risks that an individual cannot reasonably be expected to protect himself against—risks that call for governmental intervention in the form of requiring active workers to give up part of their production for the benefit of those in need? There are several such risks:

Unbridled inflation at a time when the worker does not have the protection normally afforded an active wage earner: that is, during a time when the worker is unable to be in the active work force because of old age or disability;

Abnormally long life spans that are unpredictable and that result from breakthroughs in health care; and

Misfortune, financial or health related, not reasonably controllable by the individual.

Were it not for these three risks, an individual could—in theory at least—make adequate provision for virtually every mishap that might befall him or his family. Sometimes this could be done by acting alone, but sometimes it would require joining with a group of individuals to utilize some form of voluntary pooling or risk-sharing arrangement. The techniques involved are simply:

Analyzing the risks that one must be protected against (old age, disability, death, or illness); and

Setting aside from current earnings an amount sufficient to provide for these risks. In some cases these savings can be accumulated on an individual basis; in others they must be applied to purchase some form of insurance or annuity.

The risk of unemployment is not discussed here. Unemployment can be the result of an individual's inadequacy or choice, or an employer's financial hardship, or a society's failure to provide training or retraining necessary to equip persons for the types of employment that exist from time to time. The risk of unemployment is not covered by Social Security as it is defined and discussed in this book; thus it is not discussed as part of a suggested revision in Social Security. It is believed, however, that the proposed revision in Social Security would create an environment in which future unemployment would be reduced.

Deficiencies of Present Social Security

The main deficiencies of our present Social Security program may be summarized as follows:

It is so complex that most people will never know what benefits to expect and will never know how much responsibility to assume for themselves and their families. This will lead to the individual's looking blindly to the government, hat in hand, for whatever benefits Big Brother is dispensing at the time and pressing for ever more benefits from the government cornucopia. The inevitable result will be erosion of initiative, individuality, and self-respect, as well as the loss of any sense of control over a vital aspect of our lives. Unfortunately, this process has already begun.

It trespasses upon almost every aspect of our personal lives by imposing an unnecessary straightjacket of behavioral standards: when to retire, how much to earn between ages 62 and 72, when to divorce, whether to remarry (as well as when and to whom), and so on (Chapter 22). It destroys the flexibility needed for us to manage our lives as we see fit.

It is, in effect, a rigid mechanism for dividing the population into two groups: those who work and produce goods and services, and those who are inactive but still share in such production. The particular division fostered by Social Security may have been appropriate in the past, but it will not be appropriate for tomorrow. For example, the early sixties will not be a proper age to divide the active from the inactive population as the baby boom of yesterday becomes the senior boom of tomorrow. A flexible system is needed that will permit this division of the population into active and inactive groups to adjust itself voluntarily in response to changing proportions of old and young, improved health at older ages, longer lifetimes, more women in the paid work force, and so on.

It discourages personal saving, including private pension plans, retards the capital formation necessary for a strong economy, and thus reduces the growth in national productivity that would improve the standard of living for all—active and retired alike.

It is structured to reward life patterns (for example, male breadwinner and female homemaker, and lifelong marriages) that are becoming much less representative of modern life. It is not flexible enough to accommodate the changing role of the family unit; and, in particular, of women as they move toward independence and equality. The roles of men and women will continue to evolve and will never again be as stereotyped as they once were.

It combines the elements of individual equity and social adequacy (welfare, as it is now usually called) and effectively hides any connection between the taxes an individual pays and the benefits he receives. Yet, all the while the public has been told there *is* such a connection between taxes and benefits (through the rhetoric of "contributions" paid to a "trust fund" under an "insurance" program to acquire an "earned right" to specified benefits). Indeed, the public's belief that they were buying their own benefits with their own contributions was an important element in the extraordinary public acceptance of Social Security until the mid-1970s—when they began to find out that was not the way it worked. A clear understanding of how the taxes are used and a belief that the program is fair and equitable are essential when taxes are at today's levels.

A Plan for Tomorrow

Chapters 27 through 30 present an outline of a revised Social Security program intended to overcome the deficiencies of the present Social Security program and to be consistent, insofar as practicable, with the principles listed in this chapter. The suggested plan has limitations since it is difficult to formulate a perfect program to accommodate a heterogeneous society such as exists in the United States. The best way to accommodate these diverse needs, of course, is to minimize government-dictated standards and maximize individual freedom of choice. The purpose of the following chapters is to outline a revised Social Security program in sufficient detail to demonstrate its feasibility. Refinements and more complete details concerning the transition from the present system to the revised system can be designed easily if the overall plan is considered desirable by enough of the population.

The proposed plan would be considerably different from the present one. It would provide a basic floor of protection for all citizens against fundamental economic need. It would provide additional benefits through a voluntary component. There would be a clear separation between benefits that are related directly to the individual's tax payments and those that are not. It would thus be perceived (by most people) as more equitable and fair. It would be easier to understand and administer. It would afford greater freedom of choice to the participant in the type and level of benefits provided. It would permit a more natural and flexible separation of the population into the active and inactive segments. It would accommodate the changing roles of women, as well as men, however they may evolve in the future. It would result in increased private saving and would facilitate the capital formation needed to restore and sustain a strong economy. Finally, it would encourage and reward individual initiative and self-sufficiency and would improve our standard of living, materially and spiritually. In short, the proposed new Social Security program would be based on less governmentalism and more individualism and would thus be called the Freedom Plan.

The proposed effective date of the Freedom Plan is July 4, 1984. The significance of July 4, Independence Day, is obvious.

George Orwell, in his satirical novel entitled *1984,* predicted that we would be completely engulfed by Big Brother by 1984. With a little luck and a lot of hard work we can thwart that prediction.

27
Provision for Old Age

Most of life's events for which we must make future provision usually come as a surprise: death, disability, illness. Even if the events are certain, their timing is seldom predictable. This is not true for what we frequently refer to as old age, since the majority of adults will experience it for at least a few years. Consider a group of people aged 40 to 45, an age by which most people are aware that old age is a real possibility for them. Approximately 80 percent of this group will live until at least age 65, 70 percent will live until at least age 70, and 60 percent will live until at least age 75.

Old age can be anticipated and financial plans can be made accordingly. It would not be necessary for the government to be involved in any way in our retirement planning except for the contingencies already cited—inflation, extraordinary life spans, and misfortune outside the control of an individual in financial planning for old age.

It is proposed that Social Security continue unchanged until July 4, 1984; and that for everyone aged 45 and over on July 4, 1984, Social Security continue unchanged for the balance of their lifetime with regard to the payment of old-age retirement benefits, including related dependents' benefits.

It is proposed that everyone who is less than age 45 on July 4, 1984, participate in the new Freedom Plan. The Freedom Plan would thus apply to 168 million people, or 79 percent of the population less than age 65 as of July 4, 1984. The old Social Security program would continue to apply to 46 million people, or 21 percent of such population; and, of course, it would continue to apply to some 28 million people aged 65 or older, as well as their dependents, most of whom would already be receiving Social Security benefits.

The Freedom Plan, insofar as the provision of retirement benefits is concerned, would consist of three parts:

    A mandatory Senior Citizen Benefit program;

    A Freedom Bond program of optional retirement savings bonds; and

    A Cost-of-Living Supplement for Private Pension Plans.

Senior Citizen Benefits

The proposed system of Senior Citizen Benefits would protect the individual against risks that he cannot reasonably be expected to bear: unbridled inflation at a time when he does not have the protection normally afforded an active wage earner, and breakthroughs in health care that may result in abnormally long life spans. It would also provide a genuine floor of protection against financial adversity in old age—whether caused by misfortune or poor planning.

At age 70, a monthly benefit of a uniform amount would be payable to each resident citizen of the country regardless of his previous employment, earnings history, marital status, financial need, or any other factor. The benefit would be payable to men and women alike, regardless of whether they had worked in paid employment. Residency for at least twenty-five years during the period from age 35 to age 70 could be required. The benefit would be payable for the individual's remaining lifetime.

Citizenship is relatively easy to attain and is not an onerous requirement to impose on someone who is going to derive thousands of dollars from the tax payments of the nation's working population. An applicant for citizenship must have lived in the U.S. for at least five years, must not have been a member of the Communist Party within the last ten years, and must not have been in jail more than 180 days. He or she must know basic U.S. history and civics and have a grasp of "simple" English, a standard that is very loosely interpreted.

Since the amount of the benefit would be the same for everyone, its purpose would not be to sustain varying preretirement standards of living, but rather to provide a minimum level of support. Benefits would be set at approximately the subsistence level so that every aged person could live without fear of deprivation of life's necessities, even if the vicissitudes of life should leave him with no other resources. (This presumes, of course, the existence of an appropriate health care program for the aged.) The amount of the benefit could be related to the average earnings of all workers, the average national industrial wage, or, perhaps, the minimum wage. If substantial differences continue to exist in the cost of living in various regions of the country, perhaps the amount of the benefit would vary with the geographical area of residence during retirement.

An appropriate benefit level for 1980 would probably be in the range of $225 to $275 per month. For purposes of discussion and the cost projections presented in Chapter 30, it has been assumed the Senior Citizen Benefit would be $250 per month in 1980, and an equivalent amount relative to average wages of the nation's workers in later years. By way of comparison, the following statistics for April 1980 may be of interest:

Social Security average benefit in current-payment status
Retired worker	$295.51
Aged widows and widowers	267.69

Supplemental Security Income maximum federal payment
Individual	$208.20
Couple	312.30

Aid to families with dependent children (AFDC) average family benefit $270.92

A few words of explanation may help interpret the significance of the $250 Senior Citizen Benefit relative to the benefit levels under various existing programs. For purposes of this comparison, it is assumed that the Senior Citizen Benefit program is in effect now; however, the payment of retirement benefits under the program would not actually begin until some twenty-five years hence.

Although the average monthly Social Security benefit for retired workers was $295.51 in April 1980, it does not follow that all retired workers would suffer a benefit decrease if the Senior Citizen Benefit program were in effect and they were receiving only $250. Approximately one-third of the retired workers were receiving *less* than $250 in April 1980, hence they would receive higher benefits under the Senior Citizen Benefit program; on the other hand, two-thirds of the retired workers would receive lower benefits under the program. Aged widows and widowers would be similarly affected. Benefits would be higher under the Senior Citizen Benefit program for the vast majority of dependent spouses of retired workers.

Generally speaking, it is the lower wage earners who receive the lower benefits under Social Security. It seems fair to conclude, therefore, that the Senior Citizen Benefit program would provide increased monthly retirement benefits for approximately one-third of the population—the segment with the lowest earnings. It would provide lower benefits for approximately two-thirds of the population—the segment most capable of providing supplemental benefits for its own retirement (especially, as a result of the lower future taxes that would be made possible by enactment of the Freedom Plan).

The amount of the Senior Citizen Benefit would be adjusted for changes in the average wage or other index to which it was originally related. Accordingly, all persons aged 70 or over would be receiving the same monthly benefit in any given year, regardless of when they reached age 70.

The benefit would not be subject to federal income tax—for several reasons. First, income tax is normally imposed on earnings resulting from the production of goods and services but not on transfer payments, which themselves are derived from taxes. Second, taxing the benefit would be equivalent to paying a smaller Senior Citizen Benefit to some individuals than to others and would be contrary to the intention of providing a uniform minimum benefit for every elderly person. Finally, a benefit payable in old age would offer questionable security if it were subject to taxation at rates to be determined at the whim of some future Congress.

The benefit would be financed on a "current-cost" basis: that is, taxes would be collected each year in the amount estimated to be necessary to pay benefits for that year. The tax used to provide these benefits would be some form of general revenue, as distinguished from the payroll tax currently used to finance Social Security. The essential features of the tax, whatever form it may take, are:

> That it be clearly identified so that any change in benefit levels is made with a full understanding of the cost implications;
>
> That it be spread among the population in a way that is not only "fair" but that is generally *perceived* as fair; and
>
> That it be assessed and allocated in such a way that "deficit spending" is not involved—in other words, so that we do not borrow from future production to support the current aged population. By operating this system of benefits on a current-cost basis, we would already be deferring the liability as long as is justified. Further deferral would be irresponsible.

The selection of age 70 for commencement of benefits is somewhat arbitrary, but it can be judged against the following benchmarks. Based on projected improvements in mortality, a 70-year-old person early in the twenty-first century would have a remaining life expectancy exceeding that of a 65-year-old person in the 1930s—when Social Security adopted 65 as the retirement age.[1] If the retirement age during the second quarter of the twenty-first century were about age 72, the ratio of active workers to the retired population would be about the same then as it is now.[2] Allowing for future productivity gains (increases in the productive capacity of the nation's work force), an age somewhat less than 72 may be appropriate. Whatever age is selected, it should take into account several factors, most of which are interrelated:

> The age beyond which it is presumed the majority of the population is unable to work enough to support itself completely;
>
> The general health of the elderly and their longevity;
>
> The prevailing birth rates and the growth in the size of the young work force;
>
> The general economic health of the nation, including national productive capacity; and

The nature of available work opportunities, particularly for the older population.

All of these factors, as well as several others, are determinants of the size of the active working population that is needed to produce the goods and services required to sustain the nation's total population. On balance, it seems likely that if the active working population is maintained at the requisite size, there will be a natural increase in the retirement age prevailing in the early part of the twenty-first century.

If it is appropriate for the Senior Citizen Benefit to commence at age 70 for persons reaching that age about thirty years from now, a different age—probably higher—may be appropriate for future generations reaching age 70 later in the twenty-first century. This benefit age would be subject to adjustment from time to time depending upon the circumstances. Any increase in the benefit age would be determined well in advance so as not to disrupt retirement planning. For example, by the time a group of persons reaches its forties, the benefit age should be fixed and not subject to change except under extremely unusual circumstances. Demographic projections of the relative sizes of the working and the aged populations—an important determinant of a logical benefit age—can be made with relative certainty with respect to the remaining lifetime for those who have reached their mid-forties. Most of the other factors having a bearing on the selection of a benefit age should also be determinable twenty-five or thirty years before a person's retirement.

The time of old age is different for each individual and, to a large extent, is determined by our attitudes. It is not necessary—it is not even appropriate—to have a government-imposed standard telling us when we have reached old age and when we can no longer work effectively. The establishment of the Freedom Plan with age 70 as the benefit age for the Senior Citizen Benefit does not imply that everyone should work until age 70; and it does not imply that the elderly should live out their lives on the relatively low Senior Citizen Benefit. Rather, it implies that no one has the right to demand support from one's fellow citizens except from age 70 onward and except at the subsistence level—and even this concession is made necessary only by the practicalities of life in an uncertain future environment.

If an individual chooses to retire earlier than age 70, it would be as a result of advance saving by himself or his employer. If an individual chooses to have a higher income after age 70 than the Senior Citizen Benefit, it would be as a result of advance saving by himself or his employer or a decision to work, perhaps part-time, beyond age 70. Complete freedom of choice would be afforded each person in this matter of whether to save more and retire earlier, or save less and retire later. Essential financial security would be assured for every resident beyond age 70, but no government benefits (that is, no support from fellow taxpayers) would be provided for a healthy individual before attainment of age 70, and it would clearly be the responsibility of the individual to care for himself before that time.

The cost of the system would be borne primarily by the active working population. This is a logical obligation for the relatively young, active working population to assume. Anyone who attains age 70 after having spent the majority of his adult lifetime in the United States can be presumed to have borne his share of developing the country and supporting the aged while he was actively employed. True, there will be some who reach age 70 without having contributed enough to the nation's development—at least from an economic standpoint—to warrant support in old age. There are humane considerations, however, and these same people will probably not have provided financially for their old age and will have to be supported by the active workers in any event. By holding these benefits to a minimum standard, unfair burdens on the producing taxpayer can probably be kept acceptably low.

Some would say this Senior Citizen Benefit should not be paid to those who have sufficient income without it. Why not? It is these same persons who have paid the bulk of the taxes that make the benefit possible in the first place. Paying retirement benefits only to those who need them can have several offensive characteristics: it requires too much delving by the government into the private affairs of an individual; it discourages people from striving for self-sufficiency since the reward is loss of benefits; it encourages people to hide assets since an appearance of poverty will entitle them to "government benefits." There is certainly a place in welfare planning for benefits based upon "needs" and "means," but not in the provision of basic minimum benefits for the elderly.

Payment of the Senior Citizen Benefit to all citizens, men and women alike, would go a long way toward alleviating the present special financial problems of women—an increasing proportion of the elderly population. Benefits would be paid regardless of marital status, previous attachment to the paid labor force, and other conditions imposed by the present system that have caused it to be criticized as "unfair." The vast majority of today's younger women, all of whom would be participants in the Freedom Plan, will have had an opportunity to be in the paid work force and acquire retirement benefits that are supplemental to the Senior Citizen Benefit.

The many advantages of this simplified system of Senior Citizen Benefits are significant, not the least of which is the clear separation of governmental and nongovernmental responsibility for providing for an individual's economic security at advanced ages. Under a system as complex as the present Social Security program, it is doubtful that a clear delineation of such responsibility will ever be possible—a situation almost certain to result in people's expecting more, and thus eventually receiving more, from the government (that is, the active working taxpayers), with a consequent decline in individual self-reliance and productivity of the nation as a whole.

Freedom Bond Program

The Senior Citizen Benefit is intended to provide a minimum standard of living from age 70 onward for persons who are less than age 45 on July 4, 1984, and will thus reach age 70 in the year 2009 and later. This is *not* a government-imposed standard that says everyone *must* work until age 70 or that everyone *must* have only a minimum standard of living. A person can retire whenever he pleases on any standard of living his thrift or good fortune will support.

The general social and economic environment makes it much easier to provide for retirement today than in the past. When Social Security was enacted forty-five years ago, the existing conditions included:

>　　relatively few reliable institutional channels through which an individual could invest and save for the future;

>　　an almost completely undeveloped system of private pensions and other employee benefits; and

family units that tended to be larger, with a male bread-winner and a female homemaker.

The changes that have occurred in all these areas make it much easier to provide for retirement today than in the 1930s. But a new problem has arisen: INFLATION. Continued high inflation over a long period of years makes it virtually impossible for the average individual to save for retirement.

A large proportion of the nation's employees participate in formal pension plans, usually sponsored by their employer. These private pensions, together with the Senior Citizen Benefit, often will meet a person's retirement needs adequately. In most cases, however, supplemental individual savings will be desirable, and in some cases essential.

If we believe it is healthful for individuals to take responsibility for themselves and save for their retirement, and if we believe continued high inflation is a possibility, there seems to be no alternative to getting the government involved—not to pay for anything, but to provide a mechanism by which the active working population can preserve the value of any savings that individuals accumulate for retirement.

It is proposed that the government offer retirement savings bonds—designated as Freedom Bonds—under the following general conditions to provide a supplemental mechanism for an individual to save for retirement:

The Bonds would be sold after July 4, 1984, to any resident citizen between ages 45 and 70 provided he or she was less than age 45 on July 4, 1984.

The maximum amount of Bonds an individual could purchase in any year would be 10 percent of his taxable earnings in the prior year; but any eligible individual could purchase a specified minimum amount of Bonds regardless of earnings (approximately equal to 10 percent of average earnings of the nation's employees for the prior year).

Each year the value of Bonds purchased in a prior year would be adjusted to reflect changes in the relative purchasing power that had occurred between the purchase date and the current valuation date. No interest would be payable on the Bonds, however.

No federal, state, or local taxes would be payable on the Bonds, including any increase in nominal value, when they are redeemed. The Bonds would have been purchased with funds that had already been subjected to tax.

The Bonds would be redeemed for their current value upon the individual's death. They would be redeemable, at the option of the individual, upon his bona fide disability or anytime after his attainment of age 60.

The Bonds could be redeemed in a lump sum or in a series of instalments, at the option of the individual or his survivors. If taken in instalments, the unredeemed Bonds would continue to be indexed to reflect changes in purchasing power until fully redeemed.

The rationale for these Freedom Bonds is largely self-evident; however, the following comments may add perspective.

The purpose of indexing the Bonds would be to preserve their purchasing power—no more and no less. Accordingly, the indexing factor could be based upon changes in average wages, a specially constructed cost-of-living measure, or some other element.

No interest is provided and no taxes are involved. The Bonds are not intended to be an attractive investment, but merely a hedge against inflation. During times of high inflation, purchase of the Bonds would be particularly attractive; during periods of no inflation or low inflation, alternative investments would be preferred.

The funds for adjusting the value of the Bonds would come from general revenue. This indexing procedure would not remove the nation's incentive to eliminate inflation since the population would be protecting itself against inflation by paying increased taxes as necessary.

The Bonds could be purchased only after age 45 and only in limited amounts. The purpose of the Bonds is to offer a safe and inflation-proof vehicle to accumulate a reasonable supplemental retirement income during the latter half of one's working life. The Bonds would not be available to persons aged 45 and over on July 4, 1984, since they would be continuing in the existing Social Security system and accruing benefits that are indexed to changes in average wages and prices. Perhaps an exception could be made in certain situations—such as for persons not participating in an employer-sponsored retirement plan. Special consideration could also be given to persons aged 45 and over on July 4, 1984, not participating in Social Security.

An individual who purchased Freedom Bonds worth 10 percent of his earnings every year from age 45 to age 70 would accumulate enough to provide a lifetime retirement benefit from age 70 onward of 20 to 30 percent of his average preretirement earnings (depending upon the individual's earnings pattern and sex).

The Bonds would be available to persons even though they were not in paid employment. This provision is intended primarily for spouses not working in paid employment but would include other situations also. This opportunity for individual saving together with the Senior Citizen Benefit seems to be appropriate provision for persons not working in paid employment. Of course, a spouse not in paid employment would not normally have any funds to save except funds provided by the other spouse. This proposal assumes a voluntary agreement as to sharing income between two spouses, which is preferable to some of the arbitrary, government-imposed "earnings-sharing" proposals recently advocated by some study groups.

It is proposed that the Bonds be redeemable only in the event of death, disability, and after age 60. It may be advisable to provide for their redemption also in the case of carefully defined emergencies, including long-term unemployment. The basic purpose of the Freedom Bonds, however, is to provide for retirement. Other vehicles are available to serve as ordinary savings accounts.

The purpose of the issuance of the Bonds is not to compete with private investment opportunities or to raise additional funds for the government to spend. To prevent this latter possibility, appropriate restrictions should be adopted to control the government's use of the proceeds from the Bond sales, perhaps by requiring that such proceeds be used only to refinance existing national debt. (Issuance of the Bonds would thus not *increase* the national debt.) This would make some of the funds currently invested in government securities available for private investment and thus facilitate the increased capital formation needed to revitalize the economy.

Cost-of-Living Supplement for Private Pension Plans

Ideally, the proposed Senior Citizen Benefit system and the Freedom Bond program would be the extent of government involvement in retirement planning. The majority of the nation's workers are covered by a retirement program sponsored by their employer or groups of employers. Many such programs have resulted from collective bargaining. These retirement programs are referred to here as private pension plans (to distinguish them from the federal Social Security system), but the term also includes pension plans covering employees of federal, state, and local governments. The diversity of such pension plans reflects the diversity of the circumstances of employees in various occupations; on the whole, the private pension system is well suited to the goals of maximum individual freedom of choice and minimum governmental interference.

Once again, however, the spectre of inflation rises to impede the smooth functioning of our financial institutions and suggests the need for some form of governmental intervention. As inflation erodes the purchasing power of private pensions, they are sometimes adjusted upward. It is unusual, however, for a private pension to be adjusted fully to reflect changes in the cost of living; and it is almost never that a full adjustment is guaranteed for the remaining lifetime of the pensioner.

Pensions represent promises to pay benefits for twenty-five years or more after an employee retires and leaves the employer's payroll. It is unrealistic for the average employer to attempt to assume the risk of substantial inflation that may occur many years after an employee leaves its payroll and, perhaps, many years after the employer ceases to exist. This would require the provision of retirement benefits adjusted fully for indeterminable cost-of-living changes in the distant future. Such benefits cannot be funded in advance because the extent of the liability cannot be determined in advance. Furthermore, such benefits cannot be provided by an employer *on a guaranteed basis* as the benefits become payable, since there can be no assurance the employer will still be in business and also be able to afford such a benefit twenty-five years or more after an employee retires.

It should not be surprising, therefore, that very few

employers do in fact assume the risk of adjusting retirement benefits for substantial inflation at the present time; furthermore, it appears unlikely that they will be able to do so in the future. The only notable exceptions are the retirement systems covering most federal employees, and the retirement systems of a limited number of public employers—situations where perpetual existence of the employer is presumed. This limitation of the private pension system's ability to cope with rampant inflation is not a reason to scrap the entire system. Relatively limited governmental intervention would seem to make much more sense.

It is proposed that the government provide cost-of-living supplements for all private pension plans in accordance with the following general guidelines:

> Private pension plans, including those of federal, state, and local governments, would be covered provided they met federal standards for approved plans (Internal Revenue Service requirements for "qualified" plans, for example).

> Monthly pension benefits payable for life would be covered, but only with regard to benefits payable after age 70.

> Every year, benefits payable to persons aged 70 or older would be supplemented by the amount necessary to sustain the purchasing power in the prior year in accordance with a cost-of-living index constructed especially for the elderly.

> The cost of these supplemental benefits would be paid from general revenue, that is, primarily by the active working taxpayers.

It may be worthwhile to remind ourselves that these supplemental benefits do not represent a "government subsidy" since the government does not pay the cost of anything. The government is simply formulating a standard with which the majority of the population presumably would agree (namely, the protection of the elderly population against the ravages of inflation with respect to certain monthly retirement benefits) and then providing a mechanism by which the active working taxpayer can support that standard.

This cost-of-living supplemental benefit program would need

careful study to ensure a rational formulation, but there is no need to phase it in gradually (except to mitigate the cost impact); it could be made effective as of July 4, 1984, when major changes in Social Security are proposed to take effect. Perhaps this type of cost-of-living supplement could apply to Individual Retirement Accounts and other forms of monthly retirement income as well as to private qualified pension plans.

Conclusion

Under the proposed Freedom Plan, an individual would retain principal responsibility for himself until age 70; after age 70 he would have responsibility for himself beyond the minimum standard of living provided by the Senior Citizen Benefit. He would be able to retire anytime before age 70, or enjoy any standard of living after age 70, permitted by his private saving or job-related retirement benefits. The Freedom Bond program would offer a reliable method of private saving for retirement in time of inflation.

Employer-provided retirement plans would still entail a substantial commitment, particularly if benefits are related to final average earnings. On the other hand, the most unmanageable of the retirement burdens of an employer—inflation after a worker has reached age 70—would be shifted to society as a whole, the only logical place for it. Of course, another portion of the retirement burden would be shifted from the individual and the employer to society as a whole through the Senior Citizen Benefit program and the "inflation-proofing" aspect of the Freedom Bond program (as well as through the Medicare program described in Chapter 28).

To the extent that individuals remain in the work force until higher ages than at present, both the individual and the employer must assume increased responsibilities: retraining of individuals, redesigning of jobs, finding more sophisticated methods of matching individuals and jobs, and doing whatever else is necessary to develop and utilize an individual's skills and talents during a longer proportion of his healthy lifetime.

All things considered, the proposed Freedom Plan seems a reasonable way to allocate the cost of retirement and to employ effectively the nation's most neglected asset—our human resources.

28
Provision for Illness

Illness is a certainty for most of us sometime during our life. Although we may not be able to predict when it will occur, we can make advance provision for the financial loss caused by illness—either by personal saving or the purchase of health insurance. It would not be necessary for the government to be involved in any way in our planning for illness were it not for the contingencies of inflation, extraordinary life spans, and misfortune in financial planning. These contingencies make some form of governmental intervention advisable for most of the aged population.

It is proposed that Social Security continue unchanged with regard to the provision of Medicare benefits (Hospital Insurance and Supplementary Medical Insurance benefits) until July 4, 1984; and that for everyone aged 45 and over on July 4, 1984, as well as for their dependents, Medicare continue unchanged for the balance of their lifetimes.

It is proposed that everyone who is less than age 45 on July 4, 1984, participate in a revised Medicare program with these characteristics:

Benefits, including "deductibles" and "coinsurance," provided under the present Medicare program (Hospital Insurance and Supplementary Medical Insurance) would continue substantially unchanged.

All resident citizens aged 70 and over would be eligible for Medicare benefits for the balance of their lifetimes.

323

Residency for at least twenty-five years during the period from age 35 to age 70 could be required—to be consistent with eligibility requirements for Senior Citizen Benefits.

Benefits would be provided for persons eligible for monthly cash disability benefits under the Freedom Plan during the same period that such disability benefits were payable.

Benefits would be financed on a current-cost basis from earmarked general revenue. The payroll tax currently used to finance the HI program and the monthly premiums used to finance a portion of the cost of the SMI program would be discontinued.

Benefits would continue to be nontaxable: that is, excluded from income in computing federal, state, and local income taxes.

Although no particular changes are proposed in Medicare benefits at the time of the general restructuring of Social Security on July 4, 1984, the benefit design is certainly not perfect and should be revised. Revision could begin almost immediately and continue through the years as health care practices change. On the one hand, the "deductible" and "coinsurance" features as well as the reimbursement provisions should be revised to make it mutually advantageous to the patient and the providers of health care services that costs be controlled and services not be overutilized. The net result of such changes would probably be an increase in the cost to the patient for relatively minor illnesses. On the other hand, the cost to the patient for major illnesses should be reduced by having Medicare assume an increased proportion of the cost of expensive, extended illnesses.

Medicare benefits and administrative procedures should be revised from time to time to provide an appropriate level of health care for the elderly. This will probably always require a compromise between the level of health care that is technologically possible and financially feasible.

This statement about compromise in determining health care levels should give pause for concern. The continued existence of Medicare, or any similar program, over a long period will have far-reaching effects on our lives. Under a program such as

Medicare, a governmental agency (in accordance with laws enacted by Congress) effectively defines the particular health care services that will be provided by determining whether they will be paid for by the program: the number of days in a hospital, the number of days in a skilled nursing facility, the type and level of services by hospitals and physicians that will be deemed reasonable, and so on. In theory an individual can buy any health care services desired even if they are not provided by Medicare. In practice, however, the availability of such services will be greatly influenced by the norms of Medicare.

It is not an overstatement to say that a program like Medicare places the power over our life and death in the hands of government. Witness this example: Since Medicare began providing treatment for persons with chronic kidney disease requiring dialysis or kidney transplant, regardless of their age, the health of such persons has undoubtedly improved and many are alive who would otherwise have died. Is there any reason that persons with kidney ailments should be favored over persons with hypertension, cancer, or emotional problems? Who should make such decisions and on what basis?

Medical technology already exists that would make us healthier, extend our lives, and prolong our lives in the event of a lingering final illness; however, this technology is not used uniformly throughout the population because of its high cost. It appears that medical technology will continue to advance more rapidly than our ability or willingness to pay for it. Therefore, important choices and decisions lie ahead concerning the level of health care it is feasible to provide the nation as a whole as well as any particular individual. The larger the role played by the government in providing health care services, the larger will be the role of the government in influencing the type and level of health care available to us all. Because of its important role in administering Medicare and Medicaid, the government cannot avoid being a powerful determinant of the health and longevity of the elderly population. It must be borne in mind as these decisions are being made that the purpose of Medicare should be to provide a basic level of health care to the entire population aged 70 and over regardless of an individual's financial resources. The purpose is not to inhibit continued advances in medical technology, or to set maximum standards of health care for the elderly, or to prevent an individual from utilizing alternative forms of health care—at his own expense.

The rationale for financing Medicare from some form of general revenue is the same as that applied to the financing of Senior Citizen Benefits. The Medicare benefit is not something "bought and paid for" by an individual's own contributions or premiums; it is a program of minimum health care for every aged resident citizen regardless of prior employment, marital status, financial need, or any other factor. Accordingly, the cost of Medicare should be spread over the entire active working population to the extent possible.

There is a danger in using general revenue unless it is "earmarked" in some way to ensure that the taxes needed to provide benefits are actually collected. Otherwise, there may be a temptation to borrow the necessary funds and thus shift the cost to subsequent generations. By operating Medicare on a current-cost basis, we would already be deferring the liability as long as is justified. Further deferral would be irresponsible.

Persons can arrange for health care services prior to reaching age 70 in a variety of ways: personal saving, purchase of health insurance, utilization of job-related insurance and health benefits, and so on. It is only at advanced ages after a person has left the mainstream of employment that governmental intervention may be necessary to ensure the provision of adequate health care. This is true largely because future health care costs are indeterminable—partly as a result of possible inflation and partly as a result of rapidly changing, and increasingly costly, medical technology.

Because of poor planning or genuine misfortune, some individuals under age 70 will not have adequate health care services, and other taxpayers will have to pay for such services through some form of welfare program such as Medicaid. In order to care for the truly needy, however, it is not necessary to impose on the whole of society a complex and arbitrary set of health benefits—and taxes to pay for such benefits.

29
Provision for
Death and Disability

Many of us will be disabled and unable to work sometime during our life. Some of us will be severely disabled for long periods. All of us will die. Death and disability arouse our compassion and tend to lure us into advocating government benefits for widows and orphans. But remember that "government benefits" is a euphemism for "benefits provided by other taxpayers," and that we are attempting to outline here a program of benefits that emphasizes freedom of choice and self-sufficiency—a program that calls for governmental intervention only in those instances when an individual cannot reasonably be expected to provide for himself and his family.

Provision for Death

It is proposed that Social Security continue unchanged until July 4, 1984; and that for everyone aged 45 and over on July 4, 1984, as well as their dependents, Social Security continue unchanged for the balance of their lifetimes insofar as the payment of death benefits is concerned, including both lump-sum and monthly survivors benefits. Also, everyone receiving survivors benefits on July 4, 1984, regardless of age, would continue to receive such benefits as if Social Security were unchanged. Additional transition provisions may be advisable to avoid discontinuity in some cases.

It is proposed that everyone who is less than age 45 on July 4, 1984, participate in the Freedom Plan. No death benefits would be paid under the Freedom Plan except in connection with the optional Freedom Bond program outlined in Chapter 27.

Provision for Disability

It is proposed that Social Security continue unchanged until July 4, 1984; and that for everyone aged 45 and over on July 4, 1984, as well as their dependents, Social Security continue unchanged for the balance of their lifetimes insofar as the payment of disability benefits is concerned. Also, everyone receiving disability benefits on July 4, 1984, regardless of age, would continue to receive such benefits as if Social Security were unchanged. Additional transition provisions may be necessary because of the nature of the disability risk.

It is proposed that everyone who is less than age 45 on July 4, 1984, participate in the Freedom Plan, which would have these characteristics with regard to the provision of disability benefits:

Benefits would be payable only to persons who were totally and permanently disabled, and who had been so disabled for twelve full months.

Benefits would be payable to any adult resident citizen of the country who satisfied minimum requirements of recent attachment to the paid work force. A minimum period of residency could be required if considered necessary to avoid abuse.

Benefits would be payable only to persons who agreed to participate in a qualified rehabilitation and retraining program. Substantially more emphasis would be placed on such a program than is the case with the present Social Security system.

Monthly benefits equal to the then current Senior Citizen Benefit, including adjustments to reflect changes in the cost of living, would be payable for as long as the individual remained disabled.

Medicare benefits would be provided during the same period that monthly cash disability benefits were payable.

Benefits would be financed by some form of general revenue, earmarked in such a way as to prevent deficit
financing.

Benefits would be nontaxable: that is, excluded from
income in computing federal, state, and local income
taxes.

There is no need for excessive government-imposed standards concerning the financial arrangements to be made upon a
person's death or disability. An individual can anticipate the
needs of his family and estate in the event of his death. He can
anticipate the needs of his family and himself in the event of his
disability. He can provide in advance for most of these needs by
personal saving (including participation in the Freedom Bond
program), by purchasing appropriate life insurance and disability insurance, by making arrangements with family members or
friends, and so forth. The nation's insurance companies have
adequate facilities to provide a wide range of death and disability benefits consistent with affording each individual maximum
freedom of choice.

Because of poor planning or genuine misfortune, some individuals will die without having made appropriate financial
arrangements for their survivors and some will become disabled
without having provided for themselves and their family
members. In an orderly society, the other taxpayers must
provide financial support in these unfortunate situations.
Accordingly, some form of welfare program must be continued
as a supplement to the Freedom Plan. "But help for a few
hardship cases hardly justifies putting the whole population in
a straightjacket," as so aptly stated by Milton and Rose Friedman in their book *Free to Choose: A Personal Statement.*[1]

30

Cost and Financing of Proposed Social Insurance Program

The proposed social insurance program consists of the Freedom Plan for the younger part of the population and continuation of the present Social Security program for the older part of the population. Since this proposed program covers the entire population while the existing Social Security program covers only about 90 percent of the working population and an even smaller percentage of the nonworking population, it is difficult to compare the cost of the two programs. Chart 30.A makes this comparison by illustrating the projected expenditures for benefits and administration during the next seventy-five years:

For the present Social Security program as if it remained unchanged.

For the revised social insurance program but with respect to the same limited population covered by the present Social Security program.

Projected expenditures are shown as a percentage of the taxable payroll of the population for whom benefit expenditures are shown and are based on the same intermediate assumptions used throughout the book.

331

Projected expenditures for the present Social Security program are the same as those shown in Chart 4.A and include expenditures for the OASDI, HI, and SMI programs combined. They rise from a current level of approximately 13 percent of taxable payroll to about 27 percent of taxable payroll in the middle of the twenty-first century.

Projections for the proposed social insurance program include expenditures for the mandatory part of the new program, including Senior Citizen Benefits and Medicare and disability benefits. The projected expenditures do not include the optional Freedom Bond program for discretionary retirement saving or the Cost-of-Living Supplement for Private Pension Plans, an entirely new program not related to the existing Social Security and thus not relevant to any cost comparison. Expenditures for the proposed program increase slowly for the next thirty-five years and then increase more rapidly for the following twenty years as the children of the post-World War II baby boom reach their seventies. Expenditures then level off during the middle of the twenty-first century in the range of 19 to 20 percent of taxable payroll, approximately 50 percent higher than present expenditures of 13 percent of taxable payroll.

Chart 30.A indicates with a broken line which part of the expenditures is for persons aged 45 and over and which part is for persons under age 45 on July 4, 1984, the date of introduction of the proposed new system. Not surprisingly, virtually all of the cost during the next twenty years is attributable to the group of persons aged 45 and over—the group for whom the present Social Security would continue unchanged. The cost for the large group of persons under age 45 on the date of change would increase steadily until leveling off in the middle of the twenty-first century after all these persons have begun to receive retirement benefits.

Chart 30.A is a striking illustration of the long-term nature of promises made under a social insurance system and the significance of an accrued liability. The bulk of the accrued liability of some $6 trillion under the present Social Security program as of January 1, 1979 (discussed in more detail in Chapter 7) represents promises made to persons aged 45 and older. The proposed social insurance system would honor these promises

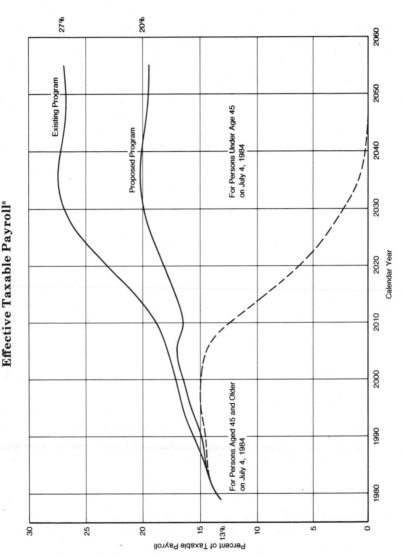

Chart 30.A

Projected Expenditures for Benefits and Administration of Existing Social Security Program and Proposed Social Insurance Program, Expressed as a Percentage of Effective Taxable Payroll[a]

[a]Projections are based on the intermediate demographic and economic assumptions described in the Appendix. Expenditures are for the same limited population covered by the present Social Security program.

completely; hence, it would take a very long time and a substantial amount of money to discharge this liability.

Although adoption of the proposed program would not result in an immediate reduction in expenditures, it would eliminate the rapid increase in cost that would begin around the year 2006 if the present Social Security program were continued. The revised social insurance program has the following characteristics that make it less costly than the present Social Security program for future generations:

> Retirement benefits and Medicare benefits begin at age 70 (instead of age 65, or even earlier for retirement benefits).
>
> Retirement benefits are basic minimum benefits that are the same for everyone (instead of increased amounts for individuals with higher earnings).
>
> Disability benefits are basic minimum benefits that are the same for everyone; and benefits are not paid until disability has lasted twelve months (instead of five months).
>
> Death benefits are not provided.

The revised social insurance program has one feature that is *more* costly than the present Social Security program: the provision of Medicare benefits after twelve months of disability (instead of approximately twenty-nine months as presently provided).

From the viewpoint of any particular individual and his employer, the lower future cost of the revised program compared with the present program may be partially offset by the higher cost of providing benefits that are supplemental to the mandatory social insurance benefits: that is, the higher cost of saving for the individual's retirement, and providing for his family in the event of death or disability. If people continue to retire in their early sixties and to arrange privately for approximately the same benefits they would have received had the present Social Security program remained unchanged, the total cost of benefits—publicly and privately provided—would be about the same as if the present Social Security program had continued. There is no way to provide the same benefits for less money—and that is not the purpose of the proposed revision in Social Security.

The purpose of the revised program is to reduce government involvement in employee benefit planning—to reduce government-imposed standards and give the individual more freedom of choice in deciding what benefits are to be provided and how they are to be financed. The difference between the expenditures shown in Chart 30.A for the existing program and the revised program represents the amount by which the revised program would shift responsibility for providing employee benefits away from a government-imposed program. The purpose of the revised program is not to set standards as to the age at which people should retire, the amount of the benefits on which they should retire, or any other aspect of employee benefits. The revised program leaves this responsibility for setting standards to the individual and provides the vehicles— where they do not already exist—by which such standards can be realized.

How would the cost of the revised program be paid? As indicated in earlier chapters, persons aged 45 and over on July 4, 1984, would continue to pay the same Social Security taxes as if the program had not changed. So would their employers and so would self-employed persons. These taxes would finance only a small portion of their benefits and the balance would be financed by general revenue paid by the entire working population, including of course this group of persons aged 45 and over. Since the revised program would pay benefits to everyone, not just to approximately 90 percent of the working population as in the present program, it would be more costly in some respects. On the other hand, the total cost of various welfare programs would be reduced since the need for welfare benefits would be lessened. For example, the cost of public assistance to survivors would probably increase, but this would be more than offset by a decline in the cost of Supplemental Security Income.

A rough estimate has been prepared of the expenditures for benefits and administration during the next seventy-five years under the revised social insurance program (excluding the optional Freedom Bond program and the Cost-of-Living Supplement for Private Pension Plans). These expenditures are shown in Chart 30.B as a percentage of the Gross National Product and thus represent the proportion of goods and

Chart 30.B

Projected Expenditures for Benefits and Administration of Proposed Social Insurance Program Expressed as a Percentage of Gross National Product—Proportion Financed by Payroll Taxes and by General Revenue[a]

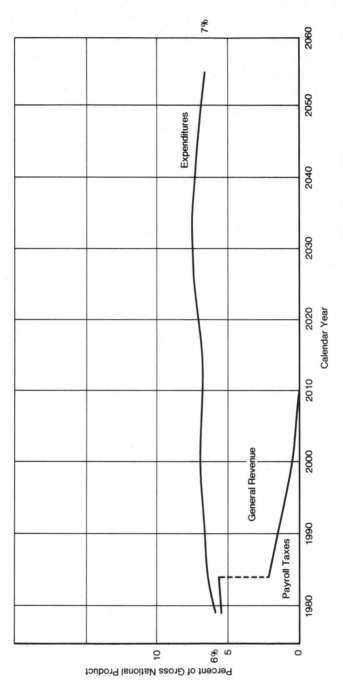

[a]Expenditures and total taxes are assumed to be equal. Projections are based on the intermediate demographic and economic assumptions described in the Appendix.

services that must be allocated to the new social insurance program. Projections are based on the same intermediate assumptions used throughout the book. The practice used earlier in the book of relating expenditures to the taxable payroll of those participating in the system is not used since the new system covers the entire population, and benefits and supporting taxes are not related to an individual's earnings. Payroll taxes show a marked decline in mid-1984 when persons under age 45 stop paying payroll taxes. A corresponding increase in general revenue must occur at that time since total taxes under the revised program will not become significantly lower than under the present program until some twenty years hence. Although expenditures for the revised social insurance program illustrated in Chart 30.A increase significantly as a percentage of taxable payroll, the expenditures illustrated in Chart 30.B, expressed as a percentage of Gross National Product, increase by a relatively smaller amount and remain in the range of 6 to 7 percent of Gross National Product throughout the projection period. This is because taxable payroll is a steadily decreasing percentage of the Gross National Product according to the assumptions used in making the projections.

Chart 30.C depicts the approximate expenditures for the proposed social insurance program based upon three alternative sets of demographic and economic assumptions described in the Appendix and employed in projections shown in earlier parts of the book. Projected expenditures are for the entire population and are shown as a percentage of the Gross National Product. Expenditures are shown for the present Social Security program from 1979 through July 4, 1984 to give a point of reference for the later expenditures under the proposed social insurance program. The projected expenditures shown in Chart 30.C are very rough estimates; the most significant conclusion to be drawn from them is that the nation can probably afford the proposed social insurance program based upon any reasonable assumptions about the future. Indeed, the nation must provide these benefits—regardless of the cost—since the proposed social insurance program calls only for minimum benefits and only for benefits an individual cannot reasonably be expected to provide for himself.

Chart 30.C

Comparison of Projected Expenditures for Benefits and Administration of Proposed Social Insurance Program Based upon Alternative Assumptions, Expressed as a Percentage of Gross National Product[a]

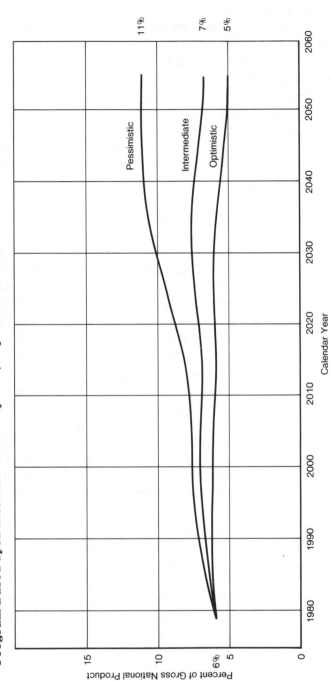

[a]Projections are based on the alternative sets of demographic and economic assumptions described in the Appendix.

This observation brings to mind a very important and basic distinction between the existing and proposed social insurance programs. The proposed program calls only for minimum benefits that are necessary in an orderly, humane society; hence, the benefits must be provided, regardless of the cost. The present program, on the other hand, calls for minimum benefits *and discretionary benefits that are not essential to an orderly, humane society.* Advocates of the present program would have us believe that all these benefits are essential and must be provided regardless of the cost. Accordingly, these advocates seem to be comfortable in ignoring the large future costs of such benefits. There appears to be no other rationale to explain this indifference by otherwise intelligent and responsible people to the probable high future benefit costs of the present social insurance program.

This basic distinction between the existing and proposed social insurance programs is also important in defining a rationale for financing. The use of general revenue, which inevitably obscures future costs, is not appropriate to finance the existing program to the extent that such program provides nonessential benefits. General revenue is appropriate, however, to finance the essential benefits provided under the existing program, just as it is appropriate to finance the mandatory part of the proposed program since it provides only essential benefits. This interrelationship between the method of financing and the level of benefits is a subtle yet quite important factor in the design of a social insurance program.

The proposed social insurance program assumes that the proceeds of the sale of Freedom Bonds would not be used to finance other portions of the revised program, and would not be used to permit additional government spending and thus increase the national debt. Instead the Freedom Bonds would refinance existing national debt; hence, Freedom Bondholders would gradually hold more of the national debt and others would hold correspondingly less, thus freeing private saving for use in developing the economy. In a sense, this procedure amounts to operating the optional Freedom Bond portion of the new Freedom Plan on an advance-funded basis. This level of advance funding appears to be feasible since it would be instituted gradually as persons attaining age 45 become eligible

to buy Freedom Bonds. Nevertheless, overall economic considerations may indicate such advance funding is not desirable,
and that part or all of the proceeds of the sale of Freedom
Bonds should be used to pay benefits under other parts of the
revised program. To the extent this practice is followed, the
amount of general revenue required for the revised program
would be less, and the existing unfunded accrued liability would
not be reduced. Instead, as Freedom Bonds were issued, the
unfunded accrued liability would be formally recognized as it
shifted to the Freedom Bondholder population.

Important questions of equity, or fairness, can be raised
about the old and new social insurance programs and how they
are financed—in the past as well as the future. The following
observations may lend perspective to these questions. There are
no simple criteria for equity that would be commonly agreed
upon by the various sectors of the population affected (Chapter
11 discusses some of the many considerations). Even if the
principles of equity could be agreed upon, it would be possible
to achieve only very rough equity in the future—particularly if
an attempt were made to balance the procedures of the past
with the proposals for the future and obtain some predeter-
mined standard of equity for the combined past and future. A
further difficulty is that participants in Social Security have
believed all along that certain principles of equity existed in the
past—but they did not.

I would consider the proposed social insurance program,
including the suggested financing arrangements, to be as fair as
is practicable under the circumstances. Of course, there is
considerable latitude in designing the exact method by which
general revenue is assessed to finance the revised program, the
details of which would be the final determinant of equity.

The cost of the proposed social insurance program presented
in this chapter is only a rough approximation intended to
demonstrate the feasibility of such a revision. No estimates
have been made of the cost effect of the revised social insurance
program on the various welfare programs, although the net
effect would be a reduction in welfare costs. Neither have cost
estimates been prepared for the Cost-of-Living Supplement for
Private Pension Plans or the adjustment to maintain the

purchasing power of the Freedom Bonds. Of course, if there is no inflation there is no cost for these two programs.

If the general approach outlined here is considered desirable by enough of the population to warrant further study, these and other cost estimates can be prepared and refinements can be developed in all the major areas of recommended change including appropriate methods of implementation.

31
Conclusion

Social Security, one of the largest single government programs in history, touches the lives of virtually everyone in the nation. Until the mid-1970s Social Security was regarded widely as the most successful government program ever enacted.

But this is not the current mood of the citizens. There is growing uneasiness and frustration about Social Security—among those who receive the benefits as well as those who pay the taxes—and it appears likely that this discontent is building to a demand for significant change.

Unfortunately, public perception of Social Security has been allowed to grow so far apart from reality that an objective appraisal of the present system by the public is difficult. The first step, then, toward rationally conceived change is increased public understanding of the present system. The second step is to obtain general agreement on a set of principles to form the underlying basis for a new Social Security. These principles may well be unique to America; ideally they will reflect the social and economic environment we desire for tomorrow, not just the environment that exists today.

Part Four of this book presents a conceptual framework for a substantial revision in Social Security that is intended to:

> preserve the rights and expectations of the 35 million persons already receiving Social Security benefits and

of the 46 million persons within twenty years of their anticipated retirement; and

permit the 168 million people who are under age 45 (almost 80 percent of the population not yet retired) the freedom to manage their own financial affairs as they see fit, but at the same time provide for their essential income security needs.

Designing and implementing a revised Social Security program may be a difficult task. But it will be no more difficult than trying to live with a program that is becoming so unpopular that its continued financial support by the working population is in serious doubt. Besides, the difficulty of the task of revising Social Security makes it no less essential to the well-being of the nation and its citizens.

We have an extraordinary opportunity to give today's youth and the youth of generations to come a matchless legacy—a social and economic environment of opportunity that will encourage and reward initiative and creativity, not one that will stifle. An appropriately designed Social Security program—such as the proposed Freedom Plan—is an essential part of this environment.

The Congress and the President, given the support of a substantial body of public opinion, can take this opportunity to restore to Americans the Freedom of Choice on which this country was founded and has prospered—and, we can hope, will continue to prosper. Such a grand opportunity may not pass this way again.

Appendix

Summary of Principal Actuarial Assumptions Used in Cost Projections

Throughout the book, reference has been made to actuarial estimates of the future financial operations of the Social Security program. The purpose of these actuarial projections is not to predict the future, since that is obviously impossible, but rather to analyze how the Social Security program would operate in the future under particular economic and demographic conditions. Because the actual future circumstances could develop in many different ways, it is only prudent to evaluate the program under a variety of different assumed conditions, any of which could be reasonably expected to occur (from today's point of view). Proper use of such projections will facilitate the design and understanding of the Social Security program, as well as help ensure that the program will be able to meet its financial obligations—and thus serve its purpose—in future years.

The official government cost projections for the Social Security program (OASDI and Medicare) are based upon assumptions and methodology explained in detail in the annual reports of the Board of Trustees of the OASI, DI, HI, and SMI trust

347

funds. The same economic and demographic assumptions employed in the 1979 annual reports were used for the financial projections contained in this book. Additional assumptions had to be made, however, in instances when the annual reports did not encompass the same period as the projections in the book. In particular, assumptions had to be made about hospital costs after the year 2000 and medical costs after the mid-1980s. In both instances it was assumed that costs would increase ultimately at about the same rate as the increase in average earnings of the nation's workers; present rates of increase were assumed to grade into these ultimate rates by about the year 1995 for medical costs and about the year 2000 for hospital costs.

Three different sets of economic and demographic assumptions were used, characterized as "optimistic," "intermediate," and "pessimistic." These characterizations refer to the effect of a given assumption on Social Security costs, not to the social desirability of a particular trend. For example, an assumption of longer life expectancy is called "pessimistic" since benefits would be paid over a longer period, thereby raising the costs. The alternative sets of assumptions were designed to illustrate a broad range within which one might reasonably expect the actual future experience to fall. Given the past volatility of such factors as inflation, hospital costs, and birth rates, however, there can be no assurance that future experience will fall within the range so defined.

The alternative sets of assumptions are summarized in Tables A.1 and A.2. It was assumed that the retirement-age patterns in the future would be substantially the same as those being experienced currently, with relatively little variation among the three alternatives. Assumptions were also made concerning variables such as migration levels, insured status, disability termination rates, marital status, administrative expenses, the timing pattern of fertility, and many others. The actual future development of all these factors will undoubtedly exhibit fluctuations and considerable variation. Since such cycles and abrupt changes cannot be foretold, the ultimate long-range values of the assumptions shown in Tables A.1 and A.2 are designed to represent the average trend levels that would result if the fluctuations were smoothed out. For the first

few years of the projection period, however, an attempt was
made to forecast cyclical behavior in the economic factors.

Appendix Table A.1

**Selected Economic Assumptions under Optimistic, Intermediate,
. and Pessimistic Alternatives, Calendar Years 1979–2055**

		Percentage Increase in Average Annual...					
Calendar Year	Real GNP[a]	Wages in Covered Employment	Consumer Price Index	In-patient Hospital Costs[b]	Real Wage Differential[c]	Average Annual Interest Rate[d]	Average Annual Unemployment Rate
(1)	(2)	(3)	(4)	(5)	(6)	(7)	(8)
1960–64	4.0	3.4	1.3	—	2.1	3.7	5.7
1965–69	4.3	5.4	3.4	15.1	1.9	5.2	3.8
1970–74	2.5	6.3	6.1	13.7	0.2	6.7	5.4
1975	−1.3	6.5	9.1	18.7	−2.5	7.4	8.5
1976	5.7	8.4	5.8	15.7	2.5	7.1	7.7
1977	4.9	6.9	6.5	13.7	0.4	7.1	7.0
1978	3.9	8.5	7.6	12.7	0.9	8.2	6.0
Alternative I (Optimistic)							
1979	3.7	8.3	9.3	12.6	−1.0	9.1	6.0
1980	2.3	8.6	7.3	13.1	1.3	8.6	6.2
1981	4.4	8.7	6.5	13.9	2.2	8.5	5.7
1982	4.9	7.9	5.2	13.4	2.7	7.8	4.9
1983	5.0	5.8	4.0	12.2	1.8	7.0	4.2
1984	3.9	4.9	3.1	9.9	1.8	6.1	4.0
1985	3.6	5.0	3.0	9.0	2.0	6.1	4.0
1986	3.9	5.1	3.0	8.8	2.1	6.1	4.0
1987	3.9	5.4	3.0	8.8	2.4	6.1	4.0
1988	4.0	5.5	3.0	8.6	2.5	6.1	4.0
1989	3.8	5.5	3.0	6.9	2.5	6.1	4.0
1990	3.8	5.5	3.0	6.7	2.5	6.1	4.0
1995	3.1	5.4	3.0	5.7	2.4	6.1	4.0
2000 and later	3.1[e]	5.25	3.0	5.7[f]	2.25	6.1	4.0
Alternative II (Intermediate)							
1979	3.7	8.3	9.4	12.6	−1.1	9.1	6.0
1980	2.0	8.0	7.4	13.1	.6	8.8	6.2
1981	4.0	9.1	6.6	14.1	2.5	8.4	6.0
1982	4.7	7.4	5.5	14.0	1.9	7.6	5.3
1983	3.6	6.0	4.5	12.8	1.5	6.9	5.0

Appendix Table A.1 (continued)

Calendar Year	Real GNP[a]	Wages in Covered Employment	Consumer Price Index	Inpatient Hospital Costs[b]	Real Wage Differential[c]	Average Annual Interest Rate[d]	Average Annual Unemployment Rate
	Percentage Increase in Average Annual...						
(1)	(2)	(3)	(4)	(5)	(6)	(7)	(8)
1984	3.0	5.4	4.0	11.3	1.4	6.6	5.0
1985	3.1	5.3	4.0	11.3	1.3	6.6	5.0
1986	3.2	5.4	4.0	11.3	1.4	6.6	5.0
1987	3.3	5.7	4.0	11.3	1.7	6.6	5.0
1988	3.3	6.0	4.0	11.4	2.0	6.6	5.0
1989	3.2	6.0	4.0	10.5	2.0	6.6	5.0
1990	3.2	6.0	4.0	10.4	2.0	6.6	5.0
1995	2.9	5.9	4.0	9.3	1.9	6.6	5.0
2000 and later	2.9[e]	5.75	4.0	9.2[f]	1.75	6.6	5.0
Alternative III (Pessimistic)							
1979	2.3	9.2	10.3	12.6	−1.1	9.1	6.3
1980	−1.1	8.7	8.9	13.1	− .2	9.0	8.2
1981	5.4	9.2	7.3	15.5	1.9	8.5	7.4
1982	4.1	7.7	6.3	15.5	1.4	8.1	6.9
1983	4.0	7.2	6.0	15.7	1.2	8.1	6.4
1984	3.7	7.1	6.0	15.6	1.1	8.1	6.0
1985	2.9	7.2	6.0	15.2	1.2	8.1	6.0
1986	2.9	7.1	6.0	15.3	1.1	8.1	6.0
1987	2.9	7.3	6.0	15.1	1.3	8.1	6.0
1988	2.9	7.5	6.0	15.1	1.5	8.1	6.0
1989	2.8	7.5	6.0	14.2	1.5	8.1	6.0
1990	2.8	7.5	6.0	14.1	1.5	8.1	6.0
1995	2.7	7.4	6.0	13.0	1.4	8.1	6.0
2000 and later	2.7[e]	7.25	6.0	12.6[f]	1.25	8.1	6.0

[a]The total output of goods and services in the Nation expressed in constant dollars.
[b]Includes hospital costs for all patients, not just HI beneficiaries. Data unavailable for years 1960–64.
[c]The difference between the percentage increase in average annual wages in covered employment and the percentage increase in the average annual CPI.
[d]The average of the interest rates determined in each of the 12 months of the year for special public-debt obligations issuable to the trust funds.
[e]This value is for the year 2000. The value for the year 2055 is 3.3, 2.4, and 0.8 for alternatives I, II, and III, respectively.
[f]Value is for 2000. Subsequent unit hospital cost increases are assumed to equal the annual increases in average wages in covered employment.

Appendix Table A.2

Selected Demographic Assumptions under Optimistic, Intermediate, and Pessimistic Alternatives, Calendar Years 1979–2055

Calendar Year	Total Fertility Rate[a]	Age-adjusted Mortality Rate[b]		Adjusted Gross Disability Incidence Rate[c]	
		Male	Female	Male	Female
(1)	(2)	(3)	(4)	(5)	(6)
1970	2,434	10.96	8.05	5.06	3.54
1971	2,249	10.66	8.06	5.92	4.10
1972	1,997	10.77	7.94	6.35	4.50
1973	1,865	10.66	7.85	6.72	4.93
1974	1,827	10.26	7.54	7.03	5.64
1975	1,771	9.88	7.17	7.76	6.06
1976	1,719	9.73	7.07	7.23	5.51
1977	1,784	9.53	6.89	7.41	5.46
1978	1,757	9.35	6.72	5.97	4.25
Alternative I (Optimistic)					
1979	1,831	9.45	6.80	5.79	4.12
1980	1,871	9.36	6.72	5.85	4.17
1981	1,911	9.32	6.68	5.92	4.22
1982	1,952	9.28	6.64	6.02	4.29
1983	1,992	9.25	6.60	6.12	4.37
1984	2,033	9.21	6.56	6.23	4.46
1985	2,074	9.17	6.52	6.34	4.55
1990	2,292	9.04	6.39	6.62	4.78
1995	2,443	8.92	6.26	6.68	4.84
2000	2,493	8.80	6.13	6.69	4.86
2005 & later	2,500	8.69[d]	6.01[d]	6.69	4.86
Alternative II (Intermediate)					
1979	1,793	9.18	6.55	5.87	4.19
1980	1,809	9.02	6.38	5.97	4.25
1981	1,824	8.85	6.22	6.09	4.34
1982	1,839	8.82	6.18	6.25	4.46
1983	1,855	8.78	6.15	6.42	4.57
1984	1,870	8.75	6.11	6.61	4.72
1985	1,887	8.72	6.08	6.79	4.86
1990	2,036	8.55	5.92	7.25	5.22
1995	2,075	8.39	5.76	7.34	5.32
2000	2,100	8.23	5.60	7.36	5.35
2005 & later	2,100	8.08[d]	5.45[d]	7.36	5.35
Alternative III (Pessimistic)					
1979	1,737	8.92	6.30	5.95	4.25
1980	1,715	8.67	6.07	6.09	4.34

Appendix Table A.2 (continued)

Calendar Year	Total Fertility Rate[a]	Age-adjusted Mortality Rate[b]		Adjusted Gross Disability Incidence Rate[c]	
		Male	Female	Male	Female
(1)	(2)	(3)	(4)	(5)	(6)
1981	1,693	8.57	5.97	6.26	4.46
1982	1,671	8.46	5.86	6.48	4.66
1983	1,649	8.36	5.76	6.71	4.78
1984	1,627	8.26	5.67	6.99	4.98
1985	1,606	8.16	5.57	7.23	5.16
1990	1,544	7.85	5.26	7.87	5.66
1995	1,524	7.58	4.97	8.01	5.79
2000	1,509	7.34	4.72	8.03	5.83
2005 & later	1,500	7.12[d]	4.48[d]	8.03	5.83

[a]The number of children that would be born to 1,000 women in their lifetimes if they were to experience the observed age-specific birth rates and were to survive the entire child-bearing period. Ultimate rates are reached in 2005.

[b]The annual number of deaths per 1,000 persons in the enumerated population as of April 1, 1970. Improvement is projected to continue throughout the projection period.

[c]The number of awards per 1,000 persons exposed to disability, adjusted for changes from the 1978 age distribution.

[d]This value is for the year 2005. Mortality rates are assumed to continue declining throughout the remainder of the projection period.

Note: Figures shown in Tables A.1 and A.2 for 1978 and earlier represent actual experience as estimated at the time the 1979 Trustees Reports were prepared. Certain of these figures have since been slightly revised based on more accurate data.

Notes

Chapter 1

1. The dollar amounts in this paragraph relate to all the benefits usually thought of as Social Security: Old-Age and Survivors Insurance, Disability Insurance, and Medicare (Hospital Insurance and Supplementary Medical Insurance).

2. There is no employer tax paid on behalf of self-employed persons; however, self-employed persons pay higher tax rates than employed persons.

3. These and other figures throughout the book are based upon the 1979 Trustees Reports (intermediate assumptions) unless noted otherwise. More recent projections based upon the 1980 Trustees Reports (intermediate assumptions) indicate the maximum Social Security tax in 1990 will be $5,118 for an employee ($10,236 for employee and employer combined) and $7,192 for a self-employed person.

Chapter 2

1. *Social Security Handbook,* U.S. Department of Health, Education, and Welfare, Social Security Administration, HEW Publication No. (SSA) 77-10135, July 1978.

2. Ibid., p. 2.

3. In addition to these noncovered employees, there are approximately 530,000 active railroad employees who are not included in Social Security but who are covered by their own railroad retirement system. For all practical purposes, however,

these railroad employees may be considered to be covered by Social Security. They generally receive benefits at least equal to those provided by Social Security as a result of the transfer of wage credits between the systems for employees with less than ten years of service and as a result of the financial interchange provisions applicable to all railroad employees.

4. "The Desirability and Feasibility of Social Security Coverage for Employees of Federal, State, and Local Governments and Private, Nonprofit Organizations," Report of the Universal Social Security Coverage Study Group, March 1980.

5. This figure includes the resident population of the fifty states and the District of Columbia, American Armed Forces and certain civilians overseas, and the residents of Puerto Rico, Guam, American Samoa, the Virgin Islands, and the Canal Zone. These groups comprise the total population eligible to participate in the Social Security program.

6. Robert M. Gibson and Charles R. Fisher, "Age Differences in Health Care Spending, Fiscal Year 1977," *Social Security Bulletin,* January 1979.

7. Subsequently, in 1980, the functions of the Department of Health, Education, and Welfare were allocated to two new departments: the Department of Education, and the Department of Health and Human Services—the Social Security Administration and the Health Care Financing Administration forming part of the latter.

8. *The Budget of the United States Government, Fiscal Year 1981.*

Chapter 3

1. According to the Omnibus Reconciliation Act of 1980 signed into law on December 5, 1980 (Pub. L. No. 96-499), some of these Medicare provisions will be liberalized as of July 1, 1981: the period within which a beneficiary must be transferred from a hospital to a skilled nursing facility and still qualify for post-hospital extended care will be increased from fourteen days to thirty days; with respect to home health visits, the three-day prior hospital stay will be eliminated under HI, the 100-visit ceiling will be removed under HI and SMI, and the $60 deductible will be eliminated under SMI.

Chapter 4

1. W. R. Williamson and R. J. Myers, "Revised Cost Estimates for Present Title II." Unpublished study, Actuarial Study No. 12, October 1938, Social Security Board, Office of the Actuary.

2. All projections were based upon the Social Security benefit provisions in effect on January 1, 1979. Most of the projections were obtained from the 1979 Trustees Reports or unpublished estimates prepared by the Social Security actuaries in conjunction with the preparation of the Trustees Reports. In cases where particular estimates were not available, the author has prepared his own estimates on the basis of the 1979 Trustees Reports assumptions.

3. As mentioned before, the SMI program is not financed by the Social Security payroll tax; it is financed primarily from general revenue (currently 70 percent) and enrollee premiums (currently 30 percent). By the year 2000, it is expected that general revenue will provide over 90 percent of SMI financing. Since SMI costs are properly included as "Social Security costs," they have been shown as a percentage of taxable payroll in order to have a uniform basis for comparison.

Chapter 5

1. J. Douglas Brown, *The Genesis of Social Security in America,* Industrial Relations Section, Princeton University, Princeton, N.J., 1969, p. 14.

2. Ibid., p. 13.

3. Arthur M. Schlesinger, Jr., *The Age of Roosevelt,* vol. 2, *The Coming of the New Deal* (Houghton-Mifflin, 1959), pp. 308–9.

Chapter 7

1. *1979 Annual Report of the Board of Trustees of the Federal Old-Age and Survivors Insurance and Disability Insurance Trust Funds* (House Document No. 96-101, 96th Congress, 1st Session), 1979.

2. In recent years the OASDI program has been operated on what may be characterized as a current-cost basis, since the

trust fund balances have been relatively low. Should the trust fund balances in fact increase as implied by Chart 7.A, the program would more properly be described as "partially advance-funded," at least for the next fifty years.

3. Based on more recent projections, scheduled OASDI tax income will not exceed expenditures until the mid-1980s; the resulting deficits will be relatively small but will necessitate corrective legislation.

4. This computation, as well as those throughout the chapter, is based on a "real rate of interest" of 2.5 percent. For example, in the case of the intermediate assumptions, the assumed 6.6 percent interest rate is comprised of a "real rate of interest" of 2.5 percent, compounded with an assumed 4.0 percent annual increase in the Consumer Price Index.

5. *1979 Annual Report of the Board of Trustees of the Federal Hospital Insurance Trust Fund* (House Document No. 96-102, 96th Congress, 1st Session), 1979.

6. Joseph A. Applebaum, "Some Effects of Fully Funding OASDI," Actuarial Note No. 97, HEW Publication No. (SSA) 79-11500, September 1979.

Chapter 11

1. Orlo R. Nichols and Richard G. Schreitmueller, "Some Comparisons of the Value of a Worker's Social Security Taxes and Benefits," Actuarial Note No. 95, HEW Publication No. (SSA) 78-11500, April 1978.

2. The calculations were based on standard actuarial mathematics, and attempted to account for each of the appropriate factors that can influence the results. For example, the probabilities that a worker would die before becoming eligible for retirement benefits, or conversely, that he would live far into old age were accounted for. Similarly, the worker's chances of becoming disabled in any given year were included. The changing value of the dollar (inflation) and the "time value of money" (interest), along with changes in average wages were also accounted for.

3. These examples were derived from the study mentioned in Note 1 but do not necessarily conform to specific examples given in the study.

Chapter 13

1. Executive Summary of *Social Security Financing and Benefits; Report of the 1979 Advisory Council on Social Security,* December 7, 1979, p. 12.

2. *Social Security Financing and Benefits; Report of the 1979 Advisory Council on Social Security,* December 7, 1979, p. 353.

Chapter 14

1. Under the new benefit provisions enacted in the 1977 Social Security Amendments, workers retiring in future years will receive somewhat smaller replacement ratios. For workers retiring at age 65, as in these examples, replacement ratios (based on the worker's benefit alone) will level off ultimately at 57 percent for the minimum wage earner, 44 percent for the average wage earner, 30 percent for the worker with maximum earnings, and 15 percent for twice-maximum earners. The corresponding figures for workers with dependent spouses are 86 percent, 66 percent, 45 percent, and 22 percent, respectively.

2. Under the "offset" method of integration, Internal Revenue Service rules allow a plan to define its benefits as a particular amount (calculated the same way for all participants) reduced by no more than 83⅓ percent of the retiring worker's Primary Insurance Amount under Social Security. Other methods of integration are allowed, provided they produce approximately the same end result.

Chapter 19

1. Persons attaining age 65 in 1982 or later will have their benefits calculated under the new indexed-earnings benefit formula. For these persons, the "delayed retirement credit" is increased from 1 percent annually to 3 percent to help offset the loss of benefits that would otherwise occur because the indexing of earnings is carried out only through age 60. Thus the net gain for retirement later than age 65 is still intended to be only about 1 percent per year.

2. According to the Omnibus Reconciliation Act of 1980 signed into law on December 5, 1980 (Pub. L. No. 96-499), some

of these Medicare provisions will be liberalized as of July 1, 1981: the period within which a beneficiary must be transferred from a hospital to a skilled nursing facility and still qualify for post-hospital extended care will be increased from fourteen days to thirty days; with respect to home health visits, the three-day prior hospital stay will be eliminated under HI, the 100-visit ceiling will be removed under HI and SMI, and the $60 deductible will be eliminated under SMI.

3. Orlo R. Nichols and Richard G. Schreitmueller, "Some Comparisons of the Value of a Worker's Social Security Taxes and Benefits," Actuarial Note No. 95, HEW Publication No. (SSA) 78-11500, April 1978.

4. Based on an unpublished study by the Social Security Administration actuaries.

Chapter 23

1. When the revisions in the earnings test enacted by the Social Security Amendments of 1977 become completely effective after 1981, references in this paragraph to age 72 should read age 70.

Chapter 27

1. In the 1930s the average remaining lifetime of persons aged 65 was about 12 years for males and 13 for females; today it is about 14 years for males and 19 years for females; for persons aged 65 in the year 2025 it is projected to be about 16 years for males and 22 years for females (based on the most recent studies by Social Security actuaries and not allowing for any major breakthroughs in health care). These same studies indicate that for persons aged 70 in the year 2025 the average remaining lifetime will be about 13 years for males and 18 years for females.

2. In mid-1981 there were approximately five persons aged 20 to 65 for every person aged 65 and over. To maintain this same ratio of "active to retired" persons during the first half of the twenty-first century, the normal retirement age of 65 would have to increase to 67 by the year 2000 and continue rising to 72 by the year 2025, after which time it would remain at about 72 for the next twenty-five years.

Chapter 29

1. Milton and Rose Friedman, *Free to Choose: A Personal Statement,* Harcourt Brace and Jovanovich, New York, 1979, p. 115.

Index

Postscript

Legislative Revisions

The Social Security law in effect in January 1981 was used throughout the book unless noted otherwise. Since then, several minor changes have been made in the law and others are being contemplated as this current edition goes to press in November 1981. None of these changes affects the substance of Social Security or of the book. The changes may affect an individual's eligibility for particular benefits, however; if in doubt, the reader should consult a local Social Security office for the exact provisions in effect at any given time.

Omnibus Reconciliation Act of 1981

This Act, signed into law on August 13, 1981, contains several provisions affecting Social Security benefits, including the following.

Earnings Test Exempt Age.   Age 72 is retained as the upper age limit beyond which the earnings test no longer applies through 1982 (rather than 1981 as under prior law), after which it drops to age 70.

Lump-Sum Death Benefit.   The lump-sum benefit in the event of a worker's death will be paid only to certain surviving spouses or children, and will no longer be paid to funeral home operators when there are no eligible survivors, effective for deaths after 1981.

Adult Student Benefits.   Benefits to persons aged 18 to 21 who are full-time students will be phased out. Persons who begin to receive such benefits before May 1982 (and who received a child's benefit for August 1981) will have their benefits reduced gradually and no benefits will be paid after April 1985. No benefits will be payable to persons first becoming eligible after July 1982.

Mother's or Father's Benefits.   Mother's or father's benefits will terminate when the youngest child attains age 16 (rather than age 18 as under prior law) effective September 1981 for new beneficiaries and September 1983 for current beneficiaries. This change does not apply in the case of a parent caring for an eligible disabled child aged 16 or over.

Disability Benefit Offsets. The current maximum of 80 percent of average earnings imposed on the combination of Social Security disability benefits and workers' compensation is extended to include certain other *publicly* provided disability benefits under federal, state and local laws. Also, the offset is extended to workers aged 62 to 65, and the "reverse offset" provision can no longer be used by states without such a provision currently in their law.

Medicare. Both deductibles and coinsurance will be increased for 1982 under Medicare. In the past, beneficiaries could count expenses incurred in the last quarter of the previous calendar year toward the SMI deductible for the current year. The new law will not allow this carryover of expenses for the 1982 deductible or for any year thereafter.

Minimum Benefit. The regular minimum benefit ($122.00 per month) was eliminated for all beneficiaries who initially become eligible for benefits after October 1981. For all other beneficiaries, the minimum was eliminated for benefits payable for months after February 1982. As noted in the following section, however, the minimum benefit will probably be reinstated for the majority of those currently eligible for benefits.

Pending Legislation

In addition to the above legislation enacted in August 1981, the Senate and the House are seriously considering (as of November 1981) Social Security legislation that would achieve approximately the following results.

Reinstate the minimum benefit to most or all current beneficiaries. Provide that no one who retires in the future, except members of certain religious orders, would qualify for the minimum benefit.

Reallocate the scheduled Social Security payroll tax rate among the OASI, DI and HI trust funds, and provide for borrowing between the OASI and DI trust funds, to enable the system to continue a few years longer without increasing the overall tax rate or decreasing benefits.

Apply the same maximum limits to retirement and survivor families that currently exist for disabled-worker families.

Subject the first six months of sick pay (except under most insured plans) to Social Security taxes.

About the Author

A. Haeworth Robertson was Chief Actuary of the United States Social Security Administration from 1975 to 1978, the period during which attention was first directed toward the alarming financial problems which lie ahead. He resigned shortly after the 1977 Amendments to Social Security were passed, believing he could more effectively provide the information necessary to bring about further rational change by working on the "outside." During the last six years he has written and lectured widely, giving special emphasis to interpreting and clarifying the financial status of Social Security.

While Chief Actuary of Social Security, he received two awards—the Commissioner's Citation and the Arthur J. Altmeyer Award—for distinguished service in managing the affairs of his office and in explaining Social Security's financial complexities in an easy-to-understand way to the Administration, the Congress, and the public.

Mr. Robertson's actuarial career began in 1953 when, as an officer in the United States Air Force, he served with a special unit of the Department of Defense appointed to prepare an actuarial study of the military retirement system for the 83rd Congress. Since then his entire career has been devoted to personal security programs of one kind or another. In addition to serving as Chief Actuary of Social Security, he worked twelve years as a consulting actuary dealing with private and public pension plans; four years in organizing, operating, and serving as president of a life insurance company; and six years as an international consultant on social insurance programs, which involved assignments in Switzerland, Barbados, Ghana, Lebanon, and the Philippines.

Mr. Robertson received his undergraduate degree in mathematics from the University of Oklahoma in 1951, where he was a Phi Beta Kappa, and his graduate degree in actuarial science from the University of Michigan in 1953. He is a Fellow of the Society of Actuaries, a Fellow of the Conference of Actuaries in Public Practice, and an Enrolled Actuary. He is also a member of the American Academy of Actuaries, the United Kingdom's Institute of Actuaries, and the International Actuarial Association. He has served as a member of the Board of Governors of the Society of Actuaries and as a member of numerous committees and advisory groups dealing with social insurance and private and public employee pension plans.

Mr. Robertson currently resides in the Washington, D.C. area, where he is a Vice President of William M. Mercer, Incorporated, an international firm of employee benefit and compensation consultants.